FAR AND WIDE

VOLUME ONE

"A blessed companion is a book"—JERROLD

BY W. SOMERSET MAUGHAM

LIZA OF LAMBETH
MRS. CRADDOCK
THE MERRY-GO-ROUND
THE EXPLORER
THE MAGICIAN
THE MOON AND SIXPENCE
OF HUMAN BONDAGE
THE TREMBLING OF A LEAF
ON A CHINESE SCREEN
THE PAINTED VEIL
THE CASUARINA TREE
ASHENDEN
THE GENTLEMAN IN THE PARLOUR
CAKES AND ALE
THE FIRST PERSON SINGULAR
THE NARROW CORNER
AH KING
DON FERNANDO
COSMOPOLITANS
THEATRE
THE SUMMING UP
CHRISTMAS HOLIDAY
THE MIXTURE AS BEFORE
BOOKS AND YOU
UP AT THE VILLA
STRICTLY PERSONAL
THE RAZOR'S EDGE
THEN AND NOW
HERE AND THERE (*Collection of Short Stories*)
CREATURES OF CIRCUMSTANCE
CATALINA
QUARTET (*Four Short Stories with Film Scripts*)
TRIO (*Three Short Stories with Film Scripts*)
ENCORE (*Three Short Stories with Film Scripts*)
A WRITER'S NOTEBOOK
THE COMPLETE SHORT STORIES (3 *Vols.*)
THE SELECTED NOVELS (3 *Vols.*)
THE PARTIAL VIEW
TEN NOVELS AND THEIR AUTHORS

The Collected Plays

VOL. 1:	VOL. 2:
LADY FREDERICK	OUR BETTERS
MRS. DOT	THE UNATTAINABLE
JACK STRAW	HOME AND BEAUTY
PENELOPE	THE CIRCLE
SMITH	THE CONSTANT WIFE
THE LAND OF PROMISE	THE BREADWINNER

VOL. 3: CÆSAR'S WIFE
EAST OF SUEZ
THE SACRED FLAME
THE UNKNOWN
FOR SERVICES RENDERED
SHEPPEY

FAR AND WIDE

Nine Novels

by

W. SOMERSET MAUGHAM

Selected by the Author

*

VOLUME ONE

THE COMPANION BOOK CLUB

LONDON

THIS edition, issued in 1955, is for members
of The Companion Book Club, 8 Long Acre,
London, W.C.2, from which address particulars
of membership may be obtained. The book
is published by arrangement with the original
publishers, William Heinemann Ltd.

PRINTED IN GREAT BRITAIN FOR THE
COMPANION BOOK CLUB (ODHAMS PRESS LTD.)
BY WILLIAM CLOWES AND SONS, LIMITED,
LONDON AND BECCLES.
S.1254.S.

Contents

VOLUME ONE

*

Contents

Preface

LIKE all authors I have had my ups and downs. Sometimes my work has pleased; sometimes it hasn't. A writer has to learn to take the rough with the smooth. But in one respect I have been uncommonly lucky: I have never had to suffer the heartbreak that many authors have to endure of sending a manuscript to publisher after publisher and having it returned time and time again with a curt note of rejection. *Liza of Lambeth* is my first novel. I sent it to Fisher Unwin, then a publisher esteemed for his enterprise, he accepted it and it was published. I was twenty-three. I wrote it while I was still a medical student at St. Thomas's Hospital. I was in my fourth year. I had spent the usual time in the out-patient departments, as clerk on the medical side and dresser on the surgical, and had passed the periods in the wards that the curriculum demanded. Then I did the obstetric work. In order to obtain the necessary certificate the student had to attend twenty confinements. I dare say all this is now changed, but in my day at St. Thomas's you were appointed obstetric clerk for a period of three weeks during which you had to be on hand day and night. You took a lodging immediately opposite the hospital, to which the porter had a key, and if you were wanted in the night he came across the street and woke you. You dressed and went to the hospital, where you found waiting for you the husband or perhaps the small son of the patient, with the card which the woman in labour had previously obtained from the hospital. For your first case you were accompanied by the Senior Obstetric Clerk, a young man recently qualified, but after that you were expected to manage by yourself and send for him only if a difficulty arose that you could not cope with. He was hard-worked and often very tired, so that if you dragged him out of bed without good reason you were very liable to hear some unpleasant truths about yourself. The messenger led you through the dark and silent streets of Lambeth, up stinking alleys and into sinister courts where the police hesitated to penetrate, but where your black bag protected you from harm. You were taken to grim houses, on each floor of which a couple of families lived, and shown into a stuffy room, ill-lit by a paraffin lamp, in which two or three women, the midwife, the mother, the "lady as lives on the floor below" were standing round the bed on which the patient lay. Sometimes you waited in that room for two or three hours, drinking a friendly cup of tea with the midwife and going down in the street below now and then to get a breath of air. The husband was sitting on the doorstep and you sat down beside him and chatted.

I attended sixty-three confinements in twenty-one days.

This was the material I used in *Liza of Lambeth*. I exercised little invention. I put down what I had seen and heard as plainly as I could. It seemed very bald and I should have liked to make my story more thrilling and picturesque by the exercise of my fancy, but I did not know how to. I was forced to stick to the facts by the miserable poverty of my imagination. I had at that time a great admiration for Guy de Maupassant and it was after the model of his tales that I tried to fashion my own. When I think of the bad examples a young writer may so easily follow I am happy to think that I took that of one who had so great a gift for telling a story clearly, straight-forwardly and effectively.

It was as a short story, and not a very long one either, that I first thought of *Cakes and Ale*. Here is the note I made when it occurred to me: "I am asked to write my reminiscences of a famous novelist, a friend of my boyhood, living at W. with a common wife very unfaithful to him. There he writes his great books. Later he marries his secretary, who guards him and makes him into a figure. My wonder whether even in old age he is not slightly restive at being made into a monument." I put the idea aside for future use and it was many years before I thought of it again, but when I did it was to discover that there was in it much more material than I could hope to get into a short story and it was borne in upon me that I could only do tolerable justice to it by turning it into a novel. I proceeded to write it.

When it appeared I was attacked in various quarters because I was supposed in the character of Edward Driffield to have drawn a portrait of Thomas Hardy. This was not my intention. He was no more in my mind than George Meredith or Anatole France. As my note suggests, I had been struck by the notion that the veneration to which an author full of years and honours is exposed must be irksome to the little alert soul within him which is still alive to the adventures of his fancy. Many odd and disconcerting ideas must cross his mind, I thought, while he maintains the dignified exterior that his admirers demand of him. I knew little of Hardy's life. I know now only enough to be certain that the points in common between his and that of Edward Driffield are negligible. They consist only in both having been born in humble circumstances and both having had two wives. I never met Hardy but once and then only for a brief period.

In point of fact I founded Edward Driffield on an obscure writer who settled with his wife and children in the small town of Whitstable (the W. of my note), of which my uncle and guardian was vicar. I do not remember his name. I don't think he ever amounted to anything and he must be long since dead. He was the first author I had ever met, and though my uncle strongly disapproved of my association with him, I used to slip away to see him whenever I had the chance. His conversation thrilled me. It was a shock to me and a satisfaction to my uncle when one day he vanished from the town leaving his debts unpaid.

At the time I was writing my novel Hugh Walpole was the most prominent member of that body of writers who attempt by seizing every opportunity to keep in the public eye, by getting on familiar terms with critics so that their books may be well reviewed, by currying favour whenever it can serve them, to attain a success which their merit scarcely deserves. It was inevitable that when I devised the character of Alroy Kear I should bear Hugh Walpole in mind. No author can create a character out of nothing. He must have a model to give him a starting point; but then his imagination goes to work, he builds him up, adding a trait here, a trait there, which his model does not possess, and when he has finished with him the complete character he presents to the reader has little in him of the person who offered the first suggestion. It is only thus that a novelist can give the creatures of his invention the intensity, the reality that make them not only plausible, but convincing. I had no wish to hurt Hugh Walpole's feelings. He was a genial creature and he had friends who, though they were apt to laugh at him, were genuinely attached to him. He was easy to like, but difficult to respect. I did all I could to cover my tracks; I made Alroy Kear a sportsman who rode to hounds, played tennis and golf much better than most of us, and an amorist who skilfully avoided the entranglement of marriage. None of this could be said of Hugh Walpole. I took these characteristics from other writers I knew whom I chanced to have run across. Unfortunately I had given Alroy Kear certain traits, certain discreditable foibles, which Walpole too notoriously had, so that few people in the literary world of London failed to see that he had been in part my model. For in this connection we are more apt to recognise persons by their defects than by their merits. Poor Hugh was bitterly affronted.

But it was not especially to write about Edward Driffield and Alroy Kear that I set to work on *Cakes and Ale*. In my youth I had been closely connected with the young woman whom in this book I have called Rosie. She had grave and maddening faults, but she was beautiful and, notwithstanding her incontinence, good. The relationship came to an end as such affairs do, but the memory of her lingered on in my mind year after year. I knew that one day I should bring her into a novel. The years went by, many years, and I could never find the occasion I was seeking. I began to fear I never should. It was not till, remembering my old note, I was seized with the desire to write about an old, distinguished novelist who, somewhat to his exasperation, was cosseted by his wife, and after his death used by her and others for their own glorification, that it occurred to me that by making Rosie his first wife I had the opportunity I had so long wanted. I must add that the model for what I consider the most engaging heroine I have ever created could never have recognised herself in my novel since by the time I wrote it she was dead. But if she had read it I don't believe she would have been displeased.

Theatre is a novel about plays and players. During the last fifty years I have seen most of the actresses who have made a name for themselves. I have seen many who had eminent gifts, many who excelled in a domain they had made their own, many who had charm, beauty and talent, but I cannot think of more than one to whom I could without hesitation ascribe greatness. This was Eleonora Duse. It may be that Mrs. Siddons had it; it may be that Rachel had it; I do not know; I never saw Sarah Bernhardt till she was past her prime; the glory that surrounded her, the extravagance of her legend, made it difficult to judge her coolly; she was often mannered and she could rant at times like any player queen; at her best she may have had greatness, I only saw its appurtenances, the crown, the sceptre and the ermine cloak—the

Emperor of China's new clothes, but no Emperor of China. With the one exception I have mentioned I have only seen actresses who could be good, sometimes very good, in certain parts. I have a notion that one's opinion in this matter depends a good deal on how much one is affected by the glamour of the stage. There are many people whom the theatre fills with an excitement which no familiarity can stale. It is to them a world of mystery and delight; it gives them entry into a realm of the imagination which increases their joy in life, and its illusion colours the ordinariness of their daily round with the golden shimmer of romance. When they watch the celebrated actress, her beauty enhanced by make-up, her significance emphasised by spot-lights, uttering fine phrases as though they came out of her own head, undergoing remarkable experiences and suffering poignant emotions, they feel that they live more fully; and it is natural enough that they should make a somewhat excessive use of hyperbole when they seek to describe the sensations which the skilful interpreter has given them. It is natural also that they should overlook the fact that the performance which has filled them with rapture owes at least something to the costumier, the scene-painter, the electrician and the author.

Even in my early youth I was never stage-struck; but whether because I am by nature of a somewhat sceptical disposition or whether because my mind was filled with private dreams which satisfied my romantic yearnings, I cannot say; and when I began to have plays acted I lost even the few illusions I had. When I discovered how much effort was put to achieving the gesture that had such a spontaneous look, when I realised how often the perfect intonation which moved an audience to tears was due not to the actress's sensibility but to the producer's expertness, when in short I learnt from the inside how complicated was the process by which a play is made ready to set before an audience, I found it impossible to regard even the most brilliant members of the profession with the same awed and admiring wonder as the general public. On the other hand I learnt that they had qualities with which the public is little inclined to credit them. I learnt, for example, that with few exceptions they were hard-working, courageous, patient and conscientious. Though dropping with fatigue after a long day's work, I saw them consent with cheerfulness to go through still once more a difficult scene which they had that very day rehearsed half a dozen times already; I saw them in illness give a performance when they could hardly stand on their feet rather than disappoint the public; and I learnt that for all the frills and airs they might put on, when it came down to the business of getting the best out of the play and themselves, they were as reasonable as anyone could wish. Behind their famous "temperament", which is a combination of selfishness and nerves more or less consciously emphasised under the erroneous impression that it is a proof of artistic sensibility, there is far oftener than the public imagines an abundance of shrewd, practical sense. I have never known a child that didn't like to show off, and in every actor there remains something of the child; it is to this that he owes many of his most charming gifts. He has more than the normal exhibitionism which is common to all but very few of us, and if he hadn't he wouldn't be an actor; it is wiser to regard this particular trait with humour than with disdain. If I had to put in a phrase the impression I formed of actors during the long time of my connection with the stage, I should say that their virtues are more solid than they pretend and their failings incidental to the hazardous and exacting profession they follow.

Thirty years elapsed between the production of my first play and the production of my last and in that period I was thrown into intimate contact with a great number of distinguished actresses. Julia Lambert, the heroine of *Theatre*, is a portrait of none of them. I have taken a trait here and a trait there and sought to create a living person. Because I was not much affected by the glamour of the brilliant creatures I had known in the flesh I drew the creature of my fancy, I dare say, with a certain coolness. I think Julia is true to life. I should like the reader of my novel to notice that though her admirers ascribe greatness to her, and though she accepts their flattery with greed, I, speaking in my own person, have not claimed that she was more than highly successful, very talented, serious and industrious. I may add that for my part I feel a great affection for her; I am not shocked by her naughtiness, nor scandalised by her absurdities; I can only consider her, whatever she does, with fond indulgence.

The Moon and Sixpence is not, of course, a life of Paul Gauguin in the form of fiction. It is founded on what I had heard about him, but I used only the main facts of his story and for the rest trusted to such gifts of invention as I was fortunate enough to possess. Fifty years ago, in 1904 to be precise, I spent a year in Paris. I had been living in London for some years, doing the same sort of things month after month, and I found myself tired of the quiet and orderliness of my daily round. I had had enough of the week-end visits to the houses of the rich and the grand and the interminable dinners in Mayfair that I was bidden to. I did not want to go to any more dances. I was growing old (I thought) and the precious years were slipping unprofitably through my fingers. I decided to make a break. I had a friend, a painter, now President of the Royal Academy, who lived on the left bank of the Seine and the life in the Latin Quarter that he described to me when we sometimes met very much took my fancy. I decided to live in Paris for a while. I had known it as a child and, even after my parents' death which sent me to England, I had often stayed there; but the Paris I knew was the Paris of the Champs Élysées and the Boulevards. The Paris I went to then was new to me. As soon as I arrived I took an apartment of three small rooms near the Lion de Belfort, on the fifth floor, with a spacious view over a cemetery. Montparnasse had at that time very much the air of a provincial town, which even now when you look at it with the eyes of fancy it still charmingly wears. The great handsome streets that have been cut through it did not exist and the Boulevard Raspail was only half built. A horse tram ran down the Rue de Rennes. The night life which for a period made it the haunt of pleasure seekers, foreign and native, had not set in. The Dome, the Rotonde, the Closerie des Lilas were there, but their patrons were the inhabitants of the Quarter. To go over to the other side of the river, in a bus drawn by three horses, was an excursion. It was rarely made except to go to the Louvre or the Salon and now and then to the theatre. As a rule if one wanted to see a show one went to the Gaîtés Montparnasse. In the Rue de Rennes there were some good shops, but in the side-streets there were the same little smelly grubby shops that had been there for a century.

Life on the Montparnasse was intense, for art seemed the most important thing in the world and, since everyone was young, love, a light love for the most part, without consequence, added zest to it, but life notwithstanding was quiet, plain and easy. It was also uncommonly cheap. That was a great advantage to me, since I was very poor. However busy one was, there was ample leisure. The air seemed fresher than in the Paris of the Boulevards and the crowd less insistent. When I look back my most vivid recollection is of a feeling of anticipation that danced in one's heart like dust in a sunbeam. It was then that I became aware of Cézanne, van Gogh and Gauguin. Cézanne was by far the greater artist, but Gauguin has a singular appeal to the man of letters. Though I do not now so much admire his pictures I still see how much there is in them to excite the literary imagination. I met men who had known him and worked with him at Pont-Avon. I heard much about him. It occurred to me that there was in what I was told the subject of a novel and I read the only life of him that at that moment had appeared. I did no more about it. I kept the idea in my mind. I kept it for over ten years. At last I had the opportunity to go to Tahiti and with the novel that had occupied my reveries off and on for so long I went there with the definite intention of finding out whatever else I could of Gauguin's life. I came across a number of persons who had been more or less closely connected with him. They were very ready to talk. Presently I found myself as ready to write the novel I had so long contemplated as one can be before one sits down to set pen to paper.

But no novelist can know everything. Sometimes he has to deal with circumstances that are completely outside his own experience. I knew that Gauguin had passed some time in Marseilles in dire poverty and it was convenient for me to have Charles Strickland, my hero, undergo the same hardships as he had. I knew something of the less reputable quarters of Marseilles, but not exactly how a man out of work would go about it to keep himself from starving. I read an interesting book of travel by Harry Franck, called *A Vagabond Journey Round the World*, and there found the very facts I needed. I used them. In a novel it would be absurd to put the source from which you obtain information, it would destroy the illusion you seek to create that your narrative is a true relation of facts; but I gave the reader a hint that I had not invented these facts myself by telling the reader of my suspicion that Captain Nichols, who in the novel told them to me as having happened to himself, had found them in the pages of a magazine. This was apparently not enough, for an angry gentleman wrote a long article condemning my reprehensible behaviour. It left me calm. I think books of facts are a legitimate quarry for the imaginative writer. I see no more reason why he should not make use of them than of the incidents that are told him in a club smoking-room or at the bar of a public-house. But I gladly take this opportunity to acknowledge my debt to Harry Franck.

The characters of fiction are strange fish. They come into your mind. They grow. They acquire suitable characteristics. An environment surrounds them. You think of them now and again. Sometimes they become an obsession so that you can think of nothing else. Then you write of them and for you they cease to be. It is odd that someone who has occupied a place, often only in the background of your thoughts, but sometimes in the very centre of them, who then perhaps for months has lived with you all the waking hours of the day and often in your dreams, should slip your consciousness so completely that you can remember neither the name you gave him nor what he looked like. You may even forget that he ever existed. But on occasion it doesn't happen like that. A character whom you thought you had done with, a character to whom you had given small heed, does not vanish into oblivion. You find yourself thinking of him again. It may be exasperating, for you have had your will of him and he is no longer of use to you. What is the good of his forcing his presence on you? He is a gate-crasher whom you do not want at your party. He is eating the food and drinking the wine prepared for others. You have no room for him. You must concern yourself with the people who are more important to you. But does he care? Unmindful of the decent sepulchre you have prepared for him, he goes on living obstinately; indeed he betrays an uncanny activity, and one day to your surprise he has forced his way to the forefront of your thoughts and you cannot help but give him your attention.

The reader of *The Narrow Corner* will find Dr. Saunders in a brief sketch in *On a Chinese Screen*. This was a little book made up of the notes I made during a sojourn of some months in China thirty years ago. Dr. Saunders was devised to act his part in a very short story called *The Stranger*. I had space there to draw him but in a few lines and I never expected to think of him again. There was no reason why he, rather than any of the many persons who made an appearance in that book, should go on living. He took the matter into his own hands. Some critics who have been sufficiently interested in me to write about my books have stated that in Dr. Saunders I drew a portrait of myself. I don't know how they got such a queer idea in their heads. It is true that I lent him one or two of my own experiences. But that is quite another matter. When a novelist has had an experience that will fit in with the characteristics of a creature of his invention he looks upon it as a

bit of luck and makes haste to use it. I founded Dr. Saunders on a
medical student I had known when I was myself one and whom I
continued to know till he died forty years later. He was never a
good doctor, but he had gaiety, a great sense of humour, a pleasant
cynicism and not a little unscrupulousness. He was a most
pleasant companion.

Captain Nichols was introduced to the reader in *The Moon and
Sixpence*. He was suggested by a beachcomber I met in the South
Seas. He was a very pretty rascal, but he took my fancy. He had
smuggled guns into South America and opium into China. He
had been engaged in the blackbird business in the Solomon
Islands and showed a scar on his forehead as the result of a wound
some scoundrelly nigger had given him who did not understand
his philanthropic intentions. Captain Nichols played but a minor
part in *The Moon and Sixpence*, but soon after I finished that book
I became aware that I was not finished with him. I went on
thinking about him and when the manuscript came back from the
typist and I was correcting errors, I was struck by an incident which
in the course of conversation he had related to me and which I had
set down as nearly as I could in his own words. It was an account
of a long cruise he had taken in the Eastern seas under peculiar
circumstances. It occupied only a page of my handwriting. As I
read it over then it was borne in upon me that here was the idea for
a novel and the more I thought of it the more I liked it. By the
time the proofs of *The Moon and Sixpence* reached me I had made
up my mind to write it and so cut out the passage in question. It
was on the foundation of that single page that twelve years later I
wrote *The Narrow Corner*.

LIZA OF LAMBETH

Liza of Lambeth

CHAPTER I

It was the first Saturday afternoon in August; it had been broiling hot all day, with a cloudless sky, and the sun had been beating down on the houses, so that the top rooms were like ovens; but now with the approach of evening it was cooler, and everyone in Vere Street was out of doors.

Vere Street, Lambeth, is a short, straight street leading out of the Westminster Bridge Road; it has forty houses on one side and forty houses on the other, and these eighty houses are very much more like one another than ever peas are like peas, or young ladies like young ladies. They are newish, three-storeyed buildings of dingy grey brick with slate roofs, and they are perfectly flat, without a bow-window or even a projecting cornice or window-sill to break the straightness of the line from one end of the street to the other.

This Saturday afternoon the street was full of life; no traffic came down Vere Street, and the cemented space between the pavements was given up to children. Several games of cricket were being played by wildly excited boys, using coats for wickets, an old tennis-ball or a bundle of rags tied together for a ball, and, generally, an old broomstick for bat. The wicket was so large and the bat so small that the man in was always getting bowled, when heated quarrels would arise, the batter absolutely refusing to go out and the bowler absolutely insisting on going in. The girls were more peaceable; they were chiefly employed in skipping, and only abused one another mildly when the rope was not properly turned or the skipper did not jump sufficiently high. Worst off of all were the very young children, for there had been no rain for weeks, and the street was as dry and clean as a covered court, and, in the lack of mud to wallow in, they sat about the road, disconsolate as poets. The number of babies was prodigious; they sprawled about everywhere, on the pavement, round the doors, and about their mothers' skirts. The grown-ups were gathered round the open doors; there were usually two women squatting

1

on the doorstep, and two or three more seated on either side on chairs; they were invariably nursing babies, and most of them showed clear signs that the present object of the maternal care would be soon ousted by a new arrival. Men were less numerous but such as there were leant against the walls, smoking, or sat on the sills of the ground-floor windows. It was the dead season in Vere Street as much as in Belgravia, and really if it had not been for babies just come or just about to come, and an opportune murder in a neighbouring doss-house, there would have been nothing whatever to talk about. As it was, the little groups talked quietly, discussing the atrocity or the merits of the local midwives, comparing the circumstances of their various confinements.

"You'll be 'avin' your little trouble soon, eh, Polly?" asked one good lady of another.

"Oh, I reckon I've got another two months ter go yet," answered Polly.

"Well," said a third, "I wouldn't 'ave thought you'd go so long by the look of yer!"

"I 'ope you'll have it easier this time, my dear," said a very stout old person, a woman of great importance.

"She said she wasn't goin' to 'ave no more, when the last one come." This remark came from Polly's husband.

"Ah," said the stout old lady, who was in the business, and boasted vast experience. "That's wot they all says; but, Lor' bless yer, they don't mean it."

"Well, I've got three, and I'm not goin' to 'ave no more, bli'me if I will; 'tain't good enough—that's wot I says."

"You're abaht right there, ole gal," said Polly. "My word, 'Arry, if you 'ave any more I'll git a divorce, that I will."

At that moment an organ-grinder turned the corner and came down the street.

"Good biz; 'ere's an organ!" cried half a dozen people at once.

The organ-man was an Italian, with a shock of black hair and a ferocious moustache. Drawing his organ to a favourable spot, he stopped, released his shoulder from the leather straps by which he dragged it, and cocking his large soft hat on the side of his head, began turning the handle. It was a lively tune, and in less than no time a little crowd had gathered round to listen, chiefly the young men and the maidens, for the married ladies were never in a fit state to dance, and therefore disinclined to trouble themselves to stand round the organ. There was a moment's hesitation at opening the ball; then one girl said to another:

"Come on, Florrie, you and me ain't shy; we'll begin, and bust it!"

The two girls took hold of one another, one acting gentleman, the other lady; three or four more pairs of girls immediately joined them, and they began a waltz. They held themselves very upright; and with an air of grave dignity which was quite impressive glided slowly about, making their steps with the utmost precision, bearing themselves with sufficient decorum for a court ball. After a while the men began to itch for a turn, and two of them, taking hold of one another in the most approved fashion, waltzed round the circle with the gravity of judges.

All at once there was a cry: "There's Liza!" And several members of the group turned and called out: "Oo, look at Liza!"

The dancers stopped to see the sight, and the organ-grinder, having come to the end of his tune, ceased turning the handle and looked to see what was the excitement.

"Oo, Liza!" they called out. "Look at Liza; oo, I sy!"

It was a young girl of about eighteen, with dark eyes, and an enormous fringe, puffed-out and curled and frizzed, covering her whole forehead from side to side, and coming down to meet her eyebrows. She was dressed in brilliant violet, with great lappets of velvet, and she had on her head an enormous black hat covered with feathers.

"I sy, ain't she got up dossy?" called out the groups at the doors, as she passed.

"Dressed ter death, and kill the fashion; that's wot I calls it."

Liza saw what a sensation she was creating; she arched her back and lifted her head, and walked down the street, swaying her body from side to side, and swaggering along as though the whole place belonged to her.

" 'Ave yer bought the street, Bill?" shouted one youth; and then half a dozen burst forth at once, as if by inspiration:

"Knocked 'em in the Old Kent Road!"

It was immediately taken up by a dozen more, and they all yelled it out:

"Knocked 'em in the Old Kent Road. Yah, ah, knocked 'em in the Old Kent Road!"

"Oo, Liza!" they shouted; the whole street joined in, and they gave long, shrill, ear-piercing shrieks and strange calls, that rung down the street and echoed back again.

"Hextra special!" called out a wag.

"Oh, Liza! Oo! Ooo!" yells and whistles, and then it thundered forth again:

"Knocked 'em in the Old Kent Road!"

Liza put on the air of a conquering hero, and sauntered on, enchanted at the uproar. She stuck out her elbows and jerked her head on one side, and said to herself as she passed through the bellowing crowd:

"This is jam!"

"Knocked 'em in the Old Kent Road!"

When she came to the group round the barrel-organ, one of the girls cried out to her:

"Is that yer new dress, Liza?"

"Well, it don't look like my old one, do it?" said Liza.

"Where did yer git it?" asked another friend, rather enviously.

"Picked it up in the street, of course!" scornfully answered Liza.

"I believe it's the same one as I saw in the pawnbroker's dahn the Road," said one of the men, to tease her.

"Thet's it; but wot was you doin' in there? Pledgin' yer shirt, or was it yer trousers?"

"Yah, I wouldn't git a second-'and dress at a pawnbroker's!"

"Garn!" said Liza indignantly. "I'll swipe yer over the snitch if yer talk ter me. I got the mayterials in the West Hend, didn't I? And I 'ad it mide up by my Court Dressmiker, so you jolly well dry up, old jelly-belly."

"Garn!" was the reply.

Liza had been so intent on her new dress and the comment it was exciting that she had not noticed the organ.

"Oo, I say, let's 'ave some dancin'," she said as soon as she saw it. "Come on, Sally," she added, to one of the girls, "you an' me'll dance togither. Grind away, old cock!"

The man turned on a new tune, and the organ began to play the Intermezzo from the *Cavalleria*; other couples quickly followed Liza's example, and they began to waltz round with the same solemnity as before; but Liza outdid them all; if the others were as stately as queens, she was as stately as an empress; the gravity and dignity with which she waltzed were something appalling, you felt that the minuet was a frolic in comparison; it would have been a fitting measure to tread round the grave of a *première danseuse,* or at the funeral of a professional humorist. And the graces she put on, the languor of the eyes, the contemptuous curl of the lips, the exquisite turn of the hand, the dainty arching of the foot! You felt there could be no questioning her right to the tyranny of Vere Street.

Suddenly she stopped short, and disengaged herself from her companion.

"Oh, I sy," she said, "this is too bloomin' slow; it gives me the sick."

That is not precisely what she said, but it is impossible always to give the exact unexpurgated words of Liza and the other personages of the story; the reader is therefore entreated with his thoughts to piece out the necessary imperfections of the dialogue.

"It's too bloomin' slow," she said again; "it gives me the sick. Let's 'ave somethin' a bit more lively than this 'ere waltz. You stand over there, Sally, an' we'll show 'em 'ow ter skirt-dance."

They all stopped waltzing.

"Talk of the ballet at the Canterbury and the South London. You just wite till you see the ballet at Vere Street, Lambeth—we'll knock 'em!"

She went up to the organ-grinder.

"Na then, Italiano," she said to him, "you buck up; give us a tune that's got some guts in it! See?"

She caught hold of his big hat and squashed it down over his eyes. The man grinned from ear to ear, and, touching the little catch at the side, began to play a lively tune such as Liza had asked for.

The men had fallen out, but several girls had put themselves in position, in couples, standing face to face; and immediately the music struck up, they began. They held up their skirts on each side, so as to show their feet, and proceeded to go through the difficult steps and motions of the dance. Liza was right; they could not have done it better in a trained ballet. But the best dancer of them all was Liza; she threw her whole soul into it; forgetting the stiff bearing which she had thought proper to the waltz, and casting off its elaborate graces, she gave herself up entirely to the present pleasure. Gradually the other couples stood aside, so that Liza and Sally were left alone. They paced it carefully, watching each other's steps, and as if by instinct performing corresponding movements, so as to make the whole a thing of symmetry.

"I'm abaht done," said Sally, blowing and puffing. "I've 'ad enough of it."

"Go on, Liza!" cried out a dozen voices when Sally stopped.

She gave no sign of having heard them other than calmly to continue her dance. She glided through the steps, and swayed about, and manipulated her skirt, all with the most charming grace imaginable; then, the music altering, she changed the style of her dancing, her feet moved more quickly, and did not keep so strictly to the ground. She was getting excited at the admiration of the onlookers, and her dance grew wilder and more daring. She lifted her skirts higher, brought in new and more difficult movements into her improvisation, kicking up her legs she did the wonderful twist, backwards and forwards, of which the dancer is proud.

"Look at 'er legs!" cried one of the men.

"Look at 'er stockin's!" shouted another; and indeed they were remarkable, for Liza had chosen them of the same brilliant hue as her dress, and was herself most proud of the harmony.

Her dance became gayer: her feet scarcely touched the ground, she whirled round madly.

"Tike care yer don't split!" cried out one of the wags, at a very audacious kick.

The words were hardly out of his mouth when Liza, with a gigantic effort, raised her foot and kicked off his hat. The feat was greeted with applause, and she went on, making turns and twists, flourishing her skirts, kicking higher and higher, and finally, among a volley of shouts, fell on her hands and turned head over heels in a magnificent catharine-wheel; then scrambling to her feet again, she tumbled into the arms of a young man standing in the front of the ring.

"That's right, Liza," he said. "Give us a kiss, now," and promptly tried to take one.

"Git aht!" said Liza, pushing him away, not too gently.

"Yus, give us a kiss," cried another, running up to her.

"I'll smack yer in the fice!" said Liza, elegantly, as she dodged him.

"Ketch 'old on 'er, Bill," cried out a third, "an' we'll all kiss her."

"Na, you won't!" shrieked Liza, beginning to run.

"Come on," they cried, "we'll ketch 'er."

She dodged in and out, between their legs, under their arms, and then, getting clear of the little crowd, caught up her skirts so that they might not hinder her, and took to her heels along the street. A score of men set in chase, whistling, shouting, yelling; the people at the doors looked up to see the fun, and cried out to her as she dashed past; she ran like the wind. Suddenly a man from the side darted into the middle of the road, stood straight in her way, and before she knew where she was, she had jumped shrieking into his arms, and he, lifting her up to him, had imprinted two sounding kisses on her cheeks.

"Oh, you ——!" she said. Her expression was quite unprintable; nor can it be euphemised.

There was a shout of laughter from the bystanders, and the young men in chase of her, and Liza, looking up, saw a big, bearded man whom she had never seen before. She blushed to the very roots of her hair, quickly extricated herself from his arms, and, amid the jeers and laughter of everyone, slid into the door of the nearest house and was lost to view.

CHAPTER II

LIZA and her mother were having supper. Mrs. Kemp was an elderly woman, short, and rather stout, with a red face, and grey hair brushed tight back over her forehead. She had been a widow for many years, and since her husband's death had lived with Liza in the ground-floor front room in which they were now sitting. Her husband had been a soldier, and from a grateful country she received a pension large enough to keep her from starvation, and by charing and doing such odd jobs as she could get she earned a little extra to supply herself with liquor. Liza was able to make her own living by working at a factory.

Mrs. Kemp was rather sulky this evening.

"Wot was yer doin' this afternoon, Liza?" she asked.

"I was in the street."

"You're always in the street when I want yer."

"I didn't know as 'ow yer wanted me, Mother," answered Liza.

"Well, yer might 'ave come ter see! I might 'ave been dead, for all you knew."

Liza said nothing.

"My rheumatics was that bad to-dy thet I didn't know wot

ter do with myself. The doctor said I was to be rubbed with that there stuff 'e give me, but yer won't never do nothin' for me."

"Well, Mother," said Liza, "your rheumatics was all right yesterday."

"I know wot you was doin'; you was showin' off thet new dress of yours. Pretty waste of money thet is, instead of givin' it me ter sive up. An' for the matter of thet, I wanted a new dress far worse than you did. But, of course, I don't matter."

Liza did not answer, and Mrs. Kemp, having nothing more to say, continued her supper in silence.

It was Liza who spoke next.

"There's some new people moved in the street. 'Ave you seen 'em?" she asked.

"Na, wot are they?"

"I dunno; I've seen a chap, a big chap with a beard. I think 'e lives up at the other end."

She felt herself blushing a little.

"No one any good you be sure," said Mrs. Kemp. "I can't swaller these new people as are comin' in; the street ain't wot it was when I fust come."

When they had done, Mrs. Kemp got up, and having finished her half-pint of beer, said to her daughter:

"Put the things awy, Liza. I'm just goin' round to see Mrs. Clayton; she's just 'ad twins, and she 'ad nine before these come. It's a pity the Lord don't see fit ter tike some on 'em—thet's wot I say."

After which pious remark Mrs. Kemp went out of the house and turned into another a few doors up.

Liza did not clear the supper things away as she was told, but opened the window and drew her chair to it. She leant on the sill, looking out into the street. The sun had set, and it was twilight, the sky was growing dark, bringing to view the twinkling stars; there was no breeze, but it was pleasantly and restfully cool. The good folk still sat at their doorsteps, talking as before on the same inexhaustible subjects, but a little subdued with the approach of night. The boys were still playing cricket, but they were mostly at the other end of the street, and their shouts were muffled before they reached Liza's ears.

She sat, leaning her head on her hands, breathing in the fresh air and feeling a certain exquisite sense of peacefulness which she was not used to. It was Saturday evening, and she thankfully remembered that there would be no factory on the morrow; she was glad to rest. Somehow she felt a little tired, perhaps it was through the excitement of the afternoon, and she enjoyed the quietness of the evening. It seemed so tranquil and still; the silence filled her with a strange delight, she felt as if she could sit there all through the night looking out into the cool, dark street, and up heavenwards at the stars. She was very happy, but yet at the same time experienced a strange new sensation of melancholy, and she almost wished to cry.

Suddenly a dark form stepped in front of the open window. She gave a little shriek.

" 'Oo's thet?" she asked, for it was quite dark, and she did not recognise the man standing in front of her.

"Me, Liza," was the answer.

"Tom?"

"Yus!"

It was a young man with light yellow hair and a little fair moustache, which made him appear almost boyish; he was light-complexioned and blue-eyed, and had a frank and pleasant look mingled with a curious bashfulness that made him blush when people spoke to him.

"Wot's up?" asked Liza.

"Come aht for a walk, Liza, will yer?"

"No!" she answered decisively.

"You promised ter yesterday, Liza."

"Yesterday an' ter-day's two different things," was her wise reply.

"Yus, come on, Liza."

"Na, I tell yer, I won't."

"I want ter talk ter yer, Liza." Her hand was resting on the window-sill, and he put his upon it. She quickly drew it back.

"Well, I don't want yer ter talk ter me."

But she did, for it was she who broke the silence.

"Say, Tom, 'oo are them new folk as 'as come into the street? It's a big chap with a brown beard."

"D'you mean the bloke as kissed yer this afternoon?"

Liza blushed again.

"Well, why shouldn't 'e kiss me?" she said, with some inconsequence.

"I never said as 'ow 'e shouldn't; I only arst yer if it was the sime."

"Yus, thet's 'oo I mean."

" 'Is nime is Blakeston—Jim Blakeston. I've only spoke to 'im once; he's took the two top rooms at No. 19 'ouse."

"Wot's 'e want two top rooms for?"

" 'Im? Oh, 'e's got a big family—five kids. Ain't yer seen 'is wife abaht the street? She's a big, fat woman, as does 'er 'air funny."

"I didn't know 'e 'ad a wife."

There was another silence; Liza sat thinking, and Tom stood at the window, looking at her.

"Won't yer come aht with me, Liza?" he asked, at last.

"Na, Tom," she said, a little more gently, "it's too lite."

"Liza," he said, blushing to the roots of his hair.

"Well?"

"Liza"—he couldn't go on, and stuttered in his shyness— "Liza, I—I—I loves yer, Liza."

"Garn awy!"

He was quite brave now, and took hold of her hand.

"Yer know, Liza, I'm earnin' twenty-three shillin's at the works now, an' I've got some furniture as Mother left me when she was took."

The girl said nothing.

"Liza, will you 'ave me? I'll make yer a good 'usband, Liza, swop me bob, I will; an' yer know I'm not a drinkin' sort. Liza, will yer marry me?"

"Na, Tom," she answered quietly.

"Oh, Liza, won't you 'ave me?"

"Na, Tom, I can't."

"Why not? You've come aht walkin' with me since Whitsun."

"Ah, things is different now."

"You're not walkin' aht with anybody else, are you, Liza?" he asked quickly.

"Na, not that."

"Well, why won't yer, Liza? Oh, Liza, I do love yer; I've never loved anybody as I love you!"

"Oh, I can't, Tom!"

"There ain't no one else?"

"Na."

"Then why not?"

"I'm very sorry, Tom, but I don't love yer so as ter marry yer."

"Oh, Liza!"

She could not see the look upon his face, but she heard the agony in his voice; and, moved with sudden pity, she bent out, threw her arms round his neck, and kissed him on both cheeks.

"Never mind, old chap!" she said. "I'm not worth troublin' abaht."

And quickly drawing back, she slammed the window to, and moved into the further part of the room.

CHAPTER III

THE following day was Sunday. Liza, when she was dressing herself in the morning, felt the hardness of fate in the impossibility of eating one's cake and having it; she wished she had reserved her new dress and had still before her the sensation of a first appearance in it. With a sigh she put on her ordinary everyday working dress, and proceeded to get the breakfast ready, for her mother had been out late the previous night, celebrating the new arrivals in the street, and had the "rheumatics" this morning.

"Oo, my 'ead!" she was saying, as she pressed her hands on each side of her forehead. "I've got the neuralgy again; wot shall I do? I dunno 'ow it is, but it always comes on Sunday mornings. Oo, an' my rheumatics, they give me sich a doin' in the night!"

"You'd better go to the 'orspital, Mother."

"Not I!" answered the worthy lady, with great decision. "You 'as a dozen young chaps messin' you abaht, and lookin' at yer; and then they tells yer ter leave off beer and spirrits. Well, wot I says, I says I can't do withaht my glass of beer." She thumped her pillow to emphasise the statement.

"Wot with the work I 'ave ter do, lookin' after you and the cookin' and gettin' everythin' ready and doin' all the 'ousework, and goin' aht charing besides—well, I says, if I don't 'ave a drop of beer, I says, ter pull me together, I should be under the turf in no time."

She munched her bread-and-butter and drank her tea.

"When you've done breakfast, Liza," she said, "you can give the grate a cleanin', an' my boots'd do with a bit of polishin'. Mrs. Tike, in the next 'ouse, 'll give yer some blackin'."

She remained silent for a bit, then said:

"I don't think I shall get up ter-day, Liza. My rheumatics is bad. You can put the room straight and cook the dinner."

"Arright, Mother; you stay where you are, an' I'll do everythin' for yer."

"Well, it's only wot yer ought to do, considerin' all the trouble you've been ter me when you was young, and considerin' thet when you was born the doctor thought I never should get through it. Wot 'ave you done with your week's money, Liza?"

"Oh, I've put it awy," answered Liza quietly.

"Where?" asked her mother.

"Where it'll be safe."

"Where's that?"

Liza was driven into a corner.

"Why d'you want ter know?" she asked.

"Why shouldn't I know; d'you think I want ter steal it from yer?"

"Na, not thet."

"Well, why won't you tell me?"

"Oh, a thing's sifer when only one person knows where it is."

This was a very discreet remark, but it set Mrs. Kemp in a whirlwind of passion. She raised herself and sat up in the bed, flourishing her clenched fist at her daughter.

"I know wot yer mean, you—you!" Her language was emphatic, her epithets picturesque, but too forcible for reproduction. "You think I'd steal it," she went on. "I know yer! D'yer think I'd go an' tike yer dirty money?"

"Well, Mother," said Liza, "when I've told yer before, the money's perspired like."

"Wot d'yer mean?"

"It got less."

"Well, I can't 'elp thet, can I? Anyone can come in 'ere and tike the money."

"If it's 'idden awy, they can't, can they, Mother?" said Liza.

Mrs. Kemp shook her fist.

"You dirty slut, you," she said, "yer think I tike yer money! Why, you ought ter give it me every week instead of savin' it up and spendin' it on all sorts of muck, while I 'ave ter grind my very bones down to keep yer."

"Yer know, Mother, if I didn't 'ave a little bit saved up, we should be rather short when you're dahn in yer luck."

Mrs. Kemp's money always ran out on Tuesday, and Liza had to keep things going till the following Saturday.

"Oh, don't talk ter me!" proceeded Mrs. Kemp. "When I was a girl I give all my money ter my mother. She never 'ad ter ask me for nothin'. On Saturday when I come 'ome with my wiges, I give it 'er every farthin'. That's wot a daughter ought ter do. I can say this for myself, I be'aved by my mother like a gal should. None of your prodigal sons for me! She didn't 'ave ter ask me for three 'apence ter git a drop of beer."

Liza was wise in her generation; she held her tongue, and put on her hat.

"Now, you're goin' aht, and leavin' me; I dunno wot you get up to in the street with all those men. No good, I'll be bound. An' 'ere am I left all alone, an' I might die for all you care."

In her sorrow at herself the old lady began to cry, and Liza slipped out of the room and into the street.

Leaning against the wall of the opposite house was Tom; he came towards her.

" 'Ulloa!" she said, as she saw him. "Wot are you doin' 'ere?"

"I was waitin' for you ter come aht, Liza," he answered.

She looked at him quickly.

"I ain't comin' aht with yer ter-day, if thet's wot yer mean," she said.

"I never thought of arskin' yer, Liza—after wot you said ter me last night."

His voice was a little sad, and she felt so sorry for him.

"But yer did want ter speak ter me, didn't yer, Tom?" she said, more gently.

"You've got a day off ter-morrow, ain't yer?"

"Bank 'Oliday. Yus! Why?"

"Why, 'cause they've got a drag startin' from the 'Red Lion' that's goin' down ter Chingford for the day—an' I'm goin'."

"Yus!" she said.

He looked at her doubtfully.

"Will yer come too, Liza? It'll be a regular beeno; there's only goin' ter be people in the street. Eh, Liza?"

"Na, I can't."

"Why not?"

"I ain't got—I ain't got the ooftish."

"I mean, won't yer come with me?"

"Na, Tom, thank yer; I can't do thet neither."

"Yer might as well, Liza; it wouldn't 'urt yer."

"Na, it wouldn't be right like; I can't come aht with yer, and then mean nothin'! It would be doin' yer aht of an outing."

"I don't see why," he said, very crestfallen.

"I can't go on keepin' company with you—after what I said last night."

"I shan't enjoy it a bit without you, Liza."

"You git somebody else, Tom. You'll do withaht me all right."

She nodded to him, and walked up the street to the house of her friend Sally. Having arrived in front of it, she put her hands to her mouth in trumpet form, and shouted:

" 'I! 'I! 'I! Sally!"

A couple of fellows standing by copied her.

" 'I! 'I! 'I! Sally!"

"Garn!" said Liza, looking round at them.

Sally did not appear, and she repeated her call. The men imitated her, and half a dozen took it up, so that there was enough noise to wake the seven sleepers.

" 'I! 'I! 'I! Sally!"

A head was put out of a top window, and Liza, taking off her hat, waved it, crying:

"Come on dahn, Sally!"

"Arright, old gal!" shouted the other. "I'm comin'!"

"So's Christmas!" was Liza's repartee.

There was a clatter down the stairs, and Sally, rushing through the passage, threw herself on to her friend. They began fooling, in reminiscence of a melodrama they had lately seen together.

"Oh, my darlin' duck!" said Liza, kissing her and pressing her, with affected rapture, to her bosom.

"My sweetest sweet!" replied Sally, copying her.

"An' 'ow does your lidyship ter-day?"

"Oh!"—with immense languor—"fust class; and is your royal 'ighness quite well?"

"I deeply regret," answered Liza, "but my royal 'ighness 'as got the collywobbles."

Sally was a small, thin girl, with sandy hair and blue eyes, and a very freckled complexion. She had an enormous mouth, with terrible, square teeth set wide apart, which looked as if they could masticate an iron bar. She was dressed like Liza, in a shortish black skirt and an old-fashioned bodice, green and grey and yellow with age; her sleeves were tucked up to the elbow, and she wore a singularly dirty apron, that had once been white.

"Wot 'ave you got yer 'air in them things for?" asked Liza, pointing to the curl-papers. "Goin' aht with yer young man ter-day?"

"Na, I'm going ter stay 'ere all day."

"Wot for, then?"

"Why, 'Arry's going ter tike me ter Chingford ter-morrer."

"Oh? In the 'Red Lion' brake?"

"Yus. Are you goin'?"

"Na!"

"Not! Well, why don't you get round Tom? 'E'll tike yer, and jolly glad 'e'll be, too."

" 'E arst me ter go with 'im, but I wouldn't."

"Swop me bob—why not?"

"I ain't keepin' company with 'im."

"Yer might 'ave gone with 'im all the sime."

"Na. You're goin' with 'Arry, ain't yer?"

"Yus!"

"An' you're goin' to 'ave 'im?"

"Right again!"

"Well, I couldn't go with Tom, an' then throw 'im over."

"Well, you are a mug!"

The two girls had strolled down towards the Westminster Bridge Road, and Sally, meeting her young man, had gone to him. Liza walked back, wishing to get home in time to cook the dinner. But she went slowly, for she knew every dweller in the street, and as she passed the groups sitting at their doors, as on the previous evening, but this time mostly engaged in peeling potatoes or shelling peas, she stopped and had a little chat. Everyone liked her, and was glad to have her company. "Good old Liza," they would say, as she left them, "she's a rare good sort, ain't she?"

She asked after the aches and pains of all the old people, and delicately inquired after the babies, past and future; the children hung on to her skirts and asked her to play with them, and she would hold one end of the rope while tiny little ragged girls skipped, invariably entangling themselves after two jumps.

She had nearly reached home, when she heard a voice cry:

"Mornin'!"

She looked round and recognised the man whom Tom had told her was called Jim Blakeston. He was sitting on a stool at the door of one of the houses, playing with two young children, to whom he was giving rides on his knee. She remembered his heavy brown beard from the day before, and she had also an impression of great size; she noticed this morning that he was, in fact, a big man, tall and broad, and she saw besides that he had large masculine features and pleasant brown eyes. She supposed him to be about forty.

"Mornin'!" he said again, as she stopped and looked at him.

Liza blushed scarlet, and was too confused to answer.

"Well, yer needn't look as if I was goin' ter eat yer up, 'cause I ain't," he said.

" 'Oo are you? I'm not afeard of yer."

"Wot are yer so bloomin' red abaht?" he asked pointedly.

"Well, I'm 'ot."

"You ain't shirty 'cause I kissed yer last night?"

"I'm not shirty; but it was pretty cool, considerin' like as I didn't know yer."

"Well, you run into my arms."

"Thet I didn't; you run aht and caught me."

"An' kissed yer before you could say 'Jack Robinson'." He laughed at the thought. "Well, Liza," he went on, "seein' as 'ow I kissed yer against yer will, the best thing you can do ter make it up is to kiss me not against yer will."

"Me?" said Liza, looking at him, open-mouthed. "Well, you are a pill!"

The children began to clamour for the riding, which had been discontinued on Liza's approach.

"Are them your kids?" she asked.

"Yes; them's two on 'em."

" 'Ow many 'ave yer got?"

"Five; the eldest gal's fifteen, and the next one 'oo's a boy's twelve, and then there are these two and baby."

"Well, you've got enough for your money."

"Too many for me—and more comin'."

"Ah, well," said Liza, laughing, "thet's your fault, ain't it?"

Then she bade him good-morning, and strolled off.

He watched her as she went, and saw half a dozen little boys surround her and beg her to join them in their game of cricket. They caught hold of her arms and skirts, and pulled her to their pitch.

"Na, I can't," she said, trying to disengage herself. "I've got the dinner ter cook."

"Dinner ter cook?" shouted one small boy. "Why, they always cooks the cats' meat at the shop."

"You little so-and-so!" said Liza, somewhat inelegantly, making a dash at him.

He dodged her and gave a whoop; then turning he caught her round the legs, and another boy catching hold of her round the neck they dragged her down, and all three struggled on the ground, rolling over and over; the other boys threw themselves on the top, so that there was a great heap of legs and arms and heads waving and bobbing up and down.

Liza extricated herself with some difficulty, and taking off her hat she began cuffing the boys with it, using all the time the most lively expressions. Then, having cleared the field, she retired victorious into her own house and began cooking the dinner.

CHAPTER IV

BANK HOLIDAY was a beautiful day: the cloudless sky threatened a stifling heat for noontide, but early in the morning, when Liza got out of bed and threw open the window, it was fresh and cool. She dressed herself, wondering how she should spend her day; she thought of Sally going off to Chingford with her lover, and of herself remaining alone in the dull street with half the people away. She almost wished it were an ordinary work-day, and that there were no such things as bank holidays. And it seemed to be a little like two Sundays running, but with the second rather worse than the first. Her mother was still sleeping, and she was in no great hurry about getting the breakfast, but stood quietly looking out of the window at the house opposite.

In a little while she saw Sally coming along. She was arrayed in purple and fine linen—a very smart red dress, trimmed with velveteen, and a tremendous hat covered with feathers. She had reaped the benefit of keeping her hair in curl-papers since Saturday, and her sandy fringe stretched from ear to ear. She was in enormous spirits.

" 'Ulloa, Liz!" she called as soon as she saw her at the window.

Liza looked at her a little enviously.

" 'Ulloa!" she answered quietly.

"I'm just goin' to the 'Red Lion' to meet 'Arry."

"At what time d'yer start?"

"The brake leaves at 'alf-past eight sharp."

"Why, it's only eight; it's only just struck at the church. 'Arry won't be there yet, will he?"

"Oh, 'e's sure ter be early. I couldn't wite. I've been witin' abaht since 'alf-past six. I've been up since five this morning."

"Since five! What 'ave you been doin'?"

"Dressin' myself and doin' my 'air. I woke up so early. I've been dreamin' all the night abaht it. I simply couldn't sleep."

"Well, you are a caution!" said Liza.

"Bust it, I don't go on the spree every day! Oh, I do 'ope I shall enjoy myself."

"Why, you simply dunno where you are!" said Liza, a little crossly.

"Don't you wish you was comin', Liza?" asked Sally.

"Na! I could if I liked, but I don't want ter."

"You are a coughdrop—thet's all I can say. Ketch me refusin' when I 'ave the chanst."

"Well, it's done now. I ain't got the chanst any more." Liza said this with just a little regret in her voice.

"Come on dahn to the 'Red Lion', Liza, and see us off," said Sally.

"No, I'm damned if I do!" answered Liza, with some warmth.

"You might as well. P'raps 'Arry won't be there, an' you can keep me company till 'e comes. An' you can see the 'orses."

Liza was really very anxious to see the brake and the horses and the people going; but she hesitated a little longer. Sally asked her once again. Then she said:

"Arright; I'll come with yer, and wite till the bloomin' old thing starts."

She did not trouble to put on a hat, but just walked out as she was, and accompanied Sally to the public-house which was getting up the expedition.

Although there was still nearly half an hour to wait, the brake was drawn up before the main entrance; it was large and long, with seats arranged crosswise, so that four people could sit on each; and it was drawn by two powerful horses, whose harness the coachman was now examining. Sally was not the first on the scene, for already half a dozen people had taken their places, but Harry had not yet arrived. The two girls stood by the public-house door, looking at the preparations. Huge baskets full of food

were brought out and stowed away; cases of beer were hoisted up
and put in every possible place—under the seats, under the driver's
legs, and even beneath the brake. As more people came up,
Sally began to get excited about Harry's non-appearance.

"I say, I wish 'e'd come!" she said. " 'E is lite."

Then she looked up and down the Westminster Bridge Road
to see if he was in view.

"Suppose 'e don't turn up! I will give it 'im when 'e comes for
keepin' me witin' like this."

"Why, there's a quarter of an hour yet," said Liza, who saw
nothing at all to get excited about.

At last Sally saw her lover, and rushed off to meet him. Liza
was left alone, rather disconsolate at all this bustle and preparation.
She was not sorry that she had refused Tom's invitation, but she
did wish that she had conscientiously been able to accept it. Sally
and her friend came up; attired in his Sunday best, he was a fit
match for his lady-love—he wore a shirt and collar, unusual
luxuries!—and he carried under his arm a concertina to make
things merry on the way.

"Ain't you goin', Liza?" he asked in surprise at seeing her without a hat and with her apron on.

"Na," said Sally, "ain't she a soft? Tom said 'e'd tike 'er, an'
she wouldn't."

"Well, I'm dashed!"

Then they climbed the ladder and took their seats, so that Liza
was left alone again. More people had come along, and the brake
was nearly full. Liza knew them all, but they were too busy taking
their places to talk to her. At last Tom came. He saw her standing
there and went up to her.

"Won't yer change yer mind, Liza, an' come along with us?"

"Na, Tom, I told yer I wouldn't—it's not right like." She felt
she must repeat that to herself often.

"I shan't enjoy it a bit without you," he said.

"Well, I can't 'elp it!" she answered, somewhat sullenly.

At that moment a man came out of the public-house with a
horn in his hand; her heart gave a great jump, for if there was anything she adored it was to drive along to the tootling of a horn.
She really felt it was very hard lines that she must stay at home
when all these people were going to have such a fine time; and
they were all so merry, and she could picture to herself so well the
delights of the drive and the picnic. She felt very much inclined

to cry. But she mustn't go, and she wouldn't go: she repeated that to herself twice as the trumpeter gave a preliminary tootle.

Two more people hurried along, and when they came near Liza saw that they were Jim Blakeston and a woman whom she supposed to be his wife.

"Are you comin', Liza?" Jim said to her.

"No," she answered. "I didn't know you was goin'."

"I wish you was comin'," he replied; "we shall 'ave a game."

She could only just keep back the sobs; she so wished she were going. It did seem hard that she must remain behind; and all because she wasn't going to marry Tom. After all, she didn't see why that should prevent her; there really was no need to refuse for that. She began to think she had acted foolishly: it didn't do anyone any good that she refused to go out with Tom, and no one thought it anything specially fine that she should renounce her pleasure. Sally merely thought her a fool.

Tom was standing by her side, silent, and looking disappointed and rather unhappy. Jim said to her, in a low voice:

"I am sorry you're not comin'!"

It was too much. She did want to go so badly, and she really couldn't resist any longer. If Tom would only ask her once more, and if she could only change her mind reasonably and decently, she would accept; but he stood silent, and she had to speak herself. It was very undignified.

"Yer know, Tom," she said, "I don't want ter spoil your day."

"Well, I don't think I shall go alone; it 'ud be so precious slow."

Supposing he didn't ask her again! What should she do? She looked up at the clock on the front of the pub, and noticed that it only wanted five minutes to the half-hour. How terrible it would be if the brake started and he didn't ask her! Her heart beat violently against her chest, and in her agitation she fumbled with the corner of her apron.

"Well, what can I do, Tom dear?"

"Why, come with me, of course. Oh, Liza, do say yes."

She had got the offer again, and it only wanted a little seemly hesitation, and the thing was done.

"I should like ter, Tom," she said. "But d'you think it 'ud be arright?"

"Yus, in course it would. Come on, Liza!" In his eagerness he clasped her hand.

"Well," she remarked, looking down, "if it'd spoil your 'oliday——"

"I won't go if you don't—swop me bob, I won't!" he answered.

"Well, if I come, it won't mean that I'm keepin' company with you."

"Na, it won't mean anythin' you don't like."

"Arright!" she said.

"You'll come?" he could hardly believe her.

"Yus!" she answered, smiling all over her face.

"You're a good sort, Liza! I say, 'Arry, Liza's comin'!" he shouted.

"Liza? 'Oorray!" shouted Harry.

" 'S'at right, Liza?" called Sally.

And Liza feeling quite joyful and light of heart called back: "Yus!"

" 'Oorray!" shouted Sally in answer.

"Thet's right, Liza," called Jim; and he smiled pleasantly as she looked at him.

"There's just room for you two 'ere," said Harry, pointing to the vacant places by his side.

"Arright!" said Tom.

"I must jest go an' get a 'at an' tell Mother," said Liza.

"There's just three minutes. Be quick!" answered Tom, and as she scampered off as hard as she could go, he shouted to the coachman: " 'Old 'ard; there's another passenger comin' in a minute."

"Arright, old cock," answered the coachman; "no 'urry!"

Liza rushed into the room, and called to her mother, who was still asleep:

"Mother! Mother! I'm going to Chingford!"

Then tearing off her old dress she slipped into her gorgeous violet one; she kicked off her old ragged shoes and put on her new boots. She brushed her hair down and rapidly gave her fringe a twirl and a twist—it was luckily still moderately in curl from the previous Saturday—and putting on her black hat with all the feathers, she rushed along the street, and scrambling up the brake steps fell panting on Tom's lap.

The coachman cracked his whip, the trumpeter tootled his horn, and with a cry and a cheer from the occupants, the brake clattered down the road.

CHAPTER V

As soon as Liza had recovered herself she started examining the people on the brake; and first of all she took stock of the woman whom Jim Blakeston had with him.

"This is my missus!" said Jim, pointing to her with his thumb.

"You ain't been dahn in the street much, 'ave yer?" said Liza, by way of making the acquaintance.

"Na," answered Mrs. Blakeston, "my youngest's been dahn with the measles, an' I've 'ad my work cut out lookin' after 'im."

"Oh, an' is 'e all right now?"

"Yus, 'e's gettin' on fine, an' Jim wanted ter go ter Chingford ter-day, an' 'e says ter me, well, 'e says, 'You come along ter Chingford, too; it'll do you good.' An' 'e says, 'You can leave Polly'—she's my eldest, yer know—'you can leave Polly,' says 'e, 'ter look after the kids.' So I says, 'Well, I don't mind if I do,' says I."

Meanwhile, Liza, was looking at her. First she noticed her dress: she wore a black cloak and a funny, old-fashioned black bonnet; then examining the woman herself, she saw a middle-sized, stout person anywhere between thirty and forty years old. She had a large, fat face with a big mouth, and her hair was curiously done, parted in the middle and plastered down on each side of the head in little plaits. One could see that she was a woman of great strength, notwithstanding evident traces of hard work and much child-bearing.

Liza knew all the other passengers, and now that everyone was settled down and had got over the excitement of departure, they had time to greet one another. They were delighted to have Liza among them, for where she was there was no dullness. Her attention was first of all taken up by a young coster who had arrayed himself in the traditional costume—grey suit, tight trousers, and shiny buttons in profusion.

"Wot cheer, Bill!" she cried to him.

"Wot cheer, Liza!" he answered.

"You are got up dossy; you'll knock 'em."

"Na then, Liza Kemp," said his companion, turning round with mock indignation, "you let my Johnny alone. If you come gettin' round 'im I'll give you wot for."

"Arright, Clary Sharp, I don't want 'im," answered Liza. "I've got one of my own, an' thet's a good 'andful—ain't it, Tom?"

Tom was delighted, and, unable to find a repartee, in his pleasure gave Liza a great nudge with his elbow.

" 'Oo, I say," said Liza, putting her hand to her side. "Tike care of my ribs; you'll brike 'em."

"Them's not yer ribs," shouted a candid friend—"them's yer whale-bones yer afraid of breakin'."

"Garn!"

" 'Ave yer got whale-bones?" said Tom, with affected simplicity, putting his arm round her waist to feel.

"Na then," she said, "keep off the grass!"

"Well, I only wanted ter know if you'd got any."

"Garn; yer don't git round me like thet."

He still kept as he was.

"Na then," she repeated, "tike yer 'and away. If yer touch me there you'll 'ave ter marry me."

"Thet's just wot I wants ter do, Liza!"

"Shut it!" she answered cruelly, and drew his arm away from her waist.

The horses scampered on, and the man behind blew his horn with vigour.

"Don't bust yerself, guv'nor!" said one of the passengers to him when he made a particularly discordant sound. They drove along eastwards, and as the hour grew later the streets became more filled and the traffic greater. At last they got on the road to Chingford, and caught up numbers of other vehicles going in the same direction—donkey-shays, pony-carts, tradesmen's carts, dog-carts, drags, brakes, every conceivable kind of wheeled thing, all filled with people, from the wretched donkey dragging along four solid rate-payers to the pair of stout horses easily managing a couple of score. They exchanged cheers and greetings as they passed, the "Red Lion" brake being noticeable above all for its uproariousness. As the day wore on the sun became hotter, and the road seemed more dusty and threw up a greater heat.

"I am getting 'ot!" was the common cry, and everyone began to puff and sweat.

The ladies removed their cloaks and capes, and the men, following their example, took off their coats and sat in their shirt-sleeves. Whereupon ensued much banter of a not particularly edifying kind respecting the garments which each person would like to remove—which showed that the innuendo of French farce is not so unknown to the upright, honest Englishman as might be supposed.

At last came in sight the half-way house, where the horses were to have a rest and a sponge down. They had been talking of it for the last quarter of a mile, and when at length it was observed on the top of a hill a cheer broke out, and some thirsty wag began to sing "Rule Britannia", whilst others burst forth with a different national ditty, "Beer, Glorious Beer!" They drew up before the pub entrance, and all climbed down as quickly as they could. The bar was besieged, and potmen and barmaids were quickly busy drawing beer and handing it over to the eager folk outside.

THE IDYLL OF CORYDON AND PHYLLIS.

Gallantry ordered that the faithful swain and the amorous shepherdess should drink out of one and the same pot.

" 'Urry up an' 'ave your whack," said Corydon, politely handing the foaming bowl for his fair one to drink from.

Phyllis, without replying, raised it to her lips and drank deep. The swain watched anxiously.

" 'Ere, give us a chanst!" he said, as the pot was raised higher and higher and its contents appeared to be getting less and less.

At this the amorous shepherdess stopped and handed the pot to her lover.

"Well, I'm dashed!" said Corydon, looking into it; and added: "I guess you know a thing or two." Then with courtly grace putting his own lips to the place where had been those of his beloved, finished the pint.

"Go' lumme!" remarked the shepherdess, smacking her lips, "that was somethin' like!" And she put out her tongue and licked her lips, and then breathed deeply.

The faithful swain, having finished, gave a long sigh, and said:

"Well, I could do with some more!"

"For the matter of thet, I could do with a gargle!"

Thus encouraged, the gallant returned to the bar, and soon brought out a second pint.

"You 'ave fust pop," amorously remarked Phyllis, and he took a long drink and handed the pot to her.

She, with maiden modesty, turned it so as to have a different part to drink from; but he remarked as he saw her:

"You are bloomin' particular."

Then, unwilling to grieve him, she turned it back again and applied her ruby lips to the place where his had been.

"Now we shan't be long!" she remarked, as she handed him back the pot.

The faithful swain took out of his pocket a short clay pipe, blew through it, filled it, and began to smoke, while Phyllis sighed at the thought of the cool liquid gliding down her throat, and with the pleasing recollection gently stroked her stomach. Then Corydon spat, and immediately his love said:

"I can spit farther than thet."

"I bet yer yer can't."

She tried, and did. He collected himself and spat again, further than before, she followed him, and in this idyllic contest they remained till the tootling horn warned them to take their places.

At last they reached Chingford, and here the horses were taken out and the drag, on which they were to lunch, drawn up in a sheltered spot. They were all rather hungry, but as it was not yet feeding-time they scattered to have drinks meanwhile. Liza and Tom, with Sally and her young man, went off together to the nearest public-house, and as they drank beer, Harry, who was a great sportsman, gave them a graphic account of a prize-fight he had seen on the previous Saturday evening, which had been rendered specially memorable by one man being so hurt that he had died from the effects. It had evidently been a very fine affair, and Harry said that several swells from the West End had been present, and he related their ludicrous efforts to get in without being seen by anyone, and their terror when someone to frighten them called out "Copper!" Then Tom and he entered into a discussion on the subject of boxing, in which Tom, being a shy and undogmatic sort of person, was entirely worsted. After this they strolled back to the brake, and found things being prepared for luncheon; the hampers were brought out and emptied, and the bottles of beer in great profusion made many a thirsty mouth thirstier.

"Come along, lidies an' gentlemen—if you are gentlemen," shouted the coachman; "the animals is now goin' ter be fed!"

"Garn awy," answered somebody, "we're not hanimals; we don't drink water."

"You're too clever," remarked the coachman; "I can see you've just come from the board school."

As the former speaker was a lady of quite mature appearance, the remark was not without its little irony. The other man blew his horn by way of grace, at which Liza called out to him:

"Don't do thet; you'll bust, I know you will, an' if you bust you'll quite spoil my dinner!"

Then they all set to. Pork-pies, saveloys, sausages, cold potatoes, hard-boiled eggs, cold bacon, veal, ham, crabs and shrimps, cheese, butter, cold suet-puddings and treacle, gooseberry-tarts, cherry-tarts, butter, bread, more sausages, and yet again pork-pies! They devoured the provisions like ravening beasts, stolidly, silently, earnestly, in large mouthfuls which they shoved down their throats unmasticated. The intelligent foreigner seeing them thus dispose of their food would have understood why England is a great nation. He would have understood why Britons never, never will be slaves. They never stopped except to drink, and then at each gulp they emptied their glass; no heel-taps! And still they ate, and still they drank—but as all things must cease, they stopped at last, and a long sigh of content broke from their two-and-thirty throats.

Then the gathering broke up, and the good folk paired themselves and separated. Harry and his lady strolled off to secluded byways in the forest, so that they might discourse of their loves and digest their dinner. Tom had all the morning been waiting for this happy moment; he had counted on the expansive effect of a full stomach to thaw his Liza's coldness, and he had pictured himself sitting on the grass with his back against the trunk of a spreading chestnut tree, with his arm round his Liza's waist, and her head resting affectionately on his manly bosom. Liza, too, had foreseen the separation into couples after dinner, and had been racking her brains to find a means of getting out of it.

"I don't want 'im slobberin' abaht me," she said; "it gives me the sick, all this kissin' an' cuddlin'!"

She scarcely knew why she objected to his caresses; but they bored her and made her cross. But luckily the blessed institution of marriage came to her rescue, for Jim and his wife naturally had no particular desire to spend the afternoon together, and Liza, seeing a little embarrassment on their part, proposed that they should go for a walk together in the forest.

Jim agreed at once, and with pleasure; but Tom was dreadfully disappointed. He hadn't the courage to say anything, but he glared at Blakeston. Jim smiled benignly at him, and Tom began to sulk. Then they began a funny walk through the woods. Jim tried to go on with Liza, and Liza was not at all disinclined to this, for she had come to the conclusion that Jim, notwithstanding his "cheek", was "not 'alf a bad sort". But Tom kept walking alongside of them, and as Jim slightly quickened his pace so as to get Liza on in front, Tom quickened his, and Mrs. Blakeston, who didn't want to be left behind, had to break into a little trot to keep up with them. Jim tried also to get Liza all to himself in the conversation, and let Tom see that he was out in the cold, but Tom would break in with cross, sulky remarks, just to make the others uncomfortable. Liza at last got rather vexed with him.

"Strikes me you got aht of bed the wrong way this mornin'," she said to him.

"Yer didn't think thet when yer said you'd come aht with me." He emphasised the "me".

Liza shrugged her shoulders.

"You give me the 'ump," she said. "If yer wants ter mike a fool of yerself, you can go elsewhere an' do it."

"I suppose yer want me ter go awy now," he said angrily.

"I didn't say I did."

"Arright, Liza, I won't stay where I'm not wanted." And turning on his heel he marched off, striking through the underwood into the midst of the forest.

He felt extremely unhappy as he wandered on, and there was a choky feeling in his throat as he thought of Liza: she was very unkind and ungrateful, and he wished he had never come to Chingford. She might so easily have come for a walk with him instead of going with that beast of a Blakeston; she wouldn't ever do anything for him, and he hated her—but all the same, he was a poor foolish thing in love, and he began to feel that perhaps he had been a little exacting and a little forward to take offence. And then he wished he had never said anything, and he wanted so much to see her and make it up. He made his way back to Chingford, hoping she would not make him wait too long.

Liza was a little surprised when Tom turned and left them.

"Wot 'as 'e got the needle abaht?" she said.

"Why, 'e's jealous," answered Jim, with a laugh.

"Tom jealous?"

"Yus; 'e's jealous of me."

"Well, 'e ain't got no cause ter be jealous of anyone—that 'e ain't!" said Liza, and continued by telling him all about Tom:

how he had wanted to marry her and she wouldn't have him, and how she had only agreed to come to Chingford with him on the understanding that she should preserve her entire freedom. Jim listened sympathetically, but his wife paid no attention; she was doubtless engaged in thought respecting her household or her family.

When they got back to Chingford they saw Tom standing in solitude looking at them. Liza was struck by the woebegone expression on his face; she felt she had been cruel to him, and leaving the Blakestons went up to him.

"I say, Tom," she said, "don't tike on so; I didn't mean it."

He was bursting to apologise for his behaviour.

"Yer know, Tom," she went on, "I'm rather 'asty, an' I'm sorry I said wot I did."

"Oh, Liza, you are good! You ain't cross with me?"

"Me? Na; it's you thet oughter be cross."

"You are a good sort, Liza!"

"You ain't vexed with me?"

"Give me Liza every time; that's wot I say," he answered, as his face lit up. "Come along an 'ave tea, an' then we'll go for a donkey-ride."

The donkey-ride was a great success. Liza was a little afraid at first, so Tom walked by her side to take care of her; she screamed the moment the beast began to trot, and clutched hold of Tom to save herself from falling, and as he felt her hand on his shoulder, and heard her appealing cry, "Oh, do 'old me! I'm fallin'!" he felt that he had never in his life been so deliciously happy. The whole party joined in, and it was proposed that they should have races; but in the first heat, when the donkeys broke into a canter, Liza fell off into Tom's arms and the donkey scampered on without her.

"I know wot I'll do," she said, when the runaway had been recovered, "I'll ride 'im straddlewyse."

"Garn!" said Sally, "yer can't with petticoats."

"Yus, I can; an' I will too!"

So another donkey was procured, this time with a man's saddle, and putting her foot in the stirrup, she cocked her leg over and took her seat triumphantly. Neither modesty nor bashfulness was to be reckoned among Liza's faults, and in this position she felt quite at ease.

"I'll git along arright now, Tom," she said; "you garn and git yerself a moke, and come an' jine in."

The next race was perfectly uproarious. Liza kicked and beat her donkey with all her might, shrieking and laughing the while, and finally came in winner by a length. After that they felt rather warm and dry, and repaired to the public-house to restore themselves and talk over the excitements of the racecourse.

When they had drunk several pints of beer Liza and Sally, with their respective adorers and the Blakestons, walked round to find other means of amusing themselves; they were arrested by a coconut-shy.

"Oh, let's 'ave a shy!" said Liza, excitedly, at which the unlucky men had to pull out their coppers, while Sally and Liza made ludicrously bad shots at the coconuts.

"It looks so bloomin' easy," said Liza, brushing up her hair, "but I can't 'it the blasted thing. You 'ave a shot, Tom."

He and Harry were equally unskilful, but Jim got three coconuts running, and the proprietors of the show began to look on him with some concern.

"You are a dab at it," said Liza, in admiration.

They tried to induce Mrs. Blakeston to try her luck, but she stoutly refused.

"I don't 'old with such foolishness. It's wiste of money ter me," she said.

"Na then, don't crack on, old tart," remarked her husband, "let's go an' eat the coconuts."

There was one for each couple, and after the ladies had sucked the juice they divided them and added their respective shares to their dinners and teas. Supper came next. Again they fell to sausage-rolls, boiled eggs, and saveloys, and countless bottles of beer were added to those already drunk.

"I dunno 'ow many bottles of beer I've drunk—I've lost count," said Liza; whereat there was a general laugh.

They still had an hour before the brake was to start back, and it was then the concertinas came in useful. They sat down on the grass, and the concert was begun by Harry, who played a solo; then there was a call for a song, and Jim stood up and sang that ancient ditty, "O dem Golden Kippers, O". There was no shyness in the company, and Liza, almost without being asked, gave another popular comic song. Then there was more concertina-playing, and another demand for a song. Liza turned to Tom, who was sitting quietly by her side.

"Give us a song, old cock," she said.

"I can't," he answered. "I'm not a singin' sort." At which Blakeston got up and offered to sing again.

"Tom is rather a soft," said Liza to herself, "not like that cove Blakeston."

They repaired to the public-house to have a few last drinks before the brake started, and when the horn blew to warn them, rather unsteadily, they proceeded to take their places.

Liza, as she scrambled up the steps, said: "Well, I believe I'm boozed."

The coachman had arrived at the melancholy stage of intoxication, and was sitting on his box holding his reins, with his head bent on his chest. He was thinking sadly of the long-lost days of his youth, and wishing he had been a better man.

Liza had no respect for such holy emotions, and she brought down her fist on the crown of his hat, and bashed it over his eyes.

"Na then, old jellybelly," she said, "wot's the good of 'avin' a fice as long as a kite?"

He turned round and smote her.

"Jellybelly yerself!" said he.

"Puddin' fice!" she cried.

"Kite fice!"

"Boss eye!"

She was tremendously excited, laughing and singing, keeping the whole company in an uproar. In her jollity she had changed hats with Tom, and he in her big feathers made her shriek with laughter. When they started they began to sing "For 'e's a jolly good feller," making the night resound with their noisy voices.

Liza and Tom and the Blakestons had got a seat together, Liza being between the two men. Tom was perfectly happy, and only wished that they might go on so for ever. Gradually as they drove along they became quieter, their singing ceased, and they talked in undertones. Some of them slept; Sally and her young man were leaning up against one another, slumbering quite peacefully. The night was beautiful, the sky still blue, very dark, scattered over with countless brilliant stars, and Liza, as she looked up at the heavens, felt a certain emotion, as if she wished to be taken in someone's arms, or feel some strong man's caresses; and there was in her heart a strange sensation as though it were growing big. She stopped speaking, and all four were silent. Then slowly she felt Tom's arm steal round her waist, cautiously, as though it were afraid of being there; this time both she and Tom were happy.

But suddenly there was a movement on the other side of her, a hand was advanced along her leg, and her hand was grasped and gently pressed. It was Jim Blakeston. She started a little and began trembling so that Tom noticed it, and whispered:

"You're cold, Liza."

"Na, I'm not, Tom; it's only a sort of shiver thet went through me."

His arm gave her waist a squeeze, and at the same time the big rough hand pressed her little one. And so she sat between them till they reached the "Red Lion" in the Westminster Bridge Road, and Tom said to himself: "I believe she does care for me after all."

When they got down they all said good-night, and Sally and Liza, with their respective slaves and the Blakestons, marched off homewards. At the corner of Vere Street Harry said to Tom and Blakeston:

"I say, you blokes, let's go an' 'ave another drink before closin' time."

"I don't mind," said Tom, "after we've took the gals 'ome."

"Then we shan't 'ave time; it's just on closin' time now," answered Harry.

"Well, we can't leave 'em 'ere."

"Yus, you can," said Sally. "No one'll run away with us."

Tom did not want to part from Liza, but she broke in with:

"Yus, go on, Tom. Sally an' me'll git along arright; an' you ain't got too much time."

"Yus, good-night, 'Arry," said Sally to settle the matter.

"Good-night, old gal," he answered, "give us another slobber."

And she, not at all unwilling, surrendered herself to him, while he imprinted two sounding kisses on her cheeks.

"Good-night, Tom," said Liza, holding out her hand.

"Good-night, Liza," he answered, taking it, but looking very wistfully at her.

She understood, and with a kindly smile lifted up her face to him. He bent down and, taking her in his arms, kissed her passionately.

"You do kiss nice, Liza," he said, making the others laugh.

"Thanks for tikin' me aht, old man," she said as they parted.

"Arright, Liza," he answered, and added, almost to himself: "God bless yer!"

" 'Ulloa, Blakeston, ain't you comin'?" said Harry, seeing that

Jim was walking off with his wife instead of joining him and Tom.

"Na," he answered, "I'm goin' 'ome. I've got ter be up at five ter-morrer."

"You are a chap!" said Harry, disgustedly, strolling off with Tom to the pub, while the others made their way down the sleeping street.

The house where Sally lived came first, and she left them; then, walking a few yards more, they came to the Blakestons', and after a little talk at the door Liza bade the couple good-night, and was left to walk the rest of the way alone. The street was perfectly silent, and the lamp-posts, far apart, threw a dim light which only served to make Liza realise her solitude. There was such a difference between the street at midday, with its swarms of people, and now, when there was neither sound nor soul besides herself, that even she was struck by it. The regular line of houses on either side, with the even pavements and straight, cemented road, seemed to her like some desert place, as if everyone were dead, or a fire had raged and left it all desolate. Suddenly she heard a footstep; she started and looked back. It was a man hurrying behind her, and in a moment she had recognised Jim. He beckoned to her, and in a low voice called:

"Liza!"

She stopped till he had come up to her.

"Wot 'ave yer come aht again for?" she said.

"I've come aht ter say good-night to you, Liza," he answered.

"But yer said good-night a moment ago."

"I wanted ter say it again—properly."

"Where's yer missus?"

"Oh, she's gone in. I said I was dry and was goin' ter 'ave a drink after all."

"But she'll know yer didn't go ter the pub."

"Na, she won't; she's gone straight upstairs to see after the kid. I wanted ter see yer alone, Liza."

"Why?"

He didn't answer, but tried to take hold of her hand. She drew it away quickly. They walked in silence till they came to Liza's house.

"Good-night," said Liza.

"Won't you come for a little walk, Liza?"

"Tike care no one 'ears you," she added, in a whisper, though why she whispered she did not know.

"Will yer?" he asked again.

"Na—you've got to get up at five."

"Oh, I only said thet not ter go inter the pub with them."

"So as yer might come 'ere with me?" asked Liza.

"Yus!"

"No, I'm not comin'. Good-night."

"Well, say good-night nicely."

"Wot d'yer mean?"

"Tom said you did kiss nice."

She looked at him without speaking, and in a moment he had clasped his arms round her, almost lifting her off her feet, and kissed her. She turned her face away.

"Give us yer lips, Liza," he whispered—"give us yer lips."

He turned her face without resistance and kissed her on the mouth.

At last she tore herself from him, and opening the door slid away into the house.

CHAPTER VI

NEXT morning on her way to the factory Liza came up with Sally. They were both of them rather stale and bedraggled after the day's outing; their fringes were ragged and untidily straying over their foreheads, their back hair, carelessly tied in a loose knot, fell over their necks and threatened completely to come down. Liza had not had time to put her hat on, and was holding it in her hand. Sally's was pinned on sideways, and she had to bash it down on her head every now and then to prevent its coming off. Cinderella herself was not more transformed than they were; but Cinderella even in her rags was virtuously tidy and patched up, while Sally had a great tear in her shabby dress, and Liza's stockings were falling over her boots.

"Wot cheer, Sal!" said Liza, when she caught her up.

"Oh, I 'ave got sich a 'ead on me this mornin'!" she remarked, turning round a pale face heavily lined under the eyes.

"I don't feel too chirpy neither," said Liza, sympathetically.

"I wish I 'adn't drunk so much beer," added Sally, as a pang shot through her head.

"Oh, you'll be arright in a bit," said Liza. Just then they heard the clock strike eight, and they began to run so that they might not miss getting their tokens and thereby their day's pay; they turned into the street at the end of which was the factory, and saw half a hundred women running like themselves to get in before it was too late.

All the morning Liza worked in a dead-and-alive sort of fashion, her head like a piece of lead with electric shocks going through it when she moved, and her tongue and mouth hot and dry. At last lunch-time came.

"Come on, Sal," said Liza; "I'm goin' to 'ave a glass o' bitter. I can't stand this no longer."

So they entered the public-house opposite, and in one draught finished their pots. Liza gave a long sigh of relief.

"That bucks you up, don't it?"

"I was dry! I ain't told yer yet, Liza, 'ave I? 'E got it aht last night."

"Who d'yer mean?"

"Why, 'Arry. 'E spit it aht at last."

"Arst yer ter nime the day?" said Liza, smiling.

"Thet's it."

"And did yer?"

"Didn't I jest!" answered Sally, with some emphasis. "I always told yer I'd git off before you."

"Yus!" said Liza, thinking.

"Yer know, Liza, you'd better tike Tom; 'e ain't a bad sort." She was quite patronising.

"I'm goin' ter tike 'oo I like; an' it ain't nobody's business but mine."

"Arright, Liza, don't get shirty over it; I don't mean no offence."

"What d'yer say it for then?"

"Well, I thought as seeing as yer'd gone aht with 'im yesterday thet yer meant ter after all."

" 'E wanted ter tike me; I didn't arsk 'im."

"Well, I didn't arsk my 'Arry, either."

"I never said yer did," replied Liza.

"Oh, you've got the 'ump, you 'ave!" finished Sally, rather angrily.

The beer had restored Liza; she went back to work without a headache, and, except for a slight languor, feeling no worse for the previous day's debauch. As she worked on she began going over in her mind the events of the preceding day, and she found entwined

in all her thoughts the burly person of Jim Blakeston. She saw
him walking by her side in the Forest, presiding over the meals,
playing the concertina, singing, joking, and finally, on the drive
back, she felt the heavy form by her side, and the big, rough hand
holding hers, while Tom's arm was round her waist. Tom! That
was the first time he had entered her mind, and he sank into a
shadow beside the other. Last of all she remembered the walk
home from the pub, the good-nights, and the rapid footstep as
Jim caught her up, and the kiss. She blushed and looked up
quickly to see whether any of the girls were looking at her; she
could not help thinking of that moment when he took her in his
arms; she still felt the roughness of his beard pressing on her
mouth. Her heart seemed to grow larger in her breast, and she
caught for breath as she threw back her head as if to receive his
lips again. A shudder ran through her from the vividness of the
thought.

"Wot are you shiverin' for, Liza?" asked one of the girls. "You
ain't cold."

"Not much," answered Liza, blushing awkwardly on her medita-
tions being broken into. "Why, I'm sweatin' so—I'm drippin'
wet."

"I expect yer caught cold in the Faurest yesterday."

"I see your mash as I was comin' along this mornin'."

Liza started a little.

"I ain't got one; 'oo d'yer mean, ay?"

"Yer only Tom, of course. 'E did look washed aht. Wot was
yer doin' with 'im yesterday?"

" 'E ain't got nothin' ter do with me, 'e ain't."

"Garn; don't you tell me!"

The bell rang, and, throwing over their work, the girls trooped
off, and after chattering in groups outside the factory gates for a
while, made their way in different directions to their respective
homes. Liza and Sally went along together.

"I sy, we are comin' aht!" cried Sally, seeing the advertisement
of a play being acted at the neighbouring theatre.

"I should like ter see thet!" said Liza, as they stood arm-in-arm
in front of the flaring poster. It represented two rooms and a
passage in between; in one room a dead man was lying on the
floor, while two others were standing horror-stricken, listening to
a youth who was in the passage, knocking at the door.

"You see, they've killed 'im," said Sally, excitedly.

"Yus, any fool can see thet! an' the one ahtside, wot's 'e doin' of?"

"Ain't 'e beautiful? I'll git my 'Arry ter tike me, I will. I should like ter see it. 'E said 'e'd tike me to the ply."

They strolled on again, and Liza, leaving Sally, made her way to her mother's. She knew she must pass Jim's house, and wondered whether she would see him. But as she walked along the street she saw Tom coming the opposite way; with a sudden impulse she turned back so as not to meet him, and began walking the way she had come. Then thinking herself a fool for what she had done, she turned again and walked towards him. She wondered if he had seen her or noticed her movement, but when she looked down the street he was nowhere to be seen; he had not caught sight of her, and had evidently gone in to see a mate in one or other of the houses. She quickened her step, and passing the house where lived Jim, could not help looking up; he was standing at the door watching her, with a smile on his lips.

"I didn't see yer, Mr. Blakeston," she said, as he came up to her.

"Didn't yer? Well, I knew yer would; an' I was witin' for yer ter look up. I see yer before ter-day."

"Na, when?"

"I passed be'ind yer as you an' thet other girl was lookin' at the advertisement of thet ply."

"I never see yer."

"Na, I know yer didn't. I 'ear yer say, you says, 'I should like to see thet.' "

"Yus, an' I should too."

"Well, I'll tike yer."

"You?"

"Yus; why not?"

"I like thet; wot would yer missus sy?"

"She wouldn't know."

"But the neighbours would!"

"No, they wouldn't; no one 'd see us."

He was speaking in a low voice so that people could not hear.

"You could meet me ahtside the theatre," he went on.

"Na, I couldn't go with you; you're a married man."

"Garn! wot's thet matter—jest ter go ter the ply? An' besides, my missus can't come if she wanted; she's got the kids ter look after."

"I should like ter see it," said Liza meditatively.

They had reached her house, and Jim said:

"Well, come aht this evenin' and tell me if yer will—eh, Liza?"

"Na, I'm not comin' aht this evening."

"Thet won't 'urt yer. I shall wite for yer."

" 'Tain't a bit of good your witin', 'cause I shan't come."

"Well, then, look 'ere, Liza; next Saturday night's the last night, an' I shall go to the theatre, any'ow. An' if you'll come, you just come to the doors at 'alf-past six, an' you'll find me there. See?"

"Na, I don't," said Liza, firmly.

"Well, I shall expect yer."

"I shan't come, so you needn't expect." And with that she walked into the house and slammed the door behind her.

Her mother had not come in from her day's charing, and Liza set about getting her tea. She thought it would be rather lonely eating it alone, so, pouring out a cup of tea and putting a little condensed milk into it, she cut a huge piece of bread-and-butter, and sat herself down outside on the doorstep. Another woman came downstairs, and seeing Liza, sat down by her side and began to talk.

"Why, Mrs. Stanley, wot 'ave yer done to your 'ead?" asked Liza, noticing a bandage round her forehead.

"I 'ad an accident last night," answered the woman, blushing uneasily.

"Oh, I am sorry! Wot did yer do to yerself?"

"I fell against the coal-scuttle and cut my 'ead open."

"Well, I never!"

"To tell yer the truth, I 'ad a few words with my old man. But one doesn't like them things ter git abaht; yer won't tell anyone, will yer?"

"Not me!" answered Liza. "I didn't know yer husband was like thet."

"Oh, 'e's as gentle as a lamb when 'e's sober," said Mrs. Stanley, apologetically. "But, Lor' bless yer, when 'e's 'ad a drop too much 'e's a demond, an' there's no two ways abaht it."

"An' you ain't been married long, neither?" said Liza.

"Na, not above eighteen months; ain't it disgriceful? Thet's wot the doctor at the 'orspital says ter me. I 'ad ter go ter the 'orspital. You should have seen 'ow it bled!—it bled all dahn my fice, and went streamin' like a bust water-pipe. Well, it fair frightened my old man, an' I says ter 'im, 'I'll charge yer,' an' although I was bleedin' like a bloomin' pig I shook my fist at 'im, an' I says, 'I'll charge ye—see if I don't!' An' 'e says, 'Na,' says 'e, 'don't do thet, for God's sike, Kitie, I'll git three months.' 'An' serve yer damn well right!' says I, an' I went aht an' left 'im. But, Lor' bless yer, I wouldn't charge 'im! I know 'e don't mean it; 'e's as gentle as a lamb when 'e's sober.'' She smiled quite affectionately as she said this.

"Wot did yer do, then?" asked Liza.

"Well, as I wos tellin' yer, I went to the 'orspital, an' the doctor 'e says ter me, 'My good woman,' says 'e, 'you might have been very seriously injured.' An' me not been married eighteen months! An' as I was tellin' the doctor all about it, 'Missus,' 'e says ter me, lookin' at me straight in the eyeball, 'Missus,' says 'e, ' 'ave you been drinkin'?' 'Drinkin'?' says I; 'no! I've 'ad a little drop, but as for drinkin'! Mind,' says I, 'I don't say I'm a teetotaller—I'm not; I 'ave my glass of beer, and I like it. I couldn't do withaht it, wot with the work I 'ave, I must 'ave somethin' ter keep me tergether. But as for drinkin' 'eavily! Well, I can say this, there ain't a soberer woman than myself in all London. Why, my first 'usband never touched a drop. Ah, my fust 'usband, 'e was a beauty, 'e was.' ''

She stopped the repetition of her conversation and addressed herself to Liza.

" 'E was thet different ter this one. 'E was a man as 'ad seen better days. 'E was a gentleman!" She mouthed the word and emphasised it with an expressive nod.

" 'E was a gentleman and a Christian. 'E'd been in good circumstances in 'is time; an' 'e was a man of education and a teetotaller, for twenty-two years."

At that moment Liza's mother appeared on the scene.

"Good-evenin', Mrs. Stanley," she said, politely.

"The sime ter you, Mrs. Kemp," replied that lady, with equal courtesy.

"An' 'ow is your poor 'ead?" asked Liza's mother, with sympathy.

"Oh, it's been achin' cruel. I've hardly known wot ter do with myself."

"I'm sure 'e ought ter be ashimed of 'imself for treatin' yer like thet."

"Oh, it wasn't 'is blows I minded so much, Mrs. Kemp," replied Mrs. Stanley, "an' don't you think it. It was wot 'e said ter me.

I can stand a blow as well as any woman. I don't mind thet, an' when 'e don't tike a mean advantage of me I can stand up for myself an' give as good as I tike; an' many's the time I give my fust husband a black eye. But the language 'e used, an' the things 'e called me! It mide me blush to the roots of my 'air; I'm not used ter bein' spoken ter like thet. I was in good circumstances when my fust 'usband was alive, 'e earned between two an' three pound a week, 'e did. As I said to 'im this mornin', ' 'Ow a gentleman can use sich language, I dunno.' "

" 'Usbands is cautions, 'owever good they are," said Mrs. Kemp, aphoristically. "But I mustn't stay aht 'ere in the night air."

" 'As yer rheumatism been troublin' yer litely?" asked Mrs. Stanely.

"Oh, cruel. Liza rubs me with embrocation every night, but it torments me cruel."

Mrs. Kemp then went into the house, and Liza remained talking to Mrs. Stanley; she, too, had to go in, and Liza was left alone. Some while she spent thinking of nothing, staring vacantly in front of her, enjoying the cool and quiet of the evening. But Liza could not be left alone long; several boys came along with a bat and a ball, and fixed upon the road just in front of her for their pitch. Taking off their coats they piled them up at the two ends, and were ready to begin.

"I say, old gal," said one of them to Liza, "come an' have a gime of cricket, will yer?"

"Na, Bob, I'm tired."

"Come on!"

"Na, I tell you I won't."

"She was on the booze yesterday, an' she ain't got over it," cried another boy.

"I'll swipe yer over the snitch!" replied Liza to him; and then on being asked again, said:

"Leave me alone, won't yer?"

"Liza's got the needle ter-night, thet's flat," commented a third member of the team.

"I wouldn't drink if I was you, Liza," added another, with mock gravity. "It's a bad 'abit ter git into," and he began rolling and swaying about like a drunken man.

If Liza had been "in form" she would have gone straight away and given the whole lot of them a sample of her strength; but she was only rather bored and vexed that they should disturb her quietness, so she let them talk. They saw she was not to be drawn, and leaving her, set to their game. She watched them for some time, but her thoughts gradually lost themselves, and insensibly her mind was filled with a burly form, and she was again thinking of Jim.

" 'E is a good sort ter want ter tike me ter the ply," she said to herself. "Tom never arst me!"

Jim had said he would come out in the evening; he ought to be here soon, she thought. Of course she wasn't going to the theatre with him, but she didn't mind talking to him; she rather enjoyed being asked to do a thing and refusing, and she would have liked another opportunity of doing so. But he didn't come, and he had said he would!

"I say, Bill," she said at last to one of the boys who was fielding close beside her, "that there Blakeston—d'you know 'im?"

"Yes, rather; why, he works at the sime plice as me."

"Wot's 'e do with 'isself in the evening; I never see 'im abaht?"

"I dunno. I see 'im this evenin' go into the 'Red Lion'. I suppose 'e's there, but I dunno."

Then he wasn't coming. Of course she had told him she was going to stay indoors, but he might have come all the same—just to see.

"I know Tom 'ud 'ave come," she said to herself, rather sulkily.

"Liza! Liza!" she heard her mother's voice calling her.

"Arright, I'm comin'," said Liza.

"I've been witin' for you this last 'alf-hour ter rub me."

"Why didn't yer call?" asked Liza.

"I did call. I've been callin' this last I dunno 'ow long; it's give me quite a sore throat."

"I never 'eard yer."

"Na, yer didn't want ter 'ear me, did yer? Yer don't mind if I dies with rheumatics, do yer? I know."

Liza did not answer, but took the bottle, and, pouring some of the liniment on her hand, began to rub it into Mrs. Kemp's rheumatic joints, while the invalid kept complaining and grumbling at everything Liza did.

"Don't rub so 'ard, Liza; you'll rub all the skin off."

Then when Liza did it as gently as she could, she grumbled again.

"If you do it like thet, it won't do no good at all. You want ter

sive yerself trouble—I know yer. When I was young girls didn't
mind a little bit of 'ard work—but, law bless yer, you don't care
abaht my rheumatics, do yer?"

At last she finished, and Liza went to bed by her mother's side.

CHAPTER VII

Two days passed, and it was Friday morning. Liza had got up
early and strolled off to her work in good time, but she did not
meet her faithful Sally on the way, nor find her at the factory
when she herself arrived. The bell rang and all the girls trooped
in, but still Sally did not come. Liza could not make it out, and
was thinking she would be shut out, when just as the man who
gave out the tokens for the day's work was pulling down the
shutter in front of his window, Sally arrived, breathless and
perspiring.

"Whew! Go' lumme, I am 'ot!" she said, wiping her face with
her apron.

"I thought you wasn't comin'," said Liza.

"Well, I only just did it; I overslep' myself. I was aht lite last
night."

"Were yer?"

"Me an' 'Arry went ter see the ply. Oh, Liza, it's simply
spiffin'! I've never see sich a good ply in my life. Lor'! Why, it
mikes yer blood run cold: they 'ang a man on the stige; oh, it mide
me creep all over!"

And then she began telling Liza all about it—the blood and
thunder, the shooting, the railway train, the murder, the bomb,
the hero, the funny man—jumbling everything up in her excitement, repeating little scraps of dialogue—all wrong—gesticulating,
getting excited and red in the face at the recollection. Liza listened
rather crossly, feeling bored at the detail into which Sally was
going; the piece really didn't much interest her.

"One 'ud think yer'd never been to a theatre in your life before,"
she said.

"I never seen anything so good, I can tell yer. You tike my tip,
and git Tom ter tike yer."

"I don't want ter go; an' if I did I'd py for myself an' go alone."

"Cheese it! That ain't 'alf so good. Me an' 'Arry, we set

together, 'im with 'is arm round my wiste and me 'oldin' 'is 'and.
It was jam, I can tell yer!"

"Well, I don't want anyone sprawlin' me abaht; thet ain't my
mark!"

"But I do like 'Arry; you dunno the little ways 'e 'as; an' we're
goin' ter be married in three weeks now. 'Arry said, well, 'e says,
'I'll git a licence.' 'Na,' says I, ' 'ave the banns read aht in church;
it seems more reg'lar like to 'ave banns; so they're goin' ter be
read aht next Sunday. You'll come with me an' 'ear them, won't
yer, Liza?"

"Yus, I don't mind."

On the way home Sally insisted on stopping in front of the
poster and explaining to Liza all about the scene represented.

"Oh, you give me the sick with your 'Fital Card', you do! I'm
goin' 'ome." And she left Sally in the midst of her explanation.

"I dunno wot's up with Liza," remarked Sally to a mutual
friend. "She's always got the needle, some'ow."

"Oh, she's barmy," answered the friend.

"Well, I do think she's a bit dotty sometimes—I do really,"
rejoined Sally.

Liza walked homewards, thinking of the play; at length she
tossed her head impatiently.

"I don't want ter see the blasted thing; an' if I see that there Jim
I'll tell 'im so; swop me bob, I will!"

She did see him; he was leaning with his back against the wall of
his house, smoking. Liza knew he had seen her, and as she walked
by pretended not to have noticed him. To her disgust, he let her
pass, and she was thinking he hadn't seen her after all, when she
heard him call her name.

"Liza!"

She turned round and started with surprise very well imitated.
"I didn't see you was there!" she said.

"Why did yer pretend not ter notice me, as yer went past—eh,
Liza?"

"Why, I didn't see her."

"Garn! But you ain't shirty with me?"

"Wot 'ave I got to be shirty abaht?"

He tried to take her hand, but she drew it away quickly. She
was getting used to the movement. They went on talking, but Jim
did not mention the theatre; Liza was surprised, and wondered
whether he had forgotten.

"Er—Sally went to the ply last night," she said, at last.

"Oh!" he said, and that was all.

She got impatient.

"Well, I'm off!" she said.

"Na, don't go yet; I want ter talk ter yer," he replied.

"Wot abaht? anythin' in partickler?" She would drag it out of him if she possibly could.

"Not thet I knows on," he said, smiling.

"Good-night!" she said, abruptly, turning away from him.

"Well, I'm damned if 'e ain't forgotten!" she said to herself, sulkily, as she marched home.

The following evening about six o'clock, it suddenly struck her that it was the last night of the "New and Sensational Drama".

"I do like thet Jim Blakeston," she said to herself; "fancy treatin' me like thet! You wouldn't catch Tom doin' sich a thing. Bli'me if I speak to 'im again, the —— Now I shan't see it at all. I've a good mind ter go on my own 'ook. Fancy 'is forgettin' all abaht it, like thet!"

She was really quite indignant; though, as she had distinctly refused Jim's offer, it was rather hard to see why.

" 'E said 'e'd wite for me ahtside the doors; I wonder if 'e's there. I'll go an' see if 'e is, see if I don't—an' then if 'e's there, I'll go in on my own 'ook, jist ter spite 'im."

She dressed herself in her best, and, so that the neighbours shouldn't see her, went up a passage between some model lodging-house buildings, and in this roundabout way got into the West-minster Bridge Road, and soon found herself in front of the theatre.

"I've been witin' for yer this 'alf-hour."

She turned round and saw Jim standing just behind her.

" 'Oo are you talkin' to? I'm not goin' to the ply with you. Wot d'yer tike me for, eh?"

" 'Oo are yer goin' with, then?"

"I'm goin' alone."

"Garn! don't be a bloomin' jackass!"

Liza was feeling very injured.

"Thet's 'ow you treat me! I shall go 'ome. Why didn't you come aht the other night?"

"Yer told me not ter."

She snorted at the ridiculous ineptitude of the reply.

"Why didn't you say nothin' abaht it yesterday?"

"Why, I thought you'd come if I didn't talk on it."

"Well, I think you're a——brute!" She felt very much inclined to cry.

"Come on, Liza, don't tike on; I didn't mean no offence." And he put his arm round her waist and led her to take their places at the gallery door. Two tears escaped from the corners of her eyes and ran down her nose, but she felt very relieved and happy, and let him lead her where he would.

There was a long string of people waiting at the door, and Liza was delighted to see a couple of niggers who were helping them to while away the time of waiting. The niggers sang and danced, and made faces, while the people looked on with appreciative gravity, like royalty listening to de Reszké, and they were very generous of applause and halfpence at the end of the performance. Then, when the niggers moved to the pit doors, paper boys came along offering *Tit-Bits* and "extra specials"; after that three little girls came round and sang sentimental songs and collected more half-pence. At last a movement ran through the serpent-like string of people, sounds were heard behind the door, everyone closed up, the men told the women to keep close and hold tight; there was a great unbarring and unbolting, the doors were thrown open, and, like a bursting river, the people surged in.

Half an hour more and the curtain went up. The play was indeed thrilling. Liza quite forgot her companion, and was intent on the scene; she watched the incidents breathlessly, trembling with excitement, almost beside herself at the celebrated hanging incident. When the curtain fell on the first act she sighed and mopped her face.

"See 'ow 'ot I am," she said to Jim, giving him her hand.

"Yus, you are!" he remarked, taking it.

"Leave go!" she said, trying to withdraw it from him.

"Not much," he answered, quite boldly.

"Garn! Leave go!" But he didn't, and she really did not struggle very violently.

The second act came, and she shrieked over the comic man; and her laughter rang higher than anyone else's, so that people turned to look at her, and said:

"She is enjoyin' 'erself."

Then when the murder came she bit her nails and the sweat stood on her forehead in great drops; in her excitement she even called out as loud as she could to the victim: "Look aht!" It caused a laugh and slackened the tension, for the whole house was holding its breath as it looked at the villains listening at the door, creeping silently forward, crawling like tigers to their prey.

Liza was trembling all over, and in her terror threw herself against Jim, who put both his arms round her, and said:

"Don't be afride, Liza; it's all right."

At last the men sprang, there was a scuffle, and the wretch was killed; then came the scene depicted on the posters—the victim's son knocking at the door, on the inside of which were the murderers and the murdered man. At last the curtain came down, and the house in relief burst forth into cheers and cheers; the handsome hero in his top hat was greeted thunderously; the murdered man, with his clothes still all disarranged, was hailed with sympathy; and the villains—the house yelled and hissed and booed, while the poor brutes bowed and tried to look as if they liked it.

"I am enjoyin' myself," said Liza, pressing herself quite close to Jim; "you are a good sort ter tike me—Jim."

He gave her a little hug, and it struck her that she was sitting just as Sally had done, and, like Sally, she found it "jam".

The *entr'actes* were short and the curtain was soon up again, and the comic man raised customary laughter by undressing and exposing his nether garments to the public view; then more tragedy, and the final act with its darkened room, its casting lots, and its explosion.

When it was all over and they had got outside Jim smacked his lips and said:

"I could do with a gargle; let's go into thet pub there."

"I'm as dry as bone," said Liza; and so they went.

When they got in they discovered they were hungry, and seeing some appetising sausage-rolls, ate of them, and washed them down with a couple of pots of beer; then Jim lit his pipe and they strolled off. They had got quite near the Westminster Bridge Road when Jim suggested that they should go and have one more drink before closing time.

"I shall be tight," said Liza.

"Thet don't matter," answered Jim, laughing. "You ain't got ter go ter work in the mornin' an' you can sleep it aht."

"Arright, I don't mind if I do then; in for a penny, in for a pound."

At the pub door she drew back.

"I say, guv'ner," she said, "there'll be some of the coves from dahn our street, and they'll see us."

"Na, there won't be nobody there, don't yer 'ave no fear."

"I don't like ter go in for fear of it."

"Well, we ain't doin' no 'arm if they does see us, an' we can go into the private bar, an' you bet your boots there won't be no one there."

She yielded, and they went in.

"Two pints of bitter, please miss," ordered Jim.

"I say, 'old 'ard. I can't drink more than 'alf a pint," said Liza.

"Cheese it," answered Jim. "You can do with all you can get, I know."

At closing time they left and walked down the broad road which led homewards.

"Let's 'ave a little sit dahn," said Jim, pointing to an empty bench between two trees.

"Na, it's gettin' lite; I want ter be 'ome."

"It's such a fine night, it's a pity ter go in already;" and he drew her unresisting towards the seat. He put his arm round her waist.

"Un'and me, villin!" she said, in apt misquotation of the melo-drama; but Jim only laughed, and she made no effort to disengage herself.

They sat there for a long while in silence; the beer had got to Liza's head, and the warm night air filled her with a double intoxication. She felt the arm round her waist, and the big, heavy form pressing against her side; she experienced again the curious sensation as if her heart were about to burst, and it choked her—a feeling so oppressive and painful that it almost made her feel sick. Her hands began to tremble, and her breathing grew rapid, as though she were suffocating. Almost fainting, she swayed over towards the man, and a cold shiver ran through her from top to toe. Jim bent over her, and, taking her in both arms, he pressed his lips to hers in a long, passionate kiss. At last, panting for breath, she turned her head away and groaned.

Then they again sat for a long while in silence, Liza full of a strange happiness, feeling as if she could laugh aloud hysterically, but restrained by the calm and silence of the night. Close behind struck a church clock—one.

"Bless my soul!" said Liza, starting, "there's one o'clock. I must get 'ome."

"It's so nice out 'ere; do sty, Liza." He pressed her closer to him. "Yer know, Liza, I love yer—fit ter kill."

"Na, I can't stay; come on." She got up from the seat, and pulled him up too. "Come on," she said.

Without speaking they went along, and there was no one to be seen either in front or behind them. He had not got his arm round her now, and they were walking side by side, slightly separated. It was Liza who spoke first.

"You'd better go dahn the Road and by the church an' git into Vere Street the other end, an' I'll go through the passage, so thet no one shouldn't see us comin' together"; she spoke almost in a whisper.

"Arright, Liza," he answered, "I'll do just as you tell me."

They came to the passage of which Liza spoke; it was a narrow way between blank walls, the backs of factories, and it led into the upper end of Vere Street. The entrance to it was guarded by two iron posts in the middle, so that horses or barrows should not be taken through.

They had just got to it when a man came out into the open road. Liza quickly turned her head away.

"I wonder if 'e see us," she said, when he had passed out of earshot. " 'E's lookin' back," she added.

"Why, 'oo is it?" asked Jim.

"It's a man aht of our street," she answered. "I dunno 'im, but I know where 'e lodges. D'yer think 'e see us?"

"Na, 'e wouldn't know 'oo it was in the dark."

"But he looked round; all the street'll know it if he see us."

"Well, we ain't doin' no 'arm."

She stretched out her hand to say good-night.

"I'll come a little wy with yer along the passage," said Jim.

"Na, you mustn't; you go straight round."

"But it's so dark; p'raps summat'll 'appen to yer."

"Not it! You go on 'ome an' leave me," she replied, and entering the passage, stood facing him with one of the iron pillars between them.

"Good-night, old cock," she said, stretching out her hand. He took it, and said:

"I wish yer wasn't goin' ter leave me, Liza."

"Garn! I must!" She tried to get her hand away from his, but he held it firm, resting it on the top of the pillar.

"Leave go my 'and," she said. He made no movement, but

looked into her eyes steadily, so that it made her uneasy. She repented having come out with him. "Leave go my 'and." And she beat down on his with her closed fist.

"Liza!" he said, at last.

"Well, wot is it?" she answered, still thumping down on his hand with her fist.

"Liza," he said in a whisper, "will yer?"

"Will I wot?" she said, looking down.

"You know, Liza. Sy, will yer?"

"Na," she said.

He bent over her and repeated—

"Will yer?"

She did not speak, but kept beating down on his hand.

"Liza," he said again, his voice growing hoarse and thick— "Liza, will yer?"

She still kept silence, looking away and continually bringing down her fist. He looked at her a moment, and she, ceasing to thump his hand, looked up at him with half-opened mouth. Suddenly he shook himself, and closing his fist gave her a violent, swinging blow in the belly.

"Come on," he said.

And together they slid down into the darkness of the passage.

CHAPTER VIII

MRS. KEMP was in the habit of slumbering somewhat heavily on Sunday mornings, or Liza would not have been allowed to go on sleeping as she did. When she woke she rubbed her eyes to gather her senses together, and gradually she remembered having gone to the theatre on the previous evening; then suddenly everything came back to her. She stretched out her legs and gave a long sigh of delight. Her heart was full; she thought of Jim, and the delicious sensation of love came over her. Closing her eyes, she imagined his warm kisses, and she lifted up her arms as if to put them round his neck and draw him down to her; she almost felt the rough beard on her face, and the strong heavy arms round her body. She smiled to herself and took a long breath; then, slipping back the sleeves of her night-dress, she looked at her own thin arms, just two pieces of bone with not a muscle on them, but very white and showing distinctly the interlacement of blue veins; she did not notice that her hands were rough and red and dirty, with the nails broken and bitten to the quick. She got out of bed and looked at herself in the glass over the mantelpiece; with one hand she brushed back her hair and smiled at herself; her face was very small and thin, but the complexion was nice, clear and white, with a delicate tint of red on the cheeks, and her eyes were big and dark like her hair. She felt very happy.

She did not want to dress yet, but rather to sit down and think, so she twisted up her hair into a little knot, slipped a skirt over her night-dress, and sat on a chair near the window and began looking around. The decorations of the room had been centred on the mantelpiece; the chief ornament consisted of a pear and an apple, a pineapple, a bunch of grapes, and several fat plums, all very beautifully done in wax, as was the fashion about the middle of this most glorious reign. They were appropriately coloured—the apple blushing red, the grapes an inky black, emerald green leaves were scattered here and there to lend finish, and the whole was mounted on an ebonised stand covered with black velvet, and protected from dust and dirt by a beautiful glass cover bordered with red plush. Liza's eyes rested on this with approbation, and the pineapple quite made her mouth water. At either end of the mantelpiece were pink jars with blue flowers on the front; round the top in Gothic letters of gold was inscribed; "A Present from a Friend"—these were products of a later but not less artistic age. The intervening spaces were taken up with little jars and cups and saucers—gold inside, with a view of a town outside, and surrounding them, "A Present from Clacton-on-Sea", or, alliteratively, "A Memento of Margate". Of these many were broken, but they had been mended with glue, and it is well known that pottery in the eyes of the connoisseur loses none of its value by a crack or two. Then there were portraits innumerable—little yellow *cartes-de-visite* in velvet frames, some of which were decorated with shells; they showed strange people with old-fashioned clothes, the women with bodices and sleeves fitting close to the figure, stern-featured females with hair carefully parted in the middle and plastered down on each side, firm chins and mouths, with small, pig-like eyes and wrinkled faces, and the men were uncomfortably clad in Sunday garments, very stiff and uneasy in their awkward postures, with large whiskers and shaved chins and upper lips and a general air of horny-handed toil. Then there were one or two daguerreotypes, little full-length figures framed in gold paper. There was one of Mrs. Kemp's father and one of her mother, and there were several photographs of betrothed or newly-married couples, the lady sitting down and the man standing behind her with his hand on the chair, or the man sitting and the woman with her hand on his shoulder. And from all sides of the room, standing on the mantelpiece, hanging above it, on the wall and over the bed, they stared full-face into the room, self-consciously fixed for ever in their stiff discomfort.

The walls were covered with dingy, antiquated paper, and ornamented with coloured supplements from Christmas Numbers —there was a very patriotic picture of a soldier shaking the hand of a fallen comrade and waving his arm in defiance of a band of advancing Arabs; there was a "Cherry Ripe", almost black with age and dirt; there were two almanacks several years old, one with a coloured portrait of the Marquess of Lorne, very handsome and elegantly dressed, the object of Mrs. Kemp's adoration since her husband's demise; the other a Jubilee portrait of the Queen, somewhat losing in dignity by a moustache which Liza in an irreverent moment had smeared on with charcoal.

The furniture consisted of a wash-hand stand and a little deal chest-of-drawers, which acted as sideboard to such pots and pans and crockery as could not find room in the grate; and besides the bed there was nothing but two kitchen chairs and a lamp. Liza looked at it all and felt perfectly satisfied; she put a pin into one corner of the noble Marquess to prevent him from falling, fiddled about with the ornaments a little, and then started washing herself. After putting on her clothes she ate some bread-and-butter, swallowed a dishful of cold tea, and went out into the street.

She saw some boys playing cricket and went up to them.

"Let me ply," she said.

"Arright, Liza," cried half a dozen of them in delight; and the captain added: "You go an' scout over by the lamp-post."

"Go an' scout my eye!" said Liza, indignantly. "When I ply cricket I does the battin'."

"Na, you're not goin' ter bat all the time: 'Oo are you gettin' at?" replied the captain, who had taken advantage of his position to put himself in first, and was still at the wicket.

"Well, then I shan't ply," answered Liza.

"Garn, Ernie, let 'er go in!" shouted two or three members of the team.

"Well, I'm busted!" remarked the captain, as she took his bat. "You won't sty in long, I lay," he said, as he sent the old bowler fielding and took the ball himself. He was a young gentleman who did not suffer from excessive backwardness.

"Aht!" shouted a dozen voices as the ball went past Liza's bat and landed in the pile of coats which formed the wicket. The captain came forward to resume his innings, but Liza held the bat away from him.

"Garn!" she said; "thet was only a trial."

"You never said trial," answered the captain indignantly.

"Yus, I did," said Liza; "I said it just as the ball was comin'— under my breath."

"Well, I am busted!" repeated the captain.

Just then Liza saw Tom among the lookers-on, and as she felt very kindly disposed to the world in general that morning, she called out to him:

" 'Ulloa, Tom!" she said. "Come an' give us a ball; this chap can't bowl."

"Well, I got yer aht, any'ow," said that person.

"Ah, yer wouldn't 'ave got me aht plyin' square. But a trial ball—well, one don't ever know wot a trial ball's goin' ter do."

Tom began bowling very slowly and easily, so that Liza could swing her bat round and hit mightily; she ran well, too, and pantingly brought up her score to twenty. Then the fielders interposed.

"I sy, look 'ere, 'e's only givin' 'er lobs; 'e's not tryin' ter git 'er aht."

"You're spoilin' our gime."

"I don't care; I've got twenty runs—thet's more than you could do. I'll go aht now of my own accord, so there! Come on, Tom."

Tom joined her, and as the captain at last resumed his bat and the game went on, they commenced talking, Liza leaning against the wall of a house, while Tom stood in front of her, smiling with pleasure.

"Where 'ave you been 'idin' yerself, Tom? I ain't seen yer for I dunno 'ow long."

"I've been abaht as usual; an' I've seen you when you didn't see me."

"Well, yer might 'ave come up and said good-mornin' when you see me."

"I didn't want ter force myself on yer, Liza."

"Garn! You are a bloomin' cuckoo, I'm blowed!"

"I thought yer didn't like me 'angin' round yer; so I kep' awy."

"Why, yer talks as if I didn't like yer. Yer don't think I'd 'ave come aht beanfeastin' with yer if I 'adn't liked yer?"

Liza was really very dishonest, but she felt so happy this morning that she loved the whole world, and of course Tom came in with the others. She looked very kindly at him, and he was so affected that a great lump came in his throat and he could not speak.

Liza's eyes turned to Jim's house, and she saw coming out of the door a girl of about her own age; she fancied she saw in her some likeness to Jim.

"Say, Tom," she asked, "thet ain't Blakeston's daughter, is it?"

"Yus, thet's it."

"I'll go an' speak to 'er," said Liza, leaving Tom and going over the road.

"You're Polly Blakeston, ain't yer?" she said.

"Thet's me!" said the girl.

"I thought you was. Your dad, 'e says ter me, 'You dunno my daughter, Polly, do yer?' says 'e. 'Na,' says I, 'I don't.' 'Well,' says 'e, 'you can't miss 'er when you see 'er.' An' right enough I didn't."

"Mother says I'm all Father, an' there ain't nothin' of 'er in me. Dad says it's lucky it ain't the other wy abaht, or 'e'd 'ave got a divorce."

They both laughed.

"Where are you goin' now?" asked Liza, looking at the slop-basin she was carrying.

"I was just goin' dahn into the Road ter get some ice-cream for dinner. Father 'ad a bit of luck last night, 'e says, and 'e'd stand the lot of us ice-cream for dinner ter-day."

"I'll come with yer if yer like."

"Come on!" And, already friends, they walked arm-in-arm to the Westminster Bridge Road. Then they went along till they came to a stall where an Italian was selling the required commodity, and having had a taste apiece to see if they liked it, Polly planked down sixpence and had her basin filled with a poisonous-looking mixture of red and white ice-cream.

On the way back, looking up the street, Polly cried:

"There's Father!"

Liza's heart beat rapidly and she turned red; but suddenly a sense of shame came over her, and casting down her head so that she might not see him, she said:

"I think I'll be off 'ome an' see 'ow Mother's gettin' on." And before Polly could say anything she had slipped away and entered her own house.

Mother was not getting on at all well.

"You've come in at last, you ——, you!" snarled Mrs. Kemp, as Liza entered the room.

"Wot's the matter, Mother?"

"Matter! I like thet—matter indeed! Go an' matter yerself an' be mattered! Nice way ter treat an old woman like me—an' yer own mother, too!"

"Wot's up now?"

"Don't talk ter me; I don't want ter listen ter you. Leavin' me all alone, me with my rheumatics, an' the neuralgy! I've 'ad the neuralgy all the mornin', and my 'ead's been simply splittin', so thet I thought the bones 'ud come apart and all my brains go streamin' on the floor. An' when I wake up there's no one ter git my tea for me, an' I lay there witin' an' witin', an' at last I 'ad ter git up and mike it myself. And, my 'ead simply cruel! Why, I might 'ave been burnt ter death, with the fire alight an' me asleep."

"Well, I am sorry, Mother; but I went aht just for a bit, an' didn't think you'd wike. An' besides, the fire wasn't alight."

"Garn with yer! I didn't treat my mother like thet. Oh, you've been a bad daughter ter me—an' I 'ad more illness carryin' you than with all the other children put togither. You was a cross at yer birth, an' you've been a cross ever since. An' now in my old age, when I've worked myself ter the bone, yer leaves me to starve and burn ter death." Here she began to cry, and the rest of her utterances was lost in sobs.

The dusk had darkened into night, and Mrs. Kemp had retired to rest with the dicky-birds. Liza was thinking of many things; she wondered why she had been unwilling to meet Jim in the morning.

"I was a bally fool," she said to herself.

It really seemed an age since the previous night, and all that had happened seemed very long ago. She had not spoken to Jim all day, and she had so much to say to him. Then, wondering whether he was about, she went to the window and looked out;

but there was nobody there. She closed the window again and sat just beside it; the time went on, and she wondered whether he would come, asking herself whether he had been thinking of her as she of him; gradually her thoughts grew vague, and a kind of mist came over them. She nodded. Suddenly she roused herself with a start, fancying she had heard something; she listened again, and in a moment the sound was repeated, three or four gentle taps on the window. She opened it quickly and whispered:

"Jim."

"Thet's me," he answered; "come aht."

Closing the window, she went into the passage and opened the street door; it was hardly unlocked before Jim had pushed his way in; partly shutting it behind him, he took her in his arms and hugged her to his breast. She kissed him passionately.

"I thought yer'd come ter-night, Jim; summat in my 'eart told me so. But you 'ave been long."

"I wouldn't come before, 'cause I thought there'd be people abaht. Kiss us!" And again he pressed his lips to hers, and Liza nearly fainted with the delight of it.

"Let's go for a walk, shall we?" he said.

"Arright!" They were speaking in whispers. "You go into the Road through the passage, an' I'll go by the street."

"Yus, thet's right," and kissing her once more, he slid out, and she closed the door behind him.

Then going back to get her hat, she came again into the passage, waiting behind the door till it might be safe for her to venture. She had not made up her mind to risk it, when she heard a key put in the lock, and she hardly had time to spring back to prevent herself from being hit by the opening door. It was a man, one of the upstairs lodgers.

" 'Ulloa!" he said, " 'oo's there?"

"Mr. 'Odges! Strike me, you did give me a turn; I was just goin' aht." She blushed to her hair, but in the darkness he could see nothing.

"Good-night," she said, and went out.

She walked close along the sides of the houses like a thief, and the policeman as she passed him turned round and looked at her, wondering whether she was meditating some illegal deed. She breathed freely on coming into the open road, and seeing Jim skulking behind a tree, ran up to him, and in the shadows they kissed again.

CHAPTER IX

THUS began a time of love and joy. As soon as her work was over and she had finished tea, Liza would slip out and at some appointed spot meet Jim. Usually it would be at the church, where the Westminster Bridge Road bends down to get to the river; and they would go off, arm-in-arm, till they came to some place where they could sit down and rest. Sometimes they would walk along the Albert Embankment to Battersea Park, and here sit on the benches, watching the children play. The female cyclist had almost abandoned Battersea for the parks on the other side of the river, but often enough one went by, and Liza, with the old-fashioned prejudice of her class, would look after the rider and make some remark about her, not seldom more forcible than ladylike. Both Jim and she liked children, and tiny, ragged urchins would gather round to have rides on the man's knees or mock fights with Liza.

They thought themselves far away from anyone in Vere Street, but twice, as they were walking along, they were met by people they knew. Once it was two workmen coming home from a job at Vauxhall: Liza did not see them till they were quite near; she immediately dropped Jim's arm, and they both cast their eyes to the ground as the men passed, like ostriches, expecting that if they did not look they would not be seen.

"D'you see 'em, Jim?" asked Liza, in a whisper, when they had gone by. "I wonder if they see us." Almost instinctively she turned round, and at the same moment one of the men turned too; then there was no doubt about it.

"Thet did give me a turn," she said.

"So it did me," answered Jim; "I simply went 'ot all over."

"We was bally fools," said Liza; "we oughter 'ave spoken to 'em! D'you think they'll let aht?"

They heard nothing of it; when Jim afterwards met one of the men in a public-house he did not mention a meeting, and they thought that perhaps they had not been recognised. But the second time was worse.

It was on the Albert Embankment again. They were met by a party of four, all of whom lived in the street. Liza's heart sank within her, for there was no chance of escape; she thought of turning quickly and walking in the opposite direction, but there was not time, for the men had already seen them. She whispered to Jim:

"Back us up," and as they met she said to one of the men:
" 'Ulloa there! Where are you off to?"

The men stopped, and one of them asked the question back.

"Where are you off to?"

"Me? Oh, I've just been to the 'orspital. One of the gals at
our plice is queer, an' so I says ter myself, 'I'll go an' see 'er.' "
She faltered a little as she began, but quickly gathered herself
together, lying fluently and without hesitation.

"An' when I come aht," she went on, " 'oo should I see just
passin' the 'orspital but this 'ere cove, an' 'e says to me, 'Wot
cheer,' says 'e, 'I'm goin' ter Vaux'all, come an' walk a bit of the
wy with us.' 'Arright,' says I, 'I don't mind if I do.' "

One man winked, and another said: "Go it, Liza!"

She fired up with the dignity of outraged innocence.

"Wot d'yer mean by thet?" she said; "d'yer think I'm kiddin'?"

"Kiddin'? No! You've only just come up from the country,
ain't yer?"

"Think I'm kidding? What d'yer think I want ter kid for?
Liars never believe anyone, thet's fact."

"Na then, Liza, don't be saucy."

"Saucy! I'll smack yer in the eye if yer sy much ter me. Come
on," she said to Jim, who had been standing sheepishly by; and
they walked away.

The men shouted: "Now we shan't be long!" and went off
laughing.

After that they decided to go where there was no chance at all
of their being seen. They did not meet till they got over Westminster Bridge, and thence they made their way into the park;
they would lie down on the grass in one another's arms, and thus
spend the long summer evenings. After the heat of the day there
would be a gentle breeze in the park, and they would take in long
breaths of the air; it seemed far away from London, it was so quiet
and cool; and Liza, as she lay by Jim's side, felt her love for him
overflowing to the rest of the world and enveloping mankind
itself in a kind of grateful happiness. If it could only have lasted!
They would stay and see the stars shine out dimly, one by one,
from the blue sky, till it grew late and the blue darkened into
black, and the stars glittered in thousands all above them. But as
the nights grew cooler, they found it cold on the grass, and the
time they had there seemed too short for the long journey they
had to make; so, crossing the bridge as before, they strolled along

the Embankment till they came to a vacant bench, and there they
would sit, with Liza nestling close up to her lover and his great
arms around her. The rain of September made no difference to
them; they went as usual to their seat beneath the trees, and Jim
would take Liza on his knee, and, opening his coat, shelter her
with it, while she, with her arms round his neck, pressed very
close to him, and occasionally gave a little laugh of pleasure and
delight. They hardly spoke at all through these evenings, for what
had they to say to one another? Often without exchanging a word
they would sit for an hour with their faces touching, the one
feeling on his cheek the hot breath from the other's mouth; while
at the end of the time the only motion was an upraising of Liza's
lips, a bending down of Jim's, so that they might meet and kiss.
Sometimes Liza fell into a light doze, and Jim would sit very still
for fear of waking her, and when she roused herself she would
smile, while he bent down again and kissed her. They were very
happy. But the hours passed by so quickly that Big Ben striking
twelve came upon them as a surprise, and unwillingly they got up
and made their way homewards; their partings were never-ending
—each evening Jim refused to let her go from his arms, and tears
stood in his eyes at the thought of the separation.

"I'd give somethin'," he would say, "if we could be togither
always."

"Never mind, old chap!" Liza would answer, herself half
crying, "it can't be 'elped, so we must jolly well lump it."

But notwithstanding all their precautions people in Vere Street
appeared to know. First of all Liza noticed that the women did
not seem quite so cordial as before, and she often fancied they
were talking of her; when she passed by they appeared to look at
her, then say something or other, and perhaps burst out laughing;
but when she approached they would immediately stop speaking,
and keep silence in a rather awkward, constrained manner. For a
long time she was unwilling to believe that there was any change
in them, and Jim, who had observed nothing, persuaded her that
it was all fancy. But gradually it became clearer, and Jim had to
agree with her that somehow or other people had found out.
Once when Liza had been talking to Polly, Jim's daughter, Mrs.
Blakeston had called ᴧer, and when the girl had come to her
mother Liza saw that she spoke angrily, and they both looked
across at her. When Liza caught Mrs. Blakeston's eye she saw in
her face a surly scowl, which almost frightened her; she wanted

to brave it out, and stepped forward a little to go and speak with the woman, but Mrs. Blakeston, standing still, looked so angrily at her that she was afraid to. When she told Jim his face grew dark, and he said: "Blast the woman! I'll give 'er wot for if she says anythin' ter you."

"Don't strike 'er, wotever 'appens, will yer, Jim?" said Liza.

"She'd better tike care then!" he answered, and he told her that lately his wife had been sulking, and not speaking to him. The previous night, on coming home after his day's work and bidding her "Good-evenin'," she had turned her back on him without answering.

"Can't you answer when you're spoke to?" he had said.

"Good-evenin'," she had replied sulkily, with her back still turned.

After that Liza noticed that Polly avoided her.

"Wot's up, Polly?" she said to her one day. "You never speaks now; 'ave you 'ad yer tongue cut aht?"

"Me? I ain't got nothin' ter speak abaht, thet I knows of," answered Polly, abruptly walking off. Liza grew very red and quickly looked to see if anyone had noticed the incident. A couple of youths, sitting on the pavement, had seen it, and she saw them nudge one another and wink.

Then the fellows about the street began to chaff her.

"You look pale," said one of a group to her one day.

"You're overworkin' yerself, you are," said another.

"Married life don't agree with Liza, thet's wot it is," added a third.

" 'Oo d'yer think yer gettin' at? I ain't married, an' never like ter be," she answered.

"Liza 'as all the pleasures of a 'usband an' none of the trouble."

"Bli'me if I know wot yer mean!" said Liza.

"Na, of course not; you don't know nothin', do yer?"

"Innocent as a bibe. Our Father which art in 'eaven!"

" 'Aven't been in London long, 'ave yer?"

They spoke in chorus, and Liza stood in front of them, bewildered, not knowing what to answer.

"Don't you mike no mistike abaht it, Liza knows a thing or two."

"O me darlin', I love yer fit to kill, but tike care your missus ain't round the corner." This was particularly bold, and they all laughed.

Liza felt very uncomfortable, and fiddled about with her apron, wondering how she should get away.

"Tike care yer don't git into trouble, thet's all," said one of the men, with burlesque gravity.

"Yer might give us a chanst, Liza; you come aht with me one evenin'. You oughter give us all a turn, jist ter show there's no ill-feelin'."

"Bli'me if I know wot yer all talkin' abaht. You're all barmy on the crumpet," said Liza indignantly, and, turning her back on them, made for home.

Among other things that had happened was Sally's marriage. One Saturday a little procession had started from Vere Street, consisting of Sally, in a state of giggling excitement, her fringe magnificent after a whole week of curling-papers, clad in a perfectly new velveteen dress of the colour known as electric blue; and Harry, rather nervous and ill at ease in the unaccustomed restraint of a collar; these two walked arm-in-arm, and were followed by Sally's mother and uncle, also arm-in-arm, and the procession was brought up by Harry's brother and a friend. They started with a flourish of trumpets and an old boot, and walked down the middle of Vere Street, accompanied by the neighbours' good wishes; but as they got into the Westminster Bridge Road and nearer to the church, the happy couple grew silent, and Harry began to perspire freely, so that his collar gave him perfect torture. There was a public-house just opposite the church, and it was suggested that they should have a drink before going in. As it was a solemn occasion they went into the private bar, and there Sally's uncle, who was a man of means, ordered six pots of beer.

"Feel a bit nervous, 'Arry?" asked his friend.

"Na," said Harry, as if he had been used to getting married every day of his life; "bit warm, thet's all."

"Your very good 'ealth, Sally," said her mother, lifting her mug; "this is the last time as I shall ever address you as miss."

"An' may she be as good a wife as you was," added Sally's uncle.

"Well, I don't think my old man ever 'ad no complaint ter mike abaht me. I did my duty by 'im, although it's me as says it," answered the good lady.

"Well, mates," said Harry's brother, "I reckon it's abaht time to go in. So 'ere's to the 'ealth of Mr. 'Enry Atkins an' 'is future missus."

"An' God bless 'em!" said Sally's mother.

Then they went into the church, and as they solemnly walked up the aisle a pale-faced young curate came out of the vestry and down to the bottom of the chancel. The beer had had a calming effect on their troubled minds, and both Harry and Sally began to think it rather a good joke. They smiled on each other, and at those parts of the service which they thought suggestive violently nudged one another in the ribs. When the ring had to be produced, Harry fumbled about in different pockets, and his brother whispered:

"Swop me bob, 'e's gone and lorst it!"

However, all went right, and, Sally having carefully pocketed the certificate, they went out and had another drink to celebrate the happy event.

In the evening Liza and several friends came into the couple's room, which they had taken in the same house as Sally had lived in before, and drank the health of the bride and bridegroom till they thought fit to retire.

CHAPTER X

It was November. The fine weather had quite gone now, and with it much of the sweet pleasure of Jim and Liza's love. When they came out at night on the Embankment they found it cold and dreary; sometimes a light fog covered the river-banks and made the lamps glow out dim and large; a light rain would be falling, which sent a chill into their very souls; foot passengers came along at rare intervals, holding up umbrellas and staring straight in front of them as they hurried along in the damp and cold; a cab would pass rapidly by, splashing up the mud on each side. The benches were deserted, except, perhaps, for some poor homeless wretch who could afford no shelter and, huddled up in a corner, with his head buried in his breast, was sleeping heavily, like a dead man. The wet mud made Liza's skirts cling about her feet, and the damp would come in and chill her legs and creep up her body, till she shivered, and for warmth pressed herself close against Jim. Sometimes they would go into the third-class waiting-rooms at Waterloo or Charing Cross and sit there, but it was not like the park or the Embankment on summer nights; they had warmth, but the heat made their wet clothes steam and smell, and the gas flared in their eyes, and they hated the people perpetually coming in and out, opening the doors and letting in a blast of cold air; they hated the noise of the guards and porters shouting out the departure of the trains, the shrill whistling of the steam-engine, the hurry and bustle and confusion. About eleven o'clock, when the trains grew less frequent, they got some quietness; but then their minds were troubled, and they felt heavy, sad and miserable.

One evening they had been sitting at Waterloo Station; it was foggy outside—a thick, yellow November fog, which filled the waiting-room, entering the lungs, and making the mouth taste nasty and the eyes smart. It was about half-past eleven, and the station was unusually quiet; a few passengers, in wraps and over-coats, were walking to and fro, waiting for the last train, and one or two porters were standing about, yawning. Liza and Jim had remained for an hour in perfect silence, filled with a gloomy unhappiness, as of a great weight on their brains. Liza was sitting forward, with her elbows on her knees, resting her face on her hands.

"I wish I was straight," she said at last, not looking up.

"Well, why won't yer come along of me altogether, an' you'll be arright then?" he answered.

"Na, that's no go; I can't do thet." He had often asked her to live with him entirely, but she had always refused.

"You can come along of me, an' I'll tike a room in a lodgin' 'ouse in 'Olloway, an' we can live there as if we was married."

"Wot abaht yer work?"

"I can get work over the other side as well as I can 'ere. I'm abaht sick of the wy things is goin' on."

"So am I; but I can't leave Mother."

"She can come, too."

"Not when I'm not married. I shouldn't like 'er ter know as I'd—as I'd gone wrong."

"Well, I'll marry yer. Swop me bob, I wants ter badly enough."

"Yer can't; yer married already."

"Thet don't matter! If I give the missus so much a week aht of my screw, she'll sign a piper ter give up all clime ter me, an' then we can get spliced. One of the men as I works with done thet, an' it was arright."

Liza shook her head.

62

"Na, yer can't do thet now; it's bigamy; an' the cop tikes yer, an' yer gits twelve months' 'ard for it."

"But swop me bob, Liza, I can't go on like this. Yer knows the missus—well, there ain't no bloomin' doubt abaht it, she knows as you an' me are carryin' on, an' she mikes no bones abaht lettin' me see it."

"She don't do thet?"

"Well, she don't exactly sy it, but she sulks an' won't speak, an' then when I says anythin' she rounds on me an' calls me all the nimes she can think of. I'd give 'er a good 'idin', but some'ow I don't like ter! She mikes the plice a 'ell ter me, an' I'm not goin' ter stand it no longer!"

"You'll 'ave ter sit it, then; yer can't chuck it."

"Yus I can, an' I would if you'd come along of me. I don't believe you like me at all, Liza, or you'd come."

She turned towards him and put her arms round his neck.

"Yer know I do, old cock," she said. "I like yer better than anyone else in the world; but I can't go awy an' leave Mother."

"Bli'me me if I see why; she's never been much ter you. She mikes yer slave awy ter pay the rent, an' all the money she earns she boozes."

"Thet's true, she ain't been wot yer might call a good mother ter me—but some'ow she's my mother, an' I don't like ter leave 'er on 'er own, now she's so old—an' she can't do much with the rheumatics. An' besides, Jim dear, it ain't only Mother, but there's yer own kids, yer can't leave them."

He thought for a while, and then said:

"You're abaht right there, Liza; I dunno if I could get on without the kids. If I could only tike them an' you too, swop me bob, I should be 'appy."

Liza smiled sadly.

"So yer see, Jim, we're in a bloomin' 'ole, an' there ain't no way aht of it thet I can see."

He took her on his knees and, pressing her to him, kissed her very long and very lovingly.

"Well, we must trust ter luck," she said again, "p'raps somethin' 'll 'appen soon, an' everythin' 'll come right in the end—when we gets four balls of worsted for a penny."

It was past twelve and, separating, they went by different ways along the dreary, wet, deserted roads till they came to Vere Street.

The street seemed quite different to Liza from what it had been three months before. Tom, the humble adorer, had quite disappeared from her life. One day, three or four weeks after the August Bank Holiday, she saw him dawdling along the pavement, and it suddenly struck her that she had not seen him for a long time; but she had been so full of her happiness that she had been unable to think of anyone but Jim. She wondered at his absence, since before wherever she had been there was he certain to be also. She passed him, but to her astonishment he did not speak to her. She thought by some wonder he had not seen her, but she felt his gaze resting upon her. She turned back, and suddenly he dropped his eyes and looked down, walking on as if he had not seen her, but blushing furiously.

"Tom," she said, "why don't yer speak ter me?"

He started and blushed more than ever.

"I didn't know yer was there," he stuttered.

"Don't tell me," she said; "wot's up?"

"Nothin' as I knows of," he answered uneasily.

"I ain't offended yer, 'ave I, Tom?"

"Na, not as I knows of," he replied, looking very unhappy.

"You don't ever come my way now," she said.

"I didn't know as yer wanted ter see me."

"Garn! Yer knows I likes you as well as anybody."

"Yer likes so many people, Liza," he said, flushing.

"What d'yer mean?" said Liza indignantly, but very red; she was afraid he knew now, and it was from him especially she would have been so glad to hide it.

"Nothin'," he answered.

"One doesn't say things like thet without any meanin', unless one's a blimed fool."

"You're right there, Liza," he answered. "I am a blimed fool."
He looked at her a little reproachfully, she thought, and then he said "Good-bye," and turned away.

At first she was horrified that he should know of her love for Jim; but then she did not care. After all, it was nobody's business, and what did anything matter as long as she loved Jim and Jim loved her? Then she grew angry that Tom should suspect her; he could know nothing but that some of the men had seen her with Jim near Vauxhall, and it seemed mean that he should condemn her for that. Thenceforward, when she ran against Tom, she cut him; he never tried to speak to her, but as she passed him, pretending to look in front of her, she could see that he always blushed, and she fancied his eyes were very sorrowful. Then several weeks went by, and as she began to feel more and more lonely in the street, she regretted the quarrel; she cried a little as she thought that she had lost his faithful, gentle love, and she would have much liked to be friends with him again. If he had only made some advance she would have welcomed him so cordially, but she was too proud to go to him herself and beg him to forgive her—and then, how could he forgive her?

She had lost Sally too, for on her marriage Harry had made her give up the factory; he was a young man with principles worthy of a Member of Parliament, and he had said:

"A woman's plice is 'er 'ome, an' if 'er old man can't afford ter keep 'er without 'er workin' in a factory—well, all I can say is thet 'e'd better go an' git single."

"Quite right, too," agreed his mother-in-law; "an' wot's more, she'll 'ave a baby ter look after soon, an' thet'll tike 'er all 'er time, an' there's no one as knows thet better than me, for I've 'ad twelve, ter sy nothin' of two stills an' one miss."

Liza quite envied Sally her happiness, for the bride was brimming over with song and laughter; her happiness overwhelmed her.

"I am 'appy," she said to Liza one day a few weeks after her marriage. "You dunno wot a good sort 'Arry is. 'E's just a darlin', an' there's no mistikin' it. I don't care wot other people sy, but wot I says is, there's nothin' like marriage. Never a cross word passes his lips, an' Mother 'as all 'er meals with us, an' 'e says all the better. Well, I'm thet 'appy I simply dunno if I'm standin' on my 'ead or on my 'eels."

But alas! it did not last too long. Sally was not so full of joy when next Liza met her, and one day her eyes looked very much as if she had been crying.

"Wot's the matter?" asked Liza, looking at her. "Wot 'ave yer been blubberin' abaht?"

"Me?" said Sally, getting very red. "Oh, I've got a bit of a toothache, an'—well, I'm rather a fool like, an' it 'urt me so much that I couldn't 'elp cryin'."

Liza was not satisfied, but could get nothing further out of her. Then one day it came out. It was a Saturday night, the time when women in Vere Street weep. Liza went up into Sally's room for a few minutes on her way to the Westminster Bridge Road, where she was to meet Jim. Harry had taken the top back room, and Liza, climbing up the second flight of stairs, called out as usual:

"Wot ho, Sally!"

The door remained shut, although Liza could see that there was a light in the room; but on getting to the door she stood still, for she heard the sound of sobbing. She listened for a minute and then knocked: there was a little flurry inside, and someone called out:

" 'Oo's there?"

"Only me," said Liza, opening the door. As she did so she saw Sally rapidly wipe her eyes and put her handkerchief away. Her mother was sitting by her side, evidently comforting her.

"Wot's up, Sal?" asked Liza.

"Nothin'," answered Sally, with a brave little gasp to stop the crying, turning her face downwards so that Liza should not see the tears in her eyes; but they were too strong for her, and, quickly taking out her handkerchief, she hid her face in it and began to sob broken-heartedly. Liza looked at the mother in interrogation.

"Oh, it's thet man again!" said the lady, snorting and tossing her head.

"Not 'Arry?" asked Liza, in surprise.

"Not 'Arry—'oo is it if it ain't 'Arry? The villin!"

"Wot's 'e been doin', then?" asked Liza again.

"Beatin' 'er, that's wot 'e's been doin'! Oh, the villin, 'e oughter be ashimed of 'isself, 'e ought!"

"I didn't know 'e was like that!" said Liza.

"Didn't yer? I thought the 'ole street knew it by now," said Mrs. Cooper indignantly. "Oh, 'e's a wrong 'un, 'e is."

"It wasn't 'is fault," put in Sally, amidst her sobs; "it's only because 'e's 'ad a little drop too much. 'E's arright when 'e's sober."

"A little drop too much! I should just think 'e'd 'ad, the beast! I'd give it 'im if I was a man. They're all like thet—'usbinds is all alike; they're arright when they're sober—sometimes—but when they've got the liquor in 'em, they're beasts, an' no mistike. I 'ad a 'usbind myself for five-an'-twenty years, an' I know 'em."

"Well, Mother," sobbed Sally, "it was all my fault. I should 'ave come 'ome earlier."

"Na, it wasn't your fault at all. Just you look 'ere, Liza: this is wot 'e done an' call 'isself a man. Just because Sally'd gone aht to 'ave a chat with Mrs. McLeod in the next 'ouse, when she come in 'e start bangin' 'er abaht. An' me, too, wot d'yer think of that!" Mrs. Cooper was quite purple with indignation.

"Yus," she went on, "thet's a man for yer. Of course, I wasn't goin' ter stand there an' see my daughter bein' knocked abaht; it wasn't likely—was it? An' 'e rounds on me, an' 'e 'its me with 'is fist. Look 'ere." She pulled up her sleeves and showed two red and brawny arms. " 'E's bruised my arms; I thought 'e'd broken it at fust. If I 'adn't put my arm up, 'e'd 'ave got me on the 'ead, an' 'e might 'ave killed me. An' I says to 'im, 'If you touch me again, I'll go ter the police-station, thet I will!' Well, that frightened 'im a bit, an' then didn't I let 'im 'ave it! 'You call yerself a man,' says I, 'an' you ain't fit ter clean the drains aht.' You should 'ave 'eard the language 'e used. 'You dirty old woman,' says 'e, 'you go away; you're always interferin' with me.' Well, I don't like ter repeat wot 'e said, and thet's the truth. An' I says ter 'im, 'I wish yer'd never married my daughter, an' if I'd known you was like this I'd 'ave died sooner than let yer.' "

"Well, I didn't know 'e was like thet!" said Liza.

" 'E was arright at fust," said Sally.

"Yus, they're always arright at fust! But ter think it should 'ave come to this now, when they ain't been married three months, an' the first child not born yet! I think it's disgraceful."

Liza stayed a little while longer, helping to comfort Sally, who kept pathetically taking to herself all the blame of the dispute; and then, bidding her good-night and better luck, she slid off to meet Jim.

When she reached the appointed spot he was not to be found. She waited for some time, and at last saw him come out of the neighbouring pub.

"Good-night, Jim," she said as she came up to him.

"So you've turned up, 'ave yer?" he answered roughly, turning round.

"Wot's the matter, Jim?" she asked, in a frightened way, for he had never before spoken to her in that manner.

"Nice thing ter keep me witin' all night for yer to come aht."

She saw that he had been drinking, and answered humbly:

"I'm very sorry, Jim, but I went in to Sally, an' 'er bloke 'ad been knockin' 'er abaht, an' so I sat with 'er a bit."

"Knockin' 'er abaht, 'ad 'e? and serve 'er damn well right too; an' there's many more as could do with a good 'idin'!"

Liza did not answer. He looked at her, and then suddenly said: "Come in an' 'ave a drink."

"Na, I'm not thirsty; I don't want a drink," she answered.

"Come on," he said angrily.

"Na, Jim, you've had quite enough already."

" 'Oo are you talkin' ter?" he said. "Don't come if yer **don't** want ter; I'll go an' 'ave one by myself."

"Na, Jim, don't." She caught hold of his arm.

"Yus I shall," he said, going towards the pub, while she held him back. "Let me go, can't yer! Let me go!" He roughly pulled his arm away from her. As she tried to catch hold of it again, he pushed her back, and in the little scuffle caught her a blow over the face.

"Oh!" she cried, "you did 'urt!"

He was sobered at once.

"Liza," he said. "I ain't 'urt yer?" She didn't answer, and he took her in his arms. "Liza, I ain't 'urt you, 'ave I? Say I ain't 'urt yer. I'm so sorry; I beg your pardon, Liza."

"Arright, old chap," she said, smiling charmingly on him. "It wasn't the blow that 'urt me much; it was the wy you was talkin'."

"I didn't mean it, Liza." He was so contrite, he could not humble himself enough. "I 'ad another bloomin' row with the missus ter-night, an' then when I didn't find you 'ere, an' I kept witin' an' witin'—well, I fair downright lost my 'air. An' I 'ad two or three pints of four 'alf, an'—well, I dunno——"

"Never mind, old cock, I can stand more than thet as long as yer loves me."

He kissed her and they were quite friends again. But the little quarrel had another effect which was worse for Liza. When she woke up next morning she noticed a slight soreness over the ridge of bone under the left eye, and on looking in the glass saw that it was black and blue and green. She bathed it, but it remained, and seemed to get more marked. She was terrified lest people should see it, and kept indoors all day; but next morning it was blacker than ever. She went to the factory with her hat over her eyes and her head bent down; she escaped observation, but on the way home she was not so lucky. The sharp eyes of some girls noticed it first.

"Wot's the matter with yer eye?" asked one of them.

"Me?" answered Liza, putting her hand up as if in ignorance. "Nothin' thet I knows of."

Two or three young men were standing by and, hearing the girl, looked up.

"Why, yer've got a black eye, Liza!"

"Me? I ain't got no black eye!"

"Yus, you 'ave; 'ow d'yer get it?"

"I dunno," said Liza. "I didn't know I 'ad one."

"Garn! tell us another!" was the answer. "One doesn't git a black eye without knowin' 'ow they got it."

"Well, I did fall against the chest-of-drawers yesterday; I suppose I must 'ave got it then."

"Oh yes, we believe thet, don't we?"

"I didn't know 'e was so 'andy with 'is dukes, did you, Ted?" asked one man of another.

Liza felt herself grow red to the tips of her toes.

"Who?" she asked.

"Never you mind; nobody you know."

At that moment Jim's wife passed and looked at her with a scowl. Liza wished herself a hundred miles away, and blushed more violently than ever.

"Wot are yer blushin' abaht?" ingenuously asked one of the girls.

And they all looked from her to Mrs. Blakeston and back again. Someone said: " 'Ow abaht our Sunday boots on now?" And a titter went through them. Liza's nerve deserted her; she could think of nothing to say, and a sob burst from her. To hide the tears which were coming from her eyes she turned away and walked homewards. Immediately a great shout of laughter broke from the group, and she heard them positively screaming till she got into her own house.

CHAPTER XI

A few days afterwards Liza was talking with Sally, who did not seem very much happier than when Liza had last seen her.

" 'E ain't wot I thought 'e wos," she said. "I don't mind sayin' thet; but 'e 'as a lot ter put up with; I expect I'm rather tryin' sometimes, an' 'e means well. P'raps 'e'll be kinder like when the biby's born."

"Cheer up, old gal," answered Liza, who had seen something of the lives of many married couples; "it won't seem so bad after yer gets used to it; it's a bit disappointin' at fust, but yer gits not ter mind it."

After a little Sally said she must go and see about her husband's tea. She said good-bye, and then rather awkwardly:

"Say, Liza, tike care of yerself!"

"Tike care of meself—why?" asked Liza, in surprise.

"Yer know wot I mean."

"Na, I'm darned if I do."

"Thet there Mrs. Blakeston, she's lookin' aht for you."

"Mrs. Blakeston!" Liza was startled.

"Yus; she says she's goin' ter give you somethin' if she can git 'old on yer. I should advise yer ter tike care."

"Me?" said Liza.

Sally looked away, so as not to see the other's face.

"She says as 'ow yer've been messin' abaht with 'er old man."

Liza didn't say anything, and Sally, repeating her good-bye, slid off.

Liza felt a chill run through her. She had several times noticed a scowl and a look of anger on Mrs. Blakeston's face, and she had avoided her as much as possible; but she had no idea that the woman meant to do anything to her. She was very frightened, a cold sweat broke out over her face. If Mrs. Blakeston got hold of her she would be helpless, she was so small and weak, while the other was strong and muscular. Liza wondered what she would do if she did catch her.

That night she told Jim, and tried to make a joke of it.

"I say, Jim, your missus—she says she's goin' ter give me socks if she catches me."

"My missus! 'Ow d'yer know?"

"She's been tellin' people in the street."

"Go' lumme," said Jim, furious, "if she dares ter touch a 'air of your 'ead, swop me dicky I'll give 'er sich a 'idin' as she never 'ad before! By God, give me the chanst, an' I would let 'er 'ave it; I'm bloomin' well sick of 'er sulks!" He clenched his fist as he spoke.

Liza was a coward. She could not help thinking of her enemy's threat; it got on her nerves, and she hardly dared go out for fear of meeting her; she would look nervously in front of her, quickly turning round if she saw in the distance anyone resembling Mrs. Blakeston. She dreamed of her at night; she saw the big, powerful form, the heavy, frowning face, and the curiously braided brown hair; and she would wake up with a cry and find herself bathed in sweat.

It was the Saturday afternoon following this, a chill November day, with the roads sloshy, and a grey, comfortless sky, that made one's spirits sink. It was about three o'clock, and Liza was coming home from work; she got into Vere Street, and was walking quickly towards her house when she saw Mrs. Blakeston coming towards her. Her heart gave a great jump. Turning, she walked rapidly in the direction she had come; with a screw round of her eyes she saw that she was being followed, and therefore went straight out of Vere Street. She went right round, meaning to get into the street from the other end and, unobserved, slip into her house, which was then quite close; but she dared not risk it immediately for fear Mrs. Blakeston should still be there; so she waited about for half an hour. It seemed an age. Finally, taking her courage in both hands, she turned the corner and entered Vere Street. She nearly ran into the arms of Mrs. Blakeston, who was standing close to the public-house door.

Liza gave a little cry, and the woman said, with a sneer:

"Yer didn't expect ter see me, did yer?"

Liza did not answer, but tried to walk past her. Mrs. Blakeston stepped forward and blocked her way.

"Yer seem ter be in a mighty fine 'urry," she said.

"Yus, I've got ter git 'ome," said Liza, again trying to pass.

"But supposin' I don't let yer?" remarked Mrs. Blakeston, preventing her from moving.

"Why don't yer leave me alone?" Liza said. "I ain't interferin' with you!"

"Not interferin' with me, aren't yer? I like thet!"

"Let me go by," said Liza. "I don't want ter talk ter you."

"Na, I know thet," said the other; "but I want ter talk ter you, an' I shan't let yer go until I've said wot I wants ter sy."

Liza looked round for help. At the beginning of the altercation the loafers about the public-house had looked up with interest, and gradually gathered round in a little circle. Passers-by had joined in, and a number of other people in the street, seeing the crowd, added themselves to it to see what was going on. Liza saw that all eyes were fixed on her, the men amused and excited, the women unsympathetic, rather virtuously indignant. Liza wanted to ask for help, but there were so many people, and they all seemed so much against her, that she had not the courage to. So, having surveyed the crowd, she turned her eyes to Mrs. Blakeston, and stood in front of her, trembling a little, and very white.

"Na, 'e ain't there," said Mrs. Blakeston, sneeringly, "so yer needn't look for 'im."

"I dunno wot yer mean," answered Liza, "an' I want ter go awy. I ain't done nothin' ter you."

"Not done nothin' ter me?" furiously repeated the woman. "I'll tell yer wot yer've done ter me—you've robbed me of my 'usbind, you 'ave. I never 'ad a word with my 'usbind until you took 'im from me. An' now it's all you with 'im. 'E's got no time for 'is wife an' family—it's all you. An' 'is money, too. I never git a penny of it; if it weren't for the little bit I 'ad saved up in the siving-bank, me an' my children 'ud be starvin' now! An' all through you!" She shook her fist at her.

"I never 'ad any money from anyone."

"Don't talk ter me; I know yer did. Yer dirty bitch! You oughter be ashimed of yourself tikin' a married man from 'is family, an' 'im old enough ter be yer father."

"She's right there!" said one or two of the onlooking women. "There can't be no good in 'er if she tikes somebody else's 'usbind."

"I'll give it yer!" proceeded Mrs. Blakeston, getting more hot and excited, brandishing her fist, and speaking in a loud voice, hoarse with rage. "Oh, I've been tryin' ter git 'old on yer this four weeks. Why, you're a prostitute—thet's wot you are!"

"I'm not!" answered Liza indignantly.

"Yus, you are," repeated Mrs. Blakeston, advancing menacingly, so that Liza shrank back. "An' wot's more, 'e treats yer like one. I know 'oo give yer thet black eye; thet shows what 'e thinks of yer! An' serve yer bloomin' well right if 'e'd give yer one in both eyes!"

Mrs. Blakeston stood close in front of her, her heavy jaw protruded and the frown of her eyebrows dark and stern. For a moment she stood silent, contemplating Liza, while the surrounders looked on in breathless interest.

"Yer dirty little bitch, you!" she said at last. "Tike that!" and with her open hand she gave her a sharp smack on the cheek.

Liza started back with a cry and put her hand up to her face.

"An' tike thet!" added Mrs. Blakeston, repeating the blow. Then, gathering up the spittle in her mouth, she spat in Liza's face.

Liza sprang on her, and with her hands spread out like claws buried her nails in the woman's face and drew them down her cheeks. Mrs. Blakeston caught hold of her hair with both hands and tugged at it as hard as she could. But they were immediately separated.

" 'Ere, 'old 'ard!" said some of the men. "Fight it aht fair and square. Don't go scratchin' and maulin' like thet."

"I'll fight 'er; I don't mind!" shouted Mrs. Blakeston, tucking up her sleeves and savagely glaring at her opponent.

Liza stood in front of her, pale and trembling; as she looked at her enemy, and saw the long red marks of her nails, with blood coming from one or two of them, she shrank back.

"I don't want ter fight," she said hoarsely.

"Na, I don't suppose yer do," hissed the other, "but yer'll damn well 'ave ter!"

"She's ever so much bigger than me; I've got no chanst," added Liza tearfully.

"You should 'ave thought of thet before. Come on!" and with these words Mrs. Blakeston rushed upon her. She hit her with both fists one after the other. Liza did not try to guard herself, but, imitating the woman's motion, hit out with her own fists; and for a minute or two they continued thus, raining blows on one another with the same windmill motion of the arms. But Liza could not stand against the other woman's weight; the blows came down heavy and rapid all over her face and head. She put up her hands to cover her face and turned her head away, while Mrs. Blakeston kept on hitting mercilessly.

"Time!" shouted some of the men—"Time!" and Mrs. Blakeston stopped to rest herself.

"It don't seem 'ardly fair to set them two on tergether. Liza's got no chanst against a big woman like thet," said a man among the crowd.

"Well, it's 'er own fault," answered a woman; "she didn't oughter mess about with 'er 'usbind."

"Well, I don't think it's right," added another man. "She's gettin' it too much."

"An' serve 'er right too!" said one of the women. "She deserves all she gets, an' a damn sight more inter the bargain."

"Quite right," put in a third; "a woman's got no right ter tike someone's 'usbind from 'er. An' if she does she's bloomin' lucky if she gits off with a 'idin'—thet's wot I think."

"So do I. But I wouldn't 'ave thought it of Liza. I never thought she was a wrong 'un."

"Pretty specimen she is!" said a little dark woman, who looked like a Jewess. "If she messed abaht with my old man, I'd stick 'er—I swear I would!"

"Now she's been carryin' on with one, she'll try an' git others—you see if she don't."

"She'd better not come round my 'ouse; I'll soon give 'er wot for."

Meanwhile Liza was standing at one corner of the ring, trembling all over and crying bitterly. One of her eyes was bunged up, and her hair, all dishevelled, was hanging down over her face. Two young fellows, who had constituted themselves her seconds, were standing in front of her, offering rather ironical comfort. One of them had taken the bottom corners of her apron and was fanning her with it, while the other was showing her how to stand and hold her arms.

"You stand up to 'er, Liza," he was saying; "there ain't no good funkin' it, you'll simply get it all the worse. You 'it 'er back. Give 'er one on the boko, like this—see; yer must show a bit of pluck, yer know."

Liza tried to check her sobs.

"Yus, 'it 'er 'ard, that's wot yer've got ter do," said the other. "An' if yer find she's gettin' the better on yer, you close on 'er and catch 'old of 'er 'air and scratch 'er."

"You've marked 'er with yer nails, Liza. By gosh, you did fly on her when she spat at yer! thet's the way ter do the job!"

Then turning to his fellow, he said:

"D'yer remember thet fight as old Mother Gregg 'ad with another woman in the street last year?"

"Na," he answered, "I never saw thet."

"It was a cawker; an' the cops come in and took 'em both off ter quod."

Liza wished the policemen would come and take her off; she would willingly have gone to prison to escape the fiend in front of her; but no help came.

"Time's up!" shouted the referee. "Fire away!"

"Tike care of the cops!" shouted a man.

"There's no fear abaht them," answered somebody else. "They always keeps out of the way when there's anythin' goin' on."

"Fire away!"

Mrs. Blakeston attacked Liza madly; but the girl stood up

bravely, and as well as she could gave back the blows she received. The spectators grew tremendously excited.

"Got 'im again!" they shouted. "Give it 'er, Liza, thet's a good 'un!—'it 'er 'ard!"

"Two ter one on the old 'un!" shouted a sporting gentleman; but Liza found no backers.

"Ain't she standin' up well now she's roused?" cried someone.

"Oh, she's got some pluck in 'er, she 'as!"

"Thet's a knock-aht!" they shouted as Mrs. Blakeston brought her fist down on to Liza's nose; the girl staggered back, and blood began to flow. Then, losing all fear, mad with rage, she made a rush on her enemy, and rained down blows all over her nose and eyes and mouth. The woman recoiled at the sudden violence of the onslaught, and the men cried:

"By God, the little 'un's gettin' the best of it!"

But quickly recovering herself the woman closed with Liza, and dug her nails into her flesh. Liza caught hold of her hair and pulled with all her might, and turning her teeth on Mrs. Blakeston tried to bite her. And thus for a minute they swayed about, scratching, tearing, biting, sweat and blood pouring down their faces, and their eyes fixed on one another, bloodshot and full of rage. The audience shouted and cheered and clapped their hands.

"Wot the 'ell's up 'ere?"

"I sy, look there," said some of the women in a whisper. "It's the 'usbind!"

He stood on tiptoe and looked over the crowd.

"My Gawd," he said, "it's Liza!"

Then roughly pushing the people aside, he made his way through the crowd into the centre, and thrusting himself between the two women, tore them apart. He turned furiously on his wife.

"By Gawd, I'll give yer somethin' for this!"

And for a moment they all three stood silently looking at one another.

Another man had been attracted by the crowd, and he, too, pushed his way through.

"Come 'ome, Liza," he said.

"Tom!"

He took hold of her arm, and led her through the people, who gave way to let her pass. They walked silently through the street, Tom very grave, Liza weeping bitterly.

"Oh, Tom," she sobbed after a while, "I couldn't 'elp it!" Then, when her tears permitted, "I did love 'im so!"

When they got to the door she plaintively said: "Come in," and he followed her to her room. Here she sank on to a chair, and gave herself up to her tears.

Tom wetted the end of a towel and began wiping her face, grimy with blood and tears. She let him do it, just moaning amid her sobs:

"You are good ter me, Tom."

"Cheer up, old gal," he said kindly, "it's all over now."

After a while the excess of crying brought its cessation. She drank some water, and then taking up a broken hand-glass she looked at herself, saying:

"I am a sight!" and proceeded to wind up her hair. "You 'ave been good ter me, Tom," she repeated, her voice still broken with sobs; and as he sat down beside her she took his hand.

"Na, I ain't," he answered; "it's only wot anybody 'ud 'ave done."

"Yer know, Tom," she said, after a little silence, "I'm so sorry I spoke cross like when I met yer in the street; you ain't spoke ter me since."

"Oh, thet's all over now, old lidy, we needn't think of thet."

"Oh, but I 'ave treated yer bad. I'm a regular wrong 'un, I am."

He pressed her hand without speaking.

"I say, Tom," she began, after another pause. "Did yer know thet—well, you know—before ter-day?"

He blushed as he answered:

"Yus."

She spoke very sadly and slowly.

"I thought yer did; yer seemed so cut up like when I used to meet yer. Yer did love me then, Tom, didn't yer?"

"I do now, dearie," he answered.

"Ah, it's too lite now," she sighed.

"D'yer know, Liza," he said, "I just abaht kicked the life aht of a feller 'cause 'e said you was messin' abaht with—with 'im."

"An' yer knew I was?"

"Yus—but I wasn't goin' ter 'ave anyone say it before me."

"They've all rounded on me except you, Tom. I'd 'ave done better if I'd tiken you when you arst me; I shouldn't be where I am now, if I 'ad."

"Well, won't yer now? Won't yer 'ave me now?"

"Me? After wot's 'appened?"

"Oh, I don't mind abaht thet. Thet don't matter ter me if you'll marry me. I fair can't live without yer, Liza—won't yer?"

She groaned.

"Na, I can't, Tom; it wouldn't be right."

"Why not, if I don't mind?"

"Tom," she said, looking down, almost whispering, "I'm like that—you know!"

"Wot d'yer mean?"

She could scarcely utter the words—

"I think I'm in the family wy."

He paused a moment; then spoke again.

"Well—I don't mind, if yer'll only marry me."

"Na, I can't, Tom," she said, bursting into tears; "I can't, but you are so good ter me; I'd do anythin' ter mike it up ter you."

She put her arms round his neck and slid on to his knees.

"Yer know, Tom, I couldn't marry yer now; but anythin' else —if yer wants me ter do anythin' else, I'll do it if it'll mike you 'appy."

He did not understand, but only said:

"You're a good gal, Liza," and bending down he kissed her gravely on the forehead.

Then with a sigh he lifted her down, and getting up left her alone. For a while she sat where he left her, but as she thought of all she had gone through her loneliness and misery overcame her, the tears welled forth, and throwing herself on the bed she buried her face in the pillows.

Jim stood looking at Liza as she went off with Tom, and his wife watched him jealously.

"It's 'er you're thinkin' abaht. Of course you'd 'ave liked ter tike 'er 'ome yerself, I know, an' leave me to shift for myself."

"Shut up!" said Jim, angrily turning upon her.

"I shan't shut up," she answered, raising her voice. "Nice 'usbind you are. Go' lumme, as good as they mike 'em! Nice thing ter go an' leave yer wife and children for a thing like thet! At your age, too! You oughter be ashimed of yerself. Why, it's like messin' abaht with yer own daughter!"

"By God!"—he ground his teeth with rage—"if yer don't leave me alone, I'll kick the life aht of yer!"

"There!" she said, turning to the crowd—"there, see 'ow 'e

treats me! Listen ter that! I've been 'is wife for twenty years, an'
yer couldn't 'ave 'ad a better wife, an' I've bore 'im nine children,
ter say nothin' of a miscarriage, an' I've got another one comin',
an' thet's 'ow 'e treats me! Nice 'usband, ain't it?'' She looked
at him scornfully, then again at the surrounders as if for their
opinion.

"Well, I ain't goin' ter stay 'ere all night; get aht of the light!''
He pushed aside the people who barred his way, and the one or
two who growled a little at his roughness, looking at his angry
face, were afraid to complain.

"Look at 'im!'' said his wife. " 'E's afraid, 'e is. See 'im
slinkin' awy like a bloomin' mongrel with 'is tail between 'is legs.
Ugh!'' She walked just behind him, shouting and brandishing her
arms.

"Yer dirty beast, you,'' she yelled; "ter go foolin' abaht with a
little girl! Ugh! I wish yer wasn't my 'usbind; I wouldn't be seen
drowned with yer, if I could 'elp it. Yer mike me sick ter look at
yer.''

The crowd followed them on both sides of the road, keeping at
a discreet distance, but still eagerly listening.

Jim turned on her once or twice and said:

"Shut up!''

But it only made her more angry. "I tell yer I shan't shut up.
I don't care 'oo knows it, you're a ——, you are! I'm ashimed the
children should 'ave such a father as you. D'yer think I didn't
know wot you was up ter them nights you was awy—courtin',
yus, courtin'? You're a nice man, you are!''

Jim did not answer her, but walked on. At last he turned round
to the people who were following and said:

"Na then, wot d'you want 'ere? You jolly well clear, or I'll
give some of you somethin'!''

They were mostly boys and women, and at his words they
shrank back.

" 'E's afraid ter sy anythin' ter me,'' jeered Mrs. Blakeston.
" 'E's a beauty!''

Jim entered his house, and she followed him till they came up
into their room. Polly was giving the children their tea. They all
started up as they saw their mother with her hair and clothes in
disorder, blotches of dried blood on her face, and the long
scratch-marks.

"Oh, Mother,'' said Polly, "wot is the matter?''

" 'E's the matter," she answered, pointing to her husband "It's through 'im I've got all this. Look at yer father, children; 'e's a father to be proud of, leavin' yer ter starve an' spendin' 'is week's money on a dirty little strumpet."

Jim felt easier now he had not got so many strange eyes on him.

"Now, look 'ere," he said, "I'm not goin' ter stand this much longer, so just you tike care."

"I ain't frightened of yer. I know yer'd like ter kill me, but yer'll get strung up if you do."

"Na, I won't kill yer, but if I 'ave any more of your sauce I'll do the next thing to it."

"Touch me if yer dare," she said; "I'll 'ave the law on you. An' I shouldn't mind 'ow many month's 'ard you got."

"Be quiet!" he said, and, closing his hand, gave her a heavy blow in the chest that made her stagger.

"Oh, you ——!" she screamed.

She seized the poker, and in a fury of rage rushed at him.

"Would yer?" he said, catching hold of it and wrenching it from her grasp. He threw it to the end of the room and grappled with her. For a moment they swayed about from side to side, then with an effort he lifted her off her feet and threw her to the ground; but she caught hold of him and he came down on the top of her. She screamed as her head thumped down on the floor, and the children, who were standing huddled up in a corner, terrified, screamed too.

Jim caught hold of his wife's head and began beating it against the floor.

She cried out: "You're killing me! Help! help!"

Polly in terror ran up to her father and tried to pull him off.

"Father, don't 'it 'er! Anythin' but thet—for God's sike!"

"Leave me alone," he said, "or I'll give you somethin' too."

She caught hold of his arm, but Jim, still kneeling on his wife, gave Polly a backhanded blow which sent her staggering back.

"Tike that!"

Polly ran out of the room, downstairs to the first-floor front, where two men and two women were sitting at tea.

"Oh, come an' stop Father!" she cried. " 'E's killin' Mother!"

"Why, wot's 'e doin'?"

"Oh, 'e's got 'er on the floor, an' 'e's bangin' 'er 'ead. 'E's payin' 'er aht for givin' Liza Kemp a 'idin'."

One of the women started up and said to her husband:

"Come on, John, you go an' stop it."

"Don't you, John," said the other man. "When a man's givin' 'is wife socks it's best not ter interfere."

"But 'e's killin' 'er," repeated Polly, trembling with fright.

"Garn!" rejoined the man; "she'll git over it; an' p'raps she deserves it, for all you know."

John sat undecided, looking now at Polly, now at his wife, and now at the other man.

"Oh, do be quick—for God's sike!" said Polly.

At that moment a sound as of something smashing was heard upstairs, and a woman's shriek. Mrs. Blakeston, in an effort to tear herself away from her husband, had knocked up against the wash-hand stand, and the whole thing had crashed down.

"Go on, John," said the wife.

"Na, I ain't goin'; I shan't do no good, an' 'e'll only round on me."

"Well, you are a bloomin' lot of cowards, thet's all I can say," indignantly answered the wife. "But I ain't goin' ter see a woman murdered; I'll go an' stop 'im."

With that she ran upstairs and threw open the door. Jim was still kneeling on his wife, hitting her furiously, while she was trying to protect her head and face with her hands.

"Leave off!" shouted the woman.

Jim looked up. " 'Oo the devil are you?" he said.

"Leave off, I tell yer. Aren't yer ashimed of yerself, knockin' a woman abaht like that?" And she sprang at him, seizing his fist.

"Let go," he said, "or I'll give you a bit."

"Yer'd better not touch me," she said. "Yer dirty coward! Why, look at 'er, she's almost senseless."

Jim stopped and gazed at his wife. He got up and gave her a kick.

"Git up!" he said; but she remained huddled up on the floor, moaning feebly. The woman from downstairs went on her knees and took her head in her arms.

"Never mind, Mrs. Blikeston. 'E's not goin' ter touch yer. 'Ere, drink this little drop of water." Then turning to Jim, with infinite disdain: "Yer dirty blackguard, you! If I was a man I'd give you something for this."

Jim put on his hat and went out, slamming the door, while the woman shouted after him: "Good riddance!"

"Lord love yer," said Mrs. Kemp, "wot is the matter?"

She had just come in, and opening the door had started back in surprise at seeing Liza on the bed, all tears. Liza made no answer, but cried as if her heart were breaking. Mrs. Kemp went up to her and tried to look at her face.

"Don't cry, dearie; tell us wot it is."

Liza sat up and dried her eyes.

"I am so un'appy!"

"Wot 'ave yer been doin' ter yer fice? My!"

"Nothin'."

"Garn! Yer can't 'ave got a fice like thet all by itself."

"I 'ad a bit of a scrimmage with a woman dahn the street," sobbed out Liza.

"She 'as give yer a doin'; an' yer all upset—an' look at yer eye! I brought in a little bit of stike for ter-morrer's dinner; you just cut a bit off an' put it over yer optic, that'll soon put it right. I always used ter do thet myself when me an' your poor father 'ad words."

"Oh, I'm all over in a tremble; an' my 'ead, oo, my 'ead does feel bad!"

"I know wot yer want," remarked Mrs. Kemp, nodding her head, "an' it so 'appens as I've got the very thing with me." She pulled a medicine bottle out of her pocket, and taking out the cork smelt it. "Thet's good stuff; none of your fire-water or your methylated spirit. I don't often indulge in sich things, but when I do I likes to 'ave the best."

She handed the bottle to Liza, who took a mouthful and gave it her back; she had a drink herself, and smacked her lips.

"Thet's good stuff. 'Ave a drop more."

"Na," said Liza, "I ain't used ter drinkin' spirits."

She felt dull and miserable, and a heavy pain throbbed through her head. If she could only forget!

"Na, I know you're not, but, bless your soul, thet won' 'urt yer. It'll do you no end of good. Why, often when I've been feelin' thet done up thet I didn't know wot ter do with myself, I've just 'ad a little drop of whisky or gin—I'm not partic'ler wot spirit it is—an' it's pulled me up wonderful."

Liza took another sip, a slightly longer one; it burnt as it went down her throat, and sent through her a feeling of comfortable warmth.

"I really do think it's doin' me good," she said, wiping her eyes and giving a sigh of relief as the crying ceased.

"I knew it would. Tike my word for it, if people took a little drop of spirits in time, there'd be much less sickness abaht."

They sat for a while in silence, then Mrs. Kemp remarked:

"Yer know, Liza, it strikes me as 'ow we could do with a drop more. You not bein' in the 'abit of tikin' anythin' I only brought just this little drop for me; an' it ain't took us long ter finish thet up. But as you're an invalid like we'll git a little more this time; it's sure ter turn aht useful."

"But you ain't got nothin' ter put it in."

"Yus, I 'ave," answered Mrs. Kemp; "there's thet bottle as they gives me at the 'orspital. Just empty the medicine aht into the pile, an' wash it aht, an' I'll tike it round to the pub myself."

Liza, when she was left alone, began to turn things over in her mind. She did not feel so utterly unhappy as before, for the things she had gone through seemed further away.

"After all," she said, "it don't so much matter."

Mrs. Kemp came in.

" 'Ave a little drop more, Liza," she said.

"Well, I don't mind if I do. I'll get some tumblers, shall I? There's no mistike abaht it," she added, when she had taken a little, "it do buck yer up."

"You're right, Liza—you're right. An' you wanted it badly. Fancy you 'avin' a fight with a woman! Oh, I've 'ad some in my day, but then I wasn't a little bit of a thing like you is. I wish I'd been there, I wouldn't 'ave stood by an' looked on while my daughter was gettin' the worst of it; although I'm turned sixty-five, an' gettin' on for sixty-six, I'd 'ave said to 'er: 'If you touch my daughter you'll 'ave me ter deal with, so just look aht!'"

She brandished her glass, and, that reminding her, she refilled it and Liza's.

"Ah, Liza," she remarked, "you're a chip of the old block. Ter see you settin' there an' 'avin' your little drop, it mikes me feel as if I was livin' a better life. Yer used ter be rather 'ard on me, Liza, 'cause I took a little drop on Saturday nights. An' mind, I don't sy I didn't tike a little drop too much sometimes—accidents will occur even in the best regulated of families; but wot I say is this—it's good stuff, I say, an' it don't 'urt yer."

"Buck up, old gal!" said Liza, filling the glasses, "no 'eel-taps. I feel like a new woman now. I was thet dahn in the dumps—

well, I shouldn't 'ave cared if I'd been at the bottom of the river, an' thet's the truth."

"You don't sy so," replied her affectionate mother.

"Yus, I do, an' I mean it too, but I don't feel like thet now. You're right, Mother, when you're in trouble there's nothin' like a bit of spirits."

"Well, if I don't know, I dunno 'oo does, for the trouble I've 'ad, it 'ud be enough to kill many women. Well, I've 'ad thirteen children, an' you can think wot thet was; every one I 'ad I used ter sy I wouldn't 'ave no more—but one does, yer know. You'll 'ave a family some day, Liza, an' I shouldn't wonder if you didn't 'ave as many as me. We come from a very prodigal family, we do, we've all gone in ter double figures, except your Aunt Mary, who only 'ad three—but then she wasn't married, so it didn't count, like."

They drank each other's health. Everything was getting blurred to Liza; she was losing her head.

"Yus," went on Mrs. Kemp, "I've 'ad thirteen children an' I'm proud of it. As your poor dear father used ter sy, it shows as 'ow one's got the blood of a Briton in one. Your poor dear father, 'e was a great 'and at speakin' 'e was: 'e used ter speak at parliamentary meetin's—I really believe 'e'd 'ave been a Member of Parliament if 'e'd been alive now. Well, as I was sayin', your father 'e used ter sy, 'None of your small families for me, I don't approve of them,' says 'e. 'E was a man of very 'igh principles, an' by politics 'e was a Radical. 'No,' says 'e, when 'e got talkin', 'when a man can 'ave a family risin' into double figures, it shows 'e's got the backbone of a Briton in 'im. That's the stuff as 'as built up England's nime and glory! When one thinks of the mighty British Hempire,' says 'e, 'on which the sun never sets from mornin' till night, one 'as ter be proud of 'isself, an' one 'as ter do one's duty in thet walk of life in which it 'as pleased Providence ter set one—an' every man's fust duty is ter get as many children as 'e bloomin' well can.' Lord love yer—'e could talk, I can tell yer."

"Drink up, Mother," said Liza. "You're not 'alf drinkin'." She flourished the bottle. "I don't care a twopenny 'ang for all them blokes; I'm quite 'appy, an' I don't want anythin' else."

"I can see you're my daughter now," said Mrs. Kemp. "When yer used ter round on me I used ter think as 'ow if I 'adn't carried yer for nine months, it must 'ave been some mistike, an' yer wasn't my daughter at all. When you come ter think of it, a man 'e don't know if it's 'is child or somebody else's, but yer can't deceive a woman like thet. Yer couldn't palm off somebody else's kid on 'er."

"I am beginnin' ter feel quite lively," said Liza. "I dunno wot it is, but I feel as if I wanted to laugh till I fairly split my sides."

And she began to sing: "For 'e's a jolly good feller—for 'e's a jolly good feller!"

Her dress was all disarranged; her face was covered with the scars of scratches, and clots of blood had fixed under her nose; her eye had swollen up so that it was nearly closed, and red; her hair was hanging over her face and shoulders, and she laughed stupidly and leered with heavy, sodden ugliness.

> "Disy, Disy! I can't afford a kerridge,
> But you'll look neat, on the seat
> Of a bicycle mide for two."

She shouted out the tunes, beating time on the table, and her mother, grinning, with her thin, grey hair hanging dishevelled over her head, joined in with her weak, cracked voice—

> "Oh, dem golden kippers, oh!"

Then Liza grew more melancholy and broke into "Auld Lang Syne".

> "Should old acquaintance be forgot
> And never brought to mind?
> . . . . . .
> For old lang syne."

Finally they both grew silent, and in a little while there came a snore from Mrs. Kemp; her head fell forward to her chest; Liza tumbled from her chair on to the bed, and sprawling across it fell asleep.

> *"Although I am drunk and bad, be you kind,*
> *Cast a glance at this heart which is bewildered and distressed.*
> *O God, take away from my mind my cry and my complaint.*
> *Offer wine, and take sorrow from my remembrance.*
> *Offer wine."*

CHAPTER XII

ABOUT the middle of the night Liza woke; her mouth was hot and dry, and a sharp, cutting pain passed through her head as she moved. Her mother had evidently roused herself, for she was lying in bed by her side, partially undressed, with all the bedclothes rolled round her. Liza shivered in the cold night, and taking off some of her things—her boots, her skirt, and jacket— got right into bed; she tried to get some of the blanket from her mother, but as she pulled Mrs. Kemp gave a growl in her sleep and drew the clothes more tightly round her. So Liza put over herself her skirt and a shawl, which was lying over the end of the bed, and tried to go to sleep.

But she could not; her head and hands were broiling hot, and she was terribly thirsty; when she lifted herself up to get a drink of water such a pang went through her head that she fell back on the bed groaning, and lay there with beating heart. And strange pains that she did not know went through her. Then a cold shiver seemed to rise in the very marrow of her bones and run down every artery and vein, freezing the blood; her skin puckered up, and drawing up her legs she lay huddled together in a heap, the shawl wrapped tightly round her, and her teeth chattering. Shivering, she whispered:

"Oh, I'm so cold, so cold. Mother, give me some clothes; I shall die of the cold. Oh, I'm freezing!"

But after a while the cold seemed to give way, and a sudden heat seized her, flushing her face, making her break out into perspiration, so that she threw everything off and loosened the things about her neck.

"Give us a drink," she said. "Oh, I'd give anythin' for a little drop of water!"

There was no one to hear; Mrs. Kemp continued to sleep heavily, occasionally breaking out into a little snore.

Liza remained there, now shivering with cold, now panting for breath, listening to the regular, heavy breathing by her side, and in her pain she sobbed. She pulled at her pillow and said:

"Why can't I go to sleep? Why can't I sleep like 'er?"

And the darkness was awful; it was a heavy, ghastly blackness, that seemed palpable, so that it frightened her, and she looked for relief at the faint light glimmering through the window from a distant street-lamp. She thought the night would never end—the minutes seemed like hours, and she wondered how she should live through till morning. And strange pains that she did not know went through her.

Still the night went on, the darkness continued, cold and horrible, and her mother breathed loudly and steadily by her side.

At last with the morning sleep came; but the sleep was almost worse than the wakefulness, for it was accompanied by ugly, disturbing dreams. Liza thought she was going through the fight with her enemy, and Mrs. Blakeston grew enormous in size, and multiplied, so that every way she turned the figure confronted her. And she began running away, and she ran and ran till she found herself reckoning up an account she had puzzled over in the morning, and she did it backwards and forwards, upwards and downwards, starting here, starting there, and the figures got mixed up with other things, and she had to begin over again, and everything jumbled up, and her head whirled, till finally, with a start, she woke.

The darkness had given way to a cold, grey dawn, her uncovered legs were chilled to the bone, and by her side she heard again the regular, nasal breathing of the drunkard.

For a long while she lay where she was, feeling very sick and ill, but better than in the night. At last her mother woke.

"Liza!" she called.

"Yus, Mother," she answered feebly.

"Git us a cup of tea, will yer?"

"I can't, Mother, I'm ill."

"Garn!" said Mrs. Kemp, in surprise. Then looking at her: "Swop me bob, wot's up with yer? Why, yer cheeks is flushed, an' yer forehead—it is 'ot! Wot's the matter with yer, gal?"

"I dunno," said Liza. "I've been thet bad all night, I thought I was goin' ter die."

"I know wot it is," said Mrs. Kemp, shaking her head; "the fact is, you ain't used ter drinkin', an' of course it's upset yer. Now me, why I'm as fresh as a disy. Tike my word, there ain't no good in teetotalism; it finds yer aht in the end, an' it's found you aht."

Mrs. Kemp considered it a judgment of Providence. She got up and mixed some whisky and water.

" 'Ere, drink this," she said. "When one's 'ad a drop too much at night, there's nothin' like havin' a drop more in the mornin' ter put one right. It just acts like magic."

"Tike it awy," said Liza, turning from it in disgust; "the smell of it gives me the sick. I'll never touch spirits again."

"Ah, thet's wot we all says sometime in our lives, but we does, an' wot's more we can't do withaht it. Why, me, the 'ard life I've 'ad——" It is unnecessary to repeat Mrs. Kemp's repetitions.

Liza did not get up all day. Tom came to inquire after her, and was told she was very ill. Liza plaintively asked whether anyone else had been, and sighed a little when her mother answered no. But she felt too ill to think much or trouble much about anything. The fever came again as the day wore on, and the pains in her head grew worse. Her mother came to bed, and quickly went off to sleep, leaving Liza to bear her agony alone. She began to have frightful pains all over her, and she held her breath to prevent herself from crying out and waking her mother. She clutched the sheets in her agony, and at last, about six o'clock in the morning, she could bear it no longer, and in the anguish of labour screamed out, and woke her mother.

Mrs. Kemp was frightened out of her wits. Going upstairs she woke the woman who lived on the floor above her. Without hesitating, the good lady put on a skirt and came down.

"She's 'ad a miss," she said, after looking at Liza. "Is there anyone you could send to the 'orspital?"

"Na, I dunno 'oo I could get at this hour?"

"Well, I'll git my old man ter go."

She called her husband, and sent him off. She was a stout, middle-aged woman, rough-visaged and strong-armed. Her name was Mrs. Hodges.

"It's lucky you came ter me," she said, when she had settled down. "I go aht nursin', yer know, so I know all abaht it."

"Well, you surprise me," said Mrs. Kemp. "I didn't know as Liza was thet way. She never told me nothin' abaht it."

"D'yer know 'oo it is 'as done it?"

"Now you ask me somethin' I don't know," replied Mrs. Kemp. "But now I come ter think of it, it must be thet there Tom. 'E's been keepin' company with Liza. 'E's a single man, so they'll be able ter get married—thet's somethin'."

"It ain't Tom," feebly said Liza.

"Not 'im; 'oo is it, then?"

Liza did not answer.

"Eh?" repeated the mother, " 'oo is it?"

Liza lay still without speaking.

"Never mind, Mrs. Kemp," said Mrs. Hodges, "don't worry 'er now; you'll be able ter find aht all abaht it when she gits better."

For a while the two women sat still, waiting the doctor's coming, and Liza lay gazing vacantly at the wall, panting for breath. Sometimes Jim crossed her mind, and she opened her mouth to call for him, but in her despair she restrained herself.

The doctor came.

"D'you think she's bad, Doctor?" asked Mrs. Hodges.

"I'm afraid she is rather," he answered. "I'll come in again this evening."

"Oh, Doctor," said Mrs. Kemp, as he was going, "could yer give me somethin' for my rheumatics? I'm a martyr to rheumatism, an' these cold days I 'ardly knows wot ter do with myself. An', Doctor, could you let me 'ave some beef-tea? My 'usbind's dead, an' of course I can't do no work with my daughter ill like this, an' we're very short——"

The day passed, and in the evening Mrs. Hodges, who had been attending to her own domestic duties, came downstairs again. Mrs. Kemp was on the bed sleeping.

"I was just 'avin' a little nap," she said to Mrs. Hodges, on waking.

" 'Ow is the girl?" asked that lady.

"Oh," answered Mrs. Kemp, "my rheumatics 'as been thet bad I really 'aven't known wot ter do with myself; an' now Liza can't rub me I'm worse than ever. It is unfortunate thet she should get ill just now when I want so much attendin' ter myself; but there, it's just my luck!"

Mrs. Hodges went over and looked at Liza; she was lying just as when she left in the morning, her cheeks flushed, her mouth open for breath, and tiny beads of sweat stood on her forehead.

" 'Ow are yer, ducky?" asked Mrs. Hodges; but Liza did not answer.

"It's my belief she's unconscious," said Mrs. Kemp. "I've been askin' 'er 'oo it was as done it, but she don't seem to 'ear wot I say. It's been a great shock ter me, Mrs. 'Odges."

"I believe you," replied that lady, sympathetically.

"Well, when you come in and said wot it was, yer might 'ave

knocked me dahn with a feather. I knew no more than the dead wot 'ad 'appened."

"I saw at once wot it was," said Mrs. Hodges, nodding her head.

"Yus, of course, you knew. I expect you've 'ad a great deal of practice one way an' another."

"You're right, Mrs. Kemp, you're right. I've been on the job now for nearly twenty years, an' if I don't know somethin' abaht it I ought."

"D'yer finds it pays well?"

"Well, Mrs. Kemp, tike it all in all, I ain't got no grounds for complaint. I'm in the 'abit of askin' five shillings, an' I will say this, I don't think it's too much for wot I do."

The news of Liza's illness had quickly spread, and more than once in the course of the day a neighbour had come to ask after her. There was a knock at the door now, and Mrs. Hodges opened it. Tom stood on the threshold asking to come in.

"Yus, you can come," said Mrs. Kemp.

He advanced on tiptoe, so as to make no noise, and for a while stood silently looking at Liza. Mrs. Hodges was by his side.

"Can I speak to 'er?" he whispered.

"She can't 'ear you."

He groaned.

"D'yer think she'll get arright?" he asked.

Mrs. Hodges shrugged her shoulders.

"I shouldn't like ter give an opinion," she said, cautiously.

Tom bent over Liza, and, blushing, kissed her; then, without speaking further, went out of the room.

"Thet's the young man as was courtin' 'er," said Mrs. Kemp, pointing over her shoulder with her thumb.

Soon after the doctor came.

"Wot do yer think of 'er, Doctor?" said Mrs. Hodges, bustling forwards authoritatively in her position of midwife and sick-nurse.

"I'm afraid she's very bad."

"D'yer think she's goin' ter die?" she asked, dropping her voice to a whisper.

"I'm afraid so!"

As the doctor sat down by Liza's side Mrs. Hodges turned round and significantly nodded to Mrs. Kemp, who put her handkerchief to her eyes. Then she went outside to the little group waiting at the door.

"Wot does the doctor sy?" they asked, among them Tom.

" 'E says just wot I've been sayin' all along; I knew she wouldn't live.

And Tom burst out: "Oh, Liza!"

As she retired a woman remarked:

"Mrs. 'Odges is very clever, I think."

"Yus," remarked another, "she got me through my last confinement simply wonderful. If it come to choosin' between 'em I'd back Mrs. 'Odges against forty doctors."

"Ter tell yer the truth, so would I. I've never known 'er wrong yet."

Mrs. Hodges sat down beside Mrs. Kemp and proceeded to comfort her.

"Why don't yer tike a little drop of brandy ter calm yer nerves, Mrs. Kemp?" she said; "you want it."

"I was just feelin' rather faint, an' I couldn't 'elp thinkin' as 'ow twopenneth of whisky 'ud do me good."

"Na, Mrs. Kemp," said Mrs. Hodges, earnestly, putting her hand on the other's arm. "You tike my tip—when you're queer there's nothin' like brandy for pullin' yer togither. I don't object to whisky myself, but as a medicine yer can't beat brandy."

"Well, I won't set up myself as knowin' better than you, Mrs. 'Odges; I'll do wot you think right."

Quite accidentally there was some in the room, and Mrs. Kemp poured it out for herself and her friend.

"I'm not in the 'abit of tikin' anythin' when I'm aht on business," she apologised, "but just ter keep you company I don't mind if I do."

"Your 'ealth, Mrs. 'Odges."

"Sime ter you, an' thank yer, Mrs. Kemp."

Liza lay still, breathing very quietly, her eyes closed. The doctor kept his fingers on her pulse.

"I've been very unfortunate of lite," remarked Mrs. Hodges, as she licked her lips; "this mikes the second death I've 'ad in the last ten days—women, I mean, of course I don't count babies."

"Yer don't sy so."

"Of course the other one—well, she was only a prostitute, so it didn't so much matter. It ain't like another woman, is it?"

"Na, you're right."

"Still, one don't like 'em ter die, even if they are thet. One mustn't be too 'ard on 'em."

"Strikes me you've got a very kind 'eart, Mrs. 'Odges," said Mrs. Kemp.

"I 'ave thet; an' I often says it 'ud be better for my peace of mind an' my business if I 'adn't. I 'ave ter go through a lot, I do; but I can say this for myself, I always gives satisfaction, an' thet's somethin' as all lidies in my line can't say."

They sipped their brandy for a while.

"It's a great trial ter me that this should 'ave 'appened," said Mrs. Kemp, coming to the subject that had been disturbing her for some time. "Mine's always been a very respectable family, an' such a thing as this 'as never 'appened before. No, Mrs. 'Odges, I was lawfully married in church, an' I've got my marriage lines now ter show I was, an' thet one of my daughters should 'ave gone wrong in this way—well, I can't understand it. I give 'er a good education, an' she 'ad all the comforts of a 'ome. She never wanted for nothin'; I worked myself to the bone ter keep 'er in luxury, an' then thet she should go an' disgrace me like this!"

"I understand wot yer mean, Mrs. Kemp."

"I can tell you my family was very respectable; an' my 'usbind, 'e earned twenty-five shillings a week, an' was in the sime plice seventeen years; an' 'is employers sent a beautiful wreath ter put on 'is coffin; an' they tell me they never 'ad such a good workman an' sich an 'onest man before. An' me! Well, I can sy this—I've done my duty by the girl, an' she's never learnt anythin' but good from me. Of course I ain't always been in wot yer might call flourishing circumstances, but I've always set her a good example, as she could tell yer so 'erself if she wasn't speechless."

Mrs. Kemp paused for a moment's reflection.

"As they sy in the Bible," she finished, "it's enough ter mike one's grey 'airs go dahn into the ground in sorrer. I can show yer my marriage certificate. Of course one doesn't like ter say much, because of course she's very bad; but if she got well I should 'ave given 'er a talkin' ter."

There was another knock.

"Do go an' see 'oo thet is; I can't, on account of my rheumatics."

Mrs. Hodges opened the door. It was Jim.

He was very white, and the blackness of his hair and beard, contrasting with the deathly pallor of his face, made him look ghastly. Mrs. Hodges stepped back.

" 'Oo's 'e?" she said, turning to Mrs. Kemp.

Jim pushed her aside and went up to the bed.

"Doctor, is she very bad?" he asked.

The doctor looked at him questioningly.

Jim whispered: "It was me as done it. She ain't goin' ter die, is she?"

The doctor nodded.

"O God! wot shall I do? It was my fault! I wish I was dead!"

Jim took the girl's head in his hands, and the tears burst from his eyes.

"She ain't dead yet, is she?"

"She's just living," said the doctor.

Jim bent down.

"Liza, Liza, speak ter me! Liza, say you forgive me! Oh, speak ter me!"

His voice was full of agony. The doctor spoke.

"She can't hear you."

"Oh, she must hear me! Liza! Liza!"

He sank on his knees by the bedside.

They all remained silent: Liza lying stiller than ever, her breast unmoved by the feeble respiration, Jim looking at her very mournfully; the doctor grave, with his fingers on the pulse. The two women looked at Jim.

"Fancy it bein' 'im!" said Mrs. Kemp. "Strike me lucky, ain't 'e a sight!"

"You 'ave got 'er insured, Mrs. Kemp?" asked the midwife. She could bear the silence no longer.

"Trust me fur thet!" replied the good lady. "I've 'ad 'er insured ever since she was born. Why, only the other dy I was sayin' ter myself thet all thet money 'ad been wisted, but you see it wasn't; yer never know yer luck, you see!"

"Quite right, Mrs. Kemp; I'm a rare one for insurin'. It's a great thing. I've always insured all my children."

"The way I look on it is this," said Mrs. Kemp—"wotever yer do when they're alive, an' we all know as children is very tryin' sometimes, you should give them a good funeral when they dies. Thet's my motto, an' I've always acted up to it."

"Do you deal with Mr. Stearman?" asked Mrs. Hodges.

"No, Mrs. 'Odges, for undertikin' give me Mr. Footley every time. In the black line 'e's fust an' the rest nowhere!"

"Well, thet's very strange now—thet's just wot I think. Mr. Footley does 'is work well, an' 'e's very reasonable. I'm a very old customer of 'is, an' 'e lets me 'ave things as cheap as anybody."

"Does 'e indeed! Well, Mrs. 'Odges, if it ain't askin' too much of yer, I should look upon it as very kind if you'd go an' mike the arrangements for Liza."

"Why, certainly, Mrs. Kemp. I'm always willin' ter do a good turn to anybody, if I can."

"I want it done very respectable," said Mrs. Kemp; "I'm not goin' ter stint for nothin' for my daughter's funeral. I like plumes, you know, although they is a bit extra."

"Never you fear, Mrs. Kemp, it shall be done as well as if it was for my own 'usbind, an' I can't say more than thet. Mr. Footley thinks a deal of me, 'e does! Why, only the other dy as I was goin' inter 'is shop, 'e says, 'Good-mornin', Mrs. 'Odges.' 'Good-mornin', Mr. Footley,' says I. 'You've jest come in the nick of time,' says 'e. 'This gentleman an' myself,' pointin' to another gentleman as was standin' there, 'we was 'avin' a bit of an argument. Now you're a very intelligent woman, Mrs. 'Odges, and a good customer too.' 'I can say thet for myself,' says I, 'I gives yer all the work I can.' 'I believe you,' says 'e. 'Well,' 'e says, 'now which do you think? Does hoak look better than helm, or does helm look better than hoak? Hoak *versus* helm, thet's the question.' 'Well, Mr. Footley,' says I, 'for my own private opinion, when you've got a nice brass plite in the middle, an' nice brass 'andles each end, there's nothin' like hoak.' 'Quite right,' says 'e, 'thet's wot I think; for coffins give me hoak any day, an' I 'ope,' says 'e, 'when the Lord sees fit ter call me to 'Imself, I shall be put in a hoak coffin myself.' 'Amen,' says I."

"I like hoak," said Mrs. Kemp. "My poor 'usbind 'e 'ad a hoak coffin. We did 'ave a job with 'im, I can tell yer. You know 'e 'ad dropsy, an' 'e swell up—oh, 'e did swell; 'is own mother wouldn't 'ave known 'im. Why, 'is leg swell up till it was as big round as 'is body, swop me bob, it did."

"Did it indeed!" ejaculated Mrs. Hodges.

"Yus, an' when 'e died they sent the coffin up. I didn't 'ave Mr. Footley at thet time; we didn't live 'ere then, we lived in Battersea, an' all our undertikin' was done by Mr. Brownin'; well, 'e sent the coffin up, an' we got my old man in, but we couldn't get the lid down, he was so swell up. Well, Mr. Brownin', 'e was a great big man, thirteen stone if 'e was a ounce. Well, 'e stood on the coffin, an' a young man 'e 'ad with 'im stood on it too, an' the lid simply wouldn't go dahn; so Mr. Brownin', 'e said, 'Jump on, missus,' so I was in my widow's weeds, yer know, but we 'ad ter git it dahn, so I stood on it, an' we all jumped, an' at last we got it to, an' screwed it; but, lor', we did 'ave a job; I shall never forget it."

Then all was silence. And a heaviness seemed to fill the air like a grey blight, cold and suffocating; and the heaviness was Death. They felt the presence in the room, and they dared not move, they dared not draw their breath. The silence was terrifying.

Suddenly a sound was heard—a loud rattle. It was from the bed and rang through the room, piercing the stillness.

The doctor opened one of Liza's eyes and touched it, then he laid on her breast the hand he had been holding, and drew the sheet over her head.

Jim turned away with a look of intense weariness on his face, and the two women began weeping silently. The darkness was sinking before the day, and a dim, grey light came through the window. The lamp spluttered out.

CAKES AND ALE

CAKES AND ALE

Cakes and Ale

CHAPTER I

I HAVE noticed that when someone asks for you on the telephone and, finding you out, leaves a message begging you to call him up the moment you come in, and it's important, the matter is more often important to him than to you. When it comes to making you a present or doing you a favour most people are able to hold their impatience within reasonable bounds. So when I got back to my lodgings with just enough time to have a drink, a cigarette, and to read my paper before dressing for dinner, and was told by Miss Fellows, my landlady, that Mr. Alroy Kear wished me to ring him up at once, I felt that I could safely ignore his request.

"Is that the writer?" she asked me.

"It is."

She gave the telephone a friendly glance.

"Shall I get him?"

"No, thank you."

"What shall I say if he rings again?"

"Ask him to leave a message."

"Very good, sir."

She pursed her lips. She took the empty siphon, swept the room with a look to see that it was tidy, and went out. Miss Fellows was a great novel reader. I was sure that she had read all Roy's books. Her disapproval of my casualness suggested that she had read them with admiration. When I got home again, I found a note in her bold, legible writing on the sideboard.

Mr. Kear rang up twice. Can you lunch with him to-morrow? If not what day will suit you?

I raised my eyebrows. I had not seen Roy for three months and then only for a few minutes at a party; he had been very friendly, he always was, and when we separated he had expressed his hearty regret that we met so seldom.

"London's awful," he said. "One never has time to see any

1

of the people one wants to. Let's lunch together one day next week, shall we?"

"I'd like to," I replied.

"I'll look at my book when I get home and ring you up."

"All right."

I had not known Roy for twenty years without learning that he always kept in the upper left-hand pocket of his waistcoat the little book in which he put down his engagements; I was therefore not surprised when I heard from him no further. It was impossible for me now to persuade myself that this urgent desire of his to dispense hospitality was disinterested. As I smoked a pipe before going to bed I turned over in my mind the possible reasons for which Roy might want me to lunch with him. It might be that an admirer of his had pestered him to introduce me to her or that an American editor, in London for a few days, had desired Roy to put me in touch with him; but I could not do my old friend the injustice of supposing him so barren of devices as not to be able to cope with such a situation. Besides, he told me to choose my own day, so it could hardly be that he wished me to meet anyone else.

Than Roy no one could show a more genuine cordiality to a fellow novelist whose name was on everybody's lips, but no one could more genially turn a cold shoulder on him when idleness, failure, or someone else's success had cast a shade on his notoriety. The writer has his ups and downs, and I was but too conscious that at the moment I was not in the public eye. It was obvious that I might have found excuses without affront to refuse Roy's invitation, though he was a determined fellow and if he was resolved for purposes of his own to see me, I well knew that nothing short of a downright "Go to hell" would check his persistence; but I was beset by curiosity. I had also a considerable affection for Roy.

I had watched with admiration his rise in the world of letters. His career might well have served as a model for any young man entering upon the pursuit of literature. I could think of no one among my contemporaries who had achieved so considerable a position on so little talent. This, like the wise man's daily dose of Bemax, might have gone into a heaped-up tablespoon. He was perfectly aware of it, and it must have seemed to him sometimes little short of a miracle that he had been able with it to compose already some thirty books. I cannot but think that he saw the white light of revelation when first he read that Thomas Carlyle in an after-dinner speech had stated that genius was an infinite capacity for taking pains. He pondered the saying. If that was all, he must have told himself, he could be a genius like the rest; and when the excited reviewer of a lady's paper, writing a notice of one of his works, used the word (and of late the critics have been doing it with agreeable frequency) he must have sighed with the satisfaction of one who after long hours of toil has completed a cross-word puzzle. No one who for years had observed his indefatigable industry could deny that at all events he deserved to be a genius.

Roy started with certain advantages. He was the only son of a civil servant who after being Colonial Secretary for many years in Hong-Kong ended his career as Governor of Jamaica. When you looked up Alroy Kear in the serried pages of *Who's Who* you saw *o. s.* of Sir Raymond Kear, K.C.M.G., K.C.V.O. *q.v.* and of Emily, *y.d.* of the late Major-General Percy Camperdown, Indian Army. He was educated at Winchester and at New College, Oxford. He was President of the Union and but for an unfortunate attack of measles might very well have got his rowing blue. His academic career was respectable rather than showy, and he left the university without a debt in the world. Roy was even then of a thrifty habit, without any inclination to unprofitable expense, and he was a good son. He knew that it had been a sacrifice to his parents to give him so costly an education. His father, having retired, lived in an unpretentious, but not mean, house near Stroud in Gloucestershire, but at intervals went to London to attend official dinners connected with the colonies he had administered, and on these occasions was in the habit of visiting the Athenæum, of which he was a member. It was through an old crony at this club that he was able to get his boy, when he came down from Oxford, appointed tutor to the delicate and only son of a very noble lord. This gave Roy a chance to become acquainted at an early age with the great world. He made good use of his opportunities. You will never find in his works any of the solecisms that disfigure the productions of those who have studied the upper circles of society only in the pages of the illustrated papers. He knew exactly how dukes spoke to one another, and the proper way they should be addressed respectively by a member of Parliament, an attorney, a bookmaker and a valet. There is something captivating in the jauntiness with which in his early novels he handles viceroys, ambassadors, prime ministers, royalties and great ladies. He is friendly without being patronising and familiar without being impertinent. He does not let you forget their rank, but shares with you his comfortable feeling that they are of the same flesh as you and I. I always think it a pity that, fashion having decided that the doings of the aristocracy are no longer a proper subject for serious fiction, Roy, always keenly sensitive to the tendency of the age, should in his later novels have confined himself to the spiritual conflicts of solicitors, chartered accountants and produce brokers. He does not move in these circles with his old assurance.

I knew him first soon after he resigned his tutorship to devote himself exclusively to literature, and he was then a fine, upstanding young man, six feet high in his stockinged feet and of an athletic build, with broad shoulders and a confident carriage. He was not handsome, but in a manly way agreeable to look at, with wide blue frank eyes and curly hair of a lightish brown; his nose was rather short and broad, his chin square. He looked honest, clean, and healthy. He was something of an athlete. No one who has read in his early books the descriptions of a run with the hounds, so vivid and so accurate, can doubt that he wrote from personal experience; and until quite lately he was willing now and then to desert his desk for a day's hunting. He published his first novel at the period when men of letters, to show their virility, drank beer and played cricket, and for some years there was seldom a literary eleven in which his name did not figure. This particular school, I hardly know why, has lost its bravery, their books are neglected and, cricketers though they have remained, they find difficulty in placing their articles. Roy ceased playing cricket a good many years ago and he has developed a fine taste for claret.

Roy was very modest about his first novel. It was short, neatly written, and, as is everything he has produced since, in perfect taste. He sent it with a pleasant letter to all the leading writers of the day, and in this he told each one how greatly he admired his works, how much he had learned from his study of them, and how ardently he aspired to follow, albeit at a humble distance, the trail his correspondent had blazed. He laid his book at the feet of a great artist as the tribute of a young man entering upon the profession of letters to one whom he would always look up to as his master. Deprecatingly, fully conscious of his audacity in asking so busy a man to waste his time on a neophyte's puny effort, he begged for criticism and guidance. Few of the replies were perfunctory. The authors he wrote to, flattered by his praise, answered at length. They commended his book; many of them asked him to luncheon. They could not fail to be charmed by his frankness and warmed by his enthusiasm. He asked for their advice with a humility that was touching and promised to act upon it with a sincerity that was impressive. Here, they felt, was someone worth taking a little trouble over.

His novel had a considerable success. It made him many friends in literary circles and in a very short while you could not go to a tea-party in Bloomsbury, Campden Hill, or Westminster without finding him handing round bread and butter or disembarrassing an elderly lady of an empty cup. He was so young, so bluff, so gay, he laughed so merrily at other people's jokes that no one could help liking him. He joined dining clubs where in the basement of a hotel in Victoria Street or Holborn men of letters young barristers and ladies in Liberty silks and strings of beads, ate a three-and-sixpenny dinner and discussed art and literature. It was soon discovered that he had a pretty gift for after-dinner speaking. He was so pleasant that his fellow writers, his rivals and contemporaries, forgave him even the fact that he was a gentleman. He was generous in his praise of their fledgeling works, and when they sent him manuscripts to criticise could never find a thing amiss. They thought him not only a good sort, but a sound judge.

He wrote a second novel. He took great pains with it and he profited by the advice his elders in the craft had given him. It was only just that more than one should at his request write a review for a paper with whose editor Roy had got into touch and only natural that the review should be flattering. His second novel was successful, but not so successful as to arouse the umbrageous susceptibilities of his competitors. In fact it confirmed them in their suspicions that he would never set the Thames on fire. He was a jolly good fellow; no side, or anything like that: they were quite content to give a leg up to a man who would never climb so high as to be an obstacle to themselves. I know some who smile bitterly now when they reflect on the mistake they made.

But when they say that he is swollen-headed they err. Roy has never lost the modesty which in his youth was his most engaging trait.

"I know I'm not a great novelist," he will tell you. "When I compare myself with the giants I simply don't exist. I used to think that one day I should write a really great novel, but I've long ceased even to hope for that. All I want people to say is that I do my best. I do work. I never let anything slipshod get past me. I think I can tell a good story and I can create characters that ring true. And, after all, the proof of the pudding is in the eating: *The Eye of the Needle* sold thirty-five thousand in England and eighty thousand in America, and for the serial rights of my next book I've got the biggest terms I've ever had yet."

And what, after all, can it be other than modesty that makes him even now write to the reviewers of his books, thanking them for their praise, and ask them to luncheon? Nay, more: when someone has written a stinging criticism and Roy, especially since his reputation became so great, has had to put up with some very virulent abuse, he does not, like most of us, shrug his shoulders, fling a mental insult at the ruffian who does not like our work, and then forget about it; he writes a long letter to his critic, telling him that he is very sorry he thought his book bad, but his review was so interesting in itself and, if he might venture to say so, showed so much critical sense and so much feeling for words, that he felt bound to write to him. No one is more anxious to improve himself than he, and he hopes he is still capable of learning. He does not want to be a bore, but if the critic has nothing to do on Wednesday or Friday will he come and lunch at the Savoy and tell him why exactly he thought his book so bad? No one can order a lunch better than Roy, and generally by the time the critic has eaten half a dozen oysters and a cut from a saddle of baby lamb, he has eaten his words too. It is only poetic justice that when Roy's next novel comes out the critic should see in the new work a very great advance.

One of the difficulties that a man has to cope with as he goes through life is what to do about the persons with whom he has once been intimate and whose interest for him has in due course subsided. If both parties remain in a modest station the break comes about naturally, and no ill-feeling subsists, but if one of them achieves eminence the position is awkward. He makes a multitude of new friends, but the old ones are inexorable; he has a thousand claims on his time, but they feel that they have the first right to it. Unless he is at their beck and call they sigh and with a shrug of the shoulders say:

"Ah, well, I suppose you're like everyone else. I must expect to be dropped now that you're a success."

That of course is what he would like to do if he had the courage. For the most part he hasn't. He weakly accepts an invitation to supper on Sunday evening. The cold roast beef is frozen and comes from Australia and was over-cooked at middle day; and the burgundy—ah, why will they call it burgundy? Have they never been to Beaune and stayed at the Hôtel de la Poste? Of course it is grand to talk of the good old days when you shared a crust of bread in a garret together, but it is a little disconcerting when you reflect how near to a garret is the room you are sitting in. You feel ill at ease when your friend tells you that his books don't sell and that he can't place his short stories; the managers won't even read his plays, and when he compares them with some of the stuff that's put on (here he fixes you with an accusing eye) it really does seem a bit hard. You are embarrassed and you look away. You exaggerate the failures you have had in order that he may realise that life has its hardships for you too. You refer to your work in the most disparaging way you can and are a trifle taken aback to find that your host's opinion of it is the same as yours. You speak of the fickleness of the public so that he may comfort himself by thinking that your popularity cannot last. He is a friendly but severe critic.

"I haven't read your last book," he says, "but I read the one before. I've forgotten its name."

You tell him.

"I was rather disappointed in it. I didn't think it was quite so good as some of the things you've done. Of course you know which my favourite is."

And you, having suffered from other hands than his, answer at once with the name of the first book you ever wrote: you were twenty then, and it was crude and ingenuous, and on every page was written your inexperience.

"You'll never do anything so good as that," he says heartily, and you feel that your whole career has been a long decadence from that one happy hit. "I always think you've never *quite* fulfilled the promise you showed then."

The gas fire roasts your feet, but your hands are icy. You look at your wrist-watch surreptitiously and wonder whether your old friend would think it offensive if you took your leave as early as ten. You have told your car to wait round the corner so that it should not stand outside the door and by its magnificence affront his poverty, but at the door he says:

"You'll find a bus at the bottom of the street. I'll just walk down with you."

Panic seizes you and you confess that you have a car. He finds it very odd that the chauffeur should wait round the corner. You answer that this is one of his idiosyncrasies. When you reach it your friend looks at it with tolerant superiority. You nervously ask him to dinner with you one day. You promise to write to him and you drive away wondering whether when he comes he will think you are swanking if you ask him to Claridge's or mean if you suggest Soho.

Roy Kear suffered from none of these tribulations. It sounds a little brutal to say that when he had got all he could get of people he dropped them; but it would take so long to put the matter more delicately, and would need so subtle an adjustment of hints, half-tones and allusions, playful or tender, that, such being at bottom the fact, I think it as well to leave it at that. Most of us when we do a caddish thing harbour resentment against the person we have done it to, but Roy's heart, always in the right place, never permitted him such pettiness. He could use a man very shabbily without afterward bearing him the slightest ill-will.

"Poor old Smith," he would say. "He is a dear; I'm so fond of him. Pity he's growing so bitter. I wish one could do something for him. No, I haven't seen him for years. It's no good trying to keep up old friendships. It's painful for both sides. The fact is, one grows out of people, and the only thing is to face it."

But if he ran across Smith at some gathering like the private view of the Royal Academy no one could be more cordial. He wrung his hand and told him how delighted he was to see him. His face beamed. He shed good fellowship as the kindly sun its rays. Smith rejoiced in the glow of this wonderful vitality and it was damned decent of Roy to say he'd give his eye-teeth to have written a book half as good as Smith's last. On the other hand, if Roy thought Smith had not seen him, he looked the other way; but Smith *had* seen him, and Smith resented being cut. Smith was very acid. He said that in the old days Roy had been glad enough to share a steak with him in a shabby restaurant and spend a month's holiday in a fisherman's cottage at St. Ives. Smith said that Roy was a time-server. He said he was a snob. He said he was a humbug.

Smith was wrong here. The most shining characteristic of Alroy Kear was his sincerity. No one can be a humbug for five-and-twenty years. Hypocrisy is the most difficult and nerve-racking vice that any man can pursue; it needs an unceasing vigilance and a rare detachment of spirit. It cannot, like adultery or gluttony, be practised at spare moments; it is a whole-time job. It needs also a cynical humour; although Roy laughed so much, I never thought he had a very quick sense of humour, and I am quite sure that he was incapable of cynicism. Though I have finished few of his novels, I have begun a good many, and to my mind his sincerity is stamped on every one of their multitudinous pages. This is clearly the chief ground of his stable popularity. Roy has always sincerely believed what everyone else believed at the moment. When he wrote novels about the aristocracy he sincerely believed that its members were dissipated and immoral, and yet had a certain nobility and an innate aptitude for governing the British Empire; when later he wrote of the middle classes he sincerely believed that they were the backbone of the country. His villains have always been villainous, his heroes heroic, and his maidens chaste.

When Roy asked the author of a flattering review to lunch it was because he was sincerely grateful to him for his good opinion, and when he asked the author of an unflattering one it was because he was sincerely concerned to improve himself. When unknown admirers from Texas or Western Australia came to London it was not only to cultivate his public that he took them to the National Gallery, it was because he was sincerely anxious to observe their reactions to art. You had only to hear him lecture to be convinced of his sincerity.

When he stood on the platform, in evening dress admirably worn, or in a loose, much used but perfectly cut lounge suit if it better fitted the occasion, and faced his audience seriously, frankly, but with an engaging diffidence you could not but realise that he was giving himself up to his task with complete earnestness. Though now and then he pretended to be at a loss for a word, it was only to make it more effective when he uttered it. His voice was full and manly. He told a story well. He was never dull. He was fond of lecturing upon the younger writers of England and America, and he explained their merits to his audience with an enthusiasm that attested his generosity. Perhaps he told almost too much, for when you had heard his lecture you felt that you really knew all you wanted to about them and it was quite unnecessary to read their books. I suppose that is why when Roy

10

had lectured in some provincial town not a single copy of the books of the authors he had spoken of was ever asked for, but there was always a run on his own. His energy was prodigious. Not only did he make successful tours of the United States, but he lectured up and down Great Britain. No club was so small, no society for the self-improvement of its members so insignificant, that Roy disdained to give it an hour of his time. Now and then he revised his lectures and issued them in neat little books. Most people who are interested in these things have at least looked through the works entitled *Modern Novelists*, *Russian Fiction*, and *Some Writers*; and few can deny that they exhibit a real feeling for literature and a charming personality.

But this by no means exhausted his activities. He was an active member of the organisations that have been founded to further the interests of authors or to alleviate their hard lot when sickness or old age has brought them to penury. He was always willing to give his help when matters of copyright were the subject of legislation and he was never unprepared to take his place in those missions to a foreign country which are devised to establish amicable relations between writers of different nationalities. He could be counted on to reply for literature at a public dinner and he was invariably on the reception committee formed to give a proper welcome to a literary celebrity from overseas. No bazaar lacked an autographed copy of at least one of his books. He never refused to grant an interview. He justly said that no one knew better than he the hardships of the author's trade and if he could help a struggling journalist to earn a few guineas by having a pleasant chat with him he had not the inhumanity to refuse. He generally asked his interviewer to luncheon and seldom failed to make a good impression on him. The only stipulation he made was that he should see the article before it was published. He was never impatient with the persons who call up the celebrated on the telephone at inconvenient moments to ask them, for the information of newspaper readers, whether they believe in God or what they eat for breakfast. He figured in every symposium and the public knew what he thought of prohibition, vegetarianism, jazz, garlic, exercise, marriage, politics and the place of women in the home.

His views on marriage were abstract, for he had successfully evaded the state which so many artists have found difficult to reconcile with the arduous pursuit of their calling. It was generally known that he had for some years cherished a hopeless passion for a married woman of rank, and though he never spoke of her but with chivalrous admiration, it was understood that she had treated him with harshness. The novels of his middle period reflected in their unwonted bitterness the strain to which he had been put. The anguish of spirit he had passed through then enabled him without offence to elude the advances of ladies of little reputation, frayed ornaments of a hectic circle, who were willing to exchange an uncertain present for the security of marriage with a successful novelist. When he saw in their bright eyes the shadow of the registry office he told them that the memory of his one great love would always prevent him from forming any permanent tie. His quixotry might exasperate, but could not affront, them. He sighed a little when he reflected that he must be for ever denied the joys of domesticity and the satisfaction of parenthood, but it was a sacrifice that he was prepared to make not only to his ideal, but also to the possible partner of his joys. He had noticed that people really do not want to be bothered with the wives of authors and painters. The artist who insisted on taking his wife wherever he went only made himself a nuisance and indeed was in consequence often not asked to places he would have liked to go to; and if he left his wife at home, he was on his return exposed to recriminations that shattered the repose so essential for him to do the best that was in him. Alroy Kear was a bachelor and now at fifty was likely to remain one.

He was an example of what an author can do, and to what heights he can rise, by industry, commonsense, honesty and the efficient combination of means and ends. He was a good fellow and none but a cross-grained carper could grudge him his success. I felt that to fall asleep with his image in my mind would insure me a good night. I scribbled a note to Miss Fellows, knocked the ashes out of my pipe, put out the light in my sitting-room and went to bed.

CHAPTER II

When I rang for my letters and the papers next morning a message was delivered to me, in answer to my note to Miss Fellows, that Mr. Alroy Kear expected me at one-fifteen at his club in St. James's

Street; so a little before one I strolled round to my own and had the cocktail, which I was pretty sure Roy would not offer me. Then I walked down St. James's Street, looking idly at the shop windows, and since I had still a few minutes to spare (I did not want to keep my appointment too punctually) I went into Christie's to see if there was anything I liked the look of. The auction had already begun and a group of dark, small men were passing round to one another pieces of Victorian silver, while the auctioneer, following their gestures with bored eyes, muttered in a drone: "Ten shillings offered, eleven, eleven and six" . . . It was a fine day, early in June, and the air in King Street was bright. It made the pictures on the walls of Christie's look very dingy. I went out. The people in the street walked with a kind of non-chalance, as though the ease of the day had entered into their souls and in the midst of their affairs they had a sudden and surprised inclination to stop and look at the picture of life.

Roy's club was sedate. In the ante-chamber were only an ancient porter and a page; and I had a sudden and melancholy feeling that the members were all attending the funeral of the head-waiter. The page, when I had uttered Roy's name, led me into an empty passage to leave my hat and stick and then into an empty hall hung with life-sized portraits of Victorian statesmen. Roy got up from a leather sofa and warmly greeted me.

"Shall we go straight up?" he said.

I was right in thinking that he would not offer me a cocktail and I commended my prudence. He led me up a noble flight of heavily carpeted stairs, and we passed nobody on the way; we entered the strangers' dining-room, and we were its only occupants. It was a room of some size, very clean and white, with an Adam window. We sat down by it and a demure waiter handed us the bill of fare. Beef, mutton and lamb, cold salmon, apple tart, rhubarb tart, gooseberry tart. As my eye travelled down the inevitable list I sighed as I thought of the restaurants round the corner where there were French cooking, the clatter of life and pretty painted women in summer frocks.

"I can recommend the veal-and-ham pie," said Roy.

"All right."

"I'll mix the salad myself," he told the waiter in an off-hand and yet commanding way, and then, casting his eye once more on the bill of fare, generously: "And what about some asparagus to follow?"

"That would be very nice."

His manner grew a trifle grander.

"Asparagus for two and tell the chef to choose them himself. Now what would you like to drink? What do you say to a bottle of hock? We rather fancy our hock here."

When I had agreed to this he told the waiter to call the wine-steward. I could not but admire the authoritative and yet perfectly polite manner in which he gave his orders. You felt that thus would a well-bred king send for one of his field-marshals. The wine-steward, portly in black, with the silver chain of his office round his neck, bustled in with the wine-list in his hand. Roy nodded to him with curt familiarity.

"Hulloa, Armstrong, we want some of the Liebfraumilch, the '21."

"Very good, sir."

"How's it holding up? Pretty well? We shan't be able to get any more of it, you know."

"I'm afraid not, sir."

"Well, it's no good meeting trouble half-way, is it, Armstrong?"

Roy smiled at the steward with breezy cordiality. The steward saw from his long experience of members that the remark needed an answer.

"No, sir."

Roy laughed and his eye sought mine. Quite a character, Armstrong.

"Well, chill it, Armstrong; not too much, you know, but just right. I want my guest to see that we know what's what here." He turned to me. "Armstrong's been with us for eight-and-forty years." And when the wine-steward had left us: "I hope you don't mind coming here. It's quiet and we can have a good talk. It's ages since we did. You're looking very fit."

This drew my attention to Roy's appearance.

"Not half so fit as you," I answered.

"The result of an upright, sober and godly life," he laughed. "Plenty of work. Plenty of exercise. How's the golf? We must have a game one of these days."

I knew that Roy was scratch and that nothing would please him less than to waste a day with so indifferent a player as myself. But I felt I was quite safe in accepting so vague an invitation. He looked the picture of health. His curly hair was getting very grey, but it suited him and made his frank, sun-burned face look younger. His eyes, which looked upon the world with such a hearty candour, were bright and clear. He was not so slim as in his youth and I was not surprised that when the waiter offered us rolls he asked for Ryvita. His slight corpulence only added to his dignity. It gave weight to his observations. Because his movements were a little more deliberate than they had been you had a comfortable feeling of confidence in him; he filled his chair with so much solidity that you had almost the impression that he sat upon a monument.

I do not know whether, as I wished, I have indicated by my report of his dialogue with the waiter that his conversation was not as a rule brilliant or witty, but it was fluent and he laughed so much that you sometimes had the illusion that what he said was funny. He was never at a loss for a remark and he could discourse on the topics of the day with an ease that prevented his hearers from experiencing any sense of strain.

Many authors from their preoccupation with words have the bad habit of choosing those they use in conversation too carefully. They form their sentences with unconscious care and say neither more nor less than they mean. It makes intercourse with them somewhat formidable to persons in the upper ranks of society whose vocabulary is limited by their simple spiritual needs, and their company consequently is sought only with hesitation. No constraint of this sort was ever felt with Roy. He could talk with a dancing guardee in terms that were perfectly comprehensible to him and with a racing countess in the language of her stable boys. They said of him with enthusiasm and relief that he was not a bit like an author. No compliment pleased him better. The wise always use a number of ready-made phrases (at the moment I write "nobody's business" is the most common), popular adjectives (like "divine" or "shy-making"), verbs that you only know the meaning of if you live in the right set (like "dunch"), which give a homely sparkle to small talk and avoid the necessity of thought. The Americans, who are the most efficient people on the earth, have carried this device to such a height of perfection and have invented so wide a range of pithy and hackneyed phrases that they can carry on an amusing and animated conversation without giving a moment's reflection to what they are saying and so leave their minds free to consider the more important matters of big business and fornication. Roy's repertory was extensive and his scent for the word of the minute unerring; it peppered his speech, but aptly, and he used it each time with a sort of bright eagerness, as though his fertile brain had just minted it.

Now he talked of this and that, of our common friends and the latest books, of the opera. He was very breezy. He was always cordial, but to-day his cordiality took my breath away. He lamented that we saw one another so seldom and told me with the frankness that was one of his pleasantest characteristics how much he liked me and what a high opinion he had of me. I felt I must not fail to meet this friendliness half-way. He asked me about the book I was writing, I asked him about the book he was writing. We told one another that neither of us had had the success he deserved. We ate the veal-and-ham pie and Roy told me how he mixed a salad. We drank the hock and smacked appreciative lips.

And I wondered when he was coming to the point.

I could not bring myself to believe that at the height of the London season Alroy Kear would waste an hour on a fellow-writer who was not a reviewer and had no influence in any quarter whatever in order to talk of Matisse, the Russian Ballet and Marcel Proust. Besides, at the back of his gaiety I vaguely felt a slight apprehension. Had I not known that he was in a prosperous state I should have suspected that he was going to borrow a hundred pounds from me. It began to look as though luncheon would end without his finding the opportunity to say what he had in mind. I knew he was cautious. Perhaps he thought that this meeting, the first after so long a separation, had better be employed in establishing friendly relations, and was prepared to look upon the pleasant, substantial meal merely as ground bait.

"Shall we go and have our coffee in the next room?" he said.

"If you like."

"I think it's more comfortable."

I followed him into another room, much more spacious, with great leather arm-chairs and huge sofas; there were papers and magazines on the tables. Two old gentlemen in a corner were talking in undertones. They gave us a hostile glance, but this did not deter Roy from offering them a cordial greeting.

"Hullo, General," he cried, nodding breezily.

I stood for a moment at the window, looking at the gaiety of the day, and wished I knew more of the historical associations of St. James's Street. I was ashamed that I did not even know the name of the club across the way and was afraid to ask Roy lest he should despise me for not knowing what every decent person knew. He called me back by asking me whether I would have a brandy with my coffee, and when I refused, insisted. The club's brandy was famous. We sat side by side on a sofa by the elegant fireplace and lit cigars.

"The last time Edward Driffield ever came to London he lunched with me here," said Roy casually. "I made the old man try our brandy and he was delighted with it. I was staying with his widow over last week-end."

"Were you?"

"She sent you all sorts of messages."

"That's very kind of her. I shouldn't have thought she remembered me."

"Oh, yes, she does. You lunched there about six years ago, didn't you? She says the old man was so glad to see you."

"I didn't think she was."

"Oh, you're quite wrong. Of course she had to be very careful. The old man was pestered with people who wanted to see him and she had to husband his strength. She was always afraid he'd do too much. It's a wonderful thing if you come to think of it that she should have kept him alive and in possession of all his faculties to the age of eighty-four. I've been seeing a good deal of her since he died. She's awfully lonely. After all, she devoted herself to looking after him for twenty-five years. Othello's occupation, you know. I really feel sorry for her."

"She's still comparatively young. I dare say she'll marry again."

"Oh, no, she couldn't do that. That would be dreadful."

There was a slight pause while we sipped our brandy.

"You must be one of the few persons still alive who knew Driffield when he was unknown. You saw quite a lot of him at one time, didn't you?"

"A certain amount. I was almost a small boy and he was a middle-aged man. We weren't boon companions, you know."

"Perhaps not, but you must know a great deal about him that other people don't."

"I suppose I do."

"Have you ever thought of writing your recollections of him?"

"Good heavens, no!"

"Don't you think you ought to? He was one of the greatest novelists of our day. The last of the Victorians. He was an enormous figure. His novels have as good a chance of surviving as any that have been written in the last hundred years."

"I wonder. I've always thought them rather boring."

Roy looked at me with eyes twinkling with laughter.

"How like you that is! Anyhow you must admit that you're in the minority. I don't mind telling you that I've read his novels not once or twice, but half a dozen times, and every time I read them I think they're finer. Did you read the articles that were written about him at his death?"

"Some of them."

"The consensus of opinion was absolutely amazing. I read every one."

"If they all said the same thing, wasn't that rather unnecessary?"

Roy shrugged his massive shoulders good-humouredly, but did not answer my question.

"I thought the *Times Lit. Sup.*, was splendid. It would have done the old man good to read it. I hear that the *Quarterly* is going to have an article in its next number."

"I still think his novels rather boring."

Roy smiled indulgently.

"Doesn't it make you slightly uneasy to think that you disagree with everyone whose opinion matters?"

"Not particularly. I've been writing for thirty-five years now, and you can't think how many geniuses I've seen acclaimed, enjoy their hour or two of glory and vanish into obscurity. I wonder what's happened to them. Are they dead, are they shut up in mad-houses, are they hidden away in offices? I wonder if they furtively lend their books to the doctor and the maiden lady in some obscure village. I wonder if they are still great men in some Italian pension."

"Oh, yes, they're the flash-in-the-pans. I've known them."

"You've even lectured about them."

"One has to. One wants to give them a leg up if one can and one knows they won't amount to anything. Hang it all, one can afford to be generous. But after all, Driffield wasn't anything like that. The collected edition of his works is in thirty-seven volumes and the last set that came up at Sotheby's sold for seventy-eight pounds. That speaks for itself. His sales have increased steadily every year and last year was the best he ever had. You can take my word for that. Mrs. Driffield showed me his accounts last time I was down there. Driffield has come to stay all right."

"Who can tell?"

"Well, you think you can," replied Roy acidly.

I was not put out. I knew I was irritating him and it gave me a pleasant sensation.

"I think the instinctive judgments I formed when I was a boy were right. They told me Carlyle was a great writer and I was ashamed that I found the *French Revolution* and *Sartor Resartus* unreadable. Can anyone read them now? I thought the opinions of others must be better than mine and I persuaded myself that I thought George Meredith magnificent. In my heart I found him affected, verbose and insincere. A good many people think so too now. Because they told me that to admire Walter Pater was to prove myself a cultured young man, I admired Walter Pater, but heavens, how *Marius* bored me!"

"Oh, well, I don't suppose anyone reads Pater now, and of course Meredith has gone all to pot and Carlyle was a pretentious windbag."

"You don't know how secure of immortality they all looked thirty years ago."

"And have you never made mistakes?"

"One or two. I didn't think half as much of Newman as I do now, and I thought a great deal more of the tinkling quatrains of Fitzgerald. I could not read Goethe's *Wilhelm Meister*; now I think it his masterpiece."

"And what did you think much of then that you think much of still?"

"Well, *Tristram Shandy* and *Amelia* and *Vanity Fair. Madame Bovary, La Chartreuse de Parme*, and *Anna Karenina*. And Wordsworth and Keats and Verlaine."

"If you don't mind my saying so, I don't think that's particularly original."

"I don't mind your saying so at all. I don't think it is. But you asked me why I believed in my own judgment, and I was trying to explain to you that, whatever I said out of timidity and in deference to the cultured opinion of the day, I didn't really admire certain authors who were then thought admirable and the event seems to show that I was right. And what I honestly and instinctively liked then has stood the test of time with me and with critical opinion in general."

Roy was silent for a moment. He looked in the bottom of his cup, but whether to see if there were any more coffee in it or to find something to say, I did not know. I gave the clock on the chimney-piece a glance. In a minute it would be fitting for me to take my leave. Perhaps I had been wrong and Roy had invited me only that we might idly chat of Shakespeare and the musical glasses. I chid myself for the uncharitable thoughts I had had of him. I looked at him with concern. If that was his only object it must be that he was feeling tired or discouraged. If he was disinterested it could only be that for the moment at least the world was too much for him. But he caught my look at the clock and spoke.

"I don't see how you can deny that there must be something in a man who's able to carry on for sixty years, writing book after book, and who's able to hold an ever-increasing public. After all, at Ferne Court there are shelves filled with the translations of Driffield's books into every language of civilised people. Of course I'm willing to admit that a lot he wrote seems a bit old-fashioned nowadays. He flourished in a bad period and he was inclined to be long-winded. Most of his plots are melodramatic; but there's one quality you must allow him: beauty."

"Yes?" I said.

"When all's said and done, that's the only thing that counts and Driffield never wrote a page that wasn't instinct with beauty."

"Yes?" I said.

"I wish you'd been there when we went down to present him with his portrait on his eightieth birthday. It really was a memorable occasion."

"I read about it in the papers."

"It wasn't only writers, you know, it was a thoroughly representative gathering—science, politics, business, art, the world; I think you'd have to go a long way to find gathered together such a collection of distinguished people as got out from that train at Blackstable. It was awfully moving when the P.M. presented the old man with the Order of Merit. He made a charming speech. I don't mind telling you there were tears in a good many eyes that day."

"Did Driffield cry?"

"No, he was singularly calm. He was like he always was, rather shy, you know, and quiet, very well-mannered, grateful, of course, but a little dry. Mrs. Driffield didn't want him to get overtired and when we went into lunch he stayed in his study, and she sent him something in on a tray. I slipped away while the others were having their coffee. He was smoking his pipe and looking at the portrait. I asked him what he thought of it. He wouldn't tell me, he just smiled a little. He asked me if I thought he could take his teeth out and I said, No, the deputation would be coming in presently to say good-bye to him. Then I asked him if he didn't think it was a wonderful moment. 'Rum,' he said, 'very rum.' The fact is, I suppose, he was shattered. He was a messy eater in his later days and a messy smoker—he scattered the tobacco all over himself when he filled his pipe; Mrs. Driffield didn't like people to see him when he was like that, but of course she didn't mind me; I tidied him up a bit and then they all came in and shook hands with him, and we went back to town."

I got up.

"Well, I really must be going. It's been awfully nice seeing you."

"I'm just going along to the private view at the Leicester Galleries. I know the people there. I'll take you in if you like."

"It's very kind of you, but they sent me a card. No, I don't think I'll come."

We walked down the stairs and I got my hat. When we came out into the street and I turned toward Piccadilly, Roy said:

"I'll just walk up to the top with you." He got into step with me. "You knew his first wife, didn't you?"

"Whose?"

"Driffield's."

"Oh!" I had forgotten him. "Yes."

"Well?"

"Fairly."

"I suppose she was awful."

"I don't recollect that."

"She must have been dreadfully common. She was a barmaid, wasn't she?"

"Yes."

"I wonder why the devil he married her. I've always been given to understand that she was extremely unfaithful to him."

"Extremely."

"Do you remember at all what she was like?"

"Yes, very distinctly," I smiled. "She was sweet."

Roy gave a short laugh.

"That's not the general impression."

I did not answer. We had reached Piccadilly, and stopping I

held out my hand to Roy. He shook it, but I fancied without his usual heartiness. I had the impression that he was disappointed with our meeting. I could not imagine why. Whatever he had wanted of me I had not been able to do, for the reason that he had given me no inkling of what it was, and as I strolled under the arcade of the Ritz Hotel and along the park railings till I came opposite Half Moon Street I wondered if my manner had been more than ordinarily forbidding. It was quite evident that Roy had felt the moment inopportune to ask me to grant him a favour.

I walked up Half Moon Street. After the gay tumult of Piccadilly it had a pleasant silence. It was sedate and respectable. Most of the houses let apartments, but this was not advertised by the vulgarity of a card; some had a brightly polished brass plate, like a doctor's, to announce the fact and others the word *Apartments* neatly painted on the fanlight. One or two with an added discretion merely gave the name of the proprietor, so that if you were ignorant you might have thought it a tailor's or a money-lender's. There was none of the congested traffic of Jermyn Street, where also they let rooms, but here and there a smart car, unattended, stood outside a door and occasionally at another a taxi deposited a middle-aged lady. You had the feeling that the people who lodged here were not gay and a trifle disreputable as in Jermyn Street, racing men who rose in the morning with headaches and asked for a hair of the dog that bit them, but respectable women from the country who came up for six weeks for the London season and elderly gentlemen who belonged to exclusive clubs. You felt that they came year after year to the same house and perhaps had known the proprietor when he was still in private service. My own Miss Fellows had been cook in some very good places, but you would never have guessed it had you seen her walking along to do her shopping in Shepherd's Market. She was not stout, red-faced and blowsy as one expects a cook to be; she was spare and very upright, neatly but fashionably dressed, a woman of middle age with determined features; her lips were rouged and she wore an eye-glass. She was businesslike, quiet, coolly cynical and very expensive.

The rooms I occupied were on the ground floor. The parlour was papered with an old marbled paper and on the walls were water-colours of romantic scenes, cavaliers bidding good-bye to their ladies and knights of old banqueting in stately halls; there were large ferns in pots, and the arm-chairs were covered with faded leather. There was about the room an amusing air of the eighteen-eighties, and when I looked out of the window I expected to see a private hansom rather than a Chrysler. The curtains were of a heavy red rep.

CHAPTER III

I HAD a good deal to do that afternoon, but my conversation with Roy and the impression of the day before yesterday, the sense of a past that still dwelt in the minds of men not yet old, that my room, I could not tell why, had given me even more strongly than usual as I entered it, inveigled my thoughts to saunter down the road of memory. It was as though all the people who had at one time and another inhabited my lodging pressed upon me with their old-fashioned ways and odd clothes, men with mutton-chop whiskers in frock-coats and women in bustles and flounced skirts. The rumble of London, which I did not know if I imagined or heard (my house was at the top of Half Moon Street), and the beauty of the sunny June day (*le vierge, le vivace et le bel aujour-d'hui*), gave my reverie a poignancy which was not quite painful. The past I looked at seemed to have lost its reality and I saw it as though it were a scene in a play and I a spectator in the back row of a dark gallery. But it was all very clear as far as it went. It was not misty like life as one leads it when the ceaseless throng of impressions seems to rob them of outline, but sharp and definite like a landscape painted in oils by a painstaking artist of the middle-Victorian era.

I fancy that life is more amusing now than it was forty years ago and I have a notion that people are more amiable. They may have been worthier then, possessed of more solid virtue as, I am told, they were possessed of more substantial knowledge; I do not know. I know they were more cantankerous; they ate too much, many of them drank too much, and they took too little exercise. Their livers were out of order and their digestions often impaired. They were irritable. I do not speak of London, of which I knew nothing till I was grown up, nor of grand people who hunted and shot, but of the countryside and of the modest persons, gentlemen of small means, clergymen, retired officers and such-like who made up the local society. The dullness of their lives was almost incredible. There were no golf links; at a few houses was an ill-kept tennis court, but it was only the very young who played; there was a dance once a year in the Assembly Rooms; carriage folk went for a drive in the afternoon; the others went for a "constitutional"! You may say that they did not miss amusements they had never thought of, and that they created excitement for themselves from the small entertainment (tea when you were asked to bring your music and you sang the songs of Maude Valérie White and Tosti) which at infrequent intervals they offered one another; the days were very long; they were bored. People who were condemned to spend their lives within a mile of one another quarrelled bitterly and, seeing each other every day in the town, cut one another for twenty years. They were vain, pig-headed and odd. It was a life that perhaps formed queer characters; people were not so like one another as now and they acquired a small celebrity by their idiosyncrasies, but they were not easy to get on with. It may be that we are flippant and careless, but we accept one another without the old suspicion; our manners, rough and ready, are kindly; we are more prepared to give and take and we are not so crabbed.

I lived with an uncle and aunt on the outskirts of a little Kentish town by the sea. It was called Blackstable and my uncle was the vicar. My aunt was a German. She came of a very noble but impoverished family, and the only portion she brought her husband was a marquetry writing-desk, made for an ancestor in the seventeenth century, and a set of tumblers. Of these only a few remained when I entered upon the scene and they were used as ornaments in the drawing-room. I liked the grand coat-of-arms with which they were heavily engraved. There were I don't know how many quarterings, which my aunt used demurely to explain to me, and the supporters were fine and the crest emerging from a crown incredibly romantic. She was a simple old lady, of a meek and Christian disposition, but she had not, though married for more than thirty years to a modest parson with very little income beyond his stipend, forgotten that she was *hochwohlgeboren*. When a rich banker from London, with a name that in these days is famous in financial circles, took a neighbouring house for the summer holidays, though my uncle called on him (chiefly, I surmise, to get a subscription to the Additional Curates Society), she refused to do so because he was in trade. No one thought her a snob. It was accepted as perfectly reasonable. The banker had a little boy of my own age, and, I forget how, I became acquainted with him. I still remember the discussion that ensued when I asked if I might bring him to the vicarage; permission was reluctantly given me, but I was not allowed to go in return to his house. My aunt said I'd be wanting to go to the coal merchant's next, and my uncle said:

"Evil communications corrupt good manners."

The banker used to come to church every Sunday morning, and he always put half a sovereign in the plate, but if he thought his generosity made a good impression he was much mistaken. All Blackstable knew, but only thought him purse-proud.

Blackstable consisted of a long winding street that led to the sea, with little two-storey houses, many of them residential but with a good many shops; and from this ran a certain number of short streets, recently built, that ended on one side in the country and on the other in the marshes. Round about the harbour was a congeries of narrow winding alleys. Colliers brought coal from Newcastle to Blackstable and the harbour was animated. When I was old enough to be allowed out by myself I used to spend hours wandering about there looking at the rough grimy men in their jerseys and watching the coal being unloaded.

It was at Blackstable that I first met Edward Driffield. I was fifteen and had just come back from school for the summer holidays. The morning after I got home I took a towel and bathing drawers and went down to the beach. The sky was unclouded and the air hot and bright, but the North Sea gave it a pleasant tang so that it was a delight just to live and breathe. In winter the natives of Blackstable walked down the empty street with a hurried gait, screwing themselves up in order to expose as little surface as possible to the bitterness of the east wind, but now they dawdled; they stood about in groups in the space between the "Duke of Kent" and the "Bear and Key". You heard a hum of their East-Anglian speech, drawling a little with an accent that may be ugly, but in which from old association I still find a leisurely charm. They were fresh-complexioned, with blue eyes and high cheek-bones, and their hair was light. They had a clean, honest and ingenuous look. I do not think they were very intelligent, but they were guileless. They looked healthy, and though not tall for the most part were strong and active. There was little wheeled traffic in Blackstable in those days and the groups that stood about the road chatting seldom had to move for any-thing but the doctor's dogcart or the baker's trap.

Passing the bank, I called in to say how-do-you-do to the manager, who was my uncle's churchwarden, and when I came out met my uncle's curate. He stopped and shook hands with me. He was walking with a stranger. He did not introduce me to him. He was a smallish man with a beard and he was dressed rather loudly in a bright brown knickerbocker suit, the breeches very tight, with navy-blue stockings, black boots and a billycock hat. Knickerbockers were uncommon then, at least in Blackstable, and being young and fresh from school I immediately set the fellow down as a cad. But while I chatted with the curate he looked at me in a friendly way, with a smile in his pale blue eyes. I felt that for two pins he would have joined in the conversation and I assumed a haughty demeanour. I was not going to run the risk of being spoken to by a chap who wore knickerbockers like a gamekeeper and I resented the familiarity of his good-humoured expression. I was myself faultlessly dressed in white flannel trousers, a blue blazer with the arms of my school on the breast pocket, and a black-and-white straw hat with a very wide brim. The curate said that he must be getting on (fortunately, for I never knew how to break away from a meeting in the street and would endure agonies of shyness while I looked in vain for an oppor-tunity), but said that he would be coming up to the vicarage that afternoon and would I tell my uncle. The stranger nodded and smiled as we parted, but I gave him a stony stare. I supposed he was a summer visitor and in Blackstable we did not mix with the summer visitors. We thought London people vulgar. We said it was horrid to have all that rag-tag and bobtail down from town every year, but of course it was all right for the tradespeople. Even they, however, gave a faint sigh of relief when September came to an end and Blackstable sank back into its usual peace.

When I went home to dinner, my hair insufficiently dried and clinging dankly to my head, I remarked that I had met the curate and he was coming up that afternoon.

"Old Mrs. Shepherd died last night," said my uncle in explanation.

The curate's name was Galloway; he was a tall, thin, ungainly man with untidy black hair and a small sallow dark face. I suppose he was quite young, but to me he seemed middle-aged. He talked very quickly and gesticulated a great deal. This made people think him rather queer and my uncle would not have kept him but that he was very energetic, and my uncle, being extremely lazy, was glad to have someone to take so much work off his shoulders. After he had finished the business that had brought him to the vicarage Mr. Galloway came in to say how-do-you-do to my aunt and she asked him to stay to tea.

"Who was that you were with this morning?" I asked him as he sat down.

"Oh, that was Edward Driffield. I didn't introduce him. I wasn't sure if your uncle would wish you to know him."

"I think it would be most undesirable," said my uncle.

"Why, who is he? He's not a Blackstable man, is he?"

"He was born in the parish," said my uncle. "His father was old Miss Wolfe's bailiff at Ferne Court. But they were chapel people."

"He married a Blackstable girl," said Mr. Galloway.

"In church, I believe," said my aunt. "Is it true that she was a barmaid at the 'Railway Arms'?"

"She looks as if she might have been something like that," said Mr. Galloway with a smile.

"Are they going to stay long?"

"Yes, I think so. They've taken one of those houses in that street where the Congregational chapel is," said the curate.

At that time in Blackstable, though the new streets doubtless had names, nobody knew or used them.

"Is he coming to church?" asked my uncle.

"I haven't actually talked to him about it yet," answered Mr. Galloway. "He's quite an educated man, you know."

"I can hardly believe that," said my uncle.

"He was at Haversham School, I understand, and he got any number of scholarships and prizes. He got a scholarship at Wadham, but he ran away to sea instead."

"I'd heard he was rather a harum-scarum," said my uncle.

"He doesn't look much like a sailor," I remarked.

"Oh, he gave up the sea many years ago. He's been all sorts of things since then."

"Jack of all trades and master of none," said my uncle.

"Now, I understand, he's a writer."

"That won't last long," said my uncle.

I had never known a writer before; I was interested.

"What does he write?" I asked. "Books?"

"I believe so," said the curate, "and articles. He had a novel published last spring. He's promised to lend it me."

"I wouldn't waste my time on rubbish in your place," said my uncle, who never read anything but *The Times* and the *Guardian*.

"What's it called?" I asked.

"He told me the title, but I forget it."

"Anyhow, it's quite unnecessary that you should know," said my uncle. "I should very much object to your reading trashy novels. During your holidays the best thing you can do is to keep out in the open air. And you have a holiday task, I presume?"

I had. It was *Ivanhoe*. I had read it when I was ten, and the notion of reading it again and writing an essay on it bored me to distraction.

When I consider the greatness that Edward Driffield afterward achieved I cannot but smile as I remember the fashion in which he was discussed at my uncle's table. When he died a little while ago and an agitation arose among his admirers to have him buried in Westminster Abbey the present incumbent at Blackstable, my uncle's successor twice removed, wrote to the *Daily Mail* pointing out that Driffield was born in the parish and not only had passed long years, especially the last twenty-five of his life, in the neighbourhood, but had laid there the scene of some of his most famous books; it was only becoming then that his bones should rest in the churchyard where under the Kentish elms his father and mother dwelt in peace. There was relief in Blackstable when, the Dean of Westminster having somewhat curtly refused the Abbey, Mrs. Driffield sent a dignified letter to the Press in which she expressed her confidence that she was carrying out the dearest wishes of her dead husband in having him buried among the simple people he knew and loved so well. Unless the notabilities of Blackstable have very much changed since my day I do not believe they vastly liked that phrase about "simple people", but, as I afterward learnt, they had never been able to "abide" the second Mrs. Driffield.

CHAPTER IV

To my surprise, two or three days after I lunched with Alroy Kear I received a letter from Edward Driffield's widow. It ran as follows:

Dear Friend,

I hear that you had a long talk with Roy last week about Edward Driffield and I am so glad to know that you spoke of him so nicely. He often talked to me of you. He had the greatest admiration for your talent and he was so very pleased to see you when you came to lunch with us. I wonder if you have in your possession any letters that he wrote to you and if so whether you would let me have copies of them. I should be very pleased if I could persuade you to come down for two or three days and stay with me. I live very quietly now and have no one here, so please choose your own time. I shall be delighted to see you again and have a talk of old times. I have a particular service I want you to do me and I am sure that for the sake of my dear dead husband you will not refuse.

Yours ever sincerely,
Amy Driffield.

I had seen Mrs. Driffield only once and she but mildly interested me; I do not like being addressed as "dear friend"; that alone would have been enough to make me decline her invitation; and I was exasperated by its general character which, however ingenious an excuse I invented, made the reason I did not go quite obvious, namely, that I did not want to. I had no letters of Driffield's. I suppose years ago he had written to me several times, brief notes, but he was then an obscure scribbler and even if I ever kept letters it would never have occurred to me to keep his. How was I to know that he was going to be acclaimed as the greatest novelist of our day? I hesitated only because Mrs. Driffield said she wanted me to do something for her. It would certainly be a nuisance, but it would be churlish not to do it if I could, and after all her husband was a very distinguished man.

The letter came by the first post and after breakfast I rang up Roy. As soon as I mentioned my name I was put through to him by his secretary. If I were writing a detective story I should immediately have suspected that my call was awaited, and Roy's virile voice calling hullo would have confirmed my suspicion. No one could naturally be quite so cheery so early in the morning.

"I hope I didn't wake you," I said.

"Good God, no." His healthy laugh rippled along the wires. "I've been up since seven. I've been riding in the park. I'm just going to have breakfast. Come along and have it with me."

"I have a great affection for you, Roy," I answered, "but I don't think you're the sort of person I'd care to have breakfast with. Besides, I've already had mine. Look here, I've just had a letter from Mrs. Driffield asking me to go down and stay."

"Yes, she told me she was going to ask you. We might go down together. She's got quite a good grass court and she does one very well. I think you'd like it."

"What is it that she wants me to do?"

"Ah, I think she'd like to tell you that herself."

There was a softness in Roy's voice such as I imagined he would use if he were telling a prospective father that his wife was about to gratify his wishes. It cut no ice with me.

"Come off it, Roy," I said. "I'm too old a bird to be caught with chaff. Spit it out."

There was a moment's pause at the other end of the telephone. I felt that Roy did not like my expression.

"Are you busy this morning?" he asked suddenly. "I'd like to come and see you."

"All right, come on. I shall be in till one."

"I'll be round in about an hour."

I replaced the receiver and relit my pipe. I gave Mrs. Driffield's letter a second glance.

I remembered vividly the luncheon to which she referred. I happened to be staying for a long week-end not far from Tercanbury with a certain Lady Hodmarsh, the clever and handsome American wife of a sporting baronet with no intelligence and charming manners. Perhaps to relieve the tedium of domestic life she was in the habit of entertaining persons connected with the arts. Her parties were mixed and gay. Members of the nobility and gentry mingled with astonishment and an uneasy awe with painters, writers and actors. Lady Hodmarsh neither read the books nor looked at the pictures of the people to whom she offered hospitality, but she liked their company and enjoyed the feeling it gave her of being in the artistic know. When on this occasion the conversation happened to dwell for a moment on Edward Driffield, her most celebrated neighbour, and I mentioned that I had at one time known him very well she proposed that we should go over and lunch with him on Monday when a number of her guests were going back to London. I demurred, for I had not seen Driffield for five and thirty years and I could not believe that he would remember me; and if he did (though this I kept to myself) I could not believe that it would be with pleasure. But

there was a young peer there, a certain Lord Scallion, with literary
inclinations so violent that, instead of ruling this country as the
laws of man and nature have decreed, he devoted his energy to
the composition of detective novels. His curiosity to see Driffield
was boundless and the moment Lady Hodmarsh made her
suggestion he said it would be too divine. The star guest of the
party was a big young fat duchess and it appeared that her
admiration for the famous writer was so intense that she was
prepared to cut an engagement in London and not go up till the
afternoon.

"That would make four of us," said Lady Hodmarsh. "I don't
think they could manage more than that. I'll wire to Mrs.
Driffield at once."

I could not see myself going to see Driffield in that company and
tried to throw cold water on the scheme.

"It'll only bore him to death," I said. "He'll hate having a lot
of strangers barging in on him like this. He's a very old man."

"That's why if they want to see him they'd better see him now.
He can't last much longer. Mrs. Driffield says he likes to meet
people. They never see anybody but the doctor and the parson
and it's a change for them. Mrs. Driffield said I could always
bring anyone interesting. Of course she has to be very careful.
He's pestered by all sorts of people who want to see him just out
of idle curiosity, and interviewers and authors who want him to
read their books, and silly hysterical women. But Mrs. Driffield
is wonderful. She keeps everyone away from him but those she
thinks he ought to see. I mean, he'd be dead in a week if he saw
everyone who wants to see him. She has to think of his strength.
Naturally we're different."

Of course I thought I was; but as I looked at them I perceived
that the duchess and Lord Scallion thought they were too; so it
seemed best to say no more.

We drove over in a bright yellow Rolls. Ferne Court was three
miles from Blackstable. It was a stucco house built, I suppose,
about 1840, plain and unpretentious, but substantial; it was the
same back and front, with two large bows on each side of a flat
piece in which was the front door, and there were two large bows
on the first floor. A plain parapet hid the low roof. It stood in
about an acre of garden, somewhat overgrown with trees, but
neatly tended, and from the drawing-room window you had a
pleasant view of woods and green downland. The drawing-room

was furnished so exactly as you felt a drawing-room in a country house of modest size should be furnished that it was slightly disconcerting. Clean bright chintzes covered the comfortable chairs and the large sofa, and the curtains were of the same bright clean chintz. On little Chippendale tables stood large Oriental bowls filled with pot-pourri. On the cream-coloured walls were pleasant water-colours by painters well known at the beginning of this century. There were great masses of flowers charmingly arranged, and on the grand piano in silver frames photographs of celebrated actresses, deceased authors and minor royalties.

It was no wonder that the duchess cried out that it was a lovely room. It was just the kind of room in which a distinguished writer should spend the evening of his days. Mrs. Driffield received us with modest assurance. She was a woman of about five-and-forty, I judged, with a small sallow face and neat sharp features. She had a black cloche hat pressed tight down on her head and wore a grey coat and skirt. Her figure was slight and she was neither tall nor short, and she looked trim, competent and alert. She might have been the squire's widowed daughter, who ran the parish and had a peculiar gift for organisation. She introduced us to a clergyman and a lady, who got up as we were shown in. They were the Vicar of Blackstable and his wife. Lady Hodmarsh and the duchess immediately assumed the cringing affability that persons of rank assume with their inferiors in order to show them that they are not in the least conscious of any difference in station between them.

Then Edward Driffield came in. I had seen portraits of him from time to time in the illustrated papers but it was with dismay that I saw him in the flesh. He was smaller than I remembered and very thin, his head was barely covered with fine silvery hair, he was clean-shaven and his skin was almost transparent. His blue eyes were very pale and the rims of his eyelids red. He looked an old, old man, hanging on to mortality by a thread; he wore very white false teeth and they made his smile seem forced and stiff. I had never seen him but bearded, and his lips were thin and pallid. He was dressed in a new, well-cut suit of blue serge and his low collar, two or three sizes too large for him, showed a wrinkled, scraggy neck. He wore a neat black tie with a pearl in it. He looked a little like a dean in mufti on his summer holiday in Switzerland.

Mrs. Driffield gave him a quick glance as he came in and smiled encouragingly; she must have been satisfied with the neatness of his appearance. He shook hands with his guests and to each said something civil. When he came to me he said:

"It's very good of a busy and successful man like you to come all this way to see an old fogey."

I was a trifle taken aback, for he spoke as though he had never seen me before, and I was afraid my friends would think I had been boasting when I claimed at one time to have known him intimately. I wondered if he had completely forgotten me.

"I don't know how many years it is since we last met," I said, trying to be hearty.

He looked at me for what I suppose was no more than a few seconds, but for what seemed to me quite a long time, and then I had a sudden shock; he gave me a little wink. It was so quick that nobody but I could have caught it, and so unexpected in that distinguished old face that I could hardly believe my eyes. In a moment his face was once more composed, intelligently benign and quietly observant. Luncheon was announced and we trooped into the dining-room.

This also was in what can only be described as the acme of good taste. On the Chippendale sideboard were silver candlesticks. We sat on Chippendale chairs and ate off a Chippendale table. In a silver bowl in the middle were roses and round this were silver dishes with chocolates in them and peppermint creams; the silver salt-cellars were brightly polished and evidently Georgian. On the cream-coloured walls were mezzotints of ladies painted by Sir Peter Lely and on the chimney-piece a garniture of blue delf. The service was conducted by two maids in brown uniform and Mrs. Driffield in the midst of her fluent conversation kept a wary eye on them. I wondered how she had managed to train these buxom Kentish girls (their healthy colour and high cheek-bones betrayed the fact that they were "local") to such a pitch of efficiency. The lunch was just right for the occasion, smart but not showy, fillets of sole rolled up and covered with a white sauce, roast chicken, with new potatoes and green peas, asparagus and gooseberry fool. It was the dining-room and the lunch and the manner which you felt exactly fitted a literary gent of great celebrity but moderate wealth.

Mrs. Driffield, like the wives of most men of letters, was a great talker and she did not let the conversation at her end of the table flag; so that, however much we might have wanted to hear what her husband was saying at the other, we had no opportunity. She was gay and sprightly. Though Edward Driffield's indifferent health and great age obliged her to live most of the year in the country, she managed notwithstanding to run up to town often enough to keep abreast of what was going on and she was soon engaged with Lord Scallion in an animated discussion of the plays in the London theatres and the terrible crowd at the Royal Academy. It had taken her two visits to look at all the pictures and even then she had not had time to see the water-colours. She liked water-colours so much; they were unpretentious; she hated things to be pretentious.

So that host and hostess should sit at the head and foot of the table, the vicar sat next to Lord Scallion and his wife next to the duchess. The duchess engaged her in conversation on the subject of working-class dwellings, a subject on which she seemed to be much more at home than the parson's lady, and my attention being thus set free I watched Edward Driffield. He was talking to Lady Hodmarsh. She was apparently telling him how to write a novel and giving him a list of a few that he really ought to read. He listened to her with what looked like polite interest, putting in now and then a remark in a voice too low for me to catch, and when she made a jest (she made them frequently and often good ones) he gave a little chuckle and shot her a quick look that seemed to say: This woman isn't such a damned fool after all. Remembering the past, I asked myself curiously what he thought of this grand company, his neatly turned-out wife, so competent and discreetly managing, and the elegant surroundings in which he lived. I wondered if he regretted his early days of adventure. I wondered if all this amused him or if the amiable civility of his manner masked a hideous boredom. Perhaps he felt my eyes upon him, for he raised his. They rested on me for a while with a thoughtful look, mild and yet oddly scrutinising, and then suddenly, unmistakably this time, he gave me another wink. The frivolous gesture in that old, withered face was more than startling, it was embarrassing; I did not know what to do. My lips outlined a dubious smile.

But the duchess joining in the conversation at the head of the table, the vicar's wife turned to me.

"You knew him many years ago, didn't you?" she asked me in a low tone.

"Yes."

She gave the company a glance to see that no one was attending to us.

"His wife is anxious that you shouldn't call up old memories that might be painful to him. He's very frail, you know, and the least thing upsets him."

"I'll be very careful."

"The way she looks after him is simply wonderful. Her devotion is a lesson to all of us. She realises what a precious charge it is. Her unselfishness is beyond words." She lowered her voice a little more. "Of course he's a very old man and old men sometimes are a little trying; I've never seen her out of patience. In her way she's just as wonderful as he is."

These were the sort of remarks to which it was difficult to find a reply, but I felt that one was expected of me.

"Considering everything I think he looks very well," I murmured.

"He owes it all to her."

At the end of luncheon we went back into the drawing-room and after we had been standing about for two or three minutes Edward Driffield joined me. I was talking with the vicar and for want of anything better to say was admiring the charming view. I turned to my host.

"I was just saying how picturesque that little row of cottages is down there."

"From here." Driffield looked at their broken outline and an ironic smile curled his thin lips. "I was born in one of them. Rum, isn't it?"

But Mrs. Driffield came up to us with bustling geniality. Her voice was brisk and melodious.

"Oh, Edward, I'm sure the duchess would like to see your writing-room. She has to go almost immediately."

"I'm so sorry, but I must catch the three-eighteen from Tercanbury," said the duchess.

We filed into Driffield's study. It was a large room on the other side of the house, looking out on the same view as the dining-room, with a bow window. It was the sort of room that a devoted wife would evidently arrange for her literary husband. It was scrupulously tidy and large bowls of flowers gave it a feminine touch.

"This is the desk at which he's written all his later works," said Mrs. Driffield, closing a book that was open face-downward on it.

"It's the frontispiece in the third volume of the *édition de luxe*. It's a period piece."

We all admired the writing-table, and Lady Hodmarsh, when she thought no one was looking, ran her fingers along its under edge to see if it was genuine. Mrs. Driffield gave us a quick, bright smile.

"Would you like to see one of his manuscripts?"

"I'd love to," said the duchess, "and then I simply must bolt."

Mrs. Driffield took from a shelf a manuscript bound in blue morocco, and while the rest of the party reverently examined it I had a look at the books with which the room was lined. As authors will, I ran my eye round quickly to see if there were any of mine, but could not find one; I saw, however, a complete set of Alroy Kear's and a great many novels in bright bindings, which looked suspiciously unread; I guessed that they were the works of authors who had sent them to the master in homage to his talent and perhaps the hope of a few words of eulogy that could be used in the publisher's advertisements. But all the books were so neatly arranged, they were so clean, that I had the impression they were very seldom read. There was the Oxford Dictionary and there were standard editions in grand bindings of most of the English classics, Fielding, Boswell, Hazlitt and so on, and there were a great many books on the sea; I recognised the variously coloured, untidy volumes of the sailing directions issued by the Admiralty, and there were a number of works on gardening. The room had the look not of a writer's workshop, but of a memorial to a great name, and you could almost see already the desultory tripper wandering in for want of something better to do and smell the rather musty, close smell of a museum that few visited. I had a suspicion that nowadays if Driffield read anything at all it was the *Gardener's Chronicle* or the *Shipping Gazette*, of which I saw a bundle on a table in the corner.

When the ladies had seen all they wanted we bade our hosts farewell. But Lady Hodmarsh was a woman of tact and it must have occurred to her that I, the excuse for the party, had scarcely had a word with Edward Driffield, for at the door, enveloping me with a friendly smile, she said to him:

"I was so interested to hear that you and Mr. Ashenden had known one another years and years ago. Was he a nice little boy?"

Driffield looked at me for a moment with that level, ironic gaze of his. I had the impression that if there had been nobody there he would have put his tongue out at me.

"Shy," he replied. "I taught him to ride a bicycle."

We got once more into the huge yellow Rolls and drove off.

"He's too sweet," said the duchess. "I'm so glad we went."

"He has such nice manners, hasn't he?" said Lady Hodmarsh.

"You didn't really expect him to eat his peas with a knife, did you?" I asked.

"I wish he had," said Scallion. "It would have been so picturesque."

"I believe it's very difficult," said the duchess. "I've tried over and over again and I can never get them to stay on."

"You have to spear them," said Scallion.

"Not at all," retorted the duchess. "You have to balance them on the flat, and they roll like the devil."

"What did you think of Mrs. Driffield?" asked Lady Hodmarsh.

"I suppose she serves her purpose," said the duchess.

"He's so old, poor darling, he must have someone to look after him. You know she was a hospital nurse?"

"Oh, was she?" said the duchess. "I thought perhaps she'd been his secretary or typist or something."

"She's quite nice," said Lady Hodmarsh, warmly defending a friend.

"Oh, quite."

"He had a long illness about twenty years ago, and she was his nurse then, and after he got well he married her."

"Funny how men will do that. She must have been years younger than him. She can't be more than—what?—forty or forty-five."

"No, I shouldn't think so. Forty-seven, say. I'm told she's done a great deal for him. I mean, she's made him quite presentable. Alroy Kear told me that before that he was almost too bohemian."

"As a rule authors' wives are odious."

"It's such a bore having to have them, isn't it?"

"Crashing. I wonder they don't see that themselves."

"Poor wretches, they often suffer from the delusion that people find them interesting," I murmured.

We reached Tercanbury, dropped the duchess at the station and drove on.

CHAPTER V

IT was true that Edward Driffield had taught me to bicycle. That
was indeed how I first made his acquaintance. I do not know how
long the safety bicycle had been invented, but I know that it was
not common in the remote part of Kent in which I lived and when
you saw someone speeding along on solid tyres you turned round
and looked till he was out of sight. It was still a matter for
jocularity on the part of middle-aged gentlemen who said Shank's
pony was good enough for them, and for trepidation on the part
of elderly ladies who made a dash for the side of the road when
they saw one coming. I had been for some time filled with envy
of the boys whom I saw riding into the school grounds on their
bicycles. It gave a pretty opportunity for showing off when you
entered the gateway without holding on to the handles. I had
persuaded my uncle to let me have one at the beginning of the
summer holidays, and though my aunt was against it, since she
said I should only break my neck, he had yielded to my pertinacity
more willingly because I was of course paying for it out of my own
money. I ordered it before school broke up and a few days later
the carrier brought it over from Tercanbury.

I was determined to learn to ride it by myself and chaps at
school had told me that they had learned in half an hour. I tried
and tried and at last came to the conclusion that I was abnormally
stupid, but even after my pride was sufficiently humbled for me to
allow the gardener to hold me up I seemed at the end of the first
morning no nearer to being able to get on by myself than at the
beginning. Next day, however, thinking that the carriage drive at
the vicarage was too winding to give a fellow a proper chance, I
wheeled the bicycle to a road not far away which I knew was
perfectly flat and straight and so solitary that no one would see
me making a fool of myself. I tried several times to mount, but
fell off each time. I barked my shins against the pedals and got
very hot and bothered. After I had been doing this for about an
hour, though I began to think that God did not intend me to ride
a bicycle, but was determined (unable to bear the thought of the
sarcasms of my uncle, his representative at Blackstable) to do so
all the same, to my disgust I saw two people on bicycles coming
along the deserted road. I immediately wheeled my machine to
the side and sat down on a stile, looking out to sea in a nonchalant

way as though I had been for a ride and were just sitting there wrapped in contemplation of the vasty ocean. I kept my eyes dreamily averted from the two persons who were advancing towards me, but I felt that they were coming nearer, and through the corner of my eye I saw that they were a man and a woman. As they passed me the woman swerved violently to my side of the road and, crashing against me, fell to the ground.

"Oh, I'm sorry," she said. "I knew I should fall off the moment I saw you."

It was impossible under the circumstances to preserve my appearance of abstraction and, blushing furiously, I said that it didn't matter at all.

The man had got off as she fell.

"You haven't hurt yourself?" he asked.

"Oh, no."

I recognised him then as Edward Driffield, the author I had seen walking with the curate a few days before.

"I'm just learning to ride," said his companion. "And I fall off whenever I see anything in the road."

"Aren't you the vicar's nephew?" said Driffield. "I saw you the other day. Galloway told me who you were. This is my wife."

She held out her hand with an oddly frank gesture and when I took it gave mine a warm and hearty pressure. She smiled with her lips and with her eyes and there was in her smile something that even then I recognised as singularly pleasant. I was confused. People I did not know made me dreadfully self-conscious, and I could not take in any of the details of her appearance. I just had an impression of a rather large blonde woman. I do not know if I noticed then or only remembered afterward that she wore a full skirt of blue serge, a pink shirt with a starched front and a starched collar, and a straw hat, called in those days, I think, a boater, perched on the top of a lot of golden hair.

"I think bicycling's lovely, don't you?" she said, looking at my beautiful new machine which leaned against the stile. "It must be wonderful to be able to ride well."

I felt that this inferred an admiration for my proficiency.

"It's only a matter of practice," I said.

"This is only my third lesson. Mr. Driffield says I'm coming on wonderful, but I feel so stupid I could kick myself. How long did it take you before you could ride?"

I blushed to the roots of my hair. I could hardly utter the shameful words.

"I can't ride," I said. "I've only just got this bike and this is the first time I've tried."

I equivocated a trifle there, but I made it all right with my conscience by adding the mental reservation: except yesterday at home in the garden.

"I'll give you a lesson if you like," said Driffield in his good-humoured way. "Come on."

"Oh, no," I said. "I wouldn't dream of it."

"Why not?" asked his wife, her blue eyes still pleasantly smiling. "Mr. Driffield would like to and it'll give me a chance to rest."

Driffield took my bicycle, and I, reluctant but unable to withstand his friendly violence, clumsily mounted. I swayed from side to side, but he held me with a firm hand.

"Faster," he said.

I pedalled and he ran by me as I wobbled from side to side. We were both very hot when, notwithstanding his efforts, I at last fell off. It was very hard under such circumstances to preserve the standoffishness befitting the vicar's nephew with the son of Miss Wolfe's bailiff, and when I started back again and for thirty or forty thrilling yards actually rode by myself and Mrs. Driffield ran into the middle of the road with her arms akimbo shouting: "Go it, go it, two to one on the favourite," I was laughing so much that I positively forgot all about my social status. I got off of my own accord, my face no doubt wearing an air of immodest triumph, and received without embarrassment the Driffields' congratulation on my cleverness in riding a bicycle the very first day I tried.

"I want to see if I can get on by myself," said Mrs. Driffield, and I sat down again on the stile while her husband and I watched her unavailing struggles.

Then, wanting to rest again, disappointed but cheerful, she sat down beside me. Driffield lit his pipe. We chatted. I did not of course realise it then, but I know now that there was a disarming frankness in her manner that put one at one's ease. She talked with a kind of eagerness, like a child bubbling over with the zest of life, and her eyes were lit all the time by her engaging smile. I did not know why I liked it. I should say it was a little sly, if slyness were not a displeasing quality; it was too innocent to be sly. It was mischievous rather, like that of a child who has done something that he thinks funny, but is quite well aware that you will think rather naughty; he knows all the same that you won't be really cross and if you don't find out about it quickly he'll come and tell you himself. But of course then I only knew that her smile made me feel at home.

Presently Driffield, looking at his watch, said that they must be going and suggested that we should all ride back together in style. It was just the time that my aunt and uncle would be coming home from their daily walk down the town and I did not like to run the risk of being seen with people whom they would not at all approve of; so I asked them to go on first, as they would go more quickly than I. Mrs. Driffield would not hear of it, but Driffield gave me a funny, amused little look, which made me think that he saw through my excuse, so that I blushed scarlet, and he said:

"Let him go by himself, Rosie. He can manage better alone."

"All right. Shall you be here to-morrow? We're coming."

"I'll try to," I answered.

They rode off, and in a few minutes I followed. Feeling very much pleased with myself, I rode all the way to the vicarage gates without falling. I think I boasted a good deal at dinner, but I did not say that I had met the Driffields.

Next day at about eleven I got my bicycle out of the coachhouse. It was so called though it held not even a pony trap and was used by the gardener to keep the mower and the roller, and by Mary-Ann for her sack of meal for the chickens. I wheeled it down to the gate and, mounting none too easily, rode along the Tercanbury Road till I came to the old turnpike and turned into Joy Lane.

The sky was blue and the air, warm and yet fresh, crackled, as it were, with the heat. The light was brilliant without harshness. The sun's beams seemed to hit the white road with a directed energy and bounce back like a rubber ball.

I rode backward and forward, waiting for the Driffields, and presently saw them come. I waved to them and turned round (getting off to do so) and we pedalled along together. Mrs. Driffield and I complimented one another on our progress. We rode anxiously, clinging like grim death to the handle-bars, but exultant, and Driffield said that as soon as we felt sure of ourselves we must go for rides all over the country.

"I want to get rubbings of one or two brasses in the neighbourhood," he said.

I did not know what he meant, but he would not explain.

"Wait and I'll show you," he said. "Do you think you could ride fourteen miles to-morrow, seven there and seven back?"

"Rather," I said.

"I'll bring a sheet of paper for you and some wax and you can make a rubbing. But you'd better ask your uncle if you can come."

"I needn't do that."

"I think you'd better all the same."

Mrs. Driffield gave me that peculiar look of hers, mischievous and yet friendly, and I blushed scarlet. I knew that if I asked my uncle he would say no. It would be much better to say nothing about it. But as we rode along I saw coming towards us the doctor in his dogcart. I looked straight in front of me as he passed in the vain hope that if I did not look at him he would not look at me. I was uneasy. If he had seen me the fact would quickly reach the ears of my uncle or my aunt and I considered whether it would not be safer to disclose myself a secret that could no longer be concealed. When we parted at the vicarage gates (I had not been able to avoid riding as far as this in their company) Driffield said that if I found I could come with them next day I had better call for them as early as I could.

"You know where we live, don't you? Next door to the Congregational Church. It's called Lime Cottage."

When I sat down to dinner I looked for an opportunity to slip in casually the information that I had by accident run across the Driffields; but news travelled fast in Blackstable.

"Who were those people you were bicycling with this morning?" asked my aunt. "We met Dr. Anstey in the town and he said he'd seen you."

My uncle, chewing his roast beef with an air of disapproval, looked sullenly at his plate.

"The Driffields," I said with nonchalance. "You know, the author. Mr. Galloway knows them."

"They're most disreputable people," said my uncle. "I don't wish you to associate with them."

"Why not?" I asked.

"I'm not going to give you my reasons. It's enough that I don't wish it."

"How did you ever get to know them?" asked my aunt.

"I was just riding along and they were riding along, and they asked me if I'd like to ride with them," I said, distorting the truth a little.

"I call it very pushing," said my uncle.

I began to sulk. And to show my indignation when the sweet was put on the table, though it was raspberry tart which I was extremely fond of, I refused to have any. My aunt asked me if I was not feeling very well.

"Yes," I said, as haughtily as I could, "I'm feeling all right."

"Have a little bit," said my aunt.

"I'm not hungry," I answered.

"Just to please me."

"He must know when he's had enough," said my uncle.

I gave him a bitter look.

"I don't mind having a small piece," I said.

My aunt gave me a generous helping, which I ate with the air of one who, impelled by a stern sense of duty, performs an act that is deeply distasteful to him. It was a beautiful raspberry tart. Mary-Ann made short pastry that melted in the mouth. But when my aunt asked me whether I could not manage a little more I refused with cold dignity. She did not insist. My uncle said grace and I carried my outraged feelings into the drawing-room.

But when I reckoned that the servants had finished their dinner I went into the kitchen. Emily was cleaning the silver in the pantry. Mary-Ann was washing up.

"I say, what's wrong with the Driffields?" I asked her.

Mary-Ann had come to the vicarage when she was eighteen. She had bathed me when I was a small boy, given me powders in plum jam when I needed them, packed my box when I went to school, nursed me when I was ill, read to me when I was bored and scolded me when I was naughty. Emily, the housemaid, was a flighty young thing, and Mary-Ann didn't know whatever would become of me if *she* had the looking after of me. Mary-Ann was a Blackstable girl. She had never been to London in her life and I do not think she had been to Tercanbury more than three or four times. She was never ill. She never had a holiday. She was paid twelve pounds a year. One evening a week she went down the town to see her mother, who did the vicarage washing; and on Sunday evenings she went to church. But Mary-Ann knew everything that went on in Blackstable. She knew who everybody was, who had married whom, what anyone's father had died of, and how many children, and what they were called, any woman had had.

I asked Mary-Ann my question and she slopped a wet clout noisily into the sink.

"I don't blame your uncle," she said. "I wouldn't let you go about with them, not if you was my nephew. Fancy their askin' you to ride your bicycle with them! Some people will do anything."

I saw that the conversation in the dining-room had been repeated to Mary-Ann.

"I'm not a child," I said.

"That makes it all the worse. The impudence of their comin' 'ere at all!" Mary-Ann dropped her aitches freely. "Takin' a house and pretendin' to be ladies and gentlemen. Now leave that pie alone."

The raspberry tart was standing on the kitchen table and I broke off a piece of crust with my fingers and put it in my mouth.

"We're goin' to eat that for our supper. If you'd wanted a second 'elpin' why didn't you 'ave one when you was 'avin' your dinner? Ted Driffield never could stick to anything. He 'ad a good education, too. The one I'm sorry for is his mother. He's been a trouble to 'er from the day he was born. And then to go an' marry Rosie Gann. They tell me that when he told his mother what he was goin' to do she took to 'er bed and stayed there for three weeks and wouldn't talk to anybody."

"Was Mrs. Driffield Rosie Gann before she married? Which Ganns were those?"

Gann was one of the commonest names at Blackstable. The churchyard was thick with their graves.

"Oh, you wouldn't 'ave known them. Old Josiah Gann was her father. He was a wild one, too. He went for a soldier and when he come back he 'ad a wooden leg. He used to go out doing painting, but he was out of work more often than not. They lived in the next 'ouse to us in Rye Lane. Me an' Rosie used to go to Sunday School together."

"But she's not as old as you are," I said with the bluntness of my age.

"She'll never see thirty again."

Mary-Ann was a little woman with a snub nose and decayed teeth, but fresh-coloured, and I do not suppose she could have been more than thirty-five.

"Rosie ain't more than four or five years younger than me, whatever she may pretend she is. They tell me you wouldn't know her now all dressed up and everything."

"Is it true that she was a barmaid?" I asked.

"Yes, at the 'Railway Arms' and then at the 'Prince of Wales's Feathers' at Haversham. Mrs. Reeves 'ad her to 'elp in the bar at the 'Railway Arms', but it got so bad she had to get rid of her."

The "Railway Arms" was a very modest little public-house just opposite the station of the London, Chatham & Dover Railway. It had a sort of sinister gaiety. On a winter's night as you passed by you saw through the glass doors men lounging about the bar. My uncle very much disapproved of it, and had for years been trying to get its licence taken away. It was frequented by the railway porters, colliers and farm labourers. The respectable residents of Blackstable would have disdained to enter it and, when they wanted a glass of bitter, went to the "Bear and Key" or the "Duke of Kent".

"Why, what did she do?" I asked, my eyes popping out of my head.

"What didn't she do?" said Mary-Ann. "What d'you think your uncle would say if he caught me tellin' you things like that? There wasn't a man who come in to 'ave a drink what she didn't carry on with. No matter who they was. She couldn't stick to anybody, it was just one man after another. They tell me it was simply 'orrible. That was when it begun with Lord George. It wasn't the sort of place he was likely to go to, he was too grand for that, but they say he went in accidental-like one day when his train was late, and he saw her. And after that he was never out of the place, mixin' with all them common rough people, and of course they all knew what he was there for, and him with a wife and three children. Oh, I was sorry for her! And the talk it made. Well, it got so Mrs. Reeves said she wasn't going to put up with it another day and she give her her wages and told her to pack her box and go. Good riddance to bad rubbish, that's what I said."

I knew Lord George very well. His name was George Kemp and the title by which he was always known had been given him ironically owing to his grand manner. He was our coal merchant, but he also dabbled in house property, and he owned a share in one or two colliers. He lived in a new brick house that stood in its own grounds and he drove his own trap. He was a stoutish man with a pointed beard, florid, with a high colour and bold blue eyes. Remembering him, I think he must have looked like some jolly rubicund merchant in an old Dutch picture. He was always very flashily dressed and when you saw him driving at a smart pace down the middle of the High Street in a fawn-coloured covert-coat with large buttons, his brown bowler on the side of his head and a red rose in his buttonhole, you could not but look at him. On Sunday he used to come to church in a lustrous topper and a frock-coat. Everyone knew that he wanted to be made churchwarden, and it was evident that his energy would have made him useful, but my uncle said not in his time, and though Lord George as a protest went to chapel for a year my uncle remained obdurate. He cut him dead when he met him in the town. A reconciliation was effected and Lord George came to church again, but my uncle only yielded so far as to appoint him sidesman. The gentry thought him vulgar and I have no doubt that he was vain and boastful. They complained of his loud voice and his strident laugh—when he was talking to somebody on one side of the street you heard every word he said from the other— and they thought his manners dreadful. He was much too friendly; when he talked to them it was as though he were not in trade at all; they said he was very pushing. But if he thought his hail-fellow-well-met air, his activity in public works, his open purse when subscriptions were needed for the annual regatta or for the harvest festival, his willingness to do anyone a good turn were going to break the barriers at Blackstable he was mistaken. His efforts at sociability were met with blank hostility.

I remember once that the doctor's wife was calling on my aunt and Emily came in to tell my uncle that Mr. George Kemp would like to see him.

"But I heard the front door ring, Emily," said my aunt.

"Yes'm, he came to the front door."

There was a moment's awkwardness. Everyone was at a loss to know how to deal with such an unusual occurrence, and even Emily, who knew who should come to the front door, who should go to the side door, and who to the back, looked a trifle flustered. My aunt, who was a gentle soul, I think felt honestly embarrassed that anyone should put himself in such a false position; but the doctor's wife gave a little sniff of contempt. At last my uncle collected himself.

"Show him into the study, Emily," he said. "I'll come as soon as I've finished my tea."

But Lord George remained exuberant, flashy, loud and boisterous. He said the town was dead and he was going to wake it up. He was going to get the company to run excursion trains. He didn't see why it shouldn't become another Margate. And why shouldn't they have a mayor? Ferne Bay had one.

"I suppose he thinks he'd be mayor himself," said the people of Blackstable. They pursed their lips. "Pride goeth before a fall," they said.

And my uncle remarked that you could take a horse to the water but you couldn't make him drink.

I should add that I looked upon Lord George with the same scornful derision as everyone else. It outraged me that he should stop me in the street and call me by my Christian name and talk to me as though there were no social difference between us. He even suggested that I should play cricket with his sons, who were of about the same age as myself. But they went to the grammar school at Haversham and of course I couldn't possibly have anything to do with them.

I was shocked and thrilled by what Mary-Ann told me, but I had difficulty in believing it. I had read too many novels and had learnt too much at school not to know a good deal about love, but I thought it was a matter that only concerned young people. I could not conceive that a man with a beard, who had sons as old as I, could have any feelings of that sort. I thought when you married all that was finished. That people over thirty should make love seemed to me rather disgusting.

"You don't mean to say they did anything?" I asked Mary-Ann.

"From what I hear there's very little that Rosie Gann didn't do. And Lord George wasn't the only one."

"But, look here, why didn't she have a baby?"

In the novels I had read whenever lovely woman stooped to folly she had a baby. The cause was put with infinite precaution, sometimes indeed suggested only by a row of asterisks, but the result was inevitable.

"More by good luck than by good management, I lay," said Mary-Ann. Then she recollected herself and stopped drying the plates she was busy with. "It seems to me you know a lot more than you ought to," she said.

"Of course I know," I said importantly. "Hang it all, I'm practically grown up, aren't I?"

"All I can tell you," said Mary-Ann, "is that when Mrs. Reeves give her the sack Lord George got her a job at the 'Prince of Wales's Feathers' at Haversham and he was always poppin' over there in his trap. You can't tell me the ale's any different over there from what it is here."

"Then why did Ted Driffield marry her?" I asked.

"Ask me another," said Mary-Ann. "It was at the 'Feathers' he saw her. I suppose he couldn't get no one else to marry him. No respectable girl would 'ave 'ad 'im."

"Did he know about her?"

"You'd better ask him."

I was silent. It was all very puzzling.

"What does she look like now?" asked Mary-Ann. "I never seen her since she married. I never even speak to 'er after I 'eard what was goin' on at the 'Railway Arms'."

"She looks all right," I said.

"Well, you ask her if she remembers me and see what she says."

CHAPTER VI

I HAD quite made up my mind that I was going out with the Driffields next morning, but knew that it was no good asking my uncle if I might. If he found out that I had been and made a row it couldn't be helped, and if Ted Driffield asked me whether I had got my uncle's permission I was quite prepared to say I had. But I had after all no need to lie. In the afternoon, the tide being high, I walked down to the beach to bathe and my uncle, having something to do in the town, walked part of the way with me. Just as we were passing the "Bear and Key", Ted Driffield stepped out of it. He saw us and came straight up to my uncle. I was startled at his coolness.

"Good-afternoon, Vicar," he said. "I wonder if you remember me. I used to sing in the choir when I was a boy. Ted Driffield. My old governor was Miss Wolfe's bailiff."

My uncle was a very timid man, and he was taken aback.

"Oh, yes, how do you do? I was sorry to hear your father died."

"I've made the acquaintance of your young nephew. I was wondering if you'd let him come for a ride with me to-morrow.

F.A.A 1F

It's rather dull for him riding alone, and I'm going to do a rubbing of one of the brasses at Ferne Church."

"It's very kind of you, but——"

My uncle was going to refuse, but Driffield interrupted him.

"I'll see he doesn't get up to any mischief. I thought he might like to make a rubbing himself. It would be an interest for him. I'll give him some paper and wax so that it won't cost him anything."

My uncle had not a consecutive mind and the suggestion that Ted Driffield should pay for my paper and wax offended him so much that he quite forgot his intention to forbid me to go at all.

"He can quite well get his own paper and wax," he said. "He has plenty of pocket money, and he'd much better spend it on something like that than on sweets and make himself sick."

"Well, if he goes to Hayward, the stationer's, and says he wants the same paper as I got and the wax they'll let him have it."

"I'll go now," I said, and to prevent any change of mind on my uncle's part dashed across the road.

CHAPTER VII

I DO not know why the Driffields bothered about me unless it was from pure kindness of heart. I was a dull little boy, not very talkative, and if I amused Ted Driffield at all it must have been unconsciously. Perhaps he was tickled by my attitude of superiority. I was under the impression that it was condescension on my part to consort with the son of Miss Wolfe's bailiff, and he what my uncle called a penny-a-liner; and when, perhaps with a trace of superciliousness, I asked him to lend me one of his books and he said it wouldn't interest me I took him at his word and did not insist. After my uncle had once consented to my going out with the Driffields he made no further objection to my association with them. Sometimes we went for sails together, sometimes we went to some picturesque spot and Driffield painted a little water-colour. I do not know if the English climate was better in those days or if it is only an illusion of youth, but I seem to remember that all through that summer the sunny days followed one another in an unbroken line. I began to feel a curious affection for the undulating, opulent and gracious country.

We went far afield, to one church after another, taking rubbings of brasses, knights in armour and ladies in stiff farthingales. Ted Driffield fired me with his own enthusiasm for this simple pursuit and I rubbed with passion. I showed my uncle proudly the results of my industry, and I suppose he thought that, whatever my company, I could not come to much harm when I was occupied in church. Mrs. Driffield used to remain in the churchyard while we were at work, not reading or sewing, but just mooning about; she seemed able to do nothing for an indefinite time without feeling bored. Sometimes I would go out and sit with her for a little on the grass. We chattered about my school, my friends there and my masters, about the people at Blackstable and about nothing at all. She gratified me by calling me Mr. Ashenden. I think she was the first person who had ever done so and it made me feel grown up. I resented it vastly when people called me Master Willie. I thought it a ridiculous name for anyone to have. In fact I did not like either of my names and spent much time inventing others that would have suited me better. The ones I preferred were Roderic Ravensworth and I covered sheets of paper with this signature in a suitably dashing hand. I did not mind Ludovic Montgomery either.

I could not get over what Mary-Ann had told me about Mrs. Driffield. Though I knew theoretically what people did when they were married, and was capable of putting the facts in the bluntest language, I did not really understand it. I thought it indeed rather disgusting and I did not quite, quite believe it. After all, I was aware that the earth was round, but I *knew* it was flat. Mrs. Driffield seemed so frank, her laugh was so open, there was in her demeanour something so young and childlike, that I could not see her "going with" sailors and above all anyone so gross and horrible as Lord George. She was not at all the type of the wicked woman I had read of in novels. Of course I knew she wasn't "good form" and she spoke with the Blackstable accent, she dropped an aitch now and then, and sometimes her grammar gave me a shock, but I couldn't help liking her. I came to the conclusion that what Mary-Ann had told me was a pack of lies.

One day I happened to tell her that Mary-Ann was our cook. "She says she lived next door to you in Rye Lane," I added, quite prepared to hear Mrs. Driffield say that she had never even heard of her.

But she smiled and her blue eyes gleamed.

"That's right. She used to take me to Sunday School. She used to have a rare job keeping me quiet. I heard she'd gone to service at the vicarage. Fancy her being there still! I haven't seen her for donkey's years. I'd like to see her again and have a chat about old days. Remember me to her, will you, and ask her to look in on her evening out. I'll give her a cup of tea."

I was taken aback at this. After all, the Driffields lived in a house that they were talking of buying and they had a "general". It wouldn't be at all the thing for them to have Mary-Ann to tea, and it would make it very awkward for me. They seemed to have no sense of the things one could do and the things one simply couldn't. It never ceased to embarrass me, the way in which they talked of incidents in their past that I should have thought they would not dream of mentioning. I do not know that the people I lived among were pretentious in the sense of making themselves out to be richer or grander than they really were, but looking back it does seem to me that they lived a life full of pretences. They dwelt behind a mask of respectability. You never caught them in their shirt-sleeves with their feet on the table. The ladies put on afternoon dresses and were not visible till then; they lived privately with rigid economy so that you could not drop in for a casual meal, but when they entertained their tables groaned with food. Though catastrophe overwhelmed the family, they held their heads high and ignored it. One of the sons might have married an actress, but they never referred to the calamity, and though the neighbours said it was dreadful, they took ostentatious care not to mention the theatre in the presence of the afflicted. We all knew that the wife of Major Greencourt who had taken the Three Gables was connected with trade, but neither she nor the major ever so much as hinted at the discreditable secret; and though we sniffed at them behind their backs, we were too polite even to mention crockery (the source of Mrs. Greencourt's adequate income) in their presence. It was still not unheard of for an angry parent to cut off his son with a shilling or to tell his daughter (who like my own mother had married a solicitor) never to darken his doors again. I was used to all this and it seemed to me natural. What did shock me was to hear Ted Driffield speak of being a waiter in a restaurant in Holborn as though it were the most ordinary thing in the world. I knew he had run away to sea; that was romantic; I knew that boys, in books at all events, often did this and had thrilling adventures before they married a fortune and an earl's daughter; but Ted Driffield had driven a cab at Maidstone and had been clerk in a booking-office at Birmingham. Once when we bicycled past the "Railway Arms", Mrs. Driffield mentioned quite casually, as though it were something that anyone might have done, that she had worked there for three years.

"It was my first place," she said. "After that I went to the 'Feathers' at Haversham. I only left there to get married."

She laughed as though she enjoyed the recollection. I did not know what to say; I did not know which way to look; I blushed scarlet. Another time when we were going through Ferne Bay on our way back from a long excursion, it being a hot day and all of us thirsty, she suggested that we should go into the "Dolphin" and have a glass of beer. She began talking to the girl behind the bar and I was horrified to hear her remark that she had been in the business herself for five years. The landlord joined us and Ted Driffield offered him a drink, and Mrs. Driffield said that the barmaid must have a glass of port, and for some time they all chatted amiably about trade and tied houses and how the price of everything was going up. Meanwhile, I stood, hot and cold all over and not knowing what to do with myself. As we went out Mrs. Driffield remarked:

"I took quite a fancy to that girl, Ted. She ought to do well for herself. As I said to her, it's a hard life but a merry one. You do see a bit of what's going on and if you play your cards right you ought to marry well. I noticed she had an engagement ring on, but she told me she just wore that because it gave the fellows a chance to tease her."

Driffield laughed. She turned to me.

"I had a rare old time when I was a barmaid, but of course you can't go on for ever. You have to think of your future."

But a great jolt awaited her. It was half-way through September and my holidays were drawing to an end. I was very full of the Driffields, but my desire to talk about them at home was snubbed by my uncle.

"We don't want your friends pushed down our throats all day long," said he. "There are other topics of conversation that are more suitable. But I do think that, as Ted Driffield was born in the parish and is seeing you almost every day, he might come to church occasionally."

One day I told Driffield: "My uncle wants you to come to church."

"All right. Let's go to church next Sunday night, Rosie."

"I don't mind," she said.

I told Mary-Ann they were going. I sat in the vicarage pew just behind the squire's and I could not look round, but I was conscious by the behaviour of my neighbours on the other side of the aisle that they were there, and as soon as I had a chance next day I asked Mary-Ann if she had seen them.

"I see 'er all right," said Mary-Ann grimly.

"Did you speak to her afterwards?"

"Me?" She suddenly burst into anger. "You get out of my kitchen. What d'you want to come bothering me all day long? How d'you expect me to do my work with you getting in my way all the time?"

"All right," I said. "Don't get in a wax."

"I don't know what your uncle's about, lettin' you go all over the place with the likes of them. All them flowers in her 'at. I wonder she ain't ashamed to show her face. Now run along, I'm busy."

I did not know why Mary-Ann was so cross. I did not mention Mrs. Driffield again. But two or three days later I happened to go into the kitchen to get something I wanted. There were two kitchens at the vicarage, a small one in which the cooking was done and a large one, built I suppose for a time when country clergymen had large families and gave grand dinners to the surrounding gentry, where Mary-Ann sat and sewed when her day's work was over. We had cold supper at eight, so that after tea she had little to do. It was getting on for seven and the day was drawing in. It was Emily's evening out and I expected to find Mary-Ann alone, but as I went along the passage I heard voices and the sound of laughter. I supposed Mary-Ann had someone in to see her. The lamp was lit, but it had a thick green shade and the kitchen was almost in darkness. I saw a teapot and cups on the table. Mary-Ann was having a late cup of tea with her friend. The conversation stopped as I opened the door, then I heard a voice.

"Good-evening."

With a start I saw that Mary-Ann's friend was Mrs. Driffield. Mary-Ann laughed a little at my surprise.

"Rosie Gann dropped in to have a cup of tea with me," she said.

"We've been having a talk about old times."

Mary-Ann was a little shy at my finding her thus, but not half so shy as I. Mrs. Driffield gave me that childlike, mischievous smile of hers; she was perfectly at her ease. For some reason I noticed her dress. I suppose because I had never seen her so grand before. It was of pale-blue cloth, very tight at the waist, with high sleeves and a long skirt with a flounce at the bottom. She wore a large black straw hat with a great quantity of roses and leaves and bows on it. It was evidently the hat she had worn in church on Sunday.

"I thought if I went on waiting till Mary-Ann came to see me I'd have to wait till doomsday, so I thought the best thing I could do was to come and see her myself."

Mary-Ann grinned self-consciously, but did not look displeased. I asked for whatever it was I wanted and as quickly as I could left them. I went out into the garden and wandered about aimlessly. I walked down to the road and looked over the gate. The night had fallen. Presently I saw a man strolling along. I paid no attention to him, but he passed backward and forward and it looked as though he were waiting for someone. At first I thought it might be Ted Driffield and I was on the point of going out when he stopped and lit a pipe; I saw it was Lord George. I wondered what he was doing there and at the same moment it struck me that he was waiting for Mrs. Driffield. My heart began to beat fast, and though I was hidden by the darkness I withdrew into the shade of the bushes. I waited a few minutes longer, then I saw the side door open and Mrs. Driffield let out by Mary-Ann. I heard her footsteps on the gravel. She came to the gate and opened it. It opened with a little click. At the sound Lord George stepped across the road and before she could come out slipped in. He took her in his arms and gave her a great hug. She gave a little laugh.

"Take care of my hat," she whispered.

I was not more than three feet away from them and I was terrified lest they should notice me. I was so ashamed for them. I was trembling with agitation. For a minute he held her in his arms.

"What about the garden?" he said, still in a whisper.

"No, there's that boy. Let's go in the fields."

They went out by the gate, he with his arm round her waist, and were lost in the night. Now I felt my heart pounding against my chest so that I could hardly breathe. I was so astonished at what I had seen that I could not think sensibly. I would have given anything to be able to tell someone, but it was a secret and I must keep it. I was thrilled with the importance it gave me. I walked slowly up to the house and let myself in by the side door. Mary-Ann, hearing it open, called me.

"Is that you, Master Willie?"

"Yes."

I looked in the kitchen. Mary-Ann was putting the supper on a tray to take it into the dining-room.

"I wouldn't say anything to your uncle about Rosie Gann 'avin' been here," she said.

"Oh, no."

"It was a surprisement to me. When I 'eard a knock at the side door and opened it and saw Rosie standing there, you could 'ave knocked me down with a feather. 'Mary-Ann,' she says, an' before I knew what she was up to she was kissing me all over me face. I couldn't but ask 'er in and when she was in I couldn't but ask her to 'ave a nice cup of tea."

Mary-Ann was anxious to excuse herself. After all she had said of Mrs. Driffield it must seem strange to me that I should find them sitting there together chatting away and laughing. I did not want to crow.

"She's not so bad, is she?" I said.

Mary-Ann smiled. Notwithstanding her black decayed teeth her smile was sweet and touching.

"I don't 'ardly know what it is, but there's somethin' you can't 'elp likin' about her. She was 'ere the best part of an hour and I will say that for 'er, she never once give 'erself airs. And she told me with 'er own lips the material of that dress she 'ad on cost thirteen and eleven a yard and I believe it. She remembers everything, how I used to brush her 'air for her when she was a tiny tot and how I used to make her wash her little 'ands before tea. You see, sometimes her mother used to send 'er in to 'ave her tea with us. She was as pretty as a picture in them days."

Mary-Ann looked back into the past and her funny crumpled face grew wistful.

"Oh, well," she said after a pause, "I dare say she's been no worse than plenty others if the truth was only known. She 'ad more temptation than most, and I dare say a lot of them as blame her would 'ave been no better than what she was if they'd 'ad the opportunity."

CHAPTER VIII

THE weather broke suddenly; it grew chilly and heavy rain fell.
It put an end to our excursions. I was not sorry, for I did not
know how I could look Mrs. Driffield in the face now that I had
seen her meeting with George Kemp. I was not so much shocked
as astonished. I could not understand how it was possible for her
to like being kissed by an old man, and the fantastic notion
passed through my mind, filled with the novels I had read, that
somehow Lord George held her in his power and forced her by
his knowledge of some fearful secret to submit to his loathsome
embraces. My imagination played with terrible possibilities.
Bigamy, murder and forgery. Very few villains in books failed
to hold the threat of exposure of one of these crimes over some
hapless female. Perhaps Mrs. Driffield had backed a bill; I never
could quite understand what this meant, but I knew that the consequences were disastrous. I toyed with the fancy of her anguish
(the long sleepless nights when she sat at her window in her night-
dress, her fair hair hanging to her knees, and watched hopelessly
for the dawn) and saw myself (not a boy of fifteen with sixpence
a week pocket money, but a tall man with a waxed moustache and
muscles of steel in faultless evening dress) with a happy blend of
heroism and dexterity rescuing her from the toils of the rascally
blackmailer. On the other hand, it had not looked as though she
had yielded quite unwillingly to Lord George's fondling and I
could not get out of my ears the sound of her laugh. It had a
note that I had never heard before. It gave me a queer feeling of
breathlessness.

During the rest of my holidays I only saw the Driffields once
more. I met them by chance in the town and they stopped and
spoke to me. I suddenly felt very shy again, but when I looked at
Mrs. Driffield I could not help blushing with embarrassment, for
there was nothing in her countenance that indicated a guilty secret.
She looked at me with those soft blue eyes of hers in which there
was a child's playful naughtiness. She often held her mouth a
little open, as though it were just going to break into a smile, and
her lips were full and red. There was honesty and innocence in
her face and an ingenuous frankness and though then I could not
have expressed this, I felt it quite strongly. If I had put it into
words at all I think I should have said: She looks as straight as a

die. It was impossible that she could be "carrying on" with Lord George. There must be an explanation; I did not believe what my eyes had seen.

Then the day came when I had to go back to school. The carter had taken my trunk and I walked to the station by myself. I had refused to let my aunt see me off, thinking it more manly to go alone, but I felt rather low as I walked down the street. It was a small branch line to Tercanbury and the station was at the other end of the town near the beach. I took my ticket and settled myself in the corner of a third-class carriage. Suddenly I heard a voice: There he is; and Mr. and Mrs. Driffield bustled gaily up.

"We thought we must come and see you off," she said. "Are you feeling miserable?"

"No, of course not."

"Oh, well, it won't last long. We'll have no end of a time when you come back for Christmas. Can you skate?"

"No."

"I can. I'll teach you."

Her high spirits cheered me, and at the same time the thought that they had come to the station to say good-bye to me gave me a lump in my throat. I tried hard not to let the emotion I felt appear on my face.

"I expect I shall be playing a lot of rugger this term," I said. "I ought to get into the second fifteen."

She looked at me with kindly shining eyes, smiling with her full red lips. There was something in her smile I had always rather liked, and her voice seemed almost to tremble with a laugh or a tear. For one horrible moment I was afraid that she was going to kiss me. I was scared out of my wits. She talked on, she was mildly facetious as grown-up people are with schoolboys, and Driffield stood there without saying anything. He looked at me with a smile in his eyes and pulled his beard. Then the guard blew a cracked whistle and waved a red flag. Mrs. Driffield took my hand and shook it. Driffield came forward.

"Good-bye," he said. "Here's something for you."

He pressed a tiny packet into my hand and the train steamed off. When I opened it I found two half-crowns wrapped in a piece of toilet-paper. I blushed to the roots of my hair. I was glad enough to have an extra five shillings, but the thought that Ted Driffield had dared to give me a tip filled me with rage and humiliation. I could not possibly accept anything from him. It

was true that I had bicycled with him and sailed with him, but he
wasn't a sahib (I had got that from Major Greencourt) and it was
an insult to give me five shillings. At first I thought of returning
the money without a word, showing by my silence how outraged
I was at the solecism he had committed, then I composed in my
head a dignified and frigid letter in which I thanked him for his
generosity, but said that he must see how impossible it was for a
gentleman to accept a tip from someone who was practically a
stranger. I thought it over for two or three days and every day it
seemed more difficult to part with the two half-crowns. I felt sure
that Driffield had meant it kindly, and of course he was very bad
form and didn't know about things; it would be rather hard to
hurt his feelings by sending the money back, and finally I spent it.
But I assuaged my wounded pride by not writing to thank Driffield
for his gift.

When Christmas came, however, and I went back to Blackstable
for the holidays, it was the Driffields I was most eager to see. In
that stagnant little place they alone seemed to have a connection
with the outside world which already was beginning to touch my
day-dreams with anxious curiosity. But I could not overcome my
shyness enough to go to their house and call, and I hoped that
I should meet them in the town. But the weather was dreadful, a
boisterous wind whistled down the street, piercing you to the
bone, and the few women who had an errand were swept along
by their full skirts like fishing boats in half a gale. The cold rain
scudded in sudden squalls and the sky, which in summer had
enclosed the friendly country so snugly, now was a great pall that
pressed upon the earth with awful menace. There was small hope
of meeting the Driffields by chance and at last I took my courage
in both hands and one day after tea slipped out. As far as the
station the road was pitch dark, but there the street lamps, few
and dim, made it easier to keep to the pavement. The Driffields
lived in a little two-storey house in a side-street; it was of dingy
yellow brick and had a bow window. I knocked and presently a
little maid opened the door; I asked if Mrs. Driffield was in. She
gave me an uncertain look and, saying she would go and see, left
me standing in the passage. I had already heard voices in the next
room, but they were stilled as she opened the door and, entering,
shut it behind her. I had a faint impression of mystery; in the
houses of my uncle's friends, even if there was no fire and the gas
had to be lit as you went in, you were shown into the drawing-

room when you called. But the door was opened and Driffield came out. There was only a speck of light in the passage and at first he could not see who it was; but in an instant he recognised me.

"Oh, it's you. We wondered when we were going to see you." Then he called out: "Rosie, it's young Ashenden."

There was a cry and before you could say knife Mrs. Driffield had come into the passage and was shaking my hands.

"Come in, come in. Take off your coat. Isn't it awful, the weather? You must be perishing."

She helped me with my coat and took off my muffler and snatched my cap out of my hand and drew me into the room. It was hot and stuffy, a tiny room full of furniture, with a fire burning in the grate; they had gas there, which we hadn't at the vicarage, and the three burners in round globes of frosted glass filled the room with harsh light. The air was grey with tobacco smoke. At first, dazzled and then taken aback by my effusive welcome, I did not see who the two men were who got up as I came in. Then I saw they were the curate, Mr. Galloway, and Lord George Kemp. I fancied that the curate shook my hand with constraint.

"How are you? I just came in to return some books that Mr. Driffield had lent me and Mrs. Driffield very kindly asked me to stay to tea."

I felt rather than saw the quizzical look that Driffield gave him. He said something about the mammon of unrighteousness, which I recognised as a quotation, but did not gather the sense of. Mr. Galloway laughed.

"I don't know about that," he said. "What about the publicans and sinners?"

I thought the remark in very bad taste, but I was immediately seized upon by Lord George. There was no constraint about him.

"Well, young fellow, home for the holidays? My word, what a big chap you're growing."

I shook hands with him rather coldly. I wished I had not come.

"Let me give you a nice strong cup of tea," said Mrs. Driffield.

"I've already had tea."

"Have some more," said Lord George, speaking as though he owned the place (that was just like him). "A big fellow like you can always tuck away another piece of bread and butter and jam and Mrs. D. will cut you a slice with her own fair hands."

The tea things were still on the table and they were sitting round it. A chair was brought up for me and Mrs. Driffield gave me a piece of cake.

"We were just trying to persuade Ted to sing us a song," said Lord George. "Come on, Ted."

"Sing, 'All Through Stickin' to a Soljer', Ted," said Mrs. Driffield. "I love that."

"No, sing 'First We Mopped the Floor with Him'."

"I'll sing 'em both if you're not careful," said Driffield.

He took his banjo, which was lying on the top of the cottage piano, tuned it and began to sing. He had a rich baritone voice. I was quite used to people singing songs. When there was a tea party at the vicarage, or I went to one at the major's or the doctor's, people always brought their music with them. They left it in the hall, so that it should not seem that they wanted to be asked to play or sing; but after tea the hostess asked them if they had brought it. They shyly admitted that they had, and if it was at the vicarage I was sent to fetch it. Sometimes a young lady would say that she had quite given up playing and hadn't brought anything with her, and then her mother would break in and say that *she* had brought it. But when they sang it was not comic songs; it was "I'll Sing Thee Songs of Araby", or "Good-Night, Beloved", or "Queen of My Heart". Once at the annual concert at the Assembly Rooms, Smithson, the draper, had sung a comic song, and though the people at the back of the hall had applauded a great deal, the gentry had seen nothing funny in it. Perhaps there wasn't. Anyhow, before the next concert he was asked to be a little more careful about what he sang ("Remember there are ladies present, Mr. Smithson") and so gave "The Death of Nelson". The next ditty that Driffield sang had a chorus and the curate and Lord George joined in lustily. I heard it a good many times afterward, but I can only remember four lines:

> *First we mopped the floor with him,*
> *Dragged him up and down the stairs;*
> *Then we lugged him round the room,*
> *Under tables, over chairs.*

When it was finished, assuming my best company manners, I turned to Mrs. Driffield.

"Don't you sing?" I asked.

"I do, but it always turns the milk, so Ted doesn't encourage me."

Driffield put down his banjo and lit a pipe.

"Well, how's the old book getting along, Ted?" said Lord George heartily.

"Oh, all right. I'm working away, you know."

"Good old Ted and his books," Lord George laughed. "Why don't you settle down and do something respectable for a change? I'll give you a job in my office."

"Oh, I'm all right."

"You let him be, George," said Mrs. Driffield. "He likes writing, and what I say is, as long as it keeps him happy, why shouldn't he?"

"Well, I don't pretend to know anything about books," began George Kemp.

"Then don't talk about them," interrupted Driffield with a smile.

"I don't think anyone need be ashamed to have written *Fairhaven*," said Mr. Galloway, "and I don't care what the critics said."

"Well, Ted, I've known you since I was a boy and I couldn't read it, try as I would."

"Oh, come on, we don't want to start talking about books," said Mrs. Driffield. "Sing us another song, Ted."

"I must be going," said the curate. He turned to me. "We might walk along together. Have you got anything for me to read, Driffield?"

Driffield pointed to a pile of new books that were heaped up on a table in the corner.

"Take your pick."

"By Jove, what a lot!" I said, looking at them greedily.

"Oh, it's all rubbish. They're sent down for review."

"What d'you do with them?"

"Take 'em into Tercanbury and sell 'em for what they'll fetch. It all helps to pay the butcher."

When we left, the curate and I, he with several books under his arm, he asked me:

"Did you tell your uncle you were coming to see the Driffields?"

"No, I just went out for a walk and it suddenly occurred to me that I might look in."

This of course was some way from the truth, but I did not care to tell Mr. Galloway that, though I was practically grown up, my uncle realised the fact so little that he was quite capable of trying to prevent me from seeing people he objected to.

"Unless you have to I wouldn't say anything about it in your place. The Driffields are perfectly all right, but your uncle doesn't quite approve of them."

"I know," I said. "It's such rot."

"Of course they're rather common, but he doesn't write half badly, and when you think what he came from it's wonderful that he writes at all."

I was glad to know how the land lay. Mr. Galloway did not wish my uncle to know that he was on friendly terms with the Driffields. I could feel sure at all events that he would not give me away.

The patronising manner in which my uncle's curate spoke of one who has been now so long recognised as one of the greater of the later Victorian novelists must arouse a smile; but it was the manner in which he was generally spoken of at Blackstable. One day we went to tea at Mrs. Greencourt's, who had staying with her a cousin, the wife of an Oxford don, and we had been told that she was very cultivated. She was a Mrs. Encombe, a little woman with an eager wrinkled face; she surprised us very much because she wore her grey hair short and a black serge skirt that only just came down below the tops of her square-toed boots. She was the first example of the New Woman that had ever been seen in Blackstable. We were staggered and immediately on the defensive, for she looked intellectual, and it made us feel shy. (Afterward we all scoffed at her, and my uncle said to my aunt: "Well, my dear, I'm thankful you're not clever, at least I've been spared that"; and my aunt in a playful mood put my uncle's slippers which were warming for him by the fire over her boots and said: "Look, I'm the new woman." And then we all said: "Mrs. Greencourt is very funny; you never know what she'll do next. But of course she isn't quite quite." We could hardly forget that her father made china and that her grandfather had been a factory hand.)

But we all found it very interesting to hear Mrs. Encombe talk of the people she knew. My uncle had been at Oxford, but everyone he asked about seemed to be dead. Mrs. Encombe knew Mrs. Humphry Ward and admired *Robert Elsmere*. My uncle considered it a scandalous work, and he was surprised that Mr. Gladstone, who at least called himself a Christian, had found a good word to say for it. They had quite an argument about it. My uncle said he thought it would unsettle people's opinions and give them all sorts of ideas that they were much better without. Mrs. Encombe answered that he wouldn't think that if he knew Mrs. Humphry Ward. She was a woman of the very highest character, a niece of Mr. Matthew Arnold, and whatever you might think of the book itself (and she, Mrs. Encombe, was quite willing to admit that there were parts which had better have been omitted) it was quite certain that she had written it from the very highest motives. Mrs. Encombe knew Miss Broughton too. She was of very good family and it was strange that she wrote the books she did.

"I don't see any harm in them," said Mrs. Hayforth the doctor's wife. "I enjoy them, especially *Red as a Rose is She*."

"Would you like your girls to read them?" asked Mrs. Encombe."

"Not just yet perhaps," said Mrs. Hayforth. "But when they're married I should have no objection."

"Then it might interest you to know," said Mrs. Encombe, "that when I was in Florence last Easter I was introduced to Ouida."

"That's quite another matter," returned Mrs. Hayforth. "I can't believe that any lady would read a book by Ouida."

"I read one out of curiosity," said Mrs. Encombe. "I must say, it's more what you'd expect from a Frenchman than from an English gentlewoman."

"Oh, but I understand she isn't really English. I've always heard her real name is Mademoiselle de la Ramée."

It was then that Mr. Galloway mentioned Edward Driffield.

"You know we have an author living here," he said.

"We're not very proud of him," said the major. "He's the son of old Miss Wolfe's bailiff and he married a barmaid."

"Can he write?" asked Mrs. Encombe.

"You can tell at once that he's not a gentleman," said the curate, "but when you consider the disadvantages he's had to struggle against it's rather remarkable that he should write as well as he does."

"He's a friend of Willie's," said my uncle.

Everyone looked at me, and I felt very uncomfortable.

"They bicycled together last summer, and after Willie had gone back to school I got one of his books from the library to see what it was like. I read the first volume and then I sent it back. I wrote a pretty stiff letter to the librarian and I was glad to hear that he'd withdrawn it from circulation. If it had been my own property I should have put it promptly in the kitchen stove."

"I looked through one of his books myself," said the doctor. "It interested me because it was set in this neighbourhood and I recognised some of the people. But I can't say I liked it; I thought it unnecessarily coarse."

"I mentioned that to him," said Mr. Galloway, "and he said the men in the colliers that run up to Newcastle and the fishermen and farm hands don't behave like ladies and gentlemen and don't talk like them."

"But why write about people of that character?" said my uncle.

"That's what I say," said Mrs. Hayforth. "We all know that there are coarse and wicked and vicious people in the world, but I don't see what good it does to write about them."

"I'm not defending him," said Mr. Galloway. "I'm only telling you what explanation he gives himself. And then of course he brought up Dickens."

"Dickens is quite different," said my uncle. "I don't see how anyone can object to the *Pickwick Papers*."

"I suppose it's a matter of taste," said my aunt. "I always found Dickens very coarse. I don't want to read about people who drop their aitches. I must say I'm very glad the weather's so bad now and Willie can't take any more rides with Mr. Driffield. I don't think he's quite the sort of person he ought to associate with."

Both Mr. Galloway and I looked down our noses.

CHAPTER IX

As often as the mild Christmas gaieties of Blackstable allowed me I went to the Driffields' little house next door to the Congregational chapel. I always found Lord George and often Mr. Galloway. Our conspiracy of silence had made us friends and when we met at the vicarage or in the vestry after church we looked at one another archly. We did not talk about our secret, but we enjoyed it; I think it gave us both a good deal of satisfaction to know that we were making a fool of my uncle. But once it occurred to me that George Kemp, meeting my uncle in the street, might remark casually that he had been seeing a lot of me at the Driffields'.

"What about Lord George?" I said to Mr. Galloway.

"Oh, I made that all right."

We chuckled. I began to like Lord George. At first I was very cold with him and scrupulously polite, but he seemed so unconscious of the social difference between us that I was forced to conclude that my haughty courtesy failed to put him in his place. He was always cordial, breezy, even boisterous; he chaffed me in his common way and I answered him back with schoolboy wit; we made the others laugh and this disposed me kindly toward him. He was forever bragging about the great schemes he had in mind, but he took in good part my jokes at the expense of his grandiose imaginations. It amused me to hear him tell stories about the swells of Blackstable that made them look foolish and when he mimicked their oddities I roared with laughter. He was blatant and vulgar and the way he dressed was always a shock to me (I had never been to Newmarket nor seen a trainer, but that was my idea of how a Newmarket trainer dressed), and his table manners were offensive, but I found myself less and less affronted by him. He gave me the *Pink 'Un* every week and I took it home, carefully tucked away in my greatcoat pocket, and read it in my bedroom.

I never went to the Driffields' till after tea at the vicarage, but I always managed to make a second tea when I got there. Afterward Ted Driffield sang comic songs, accompanying himself sometimes on the banjo and sometimes on the piano. He would sing, peering at the music with his rather short-sighted eyes, for an hour at a time; there was a smile on his lips and he liked us all to join in the chorus. We played whist. I had learned the game when I was a child and my uncle and aunt and I used to play at the vicarage during the long winter evenings. My uncle always took dummy, and though of course we played for love, when my aunt and I lost I used to retire under the dining-room table and cry. Ted Driffield did not play cards, he said he had no head for them, and when we started a game he would sit down by the fire and, pencil in hand, read one of the books that had been sent down to him from London to review. I had never played with three people before and of course I did not play well, but Mrs. Driffield had a natural card sense. Her movements as a rule were rather deliberate, but when it came to playing cards she was quick and alert. She played the rest of us right off our heads. Ordinarily she did not speak

very much and then slowly, but when, after a hand was played,
she took the trouble good-humouredly to point out to me my
mistakes, she was not only lucid but voluble. Lord George
chaffed her as he chaffed everybody; she would smile at his banter,
for she very seldom laughed, and sometimes make a neat retort.
They did not behave like lovers, but like familiar friends, and I
should have quite forgotten what I had heard about them and
what I had seen but that now and then she gave him a look that
embarrassed me. Her eyes rested on him quietly, as though he
were not a man but a chair or a table, and in them was a mischievous, childlike smile. Then I would notice that his face
seemed suddenly to swell and he moved uneasily in his chair. I
looked quickly at the curate, afraid that he would notice something, but he was intent on the cards or else was lighting his pipe.

The hour or two I spent nearly every day in that hot, poky,
smoke-laden room passed like lightning, and as the holidays drew
nearer to their end I was seized with dismay at the thought that I
must spend the next three months dully at school.

"I don't know what we shall do without you," said Mrs.
Driffield. "We shall have to play dummy."

I was glad that my going would break up the game. While I
was doing prep I did not want to think that they were sitting in
that little room and enjoying themselves just as if I did not exist.

"How long do you get at Easter?" asked Mr. Galloway.

"About three weeks."

"We'll have a lovely time then," said Mrs. Driffield. "The
weather ought to be all right. We can ride in the mornings and
then after tea we'll play whist. You've improved a lot. If we play
three or four times a week during your Easter holidays you won't
need to be afraid to play with anybody."

CHAPTER X

BUT the term came to an end at last. I was in high spirits when
once more I got out of the train at Blackstable. I had grown a
little and I had had a new suit made at Tercanbury, blue serge and
very smart, and I had bought a new tie. I meant to go and see the
Driffields immediately I had swallowed my tea and I was full of
hope that the carrier would have brought my box in time for me

to put the new suit on. It made me look quite grown up. I had already begun putting vaseline on my upper lip every night to make my moustache grow. On my way through the town I looked down the street in which the Driffields lived in the hope of seeing them. I should have liked to go in and say how-do-you-do, but I knew that Driffield wrote in the morning and Mrs. Driffield was not "presentable". I had all sorts of exciting things to tell them. I had won a heat in the hundred-yard race in the sports and I had been second in the hurdles. I meant to have a shot for the history prize in the summer and I was going to swot up my English history during the holidays. Though there was an east wind blowing, the sky was blue and there was a feeling of spring in the air. The High Street, with its colours washed clean by the wind and its lines sharp as though drawn with a new pen, looked like a picture by Samuel Scott, quiet and naïve and cosy—now, looking back; then it looked like nothing but High Street, Blackstable. When I came to the railway bridge I noticed that two or three houses were being built.

"By Jove," I said, "Lord George *is* going it."

In the fields beyond little white lambs were frisking. The elm trees were just beginning to turn green. I let myself in by the side door. My uncle was sitting in his arm-chair by the fire reading *The Times*. I shouted to my aunt and she came downstairs, a pink spot from the excitement of seeing me on each of her withered cheeks, and threw her thin old arms round my neck. She said all the right things:

"How you've grown!" and "Good gracious me, you'll be getting a moustache soon!"

I kissed my uncle on his bald forehead and I stood in front of the fire, with my legs well apart and my back to it, and was extremely grown up and rather condescending. Then I went upstairs to say how-do-you-do to Emily, and into the kitchen to shake hands with Mary-Ann, and out into the garden to see the gardener.

When I sat down hungrily to dinner and my uncle carved the leg of mutton I asked my aunt:

"Well, what's happened at Blackstable since I was here?"

"Nothing very much. Mrs. Greencourt went down to Mentone for six weeks, but she came back a few days ago. The major had an attack of gout."

"And your friends the Driffields have bolted," added my uncle.

"They've done what?" I cried.

"Bolted. They took their luggage away one night and just went up to London. They've left bills all over the place. They hadn't paid their rent and they hadn't paid for their furniture. They owed Harris the butcher the best part of thirty pounds."

"How awful," I said.

"That's bad enough," said my aunt, "but it appears they hadn't even paid the wages of the maid they had for three months."

I was flabbergasted. I thought I felt a little sick.

"I think in future," said my uncle, "you would be wiser not to consort with people whom your aunt and I don't think proper associates for you."

"One can't help feeling sorry for all those tradesmen they cheated," said my aunt.

"It serves them right," said my uncle. "Fancy giving credit to people like that! I should have thought anyone could see they were nothing but adventurers."

"I always wonder why they came down here at all."

"They just wanted to show off, and I suppose they thought as people knew who they were here it would be easier to get things on credit."

I did not think this quite logical, but was too much crushed to argue.

As soon as I had the chance I asked Mary-Ann what she knew of the incident. To my surprise she did not take it at all in the same way as my uncle and aunt. She giggled.

"They let everyone in proper," she said. "They was as free as you like with their money and everyone thought they 'ad plenty. It was always the best end of the neck for them at the butcher's and when they wanted a steak nothing would do but the undercut. Asparagus and grapes and I don't know what all. They ran up bills in every shop in the town. I don't know 'ow people can be such fools."

But it was evidently of the tradesmen she was speaking and not of the Driffields.

"But how did they manage to bunk without anyone knowing?" I asked.

"Well, that's what everybody's askin'. They do say it was Lord George 'elped them. How did they get their boxes to the station, I ask you, if 'e didn't take them in that there trap of 'is?"

"What does he say about it?"

"He says 'e knows no more about it than the man in the moon. There was a rare to-do all over the town when they found out the Driffields had shot the moon. It made me laugh. Lord George says 'e never knew they was broke, and 'e makes out 'e was as surprised as anybody. But I for one don't believe a word of it. We all know about 'im and Rosie before she was married, and between you and me and the gatepost I don't know that it ended there. They do say they was seen walkin' about the fields together last summer and 'e was in and out of the 'ouse pretty near every day."

"How did people find out?"

"Well, it's like this. They 'ad a girl there and they told 'er she could go 'ome and spend the night with her mother, but she wasn't to be back later than eight o'clock in the morning. Well, when she come back she couldn't get in. She knocked and she rung but nobody answered, and so she went in next door and asked the lady there what she'd better do, and the lady said she'd better go to the police station. The sergeant come back with 'er and 'e knocked and 'e rung, but 'e couldn't get no answer. Then he asked the girl 'ad they paid 'er 'er wages, and she said no, not for three months, and then 'e said: You take my word for it, they've shot the moon, that's what they've done. An' when they come to get inside they found they'd took all their clothes, an' their books—they say as Ted Driffield 'ad a rare lot of books—an' every blessed thing that belonged to them."

"And has nothing been heard of them since?"

"Well, not exactly, but when they'd been gone about a week the girl got a letter from London, and when she opened it there was no letter or anything, but just a postal order for 'er wages. An' if you ask me, I call that very 'andsome not to do a poor girl out of her wages."

I was much more shocked than Mary-Ann. I was a very respectable youth. The reader cannot have failed to observe that I accepted the conventions of my class as if they were the laws of Nature, and though debts on the grand scale in books had seemed to me romantic, and duns and money-lenders were familiar figures to my fancy, I could not but think it mean and paltry not to pay the tradesmen's books. I listened with confusion when people talked in my presence of the Driffields, and when they spoke of them as my friends I said: "Hang it all, I just knew them"; and when they asked: "Weren't they fearfully common?" I said:

"Well, they didn't exactly suggest the Vere de Veres, you know."
Poor Mr. Galloway was dreadfully upset.

"Of course I didn't think they were wealthy," he told me, "but
I thought they had enough to get along. The house was very nicely
furnished and the piano was new. It never struck me that they
hadn't paid for a single thing. They never stinted themselves.
What hurts me is the deceit. I used to see quite a lot of them and
I thought they liked me. They always made one welcome. You'd
hardly believe it, but the last time I saw them when they shook
hands with me Mrs. Driffield asked me to come next day and
Driffield said: 'Muffins for tea to-morrow.' And all the time they
had everything packed upstairs and that very night they took the
last train to London."

"What does Lord George say about it?"

"To tell you the truth I haven't gone out of my way to see him
lately. It's been a lesson to me. There's a little proverb about evil
communications that I've thought well to bear in mind."

I felt very much the same about Lord George, and I was a little
nervous too. If he took it into his head to tell people that at
Christmas I had been going to see the Driffields almost every day,
and it came to my uncle's ears, I foresaw an unpleasant fuss. My
uncle would accuse me of deceit and prevarication and dis-
obedience and of not behaving like a gentleman, and I did not at
the moment see what answer I could make. I knew him well
enough to be aware that he would not let the matter drop, and
that I should be reminded of my transgression for years. I was
just as glad not to see Lord George. But one day I ran into him
face to face in the High Street.

"Hulloa, youngster," he cried, addressing me in a way I
particularly resented. "Back for the holidays, I suppose."

"You suppose quite correctly," I answered with what I thought
withering sarcasm.

Unfortunately he only bellowed with laughter.

"You're so sharp you'll cut yourself if you don't look out," he
answered heartily. "Well, it looks as if there was no more whist
for you and me just yet. Now you see what comes of living
beyond your means. What I always say to my boys is: If you've
got a pound and you spend nineteen and six you're a rich man,
but if you spend twenty shillings and sixpence you're a pauper.
Look after the pence, young fellow, and the pounds'll look after
themselves."

But though he spoke after this fashion there was in his voice no note of disapproval, but a bubble of laughter as though in his heart he were tittering at these admirable maxims.

"They say you helped them to bunk," I remarked.

"Me?" His face assumed a look of extreme surprise, but his eyes glittered with sly mirth. "Why, when they came and told me the Driffields had shot the moon you could have knocked me down with a feather. They owed me four pounds seventeen and six for coal. We've all been let in, even poor old Galloway who never got his muffins for tea."

I had never thought Lord George more blatant. I should have liked to say something final and crushing, but as I could not think of anything I just said that I must be getting along and with a curt nod left him.

CHAPTER XI

MUSING thus over the past, while I waited for Alroy Kear, I chuckled when I considered this shabby incident of Edward Driffield's obscurity in the light of the immense respectability of his later years. I wondered whether it was because in my boyhood he was as a writer held in such small esteem by the people about me that I had never been able to see in him the astonishing merit that the best critical opinion eventually ascribed to him. He was for long thought to write very bad English, and indeed he gave you the impression of writing with the stub of a blunt pencil; his style was laboured, an uneasy mixture of the classical and the slangy, and his dialogue was such as could never have issued from the mouth of a human being. Toward the end of his career, when he dictated his books, his style, acquiring a conversational ease, became flowing and limpid; and then the critics, going back to the novels of his maturity, found that their English had a nervous, racy vigour that eminently suited the matter. His prime belonged to a period when the purple patch was in vogue and there are descriptive passages in his works that have found their way into all the anthologies of English prose. His pieces on the sea, and spring in the Kentish woods, and sunset on the lower reaches of the Thames are famous. It should be a mortification to me that I cannot read them without discomfort.

When I was a young man, though his books sold but little and one or two were banned by the libraries, it was very much a mark of culture to admire him. He was thought boldly realistic. He was a very good stick to beat the Philistines with. Somebody's lucky inspiration discovered that his sailors and peasants were Shakespearean, and when the advanced got together they uttered shrill cries of ecstasy over the dry and spicy humour of his yokels. This was a commodity that Edward Driffield had no difficulty in supplying. My own heart sank when he led me into the forecastle of a sailing ship or the tap-room of a public-house and I knew I was in for half a dozen pages in dialect of facetious comment on life, ethics and immortality. But, I admit, I have always thought the Shakespearean clowns tedious and their innumerable progeny insupportable.

Driffield's strength lay evidently in his depiction of the class he knew best, farmers and farm labourers, shopkeepers and bartenders, skippers of sailing ships, mates, cooks and able seamen. When he introduces characters belonging to a higher station in life even his warmest admirers, one would have thought, must experience a certain malaise; his fine gentlemen are so incredibly fine, his high-born ladies are so good, so pure, so noble that you are not surprised that they can only express themselves with polysyllabic dignity. His women hardly come to life. But here again I must add that this is only my own opinion; the world at large and the most eminent critics have agreed that they are very winsome types of English womanhood, spirited, gallant, high-souled, and they have been often compared with the heroines of Shakespeare. We know of course that women are habitually constipated, but to represent them in fiction as being altogether devoid of a back passage seems to me really an excess of chivalry. I am surprised that they care to see themselves thus limned.

The critics can force the world to pay attention to a very indifferent writer, and the world may lose its head over one who has no merit at all, but the result in neither case is lasting; and I cannot help thinking that no writer can hold the public for as long as Edward Driffield without considerable gifts. The elect sneer at popularity; they are inclined even to assert that it is a proof of mediocrity; but they forget that posterity makes its choice not from among the unknown writers of a period, but from among the known. It may be that some great masterpiece which deserves immortality has fallen still-born from the press, but posterity will never hear of it; it may be that posterity will scrap all the best sellers of our day, but it is among them that it must choose. At all events Edward Driffield is in the running. His novels happen to bore me; I find them long; the melodramatic incidents with which he sought to stir the sluggish reader's interest leave me cold; but he certainly had sincerity. There is in his best books the stir of life, and in none of them can you fail to be aware of the author's enigmatic personality. In his earlier days he was praised or blamed for his realism; according to the idiosyncrasy of his critics he was extolled for his truth or censured for his coarseness. But realism has ceased to excite remark, and the library reader will take in his stride obstacles at which a generation back he would have violently shied. The cultured reader of these pages will remember the leading article in the *Literary Supplement* of *The Times* which appeared at the moment of Driffield's death. Taking the novels of Edward Driffield as his text, the author wrote what was very well described as a hymn to beauty. No one who read it could fail to be impressed by those swelling periods, which reminded one of the noble prose of Jeremy Taylor, by that reverence and piety, by all those high sentiments, in short, expressed in a style that was ornate without excess and dulcet without effeminacy. It was itself a thing of beauty. If some suggested that Edward Driffield was by way of being a humorist and that a jest would here and there have lightened this eulogious article it must be replied that after all it was a funeral oration. And it is well known that Beauty does not look with a good grace on the timid advances of Humour. Roy Kear, when he was talking to me of Driffield, claimed that, whatever his faults, they were redeemed by the beauty that suffused his pages. Now I come to look back on our conversation, I think it was this remark that had most exasperated me.

Thirty years ago in literary circles God was all the fashion. It was good form to believe and journalists used Him to adorn a phrase or balance a sentence; then God went out (oddly enough with cricket and beer) and Pan came in. In a hundred novels his cloven hoof left its imprint on the sward; poets saw him lurking in the twilight on London commons, and literary ladies in Surrey, nymphs of an industrial age, mysteriously surrendered their virginity to his rough embrace. Spiritually they were never the same again. But Pan went out and now beauty has taken his place. People find it in a phrase, or a turbot, a dog, a day, a picture, an action, a dress. Young women in cohorts, each of whom has written so promising and competent a novel, prattle of it in every manner from allusive to arch, from intense to charming; and the young men, more or less recently down from Oxford, but still trailing its clouds of glory, who tell us in the weekly papers what we should think of art, life and the universe, fling the word with a pretty negligence about their close-packed pages. It is sadly frayed. Gosh, they have worked it hard! The ideal has many names and beauty is but one of them. I wonder if this clamour is anything more than the cry of distress of those who cannot make themselves at home in our heroic world of machines, and I wonder if their passion for beauty, the Little Nell of this shamefaced day, is anything more than sentimentality. It may be that another generation, accommodating itself more adequately to the stress of life, will look for inspiration not in a flight from reality, but in an eager acceptance of it.

I do not know if others are like myself, but I am conscious that I cannot contemplate beauty long. For me no poet made a falser statement than Keats when he wrote the first line of *Endymion*. When the thing of beauty has given me the magic of its sensation my mind quickly wanders; I listen with incredulity to the persons who tell me that they can look with rapture for hours at a view or a picture. Beauty is an ecstasy; it is as simple as hunger. There is really nothing to be said about it. It is like the perfume of a rose: you can smell it and that is all: that is why the criticism of art, except in so far as it is unconcerned with beauty and therefore with art, is tiresome. All the critic can tell you with regard to Titian's *Entombment of Christ*, perhaps of all the pictures in the world that which has most pure beauty, is to go and look at it. What else he has to say is history, or biography, or what not. But people add other qualities to beauty—sublimity, human interest, tenderness, love—because beauty does not long content them. Beauty is perfect, and perfection (such is human nature) holds our attention but for a little while. The mathematician who after seeing *Phèdre* asked: "*Qu'est-ce que ça prouve?*" was not such a fool as he has been generally made out. No one has ever been able to explain why the Doric temple of Pæstum is more beautiful than a glass of cold beer except by bringing in considerations that have nothing to do with beauty. Beauty is a blind alley. It is a mountain peak which once reached leads nowhere. That is why in the end we find more to entrance us in El Greco than in Titian, in the incomplete achievement of Shakespeare than in the consummate success of Racine. Too much has been written about beauty. That is why I have written a little more. Beauty is that which satisfies the æsthetic instinct. But who wants to be satisfied? It is only to the dullard that enough is as good as a feast. Let us face it: beauty is a bit of a bore.

But of course what the critics wrote about Edward Driffield was eye-wash. His outstanding merit was not the realism that gave vigour to his work, nor the beauty that informed it, nor his graphic portraits of seafaring men, nor his poetic descriptions of salty marshes, of storm and calm and of nestling hamlets; it was his longevity. Reverence for old age is one of the most admirable traits of the human race and I think it may safely be stated that in no other country than ours is this trait more marked. The awe and love with which other nations regard old age is often platonic; but ours is practical. Who but the English would fill Covent Garden to listen to an aged prima donna without a voice? Who but the English would pay to see dancers so decrepit that they can hardly put one foot before the other and say to one another admiringly in the intervals: "By George, sir, d'you know he's a long way past sixty?" But compared with politicians and writers these are but striplings, and I often think that a *jeune premier* must be of a singularly amiable disposition if it does not make him bitter to consider that when at the age of seventy he must end his career the public man and the author are only at their prime. A man who is a politician at forty is a statesman at three score and ten. It is at this age, when he would be too old to be a clerk or a gardener or a police-court magistrate, that he is ripe to govern a country. This is not so strange when you reflect that from the earliest times the old have rubbed it into the young that they are wiser than they, and before the young had discovered what nonsense this was they were old too, and it profited them to carry on the imposture; and besides, no one can have moved in the society of politicians without discovering that (if one may judge by results) it requires little mental ability to rule a nation. But why writers should be more esteemed the older they grow has long perplexed me. At one time I thought that the praise accorded to them when they had ceased for twenty years to write anything of interest was largely due to the fact that the younger men, having no longer to fear their competition, felt it safe to extol their merit; and it is well known that to praise someone whose rivalry you do not dread is often a very good way of putting a spoke in the wheel of someone whose rivalry you do. But this is to take a low view of human nature and I would not for the world lay myself open to a charge of cheap cynicism. After mature consideration I have come to the conclusion that the real reason for the universal applause that comforts the declining years of the author who exceeds the common span of man is that intelligent people after the age of thirty read nothing at all. As they grow older the books they read in their youth are lit with its glamour and with every year that passes they ascribe greater merit to the author that wrote them. Of course he must go on; he must keep in the public eye. It is no good his thinking that it is enough to write one or two masterpieces; he must provide a pedestal for them of forty or fifty works of no particular consequence. This needs time. His production must be such that if he cannot captivate a reader by his charm he can stun him by his weight.

If, as I think, longevity is genius, few in our time have enjoyed it in a more conspicuous degree than Edward Driffield. When he was a young fellow in the sixties (the cultured having had their way with him and passed him by) his position in the world of letters was only respectable; the best judges praised him, but with moderation; the younger men were inclined to be frivolous at his expense. It was agreed that he had talent, but it never occurred to anyone that he was one of the glories of English literature. He celebrated his seventieth birthday; an uneasiness passed over the world of letters, like a ruffling of the waters when on an Eastern sea a typhoon lurks in the distance, and it grew evident that there had lived among us all these years a great novelist and none of us had suspected it. There was a rush for Driffield's books in the various libraries and a hundred busy pens, in Bloomsbury, in Chelsea and in other places where men of letters congregate, wrote appreciations, studies, essays and works, short and chatty or long and intense, on his novels. These were reprinted, in complete editions, in select editions, at a shilling and three and six and five shillings and a guinea. His style was analysed, his philosophy was examined, his technique was dissected. At seventy-five everyone agreed that Edward Driffield had genius. At eighty he was the Grand Old Man of English Letters. This position he held till his death.

Now we look about and think sadly that there is no one to take his place. A few septuagenarians are sitting up and taking notice, and they evidently feel that they could comfortably fill the vacant niche. But it is obvious that they lack something.

Though these recollections have taken so long to narrate they took but a little while to pass through my head. They came to me higgledy-piggledy, an incident and then a scrap of conversation that belonged to a previous time, and I have set them down in order for the convenience of the reader and because I have a neat mind. One thing that surprised me was that even at that far distance I could remember distinctly what people looked like and even the gist of what they said, but only with vagueness what they wore. I knew of course that the dress, especially of women, was quite different forty years ago from what it was now, but if I recalled it at all it was not from life but from pictures and photographs that I had seen much later.

I was still occupied with my idle fancies when I heard a taxi stop at the door, the bell ring, and in a moment Alroy Kear's booming voice telling the butler that he had an appointment with me. He came in, big, bluff and hearty; his vitality shattered with a single gesture the frail construction I had been building out of the vanished past. He brought in with him, like a blustering wind in March, the aggressive and inescapable present.

"I was just asking myself," I said, "who could possibly succeed Edward Driffield as the Grand Old Man of English Letters and you arrive to answer my question."

He broke into a jovial laugh, but into his eyes came a quick look of suspicion.

"I don't think there's anybody," he said.

"How about yourself?"

"Oh, my dear boy, I'm not fifty yet. Give me another twenty-five years." He laughed, but his eyes held mine keenly. "I never know when you're pulling my leg." He looked down suddenly. "Of course one can't help thinking about the future sometimes. All the people who are at the top of the tree now are anything from fifteen to twenty years older than me. They can't last for ever, and when they're gone who is there? Of course there's Aldous; he's a good deal younger than me, but he's not very strong and I don't believe he takes great care of himself. Barring accidents, by which I mean barring some genius who suddenly springs up and sweeps the board, I don't quite see how in another twenty or twenty-five years I can help having the field pretty well to myself. It's just a question of pegging away and living on longer than the others."

Roy sank his virile bulk into one of my landlady's arm-chairs and I offered him a whisky and soda.

"No, I never drink spirits before six o'clock," he said. He looked about him. "Jolly, these digs are."

"I know. What have you come to see me about?"

"I thought I'd better have a little chat with you about Mrs. Driffield's invitation. It was rather difficult to explain over the telephone. The truth of the matter is that I've arranged to write Driffield's life."

"Oh! Why didn't you tell me the other day?"

I felt friendly disposed toward Roy. I was happy to think that I had not misjudged him when I suspected that it was not merely for the pleasure of my company that he had asked me to luncheon.

"I hadn't entirely made up my mind. Mrs. Driffield is very keen on my doing it. She's going to help me in every way she can. She's giving me all the material she has. She's been collecting it for a good many years. It's not an easy thing to do and of course I can't afford not to do it well. But if I can make a pretty good job of it, it can't fail to do me a lot of good. People have so much more respect for a novelist if he writes something serious now and then. Those critical works of mine were an awful sweat, and they sold nothing, but I don't regret them for a moment. They've given me a position I could never have got without them."

"I think it's a very good plan. You've known Driffield more intimately than most people for the last twenty years."

"I think I have. But of course he was over sixty when I first made his acquaintance. I wrote and told him how much I admired his books and he asked me to go and see him. But I know nothing about the early part of his life. Mrs. Driffield used to try to get him to talk about those days and she made very copious notes of all he said, and then there are diaries that he kept now and then, and of course a lot of the stuff in the novels is obviously autobiographical. But there are immense lacunæ. I'll tell you the sort of book I want to write, a sort of intimate life, with a lot of those little details that make people feel warm inside, you know, and then woven in with this a really exhaustive criticism of his literary work, not ponderous, of course, but, although sympathetic, searching and . . . subtle. Naturally it wants doing, but Mrs. Driffield seems to think I can do it."

"I'm sure you can," I put in.

"I don't see why not," said Roy. "I am a critic, and I'm a novelist. It's obvious that I have certain literary qualifications.

But I can't do anything unless everyone who can is willing to help me."

I began to see where I came in. I tried to make my face look quite blank. Roy leaned forward.

"I asked you the other day if you were going to write anything about Driffield yourself and you said you weren't. Can I take that as definite?"

"Certainly."

"Then have you got any objection to giving me your material?"

"My dear boy, I haven't got any."

"Oh, that's nonsense," said Roy good-humouredly, with the tone of a doctor who is trying to persuade a child to have its throat examined. "When he was living at Blackstable you must have seen a lot of him."

"I was only a boy then."

"But you must have been conscious of the unusual experience. After all, no one could be for half an hour in Edward Driffield's society without being impressed by his extraordinary personality. It must have been obvious even to a boy of sixteen, and you were probably more observant and sensitive than the average boy of that age."

"I wonder if his personality would have seemed extraordinary without the reputation to back it up. Do you imagine that if you went down to a spa in the west of England as Mr. Atkins, a chartered accountant taking the waters for his liver, you would impress the people you met there as a man of character?"

"I imagine they'd soon realise that I was not quite the common or garden chartered accountant," said Roy, with a smile that took from his remark any appearance of self-esteem.

"Well, all I can tell you is that what chiefly bothered me about Driffield in those days was that the knickerbocker suit he wore was dreadfully loud. We used to bicycle a lot together and it always made me feel a trifle uncomfortable to be seen with him."

"It sounds comic now. What did he talk about?"

"I don't know; nothing very much. He was rather keen on architecture, and he talked about farming, and if a pub looked nice he generally suggested stopping for five minutes and having a glass of bitter, and then he would talk to the landlord about the crops, and the price of coal and things like that."

I rambled on, though I could see by the look of Roy's face that

he was disappointed with me; he listened, but he was a trifle
bored, and it struck me that when he was bored he looked peevish.
But though I couldn't remember that Driffield had ever said anything significant during those long rides of ours, I had a very acute
recollection of the *feel* of them. Blackstable was peculiar in this,
that though it was on the sea, with a long shingly beach and marsh-
land at the back, you had only to go about half a mile inland to
come into the most rural country in Kent. Winding roads that
ran between the great fat green fields and clumps of huge elms,
substantial and with a homely stateliness like good old Kentish
farmers' wives, high-coloured and robust, who had grown portly
on good butter and home-made bread and cream and fresh eggs.
And sometimes the road was only a lane, with thick hawthorn
hedges, and the green elms overhung it on either side so that when
you looked up there was only a strip of blue sky between. And
as you rode along in the warm, keen air you had a sensation that
the world was standing still and life would last for ever. Although
you were pedalling with such energy you had a delicious feeling
of laziness. You were quite happy when no one spoke, and if one
of the party from sheer high spirits suddenly put on speed and
shot ahead it was a joke that everyone laughed at and for a few
minutes you pedalled as hard as you could. And we chaffed one
another innocently and giggled at our own humour. Now and
then one would pass cottages with little gardens in front of them
and in the gardens were hollyhocks and tiger lilies; and a little way
from the road were farmhouses, with their spacious barns and
oasthouses; and one would pass through hop-fields with the
ripening hops hanging in garlands. The public-houses were
friendly and informal, hardly more important than cottages, and on
the porches often honeysuckle would be growing. The names
they bore were usual and familiar: the "Jolly Sailor", the "Merry
Ploughman", the "Crown and Anchor", the "Red Lion".

But of course all that could matter nothing to Roy, and he
interrupted me.

"Did he never talk of literature?" he asked.

"I don't think so. He wasn't that sort of writer. I suppose I
thought about his writing, but he never mentioned it. He used
to lend the curate books. In the winter, one Christmas holidays,
I used to have tea at his house nearly every day and sometimes
the curate and he would talk about books, but we used to shut
them up."

"Don't you remember anything he said?"

"Only one thing. I remember it because I hadn't ever read the things he was talking about and what he said made me do so. He said that when Shakespeare retired to Stratford-on-Avon and became respectable, if he ever thought of his plays at all, probably the two that he remembered with most interest were *Measure for Measure* and *Troilus and Cressida*."

"I don't think that's very illuminating. Didn't he say anything about anyone more modern than Shakespeare?"

"Well, not then, that I can remember; but when I was lunching with the Driffields a few years ago I overheard him saying that Henry James had turned his back on one of the great events of the world's history, the rise of the United States, in order to report tittle-tattle at tea parties in English country houses. Driffield called it *il gran rifiuto*. I was surprised at hearing the old man use an Italian phrase and amused because a great big bouncing duchess who was there was the only person who knew what the devil he was talking about. He said: 'Poor Henry, he's spending eternity wandering round and round a stately park and the fence is just too high for him to peep over and they're having tea just too far away for him to hear what the countess is saying.'"

Roy listened to my little anecdote with attention. He shook his head reflectively.

"I don't think I could use that. I'd have the Henry James gang down on me like a thousand of bricks. . . . But what used you to do during those evenings?"

"Well, we played whist while Driffield read books for review, and he used to sing."

"That's interesting," said Roy, leaning forward eagerly. "Do you remember what he sang?"

"Perfectly. 'All Through Stickin' to a Soljer' and 'Come Where the Booze Is Cheaper' were his favourites."

"Oh!"

I could see that Roy was disappointed.

"Did you expect him to sing Schumann?" I asked.

"I don't know why not. It would have been rather a good point. But I think I should have expected him to sing sea chanties or old English country airs, you know, the sort of thing they used to sing at fairings—blind fiddlers and the village swains dancing with the girls on the threshing floor and all that sort of thing. I might have made something rather beautiful out of that, but I can't *see*

Edward Driffield singing music-hall songs. After all, when you're drawing a man's portrait you must get the values right; you only confuse the impression if you put in stuff that's all out of tone."

"You know that shortly after this he shot the moon. He let everybody in."

Roy was silent for fully a minute and he looked down at the carpet reflectively.

"Yes, I knew there'd been some unpleasantness. Mrs. Driffield mentioned it. I understand everything was paid up later before he finally bought Ferne Court and settled down in the district. I don't think it's necessary to dwell on an incident that is not really of any importance in the history of his development. After all, it happened nearly forty years ago. You know, there were some very curious sides to the old man. One would have thought that after a rather sordid little scandal like that the neighbourhood of Blackstable would be the last place he'd choose to spend the rest of his life in when he'd become celebrated, especially when it was the scene of his rather humble origins; but he didn't seem to mind a bit. He seemed to think the whole thing rather a good joke. He was quite capable of telling people who came to lunch about it and it was very embarrassing for Mrs. Driffield. I should like you to know Amy better. She's a very remarkable woman. Of course the old man had written all his great books before he ever set eyes on her, but I don't think anyone can deny that it was she who created the rather imposing and dignified figure that the world saw for the last twenty-five years of his life. She's been very frank with me. She didn't have such an easy job of it. Old Driffield had some very queer ways and she had to use a good deal of tact to get him to behave decently. He was very obstinate in some things and I think a woman of less character would have been discouraged. For instance, he had a habit that poor Amy had a lot of trouble to break him of: after he'd finished his meat and vegetables he'd take a piece of bread and wipe the plate clean with it and eat it."

"Do you know what that means?" I said. "It means that for long he had so little to eat that he couldn't afford to waste any food he could get."

"Well, that may be, but it's not a very pretty habit for a distinguished man of letters. And then, he didn't exactly tipple, but he was rather fond of going down to the 'Bear and Key' at Blackstable and having a few beers in the public bar. Of course there was no harm in it, but it did make him rather conspicuous, especially in summer when the place was full of trippers. He didn't mind who he talked to. He didn't seem able to realise that he had a position to keep up. You can't deny it was rather awkward after they'd been having a lot of interesting people to lunch—people like Edmund Gosse, for instance, and Lord Curzon —that he should go down to a public-house and tell the plumber and the baker and the sanitary inspector what he thought about them. But of course that could be explained away. One could say that he was after local colour and was interested in types. But he had some habits that really were rather difficult to cope with. Do you know that it was with the greatest difficulty that Amy Driffield could ever get him to take a bath?"

"He was born at a time when people thought it unhealthy to take too many baths. I don't suppose he ever lived in a house that had a bathroom till he was fifty."

"Well, he said he never had had a bath more than once a week and he didn't see why he should change his habits at his time of life. Then Amy said that he must change his under-linen every day, but he objected to that too. He said he'd always been used to wearing his vest and drawers for a week and it was nonsense, it only wore them out to have them washed so often. Mrs. Driffield did everything she could to tempt him to have a bath every day, with bath salts and perfumes, you know, but nothing would induce him to, and as he grew older he wouldn't even have one once a week. She tells me that for the last three years of his life he never had a bath at all. Of course, all this is between ourselves; I'm merely telling it to show you that in writing his life I shall have to use a good deal of tact. I don't see how one can deny that he was just a wee bit unscrupulous in money matters and he had a kink in him that made him take a strange pleasure in the society of his inferiors, and some of his personal habits were rather disagreeable, but I don't think that side of him was the most significant. I don't want to say anything that's untrue, but I do think there's a certain amount that's better left unsaid."

"Don't you think it would be more interesting if you went the whole hog and drew him warts and all?"

"Oh, I couldn't. Amy Driffield would never speak to me again. She only asked me to do the life because she felt she could trust my discretion. I must behave like a gentleman."

"It's very hard to be a gentleman and a writer."

"I don't see why. And besides, you know what the critics are. If you tell the truth they only say you're cynical and it does an author no good to get a reputation for cynicism. Of course I don't deny that if I were thoroughly unscrupulous I could make a sensation. It would be rather amusing to show the man with his passion for beauty and his careless treatment of his obligations, his fine style and his personal hatred for soap and water, his idealism and his tippling in disreputable pubs; but honestly, would it pay? They'd only say I was imitating Lytton Strachey. No, I think I shall do much better to be allusive and charming and rather subtle, you know the sort of thing, and tender. I think one ought always to *see* a book before one starts it. Well, I see this rather like a portrait by Van Dyck, with a good deal of atmosphere, you know, and a certain gravity, and with a sort of aristocratic distinction. Do you know what I mean? About eighty thousand words."

He was absorbed for a moment in the ecstasy of æsthetic contemplation. In his mind's eye he saw a book, in royal octavo, slim and light in the hand, printed with large margins on handsome paper in a type that was both clear and comely, and I think he saw a binding in smooth black cloth with a decoration in gold and gilt lettering. But being human, Alroy Kear could not, as I suggested a few pages back, hold the ecstasy that beauty yields for more than a little while. He gave me a candid smile.

"But how the devil am I to get over the first Mrs. Driffield?"

"The skeleton in the cupboard," I murmured.

"She is damned awkward to deal with. She was married to Driffield for a good many years. Amy has very decided views on the subject, but I don't see how I can possibly meet them. You see, her attitude is that Rose Driffield exerted a most pernicious influence on her husband, and that she did everything possible to ruin him morally, physically and financially; she was beneath him in every way, at least intellectually and spiritually, and it was only because he was a man of immense force and vitality that he survived. It was of course a very unfortunate marriage. It's true that she's been dead for ages and it seems a pity to rake up old scandals and wash a lot of dirty linen in public; but the fact remains that all Driffield's greatest books were written when he was living with her. Much as I admire the later books, and no one is more conscious of their genuine beauty than I am, and they have a restraint and a sort of classical sobriety which are admirable,

I must admit that they haven't the tang and the vigour and the smell and bustle of life of the early ones. It does seem to me that you can't altogether ignore the influence his first wife had on his work."

"What are you going to do about it?" I asked.

"Well, I can't see why all that part of his life shouldn't be treated with the greatest possible reserve and delicacy, so as not to offend the most exacting susceptibility, and yet with a sort of manly frankness, if you understand what I mean, that would be rather moving."

"It sounds a very tall order."

"As I see it, there's no need to dot the i's or to cross the t's. It can only be a question of getting just the right touch. I wouldn't state more than I could help, but I would suggest what was essential for the reader to realise. You know, however gross a subject is you can soften its unpleasantness if you treat it with dignity. But I can do nothing unless I am in complete possession of the facts."

"Obviously you can't cook them unless you have them."

Roy had been speaking with a fluent ease that revealed the successful lecturer. I wished (a) that I could express myself with so much force and aptness, never at a loss for a word, rolling off the sentences without a moment's hesitation; and (b) that I did not feel so miserably incompetent with my one small insignificant person to represent the large and appreciative audience that Roy was instinctively addressing. But now he paused. A genial look came over his face, which his enthusiasm had reddened and the heat of the day caused to perspire, and the eyes that had held me with a dominating brilliance softened and smiled.

"This is where you come in, old boy," he said pleasantly.

I have always found it a very good plan in life to say nothing when I had nothing to say and when I do not know how to answer a remark to hold my tongue. I remained silent and looked back at Roy amiably.

"You know more about his life at Blackstable than anybody else."

"I don't know about that. There must be a number of people at Blackstable who saw as much of him in the old days as I did."

"That may be, but after all they're presumably not people of any importance, and I don't think they matter very much."

"Oh, I see. You mean that I'm the only person who might blow the gaff."

"Roughly, that is what I do mean, if you feel that you must put it in a facetious way."

I saw that Roy was not inclined to be amused. I did not mind, for I am quite used to people not being amused at my jokes. I often think that the purest type of artist is the humorist who laughs alone at his own jests.

"And you saw a good deal of him later on in London, I believe."

"Yes."

"That is when he had an apartment somewhere in Lower Belgravia."

"Well, lodgings in Pimlico."

Roy smiled dryly.

"We won't quarrel about the exact designation of the quarter of London in which he lived. You were very intimate with him then."

"Fairly."

"How long did that last?"

"About a couple of years."

"How old were you then?"

"Twenty."

"Now look here, I want you to do me a great favour. It won't take you very long and it will be of quite inestimable value to me. I want you to jot down as fully as you can all your recollections of Driffield, and all you remember about his wife and his relations with her and so on, both at Blackstable and in London."

"Oh, my dear fellow, that's asking a great deal. I've got a lot of work to do just now."

"It needn't take you very long. You can write it quite roughly, I mean. You needn't bother about style, you know, or anything like that. I'll put the style in. All I want are the facts. After all, you know them and nobody else does. I don't want to be pompous or anything like that, but Driffield was a great man and you owe it to his memory and to English literature to tell everything you know. I shouldn't have asked you, but you told me the other day that you weren't going to write anything about him yourself. It would be rather like a dog in a manger to keep to yourself a whole lot of material that you have no intention of using."

Thus Roy appealed at once to my sense of duty, my indolence, my generosity and my rectitude.

"But why does Mrs. Driffield want me to go down and stay at Ferne Court?" I asked.

"Well, we talked it over. It's a very jolly house to stay in. She does one very well, and it ought to be divine in the country just now. She thought it would be very nice and quiet for you if you felt inclined to write your recollections there; of course, I said I couldn't promise that, but naturally being so near Blackstable would remind you of all sorts of things that you might otherwise forget. And then, living in his house, among his books and things, it would make the past seem much more real. We could all talk about him, and you know how in the heat of conversation things come back. Amy's very quick and clever. She's been in the habit of making notes of Driffield's talk for years, and after all it's quite likely that you'll say things on the spur of the moment that you wouldn't think of writing and she can just jot them down afterward. And we can play tennis and bathe."

"I'm not very fond of staying with people," I said. "I hate getting up for a nine-o'clock breakfast to eat things I have no mind to. I don't like going for walks, and I'm not interested in other people's chickens."

"She's a lonely woman now. It would be a kindness to her and it would be a kindness to me too."

I reflected.

"I'll tell you what I'll do: I'll go down to Blackstable, but I'll go down on my own. I'll put up at the 'Bear and Key' and I'll come over and see Mrs. Driffield while you're there. You can both talk your heads off about Edward Driffield, but I shall be able to get away when I'm fed up with you."

Roy laughed good-naturedly.

"All right. That'll do. And will you jot down anything you can remember that you think will be useful to me?"

"I'll try."

"When will you come? I'm going down on Friday."

"I'll come with you if you'll promise not to talk to me in the train."

"All right. The five-ten's the best one. Shall I come and fetch you?"

"I'm capable of getting to Victoria by myself. I'll meet you on the platform."

I don't know if Roy was afraid of my changing my mind, but he got up at once, shook my hand heartily and left. He begged me on no account to forget my tennis racket and bathing suit.

CHAPTER XII

My promise to Roy sent my thoughts back to my first years in London. Having nothing much to do that afternoon, it occurred to me to stroll along and have a cup of tea with my old landlady. Mrs. Hudson's name had been given to me by the secretary of the medical school at St. Luke's when, a callow youth just arrived in town, I was looking for lodgings. She had a house in Vincent Square. I lived there for five years, in two rooms on the ground floor, and over me on the drawing-room floor lived a master at Westminster School. I paid a pound a week for my rooms and he paid twenty-five shillings. Mrs. Hudson was a little, active, bustling woman, with a sallow face, a large aquiline nose and the brightest, the most vivacious black eyes that I ever saw. She had a great deal of very dark hair, in the afternoons and all day on Sunday arranged in a fringe on the forehead with a bun at the nape of the neck as you may see in old photographs of the Jersey Lily. She had a heart of gold (though I did not know it then, for when you are young you take the kindness people show you as your right) and she was an excellent cook. No one could make a better *omelette soufflée* than she. Every morning she was up betimes to get the fire lit in her gentlemen's sitting-rooms so that "they needn't eat their breakfasts simply perishin' with the cold, my word it's bitter this morning"; and if she didn't hear you having your bath, a flat tin bath that slipped under the bed, the water put in the night before to take the chill off, she'd say: "There now, there's my dining-room floor not up yet, 'e'll be late for his lecture again," and she would come tripping upstairs and thump on the door and you would hear her shrill voice: "If you don't get up at once you won't 'ave time to 'ave breakfast, an' I've got a lovely 'addick for you." She worked all day long and she sang at her work and she was gay and happy and smiling. Her husband was much older than she. He had been a butler in very good families, and wore side-whiskers and a perfect manner; he was verger at a neighbouring church, highly respected, and he waited at table and cleaned the boots and helped with the washing-up. Mrs. Hudson's only relaxation was to come up after she had served the dinners (I had mine at half-past six and the school-master at seven) and have a little chat with her gentlemen. I wish to goodness I had had the sense (like Amy Driffield with her celebrated husband) to take notes of her conversation, for Mrs. Hudson was a mistress of Cockney humour. She had a gift of repartee that never failed her, she had a racy style and an apt and varied vocabulary, she was never at a loss for the comic metaphor or the vivid phrase. She was a pattern of propriety and she would never have women in her house, you never knew what they were up to ("It's men, men, men all the time with them, and afternoon tea and thin bread and butter, and openin' the door and ringin' for 'ot water and I don't know what all"); but in conversation she did not hesitate to use what was called in those days the blue bag. One could have said of her what she said of Marie Lloyd: "What I like about 'er is that she gives you a good laugh. She goes pretty near the knuckle sometimes, but she never jumps over the fence." Mrs. Hudson enjoyed her own humour and I think she talked more willingly to her lodgers because her husband was a serious man ("It's as it should be," she said, " 'im bein' a verger and attendin' weddings and funerals and what all") and wasn't much of a one for a joke. "Wot I says to 'Udson is, laugh while you've got the chance, you won't laugh much when you're dead and buried."

Mrs. Hudson's humour was cumulative and the story of her feud with Miss Butcher who let lodgings at number fourteen was a great comic saga that went on year in and year out.

"She's a disagreeable old cat, but I give you my word I'd miss 'er if the Lord took 'er one fine day. Though what 'e'd do with 'er when 'e got 'er I can't think. Many's the good laugh she's give me in 'er time."

Mrs. Hudson had very bad teeth and the question whether she should have them taken out and have false ones was discussed by her for two or three years with an unimaginable variety of comic invention.

"But as I said to 'Udson on'y last night, when he said, 'Oh, come on, 'ave 'em out and 'ave done with it,' I shouldn't 'ave anythin' to talk about."

I had not seen Mrs. Hudson for two or three years. My last visit had been in answer to a little letter in which she asked me to come and drink a nice strong cup of tea with her and announced: "Hudson died three months ago next Saturday, aged seventy-nine, and George and Hester send their respectful compliments." George was the issue of her marriage with Hudson. He was now a man approaching middle age who worked at Woolwich Arsenal, and his mother had been repeating for twenty years that George would be bringing a wife home one of these days. Hester was the maid-of-all-work she had engaged toward the end of my stay with her, and Mrs. Hudson still spoke of her as "that dratted girl of mine". Though Mrs. Hudson must have been well over thirty when I first took her rooms, and that was five-and-thirty years ago, I had no feeling as I walked leisurely through the Green Park that I should not find her alive. She was as definitely part of the recollections of my youth as the pelicans that stood at the edge of the ornamental water.

I walked down the area steps and the door was opened to me by Hester, a woman getting on for fifty now and stoutish, but still bearing on her shyly grinning face the irresponsibility of the dratted girl. Mrs. Hudson was darning George's socks when I was shown into the front room of the basement and she took off her spectacles to look at me.

"Well, if that isn't Mr. Ashenden! Who ever thought of seeing you? Is the water boiling, 'Ester? You will 'ave a nice cup of tea, won't you?"

Mrs. Hudson was a little heavier than when I first knew her and her movements were more deliberate, but there was scarcely a white hair on her head, and her eyes, as black and shining as buttons, sparkled with fun. I sat down in a shabby little arm-chair covered with maroon leather.

"How are you getting on, Mrs. Hudson?" I asked.

"Oh, I've got nothin' much to complain of except that I'm not so young as I used to was," she answered. "I can't do so much as I could when you was 'ere. I don't give my gentlemen dinner now, only breakfast."

"Are all your rooms let?"

"Yes, I'm thankful to say."

Owing to the rise of prices Mrs. Hudson was able to get more for her rooms than in my day, and I think in her modest way she was quite well off. But of course people wanted a lot nowadays.

"You wouldn't believe it, first I 'ad to put in a bathroom, and then I 'ad to put in the electric light, and then nothin' would satisfy them but I must 'ave a telephone. What they'll want next I can't think."

"Mr. George says it's pretty near time Mrs. 'Udson thought of retiring," said Hester, who was laying the tea.

"You mind your own business, my girl," said Mrs. Hudson tartly. "When I retire it'll be to the cemetery. Fancy me livin' all alone with George and 'Ester without nobody to talk to."

"Mr. George says she ought to take a little 'ouse in the country an' take care of 'erself," said Hester, unperturbed by the reproof.

"Don't talk to me about the country. The doctor said I was to go there for six weeks last summer. It nearly killed me, I give you my word. The noise of it. All them birds singin' all the time, and the cocks crowin' and the cows mooin'. I couldn't stick it. When you've lived all the years I 'ave in peace and quietness you can't get used to all that racket goin' on all the time."

A few doors away was the Vauxhall Bridge Road and down it trams were clanging, ringing their bells as they went, motor-buses were lumbering along, taxis were tooting their horns. If Mrs. Hudson heard it, it was London she heard, and it soothed her as a mother's crooning soothes a restless child.

I looked round the cosy, shabby, homely little parlour in which Mrs. Hudson had lived so long. I wondered if there was anything I could do for her. I noticed that she had a gramophone. It was the only thing I could think of.

"Is there anything you want, Mrs. Hudson?" I asked.

She fixed her beady eyes on me reflectively.

"I don't know as there is, now you come to speak of it, except me 'ealth and strength for another twenty years so as I can go on workin'."

I do not think I am a sentimentalist, but her reply, unexpected but so characteristic, made a sudden lump come to my throat.

When it was time for me to go I asked if I could see the rooms I had lived in for five years.

"Run upstairs, 'Ester, and see if Mr. Graham's in. If he ain't, I'm sure 'e wouldn't mind you 'aving a look at them."

Hester scurried up, and in a moment, slightly breathless, came down again to say that Mr. Graham was out. Mrs. Hudson came with me. The bed was the same narrow iron bed that I had slept in and dreamed in and there was the same chest-of-drawers and the same washing-stand. But the sitting-room had the grim heartiness of the athlete; on the walls were photographs of cricket elevens and rowing men in shorts; golf clubs stood in the corner and pipes and tobacco jars, ornamented with the arms of a college, were littered on the chimney-piece. In my day we believed in art for art's sake and this I exemplified by draping the chimney-piece with a Moorish rug, putting up curtains of art serge and a bilious green, and hanging on the walls autotypes of pictures by Perugino, Van Dyck and Hobbema.

"Very artistic you was, wasn't you?" Mrs. Hudson remarked, not without irony.

"Very," I murmured.

I could not help feeling a pang as I thought of all the years that had passed since I inhabited that room, and of all that had happened to me. It was at that same table that I had eaten my hearty breakfast and my frugal dinner, read my medical books and written my first novel. It was in that same arm-chair that I had read for the first time Wordsworth and Stendhal, the Elizabethan dramatists and the Russian novelists, Gibbon, Boswell, Voltaire and Rousseau. I wondered who had used them since. Medical students, articled clerks, young fellows making their way in the City and elderly men retired from the colonies or thrown unexpectedly upon the world by the break up of an old home. The room made me, as Mrs. Hudson would have put it, go queer all over. All the hopes that had been cherished there, the bright visions of the future, the flaming passion of youth; the regrets, the disillusion, the weariness, the resignation; so much had been felt in that room, by so many, the whole gamut of human emotion, that it seemed strangely to have acquired a troubling and enigmatic personality of its own. I have no notion why, but it made me think of a woman at a cross-road with a finger on her lips, looking back and with her other hand beckoning. What I obscurely (and rather shamefacedly) felt, communicated itself to Mrs. Hudson, for she gave a laugh and with a characteristic gesture rubbed her prominent nose.

"My word, people are funny," she said. "When I think of all the gentlemen I've 'ad here, I give you my word you wouldn't believe it if I told you some of the things I know about them. One of them's funnier than the other. Sometimes I lie abed thinkin' of them, and *laugh*. Well, it would be a bad world if you didn't get a good laugh now and then, but, lor', lodgers really are the limit."

CHAPTER XIII

I LIVED with Mrs. Hudson for nearly two years before I met the Driffields again. My life was very regular. I spent all day at the hospital and about six walked back to Vincent Square. I bought the *Star* at Lambeth Bridge and read it till my dinner was served. Then I read seriously for an hour or two, works to improve my mind, for I was a strenuous, earnest and industrious youth, and after that wrote novels and plays till bedtime. I do not know for what reason it was that one day toward the end of June, happening to leave the hospital early, I thought I would walk down the Vauxhall Bridge Road. I liked it for its noisy bustle. It had a sordid vivacity that was pleasantly exciting and you felt that at any moment an adventure might there befall you. I strolled along in a daydream and was surprised suddenly to hear my name. I stopped and looked, and there to my astonishment stood Mrs. Driffield. She was smiling at me.

"Don't you know me?" she cried.

"Yes. Mrs. Driffield."

And though I was grown up I was conscious that I was blushing as furiously as when I was sixteen. I was embarrassed. With my lamentably Victorian notions of honesty I had been much shocked by the Driffields' behaviour in running away from Blackstable without paying their bills. It seemed to me very shabby. I felt deeply the shame I thought they must feel and I was astounded that Mrs. Driffield should speak to someone who knew of the discreditable incident. If I had seen her coming I should have looked away, my delicacy presuming that she would wish to avoid the mortification of being seen by me; but she held out her hand and shook mine with obvious pleasure.

"I am glad to see a Blackstable face," she said. "You know we left there in a hurry."

She laughed and I laughed too; but her laugh was mirthful and childlike, while mine, I felt, was strained.

"I hear there *was* a to-do when they found out we'd skipped. I thought Ted would never stop laughing when he heard about it. What did your uncle say?"

I was quick to get the right tone. I wasn't going to let her think that I couldn't see a joke as well as anyone.

"Oh, you know what he is. He's very old-fashioned."

"Yes, that's what's wrong with Blackstable. They want waking up." She gave me a friendly look. "You've grown a lot since I saw you last. Why, you're growing a moustache."

"Yes," I said, giving it as much of a twirl as its size allowed me. "I've had that for ages."

"How time does fly, doesn't it? You were just a boy four years ago and now you're a man."

"I ought to be," I replied somewhat haughtily. "I'm nearly twenty-one."

I was looking at Mrs. Driffield. She wore a very small hat with feathers in it, and a pale grey dress with large leg-of-mutton sleeves and a long train. I thought she looked very smart. I had always thought that she had a nice face, but I noticed now, for the first time, that she was pretty. Her eyes were bluer than I remembered and her skin was like ivory.

"You know we live just round the corner," she said.

"So do I."

"We live in Limpus Road. We've been there almost ever since we left Blackstable."

"Well, I've been in Vincent Square for nearly two years."

"I knew you were in London. George Kemp told me so, and I often wondered where you were. Why don't you walk back with me now? Ted will be so pleased to see you."

"I don't mind," I said.

As we walked along she told me that Driffield was now literary editor of a weekly paper; his last book had done much better than any of his others and he was expecting to get quite a bit as an advance on royalties for the next one. She seemed to know most of the Blackstable news, and I remembered how it had been suspected that Lord George had helped the Driffields in their flight. I guessed that he wrote to them now and then. I noticed as we walked along that sometimes the men who passed us stared at Mrs. Driffield. It occurred to me presently that they must think her pretty too. I began to walk with a certain swagger.

Limpus Road was a long, wide, straight street that ran parallel with the Vauxhall Bridge Road. The houses were all alike, of stucco, dingily painted, solid and with substantial porticos. I suppose they had been built to be inhabited by men of standing in the city of London, but the street had gone down in the world or had never attracted the right sort of tenant; and its decayed respectability had an air at once furtive and shabbily dissipated, that made you think of persons who had seen better days and now, genteelly fuddled, talked of the social distinction of their youth. The Driffields lived in a house painted a dull red, and Mrs. Driffield, letting me into a narrow dark hall, opened a door and said:

"Go in. I'll tell Ted you're here."

She walked down the hall and I entered the sitting-room. The Driffields had the basement and the ground floor of the house, which they rented from the lady who lived in the upper part. The room into which I went looked as if it had been furnished with the scourings of auction sales. There were heavy velvet curtains with great fringes, all loops and festoons, and a gilt suite, upholstered in yellow damask, heavily buttoned; and there was a great pouffe in the middle of the room. There were gilt cabinets in which were masses of little articles, pieces of china, ivory figures, wood carvings, bits of Indian brass; and on the walls hung large oil paintings of highland glens and stags and gillies. In a moment Mrs. Driffield brought her husband and he greeted me warmly. He wore a shabby alpaca coat and grey trousers; he had shaved his beard and wore now a moustache and a small imperial. I noticed for the first time how short he was; but he looked more distinguished than he used to. There was something a trifle foreign in his appearance and I thought this was much more what I should expect an author to look like.

"Well, what do you think of our new abode?" he asked. "It looks rich, doesn't it? I think it inspires confidence."

He looked round him with satisfaction.

"And Ted's got his den at the back where he can write, and we've got a dining-room in the basement," said Mrs. Driffield. "Miss Cowley was companion for many years to a lady of title and when she died she left her all her furniture. You can see everything's good, can't you? You can see it came out of a gentleman's house."

"Rosie fell in love with the place the moment we saw it," said Driffield.

"You did too, Ted."

"We've lived in sordid circumstances so long; it's a change to be surrounded by luxury. Madame de Pompadour and all that sort of thing."

When I left them it was with a very cordial invitation to come again. It appeared that they were at home every Saturday afternoon and all sorts of people whom I would like to meet were in the habit of dropping in.

CHAPTER XIV

I WENT. I enjoyed myself. I went again. When the autumn came and I returned to London for the winter session at St. Luke's I got into the habit of going every Saturday. It was my introduction into the world of art and letters; I kept it a profound secret that in the privacy of my lodgings I was busily writing; I was excited to meet people who were writing also and I listened entranced to their conversation. All sorts of persons came to these parties: at that time week-ends were rare, golf was still a subject for ridicule and few had much to do on Saturday afternoons. I do not think anyone came who was of any great importance; at all events, of all the painters, writers and musicians I met at the Driffields' I cannot remember one whose reputation has endured; but the effect was cultured and animated. You found young actors who were looking for parts and middle-aged singers who deplored the fact that the English were not a musical race, composers who played their compositions on the Driffields' cottage piano and complained in a whispered aside that they sounded nothing except on a concert grand, poets who on pressure consented to read a little thing that they had just written and painters who were looking for commissions. Now and then a person of title added a certain glamour; seldom, however, for in those days the aristocracy had not yet become bohemian and if a person of quality cultivated the society of artists it was generally because a notorious divorce or a little difficulty over cards had made life in his own station (or hers) a bit awkward. We have changed all that. One of the greatest benefits that compulsory education has conferred upon the world is the wide diffusion among the nobility and gentry of the practice of writing. Horace Walpole once wrote a *Catalogue of Royal and Noble Authors*; such a work now would have the dimensions of an encyclopædia. A title, even a courtesy one, can make a well-known author of almost anyone and it may be safely asserted that there is no better passport to the world of letters than rank.

I have indeed sometimes thought that now that the House of

Lords must inevitably in a short while be abolished, it would be a very good plan if the profession of literature were by law confined to its members and their wives and children. It would be a graceful compensation that the British people might offer the peers in return for the surrender of their hereditary privileges. It would be a means of support for those (too many) whom devotion to the public cause in keeping chorus girls and race-horses and playing *chemin de fer* has impoverished, and a pleasant occupation for the rest who by the process of natural selection have in the course of time become unfit to do anything but govern the British Empire. But this is an age of specialisation and if my plan is adopted it is obvious that it cannot but be to the greater glory of English literature that its various provinces should be apportioned among the various ranks of the nobility. I would suggest, therefore, that the humbler branches of literature should be practised by the lower orders of the peerage and that the barons and viscounts should devote themselves exclusively to journalism and the drama. Fiction might be the privileged demesne of the earls. They have already shown their aptitude for this difficult art and their numbers are so great that they would very competently supply the demand. To the marquises might safely be left the production of that part of literature which is known (I have never quite seen why) as *belles lettres*. It is perhaps not very profitable from a pecuniary standpoint, but it has a distinction that very well suits the holders of this romantic title.

The crown of literature is poetry. It is its end and aim. It is the sublimest activity of the human mind. It is the achievement of beauty. The writer of prose can only step aside when the poet passes; he makes the best of us look like a piece of cheese. It is evident then that the writing of poetry should be left to the dukes, and I should like to see their rights protected by the most severe pains and penalties, for it is intolerable that the noblest of arts should be practised by any but the noblest of men. And since here, too, specialisation must prevail, I foresee that the dukes (like the successors of Alexander) will divide the realm of poetry between them, each confining himself to that aspect with which hereditary influence and natural bent have rendered him competent to deal: thus I see the Dukes of Manchester writing poems of a didactic and moral character, the Dukes of Westminster composing stirring odes on Duty and the Responsibilities of Empire; whereas I imagine that the Dukes of Devonshire would be more likely to write love lyrics and elegies in the Propertian manner, while it is almost inevitable that the Dukes of Marlborough should pipe in an idyllic strain on such subjects as domestic bliss, conscription and content with modest station.

But if you say that this is somewhat formidable and remind me that the muse does not only stalk with majestic tread, but on occasion trips on a light fantastic toe; if, recalling the wise person who said that he did not care who made a nation's laws so long as he wrote its songs, you ask me (thinking rightly that it would ill become the dukes to do so) who shall twang those measures on the lyre that the diverse and inconstant soul of man occasionally hankers after—I answer (obviously enough, I should have thought) the duchesses. I recognise that the day is past when the amorous peasants of the Romagna sang to their sweethearts the verses of Torquato Tasso and Mrs. Humphry Ward crooned over young Arnold's cradle the choruses of Œdipus in Colonus. The age demands something more up-to-date. I suggest, therefore, that the more domestic duchesses should write our hymns and our nursery rhymes; while the skittish ones, those who incline to mingle vine leaves with the strawberry, should write the lyrics for musical comedies, humorous verse for the comic papers and mottoes for Christmas cards and crackers. Thus would they retain in the hearts of the British public that place which they have held hitherto only on account of their exalted station.

It was at these parties on Saturday afternoon that I discovered very much to my surprise that Edward Driffield was a distinguished person. He had written something like twenty books, and though he had never made more than a pittance out of them his reputation was considerable. The best judges admired them and the friends who came to his house were agreed that one of these days he would be recognised. They upbraided the public because it would not see that here was a great writer, and since the easiest way to exalt one man is to kick another in the pants, they reviled freely all the novelists whose contemporary fame obscured his. If, indeed, I had known as much of literary circles as I learned later I should have guessed by the not infrequent visits of Mrs. Barton Trafford that the time was approaching when Edward Driffield, like a runner in a long-distance race breaking away suddenly from the little knot of plodding athletes, must forge ahead. I admit that when first I was introduced to this lady her name meant nothing to me. Driffield presented me as a young neighbour of his in the country and told her that I was a medical student. She gave me a mellifluous smile, murmured in a soft voice something about Tom Sawyer, and, accepting the bread and butter I offered her, went on talking with her host. But I noticed that her arrival had made an impression and the conversation, which had been noisy and hilarious, was hushed. When in an undertone I asked who she was, I found that my ignorance was amazing; I was told that she had "made" So-and-So and So-and-So. After half an hour she rose, shook hands very graciously with such of the people as she was acquainted with, and with a sort of lithe sweetness sidled out of the room. Driffield accompanied her to the door and put her in a hansom.

Mrs. Barton Trafford was then a woman of about fifty; she was small and slight, but with rather large features, which made her head look a little too big for her body; she had crisp white hair which she wore like the Venus of Milo, and she was supposed in her youth to have been very comely. She dressed discreetly in black silk, and wore round her neck jangling chains of beads and shells. She was said to have been unhappily married in early life, but now for many years had been congenially united to Barton Trafford, a clerk in the Home Office and a well-known authority on prehistoric man. She gave you the curious impression of having no bones in her body and you felt that if you pinched her shin (which of course my respect for her sex as well as something of quiet dignity in her appearance would have never allowed me to do) your fingers would meet. When you took her hand it was like taking a fillet of sole. Her face, notwithstanding its large features, had something fluid about it. When she sat it was as though she had no backbone and were stuffed, like an expensive cushion, with swansdown.

Everything was soft about her, her voice, her smile, her laugh; her eyes, which were small and pale, had the softness of flowers; her manner was as soft as the summer rain. It was this extraordinary, and charming, characteristic that made her the wonderful friend she was. It was this that had gained her the celebrity that she now enjoyed. The whole world was aware of her friendship with the great novelist whose death a few years back had come as such a shock to the English-speaking peoples. Everyone had read the innumerable letters which he had written to her and which she was induced to publish shortly after his demise. Every page revealed his admiration for her beauty and his respect for her judgment; he could never say often enough how much he owed to her encouragement, her ready sympathy, her tact, her taste; and if certain of his expressions of passion were such as some persons might think would not be read by Mr. Barton Trafford with unmixed feelings, that only added to the human interest of the work. But Mr. Barton Trafford was above the prejudices of vulgar men (his misfortune, if such it was, was one that the greatest personages in history have endured with philosophy) and, abandoning his studies of aurignacian flints and neolithic axe heads, he consented to write a Life of the deceased novelist in which he showed quite definitely how great a part of the writer's genius was due to his wife's influence.

But Mrs. Barton Trafford's interest in literature, her passion for art, were not dead because the friend for whom she had done so much had become part, with her far from negligible assistance, of posterity. She was a great reader. Little that was noteworthy escaped her attention and she was quick to establish personal relations with any young writer who showed promise. Her fame, especially since the Life, was now such that she was sure that no one would hesitate to accept the sympathy she was prepared to offer. It was inevitable that Mrs. Barton Trafford's genius for friendship should in due course find an outlet. When she read something that struck her, Mr. Barton Trafford, himself no mean critic, wrote a warm letter of appreciation to the author and asked him to luncheon. After luncheon, having to get back to the Home Office, he left him to have a chat with Mrs. Barton Trafford. Many were called. They all had *something*, but that was not enough. Mrs. Barton Trafford had a *flair*, and she trusted her *flair*; her *flair* bade her wait.

She was so cautious indeed that with Jasper Gibbons she almost missed the bus. The records of the past tell us of writers who grew famous in a night, but in our more prudent day this is unheard of. The critics want to see which way the cat will jump, and the public has been sold a pup too often to take unnecessary chances. But in the case of Jasper Gibbons it is almost the exact truth that he did thus jump into celebrity. Now that he is so completely forgotten and the critics who praised him would willingly eat their words if they were not carefully guarded in the files of innumerable newspaper offices, the sensation he made with his first volume of poems is almost unbelievable. The most important papers gave to reviews of it as much space as they would have to the report of a prize fight, the most influential critics fell over one another in their eagerness to welcome him. They likened him to Milton (for the sonority of his blank verse), to Keats (for the opulence of his sensuous imagery), and to Shelley (for his airy fantasy); and, using him as a stick to beat idols of whom they were weary, they gave in his name many a resounding whack on the emaciated buttocks of Lord Tennyson and a few good husky smacks on the bald pate of Robert Browning. The public fell like the walls of Jericho. Edition after edition was sold, and you saw Jasper Gibbons's handsome volume in the boudoirs of countesses in Mayfair, in vicarage drawing-rooms from Land's End to John o' Groats and in the parlours of many an honest but cultured merchant in Glasgow, Aberdeen and Belfast. When it became known that Queen Victoria had accepted a specially bound copy of the book from the hands of the loyal publisher, and had given him (not the poet, the publisher) a copy of *Leaves from a Journal in the Highlands* in exchange, the national enthusiasm knew no bounds.

And all this happened as it were in the twinkling of an eye. Seven cities in Greece disputed the honour of having given birth to Homer, and though Jasper Gibbons's birthplace (Walsall) was well known, twice seven critics claimed the honour of having discovered him; eminent judges of literature who for twenty years had written eulogies of one another's works in the weekly papers quarrelled so bitterly over this matter that one cut the other dead in the Athenæum. Nor was the great world remiss in giving him its recognition. Jasper Gibbons was asked to luncheon and invited to tea by dowager duchesses, the wives of cabinet ministers and the widows of bishops. It is said that Harrison Ainsworth was the first English man of letters to move in English society on terms of equality (and I have sometimes wondered that an enterprising publisher on this account has not thought of bringing out a complete edition of his works); but I believe that Jasper Gibbons was the first poet to have his name engraved at the bottom of an At Home card as a draw as enticing as an opera singer or a ventriloquist.

It was out of the question then for Mrs. Barton Trafford to get in on the ground floor. She could only buy in the open market. I do not know what prodigious strategy she employed, what miracles of tact, what tenderness, what exquisite sympathy, what demure blandishments; I can only surmise and admire; she nobbled Jasper Gibbons. In a little while he was eating out of her soft hand. She was admirable. She had him to lunch to meet the right people; she gave At Homes where he recited his poems before the most distinguished persons in England; she introduced him to eminent actors who gave him commissions to write plays; she saw that his poems should only appear in the proper places; she dealt with the publishers and made contracts for him that would have staggered even a cabinet minister; she took care that he should accept only the invitations of which she approved; she even went so far as to separate him from his wife with whom he had lived happily for ten years, since she felt that a poet to be true to himself and his art must not be encumbered with domestic ties. When the crash came Mrs. Barton Trafford, had she chosen, might have said that she had done everything for him that it was humanly possible to do.

For there was a crash. Jasper Gibbons brought out another volume of poetry; it was neither better nor worse than the first; it was very much like the first; it was treated with respect, but the critics made reservations; some of them even carped. The book was a disappointment. Its sale also. And unfortunately Jasper Gibbons was inclined to tipple. He had never been accustomed to having money to spend, he was quite unused to the lavish entertainments that were offered him, perhaps he missed his homely, common little wife; once or twice he came to dinner at Mrs. Barton Trafford's in a condition that anyone less worldly, less simple-minded than she, would have described as blind to the world. She told her guests gently that the bard was not quite himself that evening. His third book was a failure. The critics tore him limb from limb, they knocked him down and stamped on him, and, to quote one of Edward Driffield's favourite songs, then they lugged him round the room and then they jumped upon his face: they were quite naturally annoyed that they had mistaken a fluent versifier for a deathless poet and were determined that he should suffer for their error. Then Jasper Gibbons was arrested for being drunk and disorderly in Piccadilly and Mr. Barton Trafford had to go to Vine Street at midnight to bail him out.

Mrs. Barton Trafford at this juncture was perfect. She did not repine. No harsh word escaped her lips. She might have been excused if she had felt a certain bitterness because this man for whom she had done so much had let her down. She remained tender, gentle and sympathetic. She was the woman who under-

stood. She dropped him, but not like a hot brick, or a hot
potato. She dropped him with infinite gentleness, as softly as the
tear that she doubtless shed when she made up her mind to do
something so repugnant to her nature; she dropped him with so
much tact, with such sensibility, that Jasper Gibbons perhaps
hardly knew he was dropped. But there was no doubt about it.
She would say nothing against him, indeed she would not discuss
him at all, and when mention was made of him she merely smiled,
a little sadly, and sighed. But her smile was the *coup de grâce*, and
her sigh buried him deep.

Mrs. Barton Trafford had a passion for literature too sincere to
allow a setback of this character long to discourage her; and however great her disappointment she was a woman of too disinterested a nature to let the gifts of tact, sympathy and understanding with which she was blessed by nature lie fallow. She
continued to move in literary circles, going to tea parties here and
there, to soirées and to At Homes, charming always and gentle,
listening intelligently, but watchful, critical, and determined (if I
may put it crudely) next time to back a winner. It was then that
she met Edward Driffield and formed a favourable opinion of his
gifts. It is true that he was not young, but then he was unlikely
like Jasper Gibbons to go to pieces. She offered him her friendship. He could not fail to be moved when, in that gentle way of
hers, she told him that it was a scandal that his exquisite work
remained known only in the narrow circle. He was pleased and
flattered. It is always pleasant to be assured that you are a genius.
She told him that Barton Trafford was reflecting on the possibility
of writing an important article on him for the *Quarterly Review*.
She asked him to luncheon to meet people who might be useful
to him. She wanted him to know his intellectual equals. Sometimes she took him for a walk on the Chelsea Embankment and
they talked of poets dead and gone and love and friendship, and
had tea in an A.B.C. shop. When Mrs. Barton Trafford came to
Limpus Street on Saturday afternoon she had the air of the queen
bee preparing herself for the nuptial flight.

Her manner with Mrs. Driffield was perfect. It was affable, but
not condescending. She always thanked her very prettily for
having allowed her to come and see her and complimented her on
her appearance. If she praised Edward Driffield to her, telling her
with a little envy in her tone what a privilege it was to enjoy the
companionship of such a great man, it was certainly from pure

kindness, and not because she knew that there is nothing that exasperates the wife of a literary man more than to have another woman tell her flattering things about him. She talked to Mrs. Driffield of the simple things her simple nature might be supposed to be interested in, of cooking and servants and Edward's health and how careful she must be with him. Mrs. Barton Trafford treated her exactly as you would expect a woman of very good Scotch family, which she was, to treat an ex-barmaid with whom a distinguished man of letters had made an unfortunate marriage. She was cordial, playful and gently determined to put her at her ease.

It was strange that Rosie could not bear her; indeed, Mrs. Barton Trafford was the only person that I ever knew her dislike. In those days even barmaids did not habitually use the "bitches" and "bloodys" that are part and parcel of the current vocabulary of the best-brought-up young ladies, and I never heard Rosie use a word that would have shocked my Aunt Sophie. When anyone told a story that was a little near the knuckle she would blush to the roots of her hair. But she referred to Mrs. Barton Trafford as "that damned old cat". It needed the most urgent persuasions of her more intimate friends to induce her to be civil to her.

"Don't be a fool, Rosie," they said. They all called her Rosie and presently I, though very shyly, got in the habit of doing so too. "If she wants to she can make him. He must play up to her. She can work the trick if anyone can."

Though most of the Driffields' visitors were occasional, appearing every other Saturday, say, or every third, there was a little band that, like myself, came almost every week. We were the stand-bys; we arrived early and stayed late. Of these the most faithful were Quentin Forde, Harry Retford and Lionel Hillier.

Quentin Forde was a stocky little man with a fine head of the type that was afterward for a time much admired in the moving pictures, a straight nose and handsome eyes, neatly cropped grey hair and a black moustache; if he had been four or five inches taller he would have been the perfect type of the villain of melo-drama. He was known to be very "well connected", and he was affluent; his only occupation was to cultivate the arts. He went to all the first nights and all the private views. He had the amateur's severity, and cherished for the productions of his contemporaries a polite but sweeping contempt. I discovered that he did not come to the Driffields' because Edward was a genius, but because Rosie was beautiful.

Now that I look back I cannot get over my surprise that I should have had to be told what was surely so obvious. When I first knew her it never occurred to me to ask myself whether she was pretty or plain, and when, seeing her again after five years, I noticed for the first time that she was very pretty, I was interested but did not trouble to think much about it. I took it as part of the natural order of things, just as I took the sun setting over the North Sea or the towers of Tercanbury Cathedral. I was quite startled when I heard people speak of Rosie's beauty, and when they complimented Edward on her looks and his eyes rested on her for a moment, mine followed his. Lionel Hillier was a painter and he asked her to sit for him. When he talked of the picture he wanted to paint and told me what he saw in her, I listened to him stupidly. I was puzzled and confused. Harry Retford knew one of the fashionable photographers of the period and, arranging special terms, he took Rosie to be photographed. A Saturday or two later the proofs were there and we all looked at them. I had never seen Rosie in evening dress. She was wearing a dress in white satin, with a long train and puffy sleeves, and it was cut low; her hair was more elaborately done than usual. She looked very different from the strapping young woman I had first met in Joy Lane in a boater and a starched shirt. But Lionel Hillier tossed the photographs aside impatiently.

"Rotten," he said. "What can a photograph give of Rosie? The thing about her is her colour." He turned to her. "Rosie, don't you know that your colour is *the* great miracle of the age?"

She looked at him without answering, but her full red lips broke into their childlike, mischievous smile.

"If I can only get a suggestion of it I'm made for life," he said. "All the rich stockbrokers' wives will come on their bended knees and beg me to paint them like you."

Presently I learned that Rosie was sitting to him, but when, never having been in a painter's studio and looking upon it as the gateway of romance, I asked if I might not come one day and see how the picture was getting on, Hillier said that he did not want anyone to see it yet. He was a man of five and thirty and of a flamboyant appearance. He looked like a portrait of Van Dyck in which the distinction had been replaced by good humour. He was slightly above the middle height, slim; and he had a fine mane of black hair and flowing moustaches and a pointed beard. He favoured broad-brimmed sombreros and Spanish capes. He had lived a long time in Paris and talked admiringly of painters, Monet, Sisley, Renoir, of whom we had never heard, and with contempt of Sir Frederick Leighton and Mr. Alma-Tadema and Mr. G. F. Watts, whom in our heart of hearts we very much admired. I have often wondered what became of him. He spent a few years in London trying to make his way, failed, I suppose, and then drifted to Florence. I was told that he had a drawing school there, but when, years later, chancing to be in that city, I asked about him, I could find no one who had ever heard of him. I think he must have had some talent, for I have even now a very vivid recollection of the portrait he painted of Rosie Driffield. I wonder what has happened to it. Has it been destroyed or is it hidden away, its face to the wall, in the attic of a junk shop in Chelsea? I should like to think that it has at least found a place on the walls of some provincial gallery.

When I was at last allowed to come and see it, I put my foot in it fine and proper. Hillier's studio was in the Fulham Road, one of a group at the back of a row of shops, and you went in through a dark and smelly passage. It was a Sunday afternoon in March, a fine blue day, and I walked from Vincent Square through deserted streets. Hillier lived in his studio; there was a large divan on which he slept, and a tiny little room at the back where he cooked his breakfast, washed his brushes and, I suppose, himself.

When I arrived Rosie still wore the dress in which she had been sitting and they were having a cup of tea. Hillier opened the door for me, and still holding my hand led me up to the large canvas.

"There she is," he said.

He had painted Rosie full length, just a little less than life-size, in an evening dress of white silk. It was not at all like the Academy portraits I was accustomed to. I did not know what to say, so I said the first thing that came into my head.

"When will it be finished?"

"It is finished," he answered.

I blushed furiously. I felt a perfect fool. I had not then acquired the technique that I flatter myself now enables me to deal competently with the works of modern artists. If this were the place I could write a very neat little guide to enable the amateur of pictures to deal to the satisfaction of their painters with the most diverse manifestations of the creative instinct.

There is the intense "By God" that acknowledges the power of the ruthless realist, the "It's so awfully sincere" that covers your embarrassment when you are shown the coloured photograph of an alderman's widow, the low whistle that exhibits your admiration for the post-impressionist, the "Terribly amusing" that expresses what you feel about the cubist, the "Oh!" of one who is overcome, the "Ah!" of him whose breath is taken away.

"It's awfully like," was all that then I could lamely say.

"It's not chocolate-boxy enough for you," said Hillier.

"I think it's awfully good," I answered quickly, defending myself. "Are you going to send it to the Academy?"

"Good God, no! I might send it to the Grosvenor."

I looked from the painting to Rosie and from Rosie to the painting.

"Get into the pose, Rosie," said Hillier, "and let him see you."

She got up on to the model stand. I stared at her and I stared at the picture. I had such a funny little feeling in my heart. It was as though someone softly plunged a sharp knife into it, but it was not an unpleasant sensation at all, painful but strangely agreeable; and then suddenly I felt quite weak at the knees. But now I do not know if I remember Rosie in the flesh or in the picture. For when I think of her it is not in the shirt and boater that I first saw her in, nor in any of the other dresses I saw her in then or later, but in the white silk that Hillier painted, with a black velvet bow in her hair, and in the pose he had made her take.

I never exactly knew Rosie's age, but reckoning the years out as well as I can, I think she must have been then thirty-five. She did not look anything like it. Her face was quite unlined and her skin as smooth as a child's. I do not think she had very good features. They certainly had none of the aristocratic distinction of the great ladies whose photographs were at that time sold in all the shops; they were rather blunt. Her short nose was a little thick, her eyes were smallish, her mouth was large; but her eyes had the blue of cornflowers, and they smiled with her lips, very red and sensual, and her smile was the gayest, the most friendly, the sweetest thing I ever saw. She had by nature a heavy, sullen look, but when she smiled this sullenness became on a sudden infinitely attractive. She had no colour in her face; it was of a very pale brown except under the eyes, where it was faintly blue. Her hair was pale gold and it was done in the fashion of the day high on the head with an elaborate fringe.

"She's the very devil to paint," said Hillier, looking at her and at his picture. "You see, she's all gold, her face and her hair, and yet she doesn't give you a golden effect, she gives you a silvery effect."

I knew what he meant. She glowed, but palely, like the moon rather than the sun, or if it was like the sun it was like the sun in the white mist of dawn. Hillier had placed her in the middle of his canvas and she stood, with her arms by her sides, the palms of her hands toward you and her head a little thrown back, in an attitude that gave value to the pearly beauty of her neck and bosom. She stood like an actress taking a call, confused by unexpected applause, but there was something so virginal about her, so exquisitely spring-like, that the comparison was absurd. This artless creature had never known grease-paint or footlights. She stood like a maiden apt for love offering herself guilelessly, because she was fulfilling the purposes of Nature, to the embraces of a lover. She belonged to a generation that did not fear a certain opulence of line, she was slender, but her breasts were ample and her hips well marked. When, later, Mrs. Barton Trafford saw the picture she said it reminded her of a sacrificial heifer.

CHAPTER XV

EDWARD DRIFFIELD worked at night, and Rosie, having nothing to do, was glad to go out with one or other of her friends. She liked luxury and Quentin Forde was well-to-do. He would fetch her in a cab and take her to dine at Kettner's or the Savoy, and she would put on her grandest clothes for him; and Harry Retford, though he never had a bob, behaved as if he had, and took her about in hansoms too and gave her dinner at Romano's or in one or other of the little restaurants that were becoming modish in Soho. He was an actor and a clever one, but he was difficult to suit and so was often out of work. He was about thirty, a man with a pleasantly ugly face and a clipped way of speaking that made what he said sound funny. Rosie liked his devil-may-care attitude toward life, the swagger with which he wore clothes made by the best tailor in London and unpaid for, the recklessness with which he would put a fiver he hadn't got on a horse, and the generosity with which he flung his money about when a lucky win put him in funds. He was gay, charming, vain, boastful and unscrupulous. Rosie told me that once he had pawned his watch to take her out to dinner and then borrowed a couple of pounds from the actor manager who had given them seats for the play in order to take him out to supper with them afterward.

But she was just as well pleased to go with Lionel Hillier to his studio and eat a chop that he and she cooked between them and spend the evening talking, and it was only very rarely that she would dine with me at all. I used to fetch her after I had had my dinner in Vincent Square and she hers with Driffield, and we would get on a bus and go to a music-hall. We went here and there, to the Pavilion or the Tivoli, sometimes to the Metropolitan if there was a particular turn we wanted to see; but our favourite was the Canterbury. It was cheap and the show was good. We ordered a couple of beers and I smoked my pipe. Rosie looked round with delight at the great dark smoky house, crowded to the ceiling with the inhabitants of South London.

"I like the Canterbury," she said. "It's so homey."

I discovered that she was a great reader. She liked history, but only history of a certain kind, the lives of queens and of mistresses of royal personages; and she would tell me with a childlike wonder of the strange things she read. She had a wide acquaintance with the six consorts of King Henry VIII and there was little she did not know about Mrs. Fitzherbert and Lady Hamilton. Her appetite was prodigious and she ranged from Lucrezia Borgia to the wives of Philip of Spain; then there was the long list of the royal mistresses of France. She knew them all, and all about them, from Agnes Sorel down to Madame du Barry.

"I like to read about real things," she said. "I don't much care for novels."

She liked to gossip about Blackstable and I thought it was on account of my connection with it that she liked to come out with me. She seemed to know all that was going on there.

"I go down every other week or so to see my mother," she said. "Just for the night, you know."

"To Blackstable?"

I was surprised.

"No, not to Blackstable," Rosie smiled. "I don't know that I'd care to go there just yet. To Haversham. Mother comes over to meet me. I stay at the hotel where I used to work."

She was never a great talker. Often when, the night being fine, we decided to walk back from the music-hall at which we had been spending the evening, she never opened her mouth. But her silence was intimate and comfortable. It did not exclude you from thoughts that engaged her apart from you; it included you in a pervasive well-being.

I was talking about her once to Lionel Hillier and I said to him that I could not understand how she had turned from the fresh pleasant-looking young woman I had first known at Blackstable into the lovely creature whose beauty now practically everyone acknowledged. (There were people who made reservations. "Of course she has a very good figure," they said, "but it's not the sort of face I very much admire personally." And others said: "Oh, yes, a very pretty woman; but it's a pity she hasn't a little more distinction.")

"I can explain that to you in half a jiffy," said Lionel Hillier. "She was only a fresh, buxom wench when you first met her. I made her beauty."

I forget what my answer was, but I know it was ribald.

"All right. That just shows you don't know anything about beauty. No one ever thought very much of Rosie till I saw her like the sun shining silver. It wasn't till I painted it that anyone knew that her hair was the most lovely thing in the world."

"Did you make her neck and her breasts and her carriage and her bones?" I asked.

"Yes, damn you, that's just what I did do."

When Hillier talked of Rosie in front of her she listened to him with a smiling gravity. A little flush came into her pale cheeks. I think that at first when he spoke to her of her beauty she believed he was just making game of her; but when she found out that he wasn't, when he painted her silvery gold, it had no particular effect on her. She was a trifle amused, pleased of course, and a little surprised, but it did not turn her head. She thought him a little mad. I often wondered whether there was anything between them. I could not forget all I had heard of Rosie at Blackstable and what I had seen in the vicarage garden; I wondered about Quentin Forde, too, and Harry Retford. I used to watch them with her. She was not exactly familiar with them, comradely rather; she used to make her appointments with them quite openly in anybody's hearing; and when she looked at them it was with that mischievous, childlike smile which I had now discovered held such a mysterious beauty. Sometimes when we were sitting side by side in a music-hall I looked at her face; I do not think I was in love with her, I merely enjoyed the sensation of sitting quietly beside her and looking at the pale gold of her hair and the pale gold of her skin. Of course Lionel Hillier was right; the strange thing was that this gold did give one a strange moonlight feeling. She had the serenity of a summer evening when the light fades slowly from the unclouded sky. There was nothing dull in her immense placidity; it was as living as the sea when under the August sun it lay calm and shining along the Kentish coast. She reminded me of a sonatina by an old Italian composer with its wistfulness in which there is yet an urbane flippancy and its light rippling gaiety in which echoes still the trembling of a sigh. Sometimes, feeling my eyes on her, she would turn round and for a moment or two look me full in the face. She did not speak. I did not know of what she was thinking.

Once, I remember, I fetched her at Limpus Road, and the maid, telling me she was not ready, asked me to wait in the parlour. She came in. She was in black velvet, with a picture hat covered with ostrich feathers (we were going to the Pavilion and she had dressed up for it) and she looked so lovely that it took my breath away. I was staggered. The clothes of that day gave a woman dignity and there was something amazingly attractive in the way her virginal beauty (sometimes she looked like the exquisite statue of Psyche in the museum at Naples) contrasted with the stateliness of her gown. She had a trait that I think must be very rare: the skin under her eyes, faintly blue, was all dewy. Sometimes I could not persuade myself that it was natural, and once I asked her if she had rubbed vaseline under her eyes. That was just the effect it gave. She smiled, took a handkerchief and handed it to me.

"Rub them and see," she said.

Then one night when we had walked home from the Canterbury, and I was leaving her at her door, when I held out my hand she laughed a little, a low chuckle it was, and leaned forward.

"You old silly," she said.

She kissed me on the mouth. It was not a hurried peck, nor was it a kiss of passion. Her lips, those very full red lips of hers, rested on mine long enough for me to be conscious of their shape and their warmth and their softness. Then she withdrew them, but without hurry, in silence pushed open the door, slipped inside and left me. I was so startled that I had not been able to say anything. I accepted her kiss stupidly. I remained inert. I turned away and walked back to my lodgings. I seemed to hear still in my ears Rosie's laughter. It was not contemptuous or wounding, but frank and affectionate; it was as though she laughed because she was fond of me.

CHAPTER XVI

I DID not go out with Rosie again for more than a week. She was going down to Haversham to spend a night with her mother. She had various engagements in London. Then she asked me if I would go to the Haymarket Theatre with her. The play was a success and free seats were not to be had, so we made up our minds to go in the pit. We had a steak and a glass of beer at the Café Monico and then stood with the crowd. In those days there was no orderly queue and when the doors were opened there was a mad rush and scramble to get in. We were hot and breathless and somewhat battered when at last we pushed our way into our seats.

We walked back through St. James's Park. The night was so lovely that we sat down on a bench. In the starlight Rosie's face and her fair hair glowed softly. She was suffused, as it were (I express it awkwardly, but I do not know how to describe the emotion she gave me) with a friendliness at once candid and tender. She was like a silvery flower of the night that only gave its perfume to the moonbeams. I slipped my arm round her waist and she turned her face to mine. This time it was I who kissed. She did not move; her soft red lips submitted to the pressure of mine with a calm, intense passivity as the water of a lake accepts the light of the moon. I don't know how long we stayed there.

"I'm awfully hungry," she said suddenly.

"So am I," I laughed.

"Couldn't we go and have some fish and chips somewhere?"

"Rather."

In those days I knew my way very well about Westminster, not yet a fashionable quarter for parliamentary and otherwise cultured persons, but slummy and down-at-heel; and after we had come out of the park, crossing Victoria Street, I led Rosie to a fried fish shop in Horseferry Row. It was late and the only other person there was the driver of a four-wheeler waiting outside. We ordered our fish and chips and a bottle of beer. A poor woman came in and bought two penn'orth of mixed and took it away with her in a piece of paper. We ate with appetite.

Our way back to Rosie's led through Vincent Square and as we passed my house I asked her:

"Won't you come in for a minute? You've never seen my rooms."

"What about your landlady? I don't want to get you into trouble."

"Oh, she sleeps like a rock."

"I'll come in for a little."

I slipped my key into the lock and because the passage was dark took Rosie's hand to lead her in. I lit the gas in my sitting-room. She took off her hat and vigorously scratched her head. Then she looked for a glass, but I was very artistic and had taken down the mirror that was over the chimney-piece and there was no means in the room for anyone to see what he looked like.

"Come into my bedroom," I said. "There's a glass there."

I opened the door and lit the candle. Rosie followed me in and I held it up so that she should be able to see herself. I looked at her in the glass as she arranged her hair. She took two or three pins out, which she put in her mouth, and, taking one of my brushes, brushed her hair up from the nape of her neck. She twisted it, patted it, and put back the pins, and as she was intent on this her eyes caught mine in the glass and she smiled at me. When she had replaced the last pin she turned and faced me; she did not say anything; she looked at me tranquilly, still with that little friendly smile in her blue eyes. I put down the candle. The room was very small and the dressing-table was by the bed. She raised her hand and softly stroked my cheek.

I wish now that I had not started to write this book in the first person singular. It is all very well when you can show yourself in an amiable or touching light, and nothing can be more effective than the modest heroic or pathetic humorous which in this mode is much cultivated; it is charming to write about yourself when you see on the reader's eyelash the glittering tear and on his lips the tender smile; but it is not so nice when you have to exhibit yourself as a plain damned fool.

A little while ago I read in the *Evening Standard* an article by Mr. Evelyn Waugh in the course of which he remarked that to write novels in the first person was a contemptible practice. I wish he had explained why, but he merely threw out the statement with just the same take-it-or-leave-it casualness as Euclid used when he made his celebrated observation about parallel straight lines. I was much concerned and forthwith asked Alroy Kear (who reads everything, even the books he writes prefaces for) to recommend to me some works on the art of fiction. On his advice I read *The Craft of Fiction* by Mr. Percy Lubbock, from which I learned that the only way to write novels was like Henry James; after that I read *Aspects of the Novel* by Mr. E. M. Forster, from which I learned that the only way to write novels was like Mr. E. M. Forster; then I read *The Structure of the Novel* by Mr. Edwin Muir, from which I learned nothing at all. In none of them could I discover anything to the point at issue. All the same I can find one reason why certain novelists, such as Defoe, Sterne, Thackeray, Dickens, Emily Brontë and Proust, well known in their day but now doubtless forgotten, have used the method that Mr. Evelyn Waugh reprehends. As we grow older we become more conscious of the complexity, incoherence and unreasonableness of human beings; this indeed is the only excuse that offers for the middle-aged or elderly writer, whose thoughts should more properly be turned to graver matters, occupying himself with the trivial concerns of imaginary people. For if the proper study of mankind is man it is evidently more sensible to occupy yourself with the coherent, substantial and significant creatures of fiction than with the irrational and shadowy figures of real life. Sometimes the novelist feels himself like God and is prepared to tell you everything about his characters; sometimes, however, he does not; and then he tells you not everything that is to be known about them but the little he knows himself; and since as we grow older we feel ourselves less and less like God I should not be surprised to learn that with advancing years the novelist grows less and less inclined to describe more than his own experience has given him. The first person singular is a very useful device for this limited purpose.

Rosie raised her hand and softly stroked my face. I do not know why I should have behaved as I then did; it was not at all how I had seen myself behaving on such an occasion. A sob broke from my tight throat. I do not know whether it was because I was shy and lonely (not lonely in the body, for I spent all day at the hospital with all kinds of people, but lonely in the spirit) or because my desire was so great, but I began to cry. I felt terribly ashamed of myself; I tried to control myself, I couldn't; the tears welled up in my eyes and poured down my cheeks. Rosie saw them and gave a little gasp.

"Oh, honey, what is it? What's the matter? Don't. Don't!"

She put her arms round my neck and began to cry too, and she kissed my lips and my eyes and my wet cheeks. She undid her bodice and lowered my head till it rested on her bosom. She stroked my smooth face. She rocked me back and forth as though I were a child in her arms. I kissed her breasts and I kissed the white column of her neck; and she slipped out of her bodice and out of her skirt and her petticoats and I held her for a moment by her corseted waist; then she undid it, holding her breath for an instant to enable her to do so, and stood before me in her shift. When I put my hands on her sides I could feel the ribbing of the skin from the pressure of the corsets.

"Blow out the candle," she whispered.

It was she who awoke me when the dawn peering through the curtains revealed the shape of the bed and of the wardrobe against the darkness of the lingering night. She woke me by kissing me on the mouth and her hair falling over my face tickled me.

"I must get up," she said. "I don't want your landlady to see me."

"There's plenty of time."

Her breasts when she leaned over me were heavy on my chest. In a little while she got out of bed. I lit the candle. She turned to the glass and tied up her hair and then she looked for a moment at her naked body. Her waist was naturally small; though so well developed she was very slender; her breasts were straight and firm and they stood out from the chest as though carved in marble. It was a body made for the act of love. In the light of the candle, struggling now with the increasing day, it was all silvery gold; and the only colour was the rosy pink of the hard nipples.

We dressed in silence. She did not put on her corsets again, but rolled them up and I wrapped them in a piece of newspaper. We tiptoed along the passage and when I opened the door and we stepped out into the street the dawn ran to meet us like a cat leaping up the steps. The square was empty; already the sun was shining on the eastern windows. I felt as young as the day. We walked arm-in-arm till we came to the corner of Limpus Road.

"Leave me here," said Rosie. "One never knows."

I kissed her and I watched her walk away. She walked rather

slowly, with the firm tread of the country woman who likes to feel the good earth under her feet, and held herself erect. I could not go back to bed. I strolled on till I came to the Embankment. The river had the bright hues of the early morning. A brown barge came down-stream and passed under Vauxhall Bridge. In a dinghy two men were rowing close to the side. I was hungry.

CHAPTER XVII

AFTER that for more than a year whenever Rosie came out with me she used on the way home to drop into my rooms, sometimes for an hour, sometimes till the breaking day warned us that the slaveys would soon be scrubbing the doorsteps. I have a recollection of warm sunny mornings when the tired air of London had a welcome freshness, and of our footfalls that seemed so noisy in the empty streets, and then of scurrying along huddled under an umbrella, silent but gay, when the winter brought cold and rain. The policeman on point duty gave us a stare as we passed, sometimes of suspicion; but sometimes also there was a twinkle of comprehension in his eyes. Now and then we would see a homeless creature huddled up asleep in a portico and Rosie gave my arm a friendly little pressure when (chiefly for show and because I wanted to make a good impression on her, for my shillings were scarce) I placed a piece of silver on a shapeless lap or in a skinny fist. Rosie made me very happy. I had a great affection for her. She was easy and comfortable. She had a placidity of temper that communicated itself to the people she was with; you shared her pleasure in the passing moment.

Before I became her lover I had often asked myself if she was the mistress of the others, Forde, Harry Retford and Hillier, and afterward I questioned her. She kissed me.

"Don't be so silly. I like them, you know that. I like to go out with them, but that's all."

I wanted to ask her if she had been the mistress of George Kemp, but I did not like to. Though I had never seen her in a temper, I had a notion that she had one and I vaguely felt that this was a question that might anger her. I did not want to give her the opportunity of saying things so wounding that I could not forgive her. I was young, only just over one-and-twenty, Quentin

Forde and the others seemed old to me; it did not seem unnatural to me that to Rosie they were only friends. It gave me a little thrill of pride to think that I was her lover. When I used to look at her chatting and laughing with all and sundry at tea on Saturday afternoons, I glowed with self-satisfaction. I thought of the nights we passed together and I was inclined to laugh at the people who were so ignorant of my great secret. But sometimes I thought that Lionel Hillier looked at me in a quizzical way, as if he were enjoying a good joke at my expense, and I asked myself uneasily if Rosie had told him that she was having an affair with me. I wondered if there was anything in my manner that betrayed me. I told Rosie that I was afraid Hillier suspected something; she looked at me with those blue eyes of hers that always seemed ready to smile.

"Don't bother about it," she said. "He's got a nasty mind."

I had never been intimate with Quentin Forde. He looked upon me as a dull and insignificant young man (which of course I was) and though he had always been civil he had never taken any notice of me. I thought it could only be my fancy that now he began to be a little more frigid with me than before. But one day Harry Retford to my surprise asked me to dine with him and go to the play. I told Rosie.

"Oh, of course you must go. He'll give you an awfully good time. Good old Harry, he always makes me laugh."

So I dined with him. He made himself very pleasant and I was impressed to hear him talk of actors and actresses. He had a sarcastic humour and was very funny at the expense of Quentin Forde, whom he did not like; I tried to get him to talk of Rosie, but he had nothing to say of her. He seemed to be a gay dog. With leers and laughing innuendoes he gave me to understand that he was a devil with the girls. I could not but ask myself if he was standing me this dinner because he knew I was Rosie's lover and so felt friendly disposed toward me. But if he knew, of course the others knew too. I hope I did not show it, but in my heart I certainly felt somewhat patronising toward them.

Then in winter, toward the end of January, someone new appeared at Limpus Road. This was a Dutch Jew named Jack Kuyper, a diamond merchant from Amsterdam, who was spending a few weeks in London on business. I do not know how he had come to know the Driffields and whether it was esteem for the author that brought him to the house, but it was certainly not that

which caused him to come again. He was a tall, stout, dark man
with a bald head and a big hooked nose, a man of fifty, but of a
powerful appearance, sensual, determined and jovial. He made no
secret of his admiration for Rosie. He was rich apparently, for he
sent her roses every day; she chid him for his extravagance, but
was flattered. I could not bear him. He was blatant and loud.
I hated his fluent conversation in perfect but foreign English; I
hated the extravagant compliments he paid Rosie; I hated the
heartiness with which he treated her friends. I found that Quentin
Forde liked him as little as I; we almost became cordial with one
another.

"Mercifully he's not staying long." Quentin Forde pursed his
lips and raised his black eyebrows; with his white hair and long
sallow face he looked incredibly gentlemanly. "Women are
always the same; they adore a bounder."

"He's so frightfully vulgar," I complained.

"That is his charm," said Quentin Forde.

For the next two or three weeks I saw next to nothing of Rosie.
Jack Kuyper took her out night after night, to this smart restaurant
and that, to one play after another. I was vexed and hurt.

"He doesn't know anyone in London," said Rosie, trying to
soothe my ruffled feelings. "He wants to see everything he can
while he's here. It wouldn't be very nice for him to go alone all
the time. He's only here for a fortnight more."

I did not see the object of this self-sacrifice on her part.

"But don't you think he's awful?" I said.

"No. I think he's fun. He makes me laugh."

"Don't you know that he's absolutely gone on you?"

"Well, it pleases him and it doesn't do me any harm."

"He's old and fat and horrible. It gives me the creeps to look
at him."

"I don't think he's so bad," said Rosie.

"You couldn't have anything to do with him," I protested. "I
mean, he's such an awful cad."

Rosie scratched her head. It was an unpleasant habit of hers.

"It's funny how different foreigners are from English people,"
she said.

I was thankful when Jack Kuyper went back to Amsterdam.
Rosie had promised to dine with me the day after and as a treat
we arranged to dine in Soho. She fetched me in a hansom and we
drove on.

"Has your horrible old man gone?" I asked.

"Yes," she laughed.

I put my arm round her waist. (I have elsewhere remarked how much more convenient the hansom was for this pleasant and indeed almost essential act in human intercourse than the taxi of the present day, so unwillingly refrain from labouring the point.) I put my arm round her waist and kissed her. Her lips were like spring flowers. We arrived. I hung my hat and my coat (it was very long and tight at the waist, with a velvet collar and velvet cuffs; very smart) on a peg and asked Rosie to give me her cape.

"I'm going to keep it on," she said.

"You'll be awfully hot. You'll only catch cold when we go out."

"I don't care. It's the first time I've worn it. Don't you think it's lovely. And look: the muff matches."

I gave the cape a glance. It was of fur. I did not know it was sable.

"It looks awfully rich. How did you get that?"

"Jack Kuyper gave it to me. We went and bought it yesterday just before he went away." She stroked the smooth fur; she was as happy with it as a child with a toy. "How much d'you think it cost?"

"I haven't an idea."

"Two hundred and sixty pounds. Do you know I've never had anything that cost so much in my life? I told him it was far too much, but he wouldn't listen. He made me have it."

Rosie chuckled with glee and her eyes shone. But I felt my face go stiff and a shiver run down my spine.

"Won't Driffield think it's rather funny, Kuyper giving you a fur cape that costs all that?" said I, trying to make my voice sound natural.

Rosie's eyes danced mischievously.

"You know what Ted is, he never notices anything; if he says anything about it I shall tell him I gave twenty pounds for it in a pawnshop. He won't know any better." She rubbed her face against the collar. "It's so soft. And everyone can see it cost money."

I tried to eat and in order not to show the bitterness in my heart I did my best to keep the conversation going on one topic or another. Rosie did not much mind what I said. She could only think of her new cape and every other minute her eyes returned

to the muff that she insisted on holding on her lap. She looked
at it with an affection in which there was something lazy, sensual
and self-complacent. I was angry with her. I thought her stupid
and common.

"You look like a cat that's swallowed a canary," I could not
help snapping.

She only giggled.

"That's what I feel like."

Two hundred and sixty pounds was an enormous sum to me.
I did not know one *could* pay so much for a cape. I lived on
fourteen pounds a month and not at all badly either; and in case
any reader is not a ready reckoner I will add that this is one
hundred and sixty-eight pounds a year. I could not believe that
anyone would make as expensive a present as that from pure
friendship; what did it mean but that Jack Kuyper had been
sleeping with Rosie, night after night, all the time he was in
London, and now when he went away was paying her? How could
she accept it? Didn't she see how it degraded her? Didn't she see
how frightfully vulgar it was of him to give her a thing that cost
so much? Apparently not, for she said to me:

"It was nice of him, wasn't it? But then Jews are always
generous."

"I suppose he could afford it," I said.

"Oh, yes, he's got lots of money. He said he wanted to give
me something before he went away and asked me what I wanted.
Well, I said, I could do with a cape and a muff to match, but I
never thought he'd buy me anything like this. When we went
into the shop I asked them to show me something in astrakhan,
but he said: No, sable, and the best money can buy. And when
we saw this he absolutely insisted on my having it."

I thought of her with her white body, her skin so milky, in the
arms of that old fat gross man and his thick loose lips kissing hers.
And then I knew that the suspicion that I had refused to believe
was true; I knew that when she went out to dinner with Quentin
Forde and Harry Retford and Lionel Hillier she went to bed with
them just as she came to bed with me. I could not speak; I knew
that if I did I should insult her. I do not think I was jealous so
much as mortified. I felt that she had been making a damned fool
of me. I used all my determination to prevent the bitter gibes
from passing my lips.

We went on to the theatre. I could not listen to the play. I could only feel against my arm the smoothness of the sable cape; I could only see her fingers forever stroking the muff. I could have borne the thought of the others; it was Jack Kuyper who horrified me. How could she? It was abominable to be poor. I longed to have enough money to tell her that if she would send the fellow back his beastly furs I would give her better ones instead. At last she noticed that I did not speak.

"You're very silent to-night."

"Am I?"

"Aren't you well?"

"Perfectly."

She gave me a sidelong look. I did not meet her eyes, but I knew they were smiling with that smile at once mischievous and childlike that I knew so well. She said nothing more. At the end of the play, since it was raining, we took a hansom and I gave the driver her address in Limpus Road. She did not speak till we got to Victoria Street, then she said:

"Don't you want me to come home with you?"

"Just as you like."

She lifted up the trap and gave the driver my address. She took my hand and held it, but I remained inert. I looked straight out of the window with angry dignity. When we reached Vincent Square I handed her out of the cab and let her into the house without a word. I took off my hat and coat. She threw her cape and her muff on the sofa.

"Why are you so sulky?" she asked, coming up to me.

"I'm not sulky," I answered, looking away.

She took my face in her two hands.

"How can you be so silly? Why should you be angry because Jack Kuyper gives me a fur cape? You can't afford to give me one, can you?"

"Of course I can't."

"And Ted can't either. You can't expect me to refuse a fur cape that cost two hundred and sixty pounds. I've wanted a fur cape all my life. It means nothing to Jack."

"You don't expect me to believe that he gave it you just out of friendship."

"He might have. Anyhow, he's gone back to Amsterdam, and who knows when he'll come back?"

"He isn't the only one, either."

I looked at Rosie now, with angry, hurt, resentful eyes; she smiled at me, and I wish I knew how to describe the sweet kindliness of her beautiful smile; her voice was exquisitely gentle.

"Oh, my dear, why d'you bother your head about any others? What harm does it do you? Don't I give you a good time? Aren't you happy when you're with me?"

"Awfully."

"Well, then. It's so silly to be fussy and jealous. Why not be happy with what you can get? Enjoy yourself while you have the chance, I say; we shall all be dead in a hundred years and what will anything matter then? Let's have a good time while we can."

She put her arms round my neck and pressed her lips against mine. I forgot my wrath. I only thought of her beauty and her enveloping kindness.

"You must take me as I am, you know," she whispered.

"All right," I said.

CHAPTER XVIII

During all this time I saw really very little of Driffield. His editorship occupied much of his day and in the evening he wrote. He was, of course, there every Saturday afternoon, amiable and ironically amusing; he appeared glad to see me and chatted with me for a little while pleasantly of indifferent things; but naturally most of his attention was given to guests older and more important than I. But I had a feeling that he was growing more aloof; he was no longer the jolly, rather vulgar companion that I had known at Blackstable. Perhaps it was only my increasing sensibility that discerned as it were an invisible barrier that existed between him and the people he chaffed and joked with. It was as though he lived a life of the imagination that made the life of every day a little shadowy. He was asked to speak now and then at public dinners. He joined a literary club. He began to know a good many people outside the narrow circle into which his writing had drawn him, and he was increasingly asked to luncheon and tea by the ladies who like to gather about them distinguished authors. Rosie was asked too, but seldom went; she said she didn't care for parties, and after all they didn't want her, they only wanted Ted. I think she was shy and felt out of it. It may be that hostesses had more than once let her see how tiresome they thought it that she must be included; and after inviting her because it was polite, ignored her because to be polite irked them.

It was just about then that Edward Driffield published *The Cup of Life*. It is not my business to criticise his works, and of late as much has been written about them as must satisfy the appetite of any ordinary reader; but I will permit myself to say that *The Cup of Life*, though certainly not the most celebrated of his books, nor the most popular, is to my mind the most interesting. It has a cold ruthlessness that in all the sentimentality of English fiction strikes an original note. It is refreshing and astringent. It tastes of tart apples. It sets your teeth on edge, but it has a subtle, bitter-sweet savour that is very agreeable to the palate. Of all Driffield's books it is the only one I should like to have written. The scene of the child's death, terrible and heartrending, but written without slop or sickliness, and the curious incident that follows it, cannot easily be forgotten by anyone who has read them.

It was this part of the book that caused the sudden storm that burst on the wretched Driffield's head. For a few days after publication it looked as though it would run its course like the rest of his novels, namely that it would have substantial reviews, laudatory on the whole but with reservations, and that the sales would be respectable, but modest. Rosie told me that he expected to make three hundred pounds out of it and was talking of renting a house on the river for the summer. The first two or three notices were noncommittal; then in one of the morning papers appeared a violent attack. There was a column of it. The book was described as gratuitously offensive, obscene, and the publishers were rated for putting it before the public. Harrowing pictures were drawn of the devastating effect it must have on the youth of England. It was described as an insult to womanhood. The reviewer protested against the possibility of such a work falling into the hands of young boys and innocent maidens. Other papers followed suit. The more foolish demanded that the book should be suppressed and some asked themselves gravely if this was not a case where the public prosecutor might with fitness intervene. Condemnation was universal; if here and there a courageous writer, accustomed to the more realistic tone of continental fiction, asserted that Edward Driffield had never written anything better, he was ignored. His honest opinion was ascribed to a base desire to play to the gallery. The libraries barred the book and the lessors of the railway bookstalls refused to stock it.

All this was naturally very unpleasant for Edward Driffield, but he bore it with philosophic calm. He shrugged his shoulders.

"They say it isn't true," he smiled. "They can go to hell. It is true."

He was supported in this trial by the fidelity of his friends. To admire *The Cup of Life* became a mark of æsthetic acumen: to be shocked by it was to confess yourself a philistine. Mrs. Barton Trafford had no hesitation in saying that it was a masterpiece, and though this wasn't quite the moment for Barton's article in the *Quarterly*, her faith in Edward Driffield's future remained unshaken. It is strange (and instructive) to read now, the book that created such a sensation; there is not a word that could bring a blush to the cheek of the most guileless, not an episode that could cause the novel reader of the present day to turn a hair.

CHAPTER XIX

ABOUT six months later, when the excitement over *The Cup of Life* had subsided and Driffield had already begun the novel which he published under the name of *By Their Fruits*, I, being then an in-patient dresser and in my fourth year, in the course of my duties went one day into the main hall of the hospital to await the surgeon whom I was accompanying on his round of the wards. I glanced at the rack in which letters were placed, for sometimes people, not knowing my address in Vincent Square, wrote to me at the hospital. I was surprised to find a telegram for me. It ran as follows:

Please come and see me at five o'clock this afternoon without fail. Important.   *Isabel Trafford.*

I wondered what she wanted me for. I had met her perhaps a dozen times during the last two years, but she had never taken any notice of me, and I had never been to her house. I knew that men were scarce at tea-time and a hostess, short of them at the last moment, might think that a young medical student was better than nothing; but the wording of the telegram hardly suggested a party.

The surgeon for whom I dressed was prosy and verbose. It was not till past five that I was free and then it took me a good twenty minutes to get down to Chelsea. Mrs. Barton Trafford lived in a block of flats on the Embankment. It was nearly six when I rang at her door and asked if she was at home. But when I was ushered into her drawing-room and began to explain why I was late she cut me short.

"We supposed you couldn't get away. It doesn't matter."

Her husband was there.

"I expect he'd like a cup of tea," he said.

"Oh, I think it's rather late for tea, isn't it?" She looked at me gently, her mild, rather fine eyes full of kindness. "You don't want any tea, do you?"

I was thirsty and hungry, for my lunch had consisted of a scone and butter and a cup of coffee, but I did not like to say so. I refused tea.

"Do you know Allgood Newton?" asked Mrs. Barton Trafford, with a gesture towards a man who had been sitting in a big arm-chair when I was shown in, and now got up. "I expect you've met him at Edward's."

I had. He did not come often, but his name was familiar to me and I remembered him. He made me very nervous and I do not think I had ever spoken to him. Though now completely forgotten, in those days he was the best-known critic in England. He was a large, fat, blond man, with a fleshy white face, pale blue eyes and greying fair hair. He generally wore a pale blue tie to bring out the colour of his eyes. He was very amiable to the authors he met at Driffield's and said charming and flattering things to them, but when they were gone he was very amusing at their expense. He spoke in a low, even voice, with an apt choice of words: no one could with more point tell a malicious story about a friend.

Allgood Newton shook hands with me and Mrs. Barton Trafford, with her ready sympathy, anxious to put me at my ease, took me by the hand and made me sit on the sofa beside her. The tea was still on the table and she took a jam sandwich and delicately nibbled it.

"Have you seen the Driffields lately?" she asked me as though making conversation.

"I was there last Saturday."

"You haven't seen either of them since?"

"No."

Mrs. Barton Trafford looked from Allgood Newton to her husband and back again as though mutely demanding their help.

"Nothing will be gained by circumlocution, Isabel," said Newton, a faintly malicious twinkle in his eye, in his fat precise way.

Mrs. Barton Trafford turned to me.

"Then you don't know that Mrs. Driffield has run away from her husband."

"What!"

I was flabbergasted. I could not believe my ears.

"Perhaps it would be better if you told him the facts, Allgood," said Mrs. Trafford.

The critic leaned back in his chair and placed the tips of the fingers of one hand against the tips of the fingers of the other. He spoke with unction.

"I had to see Edward Driffield last night about a literary article that I am doing for him and after dinner, since the night was fine, I thought I would walk round to his house. He was expecting me; and I knew besides that he never went out at night except for some function as important as the Lord Mayor's banquet or the Academy dinner. Imagine my surprise then, nay, my utter and complete bewilderment, when as I approached I saw the door of his house open and Edward in person emerge. You know of course that Immanuel Kant was in the habit of taking his daily walk at a certain hour with such punctuality that the inhabitants of Königsberg were accustomed to set their watches by the event and when once he came out of his house an hour earlier than usual they turned pale, for they knew that this could only mean that some terrible thing had happened. They were right; Immanuel Kant had just received intelligence of the fall of the Bastille."

Allgood Newton paused for a moment to mark the effect of his anecdote. Mrs. Barton Trafford gave him her understanding smile.

"I did not envisage so world-shaking a catastrophe as this when I saw Edward hurrying towards me, but it immediately occurred to me that something untoward was afoot. He carried neither cane nor gloves. He wore his working coat, a venerable garment in black alpaca, and a wide-awake hat. There was something wild in his mien and distraught in his bearing. I asked myself, knowing the vicissitudes of the conjugal state, whether a matrimonial difference had driven him headlong from the house or whether he was hastening to a letter-box in order to post a letter. He sped like Hector flying the noblest of the Greeks. He did not seem to see me and the suspicion flashed across my mind that he did not want to. I stopped him. 'Edward,' I said. He looked startled. For a moment I could have sworn he did not know who I was. 'What avenging furies urge you with such hot haste through the rakish purlieus of Pimlico?' I asked. 'Oh, it's you,' he said. 'Where are you going?' I asked. 'Nowhere,' he replied."

At this rate I thought Allgood Newton would never finish his story and Mrs. Hudson would be vexed with me for turning up to dinner half an hour late.

"I told him on what errand I had come, and proposed that we should return to his house where we could more conveniently discuss the question that perturbed me. 'I'm too restless to go home,' he said; 'let's walk. You can talk to me as we go along.' Assenting, I turned round and we began to walk; but his pace was so rapid that I had to beg him to moderate it. Even Dr. Johnson could not have carried on a conversation when he was walking down Fleet Street at the speed of an express train. Edward's appearance was so peculiar and his manner so agitated that I thought it wise to lead him through the less frequented streets. I talked to him of my article. The subject that occupied me was more copious than had at first sight appeared, and I was doubtful whether after all I could do justice to it in the columns of a weekly journal. I put the matter before him fully and fairly and asked him his opinion. 'Rosie has left me,' he answered. For a moment I did not know what he was talking about, but in a trice it occurred to me that he was speaking of the buxom and not unprepossessing female from whose hands I had on occasion accepted a cup of tea. From his tone I divined that he expected condolence from me rather than felicitation."

Allgood Newton paused again and his blue eyes twinkled.

"You're wonderful, Allgood," said Mrs. Barton Trafford.

"Priceless," said her husband.

"Realising that the occasion demanded sympathy, I said: 'My dear fellow.' He interrupted me. 'I had a letter by the last post,' he said. 'She's run away with Lord George Kemp.' "

I gasped, but said nothing. Mrs. Trafford gave me a quick look.

" 'Who is Lord George Kemp?' 'He's a Blackstable man,' he replied. I had little time to think. I determined to be frank.

'You're well rid of her,' I said. 'Allgood!' he cried. I stopped and put my hand on his arm. 'You must know that she was deceiving you with all your friends. Her behaviour was a public scandal. My dear Edward, let us face the fact: your wife was nothing but a common strumpet.' He snatched his arm away from me and gave a sort of low roar, like an orang-utan in the forests of Borneo forcibly deprived of a coconut, and before I could stop him he broke away and fled. I was so startled that I could do nothing but listen to his cries and his hurrying footsteps."

"You shouldn't have let him go," said Mrs. Barton Trafford. "In the state he was he might have thrown himself in the Thames."

"The thought occurred to me, but I noticed that he did not run in the direction of the river, but plunged into the meaner streets of the neighbourhood in which we had been walking. And I reflected also that there is no example in literary history of an author committing suicide while engaged on the composition of a literary work. Whatever his tribulations, he is unwilling to leave to posterity an uncompleted opus."

I was astounded at what I heard and shocked and dismayed; but I was worried too because I could not make out why Mrs. Trafford had sent for me. She knew me much too little to think that the story could be of any particular interest to me; nor would she have troubled to let me hear it as a piece of news.

"Poor Edward," she said. "Of course no one can deny that it is a blessing in disguise, but I'm afraid he'll take it very much to heart. Fortunately he's done nothing rash." She turned to me. "As soon as Mr. Newton told us about it I went round to Limpus Road. Edward was out, but the maid said he'd only just left; that means that he must have gone home between the time he ran away from Allgood and this morning. You'll wonder why I asked you to come and see me."

I did not answer. I waited for her to go on.

"It was at Blackstable you first knew the Driffields, wasn't it? You can tell us who is this Lord George Kemp. Edward said he was a Blackstable man."

"He's middle-aged. He's got a wife and two sons. They're as old as I am."

"But I don't understand who he can be. I can't find him in Debrett."

I almost laughed.

"Oh, he's not really a lord. He's the local coal merchant. They call him Lord George at Blackstable because he's so grand. It's just a joke."

"The quiddity of bucolic humour is often a trifle obscure to the uninitiated," said Allgood Newton.

"We must all help dear Edward in every way we can," said Mrs. Barton Trafford. Her eyes rested on me thoughtfully. "If Kemp has run away with Rosie Driffield he must have left his wife."

"I suppose so," I replied.

"Will you do something very kind?"

"If I can."

"Will you go down to Blackstable and find out exactly what has happened? I think we ought to get in touch with the wife."

I have never been very fond of interfering in other people's affairs.

"I don't know how I could do that," I answered.

"Couldn't you see her?"

"No, I couldn't."

If Mrs. Barton Trafford thought my reply blunt she did not show it. She smiled a little.

"At all events that can be left over. The urgent thing is to go down and find out about Kemp. I shall try to see Edward this evening. I can't bear the thought of his staying on in that odious house by himself. Barton and I have made up our minds to bring him here. We have a spare room and I'll arrange it so that he can work there. Don't you agree that that would be the best thing for him, Allgood?"

"Absolutely."

"There's no reason why he shouldn't stay here indefinitely, at all events for a few weeks, and then he can come away with us in the summer. We're going to Brittany. I'm sure he'd like that. It would be a thorough change for him."

"The immediate question," said Barton Trafford, fixing on me an eye nearly as kindly as his wife's, "is whether this young sawbones will go to Blackstable and find out what he can. We must know where we are. That is essential."

Barton Trafford excused his interest in archæology by a hearty manner and a jocose, even slangy way of speech.

"He couldn't refuse," said his wife, giving me a soft, appealing glance. "You won't refuse, will you? It's so important and you're the only person who can help us."

Of course she did not know that I was as anxious to find out what had happened as she; she could not tell what a bitter jealous pain stabbed my heart.

"I couldn't possibly get away from the hospital before Saturday," I said.

"That'll do. It's very good of you. All Edward's friends will be grateful to you. When shall you return?"

"I have to be back in London early on Monday morning."

"Then come and have tea with me in the afternoon. I shall await you with impatience. Thank God, that's settled. Now I must try and get hold of Edward."

I understood that I was dismissed. Allgood Newton took his leave and came downstairs with me.

"Our Isabel has *un petit air* of Catherine of Aragon to-day that I find vastly becoming," he murmured when the door was closed behind us. "This is a golden opportunity and I think we may safely trust our friend not to miss it. A charming woman with a heart of gold. *Vénus toute entière à sa proie attachée.*"

I did not understand what he meant, for what I have already told the reader about Mrs. Barton Trafford I only learned much later, but I realised that he was saying something vaguely malicious about her, and probably amusing, so I sniggered.

"I suppose your youth inclines you to what my good Dizzy named in an unlucky moment the gondola of London."

"I'm going to take a bus," I answered.

"Oh? Had you proposed to go by hansom I was going to ask you to be good enough to drop me on your way, but if you are going to use the homely conveyance which I in my old-fashioned manner still prefer to call an omnibus, I shall hoist my unwieldy carcase into a four-wheeler."

He signalled to one and gave me two flabby fingers to shake.

"I shall come on Monday to hear the result of what dear Henry would call your so exquisitely delicate mission."

CHAPTER XX

But it was years before I saw Allgood Newton again, for when I got to Blackstable I found a letter from Mrs. Barton Trafford (who had taken the precaution to note my address) asking me, for reasons that she would explain when she saw me, not to come to her flat but to meet her at six o'clock in the first-class waiting-room at Victoria Station. As soon then as I could get away from the hospital on Monday I made my way there, and after waiting for a while saw her come in. She came towards me with little tripping steps.

"Well, have you anything to tell me? Let us find a quiet corner and sit down."

We sought a place and found it.

"I must explain why I asked you to come here," she said. "Edward is staying with me. At first he did not want to come, but I persuaded him. But he's nervous and ill and irritable. I did not want to run the risk of his seeing you."

I told Mrs. Trafford the bare facts of my story and she listened attentively. Now and then she nodded her head. But I could not hope to make her understand the commotion I had found at Blackstable. The town was beside itself with excitement. Nothing so thrilling had happened there for years and no one could talk of anything else. Humpty-dumpty had had a great fall. Lord George Kemp had absconded. About a week before he had announced that he had to go up to London on business, and two days later a petition in bankruptcy was filed against him. It appeared that his building operations had not been successful, his attempt to make Blackstable into a frequented seaside resort meeting with no response, and he had been forced to raise money in every way he could. All kinds of rumours ran through the little town. Quite a number of small people who had entrusted their savings to him were faced with the loss of all they had. The details were vague, for neither my uncle nor my aunt knew anything of business matters, nor had I the knowledge to make what they told me comprehensible. But there was a mortgage on George Kemp's house and a bill of sale on his furniture. His wife was left without a penny. His two sons, lads of twenty and twenty-one, were in the coal business, but that too was involved in the general ruin. George Kemp had gone off with all the cash he could lay hands on, something like fifteen hundred pounds, they said, though how they knew I cannot imagine; and it was reported that a warrant had been issued for his arrest. It was supposed that he had left the country; some said he had gone to Australia and some to Canada.

"I hope they catch him," said my uncle. "He ought to get penal servitude for life."

The indignation was universal. They could not forgive him because he had always been so noisy and boisterous, because he had chaffed them and stood them drinks and given them garden parties, because he had driven such a smart trap and worn his brown billycock hat at such a rakish angle. But it was on Sunday night after church in the vestry that the churchwarden told my uncle the worst. For the last two years he had been meeting Rosie Driffield at Haversham almost every week and they had been spending the night together at a public-house. The licensee of this had put money into one of Lord George's wildcat schemes, and on discovering that he had lost it blurted out the whole story. He could have borne it if Lord George had defrauded others, but that he should defraud him who had done him a good turn and whom he looked upon as a chum, that was the limit.

"I expect they've run away together," said my uncle.

"I shouldn't be surprised," said the churchwarden.

After supper, while the housemaid was clearing away, I went into the kitchen to talk to Mary-Ann. She had been at church and had heard the story too. I cannot believe that the congregation had listened very attentively to my uncle's sermon.

"The vicar says they've run away together," I said. I had not breathed a word of what I knew.

"Why, of course they 'ave," said Mary-Ann. "He was the only man she ever really fancied. He only 'ad to lift 'is little finger and she'd leave anyone no matter who it was."

I lowered my eyes. I was suffering from bitter mortification; and I was angry with Rosie; I thought she had behaved very badly to me.

"I suppose we shall never see her again," I said.

It gave me a pang to utter the words.

"I don't suppose we shall," said Mary-Ann cheerfully.

When I had told Mrs. Barton Trafford as much of this story as I thought she need know, she sighed, but whether from satisfaction or distress I had no notion.

"Well, that's the end of Rosie at all events," she said. She got up and held out her hand. "Why will these literary men make these unfortunate marriages? It's all very sad, very sad. Thank you so much for what you've done. We know where we are now. The great thing is that it shouldn't interfere with Edward's work."

Her remarks seemed a trifle disconnected to me. The fact was,

I have no doubt, that she was giving me not the smallest thought. I led her out of Victoria Station and put her into a bus that went down the King's Road, Chelsea; then I walked back to my lodgings.

CHAPTER XXI

I lost touch with Driffield. I was too shy to seek him out; I was busy with my examinations, and when I had passed them I went abroad. I remember vaguely to have seen in the paper that he had divorced Rosie. Nothing more was heard of her. Small sums reached her mother occasionally, ten or twenty pounds, and they came in a registered letter with a New York postmark; but no address was given, no message enclosed, and they were presumed to come from Rosie only because no one else could possibly send Mrs. Gann money. Then in the fullness of years Rosie's mother died, and it may be supposed that in some way the news reached her, for the letters ceased to come.

CHAPTER XXII

Alroy Kear and I, as arranged, met on Friday at Victoria Station to catch the five-ten to Blackstable. We made ourselves comfortable in opposite corners of a smoking compartment. From him I now learned roughly what had happened to Driffield after his wife ran away from him. Roy had in due course become very intimate with Mrs. Barton Trafford. Knowing him and remembering her, I realised that this was inevitable. I was not surprised to hear that he had travelled with her and Barton on the continent, sharing with them to the full their passion for Wagner, post-impressionist painting and baroque architecture. He had lunched assiduously at the flat in Chelsea and when advancing years and failing health had imprisoned Mrs. Trafford to her drawing-room, notwithstanding the many claims on his time he had gone regularly once a week to sit with her. He had a good heart. After her death he wrote an article about her in which with admirable emotion he did justice to her great gifts of sympathy and discrimination.

It pleased me to think that his kindliness should receive its due and unexpected reward, for Mrs. Barton Trafford had told him much about Edward Driffield that could not fail to be of service to him in the work of love on which he was now engaged. Mrs. Barton Trafford, exercising a gentle violence, not only took Edward Driffield into her house when the flight of his faithless wife left him what Roy could only describe by the French word *désemparé*, but persuaded him to stay for nearly a year. She gave him the loving care, the unfailing kindness and the intelligent understanding of a woman who combined feminine tact with masculine vigour, a heart of gold with an unerring eye for the main chance. It was in her flat that he finished *By Their Fruits*. She was justified in looking upon it as her book and the dedication to her is a proof that Driffield was not unmindful of his debt. She took him to Italy (with Barton of course, for Mrs. Trafford knew too well how malicious people were, to give occasion for scandal) and with a volume of Ruskin in her hand revealed to Edward Driffield the immortal beauties of that country. Then she found him rooms in the Temple and arranged little luncheons there, she acting very prettily the part of hostess, where he could receive the persons whom his increasing reputation attracted.

It must be admitted that this increasing reputation was very largely due to her. His great celebrity came only during his last years when he had long ceased to write, but the foundations of it were undoubtedly laid by Mrs. Trafford's untiring efforts. Not only did she inspire (and perhaps write not a little, for she had a dexterous pen) the article that Barton at last contributed to the *Quarterly* in which the claim was first made that Driffield must be ranked with the masters of British fiction, but as each book came out she organised its reception. She went here and there, seeing editors and, more important still, proprietors of influential organs; she gave soirées to which everyone was invited who could be of use. She persuaded Edward Driffield to give readings at the houses of the very great for charitable purposes; she saw to it that his photographs should appear in the illustrated weeklies; she revised personally any interview he gave. For ten years she was an indefatigable Press agent. She kept him steadily before the public.

Mrs. Barton Trafford had a grand time, but she did not get above herself. It was useless indeed to ask him to a party without her; he refused. And when she and Barton and Driffield were invited anywhere to dinner they came together and went together.

She never let him out of her sight. Hostesses might rave; they could take it or leave it. As a rule they took it. If Mrs. Barton Trafford happened to be a little out of temper it was through him she showed it, for while she remained charming, Edward Driffield would be uncommonly gruff. But she knew exactly how to draw him out and when the company was distinguished could make him brilliant. She was perfect with him. She never concealed from him her conviction that he was the greatest writer of his day; she not only referred to him invariably as the master, but, perhaps a little playfully and yet how flatteringly, addressed him always as such. To the end she retained something kittenish.

Then a terrible thing happened. Driffield caught pneumonia and was extremely ill; for some time his life was despaired of. Mrs. Barton Trafford did everything that such a woman could do, and would willingly have nursed him herself, but she was frail, she was indeed over sixty, and he had to have professional nurses. When at last he pulled through, the doctors said that he must go into the country, and since he was still extremely weak insisted that a nurse should go with him. Mrs. Trafford wanted him to go to Bournemouth so that she could run down for week-ends and see that everything was well with him, but Driffield had a fancy for Cornwall, and the doctors agreed that the mild airs of Penzance would suit him. One would have thought that a woman of Isabel Trafford's delicate intuition would have had some foreboding of ill. No. She let him go. She impressed on the nurse that she entrusted her with a grave responsibility; she placed in her hands, if not the future of English literature, at least the life and welfare of its most distinguished living representative. It was a priceless charge.

Three weeks later Edward Driffield wrote and told her that he had married his nurse by special licence.

I imagine that never did Mrs. Barton Trafford exhibit more preeminently her greatness of soul than in the manner in which she met this situation. Did she cry, Judas, Judas? Did she tear her hair and fall on the floor and kick her heels in an attack of hysterics? Did she turn on the mild and learned Barton and call him a blithering old fool? Did she inveigh against the faithlessness of men and the wantonness of women or did she relieve her wounded feelings by shouting at the top of her voice a string of those obscenities with which the alienists tell us the chastest females are surprisingly acquainted? Not at all. She wrote a charming letter of congratulation to Driffield and she wrote to his bride telling her that she was glad to think that now she would have two loving friends instead of one. She begged them both to come and stay with her on their return to London. She told everyone she met that the marriage had made her very, very happy, for Edward Driffield would soon be an old man and must have someone to take care of him; who could do this better than a hospital nurse? She never had anything but praise for the new Mrs. Driffield; she was not exactly pretty, she said, but she had a very nice face; of course she wasn't quite, quite a lady, but Edward would only have been uncomfortable with anyone too grand. She was just the sort of wife for him. I think it may be not unjustly said that Mrs. Barton Trafford fairly ran over with the milk of human kindness, but all the same I have an inkling that if ever the milk of human kindness was charged with vitriol, here was a case in point.

CHAPTER XXIII

WHEN we arrived at Blackstable, Roy and I, a car, neither ostentatiously grand nor obviously cheap, was waiting for him and the chauffeur had a note for me asking me to lunch with Mrs. Driffield next day. I got into a taxi and went to the "Bear and Key". I had learned from Roy that there was a new Marine Hotel on the front, but I did not propose for the luxuries of civilisation to abandon a resort of my youth. Change met me at the railway station, which was not in its old place, but up a new road, and of course it was strange to be driven down the High Street in a car. But the "Bear and Key" was unaltered. It received me with its old churlish indifference: there was no one at the entrance, the driver put my bag down and drove away; I called, no one answered; I went into the bar and found a young lady with shingled hair reading a book by Mr. Compton Mackenzie. I asked her if I could have a room. She gave me a slightly offended look and said she thought so, but as that seemed to exhaust her interest in the matter I asked politely whether there was anyone who could show it to me. She got up and, opening a door, in a shrill voice called: "Katie."

"What is it?" I heard.

"There's a gent wants a room."

In a little while appeared an ancient and haggard female in a very dirty print dress, with an untidy mop of grey hair, and showed me, two flights up, a very small grubby room.

"Can't you do something better than that for me?" I asked.

"It's the room commercials generally 'ave," she answered with a sniff.

"Haven't you got any others?"

"Not single."

"Then give me a double room."

"I'll go and ask Mrs. Brentford."

I accompanied her down to the first floor and she knocked at a door. She was told to come in, and when she opened it I caught sight of a stout woman with grey hair elaborately marcelled. She was reading a book. Apparently everyone at the "Bear and Key" was interested in literature. She gave me an indifferent look when Katie said I wasn't satisfied with number seven.

"Show him number five," she said.

I began to feel that I had been a trifle rash in declining so haughtily Mrs. Driffield's invitation to stay with her and then putting aside in my sentimental way Roy's wise suggestion that I should stay at the Marine Hotel. Katie took me upstairs again and ushered me into a largish room looking on the High Street. Most of its space was occupied by a double bed. The windows had certainly not been opened for a month.

I said that would do and asked about dinner.

"You can 'ave what you like," said Katie. "We 'aven't got nothing in, but I'll run round and get it."

Knowing English inns, I ordered a fried sole and a grilled chop. Then I went for a stroll. I walked down to the beach and found that they had built an esplanade and there was a row of bungalows and villas where I remembered only windswept fields. But they were seedy and bedraggled and I guessed that even after all these years Lord George's dream of turning Blackstable into a popular seaside resort had not come true. A retired military man, a pair of elderly ladies walked along the crumbling asphalt. It was incredibly dreary. A chill wind was blowing and a light drizzle swept over from the sea.

I went back into the town and here, in the space between the "Bear and Key" and the "Duke of Kent", were little knots of men standing about notwithstanding the inclement weather; and their eyes had the same pale blue, their high cheek-bones the same

ruddy colour as that of their fathers before them. It was strange
to see that some of the sailors in blue jerseys still wore little gold
rings in their ears; and not only old ones but boys scarcely out of
their teens. I sauntered down the street and there was the bank
refronted, but the stationery shop where I had bought paper and
wax to make rubbings with an obscure writer whom I had met by
chance was unchanged; there were two or three cinemas and their
garish posters suddenly gave the prim street a dissipated air so that
it looked like a respectable elderly woman who had taken a drop
too much.

It was cold and cheerless in the commercial room where I ate
my dinner alone at a large table laid for six. I was served by the
slatternly Katie. I asked if I could have a fire.

"Not in June," she said. "We don't 'ave fires after April."

"I'll pay for it," I protested.

"Not in June. In October, yes, but not in June."

When I had finished I went into the bar to have a glass of port.

"Very quiet," I said to the shingled barmaid.

"Yes, it is quiet," she answered.

"I should have thought on a Friday night you'd have quite a lot
of people in here."

"Well, one would think that, wouldn't one?"

Then a stout red-faced man with a close-cropped head of grey
hair came in from the back and I guessed that this was my host.

"Are you Mr. Brentford?" I asked him.

"Yes, that's me."

"I knew your father. Will you have a glass of port?"

I told him my name, in the days of his boyhood better known
than any other at Blackstable, but somewhat to my mortification
I saw that it aroused no echo in his memory. He consented, however, to let me stand him a glass of port.

"Down here on business?" he asked me. "We get quite a few
commercial gents at one time and another. We always like to do
what we can for them."

I told him that I had come down to see Mrs. Driffield and left
him to guess on what errand.

"I used to see a lot of the old man," said Mr. Brentford. "He
used to be very partial to dropping in here and having his glass of
bitter. Mind you, I don't say he ever got tiddly, but he used to
like to sit in the bar and talk. My word, he'd talk by the hour
and he never cared who he talked to. Mrs. Driffield didn't half

like his coming here. He'd slip away, out of the house, without saying a word to anybody, and come toddling down. You know it's a bit of a walk for a man of that age. Of course when they missed him Mrs. Driffield knew where he was, and she used to telephone and ask if he was here. Then she'd drive over in the car and go in and see my wife. 'You go in and fetch him, Mrs. Brentford,' she'd say; 'I don't like to go in the bar meself, not with all those men hanging about'; so Mrs. Brentford would come in and she'd say: 'Now Mr. Driffield, Mrs. Driffield's come for you in the car, so you'd better finish your beer and let her take you home.' He used to ask Mrs. Brentford not to say he was here when Mrs. Driffield rang up, but of course we couldn't do that. He was an old man and all that and we didn't want to take the responsibility. He was born in this parish, you know, and his first wife, she was a Blackstable girl. She's been dead these many years. I never knew her. He was a funny old fellow. No side, you know; they tell me they thought a rare lot of him in London and when he died the papers were full of him, but you'd never have known it to talk to him. He might have been just nobody, like you and me. Of course we always tried to make him comfortable; we tried to get him to sit in one of them easy chairs, but no, he must sit up at the bar; he said he liked to feel his feet on a rail. My belief is he was happier here than anywhere. He always said he liked a bar. He said you saw life there and he said he'd always loved life. Quite a character he was. Reminded me of my father, except that my old governor never read a book in his life and he drank a bottle of French brandy a day and he was seventy-eight when he died and his last illness was his first. I quite missed old Driffield when he popped off. I was only saying to Mrs. Brentford the other day, I'd like to read one of his books some time. They tell me he wrote several about these parts."

CHAPTER XXIV

NEXT morning it was cold and raw, but it was not raining, and I walked down the High Street towards the vicarage. I recognised the names over the shops, the Kentish names that have been borne for centuries—the Ganns, the Kemps, the Cobbs, the Igguldens—but I saw no one that I knew. I felt like a ghost walking down that street where I had once known nearly everyone, if not to speak to, at least by sight. Suddenly a very shabby little car passed me, stopped and backed, and I saw someone looking at me curiously. A tall, heavy, elderly man got out and came towards me.

"Aren't you Willie Ashenden?" he asked.

Then I recognised him. He was the doctor's son, and I had been at school with him; we had passed from form to form together, and I knew that he had succeeded his father in his practice.

"Hullo, how are you?" he asked. "I've just been along to the vicarage to see my grandson. It's a preparatory school now, you know, and I put him there at the beginning of this term."

He was shabbily dressed and unkempt, but he had a fine head and I saw that in youth he must have had unusual beauty. It was funny that I had never noticed it.

"Are you a grandfather?" I asked.

"Three times over," he laughed.

It gave me a shock. He had drawn breath, walked the earth and presently grown to man's estate, married, had children and they in turn had had children; I judged from the look of him that he had lived, with incessant toil, in penury. He had the peculiar manner of the country doctor, bluff, hearty and unctuous. His life was over. I had plans in my head for books and plays, I was full of schemes for the future; I felt that a long stretch of activity and fun still lay before me; and yet, I supposed, to others I must seem the elderly man that he seemed to me. I was so shaken that I had not the presence of mind to ask about his brothers whom as a child I had played with, or about the old friends who had been my companions; after a few foolish remarks I left him. I walked on to the vicarage, a roomy, rambling house too far out of the way for the modern incumbent who took his duties more seriously than did my uncle and too large for the present cost of living. It stood in a big garden and was surrounded by green fields. There was a great square notice-board that announced that it was a preparatory school for the sons of gentlemen and gave the name and the degrees of the headmaster. I looked over the paling; the garden was squalid and untidy and the pond in which I used to fish for roach was choked up. The glebe fields had been cut up into building lots. There were rows of little brick houses with bumpy ill-made roads. I walked along Joy Lane and there were houses here too, bungalows facing the sea; and the old turnpike house was a trim tea shop.

I wandered about here and there. There seemed innumerable streets of little houses of yellow brick, but I do not know who lived in them for I saw no one about. I went down to the harbour. It was deserted. There was but one tramp lying a little way out from the pier. Two or three sailormen were sitting outside a warehouse and they stared at me as I passed. The bottom had fallen out of the coal trade and colliers came to Blackstable no longer.

Then it was time for me to go to Ferne Court and I went back to the "Bear and Key". The landlord had told me that he had a Daimler for hire and I had arranged that it should take me to my luncheon. It stood at the door when I came up, a brougham, but the oldest, most dilapidated car of its make that I had ever seen; it panted along with squeaks and thumps and rattlings, with sudden angry jerks, so that I wondered if I should ever reach my destination. But the extraordinary, the amazing thing about it was that it smelled exactly like the old landau which my uncle used to hire every Sunday morning to go to church in. This was a rank odour of stables and of stale straw that lay at the bottom of the carriage; and I wondered in vain why, after all these years, the motor-car should have it too. But nothing can bring back the past like a perfume or a stench, and, oblivious to the country I was trundling through, I saw myself once more a little boy on the front seat with the communion plate beside me and, facing me, my aunt, smelling slightly of clean linen and eau-de-Cologne, in her black silk cloak and her little bonnet with a feather, and my uncle in his cassock, a broad band of ribbed silk round his ample waist and a gold cross hanging over his stomach from the gold chain round his neck.

"Now, Willie, mind you behave nicely to-day. You're not to turn round, and sit up properly in your seat. The Lord's House isn't the place to loll in and you must remember that you should set an example to other little boys who haven't had your advantages."

When I arrived at Ferne Court, Mrs. Driffield and Roy were walking round the garden and they came up to me as I got out of the car.

"I was showing Roy my flowers," said Mrs. Driffield, as she shook hands with me. And then with a sigh: "They're all I have now."

She looked no older than when last I saw her six years before.

She wore her weeds with quiet distinction. At her neck was a
collar of white crêpe and at her wrists cuffs of the same. Roy, I
noticed, wore with his neat blue suit a black tie; I supposed it was
a sign of respect for the illustrious dead.

"I'll just show you my herbaceous borders," said Mrs. Driffield,
"and then we'll go in to lunch."

We walked round and Roy was very knowledgeable. He knew
what all the flowers were called, and the Latin names tripped off
his tongue like cigarettes out of a cigarette-making machine. He
told Mrs. Driffield where she ought to get certain varieties that
she absolutely must have and how perfectly lovely were certain
others.

"Shall we go in through Edward's study?" suggested Mrs.
Driffield. "I keep it exactly as it was when he was here. I haven't
changed a thing. You'd be surprised how many people come over
to see the house, and of course above all they want to see the
room he worked in."

We went in through an open window. There was a bowl of
roses on the desk and on a little round table by the side of the
arm-chair a copy of the *Spectator*. In the ash-trays were the master's
pipes and there was ink in the inkstand. The scene was perfectly
set. I do not know why the room seemed so strangely dead; it
had already the mustiness of a museum. Mrs. Driffield went to
the bookshelves and with a little smile, half playful, half sad,
passed a rapid hand across the back of half a dozen volumes
bound in blue.

"You know that Edward admired your work so much," said
Mrs. Driffield. "He re-read your books quite often."

"I'm very glad to think that," I said politely.

I knew very well that they had not been there on my last visit
and in a casual way I took one of them out and ran my fingers
along the top to see whether there was dust on it. There was not.
Then I took another book down, one of Charlotte Brontë's, and
making a little plausible conversation tried the same experiment.
No, there was no dust there either. All I learned was that Mrs.
Driffield was an excellent housekeeper and had a conscientious
maid.

We went in to luncheon, a hearty British meal of roast beef
and Yorkshire pudding, and we talked of the work on which Roy
was engaged.

"I want to spare dear Roy all the labour I can," said Mrs.

Driffield, "and I've been gathering together as much of the material as I could myself. Of course it's been rather painful, but it's been very interesting, too. I came across a lot of old photographs that I must show you."

After luncheon we went into the drawing-room and I noticed again with what perfect tact Mrs. Driffield had arranged it. It suited the widow of a distinguished man of letters almost more than it had suited the wife. Those chintzes, those bowls of pot-pourri, those Dresden China figures—there was about them a faint air of regret; they seemed to reflect pensively upon a past of distinction. I could have wished on this chilly day that there were a fire in the grate, but the English are a hardy as well as a conservative race; and it is not difficult for them to maintain their principles at the cost of the discomfort of others. I doubted whether Mrs. Driffield would have conceived the possibility of lighting a fire before the first of October. She asked me whether I had lately seen the lady who had brought me to lunch with the Driffields, and I surmised from her faint acerbity that since the death of her eminent husband the great and fashionable had shown a distinct tendency to take no further notice of her. We were just settling down to talk about the defunct; Roy and Mrs. Driffield were putting artful questions to incite me to disclose my recollections and I was gathering my wits about me so that I should not in an unguarded moment let slip anything that I had made up my mind to keep to myself; when suddenly the trim parlour-maid brought in two cards on a small salver.

"Two gentlemen in a car, mum, and they say, could they look at the house and garden?"

"What a bore!" cried Mrs. Driffield, but with astonishing alacrity. "Isn't it funny I should have been speaking just now about the people who want to see the house? I never have a moment's peace."

"Well, why don't you say you're sorry you can't see them?" said Roy, with what I thought a certain cattiness.

"Oh, I couldn't do that. Edward wouldn't have liked me to." She looked at the cards. "I haven't got my glasses on me."

She handed them to me, and on one I read "Henry Beard MacDougal, University of Virginia"; and in pencil was written: "Assistant professor in English Literature". The other was "Jean-Paul Underhill", and there was at the bottom an address in New York.

"Americans," said Mrs. Driffield. "Say I shall be very pleased if they'll come in."

Presently the maid ushered the strangers in. They were both tall young men and broad-shouldered, with heavy, clean-shaven, swarthy faces and handsome eyes; they both wore horn-rimmed spectacles and they both had thick black hair combed straight back from their foreheads. They both wore English suits that were evidently brand-new; they were both slightly embarrassed, but verbose and extremely civil. They explained that they were making a literary tour of England and, being admirers of Edward Driffield, had taken the liberty of stopping off on their way to Rye to visit Henry James's house in the hope that they would be permitted to see a spot sanctified by so many associations. The reference to Rye did not go down very well with Mrs. Driffield.

"I believe they have some very good links there," she said.

She introduced the Americans to Roy and me. I was filled with admiration for the way in which Roy rose to the occasion. It appeared that he had lectured before the University of Virginia and had stayed with a distinguished member of the faculty. It had been an unforgettable experience. He did not know whether he had been more impressed by the lavish hospitality with which those charming Virginians had entertained him or by their intelligent interest in art and literature. He asked how So-and-So was, and So-and-So; he had made lifelong friends there, and it looked as though everyone he had met was good and kind and clever. Soon the young professor was telling Roy how much he liked his books, and Roy was modestly telling him what in this one and the other his aim had been and how conscious he was that he had come far short of achieving it. Mrs. Driffield listened with smiling sympathy, but I had a feeling that her smile was growing a trifle strained. It may be that Roy had too, for he suddenly broke off.

"But you don't want me to bore you with my stuff," he said in his loud hearty way. "I'm only here because Mrs. Driffield has entrusted to me the great honour of writing Edward Driffield's Life."

This of course interested the visitors very much.

"It's some job, believe me," said Roy, playfully American. "Fortunately I have the assistance of Mrs. Driffield, who was not only a perfect wife, but an admirable amanuensis and secretary; the materials she has placed at my disposal are so amazingly full that really little remains for me to do but take advantage of her industry and her—her affectionate zeal."

Mrs. Driffield looked down demurely at the carpet and the two young Americans turned on her their large dark eyes in which you could read their sympathy, their interest and their respect. After a little more conversation—partly literary but also about golf, for the visitors admitted that they hoped to get a round or two at Rye, and here again Roy was on the spot, for he told them to look out for such and such a bunker and when they came to London hoped they would play with him at Sunningdale—after this, I say, Mrs. Driffield got up and offered to show them Edward's study and bedroom, and of course the garden. Roy rose to his feet, evidently bent on accompanying them, but Mrs. Driffield gave him a little smile; it was pleasant but firm.

"Don't you bother to come, Roy," she said. "I'll take them round. You stay here and talk to Mr. Ashenden."

"Oh, all right. Of course."

The strangers bade us farewell and Roy and I settled down again in the chintz arm-chairs.

"Jolly room this is," said Roy.

"Very."

"Amy had to work hard to get it. You know the old man bought this house two or three years before they were married. She tried to make him sell it, but he wouldn't. He was very obstinate in some ways. You see, it belonged to a certain Miss Wolfe, whose bailiff his father was, and he said that when he was a little boy his one idea was to own it himself and now he'd got it he was going to keep it. One would have thought the last thing he'd want to do was to live in a place where everyone knew all about his origins and everything. Once poor Amy very nearly engaged a housemaid before she discovered she was Edward's great-niece. When Amy came here the house was furnished from attic to cellar in the best Tottenham Court Road manner; you know the sort of thing, Turkey carpets and mahogany sideboards, and a plush-covered suite in the drawing-room, and modern marquetry. It was his idea of how a gentleman's house should be furnished. Amy says it was simply awful. He wouldn't let her change a thing and she had to go to work with the greatest care; she says she simply couldn't have lived in it and she was determined to have things right, so she had to change things one by one so that he didn't pay any attention. She told me the hardest job she had was with his writing-desk. I don't know whether you've noticed the one there is in his study now. It's a very good period piece; I wouldn't mind having it myself. Well, he had a horrible American roll-top desk. He'd had it for years and he'd written a dozen books on it and he simply wouldn't part with it, he had no feeling for things like that; he just happened to be attached to it because he'd had it so long. You must get Amy to tell you the story how she managed to get rid of it in the end. It's really priceless. She's a remarkable woman, you know; she generally gets her own way."

"I've noticed it," I said.

It had not taken her long to dispose of Roy when he showed signs of wishing to go over the house with the visitors. He gave me a quick look and laughed. Roy was not stupid.

"You don't know America as well as I do," he said. "They always prefer a live mouse to a dead lion. That's one of the reasons why I like America."

CHAPTER XXV

WHEN Mrs. Driffield, having sent the pilgrims on their way, came back she bore under her arm a portfolio.

"What very nice young men!" she said. "I wish young men in England took such a keen interest in literature. I gave them that photo of Edward when he was dead and they asked me for one of mine, and I signed it for them." Then very graciously: "You made a great impression on them, Roy. They said it was a real privilege to meet you."

"I've lectured in America so much," said Roy, with modesty.

"Oh, but they've read your books. They say that what they like about them is that they're so virile."

The portfolio contained a number of old photographs, groups of schoolboys among whom I recognised an urchin with untidy hair as Driffield only because his widow pointed him out, Rugby fifteens with Driffield a little older, and then one of a young sailor in a jersey and a reefer jacket, Driffield when he ran away to sea.

"Here's one taken when he was first married," said Mrs. Driffield.

He wore a beard and black-and-white check trousers; in his

buttonhole was a large white rose backed by maidenhair and on the table beside him a chimney-pot hat.

"And here is the bride," said Mrs. Driffield, trying not to smile.

Poor Rosie, seen by a country photographer over forty years ago, was grotesque. She was standing very stiffly against a background of baronial hall, holding a large bouquet; her dress was elaborately draped, pinched at the waist, and she wore a bustle. Her fringe came down to her eyes. On her head was a wreath of orange blossoms, perched high on a mass of hair, and from it was thrown back a long veil. Only I knew how lovely she must have looked.

"She looks fearfully common," said Roy.

"She was," murmured Mrs. Driffield.

We looked at more photographs of Edward, photographs that had been taken of him when he began to be known, photographs when he wore only a moustache and others, all the later ones, when he was clean-shaven. You saw his face grown thinner and more lined. The stubborn commonplace of the early portraits melted gradually into a weary refinement. You saw the change in him wrought by experience, thought and achieved ambition. I looked again at the photograph of the young sailorman and fancied that I saw in it already a trace of that aloofness that seemed to me so marked in the older ones and that I had had years before the vague sensation of in the man himself. The face you saw was a mask and the actions he performed were without significance. I had an impression that the real man, to his death unknown and lonely, was a wraith that went a silent way unseen between the writer of his books and the man who led his life, and smiled with ironical detachment at the two puppets that the world took for Edward Driffield. I am conscious that in what I have written of him I have not presented a living man, standing on his feet, rounded, with comprehensible motives and logical activities; I have not tried to: I am glad to leave that to the abler pen of Alroy Kear.

I came across the photographs that Harry Retford, the actor, had had taken of Rosie, and then a photograph of the picture that Lionel Hillier had painted of her. It gave me a pang. That was how I best remembered her. Notwithstanding the old-fashioned gown, she was alive there and tremulous with the passion that filled her. She seemed to offer herself to the assault of love.

"She gives you the impression of a hefty wench," said Roy.

"If you like the milkmaid type," answered Mrs. Driffield. "I've always thought she looked rather like a white nigger."

That was what Mrs. Barton Trafford had been fond of calling her, and with Rosie's thick lips and broad nose there was indeed a hateful truth in the description. But they did not know how silvery golden her hair was, nor how golden silver her skin; they did not know her enchanting smile.

"She wasn't a bit like a white nigger," I said. "She was virginal like the dawn. She was like Hebe. She was like a tea rose."

Mrs. Driffield smiled and exchanged a meaning glance with Roy.

"Mrs. Barton Trafford told me a great deal about her. I don't wish to seem spiteful, but I'm afraid I don't think that she can have been a very nice woman."

"That's where you make a mistake," I replied. "She was a very nice woman. I never saw her in a bad temper. You only had to say you wanted something for her to give it to you. I never heard her say a disagreeable thing about anyone. She had a heart of gold."

"She was a terrible slattern. Her house was always in a mess; you didn't like to sit down in a chair because it was so dusty and you dared not look in the corners. And it was the same with her person. She could never put a skirt on straight and you'd see about two inches of petticoat hanging down on one side."

"She didn't bother about things like that. They didn't make her any the less beautiful. And she was as good as she was beautiful."

Roy burst out laughing and Mrs. Driffield put her hand up to her mouth to hide her smile.

"Oh, come, Mr. Ashenden, that's really going too far. After all, let's face it, she was a nymphomaniac."

"I think that's a very silly word," I said.

"Well, then, let me say that she can hardly have been a very good woman to treat poor Edward as she did. Of course it was a blessing in disguise. If she hadn't run away from him he might have had to bear that burden for the rest of his life, and with such a handicap he could never have reached the position he did. But the fact remains that she was notoriously unfaithful to him. From what I hear she was absolutely promiscuous."

"You don't understand," I said. "She was a very simple

woman. Her instincts were healthy and ingenuous. She loved to make people happy. She loved love."

"Do you call that love?"

"Well, then, the act of love. She was naturally affectionate. When she liked anyone it was quite natural for her to go to bed with him. She never thought twice about it. It was not vice; it wasn't lasciviousness; it was her nature. She gave herself as naturally as the sun gives heat or the flowers their perfume. It was a pleasure to her and she liked to give pleasure to others. It had no effect on her character; she remained sincere, unspoiled and artless."

Mrs. Driffield looked as though she had taken a dose of castor oil and had just been trying to get the taste of it out of her mouth by sucking a lemon.

"I don't understand," she said. "But then I'm bound to admit that I never understood what Edward saw in her."

"Did he know that she was carrying on with all sorts of people?" asked Roy.

"I'm sure he didn't," she replied quickly.

"You think him a bigger fool than I do, Mrs. Driffield," I said.

"Then why did he put up with it?"

"I think I can tell you. You see, she wasn't a woman who ever inspired love. Only affection. It was absurd to be jealous over her. She was like a clear deep pool in a forest glade into which it's heavenly to plunge, but it is neither less cool nor less crystalline because a tramp and a gipsy and a gamekeeper have plunged into it before you."

Roy laughed again and this time Mrs. Driffield without concealment smiled thinly.

"It's comic to hear you so lyrical," said Roy.

I stifled a sigh. I have noticed that when I am most serious people are apt to laugh at me, and indeed when after a lapse of time I have read passages that I wrote from the fullness of my heart I have been tempted to laugh at myself. It must be that there is something naturally absurd in a sincere emotion, though why there should be I cannot imagine, unless it is that man, the ephemeral inhabitant of an insignificant planet, with all his pain and all his striving is but a jest in an eternal mind.

I saw that Mrs. Driffield wished to ask me something. It caused her a certain embarrassment.

"Do you think he'd have taken her back if she'd been willing to come?"

"You knew him better than I. I should say no. I think that when he had exhausted an emotion he took no further interest in the person who had aroused it. I should say that he had a peculiar combination of strong feeling and extreme callousness."

"I don't know how you can say that," cried Roy. "He was the kindest man I ever met."

Mrs. Driffield looked at me steadily and then dropped her eyes.

"I wonder what happened to her when she went to America," he asked.

"I believe she married Kemp," said Mrs. Driffield. "I heard they had taken another name. Of course they couldn't show their faces over here again."

"When did she die?"

"Oh, about ten years ago."

"How did you hear?" I asked.

"From Harold Kemp, the son; he's in some sort of business at Maidstone. I never told Edward. She'd been dead to him for many years and I saw no reason to remind him of the past. It always helps you if you put yourself in other people's shoes and I said to myself that if I were he I shouldn't want to be reminded of an unfortunate episode of my youth. Don't you think I was right?"

CHAPTER XXVI

MRS. DRIFFIELD very kindly offered to send me back to Blackstable in her car, but I preferred to walk. I promised to dine at Ferne Court next day and meanwhile to write down what I could remember of the two periods during which I had been in the habit of seeing Edward Driffield. As I walked along the winding road, meeting no one by the way, I mused upon what I should say. Do they not tell us that style is the art of omission? If that is so I should certainly write a very pretty piece, and it seemed almost a pity that Roy should use it only as material. I chuckled when I reflected what a bombshell I could throw if I chose. There was one person who could tell them all they wanted to know about Edward Driffield and his first marriage; but this fact I proposed to keep to myself. They thought Rosie was dead; they erred; Rosie was very much alive.

Being in New York for the production of a play and my arrival having been advertised to all and sundry by my manager's energetic Press representative, I received one day a letter addressed in a handwriting I knew but could not place. It was large and round, firm but uneducated. It was so familiar to me that I was exasperated not to remember whose it was. It would have been more sensible to open the letter at once, but instead I looked at the envelope and racked my brain. There are handwritings I cannot see without a little shiver of dismay and some letters that look so tiresome that I cannot bring myself to open them for a week. When at last I tore open the envelope what I read gave me a strange feeling. It began abruptly:

I have just seen that you are in New York and would like to see you again. I am not living in New York any more, but Yonkers is quite close and if you have a car you can easily do it in half an hour. I expect you are very busy so leave it to you to make a date. Although it is many years since we last met I hope you have not forgotten your old friend

ROSE IGGULDEN (*formerly Driffield*)

I looked at the address; it was the Albemarle, evidently a hotel or an apartment house, then there was the name of a street, and Yonkers. A shiver passed through me as though someone had walked over my grave. During the years that had passed I had sometimes thought of Rosie, but of late I had said to myself that she must surely be dead. I was puzzled for a moment by the name. Why Iggulden and not Kemp? Then it occurred to me that they had taken this name, a Kentish one too, when they fled from England. My first impulse was to make an excuse not to see her; I am always shy of seeing again people I have not seen for a long time; but then I was seized with curiosity. I wanted to see what she was like and to hear what had happened to her. I was going down to Dobb's Ferry for the week-end, to reach which I had to pass through Yonkers, and so answered that I would come at about four on the following Saturday.

The Albemarle was a huge block of apartments, comparatively new, and it looked as though it were inhabited by persons in easy circumstances. My name was telephoned up by a negro porter in uniform and I was taken up in the elevator by another. I felt uncommonly nervous. The door was opened for me by a coloured maid.

"Come right in," she said. "Mrs. Iggulden's expecting you."

I was ushered into a living-room that served also as dining-room, for at one end of it was a square table of heavily carved oak, a dresser and four chairs of the kind that the manufacturers in Grand Rapids would certainly describe as Jacobean. But the other end was furnished with a Louis XV suite, gilt and upholstered in pale blue damask; there were a great many small tables, richly carved and gilt, on which stood Sèvres vases with ormolu decorations and nude bronze ladies with draperies flowing as though in a howling gale that artfully concealed those parts of their bodies that decency required; and each one held at the end of a playfully outstretched arm an electric lamp. The gramophone was the grandest thing I had ever seen out of a shop window, all gilt and shaped like a sedan chair and painted with Watteau courtiers and their ladies.

After I had waited for about five minutes a door was opened and Rosie came briskly in. She gave me both her hands.

"Well, this is a surprise," she said. "I hate to think how many years it is since we met. Excuse me one moment." She went to the door and called: "Jessie, you can bring the tea in. Mind the water's boiling properly." Then, coming back: "The trouble I've had to teach that girl to make tea properly, you'd never believe."

Rosie was at least seventy. She was wearing a very smart sleeveless frock of green chiffon, heavily *diamanté*, cut square at the neck and very short; it fitted like a bursting glove. By her shape I gathered that she wore rubber corsets. Her nails were blood-coloured and her eyebrows plucked. She was stout, and she had a double chin; the skin of her bosom, although she had powdered it freely, was red, and her face was red too. But she looked well and healthy and full of beans. Her hair was still abundant, but it was quite white, shingled and permanently waved. As a young woman she had had soft, naturally waving hair and these stiff undulations, as though she had just come out of a hairdresser's, seemed more than anything else to change her. The only thing that remained was her smile, which had still its old childlike and mischievous sweetness. Her teeth had never been very good, irregular and of bad shape; but these now were replaced by a set of perfect evenness and snowy brilliance; they were obviously the best money could buy.

The coloured maid brought in an elaborate tea with *pâté* sandwiches and cookies and candy and little knives and forks and tiny napkins. It was all very neat and smart.

"That's one thing I've never been able to do without—my tea," said Rosie, helping herself to a hot buttered scone. "It's my best meal, really, though I know I shouldn't eat it. My doctor keeps on saying to me: 'Mrs. Iggulden, you can't expect to get your weight down if you will eat half a dozen cookies at tea.'" She gave me a smile, and I had a sudden inkling that, notwithstanding the marcelled hair and the powder and the fat, Rosie was the same as ever. "But what I say is: A little of what you fancy does you good."

I had always found her easy to talk to. Soon we were chatting away as though it were only a few weeks since we had last seen one another.

"Were you surprised to get my letter? I put Driffield so as you should know who it was from. We took the name of Iggulden when we came to America. George had a little unpleasantness when he left Blackstable, perhaps you heard about it, and he thought in a new country he'd better start with a new name, if you understand what I mean."

I nodded vaguely.

"Poor George, he died ten years ago, you know."

"I'm sorry to hear that."

"Oh, well, he was getting on in years. He was past seventy, though you'd never have guessed it to look at him. It was a great blow to me. No woman could want a better husband than what he made me. Never a cross word from the day we married till the day he died. And I'm pleased to say he left me very well provided for."

"I'm glad to know that."

"Yes, he did very well over here. He went into the building trade, he always had a fancy for it, and he got in with Tammany. He always said the greatest mistake he ever made was not coming here over twenty years before. He liked the country from the first day he set foot in it. He had plenty of go and that's what you want here. He was just the sort to get on."

"Have you never been back to England?"

"No, I've never wanted to. George used to talk about it sometimes, just for a trip, you know, but we never got down to it, and now he's gone I haven't got the inclination. I expect London would seem very dead and alive to me after New York. We used to live in New York, you know. I only came here after his death."

"What made you choose Yonkers?"

"Well, I always fancied it. I used to say to George, when we retire we'll go and live at Yonkers. It's like a little bit of England to me, you know. Maidstone or Guildford or some place like that."

I smiled, but I understood what she meant. Notwithstanding its trams and its tootling cars, its cinemas and electric signs, Yonkers, with its winding main street, has a faint air of an English market town gone jazz.

"Of course I sometimes wonder what's happened to all the folks at Blackstable. I suppose they're most of them dead by now and I expect they think I am too."

"I haven't been there for thirty years."

I did not know then that the rumour of Rosie's death had reached Blackstable. I dare say that someone had brought back the news that George Kemp was dead and thus a mistake had arisen.

"I suppose nobody knows here that you were Edward Driffield's first wife?"

"Oh, no; why, if they had I should have had the reporters buzzing around my apartment like a swarm of bees. You know sometimes I've hardly been able to help laughing when I've been out somewhere playing bridge and they've started talking about Ted's books. They like them no end in America. I never thought so much of them myself."

"You never were a great novel reader, were you?"

"I used to like history better, but I don't seem to have much time for reading now. Sunday's my great day. I think the Sunday papers over here are lovely. You don't have anything like them in England. Then of course I play a lot of bridge; I'm crazy about contract."

I remembered that when as a young boy I had first met Rosie her uncanny skill at whist had impressed me. I felt that I knew the sort of bridge player she was, quick, bold and accurate: a good partner and a dangerous opponent.

"You'd have been surprised at the fuss they made over here when Ted died. I knew they thought a lot of him, but I never

knew he was such a big bug as all that. The papers were full of
him, and they had pictures of him and Ferne Court; he always
said he meant to live in that house some day. Whatever made him
marry that hospital nurse? I always thought he'd marry Mrs.
Barton Trafford. They never had any children, did they?"

"No."

"Ted would have liked to have some. It was a great blow to
him that I couldn't have any more after the first."

"I didn't know you'd ever had a child," I said with surprise.

"Oh, yes. That's why Ted married me. But I had a very bad
time when it came and the doctors said I couldn't have another.
If she'd lived, poor little thing, I don't suppose I'd ever have run
away with George. She was six when she died. A dear little thing
she was and as pretty as a picture."

"You never mentioned her."

"No, I couldn't bear to speak about her. She got meningitis and
we took her to the hospital. They put her in a private room and
they let us stay with her. I shall never forget what she went
through, screaming, screaming all the time, and nobody able to do
anything."

Rosie's voice broke.

"Was it that death Driffield described in *The Cup of Life?*"

"Yes, that's it. I always thought it so funny of Ted. He
couldn't bear to speak of it, any more than I could, but he wrote
it all down; he didn't leave out a thing; even little things I hadn't
noticed at the time he put in and then I remembered them. You'd
think he was just heartless, but he wasn't, he was upset just as
much as I was. When we used to go home at night he'd cry like
a child. Funny chap, wasn't he?"

It was *The Cup of Life* that had raised such a storm of protest;
and it was the child's death and the episode that followed it that
had especially brought down on Driffield's head such virulent
abuse. I remembered the description very well. It was harrowing.
There was nothing sentimental in it; it did not excite the reader's
tears, but his anger rather that such cruel suffering should be
inflicted on a little child. You felt that God at the Judgment Day
would have to account for such things as this. It was a very
powerful piece of writing. But if this incident was taken from
life, was the one that followed it also? It was this that had shocked
the public of the 'nineties and this that the critics had condemned
as not only indecent but incredible. In *The Cup of Life* the husband

and wife (I forget their names now) had come back from the hospital after the child's death—they were poor people and they lived from hand to mouth in lodgings—and had their tea. It was latish: about seven o'clock. They were exhausted by the strain of a week's ceaseless anxiety and shattered by their grief. They had nothing to say to one another. They sat in a miserable silence. The hours passed. Then on a sudden the wife got up and going into their bedroom put on her hat.

"I'm going out," she said.

"All right."

They lived near Victoria Station. She walked along the Buckingham Palace Road and through the park. She came into Piccadilly and went slowly towards the Circus. A man caught her eye, paused and turned round.

"Good-evening," he said.

"Good-evening."

She stopped and smiled.

"Will you come and have a drink?" he asked.

"I don't mind if I do."

They went into a tavern in one of the side-streets of Piccadilly, where harlots congregated and men came to pick them up, and they drank a glass of beer. She chatted with the stranger and laughed with him. She told him a cock-and-bull story about herself. Presently he asked if he could go home with her; no, she said, he couldn't do that, but they could go to a hotel. They got into a cab and drove to Bloomsbury and there they took a room for the night. And next morning she took a bus to Trafalgar Square and walked through the park; when she got home her husband was just sitting down to breakfast. After breakfast they went back to the hospital to see about the child's funeral.

"Will you tell me something, Rosie?" I asked. "What happened in the book after the child's death—did that happen too?"

She looked at me for a moment doubtfully; then her lips broke into her still beautiful smile.

"Well, it's all so many years ago, what odds does it make? I don't mind telling you. He didn't get it quite right. You see, it was only guesswork on his part. I was surprised that he knew as much as he did; I never told him anything."

Rosie took a cigarette and pensively tapped its end on the table, but she did not light it.

"We came back from the hospital just like he said. We walked back; I felt I couldn't sit still in a cab, and I felt all dead inside me. I'd cried so much I couldn't cry any more, and I was tired. Ted tried to comfort me, but I said: 'For God's sake shut up.' After that he didn't say any more. We had rooms in the Vauxhall Bridge Road then, on the second floor, just a sitting-room and a bedroom, that's why we'd had to take the poor little thing to the hospital; we couldn't nurse her in lodgings; besides, the landlady said she wouldn't have it, and Ted said she'd be looked after better at the hospital. She wasn't a bad sort, the landlady; she'd been a tart and Ted used to talk to her by the hour together. She came up when she heard us come in.

" 'How's the little girl to-night?' she said.

" 'She's dead,' said Ted.

"I couldn't say anything. Then she brought up the tea. I didn't want anything, but Ted made me eat some ham. Then I sat at the window. I didn't look round when the landlady came up to clear away, I didn't want anyone to speak to me. Ted was reading a book; at least he was pretending to, but he didn't turn the pages, and I saw the tears dropping on it. I kept on looking out of the window. It was the end of June, the twenty-eighth, and the days were long. It was just near the corner where we lived and I looked at the people going in and out of the public-house and the trams going up and down. I thought the day would never come to an end; then all of a sudden I noticed that it was night. All the lamps were lit. There was an awful lot of people in the street. I felt so tired. My legs were like lead.

" 'Why don't you light the gas?' I said to Ted.

" 'Do you want it?' he said.

" 'It's no good sitting in the dark,' I said.

"He lit the gas. He began smoking his pipe. I knew that would do him good. But I just sat and looked at the street. I don't know what came over me. I felt that if I went on sitting in that room I'd go mad. I wanted to go somewhere where there were lights and people. I wanted to get away from Ted; no, not so much that, I wanted to get away from all that Ted was thinking and feeling. We only had two rooms. I went into the bedroom; the child's cot was still there, but I wouldn't look at it. I put on my hat and a veil and I changed my dress and then I went back to Ted.

" 'I'm going out,' I said.

"Ted looked at me. I dare say he noticed I'd got my new dress on and perhaps something in the way I spoke made him see I didn't want him.

"'All right,' he said.

"In the book he made me walk through the park, but I didn't do that really. I went down to Victoria and I took a hansom to Charing Cross. It was only a shilling fare. Then I walked up the Strand. I'd made up my mind what I wanted to do before I came out. Do you remember Harry Retford? Well, he was acting at the Adelphi then, he had the second comedy part. Well, I went to the stage door, and sent up my name. I always liked Harry Retford. I expect he was a bit unscrupulous and he was rather funny over money matters, but he could make you laugh and with all his faults he was a rare good sort. You know he was killed in the Boer War, don't you?"

"I didn't. I only knew he'd disappeared and one never saw his name on playbills; I thought perhaps he'd gone into business or something."

"No, he went out at once. He was killed at Ladysmith. After I'd been waiting a bit he came down and I said: 'Harry, let's go on the razzle to-night. What about a bit of supper at Romano's?' 'Not 'alf,' he said. 'You wait here and the minute the show's over and I've got my make-up off I'll come down.' It made me feel better just to see him; he was playing a racing tout and it made me laugh just to look at him in his check suit and his billycock hat and his red nose. Well, I waited till the end of the show and then he came down and we walked along to Romano's.

"'Are you hungry?' he said to me.

"'Starving,' I said; and I was.

"'Let's have the best,' he said, 'and blow the expense. I told Bill Terris I was taking my best girl out to supper and I touched him for a couple of quid.'

"'Let's have champagne,' I said.

"'Three cheers for the widow!' he said.

"I don't know if you ever went to Romano's in the old days. It was fine. You used to see all the theatrical people and the racing men, and the girls from the Gaiety used to go there. It was the place. And the Roman. Harry knew him and he came up to our table; he used to talk in funny broken English; I believe he put it on because he knew it made people laugh. And if someone he knew was down and out he'd always lend him a fiver.

"'How's the kid?' said Harry.

" 'Better,' I said.

"I didn't want to tell him the truth. You know how funny men are; they don't understand some things. I knew Harry would think it dreadful of me to come out to supper when the poor child was lying dead in the hospital. He'd be awfully sorry and all that, but that's not what I wanted; I wanted to laugh."

Rosie lit the cigarette that she had been playing with.

"You know how when a woman is having a baby, sometimes the husband can't stand it any more and he goes out and has another woman. And then when she finds out, and it's funny how often she does, she kicks up no end of a fuss; she says, that the man should go and do it just then, when she's going through hell, well, it's the limit. I always tell her not to be silly. It doesn't mean he doesn't love her, and isn't terribly upset, it doesn't mean anything, it's just nerves; if he wasn't so upset he wouldn't think of it. I know, because that's how I felt then.

"When we'd finished our supper Harry said: 'Well, what about it?'

" 'What about what?' I said.

"There wasn't any dancing in those days and there was nowhere to go.

" 'What about coming round to my flat and having a look at my photograph album?' said Harry.

" 'I don't mind if I do,' I said.

"He had a little bit of a flat in the Charing Cross Road, just two rooms and a bath and a kitchenette, and we drove round there, and I stayed the night.

"When I got back next morning the breakfast was already on the table and Ted had just started. I'd made up my mind that if he said anything I was going to fly out at him. I didn't care what happened. I'd earned my living before, and I was ready to earn it again. For two pins I'd have packed my box and left him there and then. But he just looked up as I came in.

" 'You've just come in time,' he said. 'I was going to eat your sausage.'

"I sat down and poured him out his tea. And he went on reading the paper. After we'd finished breakfast we went to the hospital. He never asked me where I'd been. I didn't know what he thought. He was terribly kind to me all that time. I was miserable, you know. Somehow I felt that I just couldn't get over it, and there was nothing he didn't do to make it easier for me."

"What did you think when you read the book?" I asked.

"Well, it did give me a turn to see that he did know pretty well what had happened that night. What beat me was his writing it at all. You'd have thought it was the last thing he'd put in a book. You're queer fish, you writers."

At that moment the telephone bell rang. Rosie took up the receiver and listened.

"Why, Mr. Vanuzzi, how very nice of you to call me up! Oh, I'm pretty well, thank you. Well, pretty and well, if you like. When you're my age you take all the compliments you can get."

She embarked upon a conversation which, I gathered from her tone, was of a facetious and even flirtatious character. I did not pay much attention, and since it seemed to prolong itself I began to meditate upon the writer's life. It is full of tribulation. First he must endure poverty and the world's indifference; then, having achieved a measure of success, he must submit with a good grace to its hazards. He depends upon a fickle public. He is at the mercy of journalists who want to interview him and photographers who want to take his picture, of editors who harry him for copy and tax gatherers who harry him for income tax, of persons of quality who ask him to lunch and secretaries of institutes who ask him to lecture, of women who want to marry him and women who want to divorce him, of youths who want his autograph, actors who want parts and strangers who want a loan, of gushing ladies who want advice on their matrimonial affairs and earnest young men who want advice on their compositions, of agents, publishers, managers, bores, admirers, critics, and his own conscience. But he has one compensation. Whenever he has anything on his mind, whether it be a harassing reflection, grief at the death of a friend, unrequited love, wounded pride, anger at the treachery of someone to whom he has shown kindness, in short any emotion or any perplexing thought, he has only to put it down in black and white, using it as a theme of a story or the decoration of an essay, to forget all about it. He is the only free man.

Rosie put back the receiver and turned to me.

"That was one of my beaux. I'm going to play bridge to-night and he rang up to say he'd call round for me in his car. Of course he's a Wop, but he's real nice. He used to run a big grocery store down-town, in New York, but he's retired now."

"Have you never thought of marrying again, Rosie?"

"No." She smiled. "Not that I haven't had offers. I'm quite

happy as I am. The way I look on it is this: I don't want to marry an old man, and it would be silly at my age to marry a young one. I've had my time and I'm ready to call it a day."

"What made you run away with George Kemp?"

"Well, I'd always liked him. I knew him long before I knew Ted, you know. Of course, I never thought there was any chance of marrying him. For one thing, he was married already, and then he had his position to think of. And then when he came to me one day and said that everything had gone wrong and he was bust and there'd be a warrant out for his arrest in a few days and he was going to America and would I go with him, well, what could I do? I couldn't let him go all that way by himself, with no money perhaps, and him having been always so grand and living in his own house and driving his own trap. It wasn't as if I was afraid of work."

"I sometimes think he was the only man you ever cared for," I suggested.

"I dare say there's some truth in that."

"I wonder what it was you saw in him."

Rosie's eyes travelled to a picture on the wall that for some reason had escaped my notice. It was an enlarged photograph of Lord George in a carved gilt frame. It looked as if it might have been taken soon after his arrival in America; perhaps at the time of their marriage. It was a three-quarter length. It showed him in a long frock-coat, tightly buttoned, and a tall silk hat cocked rakishly on one side of his head; there was a large rose in his buttonhole; under one arm he carried a silver-headed cane and smoke curled from a big cigar that he held in his right hand. He had a heavy moustache, waxed at the ends, a saucy look in his eye, and in his bearing an arrogant swagger. In his tie was a horse-shoe in diamonds. He looked like a publican dressed up in his best to go to the Derby.

"I'll tell you," said Rosie. "He was always such a perfect gentleman."

THEATRE

Theatre

CHAPTER I

The door opened and Michael Gosselyn looked up. Julia came in.

"Hulloa! I won't keep you a minute. I was just signing some letters."

"No hurry. I only came to see what seats had been sent to the Dennorants. What's that young man doing here?"

With the experienced actress's instinct to fit the gesture to the words by a movement of her neat head she indicated the room through which she had just passed.

"He's the accountant. He comes from Lawrence and Hamphreys. He's been here three days."

"He looks very young."

"He's an articled clerk. He seems to know his job. He can't get over the way our accounts are kept. He told me he never expected a theatre to be run on such business-like lines. He says the way some of those firms in the City keep their accounts is enough to turn your hair grey."

Julia smiled at the complacency on her husband's handsome face.

"He's a young man of tact."

"He finishes to-day. I thought we might take him back with us and give him a spot of lunch. He's quite a gentleman."

"Is that a sufficient reason to ask him to lunch?"

Michael did not notice the faint irony of her tone.

"I won't ask him if you don't want him. I merely thought it would be a treat for him. He admires you tremendously. He's been to see the play three times. He's crazy to be introduced to you."

Michael touched a button and in a moment his secretary came in.

"Here are the letters, Margery. What appointments have I got for this afternoon?"

Julia with half an ear listened to the list Margery read out and, though she knew the room so well, idly looked about her. It was a very proper room for the manager of a first-class theatre. The walls had been panelled (at cost price) by a good decorator and on them hung engravings of theatrical pictures by Zoffany and de Wilde. The arm-chairs were large and comfortable. Michael sat in a heavily-carved Chippendale chair, a reproduction but made by a well-known firm, and his Chippendale table, with heavy ball and claw feet, was immensely solid. On it stood in a massive silver frame a photograph of herself and to balance it a photograph of Roger, their son. Between these was a magnificent silver ink-stand that she had herself given him on one of his birthdays and behind it a rack in red morocco, heavily gilt, in which he kept his private paper in case he wanted to write a letter in his own hand. The paper bore the address, Siddons Theatre, and the envelope his crest, a boar's head with the motto underneath: *Nemo me impune lacessit.* A bunch of yellow tulips in a silver bowl, which he had got through winning the theatrical golf tournament three times running, showed Margery's care. Julia gave her a reflective glance. Notwithstanding her cropped peroxide hair and her heavily-painted lips she had the neutral look that marks the perfect secretary. She had been with Michael for five years. In that time she must have got to know him inside and out. Julia wondered if she could be such a fool as to be in love with him.

But Michael rose from his chair.

"Now, darling, I'm ready for you."

Margery gave him his black Homburg hat and opened the door for Julia and Michael to go out. As they entered the office the young man Julia had noticed turned round and stood up.

"I should like to introduce you to Miss Lambert," said Michael. Then with the air of an ambassador presenting an attaché to the sovereign of the court to which he is accredited: "This is the gentleman who is good enough to put some order into the mess we make of our accounts."

The young man went scarlet. He smiled stiffly in answer to Julia's warm, ready smile and she felt the palm of his hand wet with sweat when she cordially grasped it. His confusion was touching. That was how people had felt when they were presented to Sarah Siddons. She thought that she had not been very gracious to Michael when he had proposed asking the boy to luncheon. She looked straight into his eyes. Her own were large, of a very dark brown, and starry. It was no effort to her, it was as instinctive as brushing away a fly that was buzzing round her, to suggest now a faintly amused, friendly tenderness.

"I wonder if we could persuade you to come and eat a chop with us. Michael will drive you back after lunch."

The young man blushed again and his adam's apple moved in his thin neck.

"It's awfully kind of you." He gave his clothes a troubled look. "I'm absolutely filthy."

"You can have a wash and brush up when we get home."

The car was waiting for them at the stage door, a long car in black and chromium, upholstered in silver leather, and with Michael's crest discreetly emblazoned on the doors. Julia got in.

"Come and sit with me. Michael is going to drive."

They lived in Stanhope Place, and when they arrived Julia told the butler to show the young man where he could wash his hands. She went up to the drawing-room. She was painting her lips when Michael joined her.

"I've told him to come up as soon as he's ready."

"By the way, what's his name?"

"I haven't a notion."

"Darling, we must know. I'll ask him to write in our book."

"Damn it, he's not important enough for that." Michael asked only very distinguished people to write in their book. "We shall never see him again."

At that moment the young man appeared. In the car Julia had done all she could to put him at his ease, but he was still very shy. The cocktails were waiting and Michael poured them out. Julia took a cigarette and the young man struck a match for her, but his hand was trembling so much that she thought he would never be able to hold the light near enough to her cigarette, so she took his hand and held it.

"Poor lamb," she thought, "I suppose this is the most wonderful moment in his whole life. What fun it'll be for him when he tells his people. I expect he'll be a blasted little hero in his office."

Julia talked very differently to herself and to other people: when she talked to herself her language was racy. She inhaled the first whiff of her cigarette with delight. It was really rather wonderful, when you came to think of it, that just to have lunch with her and talk to her for three-quarters of an hour, perhaps, could make a man quite important in his own scrubby little circle.

The young man forced himself to make a remark.

"What a stunning room this is."

She gave him the quick, delightful smile, with a slight lift of her fine eyebrows, which he must often have seen her give on the stage.

"I'm so glad you like it." Her voice was rather low and ever so slightly hoarse. You would have thought his observation had taken a weight off her mind. "We think in the family that Michael has such perfect taste."

Michael gave the room a complacent glance.

"I've had a good deal of experience. I always design the sets myself for our plays. Of course, I have a man to do the rough work for me, but the ideas are mine."

They had moved into that house two years before, and he knew, and Julia knew, that they had put it into the hands of an expensive decorator when they were going on tour, and he had agreed to have it completely ready for them, at cost price in return for the work they promised him in the theatre, by the time they came back. But it was unnecessary to impart such tedious details to a young man whose name even they did not know. The house was furnished in extremely good taste, with a judicious mixture of the antique and the modern, and Michael was right when he said that it was quite obviously a gentleman's house. Julia, however, had insisted that she must have her bedroom as she liked, and having had exactly the bedroom that pleased her in the old house in Regent's Park which they had occupied since the end of the war she brought it over bodily. The bed and the dressing-table were upholstered in pink silk, the chaise-longue and the arm-chair in Nattier-blue; over the bed there were fat little gilt cherubs who dangled a lamp with a pink shade, and fat little gilt cherubs swarmed all round the mirror on the dressing-table. On satin-wood tables were signed photographs, richly framed, of actors and actresses and members of the royal family. The decorator had raised his supercilious eyebrows, but it was the only room in the house in which Julia felt completely at home. She wrote her letters at a satinwood desk, seated on a gilt Hamlet stool.

Luncheon was announced and they went downstairs.

"I hope you'll have enough to eat," said Julia. "Michael and I have very small appetites."

In point of fact there was grilled sole, grilled cutlets and spinach, and stewed fruit. It was a meal designed to satisfy legitimate hunger, but not to produce fat. The cook, warned by Margery that there was a guest to luncheon had hurriedly made some fried potatoes. They looked crisp and smelt appetising. Only the young man took them. Julia gave them a wistful look before she shook her head in refusal. Michael stared at them gravely for a moment as though he could not quite tell what they were, and then with a little start, breaking out of a brown study, said No, thank you. They sat at a refectory table, Julia and Michael at either end in very grand Italian chairs, and the young man in the middle on a chair that was not at all comfortable, but perfectly in character. Julia noticed that he seemed to be looking at the sideboard and, with her engaging smile, leaned forward.

"What is it?"

He blushed scarlet.

"I was wondering if I might have a piece of bread."

"Of course."

She gave the butler a significant glance; he was at that moment helping Michael to a glass of dry white wine, and he left the room.

"Michael and I never eat bread. It was stupid of Jevons not to realise that you might want some."

"Of course bread is only a habit," said Michael. "It's wonderful how soon you can break yourself of it if you set your mind to it."

"The poor lamb's as thin as a rail, Michael."

"I don't eat bread because I'm afraid of getting fat. I don't eat it because I see no point in it. After all, with the exercise I take I can eat anything I like."

He still had at fifty-two a very good figure. As a young man, with a great mass of curling chestnut hair, with a wonderful skin and large deep blue eyes, a straight nose and small ears, he had been the best-looking actor on the English stage. The only thing that slightly spoiled him was the thinness of his mouth. He was just six foot tall and he had a gallant bearing. It was his obvious beauty that had engaged him to go on the stage rather than to become a soldier like his father. Now his chestnut hair was very grey, and he wore it much shorter; his face had broadened and was a good deal lined; his skin no longer had the soft bloom of a peach and his colour was high. But with his splendid eyes and his fine figure he was still a very handsome man. Since his five years at the war he had adopted a military bearing, so that if you had not known who he was (which was scarcely possible, for in one way and another his photograph was always appearing in the illustrated papers) you might have taken him for an officer of high rank. He boasted that his weight had not changed since he was twenty, and for years, wet or fine, he had got up every morning at eight to put on shorts and a sweater and have a run round Regent's Park.

"The secretary told me you were rehearsing this morning, Miss Lambert," the young man remarked. "Does that mean you're putting on a new play?"

"Not a bit of it," answered Michael. "We're playing to capacity."

"Michael thought we were getting a bit ragged, so he called a rehearsal."

"I'm very glad I did. I found little bits of business had crept in that I hadn't given them and a good many liberties were being taken with the text. I'm a great stickler for saying the author's exact words, though, God knows, the words authors write nowadays aren't much."

"If you'd like to come and see our play," Julia said graciously, "I'm sure Michael will be delighted to give you some seats."

"I'd love to come again," the young man answered eagerly. "I've seen it three times already."

"You haven't?" cried Julia, with surprise, though she remembered perfectly that Michael had already told her so. "Of course it's not a bad little play, it's served our purpose very well, but I can't imagine anyone wanting to see it three times."

"It's not so much the play I went to see, it was your performance."

"I dragged that out of him all right," thought Julia, and then aloud: "When we read the play Michael was rather doubtful about it. He didn't think my part was very good. You know, it's not really a star part. But I thought I could make something out of it. Of course we had to cut the other woman a lot in rehearsals."

"I don't say we re-wrote the play," said Michael, "but I can tell you it was a very different play we produced from the one the author submitted to us."

"You're simply wonderful in it," the young man said.

("He has a certain charm.") "I'm glad you liked me," she answered.

"If you're very nice to Julia I dare say she'll give you a photograph of herself when you go."

"Would you?"

He blushed again and his blue eyes shone ("He's really rather sweet.") He was not particularly good-looking, but he had a frank, open face and his shyness was attractive. He had curly light brown hair, but it was plastered down and Julia thought how much better he would look if, instead of trying to smoothe out the wave with brilliantine, he made the most of it. He had a fresh colour, a good skin and small well-shaped teeth. She noticed with approval that his clothes fitted and that he wore them well. He looked nice and clean.

"I suppose you've never had anything to do with the theatre from the inside before?" she said.

"Never. That's why I was so crazy to get this job. You can't think how it thrills me."

Michael and Julia smiled on him kindly. His admiration made them feel a little larger than life-size.

"I never allow outsiders to come to rehearsals, but as you're our accountant you almost belong to the theatre, and I wouldn't mind making an exception in your favour if it would amuse you to come."

"That would be terribly kind of you. I've never been to a rehearsal in my life. Are you going to act in the next play?"

"Oh, I don't think so. I'm not very keen about acting any more. I find it almost impossible to find a part to suit me. You see, at my time of life I can't very well play young lovers, and authors don't seem to write the parts they used to write when I was a young fellow. What the French call a *raisonneur*. You know the sort of thing I mean, a duke, or a cabinet minister, or an eminent K.C. who says clever, witty things and turns people round his little finger. I don't know what's happened to authors. They don't seem able to write good lines any more. Bricks without straw; that's what we actors are expected to make nowadays. And are they grateful to us? The authors, I mean. You'd be surprised if I told you the terms some of them have the nerve to ask."

"The fact remains, we can't do without them," smiled Julia. "If the play's wrong no acting in the world will save it."

"That's because the public isn't really interested in the theatre. In the great days of the English stage people didn't go to see the plays, they went to see the players. It didn't matter what Kemble and Mrs. Siddons acted. The public went to see them. And even now, though I don't deny that if the play's wrong you're dished, I do contend that if the play's right, it's the actors the public go to see, not the play."

"I don't think anyone can deny that," said Julia.

"All an actress like Julia wants is a vehicle. Give her that and she'll do the rest."

Julia gave the young man a delightful, but slightly deprecating smile.

"You mustn't take my husband too seriously. I'm afraid we must admit that he's partial where I'm concerned."

"Unless this young man is a much bigger fool than I think him he must know that there's nothing in the way of acting that you can't do."

"Oh, that's only an idea that people have got because I take care never to do anything but what I can do."

Presently Michael looked at his watch.

"I think when you've finished your coffee, young man, we ought to be going."

The boy gulped down what was left in his cup and Julia rose from the table.

"You won't forget my photograph?"

"I think there are some in Michael's den. Come along and we'll choose one."

She took him into a fair-sized room behind the dining-room. Though it was supposed to be Michael's private sitting-room—"a fellow wants a room where he can get away by himself and smoke his pipe"—it was chiefly used as a cloak-room when they had guests. There was a noble mahogany desk on which were signed photographs of George V and Queen Mary. Over the chimney-piece was an old copy of Lawrence's portrait of Kemble as Hamlet. On a small table was a pile of typescript plays. The room was surrounded by bookshelves under which were cupboards, and from one of these Julia took a bundle of her latest photographs. She handed one to the young man.

"This one is not so bad."

"It's lovely."

"Then it can't be as like me as I thought."

"But it is. It's exactly like you."

She gave him another sort of smile, just a trifle roguish; she lowered her eyelids for a second and then raising them gazed at him for a little with that soft expression that people described as her velvet look. She had no object in doing this. She did it, if not mechanically, from an instinctive desire to please. The boy was so young, so shy, he looked as if he had such a nice nature, and she would never see him again; she wanted him to have his money's worth; she wanted him to look back on this as one of the great moments of his life. She glanced at the photograph again. She liked to think she looked like that. The photographer had so posed her, with her help, as to show her at her best. Her nose was slightly thick, but he had managed by his lighting to make it look very delicate, not a wrinkle marred the smoothness of her skin, and there was a melting look in her fine eyes.

"All right. You shall have this one. You know I'm not a beautiful woman, I'm not even a very pretty one; Coquelin always used to say I had the *beauté du diable*. You understand French, don't you?"

"Enough for that."

"I'll sign it for you."

She sat at the desk and with her bold, flowing hand wrote: Yours sincerely, Julia Lambert.

CHAPTER II

WHEN the two men had gone she looked through the photographs again before putting them back.

"Not bad for a woman of forty-six," she smiled. "They are like me, there's no denying that." She looked round the room for a mirror, but there wasn't one. "These damned decorators. Poor Michael, no wonder he never uses this room. Of course I never have photographed well."

She had an impulse to look at some of her old photographs. Michael was a tidy, business-like man, and her photographs were kept in large cardboard cases, dated and chronologically arranged. His were in other cardboard cases in the same cupboard.

"When someone comes along and wants to write the story of our careers he'll find all the material ready to his hand," he said.

With the same laudable object he had had all their Press cuttings from the very beginning pasted in a series of large books.

There were photographs of Julia when she was a child, and photographs of her as a young girl, photographs of her in her first parts, photographs of her as a young married woman, with Michael, and then with Roger, her son, as a baby. There was one photograph of the three of them, Michael very manly and incredibly handsome, herself all tenderness looking down at Roger with maternal feeling, and Roger a little boy with a curly head, which had been an enormous success. All the illustrated papers had given it a full page and they had used it on the programmes. Reduced to picture-postcard size it had sold in the provinces for years. It was such a bore that Roger when he got to Eton refused to be photographed with her any more. It seemed so funny of him not to want to be in the papers.

"People will think you're deformed or something," she told him. "And it's not as if it weren't good form. You should just go to a first night and see the society people, how they mob the photographers, cabinet ministers and judges and everyone. They may pretend they don't like it, but just see them posing when they think the camera man's got his eye on them."

But he was obstinate.

Julia came across a photograph of herself as Beatrice. It was the only Shakespearean part she had ever played. She knew that she didn't look well in costume; she could never understand why, because no one could wear modern clothes as well as she could. She had her clothes made in Paris, both for the stage and for private life, and the dressmakers said that no one brought them more orders. She had a lovely figure, everyone admitted that; she was fairly tall for a woman, and she had long legs. It was a pity she had never had a chance of playing Rosalind, she would have looked all right in boy's clothes; of course it was too late now, but perhaps it was just as well she hadn't risked it. Though you would have thought, with her brilliance, her roguishness, her sense of comedy she would have been perfect. The critics hadn't really liked her Beatrice. Her voice, her rather low rich voice, with that effective hoarseness, which wrung your heart in an emotional passage or gave so much humour to a comedy line, when she came to play *Much Ado* proved surprisingly ineffective. Her articulation was so distinct that, without raising her voice, she could make you hear her every word in the last row of the gallery; she had always found blank verse difficult to cope with and though there was little of it in the part of Beatrice, the critics had pointed out with asperity that such as there was had evidently escaped her notice.

Michael had started with Shakespeare. That was before she knew him. He had played Romeo at Cambridge, and when he came down, after a year at a dramatic school, Benson had engaged him. He toured the country and played a great variety of parts. But he realised that Shakespeare would get him nowhere and that if he wanted to become a leading actor he must gain experience in modern plays. A man called James Langton was running a repertory theatre at Middlepool that was attracting a good deal of attention; and after Michael had been with Benson for three years, when the company was going to Middlepool on its annual visit, he wrote to Langton and asked whether he would see him. Jimmie Langton, a fat, bald-headed, rubicund man of forty-five, who looked like one of Rubens' prosperous burghers, had a passion for the theatre. He was an eccentric, arrogant, exuberant, vain and charming fellow. He loved acting, but his physique prevented him from playing any but a few parts, which was fortunate, for he was a bad actor. He could not subdue his natural flamboyance, and every part he played, though he studied it with care and gave it thought, he turned into a grotesque. He broadened every gesture, he exaggerated every intonation. But it was a very different matter when he rehearsed his cast; then he would suffer nothing artificial. His ear was perfect, and though he could not produce the right intonation himself he would never let a false one pass in anyone else.

"Don't *be* natural," he told his company. "The stage isn't the place for that. The stage is make-believe. But *seem* natural."

He worked his company hard. They rehearsed every morning from ten till two, when he sent them home to learn their parts and rest before the evening's performance. He bullied them, he screamed at them, he mocked them. He underpaid them. But if they played a moving scene well he cried like a child, and when they said an amusing line as he wanted it said he bellowed with laughter. He would skip about the stage on one leg if he was pleased, and if he was angry would throw the script down and stamp on it while tears of rage ran down his cheeks. The company laughed at him and abused him and did everything they could to please him. He aroused a protective instinct in them, so that one and all they felt that they couldn't let him down. Though they said he drove them like slaves, and they never had a moment to themselves, flesh and blood couldn't stand it, it gave them a sort of horrible satisfaction to comply with his outrageous demands. When he wrung an old trouper's hand, who was getting seven pounds a week, and said: By God, laddie, you're stupendous, the old trouper felt like Charles Kean.

It happened that when Michael kept the appointment he had asked for, Jimmie Langton was in need of a leading juvenile. He had guessed why Michael wanted to see him, and had gone the night before to see him play. Michael was playing Mercutio and he had not thought him very good, but when he came into the office he was staggered by his beauty. In a brown coat and grey flannel trousers, even without make-up, he was so handsome it took your breath away. He had an easy manner and he talked like a gentleman. While Michael explained the purpose of his visit Jimmie Langton observed him shrewdly. If he could act at all, with those looks that young man ought to go far.

"I saw your Mercutio last night," he said. "What d'you think of it yourself?"

"Rotten."

"So do I. How old are you?"

"Twenty-five."

"I suppose you've been told you're good-looking?"

"That's why I went on the stage. Otherwise I'd have gone into the army like my father."

"By gum, if I had your looks what an actor I'd have been."

The result of the interview was that Michael got an engagement. He stayed at Middlepool for two years. He soon grew popular with the company. He was good-humoured and kindly; he would take any amount of trouble to do anyone a service. His beauty created a sensation in Middlepool and the girls used to hang about the stage door to see him go out. They wrote him love letters and sent him flowers. He took it as a natural homage, but did not allow it to turn his head. He was eager to get on and seemed determined not to let any entanglement interfere with his career. It was his beauty that saved him, for Jimmie Langton quickly came to the conclusion that, notwithstanding his perseverance and desire to excel, he would never be more than a competent actor. His voice was a trifle thin and in moments of vehemence was apt to go shrill. It gave then more the effect of hysteria than of passion. But his gravest fault as a juvenile lead was that he could not make love. He was easy enough in ordinary dialogue and could say his lines with point, but when it came to making protestations of passion something seemed to hold him back. He felt embarrassed and looked it.

"Damn you, don't hold that girl as if she was a sack of potatoes," Jimmie Langton shouted at him. "You kiss her as if you were afraid you were standing in a draught. You're in love with that girl. You must feel that you're in love with her. Feel as if your bones were melting inside you, and if an earthquake were going to swallow you up next minute, to hell with the earthquake."

But it was no good. Notwithstanding his beauty, his grace and his ease of manner, Michael remained a cold lover. This did not prevent Julia from falling madly in love with him. For it was when he joined Langton's repertory company that they met.

Her own career had been singularly lacking in hardship. She was born in Jersey, where her father, a native of that island, practised as a veterinary surgeon. Her mother's sister was married to a Frenchman, a coal merchant, who lived at St. Malo, and Julia had been sent to live with her while she attended classes at the local *lycée*. She learnt to speak French like a Frenchwoman. She was a born actress and it was an understood thing for as long as she could remember that she was to go on the stage. Her aunt, Madame Falloux, was *en relations* with an old actress who had been a *sociétaire* of the Comédie Française and who had retired to St. Malo to live on the small pension that one of her lovers had settled on her when after many years of faithful concubinage they had parted. When Julia was a child of twelve this actress was a boisterous, fat old woman of more than sixty, but of great vitality, who loved food more than anything else in the world. She had a great, ringing laugh, like a man's, and she talked in a deep, loud voice. It was she who gave Julia her first lessons. She taught her all the arts that she had herself learnt at the Conservatoire and she talked to her of Reichenberg who had played *ingénues* till she was seventy, of Sarah Bernhardt and her golden voice, of Mounet-Sully and his majesty, and of Coquelin the greatest actor of them all. She recited to her the great tirades of Corneille and Racine as she had learnt to say them at the Française and taught her to say them in the same way. It was charming to hear Julia in her childish voice recite those languorous, passionate speeches of Phèdre, emphasising the beat of the Alexandrines and mouthing her words in that manner which is so artificial and yet so wonderfully dramatic. Jane Taitbout must always have been a very stagy actress, but she taught Julia to articulate with extreme distinctness, she taught her how to walk and how to hold herself, she taught her not to be afraid of her own voice, and she made deliberate that wonderful sense of timing which Julia had by instinct and which afterwards was one of her greatest gifts.

"Never pause unless you have a reason for it," she thundered,
banging with her clenched fist on the table at which she sat, "but
when you pause, pause as long as you can."

When Julia was sixteen and went to the Royal Academy of
Dramatic Art in Gower Street she knew already much that they
could teach her there. She had to get rid of a certain number of
tricks that were out of date and she had to acquire a more conversational style. But she won every prize that was open to her,
and when she was finished with the school her good French got
her almost immediately a small part in London as a French maid.
It looked for a while as though her knowledge of French would
specialise her in parts needing a foreign accent, for after this she
was engaged to play an Austrian waitress. It was two years later
that Jimmie Langton discovered her. She was on tour in a melo-
drama that had been successful in London; in the part of an
Italian adventuress, whose machinations were eventually exposed,
she was trying somewhat inadequately to represent a woman of
forty. Since the heroine, a blonde person of mature years, was
playing a young girl, the performance lacked verisimilitude.
Jimmie was taking a short holiday which he spent in going every
night to the theatre in one town after another. At the end of the
piece he went round to see Julia. He was well enough known in
the theatrical world for her to be flattered by the compliments he
paid her, and when he asked her to lunch with him next day
she accepted.

They had no sooner sat down to table than he went straight to
the point.

"I never slept a wink all night for thinking of you," he said.

"This is very sudden. Is your proposal honourable or dis-
honourable?"

He took no notice of the flippant rejoinder.

"I've been at this game for twenty-five years. I've been a call-
boy, a stage-hand, a stage-manager, an actor, a publicity man,
damn it, I've even been a critic. I've lived in the theatre since I
was a kid just out of a board school, and what I don't know about
acting isn't worth knowing. I think you're a genius."

"It's sweet of you to say so."

"Shut up. Leave me to do the talking. You've got everything.
You're the right height, you've got a good figure, you've got an
indiarubber face."

"Flattering, aren't you?"

"That's just what I am. That's the face an actress wants. The face that can look anything, even beautiful, the face that can show every thought that passes through the mind. That's the face Duse's got. Last night even though you weren't really thinking about what you were doing every now and then the words you were saying wrote themselves on your face."

"It's such a rotten part. How could I give it my attention? Did you hear the things I had to say?"

"Actors are rotten, not parts. You've got a wonderful voice, the voice that can wring an audience's heart; I don't know about your comedy, I'm prepared to risk that."

"What d'you mean by that?"

"Your timing is almost perfect. That couldn't have been taught, you must have that by nature. That's the far, far better way. Now let's come down to brass tacks. I've been making enquiries about you. It appears you speak French like a French-woman and so they give you broken English parts. That's not going to lead you anywhere, you know."

"That's all I can get."

"Are you satisfied to go on playing those sort of parts for ever? You'll get stuck in them and the public won't take you in any-thing else. Seconds, that's all you'll play. Twenty pounds a week at the outside and a great talent wasted."

"I've always thought that some day or other I should get a chance of a straight part."

"When? You may have to wait ten years. How old are you now?"

"Twenty."

"What are you getting?"

"Fifteen pounds a week."

"That's a lie. You're getting twelve, and it's a damned sight more than you're worth. You've got everything to learn. Your gestures are commonplace. You don't know that every gesture must mean something. You don't know how to get an audience to look at you before you speak. You make up too much. With your sort of face the less make-up the better. Wouldn't you like to be a star?"

"Who wouldn't?"

"Come to me and I'll make you the greatest actress in England. Are you a quick study? You ought to be at your age."

"I think I can be word-perfect in any part in forty-eight hours."

"It's experience you want and me to produce you. Come to

me and I'll let you play twenty parts a year. Ibsen, Shaw, Barker, Sudermann, Hankin, Galsworthy. You've got magnetism and you don't seem to have an idea how to use it." He chuckled. "By God, if you had, that old hag would have had you out of the play you're in now before you could say knife. You've got to take an audience by the throat and say: Now, you dogs, you pay attention to me. You've got to dominate them. If you haven't got the gift no one can give it you, but if you have you can be taught how to use it. I tell you, you've got the makings of a great actress. I've never been so sure of anything in my life."

"I know I want experience. I'd have to think it over of course. I wouldn't mind coming to you for a season."

"Go to hell. Do you think I can make an actress of you in a season? Do you think I'm going to work my guts out to make you give a few decent performances and then have you go away to play some twopenny-halfpenny part in a commercial play in London? What sort of a bloody fool do you take me for? I'll give you a three years' contract, I'll give you eight pounds a week and you'll have to work like a horse."

"Eight pounds a week's absurd. I couldn't possibly take that."

"Oh yes, you could. It's all you're worth and it's all you're going to get."

Julia had been on the stage for three years and had learnt a good deal. Besides, Jane Taitbout, no strict moralist, had given her a lot of useful information.

"And are you under the impression by any chance, that for that I'm going to let you sleep with me as well?"

"My God, do you think I've got time to go to bed with the members of my company? I've got much more important things to do than that, my girl. And you'll find that after you've rehearsed for four hours and played a part at night to my satisfaction, besides a couple of matinées, you won't have much time or much inclination to make love to anybody. When you go to bed all you'll want to do is to sleep."

But Jimmie Langton was wrong there.

CHAPTER III

JULIA, taken by his enthusiasm and his fantastic exuberance, accepted his offer. He started her in modest parts which under his direction she played as she had never played before. He interested the critics in her, he flattered them by letting them think that they had discovered a remarkable actress, and allowed the suggestion to come from them that he should let the public see her as Magda. She was a great hit and then in quick succession he made her play Nora in *The Doll's House*, Ann in *Man and Superman*, and Hedda Gabler. Middlepool was delighted to discover that it had in its midst an actress who it could boast was better than any star in London, and crowded to see her in plays that before it had gone to only from local patriotism. The London paragraphers mentioned her now and then, and a number of enthusiastic patrons of the drama made the journey to Middlepool to see her. They went back full of praise, and two or three London managers sent representatives to report on her. They were doubtful. She was all very well in Shaw and Ibsen, but what would she do in an ordinary play? The managers had had bitter experiences. On the strength of an outstanding performance in one of these queer plays they had engaged an actor, only to discover that in any other sort of play he was no better than anybody else.

When Michael joined the company Julia had been playing in Middlepool for a year. Jimmie started him with Marchbanks in *Candida*. It was the happy choice one would have expected him to make, for in that part his great beauty was an asset and his lack of warmth no disadvantage.

Julia reached over to take out the first of the cardboard cases in which Michael's photographs were kept. She was sitting comfortably on the floor. She turned the early photographs over quickly, looking for that which he had had taken when first he came to Middlepool; but when she came upon it, it gave her a pang. For a moment she felt inclined to cry. It had been just like him then. Candida was being played by an older woman, a sound actress who was cast generally for mothers, maiden aunts or character parts, and Julia with nothing to do but act eight times a week attended the rehearsals. She fell in love with Michael at first sight. She had never seen a more beautiful young man, and she pursued him relentlessly. In due course Jimmie put on *Ghosts*, braving the censure of respectable Middlepool, and Michael played the boy and she played Regina. They heard one another their parts and after rehearsals lunched, very modestly, together so that they might talk of them. Soon they were inseparable. Julia had little reserve; she flattered Michael outrageously. He was not vain of his good looks, he knew he was handsome and accepted compliments, not exactly with indifference, but as he might have accepted a compliment on a fine old house that had been in his family for generations. It was a well-known fact that it was one of the best houses of its period, one was proud of it and took care of it, but it was just there, as natural to possess as the air one breathed. He was shrewd and ambitious. He knew that his beauty was at present his chief asset, but he knew it could not last for ever and was determined to become a good actor so that he should have something besides his looks to depend on. He meant to learn all he could from Jimmie Langton and then go to London.

"If I play my cards well I can get some old woman to back me and go into management. One's got to be one's own master. That's the only way to make a packet."

Julia soon discovered that he did not much like spending money, and when they ate a meal together, or on a Sunday went for a small excursion, she took care to pay her share of the expenses. She did not mind this. She liked him for counting the pennies, and, inclined to be extravagant herself and always a week or two behind with her rent, she admired him because he hated to be in debt and even with the small salary he was getting managed to save up a little every week. He was anxious to have enough put by so that when he went to London he need not accept the first part that was offered him, but could afford to wait till he got one that gave him a real chance. His father had little more than his pension to live on, and it had been a sacrifice to send him to Cambridge. His father, not liking the idea of his going on the stage, had insisted on this.

"If you want to be an actor I suppose I can't stop you," he said, "but damn it all, I insist on your being educated like a gentleman."

It gave Julia a good deal of satisfaction to discover that Michael's father was a colonel, it impressed her to hear him speak of an ancestor who had gambled away his fortune at White's during the

Regency, and she liked the signet ring Michael wore with the boar's head on it and the motto: *Nemo me impune lacessit.*

"I believe you're prouder of your family than of looking like a Greek god," she told him fondly.

"Anyone can be good-looking," he answered, with his sweet smile, "but not everyone can belong to a decent family. To tell you the truth I'm glad my governor's a gentleman."

Julia took her courage in both hands.

"My father's a vet."

For an instant Michael's face stiffened, but he recovered himself immediately and laughed.

"Of course it doesn't really matter what one's father is. I've often heard my father talk of the vet in his regiment. He counted as an officer of course. Dad always said he was one of the best."

And she was glad he'd been to Cambridge. He had rowed for his College and at one time there was some talk of putting him in the University boat.

"I should have liked to get my blue. It would have been useful to me on the stage. I'd have got a lot of advertisement out of it."

Julia could not tell if he knew that she was in love with him. He never made love to her. He liked her society and when they found themselves with other people scarcely left her side. Sometimes they were asked to parties on Sunday, dinner at midday or a cold, sumptuous supper, and he seemed to think it natural that they should go together and come away together. He kissed her when he left her at her door, but he kissed her as he might have kissed the middle-aged woman with whom he had played *Candida.* He was friendly, good-humoured and kind, but it was distressingly clear that she was no more to him than a comrade. Yet she knew that he was not in love with anybody else. The love-letters that women wrote to him he read out to Julia with a chuckle, and when they sent him flowers he immediately gave them to her.

"What blasted fools, they are," he said. "What the devil do they think they're going to get out of it?"

"I shouldn't have thought it very hard to guess that," said Julia dryly.

Although she knew he took these attentions so lightly she could not help feeling angry and jealous.

"I should be a damned fool if I got myself mixed up with some woman in Middlepool. After all, they're mostly flappers. Before

I knew where I was I'd have some irate father coming along and saying. Now you must marry the girl."

She tried to find out whether he had had any adventures while he was playing with Benson's company. She gathered that one or two of the girls had been rather inclined to make nuisances of themselves, but he thought it was a terrible mistake to get mixed up with any of the actresses a chap was playing with. It was bound to lead to trouble.

"And you know how people gossip in a company. Everyone would know everything in twenty-four hours. And when you start a thing like that you don't know what you're letting yourself in for. I wasn't risking anything."

When he wanted a bit of fun he waited till they were within a reasonable distance of London and then he would race up to town and pick up a girl at the Globe Restaurant. Of course it was expensive, and when you came to think of it, it wasn't really worth the money; besides, he played a lot of cricket in Benson's company, and golf when he got the chance, and that sort of thing was rotten for the eye.

Julia told a thumping lie.

"Jimmie always says I'd be a much better actress if I had an affair."

"Don't you believe it. He's just a dirty old man. With him, I suppose. I mean, you might just as well say that I'd give a better performance of Marchbanks if I wrote poetry."

They talked so much together that it was inevitable for her at last to learn his views on marriage.

"I think an actor's a perfect fool to marry young. There are so many cases in which it absolutely ruins a chap's career. Especially if he marries an actress. He becomes a star and then she's a millstone round his neck. She insists on playing with him, and if he's in management he has to give her leading parts, and if he engages someone else there are most frightful scenes. And of course, for an actress it's insane. There's always the chance of her having a baby and she may have to refuse a damned good part. She's out of the public eye for months, and you know what the public is, unless they see you all the time they forget that you ever existed."

Marriage? What did she care about marriage? Her heart melted within her when she looked into his deep, friendly eyes, and she shivered with delightful anguish when she considered his shining, russet hair. There was nothing that he could have asked her that she would not gladly have given him. The thought never entered his lovely head.

"Of course he likes me," she said to herself. "He likes me better than anyone, he even admires me, but I don't attract him that way."

She did everything to seduce him except slip into bed with him, and she only did not do that because there was no opportunity. She began to fear that they knew one another too well for it to seem possible that their relations should change, and she reproached herself bitterly because she had not rushed to a climax when first they came in contact with one another. He had too sincere an affection for her now ever to become her lover. She found out when his birthday was and gave him a gold cigarette-case which she knew was the thing he wanted more than anything in the world. It cost a good deal more than she could afford and he smilingly reproached her for her extravagance. He never dreamt what ecstatic pleasure it gave her to spend her money on him. When her birthday came along he gave her half a dozen pairs of silk stockings. She noticed at once that they were not of very good quality—poor lamb, he had not been able to bring himself to spring to that—but she was so touched that he should give her anything that she could not help crying.

"What an emotional little thing you are," he said, but he was pleased and touched to see her tears.

She found his thrift rather an engaging trait. He could not bear to throw his money about. He was not exactly mean, but he was not generous. Once or twice at restaurants she thought he under-tipped the waiter, but he paid no attention to her when she ventured to remonstrate. He gave the exact ten per cent, and when he could not make the exact sum to a penny asked the waiter for change.

"Neither a borrower nor a lender be," he quoted from Polonius.

When some member of the company, momentarily hard up, tried to borrow from him it was in vain. But he refused so frankly, with so much heartiness, that he did not affront.

"My dear old boy, I'd love to lend you a quid, but I'm absolutely stony. I don't know how I'm going to pay my rent at the end of the week."

For some months Michael was so much occupied with his own parts that he failed to notice how good an actress Julia was. Of course he read the reviews, and their praise of Julia, but he read summarily, without paying much attention till he came to the remarks the critics made about him. He was pleased by their approval, but not cast down by their censure. He was too modest to resent an unfavourable criticism.

"I suppose I was rotten," he would say ingenuously.

His most engaging trait was his good humour. He bore Jimmie Langton's abuse with equanimity. When tempers grew frayed during a long rehearsal he remained serene. It was impossible to quarrel with him. One day he was sitting in front watching the rehearsal of an act in which he did not appear. It ended with a powerful and moving scene in which Julia had the opportunity to give a fine display of acting. When the stage was being set for the next act Julia came through the pass door and sat down beside Michael. He did not speak to her, but looked sternly in front of him. She threw him a surprised look. It was unlike him not to give her a smile and a friendly word. Then she saw that he was clenching his jaw to prevent its trembling and that his eyes were heavy with tears.

"What's the matter, darling?"

"Don't talk to me. You dirty little bitch, you've made me cry."

"Angel!"

The tears came to her own eyes and streamed down her face. She was so pleased, so flattered.

"Oh, damn it," he sobbed. "I can't help it."

He took a handkerchief out of his pocket and dried his eyes.

("I love him, I love him, I love him.")

Presently he blew his nose.

"I'm beginning to feel better now. But, my God, you shattered me."

"It's not a bad scene, is it?"

"The scene be damned, it was you. You just wrung my heart. The critics are right, damn it, you're an actress and no mistake."

"Have you only just discovered it?"

"I knew you were pretty good, but I never knew you were as good as all that. You make the rest of us look like a piece of cheese. You're going to be a star. Nothing can stop you."

"Well then, you shall be my leading man."

"Fat chance I'd have of that with a London manager."

Julia had an inspiration.

"Then you must go into management yourself and make me your leading lady."

He paused. He was not a quick thinker and needed a little time to let a notion sink into his mind. He smiled.

"You know, that's not half a bad idea."

They talked it over at luncheon. Julia did most of the talking while he listened to her with absorbed interest.

"Of course the only way to get decent parts consistently is to run one's own theatre," he said. "I know that."

The money was the difficulty. They discussed how much was the least they could start on. Michael thought five thousand pounds was the minimum. But how in heaven's name could they raise a sum like that? Of course some of those Middlepool manufacturers were rolling in money, but you could hardly expect them to fork out five thousand pounds to start a couple of young actors who had only a local reputation. Besides, they were jealous of London.

"You'll have to find your rich old woman," said Julia gaily.

She only half believed all she had been saying, but it excited her to discuss a plan that would bring her into a close and constant relation with Michael. But he was being very serious.

"I don't believe one could hope to make a success in London unless one were pretty well known already. The thing to do would be to act there in other managements for three or four years first; one's got to know the ropes. And the advantage of that would be that one would have had time to read plays. It would be madness to start in management unless one had at least three plays. One of them ought to be a winner."

"Of course if one did that, one ought to make a point of acting together so that the public got accustomed to seeing the two names on the same bill."

"I don't know that there's much in that. The great thing is to have good, strong parts. There's no doubt in my mind that it would be much easier to find backers if one had made a bit of a reputation in London."

CHAPTER IV

IT was getting on for Easter, and Jimmie Langton always closed his theatre for Holy Week. Julia did not quite know what to do with herself; it seemed hardly worth while to go to Jersey. She was surprised to receive a letter one morning from Mrs. Gosselyn, Michael's mother, saying that it would give the colonel and herself so much pleasure if she would come with Michael to spend the week at Cheltenham. When she showed the letter to Michael he beamed.

"I asked her to invite you. I thought it would be more polite than if I just took you along."

"You are sweet. Of course I shall love to come."

Her heart beat with delight. The prospect of spending a whole week with Michael was enchanting. It was just like his good nature to come to the rescue when he knew she was at a loose end. But she saw there was something he wanted to say, yet did not quite like to.

"What is it?"

He gave a little laugh of embarrassment.

"Well, dear, you know, my father's rather old-fashioned, and there are some things he can't be expected to understand. Of course I don't want you to tell a lie or anything like that, but I think it would seem rather funny to him if he knew your father was a vet. When I wrote and asked if I could bring you down I said he was a doctor."

"Oh, that's all right."

Julia found the colonel a much less alarming person than she had expected. He was thin and rather small, with a lined face and close-cropped white hair. His features had a worn distinction. He reminded you of a head on an old coin that had been in circulation too long. He was civil, but reserved. He was neither peppery nor tyrannical as Julia, from her knowledge of the stage, expected a colonel to be. She could not imagine him shouting out words of command in that courteous, rather cold voice. He had in point of fact retired with honorary rank after an entirely un-distinguished career, and for many years had been content to work in his garden and play bridge at his club. He read *The Times*, went to church on Sunday and accompanied his wife to tea-parties. Mrs. Gosselyn was a tall, stoutish, elderly woman, much taller than her husband, who gave you the impression that she was always trying to diminish her height. She had the remains of good looks, so that you said to yourself that when young she must have been beautiful. She wore her hair parted in the middle with a bun on the nape of her neck. Her classic features and her size made her at first meeting somewhat imposing, but Julia quickly discovered that she was very shy. Her movements were stiff and awkward. She was dressed fussily, with a sort of old-fashioned richness which did not suit her. Julia, who was entirely without self-consciousness, found the elder woman's deprecating attitude rather touching. She had never known an actress to speak to and did not quite know how to deal with the predicament in which she now found herself. The house was not at all grand, a small detached stucco house in a garden with a laurel hedge, and since the Gosselyns had been for some years in India there were great trays of brass ware and brass bowls, pieces of Indian embroidery and highly-carved Indian tables. It was cheap bazaar stuff, and you wondered how anyone had thought it worth bringing home.

Julia was quick-witted. It did not take her long to discover that the colonel, notwithstanding his reserve, and Mrs. Gosselyn, notwithstanding her shyness, were taking stock of her. The thought flashed through her mind that Michael had brought her down for his parents to inspect her. Why? There was only one possible reason, and when she thought of it her heart leaped. She saw that he was anxious for her to make a good impression. She felt instinctively that she must conceal the actress, and without effort, without deliberation, merely because she felt it would please, she played the part of the simple, modest, ingenuous girl who had lived a quiet country life. She walked round the garden with the colonel and listened intelligently while he talked of peas and asparagus; she helped Mrs. Gosselyn with the flowers and dusted the ornaments with which the drawing-room was crowded. She talked to her of Michael. She told her how cleverly he acted and how popular he was and she praised his looks. She saw that Mrs. Gosselyn was very proud of him, and with a flash of intuition saw that it would please her if she let her see, with the utmost delicacy, as though she would have liked to keep it a secret but betrayed herself unwittingly, that she was head over ears in love with him.

"Of course we hope he'll do well," said Mrs. Gosselyn. "We didn't much like the idea of his going on the stage; you see, on both sides of the family, we're army, but he was set on it."

"Yes, of course I see what you mean."

"I know it doesn't mean so much as when I was a girl, but after all he was born a gentleman."

"Oh, but some very nice people go on the stage nowadays, you know. It's not like in the old days."

"No, I suppose not. I'm so glad he brought you down here. I was a little nervous about it. I thought you'd be made-up and . . . perhaps a little loud. No one would dream you were on the stage."

("I should damn well think not. Haven't I been giving a perfect performance of the village maiden for the last forty-eight hours?")

The colonel began to make little jokes with her and sometimes he pinched her ear playfully.

"Now you mustn't flirt with me, Colonel," she cried, giving him a roguish, delicious glance. "Just because I'm an actress you think you can take liberties with me."

"George, George," smiled Mrs. Gosselyn. And then to Julia: "He always was a terrible flirt."

("Gosh, I'm going down like a barrel of oysters.")

Mrs. Gosselyn told her about India, how strange it was to have all those coloured servants, but how nice the society was, only army people and Indian civilians, but still it wasn't like home, and how glad she was to get back to England.

They were to leave on Easter Monday because they were playing that night, and on Sunday evening after supper Colonel Gosselyn said he was going to his study to write letters; a minute or two later Mrs. Gosselyn said she must go and see the cook. When they were left alone Michael, standing with his back to the fire, lit a cigarette.

"I'm afraid it's been very quiet down here; I hope you haven't had an awfully dull time."

"It's been heavenly."

"You've made a tremendous success with my people. They've taken an enormous fancy to you."

"God, I've worked for it," thought Julia, but aloud said: "How d'you know?"

"Oh, I can see it. Father told me you were very ladylike, and not a bit like an actress, and Mother says you're so sensible."

Julia looked down as though the extravagance of these compliments was almost more than she could bear. Michael came over and stood in front of her. The thought occurred to her that he looked like a handsome young footman applying for a situation. He was strangely nervous. Her heart thumped against her ribs.

"Julia dear, will you marry me?"

For the last week she had asked herself whether or not he was going to propose to her, and now that he had at last done so, she was strangely confused.

"Michael!"

"Not immediately, I don't mean. But when we've got our feet on the ladder. I know that you can act me off the stage, but we get on together like a house on fire, and when we do go into management I think we'd make a pretty good team. And you know I do like you most awfully. I mean, I've never met anyone who's a patch on you."

("The blasted fool, why does he talk all that rot? Doesn't he know I'm crazy to marry him? Why doesn't he kiss me, kiss me, kiss me? I wonder if I dare tell him I'm absolutely sick with love for him.")

"Michael, you're so handsome. No one could refuse to marry you!"

"Darling!"

("I'd better get up. He wouldn't know how to sit down. God, that scene that Jimmie made him do over and over again!")

She got on her feet and put up her face to his. He took her in his arms and kissed her lips.

"I must tell Mother."

He broke away from her and went to the door.

"Mother, Mother!"

In a moment the colonel and Mrs. Gosselyn came in. They bore a look of happy expectancy.

("By God, it was a put-up job.")

"Mother, Father, we're engaged."

Mrs. Gosselyn began to cry. With her awkward, lumbering gait she came up to Julia, flung her arms round her and, sobbing, kissed her. The colonel wrung his son's hand in a manly way and releasing Julia from his wife's embrace kissed her too. He was deeply moved. All this emotion worked on Julia and, though she smiled happily, the tears coursed down her cheeks. Michael watched the affecting scene with sympathy.

"What d'you say to a bottle of pop to celebrate?" he said. "It looks to me as though Mother and Julia were thoroughly upset."

"The ladies, God bless 'em," said the colonel when their glasses were filled.

CHAPTER V

JULIA now was looking at the photograph of herself in her wedding-dress.

"Christ, what a sight I looked."

They decided to keep their engagement to themselves, and Julia told no one about it but Jimmie Langton, two or three girls in the company and her dresser. She vowed them to secrecy and could not understand how within forty-eight hours everyone in the theatre seemed to know all about it. Julia was divinely happy. She loved Michael more passionately than ever and would gladly have married him there and then, but his good sense prevailed. They were at present no more than a couple of provincial actors, and to start their conquest of London as a married couple would jeopardise their chances. Julia showed him as clearly as she knew how, and this was very clearly indeed, that she was quite willing to become his mistress, but this he refused. He was too honourable to take advantage of her.

"I could not love thee, dear, so much, loved I not honour more," he quoted.

He felt sure that when they were married they would bitterly regret it if they had lived together before as man and wife. Julia was proud of his principles. He was a kind and affectionate lover, but in a very short while seemed to take her a trifle for granted; by his manner, friendly but casual, you might have thought they had been married for years. But he showed great good nature in allowing Julia to make love to him. She adored to sit cuddled up to him with his arm round her waist, her face against his, and it was heaven when she could press her eager mouth against his rather thin lips. Though when they sat side by side like that he preferred to talk of the parts they were studying or make plans for the future, he made her very happy. She never tired of praising his beauty. It was heavenly, when she told him how exquisite his nose was and how lovely his russet, curly hair, to feel his hold on her tighten a little and to see the tenderness in his eyes.

"Darling, you'll make me as vain as a peacock."

"It would be so silly to pretend you weren't divinely hand-some."

Julia thought he was, and she said it because she liked saying it, but she said it also because she knew he liked to hear it. He had affection and admiration for her, he felt at ease with her, and he had confidence in her, but she was well aware that he was not in love with her. She consoled herself by thinking that he loved her as much as he was capable of loving, and she thought that when they were married, when they slept together, her own passion would excite an equal passion in him. Meanwhile she exercised all her tact and all her self-control. She knew she could not afford to bore him. She knew she must never let him feel that she was a burden or a responsibility. He might desert her for a game of golf, or to lunch with a casual acquaintance, she never let him see for a moment that she was hurt. And with an inkling that her success as an actress strengthened his feeling for her she worked like a dog to play well.

When they had been engaged for rather more than a year an American manager, looking for talent and having heard of Jimmie Langton's repertory company, came to Middlepool and was greatly taken by Michael. He sent him round a note asking him to come to his hotel on the following afternoon. Michael, breathless with excitement, showed it to Julia; it could only mean that he was going to offer him a part. Her heart sank, but she pretended that she was as excited as he, and went with him next day to the hotel. She was to wait in the lobby while Michael saw the great man.

"Wish me luck," he whispered, as he turned from her to enter the lift. "It's almost too good to be true."

Julia sat in a great leather arm-chair willing with all her might the American manager to offer a part that Michael would refuse or a salary that he felt it would be beneath his dignity to accept. Or alternatively that he should get Michael to read the part he had in view and come to the conclusion that he could not touch it. But when she saw Michael coming towards her half an hour later, his eyes bright and his step swinging, she knew he had clicked. For a moment she thought she was going to be sick, and when she forced on her face an eager, happy smile, she felt that her muscles were stiff and hard.

"It's all right. He says it's a damned good part, a boy's part, nineteen. Eight or ten weeks in New York and then on the road. It's a safe forty weeks with John Drew. Two hundred and fifty dollars a week."

"Oh, darling, how wonderful for you."

It was quite clear that he had accepted with alacrity. The thought of refusing had never even occurred to him.

"And I—I," she thought, "if they'd offered me a thousand dollars a week I wouldn't have gone if it meant being separated from Michael."

Black despair seized her. She could do nothing. She must pretend to be as delighted as he was. He was too much excited to sit still and took her out into the crowded street to walk.

"It's a wonderful chance. Of course America's expensive, but I ought to be able to live on fifty dollars a week at the outside, they say the Americans are awfully hospitable and I shall get a lot of free meals. I don't see why I shouldn't save eight thousand dollars in the forty weeks and that's sixteen hundred pounds."

("He doesn't love me. He doesn't care a damn about me. I hate him. I'd like to kill him. Blast that American manager.")

"And if he takes me on for a second year I'm to get three hundred. That means that in two years I'd have the best part of four thousand pounds. Almost enough to start management on."

"A second year!" For a moment Julia lost control of herself and her voice was heavy with tears. "D'you mean to say you'll be gone two years?"

"Oh, I should come back next summer of course. They pay my fare back and I'd go and live at home so as not to spend any money."

"I don't know how I'm going to get on without you."

She said the words very brightly, so that they sounded polite, but somewhat casual.

"Well, we can have a grand time together in the summer and, you know, a year, two years at the outside, well, it passes like a flash of lightning."

Michael had been walking at random, but Julia without his noticing had guided him in the direction she wished, and now they arrived in front of the theatre. She stopped.

"I'll see you later. I've got to pop up and see Jimmie." His face fell.

"You're not going to leave me now! I must talk to somebody. I thought we might go and have a snack together before the show."

"I'm terribly sorry. Jimmie's expecting me and you know what he is."

Michael gave her his sweet, good-natured smile.

"Oh, well, go on then. I'm not going to hold it up against you because for once you've let me down."

He walked on and she went in by the stage door. Jimmie Langton had arranged himself a tiny flat under the roof to which you gained access through the balcony. She rang the bell of his front door and he opened it himself. He was surprised, but pleased, to see her.

"Hulloa, Julia, come in."

She walked past him without a word, and when they got into his sitting-room, untidy, littered with typescript plays, books and other rubbish, the remains of his frugal luncheon still on a tray by his desk, she turned and faced him. Her jaw was set and her eyes were frowning.

"You devil!"

With a swift gesture she went up to him, seized him by his loose shirt collar with both hands and shook him. He struggled to get free of her, but she was strong and violent.

"Stop it. Stop it."

"You devil, you swine, you filthy low-down cad."

He took a swing and with his open hand gave her a great smack on the face. She instinctively loosened her grip on him and put her own hand up to her cheek, for he had hurt her. She burst out crying.

"You brute. You rotten hound to hit a woman."

"You put that where the monkey put the nuts, dearie. Didn't you know that when a woman hits me I always hit back?"

"I didn't hit you."

"You damned near throttled me."

"You deserved it. Oh, my God, I'd like to kill you."

"Now sit down, duckie, and I'll give you a drop of Scotch to pull you together. And then you can tell me all about it."

Julia looked round for a big chair into which she could conveniently sink.

"Christ, the place is like a pig-sty. Why the hell don't you get a charwoman in?"

With an angry gesture she swept the books on to the floor from an arm-chair, threw herself in it, and began to cry in earnest. He poured her out a stiff dose of whisky, added a drop of soda, and made her drink it.

"Now what's all this Tosca stuff about?"

"Michael's going to America."

"Is he?"

She wrenched herself away from the arm he had round her shoulder.

"How could you? How could you?"

"I had nothing to do with it."

"That's a lie. I suppose you didn't even know that filthy American manager was in Middlepool. Of course it's your doing. You did it deliberately to separate us."

"Oh, dearie, you're doing me an injustice. In point of fact I don't mind telling you that I said to him he could have anyone in the company he liked with the one exception of Michael Gosselyn."

Julia did not see the look in Jimmie's eyes when he told her this, but if she had would have wondered why he was looking as pleased as if he had pulled off a very clever little trick.

"Even me?" she said.

"I knew he didn't want women. They've got plenty of their own. It's men they want who know how to wear their clothes and don't spit in the drawing-room."

"Oh, Jimmie, don't let Michael go. I can't bear it."

"How can I prevent it? His contract's up at the end of the season. It's a wonderful chance for him."

"But I love him. I want him. Supposing he sees someone else in America. Supposing some American heiress falls in love with him."

"If he doesn't love you any more than that I should have thought you'd be well rid of him."

The remark revived Julia's fury.

"You rotten old eunuch, what do you know about love?"

"These women," Jimmie sighed. "If you try to go to bed with them they say you're a dirty old man, and if you don't they say you're a rotten old eunuch."

"Oh, you don't understand. He's so frightfully handsome, they'll fall for him like a row of ninepins, and, poor lamb, he's so susceptible to flattery. Anything can happen in two years."

"What's this about two years?"

"If he's a success he's to stay another year."

"Well, don't worry your head about that. He'll be back at the end of the season and back for good. That manager only saw him in *Candida*. It's the only part he's half-way decent in. Take my word for it, it won't be long before they find out they've been sold a pup. He's going to be a flop."

"What do you know about acting?"

"Everything."

"I'd like to scratch your eyes out."

"I warn you that if you attempt to touch me I shan't give you a little bit of a slap, I shall give you such a biff on the jaw that you won't be able to eat in comfort for a week."

"By God, I believe you'd do it. Do you call yourself a gentleman?"

"Not even when I'm drunk."

Julia giggled, and Jimmie felt the worst of the scene was over.

"Now you know just as well as I do that you can act him off his head. I tell you, you're going to be the greatest actress since Mrs. Kendal. What do you want to go and hamper yourself with a man who'll always be a mill-stone round your neck? You want to go into management; he'll want to play opposite you. He'll never be good enough, my dear."

"He's got looks. I can carry him."

"You've got a pretty good opinion of yourself, haven't you? But you're wrong. If you want to make a success you can't afford to have a leading man who's not up to the mark."

"I don't care. I'd rather marry him and be a failure than be a success and married to somebody else."

"Are you a virgin?"

Julia giggled again.

"I don't know that it's any business of yours, but in point of fact I am."

"I thought you were. Well, unless it means something to you, why don't you go over to Paris with him for a fortnight when we close? He won't be sailing till August. It might get him out of your system."

"Oh, he wouldn't. He's not that sort of man. You see, he's by way of being a gentleman."

"Even the upper classes propagate their species."

"You don't understand," said Julia haughtily.

"I bet you don't either."

Julia did not condescend to reply. She was really very unhappy.

"I can't live without him, I tell you. What am I to do with myself when he's away?"

"Stay on with me. I'll give you a contract for another year. I've got a lot of new parts I want to give you and I've got a juvenile in my eye who's a find. You'll be surprised how much easier you'll find it when you've got a chap opposite you who'll really give you something. You can have twelve pounds a week."

Julia went up to him and stared into his eyes searchingly.

"Have you done all this to get me to stay on for another year? Have you broken m yheart and ruined my whole life just to keep me in your rotten theatre?"

"I swear I haven't. I like you and I admire you. And we've done better business the last two years than we've ever done before. But, damn it, I wouldn't play you a dirty trick like that."

"You liar, you filthy liar."

"I swear it's the truth."

"Prove it then," she said violently.

"How can I prove it? You know I'm decent really."

"Give me fifteen pounds a week and I'll believe you."

"Fifteen pounds a week? You know what our takings are. How can I? Oh well, all right. But I shall have to pay three pounds out of my own pocket."

"A fat lot I care."

CHAPTER VI

AFTER a fortnight of rehearsals, Michael was thrown out of the part for which he had been engaged, and for three or four weeks was left to kick his heels about till something else could be found for him. He opened in due course in a play that ran less than a month in New York. It was sent on the road; but languished and was withdrawn. After another wait he was given a part in a costume play where his good looks shone to such advantage that his indifferent acting was little noticed, and in this he finished the season. There was no talk of renewing his contract. Indeed the manager who had engaged him was caustic in his comments.

"Gee, I'd give something to get even with that fellow Langton, the son of a bitch," he said. "He knew what he was doing all right when he landed me with that stick."

Julia wrote to Michael constantly, pages and pages of love and gossip, while he answered once a week, four pages exactly in a neat, precise hand. He always ended up by sending her his best love and signing himself hers very affectionately, but the rest of his letter was more informative than passionate. Yet she awaited its coming in an agony of impatience and read it over and over again. Though he wrote cheerfully, saying little about the theatre except that the parts they gave him were rotten and the plays in which he was expected to act beneath contempt, news travels in the theatrical world, and Julia knew that he had not made good.

"I suppose it's beastly of me," she thought, "but thank God, thank God."

When he announced the date of his sailing she could not contain her joy. She got Jimmie so to arrange his programme that she might go and meet him at Liverpool.

"If the boat comes in late I shall probably stay the night," she told Jimmie.

He smiled ironically.

"I suppose you think that in the excitement of home-coming you may work the trick."

"What a beastly little man you are."

"Come off it, dear. My advice to you is, get him a bit tight and then lock yourself in a room with him and tell him you won't let him out till he's made a dishonest woman of you."

But when she was starting he came to the station with her. As she was getting into the carriage he took her hand and patted it.

"Feeling nervous, dear?"

"Oh, Jimmie dear, wild with happiness and sick with anxiety."

"Well, good luck to you. And don't forget you're much too good for him. You're young and pretty and you're the greatest actress in England."

When the train steamed out Jimmie went to the station bar and had a whisky and soda. "Lord, what fools these mortals be," he sighed. But Julia stood up in the empty carriage and looked at herself in the glass.

"Mouth too large, face too puddingy, nose too fleshy. Thank God, I've got good eyes and good legs. Exquisite legs. I wonder if I've got too much make-up on. He doesn't like make-up off the stage. I look bloody without rouge. My eyelashes are all right. Damn it all, I don't look so bad."

Uncertain till the last moment whether Jimmie would allow her to go, Julia had not been able to let Michael know that she was meeting him. He was surprised and frankly delighted to see her. His beautiful eyes beamed with pleasure.

"You're more lovely than ever," she said.

"Oh, don't be so silly," he laughed, squeezing her arm affectionately. "You haven't got to go back till after dinner, have you?"

"I haven't got to go back till to-morrow. I've taken a couple of rooms at the Adelphi, so that we can have a real talk."

"The Adelphi's a bit grand, isn't it?"

"Oh, well, you don't come back from America every day. Damn the expense."

"Extravagant little thing, aren't you? I didn't know when we'd dock, so I told my people I'd wire when I was getting down to Cheltenham. I'll tell them I'll be coming along to-morrow."

When they got to the hotel Michael came to Julia's room, at her suggestion, so that they could talk in peace and quiet. She sat on his knees, with her arm round his neck, her cheek against his.

"Oh, it's so good to be home again," she sighed.

"You don't have to tell me that," he said, not understanding that she referred to his arms and not to his arrival.

"D'you still like me?"

"Rather."

She kissed him fondly.

"Oh, you don't know how I've missed you."

"I was an awful flop in America," he said. "I didn't tell you in my letters, because I thought it would only worry you. They thought me rotten."

"Michael!" she cried, as though she could not believe him.

"The fact is, I suppose, I'm too English. They don't want me another year. I didn't think they did, but just as a matter of form I asked them if they were going to exercise their option and they said no, not at any price."

Julia was silent. She looked deeply concerned, but her heart was beating with exultation.

"I honestly don't care, you know. I didn't like America. It's a smack in the eye of course, it's no good denying that, but the only thing is to grin and bear it. If you only knew the people one has to deal with! Why, compared with some of them, Jimmie Langton's a great gentleman. Even if they had wanted me to stay I should have refused."

Though he put a brave face on it, Julia felt that he was deeply mortified. He must have had to put up with a good deal of unpleasantness. She hated him to have been made unhappy, but, oh, she was so relieved.

"What are you going to do now?" she asked quietly.

"Well, I shall go home for a bit and think things over. Then I shall go to London and see if I can't get a part."

She knew that it was no good suggesting that he should come back to Middlepool. Jimmie Langton would not have him.

"You wouldn't like to come with me, I suppose?"

Julia could hardly believe her ears.

"Me? Darling, you know I'd go anywhere in the world with you."

"Your contract's up at the end of this season, and if you want to get anywhere you've got to make a stab at London soon. I saved every bob I could in America, they all called me a tight-wad but I just let them talk, I've brought back between twelve and fifteen hundred pounds."

"Michael, how on earth can you have done that?"

"I didn't give much away, you know," he smiled happily. "Of course it's not enough to start management on, but it's enough to get married on, I mean we'd have something to fall back on if we didn't get parts right away or happened to be out of a job for a few months."

It took Julia a second or two to understand what he meant.

"D'you mean to say, get married now?"

"Of course it's a risk, without anything in prospect, but one has to take a risk sometimes."

Julia took his head in both her hands and pressed his lips with hers. Then she gave a sigh.

"Darling, you're wonderful and you're as beautiful as a Greek god, but you're the biggest damned fool I've ever known in my life."

They went to a theatre that night and at supper drank champagne to celebrate their reunion and toast their future. When Michael accompanied her to her room she held up her face to his.

"D'you want me to say good-night to you in the passage? I'll just come in for a minute."

"Better not, darling," she said with quiet dignity.

She felt like a high-born damsel, with all the traditions of a great and ancient family to keep up; her purity was a pearl of great price; she also felt that she was making a wonderfully good impression: of course he was a great gentleman, and "damn it all" it behoved her to be a great lady. She was so pleased with her performance that when she had got into her room and somewhat noisily locked the door, she paraded up and down bowing right and left graciously to her obsequious retainers. She stretched out her lily-white hands for the trembling old steward to kiss (as a baby he had often dandled her on his knee), and when he pressed it with his pallid lips she felt something fall upon it. A tear.

CHAPTER VII

THE first year of their marriage would have been stormy except for Michael's placidity. It needed the excitement of getting a part or a first night, the gaiety of a party where he had drunk several glasses of champagne, to turn his practical mind to thoughts of love. No flattery, no allurements, could tempt him when he had an engagement next day for which he had to keep his brain clear or a round of golf for which he needed a steady eye. Julia made him frantic scenes. She was jealous of his friends at the Green Room Club, jealous of the games that took him away from her, and jealous of the men's luncheons he went to under the pretext that he must cultivate people who might be useful to them. It infuriated her that when she worked herself up into a passion of tears he should sit there quite calmly, with his hands crossed and a good-humoured smile on his handsome face, as though she were merely making herself ridiculous.

"You don't think I'm running after any other woman, do you?" he asked.

"How do I know? It's quite obvious that you don't care two straws for me."

"You know you're the only woman in the world for me."

"My God!"

"I don't know what you want."

"I want love. I thought I'd married the handsomest man in England and I've married a tailor's dummy."

"Don't be so silly. I'm just the ordinary normal Englishman. I'm not an Italian organ-grinder."

She swept up and down the room. They had a small flat at Buckingham Gate and there was not much space, but she did her best. She threw up her hands to heaven.

"I might be squint-eyed and hump-backed. I might be fifty. Am I so unattractive as all that? It's so humiliating to have to beg for love. Misery, misery."

"That was a good movement, dear. As if you were throwing a cricket ball. Remember that."

She gave him a look of scorn.

"That's all you can think of. My heart is breaking, and you can talk of a movement that I made quite accidentally."

But he saw by the expression of her face that she was registering it in her memory, and he knew that when the occasion arose she would make effective use of it.

"After all, love isn't everything. It's all very well at its proper time and in its proper place. We had a lot of fun on our honeymoon, that's what a honeymoon's for, but now we've got to get down to work."

They had been lucky. They had managed to get fairly good parts together in a play that had proved a success. Julia had one good acting scene in which she had brought down the house, and Michael's astonishing beauty had made a sensation. Michael with his gentlemanly push, with his breezy good-nature, had got them both a lot of publicity and their photographs appeared in the illustrated papers. They were asked to a number of parties and Michael, notwithstanding his thriftiness, did not hesitate to spend money on entertaining people who might be of service. Julia was impressed by his lavishness on these occasions. An actor-manager offered Julia the leading part in his next play, and though there was no part for Michael and she was anxious to refuse it, he would not let her. He said they could not afford to let sentiment stand in the way of business. He eventually got a part in a costume play.

They were both acting when the war broke out. To Julia's pride and anguish Michael enlisted at once, but with the help of his father, one of whose old brother officers was an important personage at the War Office, he very soon got a commission. When he went out to France Julia bitterly regretted the reproaches she had so often heaped upon him, and made up her mind that if he were killed she would commit suicide. She wanted to become a nurse so that she could go out to France too and at least be on the same soil as he, but he made her understand that patriotism demanded that she should go on acting, and she could not resist what might very well be his dying request. Michael thoroughly enjoyed the war. He was popular in the regimental mess, and the officers of the old army accepted him almost at once, even though he was an actor, as one of themselves. It was as though the family of soldiers from which he was born had set a seal on him so that he fell instinctively into the manner and way of thinking of the professional soldier. He had tact and a pleasant manner, and he knew how to pull strings adroitly; it was inevitable that he should get on the staff of some general. He showed himself possessed of considerable organising capacity and the last three years of the war he passed at G.H.Q. He ended it as a major, with the Military Cross and the Legion of Honour.

Meanwhile Julia had been playing a succession of important parts and was recognised as the best of the younger actresses. Throughout the war the theatre was very prosperous, and she profited by being seen in plays that had long runs. Salaries went up, and with Michael to advise her she was able to extort eighty pounds a week from reluctant managers. Michael came over to England on his leaves and Julia was divinely happy. Though he was in no more danger than if he had been sheep-farming in New Zealand, she acted as though the brief periods he spent with her were the last days the doomed man would ever enjoy on earth. She treated him as though he had just come from the horror of the trenches and was tender, considerate, and unexacting.

It was just before the end of the war that she fell out of love with him.

She was pregnant at the time. Michael had judged it imprudent to have a baby just then, but she was nearly thirty and thought that if they were going to have one at all they ought to delay no longer; she was so well established on the stage that she could afford not to appear for a few months, and with the possibility that Michael might be killed at any moment—it was true he said he was as safe as a house, he only said that to reassure her, and even generals were killed sometimes—if she was to go on living she must have a child by him. The baby was expected at the end of the year. She looked forward to Michael's next leave as she had never done before. She was feeling very well, but she had a great yearning to feel his arms around her, she felt a little lost, a little helpless, and she wanted his protective strength. He came, looking wonderfully handsome in his well-cut uniform, with the red tabs and the crown on his shoulder-straps. He had filled out a good deal as the result of the hardships of G.H.Q. and his skin was tanned. With his close-cropped hair, breezy manner and military carriage he looked every inch a soldier. He was in great spirits, not only because he was home for a few days, but because the end of the war was in sight. He meant to get out of the army as quickly as possible. What was the good of having a bit of influence if you didn't use it? So many young men had left the stage, either from patriotism or because life was made intolerable for them by the patriotic who stayed at home, and finally owing to conscription, that leading parts had been in the hands either of people who were inapt for military service or those who had been so badly wounded that they had got their discharge. There was a wonderful opening, and Michael saw that if he were available quickly he could get his choice of parts. When he had recalled himself to the recollection of the public they could look about for a theatre, and with the reputation Julia had now acquired it would be safe to start in management.

They talked late into the night and then they went to bed. She cuddled up to him voluptuously and he put his arms round her. After three months of abstinence he was amorous.

"You're the most wonderful little wife," he whispered.

He pressed his mouth to hers. She was filled on a sudden with a faint disgust. She had to resist an inclination to push him away. Before, to her passionate nostrils his body, his young beautiful body, had seemed to have a perfume of flowers and honey, and this had been one of the things that had most enchained her to him, but now in some strange way it had left him. She realised that he no longer smelt like a youth, he smelt like a man. She felt a little sick. She could not respond to his ardour, she was eager that he should get his desire satisfied quickly, turn over on his side, and go to sleep. For long she lay awake. She was dismayed. Her heart sank because she knew she had lost something that was infinitely precious to her, and pitying herself she was inclined to cry; but at the same time she was filled with a sense of triumph, it seemed a revenge that she enjoyed for the unhappiness he had caused her; she was free of the bondage in which her senses had held her to him and she exulted. Now she could deal with him on equal terms. She stretched her legs out in bed and sighed with relief.

"By God, it's grand to be one's own mistress."

They had breakfast in their room. Julia in bed and Michael seated at a little table by her side. She looked at him while he read the paper. Was it possible that three months had made so much difference in him, or was it merely that for years she had still seen him with the eyes that had seen him when he came on the stage to rehearse at Middlepool in the glorious beauty of his youth and she had been stricken as with a mortal sickness? He was wonderfully handsome still—after all he was only thirty-six—but he was not a boy any more; with his close-cropped hair and weather-beaten skin, little lines beginning to mark the smoothness of his forehead and to show under his eyes, he was definitely a man. He had lost his coltish grace and his movements were set. Each difference was very small, but taken altogether they amounted, in her shrewd, calculating eyes, to all the difference in the world. He was a middle-aged man.

They still lived in the small flat that they had taken when first they came to London. Though Julia had been for some time earning a good income it had not seemed worth while to move while Michael was on active service, but now that a baby was coming the flat was obviously too small. Julia had found a house in Regent's Park that she liked very much. She wanted to be settled down in good time for her confinement.

The house faced the gardens. Above the drawing-room floor were two bedrooms and above these, two rooms that could be made into a day and a night nursery. Michael was pleased with everything; even the price seemed to him reasonable. Julia had, during the last four years, been earning so much more money than he that she had offered to furnish the house herself. They stood in one of the bedrooms.

"I can make do with a good deal of what we've got for my bedroom," she said. "I'll get you a nice suite at Maple's."

"I wouldn't go to much expense," he smiled. "I don't suppose I shall use it much, you know."

He liked to share a bed with her. Though not passionate he was affectionate, and he had an animal desire to feel her body against his. For long it had been her greatest comfort. The thought now filled her with irritation.

"Oh, I don't think there should be any more nonsense till after the baby's born. Until all that's over and done with I'm going to make you sleep by yourself."

"I hadn't thought of that. If you think it's better for the kid . . ."

CHAPTER VIII

MICHAEL got himself demobbed the moment the war was finished and stepped straight into a part. He returned to the stage a much better actor than he left it. The breeziness he had acquired in the army was effective. He was a well set-up, normal, high-spirited fellow, with a ready smile and a hearty laugh. He was well suited to drawing-room comedy. His light voice gave a peculiar effect to a flippant line, and though he never managed to make love convincingly he could carry off a chaffing love scene, making a proposal as if it were rather a joke, or a declaration as though he were laughing at himself, in a manner that the audience found engaging. He never attempted to play anyone but himself. He specialised in men about town, gentlemanly gamblers, guardsmen and young scamps with a good side to them. Managers liked him. He worked hard and was amenable to direction. So long as he could get work he didn't mind much what sort of part it was. He stuck out for the salary he thought he was worth, but if he couldn't get it was prepared to take less rather than be idle.

He was making his plans carefully. During the winter that followed the end of the war there was an epidemic of influenza. His father and mother died. He inherited nearly four thousand pounds, and this with his own savings and Julia's brought up their joint capital to seven thousand. But the rent of theatres had gone up enormously, the salaries of actors and the wages of stage-hands had increased, so that the expense of running a theatre was very much greater than it had been before the war. A sum that would then have been amply sufficient to start management on was now inadequate. The only thing was to find some rich man to go in with them so that a failure or two to begin with would not drive them from the field. It was said that you could always find a mug in the City to write a fat cheque for the production of a play, but when you came down to business you discovered that the main condition was that the leading part should be played by some pretty lady in whom he was interested. Years before, Michael and Julia had often joked about the rich old woman who would fall in love with him and set him up in management. He had long since learnt that no rich old woman was to be found to set up in management a young actor whose wife was an actress to whom he was perfectly faithful. In the end the money was found by a rich woman, and not an old one either, but who was interested not in him but in Julia.

Mrs. de Vries was a widow. She was a short stout woman with a fine Jewish nose and fine Jewish eyes, a great deal of energy, a manner at once effusive and timid, and a somewhat virile air. She had a passion for the stage. When Julia and Michael had decided to try their luck in London, Jimmie Langton, to whose rescue she had sometimes come when it looked as though he would be forced to close his repertory theatre, had written to her asking her to do what she could for them. She had seen Julia act in Middlepool. She gave parties so that the young actors might get to know managers, and asked them to stay at her grand house near Guildford, where they enjoyed a luxury they had never dreamt of. She did not much like Michael. Julia accepted the flowers with which Dolly de Vries filled her flat and her dressing-room, she was properly delighted with the presents she gave her, bags, vanity cases, strings of beads in semi-precious stones, brooches; but appeared to be unconscious that Dolly's generosity was due to anything but admiration for her talent. When Michael went away to the war Dolly pressed her to come and live in her house in Montagu Square, but Julia, with protestations of extravagant gratitude, refused in such a way that Dolly, with a sigh and a tear, could only admire her the more. When Roger was born Julia asked her to be his godmother.

For some time Michael had been turning over in his mind the possibility that Dolly de Vries might put up the money they needed, but he was shrewd enough to know that while she might do it for Julia she would not do it for him. Julia refused to approach her.

"She's already been so kind to us I really couldn't ask her, and it would be so humiliating if she refused."

"It's a good gamble, and even if she lost the money she wouldn't feel it. I'm quite sure you could get round her if you tried."

Julia was pretty sure she could too. Michael was very simple-minded in some ways; she did not feel called upon to point out to him the obvious facts.

But he was not a man who let a thing drop when he had set his mind to it. They were going to Guildford to spend the week-end with Dolly, and were driving down after the Saturday night's performance in the new car that Julia had given Michael for his birthday. It was a warm beautiful night. Michael had bought options, though it wrung his heart to write the cheques, on three plays that they both liked, and he had heard of a theatre that they could get on reasonable terms. Everything was ready for the venture except the capital. He urged Julia to seize the opportunity that the week-end presented.

"Ask her yourself then," said Julia impatiently. "I tell you, I'm not going to."

"She wouldn't do it for me. You can twist her round your little finger."

"We know a thing or two about financing plays now. People finance plays for two reasons, either because they want notoriety, or because they're in love with someone. A lot of people talk about art, but you don't often find them paying out hard cash unless they're going to get something out of it for themselves."

"Well, we'll give Dolly all the notoriety she wants."

"That doesn't happen to be what she's after."

"What do you mean?"

"Can't you guess?"

Light dawned on him, and he was so surprised that he slowed down. Was it possible that what Julia suspected was true? He had never even thought that Dolly liked him much, and as for supposing she was in love with him—why, the notion had never crossed his mind. Of course Julia had sharp eyes, not much got by her, but she was a jealous little thing, she was always thinking women were making a dead set at him. It was true that Dolly had given him a pair of cuff-links at Christmas, but he thought that was only so that he shouldn't feel left out in the cold because she had given Julia a brooch that must have cost at least two hundred pounds. That might be only her cunning. Well, he could honestly say he'd never done a thing to make her think there was anything doing. Julia giggled.

"No, darling, it's not you she's in love with."

It was disconcerting the way Julia knew what he was thinking. You couldn't hide a thing from that woman.

"Then why did you put the idea into my head? I wish to goodness you'd express yourself so that a fellow can understand." Julia did.

"I never heard such nonsense," he cried. "What a filthy mind you've got, Julia!"

"Come off it, dear."

"I don't believe there's a word of truth in it. After all I've got eyes in my head. Do you mean to say I shouldn't have noticed it?" He was more irritable than she had ever known him. "And even if it were true I suppose you can take care of yourself. It's a chance in a thousand, and I think it would be madness not to take it."

"Claudio and Isabella in *Measure for Measure*."

"That's a rotten thing to say, Julia. God damn it, I am a gentleman."

"*Nemo me impune lacessit.*"

They drove the rest of the journey in stormy silence. Mrs. de Vries was waiting up for them.

"I didn't want to go to bed till I'd seen you," she said as she folded Julia in her arms and kissed her on both cheeks. She gave Michael a brisk handshake.

Julia spent a happy morning in bed reading the Sunday papers. She read first the theatrical news, then the gossip columns, after that the woman's pages, and finally cast an eye over the headlines of the world's news. The book reviews she ignored; she could never understand why so much space was wasted on them. Michael, who had the room next hers, had come in to say goodmorning, and then gone out into the garden. Presently there was a timid little knock at her door and Dolly came in. Her great black eyes were shining. She sat on the bed and took Julia's hand.

"Darling, I've been talking to Michael. I'm going to put up the money to start you in management."

Julia's heart gave a sudden beat.

"Oh, you mustn't. Michael shouldn't have asked you. I won't have it. You've been far, far too kind to us already."

Dolly leant over and kissed Julia on the lips. Her voice was lower than usual and there was a little tremor in it.

"Oh, my love, don't you know there isn't anything in the world I wouldn't do for you? It'll be so wonderful; it'll bring us so close together and I shall be so proud of you."

They heard Michael come whistling along the passage, and when he came into the room Dolly turned to him with her great eyes misty with tears.

"I've just told her."

He was brimming over with excitement.

"What a grand woman!" He sat down on the other side of the bed and took Julia's disengaged hand. "What d'you say, Julia?"

She gafe him a little reflective look.

"*Vous l'avez voulu*, Georges Dandin."

"What's that?"

"Molière."

As soon as the deed of partnership had been signed and Michael had got his theatre booked for the autumn he engaged a publicity agent. Paragraphs were sent to the papers announcing the new venture and Michael and the publicity agent prepared interviews for him and Julia to give to the Press. Photographs of them, singly and together, with and without Roger, appeared in the weeklies. The domestic note was worked for all it was worth. They could not quite make up their minds which of the three plays they had it would be best to start with. Then one afternoon when Julia was sitting in her bedroom reading a novel, Michael came in with a manuscript in his hand.

"Look here, I want you to read this play at once. It's just come in from an agent. I think it's a knockout. Only we've got to give an answer right away."

Julia put down her novel.

"I'll read it now."

"I shall be downstairs. Let me know when you've finished and I'll come up and talk it over with you. It's got a wonderful part for you."

Julia read quickly, skimming over the scenes in which she was not concerned, but the principal woman's part, the part of course she would play, with concentration. When she had turned the last page she rang the bell and asked her maid (who was also her dresser) to tell Michael she was ready for him.

"Well, what d'you think?"

"The play's all right. I don't see how it can fail to be a success."

He caught something doubtful in her tone.

"What's wrong then? The part's wonderful. I mean, it's the sort of thing that you can do better than anyone in the world. There's a lot of comedy and all the emotion you want."

"It's a wonderful part, I know that; it's the man's part."

"Well, that's a damned good part too."

"I know; but he's fifty, and if you make him younger you take all the point out of the play. You don't want to take the part of a middle-aged man."

"But I wasn't thinking of playing that. There's only one man for that. Monte Vernon. And we can get him. I'll play George."

"But it's a tiny part. You can't play that."

"Why not?"

"But I thought the point of going into management was that we should both play leads."

"Oh, I don't care a hang about that. As long as we can find

plays with star parts for you I don't matter. Perhaps in the next play there'll be a good part for me too."

Julia leant back in her chair, and the ready tears filled her eyes and ran down her cheeks.

"Oh, what a beast I am."

He smiled, and his smile was as charming as ever. He came over to her and kneeling by her side put his arms round her.

"Lor lumme, what's the matter with the old lady now?"

When she looked at him now she wondered what there was in him that had ever aroused in her such a frenzy of passion. The thought of having sexual relations with him nauseated her. Fortunately he found himself very comfortable in the bedroom she had furnished for him. He was not a man to whom sex was important, and he was relieved when he discovered that Julia no longer made any demands on him. He thought with satisfaction that the birth of the baby had calmed her down, he was bound to say that he had thought it might, and he was only sorry they had not had one before. When he had two or three times, more out of amiability than out of desire, suggested that they should resume marital relations and she had made excuses, either that she was tired, not very well, or had two performances next day, to say nothing of a fitting in the morning, he accepted the situation with equanimity. Julia was much easier to get on with, she never made scenes any more, and he was happier than he had ever been before. It was a damned satisfactory marriage he had made, and when he looked at other people's marriages he couldn't help seeing he was one of the lucky ones. Julia was a damned good sort and clever, as clever as a bagful of monkeys; you could talk to her about anything in the world. The best companion a chap ever had, my boy. He didn't mind saying this: he'd rather spend a day alone with her than play a round of golf.

Julia was surprised to discover in herself a strange feeling of pity for him because she no longer loved him. She was a kindly woman, and she realised that it would be a bitter blow to his pride if he ever had an inkling how little he meant to her. She continued to flatter him. She noticed that for long now he had come to listen complacently to her praise of his exquisite nose and beautiful eyes. She got a little private amusement by seeing how much he could swallow. She laid it on with a trowel. But now she looked more often at his straight thin-lipped mouth. It grew meaner as he grew older, and by the time he was an old man it would be no more than a cold hard line. His thrift, which in the early days had seemed an amusing, rather touching trait, now revolted her. When people were in trouble, and on the stage they too often are, they got sympathy and kind friendly words from Michael, but very little cash. He looked upon himself as devilish generous when he parted with a guinea, and a five-pound note was to him the extreme of lavishness. He had soon discovered that Julia ran the house extravagantly, and insisting that he wanted to save her trouble took the matter in his own hands. After that nothing was wasted. Every penny was accounted for. Julia wondered why servants stayed with them. They did because Michael was so nice to them. With his hearty, jolly, affable manner he made them anxious to please him, and the cook shared his satisfaction when she had found a butcher from whom they could get meat a penny a pound cheaper than elsewhere. Julia could not but laugh when she thought how strangely his passion for economy contrasted with the devil-may-care, extravagant creatures he portrayed so well on the stage. She had often thought that he was incapable of a generous impulse; and now, as though it were the most natural thing in the world, he was prepared to stand aside so that she might have her chance. She was too deeply moved to speak. She reproached herself bitterly for all the unkind things she had for so long been thinking of him.

CHAPTER IX

THEY put on the play, and it was a success. After that they continued to produce plays year after year. Because Michael ran the theatre with the method and thrift with which he ran his home they lost little over the failures, which of course they sometimes had, and made every possible penny out of their successes. Michael flattered himself that there was not a management in London where less money was spent on the productions. He exercised great ingenuity in disguising old sets so that they looked new, and by ringing the changes on the furniture that he gradually collected in the store-room saved the expense of hiring. They gained the reputation of being an enterprising management because Michael in order not to pay the high royalties of well-known authors was always willing to give an unknown one a trial.

He sought out actors who had never been given a chance and whose salaries were small. He thus made some very profitable discoveries.

When they had been in management for three years they were sufficiently well established for Michael to be able to borrow from the bank enough money to buy the lease of a theatre that had just been built. After much discussion they decided to call it the Siddons Theatre. They opened with a failure and this was succeeded by another. Julia was frightened and discouraged. She thought that the theatre was unlucky and that the public were getting sick of her. It was then that Michael showed himself at his best. He was unperturbed.

"In this business you have to take the rough with the smooth. You're the best actress in England. There are only three people who bring money into the theatre regardless of the play, and you're one of them. We've had a couple of duds. The next play's bound to be all right and then we shall get back all we've lost and a packet into the bargain."

As soon as Michael had felt himself safe he had tried to buy Dolly de Vries out, but she would not listen to his persuasion and was indifferent to his coldness. For once his cunning found its match. Dolly saw no reason to sell out an investment that seemed sound, and her half share in the partnership kept her in close touch with Julia. But now with great courage he made another effort to get rid of her. Dolly indignantly refused to desert them when they were in difficulties, and he gave it up as a bad job. He consoled himself by thinking that Dolly might leave Roger, her godson, a great deal of money. She had no one belonging to her but nephews in South Africa, and you could not look at her without suspecting that she had a high blood pressure. Meanwhile it was convenient to have the house near Guildford to go to whenever they wished. It saved the expense of having a country house of their own. The third play was a winner, and Michael did not hesitate to point out how right he had been. He spoke as though he was directly responsible for its success. Julia could almost have wished that it had failed like the others in order to take him down a peg or two. For his conceit was outrageous. Of course you had to admit that he had a sort of cleverness, shrewdness rather, but he was not nearly so clever as he thought himself. There was nothing in which he did not think that he knew better than anybody else.

As time went on he began to act less frequently. He found himself much more interested in management.

"I want to run my theatre in as businesslike a way as a City office," he said.

And he felt that he could more profitably spend his evenings, when Julia was acting, by going to outlying theatres and trying to find talent. He kept a little book in which he made a note of every actor who seemed to show promise. Then he had taken to directing. It had always grizzled him that directors should ask so much money for rehearsing a play, and of late some of them had even insisted on a percentage on the gross. At last an occasion came when the two directors Julia liked best were engaged and the only other one she trusted was acting and thus could not give them all his time.

"I've got a good mind to have a shot at it myself," said Michael.

Julia was doubtful. He had no fantasy and his ideas were commonplace. She was not sure that he would have authority over the cast. But the only available director demanded a fee that they both thought exorbitant and there was nothing left but to let Michael try. He made a much better job of it than Julia expected. He was thorough; he worked hard. Julia, strangely enough, felt that he was getting more out of her than any other director had done. He knew what she was capable of, and, familiar with her every inflection, every glance of her wonderful eyes, every graceful movement of her body, he was able to give her suggestions out of which she managed to build up the best performance of her career. With the cast he was at once conciliatory and exacting. When tempers were frayed his good humour, his real kindliness, smoothed things over. After that there was no question but that he should continue to direct their plays. Authors liked him because, being unimaginative, he was forced to let the plays speak for themselves and often not being quite sure what they meant he was obliged to listen to them.

Julia was now a rich woman. She could not but admit that Michael was as careful of her money as of his own. He watched her investments and was as pleased when he could sell stocks at a profit on her account as if he had made the money for himself. He put her down for a very large salary, and was proud to be able to say that she was the most highly-paid actress in London, but when he himself acted he never put himself down for a higher salary than he thought the part was worth. When he directed a play he put down on the expense account the fee that a director of the second rank would have received. They shared the expenses of the house and the cost of Roger's education. Roger had been entered for Eton within a week of his birth. It was impossible to deny that Michael was scrupulously fair and honest. When Julia realised how much richer she was than he, she wanted to pay all these expenses herself.

"There's no reason why you should," said Michael. "As long as I can pay my whack I'll pay it. You earn more than I do because you're worth more. I put you down for a good salary because you draw it."

No one could do other than admire the self-abnegation with which he sacrificed himself for her sake. Any ambition he may have had for himself he had abandoned in order to foster her career. Even Dolly, who did not like him, acknowledged his unselfishness. A sort of modesty had always prevented Julia from discussing him with Dolly, but Dolly, with her shrewdness, had long seen how intensely Michael exasperated his wife, and now and then took the trouble to point out how useful he was to her. Everybody praised him. A perfect husband. It seemed to her that none but she knew what it was like to live with a man who was such a monster of vanity. His complacency when he had beaten an opponent at golf or got the better of someone in a business deal was infuriating. He gloried in his artfulness. He was a bore, a crashing bore. He liked to tell Julia everything he did and every scheme that passed through his head; it had been charming when merely to have him with her was a delight, but for years she had found his prosiness intolerable. He could describe nothing without circumstantial detail. Nor was he only vain of his business acumen; with advancing years he had become outrageously vain of his person. As a youth he had taken his beauty for granted: now he began to pay more attention to it and spared no pains to keep what was left of it. It became an obsession. He devoted anxious care to his figure. He never ate a fattening thing and never forgot his exercises. He consulted hair specialists when he thought his hair was thinning, and Julia was convinced that had it been possible to get the operation done secretly he would have had his face lifted. He had got into the way of sitting with his chin slightly thrust out so that the wrinkles in his neck should not show and he held himself with an arched back to keep his belly from sagging. He could not pass a mirror without looking into it. He

hankered for compliments and beamed with delight when he had
managed to extract one. They were food and drink to him. Julia
laughed bitterly when she remembered that it was she who had
accustomed him to them. For years she had told him how
beautiful he was and now he could not live without flattery. It
was the only chink in his armour. An actress out of a job had only
to tell him to his face that he was too handsome to be true, for him
to think that she might do for a part he had in mind. For years, so
far as Julia knew, Michael had not bothered with women, but
when he reached the middle forties he began to have little
flirtations. Julia suspected that nothing much came of them. He
was prudent, and all he wanted was admiration. She had heard
that when women became pressing he used her as a pretext to get
rid of them. Either he couldn't risk doing anything to hurt her, or
she was jealous or suspicious and it seemed better that the friendship should cease.

"God knows what they see in him," Julia exclaimed to the
empty room.

She took up half a dozen of his later photographs at random and
looked at them carefully one by one. She shrugged her shoulders.

"Well, I suppose I can't blame them. I fell in love with him too.
Of course he was better-looking in those days."

It made Julia a little sad to think how much she had loved him.
Because her love had died she felt that life had cheated her. She
sighed.

"And my back's aching," she said.

CHAPTER X

THERE was a knock at the door.

"Come in," said Julia.

Evie entered.

"Aren't you going to bed to-day, Miss Lambert?" She saw
Julia sitting on the floor surrounded by masses of photographs.
"Whatever are you doing?"

"Dreaming." She took up two of the photographs. "Look
here upon this picture, and on this."

One was of Michael as Mercutio in all the radiant beauty
of his youth and the other of Michael in the last part he had

played, in a white topper and a morning coat, with a pair of field-
glasses slung over his shoulder. He looked unbelievably self-
satisfied.

Evie sniffed.

"Oh, well, it's no good crying over spilt milk."

"I've been thinking of the past and I'm as blue as the devil."

"I don't wonder. When you start thinking of the past it means
you ain't got no future, don't it?"

"You shut your trap, you old cow," said Julia, who could be
very vulgar when she chose.

"Come on now, or you'll be fit for nothing to-night. I'll clear
up all this mess."

Evie was Julia's dresser and maid. She had come to her first at
Middlepool and had accompanied her to London. She was a
Cockney, a thin, raddled, angular woman, with red hair which was
always untidy and looked as if it much needed washing; two of
her front teeth were missing but, notwithstanding Julia's offer,
repeated for years, to provide her with new ones she would not
have them replaced.

"For the little I eat I've got all the teeth I want. It'd only fidget
me to 'ave a lot of elephant's tusks in me mouth."

Michael had long wanted Julia at least to get a maid whose
appearance was more suitable to their position, and he had tried
to persuade Evie that the work was too much for her, but Evie
would not hear of it.

"You can say what you like, Mr. Gosselyn, but no one's going
to maid Miss Lambert as long as I've got me 'ealth and strength."

"We're all getting on, you know, Evie. We're not so young as
we were."

Evie drew her forefinger across the base of her nostrils and
sniffed.

"As long as Miss Lambert's young enough to play women of
twenty-five, I'm young enough to dress 'er. And maid 'er." Evie
gave him a sharp look. "An' what d'you want to pay two lots of
wages for, when you can get the work done for one?"

Michael chuckled in his good-humoured way.

"There's something in that, Evie dear."

She bustled Julia upstairs. When she had no matinée Julia went
to bed for a couple of hours in the afternoon and then had a light
massage. She undressed now and slipped between the sheets.

"Damn, my hot-water bottle's nearly stone-cold."

She looked at the clock on the chimney-piece. It was no wonder. It must have been there an hour. She had no notion that she had stayed so long in Michael's room, looking at those photographs and idly thinking of the past.

"Forty-six. Forty-six. Forty-six. I shall retire when I'm sixty. At fifty-eight South Africa and Australia. Michael says we can clean up there. Twenty thousand pounds. I can play all my old parts. Of course even at sixty I could play women of forty-five. But what about parts? Those bloody dramatists."

Trying to remember any plays in which there was a first-rate part for a woman of five-and-forty she fell asleep. She slept soundly till Evie came to awake her because the masseuse was there. Evie brought her the evening paper, and Julia, stripped, while the masseuse rubbed her long slim legs and her belly, putting on her spectacles, read the same theatrical intelligence she had read that morning, the gossip column and the woman's page. Presently Michael came in and sat on her bed. He often came at that hour to have a little chat with her.

"Well, what was his name?" asked Julia.

"Whose name?"

"The boy who came to lunch?"

"I haven't a notion. I drove him back to the theatre. I never gave him another thought."

Miss Phillips, the masseuse, liked Michael. You knew where you were with him. He always said the same things and you knew exactly what to answer. No side to him. And terribly good-looking. My word!

"Well, Miss Phillips, fat coming off nicely?"

"Oh, Mr. Gosselyn, there's not an ounce of fat on Miss Lambert. I think it's wonderful the way she keeps her figure."

"Pity I can't have you to massage me, Miss Phillips. You might be able to do something about mine."

"How you talk, Mr. Gosselyn. Why, you've got the figure of a boy of twenty. I don't know how you do it, upon my word I don't."

"Plain living and high thinking, Miss Phillips."

Julia was paying no attention to what they said, but Miss Phillips's reply reached her.

"Of course there's nothing like massage, I always say that, but you've got to be careful of your diet. That there's no doubt about at all."

"Diet!" she thought. "When I'm sixty I shall let myself go. I shall eat all the bread and butter I like. I'll have hot rolls for breakfast, I'll have potatoes for lunch and potatoes for dinner. And beer. God, how I like beer. Pea soup and tomato soup; treacle pudding and cherry tart. Cream, cream, cream. And so help me God, I'll never eat spinach again as long as I live."

When the massage was finished Evie brought her a cup of tea, a slice of ham from which the fat had been cut, and some dry toast. Julia got up, dressed, and went down with Michael to the theatre. She liked to be there an hour before the curtain rang up. Michael went on to dine at his club. Evie had preceded her in a cab and when she got into her dressing-room everything was ready for her. She undressed once more and put on a dressing-gown. As she sat down at her dressing-table to make up she noticed some fresh flowers in a vase.

"Hulloa, who sent them? Mrs. de Vries?"

Dolly always sent her a huge basket on her first nights, and on the hundredth night, and the two hundredth if there was one, and in between, whenever she ordered flowers for her own house, had some sent to Julia.

"No, miss."

"Lord Charles?"

Lord Charles Tamerley was the oldest and the most constant of Julia's admirers, and when he passed a florist's he was very apt to drop in and order some roses for her.

"Here's the card," said Evie.

Julia looked at it. Mr. Thomas Fennell. Tavistock Square.

"What a place to live. Who the hell d'you suppose he is, Evie?"

"Some feller knocked all of a heap by your fatal beauty, I expect."

"They must have cost all of a pound. Tavistock Square doesn't look very prosperous to me. For all you know he may have gone without his dinner for a week to buy them."

"I don't think."

Julia plastered her face with grease-paint.

"You're so damned unromantic, Evie. Just because I'm not a chorus girl you can't understand why anyone should send me flowers. And God knows, I've got better legs than most of them."

"You and your legs," said Evie.

"Well, I don't mind telling you I think it's a bit of all right having an unknown young man sending me flowers at my time of life. I mean it just shows you."

"If he saw you now 'e wouldn't, not if I know anything about men."

"Go to hell," said Julia.

But when she was made up to her satisfaction, and Evie had put on her stockings and her shoes, having a few minutes still to spare she sat down at her desk and in her straggling bold hand wrote to Mr. Thomas Fennell a gushing note of thanks for his beautiful flowers. She was naturally polite and it was, besides, a principle with her to answer all fan letters. That was how she kept in touch with her public. Having addressed the envelope she threw the card in the wastepaper basket and was ready to slip into her first-act dress. The call-boy came round knocking at the dressing-room doors.

"Beginners, please."

Those words, though heaven only knew how often she had heard them, still gave her a thrill. They braced her like a tonic. Life acquired significance. She was about to step from the world of make-believe into the world of reality.

CHAPTER XI

NEXT day Julia had luncheon with Charles Tamerley. His father, the Marquess of Dennorant, had married an heiress and he had inherited a considerable fortune. Julia often went to the luncheon parties he was fond of giving at his house in Hill Street. At the bottom of her heart she had a profound contempt for the great ladies and the noble lords she met there, because she was a working woman and an artist, but she knew the connection was useful. It enabled them to have first nights at the Siddons which the papers described as brilliant, and when she was photographed at week-end parties among a number of aristocratic persons, she knew that it was good publicity. There were one or two leading ladies, younger than she, who did not like her any better because she called at least two duchesses by their first names. This caused her no regret. Julia was not a brilliant conversationalist, but her eyes were so bright, her manner so intelligent, that once she had learnt the language of society she passed for a very amusing woman. She had a great gift of mimicry, which ordinarily she kept in check thinking it was bad for her acting, but in these circles she turned it to good account and by means of it acquired the reputation of a wit. She was pleased that they liked her, these smart, idle women, but she laughed at them up her sleeve because they were dazzled by her glamour. She wondered what they would think if they really knew how unromantic the life of a successful actress was, the hard work it entailed, the constant care one had to take of oneself and the regular, monotonous habits which were essential. But she good-naturedly offered them advice on make-up and let them copy her clothes. She was always beautifully dressed. Even Michael, fondly thinking she got her clothes for nothing, did not know how much she really spent on them.

Morally she had the best of both worlds. Everyone knew that her marriage with Michael was exemplary. She was a pattern of conjugal fidelity. At the same time many people in that particular set were convinced that she was Charles Tamerley's mistress. It was an affair that was supposed to have been going on so long that it had acquired respectability, and tolerant hostesses when they were asked to the same house for a week-end gave them adjoining rooms. This belief had been started by Lady Charles, from whom Charles Tamerley had been long separated, and in point of fact there was not a word of truth in it. The only foundation for it was that Charles had been madly in love with her for twenty years, and it was certainly on Julia's account that the Tamerleys, who had never got on very well, agreed to separate. It was indeed Lady Charles who had first brought Julia and Charles together. They happened, all three, to be lunching at Dolly de Vries' when Julia, a young actress, had made her first great success in London. It was a large party and she was being made much of. Lady Charles, a woman of over thirty then, who had the reputation of being a beauty, though except for her eyes she had not a good feature but by a sort of brazen audacity managed to produce an effective appearance, leant across the table with a gracious smile.

"Oh, Miss Lambert, I think I used to know your father in Jersey. He was a doctor, wasn't he? He used to come to our house quite often."

Julia felt a slight sickness in the pit of her stomach; she remembered now who Lady Charles was before she married, and she saw the trap that was being set for her. She gave a rippling laugh.

"Not at all," she answered. "He was a vet. He used to go to your house to deliver the bitches. The house was full of them."

Lady Charles for a moment did not quite know what to say.

"My mother was very fond of dogs," she answered.

Julia was glad that Michael was not there. Poor lamb, he would have been terribly mortified. He always referred to her father as Dr. Lambert, pronouncing it as though it were a French name, and when soon after the war he died and her mother went to live with her widowed sister at St. Malo he began to speak of her as Madame de Lambert. At the beginning of her career Julia had been somewhat sensitive on the point, but when once she was established as a great actress she changed her mind. She was inclined, especially among the great, to insist on the fact that her father had been a vet. She could not quite have explained why, but she felt that by so doing she put them in their place.

But Charles Tamerley knew that his wife had deliberately tried to humiliate the young woman and, angered, went out of his way to be nice to her. He asked her if he might be allowed to call and brought her some beautiful flowers.

He was then a man of nearly forty, with a small head on an elegant body, not very good-looking but of distinguished appearance. He looked very well-bred, which indeed he was, and he had exquisite manners. He was an amateur of the arts. He bought modern pictures and collected old furniture. He was a lover of music and exceedingly well read. At first it amused him to go to the tiny flat off the Buckingham Palace Road in which these two young actors lived. He saw that they were poor and it excited him to get into touch with what he fondly thought was Bohemia. He came several times and he thought it quite an adventure when they asked him to have a luncheon with them which was cooked and served by a scarecrow of a woman whom they called Evie. This was life. He did not pay much attention to Michael, who seemed to him, notwithstanding his too obvious beauty, a somewhat ordinary young man, but he was taken by Julia. She had a warmth, a force of character, and a bubbling vitality which were outside his experience. He went to see her act several times and compared her performance with his recollections of the great foreign actresses. It seemed to him that she had in her something quite individual. Her magnetism was incontestable. It gave him quite a thrill to realise on a sudden that she had genius.

"Another Siddons perhaps. A greater Ellen Terry."

In those days Julia did not think it necessary to go to bed in the afternoons, she was as strong as a horse and never tired, so he used often to take her for walks in the Park. She felt that he wanted her to be a child of nature. That suited her very well. It was no effort for her to be ingenuous, frank and girlishly delighted with everything. He took her to the National Gallery, and the Tate, and the British Museum, and she really enjoyed it almost as much as she said. He liked to impart information and she was glad to receive it. She had a retentive memory and learnt a great deal from him. If later she was able to talk about Proust and Cézanne with the best of them, so that you were surprised and pleased to find so much culture in an actress, it was to him she owed it. She knew that he had fallen in love with her some time before he knew it himself. She found it rather comic. From her standpoint he was a middle-aged man, and she thought of him as a nice old thing. She was madly in love with Michael. When Charles realised that he loved her his manner changed a little, he seemed struck with shyness and when they were together was often silent.

"Poor lamb," she said to herself, "he's such a hell of a gentleman he doesn't know what to do about it."

But she had already prepared her course of conduct for the declaration which she felt he would sooner or later bring himself to make. One thing she was going to make quite clear to him. She wasn't going to let him think that because he was a lord and she was an actress he had only to beckon and she would hop into bed with him. If he tried that sort of thing she'd play the outraged heroine on him, with the outflung arm and the index extended in the same line, as Jane Taitbout had taught her to make the gesture, pointed at the door. On the other hand if he was shattered and tongue-tied, she'd be all tremulous herself, sobs in the voice and all that, and she'd say it had never dawned on her that he felt like that about her, and no, no, it would break Michael's heart. They'd have a good cry together and then everything would be all right. With his beautiful manners she could count upon him not making a nuisance of himself when she had once got it into his head that there was nothing doing.

But when it happened it did not turn out in the least as she had expected. Charles Tamerley and Julia had been for a walk in St. James's Park, they had looked at the pelicans, and, the scene suggesting it, they had discussed the possibility of her playing Millamant on a Sunday evening. They went back to Julia's flat to have a cup of tea. They shared a crumpet. Then Charles got up to go. He took a miniature out of his pocket and gave it to her.

"It's a portrait of Clairon. She was an eighteenth-century actress and she had many of your gifts."

Julia looked at the pretty, clever face, with the powdered hair, and wondered whether the stones that framed the little picture were diamonds or only paste.

"Oh, Charles, how can you! You are sweet."

"I thought you might like it. It's by way of being a parting present."

"Are you going away?"

She was surprised, for he had said nothing about it. He looked at her with a faint smile.

"No. But I'm not going to see you any more."

"Why?"

"I think you know just as well as I do."

Then Julia did a disgraceful thing. She sat down and for a minute looked silently at the miniature. Timing it perfectly, she raised her eyes till they met Charles's. She could cry almost at will, it was one of her most telling accomplishments, and now without a sound, without a sob, the tears poured down her cheeks. With her mouth slightly open, with the look in her eyes of a child that has been deeply hurt and does not know why, the effect was unbearably pathetic. His face was crossed by a twinge of agony. When he spoke his voice was hoarse with emotion.

"You're in love with Michael, aren't you?"

She gave a little nod. She tightened her lips as though she were trying to control herself, but the tears rolled down her cheeks.

"There's no chance for me at all?" He waited for some answer from her, but she gave none, she raised her hand to her mouth and seemed to bite a nail, and still she stared at him with those streaming eyes. "Don't you know what torture it is to go on seeing you? D'you want me to go on seeing you?"

Again she gave a little nod.

"Clara's making me scenes about you. She's found out I'm in love with you. It's only common sense that we shouldn't see one another any more."

This time Julia slightly shook her head. She gave a sob. She leant back in the chair and turned her head aside. Her whole body seemed to express the hopelessness of her grief. Flesh and blood couldn't stand it. Charles stepped forward and sinking to his knees took that broken woebegone body in his arms.

"For God's sake don't look so unhappy. I can't bear it. Oh, Julia, Julia, I love you so much, I can't make you so miserable. I'll accept anything. I'll make no demands on you."

She turned her tear-stained face to him ("God, what a sight I must look now") and gave him her lips. He kissed her tenderly. It was the first time he had ever kissed her.

"I don't want to lose you," she muttered huskily.

"Darling, darling!"

"It'll be just as it was before?"

"Just."

She gave a deep sigh of contentment and for a minute or two rested in his arms. When he went away she got up and looked in the glass.

"You rotten bitch," she said to herself.

But she giggled as though she were not in the least ashamed and then went into the bathroom to wash her face and eyes. She felt wonderfully exhilarated. She heard Michael come in and called out to him.

"Michael, look at that miniature Charles has just given me. It's on the chimney-piece. Are those diamonds or paste?"

Julia was somewhat nervous when Lady Charles left her husband. She threatened to bring proceedings for divorce, and Julia did not at all like the idea of appearing as intervener. For two or three weeks she was very jittery. She decided to say nothing to Michael till it was necessary, and she was glad she had not, for in due course it appeared that the threats had been made only to extract more substantial alimony from the innocent husband. Julia managed Charles with wonderful skill. It was understood between them that her great love for Michael made any close relation between them out of the question, but so far as the rest was concerned he was everything to her, her friend, her adviser, her confidant, the man she could rely on in any emergency to go to for comfort in any disappointment. It was a little more difficult when Charles, with his fine sensitiveness, saw that she was no longer in love with Michael. Then Julia had to exercise a great deal of tact. It was not that she had any scruples about being his mistress; if he had been an actor who loved her so much and had loved her so long she would not have minded popping into bed with him out of sheer good nature; but she just did not fancy him. She was very fond of him, but he was so elegant, so well-bred, so cultured, she could not think of him as a lover. It would be like going to bed with an *objet d'art*. And his love of art filled her with a faint derision; after all she was a creator, when all was said and done he was only the public. He wished her to elope with him. They would buy a villa at Sorrento on the bay of Naples, with a large garden, and they would have a schooner so that they could spend long days on the beautiful wine-coloured sea. Love and beauty and art; the world well lost.

"The damned fool," she thought. "As if I'd give up my career to bury myself in some hole in Italy!"

She persuaded him that she had a duty to Michael, and then there was the baby; she couldn't let him grow up with the burden on his young life that his mother was a bad woman. Orange trees or no orange trees, she would never have a moment's peace in that beautiful Italian villa if she was tortured by the thought of Michael's unhappiness and her baby being looked after by strangers. One couldn't only think of oneself, could one? One had to think of others too. She was very sweet and womanly. She sometimes asked Charles why he did not arrange a divorce with his wife and marry some nice woman. She could not bear the thought of his wasting his life over her. He told her that she was the only woman he had ever loved and that he must go on loving her till the end.

"It seems so sad," said Julia.

All the same she kept her eyes open, and if she noticed that any woman had predatory intentions on Charles she took care to queer her pitch. She did not hesitate if the danger seemed to warrant it to show herself extremely jealous. It had been long agreed, with all the delicacy that might be expected from his good-breeding and Julia's good heart, in no definite words, but with guarded hints and remote allusiveness, that if anything happened to Michael, Lady Charles should somehow or other be disposed of and they would then marry. But Michael had perfect health.

On this occasion Julia had much enjoyed lunching at Hill Street. The party had been very grand. Julia had never encouraged Charles to entertain any of the actors or authors he sometimes came across, and she was the only person there who had ever had to earn a living. She had sat between an old, fat, bald and loquacious cabinet minister who took a great deal of trouble to entertain her, and a young Duke of Westreys who looked like a stable-boy and who flattered himself that he knew French slang better than a Frenchman. When he discovered that Julia spoke

French he insisted on conversing with her in that language. After luncheon she was persuaded to recite a tirade from *Phèdre* as it was done at the Comédie Française and the same tirade as an English student at the Royal Academy of Dramatic Art would deliver it. She made the company laugh very much and came away from the party flushed with success. It was a fine bright day and she made up her mind to walk from Hill Street to Stanhope Place. A good many people recognised her as she threaded her way through the crowd in Oxford Street, and though she looked straight ahead of her she was conscious of their glances.

"What a hell of a nuisance it is that one can't go anywhere without people staring at one."

She slackened her pace a little. It certainly was a beautiful day.

She let herself into her house with a latch-key and as she got in heard the telephone ringing. Without thinking she took up the receiver.

"Yes?"

She generally disguised her voice when she answered, but for once forgot to.

"Miss Lambert?"

"I don't know if Miss Lambert's in. Who is it, please?" she asked, assuming quickly a Cockney accent.

The monosyllable had betrayed her. A chuckle travelled over the wire.

"I only wanted to thank you for writing to me. You know, you needn't have troubled. It was so nice of you to ask me to lunch, I thought I'd like to send you a few flowers."

The sound of his voice and the words told her who it was. It was the blushing young man whose name she did not know. Even now, though she had looked at his card, she could not remember it. The only thing that had struck her was that he lived in Tavistock Square.

"It was very sweet of you," she answered, in her own voice.

"I suppose you wouldn't come to tea with me one day, would you?"

The nerve of it! She wouldn't go to tea with a duchess; he was treating her like a chorus girl. It was rather funny when you came to think of it.

"I don't know why not."

"Will you, really?" his voice sounded eager. He had a pleasant voice. "When?"

She did not feel at all like going to bed that afternoon.

"To-day."

"O.K. I'll get away from the office. Half-past four? 138, Tavistock Square."

It was nice of him to have suggested that. He might so easily have mentioned some fashionable place where people would stare at her. It proved that he didn't just want to be seen with her.

She took a taxi to Tavistock Square. She was pleased with herself. She was doing a good action. It would be wonderful for him in after years to be able to tell his wife and children that Julia Lambert had been to tea with him when he was just a little insignificant clerk in an accountant's office. And she had been so simple and so natural. No one, to hear her prattling away, would have guessed that she was the greatest actress in England. And if they didn't believe him he'd have her photograph to prove it, signed "Yours sincerely." He'd laugh and say that of course if he hadn't been such a kid he'd never have had the cheek to ask her.

When she arrived at the house and had paid off the taxi she suddenly remembered that she did not know his name and when the maid answered the door would not know whom to ask for. But on looking for the bell she noticed that there were eight of them, four rows of two, and by the side of each was a card or a name written in ink on a piece of paper. It was an old house that had been divided up into flats. She began looking, rather hopelessly, at the names wondering whether one of them would recall something, when the door opened and he stood before her.

"I saw you drive up and I ran down. I'm afraid I'm on the third floor. I hope you don't mind."

"Of course not."

She climbed the uncarpeted stairs. She was a trifle out of breath when she came to the third landing. He had skipped up eagerly, like a young goat, she thought, and she had not liked to suggest that she would prefer to go more leisurely. The room into which he led her was fairly large, but dingily furnished. On the table was a plate of cakes and two cups, a sugar-basin and a milk-jug. The crockery was of the cheapest sort.

"Take a pew," he said. "The water's just on the boil. I'll only be a minute. I've got a gas-ring in the bathroom."

He left her and she looked about.

"Poor lamb, he must be as poor as a church mouse."

The room reminded her very much of some of the lodgings she

had lived in when she was first on the stage. She noticed the pathetic attempts he had made to conceal the fact that it was a bedroom as well as a sitting-room. The divan against the wall was evidently his bed at night. The years slipped away from her in fancy and she felt strangely young again. What fun they had had in rooms very like that and how they had enjoyed the fantastic meals they had had, things in paper bags and eggs and bacon fried on the gas-ring! He came in with the tea in a brown pot. She ate a square sponge-cake with pink icing on it. That was a thing she had not done for years. The Ceylon tea, very strong, with milk and sugar in it, took her back to days she thought she had forgotten. She saw herself as a young, obscure, struggling actress. It was rather delicious. It needed a gesture, but she could only think of one: she took off her hat and gave her head a shake.

They talked. He seemed shy, much shyer than he had seemed over the telephone; well, that was not to be wondered at, now she was there he must be rather overcome, and she set herself to put him at his ease. He told her that his parents lived at Highgate, his father was a solicitor, and he had lived there too, but he wanted to be his own master and now in the last year of his articles he had broken away and taken this tiny flat. He was working for his final examination. They talked of the theatre. He had seen her in every play she had acted in since he was twelve years old. He told her that once when he was fourteen he had stood outside the stage door after a matinée and when she came out had asked her to sign her name in his autograph-book. He was sweet, with his blue eyes and pale brown hair. It was a pity he plastered it down like that. He had a white skin and rather a high colour; she wondered if he was consumptive. Although his clothes were cheap he wore them well—she liked that—and he looked incredibly clean.

She asked him why he had chosen Tavistock Square. It was central, he explained, and he liked the trees. It was quite nice when you looked out of the window. She got up to look, that would be a good way to make a move, then she would put on her hat and say good-bye to him.

"Yes, it is rather charming, isn't it. It's so London; it gives one a sort of jolly feeling."

She turned to him, standing by her side, as she said this. He put his arm round her waist and kissed her full on the lips. No woman was ever more surprised in her life. She was so taken aback that she never thought of doing anything. His lips were soft and there was a perfume of youth about him which was really rather delightful. But what he was doing was preposterous. He was forcing her lips apart with the tip of his tongue and now he had both arms round her. She did not feel angry, she did not feel inclined to laugh, she did not know what she felt. And now she had a notion that he was gently drawing her along, his lips still pressing hers, she felt quite distinctly the glow of his body, it was as though there was a furnace inside him, it was really remarkable; and then she found herself laid on the divan and he was beside her, kissing her mouth and her neck and her cheeks and her eyes. Julia felt a strange pang in her heart. She took his head in her hands and kissed his lips.

A few minutes later she was standing at the chimney-piece, in front of the looking-glass, making herself tidy.

"Look at my hair."

He handed her a comb and she ran it through. Then she put on her hat. He was standing just behind her, and over her shoulder she saw his face with those eager blue eyes and a faint smile in them.

"And I thought you were such a shy young man," she said to his reflection.

He chuckled.

"When am I going to see you again?"

"Do you want to see me again?"

"Rather."

She thought rapidly. It was too absurd, of course she had no intention of seeing him again, it was stupid of her to have let him behave like that, but it was just as well to temporise. He might be tiresome if she told him that the incident would have no sequel.

"I'll ring up one of these days."

"Swear."

"On my honour."

"Don't be too long."

He insisted on coming downstairs with her and putting her into a cab. She had wanted to go down alone, so that she could have a look at the cards attached to the bells on the lintel.

"Damn it all, I ought at least to know his name."

But he gave her no chance. When the taxi drove off she sank into one corner of it and gurgled with laughter.

"Raped, my dear. Practically raped. At my time of life. And

without so much as a by your leave. Treated me like a tart. Eighteenth-century comedy, that's what it is. I might have been a waiting-maid. In a hoop, with those funny puffy things—what the devil are they called?—that they wore to emphasise their hips, an apron and a scarf round me neck." Then with vague memories of Farquhar and Goldsmith she invented the dialogue. "La, sir, 'tis shame to take advantage of a poor country girl. What would Mrs. Abigail, her ladyship's woman, say an she knew her ladyship's brother had ravished me of the most precious treasure a young woman in my station of life can possess, videlicet her innocence. Fie, o fie, sir."

When Julia got home the masseuse was already waiting for her. Miss Phillips and Evie were having a chat.

"Wherever 'ave you been, Miss Lambert?" said Evie. "An' what about your rest, I should like to know."

"Damn my rest."

Julia tore off her clothes, and flung them with ample gestures all over the room. Then, stark naked, she skipped on to the bed, stood up on it for a moment, like Venus rising from the waves, and then throwing herself down stretched herself out.

"What's the idea?" said Evie.

"I feel good."

"Well, if I behaved like that people'd say I'd been drinkin'."

Miss Phillips began to massage her feet. She rubbed gently, to rest and not to tire her.

"When you came in just now, like a whirlwind," she said, "I thought you looked twenty years younger. Your eyes were shining something wonderful."

"Oh, keep that for Mr. Gosselyn, Miss Phillips." And then as an afterthought, "I feel like a two-year-old."

And it was the same at the theatre later on. Archie Dexter, who was her leading man, came into her dressing-room to speak about something. She had just finished making-up. He was startled.

"Hulloa, Julia, what's the matter with you to-night? Gosh, you look swell. Why, you don't look a day more than twenty-five."

"With a son of sixteen it's no good pretending I'm so terribly young any more. I'm forty and I don't care who knows it."

"What have you done to your eyes? I've never seen them shine like that before."

She felt in tremendous form. They had been playing the play, it was called *The Powder Puff*, for a good many weeks, but to-night

Julia played it as though it were the first time. Her performance was brilliant. She got laughs that she had never got before. She always had magnetism, but on this occasion it seemed to flow over the house in a great radiance. Michael happened to be watching the last two acts from the corner of a box and at the end he came into her dressing-room.

"D'you know the prompter says we played nine minutes longer to-night, they laughed so much."

"Seven curtain calls. I thought the public were going on all night."

"Well, you've only got to blame yourself, darling. There's no one in the world who could have given the performance you gave to-night."

"To tell you the truth I was enjoying myself. Christ, I'm hungry. What have we got for supper?"

"Tripe and onions."

"Oh, how divine!" She flung her arms round his neck and kissed him. "I adore tripe and onions. Oh, Michael, Michael, if you love me, if you've got any spark of tenderness in that hard heart of yours, let me have a bottle of beer."

"Julia!"

"Just this once. It's not often I ask you to do anything for me."

"Oh well, after the performance you gave to-night I suppose I can't say no, but, by God, I'll see that Miss Phillips pitches into you to-morrow."

CHAPTER XII

WHEN Julia got to bed and slipped her feet down to the comfort of her hot-water bottle, she took a happy look at her room, rose-pink and Nattier-blue, with the gold cherubs of her dressing-table, and sighed with satisfaction. She thought how very Madame de Pompadour it was. She put out the light but she did not feel at all sleepy. She would have liked really to go to Quag's and dance, but not to dance with Michael, to dance with Louis XV or Ludwig of Bavaria or Alfred de Musset. Clairon and the Bal de l'Opéra. She remembered the miniature Charles had once given her. That was how she felt to-night. Such an adventure had not happened to her for ages. The last was eight years before. That was an episode that she ought to have been thoroughly ashamed of; goodness, how scared she'd been afterwards, but she had in point of fact never been able to think of it since without a chuckle.

That had been an accident too. She had been acting for a long time without a rest and she badly needed one. The play she was in was ceasing to attract and they were about to start rehearsing a new one when Michael got the chance of letting the theatre to a French company for six weeks. It seemed a good opportunity for Julia to get away. Dolly had rented a house at Cannes for the season and Julia could stay with her. It was just before Easter when she started off, and the trains south were so crowded that she had not been able to get a sleeper, but at a travel agency they had said that it would be quite all right and there would be one waiting for her at the station in Paris. To her consternation she found when they got to Paris that nothing seemed to be known about her, and the chef de train told her that every sleeper was engaged. The only chance was that someone should not turn up at the last moment. She did not like the idea of sitting up all night in the corner of a first-class carriage, and went in to dinner with a perturbed mind. She was given a table for two, and soon a man came and sat down opposite her. She paid no attention to him. Presently the chef de train came along and told her that he was very sorry, but he could do nothing for her. She made a useless scene. When the official had gone, the man at her table addressed her. Though he spoke fluent, idiomatic French, she recognised by his accent that he was not a Frenchman. She told him in answer to his polite enquiry the whole story and gave him her opinion of the travel agency, the railway company, and the general inefficiency of the human race. He was very sympathetic. He told her that after dinner he would go along the train and see for himself if something could not be arranged. One never knew what one of the conductors could not manage for a tip.

"I'm simply tired out," she said. "I'd willingly give five hundred francs for a sleeper."

The conversation thus started, he told her that he was an attaché at the Spanish Embassy in Paris and was going down to Cannes for Easter. Though she had been talking to him for a quarter of an hour she had not troubled to notice what he was like. She observed now that he had a beard, a black curly beard and a black curly moustache, but the beard grew rather oddly on his face;

there were two bare patches under the corners of his mouth. It gave him a curious look. With his black hair, drooping eyelids and rather long nose, he reminded her of someone she had seen. Suddenly she remembered, and it was such a surprise that she blurted out:

"D'you know, I couldn't think who you reminded me of. You're strangely like Titian's portrait of Francis I in the Louvre."

"With his little pig's eyes?"

"No, not them, yours are large, I think it's the beard chiefly."

She glanced at the skin under his eyes; it was faintly violet and unwrinkled. Notwithstanding the ageing beard he was quite a young man; he could not have been more than thirty. She wondered if he was a Spanish Grandee. He was not very well dressed, but then foreigners often weren't; his clothes might have cost a lot even if they were badly cut, and his tie, though rather loud, she recognised as a Charvet. When they came to the coffee he asked her whether he might offer her a liqueur.

"That's very kind of you. Perhaps it'll make me sleep better."

He offered her a cigarette. His cigarette-case was silver—that put her off a little, but when he closed it she saw that in the corner was a small crown in gold. He must be a count or something. It was rather chic, having a silver cigarette-case with a gold crown on it. Pity he had to wear those modern clothes! If he'd been dressed like Francis I he would really look very distinguished. She set herself to be as gracious as she knew how.

"I think I should tell you," he said presently, "that I know who you are. And may I add that I have a great admiration for you?"

She gave him a lingering look of her splendid eyes.

"You've seen me act?"

"Yes, I was in London last month."

"An interesting little play, wasn't it?"

"Only because you made it so."

When the man came round to collect the money she had to insist on paying her own bill. The Spaniard accompanied her to the carriage and then said he would go along the train to see if he could find a sleeper for her. He came back in a quarter of an hour with a conductor and told her that he had got her a compartment and if she would give the conductor her things he would take her to it. She was delighted. He threw down his hat on the seat she vacated and she followed him along the corridor. When they reached the compartment he told the conductor to take the portmanteau and the dispatch-case that were in the rack to the carriage madame had just left.

"But it's not your own compartment you're giving up to me?" cried Julia.

"It's the only one on the train."

"Oh, but I won't hear of it."

"*Allez*," the Spaniard said to the conductor.

"No, no."

The conductor, on a nod from the stranger, took the luggage away.

"I don't matter. I can sleep anywhere, but I shouldn't sleep a wink if I thought that such a great artist was obliged to spend the night in a stuffy carriage with three other people."

Julia continued to protest, but not too much. It was terribly sweet of him. She didn't know how to thank him. He would not even let her pay for the sleeper. He begged her, almost with tears in his eyes, to let him have the great privilege of making her that trifling present. She had with her only a dressing-bag, in which were her face creams, her night-dress and her toilet things, and this he put on the table for her. All he asked was that he might be allowed to sit with her and smoke a cigarette or two till she wanted to go to bed. She could hardly refuse him that. The bed was already made up and they sat down on it. In a few minutes the conductor came back with a bottle of champagne and a couple of glasses. It was an odd little adventure and Julia was enjoying it. It was wonderfully polite of him, all that, ah, those foreigners, they knew how to treat a great actress. Of course that was the sort of thing that happened to Bernhardt every day. And Siddons, when she went into a drawing-room everyone stood up as though she were royalty. He complimented her on her beautiful French. Born in Jersey and educated in France? Ah, that explained it. But why hadn't she chosen to act in French rather than in English? She would have as great a reputation as Duse if she had. She reminded him of Duse, the same magnificent eyes and the pale skin, and in her acting the same emotion and the wonderful naturalness.

They half finished the bottle of champagne and Julia realised that it was very late.

"I really think I ought to go to bed now."

"I'll leave you."

He got up and kissed her hand. When he was gone Julia bolted the door and undressed. Putting out all the lights except the one just behind her head she began to read. Presently there was a knock at the door.

"Yes?"

"I'm sorry to disturb you. I left my toothbrush in the *lavabo.* May I get it?"

"I'm in bed."

"I can't go to sleep unless I brush my teeth."

("Oh well, he's clean anyway.")

With a little shrug of her shoulders Julia slipped her hand to the door and drew back the bolt. It would be stupid in the circumstances to be prudish. He came in, went into the lavatory and in a moment came out, brandishing a toothbrush. She had noticed it when she brushed her own teeth, but thought it belonged to the person who had the compartment next door. At that period adjoining compartments shared a lavatory. The Spaniard seemed to catch sight of the bottle.

"I'm so thirsty, do you mind if I have a glass of champagne?"

Julia was silent for a fraction of a second. It was his champagne and his compartment. Oh, well, in for a penny, in for a pound.

"Of course not."

He poured himself out a glass, lit a cigarette and sat down on the edge of her bed. She moved a little to give him more room. He accepted the situation as perfectly natural.

"You couldn't possibly have slept in that carriage," he said. "There's a man there who's a heavy breather. I'd almost rather he snored. If he snored one could wake him."

"I'm so sorry."

"Oh, it doesn't matter. If the worst comes to the worst I'll curl up in the corridor outside your door."

"He can hardly expect me to ask him to come and sleep in here," Julia said to herself. "I'm beginning to think this was all a put-up job. Nothing doing, my lad." And then aloud: "Romantic, of course, but uncomfortable."

"You're a terribly attractive woman."

She was just as glad that her night-dress was pretty and that she had put no cream on her face. She had in point of fact not troubled to take off her make-up. Her lips were brightly scarlet, and with the reading light behind her she well knew that she did not look her worst. But she answered ironically:

"If you think that because you've given up your compartment

to me I'm going to let you sleep with me, you're mistaken."

"Just as you say, of course. But why not?"

"I'm not that sort of terribly attractive woman."

"What sort of woman are you then?"

"A faithful wife and a devoted mother."

He gave a little sigh.

"Very well. Then I'll say good-night to you."

He crushed the stub of his cigarette on the ash-tray and took her hand and kissed it. He slowly ran his lips up her arm. It gave Julia a funny little sensation. The beard slightly tickled her skin. Then he leant over and kissed her lips. His beard had a somewhat musty smell, which she found peculiar; she was not sure if it revolted or thrilled her. It was odd when she came to think of it, she had never been kissed by a man with a beard before. It seemed strangely indecent. He snapped out the light.

He did not leave her till a chink of light through the drawn blind warned them that day had broken. Julia was shattered morally and physically.

"I shall look a perfect wreck when we get to Cannes."

And what a risk to take! He might have murdered her or stolen her pearl necklace. She went hot and cold all over as she pictured to herself the danger she had incurred. He was going to Cannes too. Supposing he claimed acquaintance with her there, how on earth was she going to explain him to her friends? She felt sure Dolly wouldn't like him. He might try to blackmail her. And what should she do if he wanted to repeat the experience? He was passionate, there was no doubt about that; he had asked her where she was staying, and though she had not told him, he could certainly find out if he tried; in a place like Cannes, it would be almost impossible not to run across him. He might pester her. If he loved her as much as he said it was inconceivable that he should let her alone, and foreigners were so unreliable, he might make frightful scenes. The only comfort was that he was only staying over Easter; she would pretend she was tired and tell Dolly that she preferred to stay quietly at the villa.

"How could I have been such a fool?" she cried angrily.

Dolly would be there to meet her at the station, and if he was tactless enough to come up and say good-bye to her she would tell Dolly that he had given up his compartment to her. There was no harm in that. It was always best to tell as much of the truth as you could. But there was quite a crowd of passengers getting out at

Cannes, and Julia got out of the station and into Dolly's car without catching a glimpse of him.

"I've arranged nothing for to-day," said Dolly. "I thought you'd be tired and I wanted to have you all to myself just for twenty-four hours."

Julia gave her arm an affectionate squeeze.

"That'll be too wonderful. We'll just sit about the villa and grease our faces and have a good old gossip."

But next day Dolly had arranged that they should go out to luncheon, and they were to meet their hosts at one of the bars on the Croisette to have cocktails. It was a beautiful day, clear, warm and sunny. When they got out of the car Dolly stopped to give the chauffeur instructions about fetching them and Julia waited for her. Suddenly her heart gave a great jump, for there was the Spaniard walking towards her, with a woman on one side of him clinging to his arm and on the other a little girl whose hand he held. She had not time to turn away. At that moment Dolly joined her to walk across the pavement. The Spaniard came, gave her a glance in which there was no sign of recognition, he was in animated conversation with the woman on his arm, and walked on. In a flash Julia understood that he was just as little anxious to see her as she was to see him. The woman and the child were obviously his wife and daughter whom he had come down to Cannes to spend Easter with. What a relief! Now she could enjoy herself without fear. But as she accompanied Dolly to the bar, Julia thought how disgusting men were. You simply couldn't trust them for a minute. It was really disgraceful that a man with a charming wife and such a sweet little girl should be willing to pick up a woman in the train. You would think they'd have some sense of decency.

But as time passed Julia's indignation was mitigated, and she had often thought of the adventure since with a good deal of pleasure. After all it had been fun. Sometimes she allowed her reveries to run away with her and she went over in her fancy the incidents of that singular night. He had been a most agreeable lover. It would be something to look back on when she was an old woman. It was the beard that had made such an impression on her, the odd feeling of it on her face and that slightly musty smell which was repulsive and yet strangely exciting. For years she looked out for men with beards, and she had a feeling that if one of them made proposals to her she simply wouldn't be able to resist him. But few men wore beards any more, luckily for her because the sight made her go a little weak at the knees, and none of those that did ever made any advance to her. She would have liked to know who the Spaniard was. She saw him a day or two later playing *chemin de fer* at the Casino and asked two or three people if they knew him. Nobody did, and he remained in her recollection, and in her bones, without a name. It was an odd coincidence that she didn't know the name either of the young man who had that afternoon behaved in so unexpected a manner. It struck her as rather comic.

"If I only knew beforehand that they were going to take liberties with me I'd at least ask for their cards."

With this thought she fell happily asleep.

CHAPTER XIII

SOME days passed, and one morning, while Julia was lying in bed reading a play, they rang through from the basement to ask if she would speak to Mr. Fennell. The name meant nothing to her and she was about to refuse when it occurred to her that it might be the young man of her adventure. Her curiosity induced her to tell them to connect him. She recognised his voice.

"You promised to ring me up," he said. "I got tired of waiting, so I've rung you up instead."

"I've been terribly busy the last few days."

"When am I going to see you?"

"As soon as I have a moment to spare."

"What about this afternoon?"

"I've got a matinée to-day."

"Come to tea after the matinée."

She smiled. ("No, young feller-me-lad, you don't catch me a second time like that.")

"I can't possibly," she answered. "I always stay in my dressing-room and rest till the evening performance."

"Can't I come and see you while you're resting?"

She hesitated for an instant. Perhaps the best thing would be to let him come; with Evie popping in and out and Miss Phillips due at seven, there would be no chance of any nonsense, and it would be a good opportunity to tell him, amiably, because he was really a sweet little thing, but firmly, that the incident of the other afternoon was to have no sequel. With a few well-chosen words she would explain to him that it was quite unreasonable and that he must oblige her by erasing the episode from his memory.

"All right. Come at half-past five and I'll give you a cup of tea."

There was no part of her busy life that she enjoyed more than those three hours that she spent in her dressing-room between the afternoon and the evening performances. The other members of the cast had gone away; and Evie was there to attend to her wants and the door-keeper to guard her privacy. Her dressing-room was like the cabin of a ship. The world seemed a long way off, and she relished her seclusion. She felt an enchanting freedom. She dozed a little, she read a little, or lying on the comfortable sofa she let her thoughts wander. She reflected on the part she was playing and the favourite parts she had played in the past. She thought of Roger her son. Pleasant reveries sauntered through her mind like lovers wandering in a green wood. She was fond of French poetry, and sometimes she repeated to herself verses of Verlaine.

Punctually at half-past five Evie brought her in a card. "Mr. Thomas Fennell," she read.

"Send him in and bring some tea."

She had decided how she was going to treat him. She would be amiable, but distant. She would take a friendly interest in his work and ask him about his examination. Then she would talk to him about Roger. Roger was seventeen now and in a year would be going to Cambridge. She would insinuate the fact that she was old enough to be his mother. She would act as if there had never been anything between them and he would go away, never to see her again except across the footlights, half convinced that the while thing had been a figment of his fancy. But when she saw him, so slight, with his hectic flush and his blue eyes, so charmingly boyish, she felt a sudden pang. Evie closed the door behind him. She was lying on the sofa and she stretched out her arm to give him her hand, the gracious smile of Madame Récamier on her lips, but he flung himself on his knees and passionately kissed her mouth. She could not help herself, she put her arms round his neck, and kissed him as passionately.

("Oh, my good resolutions. My God, I can't have fallen in love with him.")

"For goodness' sake, sit down. Evie's coming in with the tea."

"Tell her not to disturb us."

"What do you mean?" But what he meant was obvious. Her heart began to beat quickly. "It's ridiculous. I can't. Michael might come in."

"I want you."

"What d'you suppose Evie would think? It'd be idiotic to take such a risk. No, no, no."

There was a knock at the door and Evie came in with the tea. Julia gave her instructions to put the table by the side of her sofa and a chair for the young man on the other side of the table. She kept Evie with unnecessary conversation. She felt him looking at her. His eyes moved quickly, following her gestures and the expression of her face; she avoided them, but she felt their anxiety and the eagerness of his desire. She was troubled. It seemed to her that her voice did not sound quite natural.

("What the devil's the matter with me? God, I can hardly breathe.")

When Evie reached the door the boy made a gesture that was so instinctive that her sensitiveness rather than her sight caught it. She could not but look at him. His face had gone quite pale.

"Oh, Evie," she said. "This gentleman wants to talk to me about a play. See that no one disturbs me. I'll ring when I want you."

"Very good, miss."

Evie went out and closed the door.

("I'm a fool. I'm a bloody fool.")

But he had moved the table, and he was on his knees, and she was in his arms.

She sent him away a little before Miss Phillips was due, and when he was gone rang for Evie.

"Play any good?" asked Evie.

"What play?"

"The play 'e was talkin' to you abaht."

"He's clever. Of course he's young."

Evie was looking down at the dressing-table. Julia liked everything always to be in the same place, and if a pot of grease or her eye-black was not exactly where it should be made a scene.

"Where's your comb?"

He had used it to comb his hair and had carelessly placed it on the tea-table. When Evie caught sight of it she stared at it for a moment reflectively.

"How on earth did it get there?" cried Julia lightly.

"I was just wondering."

It gave Julia a nasty turn. Of course it was madness to do that sort of thing in the dressing-room. Why, there wasn't even a key in the lock. Evie kept it. All the same the risk had given it a spice. It was fun to think that she could be so crazy. At all events they'd made a date now. Tom—she'd asked him what they called him at home and he said Thomas, she really couldn't call him that—Tom wanted to take her to supper somewhere so that they could dance, and it happened that Michael was going up to Cambridge for a night to rehearse a series of one-act plays written by under-graduates. They would be able to spend hours together.

"You can get back with the milk," he'd said.

"And what about my performance next day?"

"We can't bother about that."

She had refused to let him fetch her at the theatre, and when she got to the restaurant they had chosen he was waiting for her in the lobby. His face lit up as he saw her.

"It was getting so late, I was afraid you weren't coming."

"I'm sorry, some tiresome people came round after the play and I couldn't get rid of them."

But it wasn't true. She had been as excited all the evening as a girl going to her first ball. She could not help thinking how absurd she was. But when she had taken off her theatrical make-up and made up again for supper she could not satisfy herself. She put blue on her eyelids and took it off again, she rouged her cheeks, rubbed them clean and tried another colour.

"What are you trying to do?" said Evie.

"I'm trying to look twenty, you fool."

"If you try much longer you'll look your age."

She had never seen him in evening clothes before. He shone like a new pin. Though he was of no more than average height his slimness made him look tall. She was a trifle touched to see that for all his airs of the man of the world he was shy with the head-waiter when it came to ordering supper. They danced and he did not dance very well, but she found his slight awkwardness rather charming. People recognised her, and she was conscious that he enjoyed the reflected glory of their glances. A pair of young things who had been dancing came up to their table to say how-do-you-do to her. When they had left he asked:

"Wasn't that Lord and Lady Dennorant?"

"Yes. I've known George since he was at Eton."

He followed them with his eyes.

"She was Lady Cecily Laweston, wasn't she?"

"I've forgotten. Was she?"

It seemed a matter of no interest to her. A few minutes later another couple passed them.

"Look, there's Lady Lepard."

"Who's she?"

"Don't you remember, they had a big party at their place in Cheshire a few weeks ago and the Prince of Wales was there. It was in the *Bystander*."

Oh, that was how he got all his information. Poor sweet. He read about grand people in the papers and now and then, at a restaurant or a theatre, saw them in the flesh. Of course it was a thrill for him. Romance. If he only knew how dull they were really! This innocent passion for the persons whose photographs appear in the illustrated papers made him seem incredibly naïve, and she looked at him with tender eyes.

"Have you ever taken an actress out to supper before?"

He blushed scarlet.

"Never."

She hated to let him pay the bill, she had an inkling that it was costing pretty well his week's salary, but she knew it would hurt his pride if she offered to pay it herself. She asked casually what the time was and instinctively he looked at his wrist.

"I forgot to put on my watch."

She gave him a searching look.

"Have you pawned it?"

He reddened again.

"No. I dressed in rather a hurry to-night."

She only had to look at his tie to know that he had done no such thing. He was lying to her. She knew that he had pawned his watch in order to take her out to supper. A lump came into her throat. She could have taken him in her arms then and there and kissed his blue eyes. She adored him.

"Let's go," she said.

They drove back to his bed-sitting-room in Tavistock Square.

CHAPTER XIV

NEXT day Julia went to Cartier's and bought a watch to send to Tom Fennell instead of the one he had pawned, and two or three weeks later, discovering that it was his birthday, she sent him a gold cigarette-case.

"D'you know, that's the one thing I've wanted all my life."

She wondered if there were tears in his eyes. He kissed her passionately.

Then, on one excuse and another, she sent him pearl studs and sleeve-links and waistcoat buttons. It thrilled her to make him presents.

"It's so awful that I can't give you anything in return," he said.

"Give me the watch you pawned to stand me a supper."

It was a little gold watch that could not have cost more than ten pounds, but it amused her to wear it now and then.

It was not till after that night when they had first supped together that Julia confessed to herself that she had fallen in love with Tom. It came to her as a shock. But she was exhilarated.

"I who thought I could never be in love again. Of course it can't last. But why shouldn't I get what fun out of it I can?"

She decided that he must come again to Stanhope Place. It was not long before an opportunity presented itself.

"You know that young accountant of yours," she said to Michael. "Tom Fennell's his name. I met him out at supper the other night and I've asked him to dinner next Sunday. We want an extra man."

"Oh, d'you think he'll fit in?"

It was rather a grand party. It was on that account she had asked him. She thought it would please him to meet some of the people he had known only from their pictures. She had realised already that he was a bit of a snob. Well, that was all to the good; she could give him all the smart people he wanted. For Julia was shrewd, and she knew very well that Tom was not in love with her. To have an affair with her flattered his vanity. He was a highly-sexed young man and enjoyed sexual exercise. From hints, from stories that she had dragged out of him, she discovered that since he was seventeen he had had a great many women. He loved the act rather than the person. He looked upon it as the greatest lark in the world. And she could understand why he had so much success. There was something appealing in his slightness—his body was just skin and bone, that was why his clothes sat on him so well—and something charming in his clean freshness. His shyness and his effrontery combined to make him irresistible. It was strangely flattering for a woman to be treated as a little bit of fluff that you just tumbled on to a bed.

"What he's got, of course, is sex appeal."

She knew that his good looks were due to his youth. He would grow wizened as he grew older, dried up and haggard; that charming flush on his cheeks would turn into a purple glow and his delicate skin would go lined and sallow; but the feeling that what she loved in him would endure so short a time increased her tenderness. She felt a strange compassion for him. He had the high spirits of youth, and she lapped them up as a kitten laps up milk. But he was not amusing. Though he laughed when Julia said a funny thing he never said one himself. She did not mind. She found his dullness restful. She never felt so light-hearted as in his company, and she could be brilliant enough for two.

People kept on telling Julia that she was looking ten years younger and that she had never acted better. She knew it was true and she knew the reason. But it behoved her to walk warily. She must keep her head. Charles Tamerley always said that what an actress needed was not intelligence, but sensibility, and he might be right; perhaps she wasn't clever, but her feelings were alert and she trusted them. They told her now that she must never tell Tom that she loved him. She was careful to make it plain to him that she laid no claims on him and that he was free to do whatever he liked. She took up the attitude that the whole thing was a bit of nonsense to which neither of them must attach importance. But she left nothing undone to bind him to her. He liked parties and she took him to parties. She got Dolly and Charles Tamerley to ask him to luncheon. He was fond of dancing and she got him cards for balls. For his sake she would go to them herself for an hour, and she was conscious of the satisfaction he got out of seeing how much fuss people made of her. She knew that he was dazzled by the great, and she introduced him to eminent persons. Fortunately Michael took a fancy to him. Michael liked to talk, and Tom was a good listener. He was clever at his business. One day Michael said to her:

"Smart fellow, Tom. He knows a lot about income tax. I

believe he's shown me a way of saving two or three hundred pounds on my next return."

Michael, looking for new talent, often took him to the play in the evenings, either in London or the suburbs; they would fetch Julia after the performance, and the three of them supped together. Now and then Michael asked Tom to play golf with him on Sundays and then if there was no party would bring him home to dinner.

"Nice to have a young fellow like that around," he said. "It keeps one from growing rusty."

Tom was very pleasant about the house. He would play back-gammon with Michael, or patience with Julia, and when they turned on the gramophone he was always there to change the records.

"He'll be a nice friend for Roger," said Michael. "Tom's got his head screwed on his shoulders the right way, and he's a lot older than Roger. He ought to have a good influence on him. Why don't you ask him to come and spend his holiday with us?"

("Lucky I'm a good actress.") But it wanted an effort to keep the joy out of her voice and to prevent her face from showing the exultation that made her heart beat so violently. "That's not a bad idea," she answered. "I'll ask him if you like."

Their play was running through August, and Michael had taken a house at Taplow so that they could spend the height of the summer there. Julia was to come up for her performances and Michael when business needed it, but she would have the day in the country and Sundays. Tom had a fortnight's holiday; he accepted the invitation with alacrity.

But one day Julia noticed that he was unusually silent. He looked pale and his buoyant spirits had deserted him. She knew that something was wrong, but he would not tell her what it was; he would only say that he was worried to death. At last she forced him to confess that he had got into debt and was being dunned by tradesmen. The life into which she had led him had made him spend more money than he could afford, and, ashamed of his cheap clothes at the grand parties to which she took him, he had gone to an expensive tailor and ordered himself new suits. He had backed a horse hoping to make enough money to get square and the horse was beaten. To Julia it was a very small sum that he owed, a hundred and twenty-five pounds, and she found it absurd that anyone should allow a trifle like that to upset him. She said at once that she would give it to him.

"Oh, I couldn't. I couldn't take money from a woman."

He went scarlet; the mere thought of it made him ashamed. Julia used all her arts of cajolery. She reasoned, she pretended to be affronted, she even cried a little, and at last as a great favour he consented to borrow the money from her. Next day she sent him a letter in which were bank-notes to the value of two hundred pounds. He rang her up and told her that she had sent far more than he wanted.

"Oh, I know people always lie about their debts," she said with a laugh. "I'm sure you owe more than you said."

"I promise you I don't. You're the last person I'd lie to."

"Then keep the rest for anything that turns up. I hate seeing you pay the bill when we go out to supper. And taxis and all that sort of thing."

"No, really. It's so humiliating."

"What nonsense! You know I've got more money than I know what to do with. Can you grudge me the happiness it gives me to get you out of a hole?"

"It's awfully kind of you. You don't know what a relief it is. I don't know how to thank you."

But his voice was troubled. Poor lamb, he was so conventional. But it was true, it gave her a thrill she had never known before to give him money; it excited in her a surprising passion. And she had another scheme in her head which during the fortnight Tom was to spend at Taplow she thought she could easily work. Tom's bed-sitting-room in Tavistock Square had at first seemed to her charming in its sordidness, and the humble furniture had touched her heart. But time had robbed it of these moving characteristics. Once or twice she had met people on the stairs and thought they stared at her strangely. There was a slatternly housekeeper who made Tom's room and cooked his breakfast, and Julia had a feeling that she knew what was going on and was spying on her. Once the locked door had been tried while Julia was in the room, and when she went out the housekeeper was dusting the banisters. She gave Julia a sour look. Julia hated the smell of stale food that hung about the stairs and with her quick eyes she soon discovered that Tom's room was none too clean. The dingy curtains, the worn carpet, the shoddy furniture; it all rather disgusted her. Now it happened that a little while before, Michael, always on the look-out for a good investment, had bought a block of garages near

Stanhope Place. By letting off those he did not want he found that he could get their own for nothing. There were a number of rooms over. He divided them into two small flats, one for their chauffeur and one which he proposed to let. This was still vacant and Julia suggested to Tom that he should take it. It would be wonderful. She could slip along and see him for an hour when he got back from the office; sometimes she could drop in after the theatre and no one would be any the wiser. They would be free there. She talked to him of the fun they would have furnishing it; she was sure they had lots of things in their house that they did not want, and by storing them he would be doing them a kindness. The rest they would buy together. He was tempted by the idea of having a flat of his own, but it was out of the question; the rent, though small, was beyond his means. Julia knew that. She knew also that if she offered to pay it herself he would indignantly refuse. But she had a notion that during that idle, luxurious fortnight by the river she would be able to overcome his scruples. She saw how much the idea tempted him, and she had little doubt that she could devise some means to persuade him that by falling in with her proposal he was really doing her a service.

"People don't want reasons to do what they'd like to," she reflected. "They want excuses."

Julia looked forward to Tom's visit to Taplow with excitement. It would be lovely to go on the river with him in the morning and in the afternoon sit about the garden with him. With Roger in the house she was determined that there should be no nonsense between her and Tom; decency forbade. But it would be heaven to spend nearly all day with him. When she had matinées he could amuse himself with Roger.

But things did not turn out at all as she expected. It had never occurred to her that Roger and Tom would take a great fancy to one another. There were five years between them and she thought, or would have if she had thought about it at all, that Tom would look upon Roger as a hobbledehoy, quite nice of course, but whom you treated as such, who fetched and carried for you and whom you told to go and play when you did not want to be bothered with him. Roger was seventeen. He was a nice-looking boy, with reddish hair and blue eyes, but that was the best you could say of him. He had neither his mother's vivacity and changing expression nor his father's beauty of feature. Julia was somewhat disappointed in him. As a child when she had been so constantly photographed with him he was lovely. He was rather stolid now and he had a serious look. Really when you came to examine him his only good features were his teeth and his hair. Julia was very fond of him, but she could not but find him a trifle dull. When she was alone with him the time hung somewhat heavily on her hands. She exhibited a lively interest in the things she supposed must interest him, cricket and such like, but he did not seem to have much to say about them. She was afraid he was not very intelligent.

"Of course he's young," she said hopefully. "Perhaps he'll improve as he grows older."

From the time that he first went to his preparatory school she had seen little of him. During the holidays she was always acting at night and he went out with his father or with a boy friend, and on Sundays he and his father played golf together. If she happened to be lunching out it often happened that she did not see him for two or three days together except for a few minutes in the morning when he came to her room. It was a pity he could not always have remained a sweetly pretty little boy who could play in her room without disturbing her and be photographed, smiling into the camera, with his arm round her neck. She went down to see him at Eton occasionally and had tea with him. It flattered her that there were several photographs of her in his room. She was conscious that when she went to Eton it created quite a little excitement, and Mr. Brackenbridge, in whose house he was, made a point of being very polite to her. When the half ended Michael and Julia had already moved to Taplow and Roger came straight there. Julia kissed him emotionally. He was not so much excited at getting home as she had expected him to be. He was rather casual. He seemed suddenly to have grown very sophisticated.

He told Julia at once that he desired to leave Eton at Christmas, he thought he had got everything out of it that he could, and he wanted to go to Vienna for a few months and learn German before going up to Cambridge. Michael had wished him to go into the army, but this he had set his face against. He did not yet know what he wanted to be. Both Julia and Michael had from the first been obsessed by the fear that he would go on the stage, but for this apparently he had no inclination.

"Anyhow he wouldn't be any good," said Julia.

He led his own life. He went out on the river and lay about the garden reading. On his seventeenth birthday Julia had given him a very smart roadster, and in this he careered about the country at breakneck speeds.

"There's one comfort," said Julia. "He's no bother. He seems quite capable of amusing himself."

On Sundays they had a good many people down for the day, actors and actresses, an occasional writer, and a sprinkling of some of their grander friends. Julia found these parties very amusing and she knew that people liked to come to them. On the first Sunday after Roger's arrival there was a great mob. Roger was very polite to the guests. He did his duty as part host like a man of the world. But it seemed to Julia that he held himself in some curious way aloof, as though he were playing a part in which he had not lost himself, and she had an uneasy feeling that he was not accepting all these people, but coolly judging them. She had an impression that he took none of them very seriously.

Tom had arranged to come on the following Saturday and she drove him down after the theatre. It was a moonlit night and at that hour the roads were empty. The drive was enchanting. Julia would have liked it to go on for ever. She nestled against him and every now and then in the darkness he kissed her.

"Are you happy?" she asked.

"Absolutely."

Michael and Roger had gone to bed, but supper was waiting for them in the dining-room. The silent house gave them the feeling of being there without leave. They might have been a couple of wanderers who had strolled out of the night into a strange house and found a copious repast laid out for them. It was romantic. It had a little the air of a tale in the Arabian Nights. Julia showed him his room, which was next door to Roger's, and then went to bed. She did not wake till late next morning. It was a lovely day. So that she might have Tom all to herself she had not asked anybody down. When she was dressed they would go on the river together. She had her breakfast and her bath. She put on a little white frock that suited the sunny riverside and her, and a large-brimmed red straw hat whose colour threw a warm glow on her face. She was very little made-up. She looked at herself in the glass and smiled with satisfaction. She really looked very pretty and young. She strolled down into the garden. There was a lawn that stretched down to the river, and here she saw Michael surrounded by the Sunday papers. He was alone.

"I thought you'd gone to play golf."

"No, the boys have gone. I thought they'd have more fun if I let them go alone." He smiled in his friendly way. "They're a bit too active for me. They were bathing at eight o'clock this morning, and as soon as they'd swallowed their breakfast they bolted off in Roger's car."

"I'm glad they've made friends."

Julia meant it. She was slightly disappointed that she would not be able to go on the river with Tom, but she was anxious that Roger should like him, she had a feeling that Roger did not like people indiscriminately; and after all she had the next fortnight to be with Tom.

"They make me feel damned middle-aged, I don't mind telling you that," Michael remarked.

"What nonsense. You're much more beautiful than either of them, and well you know it, my pet."

Michael thrust out his jaw a little and pulled in his belly.

The boys did not come back till luncheon was nearly ready.

"Sorry we're so late," said Roger. "There was a filthy crowd and we had to wait on nearly every tee. We halved the match."

They were hungry and thirsty, excited and pleased with themselves.

"It's grand having no one here to-day," said Roger. "I was afraid you'd got a whole gang coming and we'd have to behave like little gentlemen."

"I thought a rest would be rather nice," said Julia.

Roger gave her a glance.

"It'll do you good, Mummy. You're looking awfully fagged."

("Blast his eyes. No, I mustn't show I mind. Thank God, I can act.")

She laughed gaily.

"I had a sleepless night wondering what on earth we were going to do about your spots."

"I know, aren't they sickening? Tom says he used to have them too."

Julia looked at Tom. In his tennis shirt open at the neck, with his hair ruffled, his face already caught by the sun, he looked incredibly young. He really looked no older than Roger.

"Anyhow, his nose is going to peel," Roger went on with a chuckle. "He'll look a sight then."

Julia felt slightly uneasy. It seemed to her that Tom had shed the years so that he was become not only in age Roger's contemporary. They talked a great deal of nonsense. They ate enormously and drank tankards of beer. Michael, eating and drinking as sparingly as usual, watched them with amusement. He was enjoying their youth and their high spirits. He reminded Julia of an old dog lying in the sun and gently beating his tail on the ground as he looked at a pair of puppies gambolling about him. They had coffee on the lawn. Julia found it very pleasant to sit there in the shade, looking at the river. Tom was slim and graceful in his long white trousers. She had never seen him smoke a pipe before. She found it strangely touching. But Roger mocked him.

"Do you smoke it because it makes you feel manly or because you like it?"

"Shut up," said Tom.

"Finished your coffee?"

"Yes."

"Come on then, let's go on the river."

Tom gave her a doubtful look. Roger saw it.

"Oh, it's all right, you needn't bother about my respected parents, they've got the Sunday papers. Mummy's just given me a racing punt."

("I must keep my temper. I must keep my temper. Why was I such a fool as to give him a racing punt?")

"All right," she said, with an indulgent smile, "go on the river, but don't fall in."

"It won't hurt us if we do. We'll be back for tea. Is the court marked out, Daddy? We're going to play tennis after tea."

"I dare say your father can get hold of somebody and you can have a four."

"Oh, don't bother. Singles are better fun really and one gets more exercise." Then to Tom. "I'll race you to the boat-house."

Tom leapt to his feet and dashed off with Roger in quick pursuit. Michael took up one of the papers and looked for his spectacles.

"They've clicked all right, haven't they?"

"Apparently."

"I was afraid Roger would be rather bored alone here with us. It'll be fine for him to have someone to play around with."

"Don't you think Roger's rather inconsiderate?"

"You mean about the tennis? Oh, my dear, I don't really care if I play or not. It's only natural that those two boys should want to play together. From their point of view I'm an old man, and they think I'll spoil their game. After all, the great thing is that they should have a good time."

Julia had a pang of remorse. Michael was prosy, near with his money, self-complacent, but how extraordinarily kind he was and how unselfish! He was devoid of envy. It gave him a real satisfaction, so long as it did not cost money, to make other people happy. She read his mind like an open book. It was true that he never had any but a commonplace thought; on the other hand he never had a shameful one. It was exasperating that, with so much to make him worthy of her affection, she should be so excruciatingly bored by him.

"I think you're a much better man than I am a woman, my sweet," she said.

He gave her his good, friendly smile and slightly shook his head.

"No, dear, I had a wonderful profile, but you've got genius."

Julia giggled. There was a certain fun to be got out of a man who never knew what you were talking about. But what did they mean when they said an actress had genius? Julia had often asked herself what it was that had placed her at last head and shoulders above her contemporaries. She had had detractors. At one time people had compared her unfavourably with some actress or other who at the moment enjoyed the public favour, but now no one disputed her supremacy. It was true that she had not the world-wide notoriety of the film-stars; she had tried her luck on the pictures, but had achieved no success; her face, on the stage so mobile and expressive, for some reason lost on the screen, and after one trial she had with Michael's approval refused to accept any of the offers that were from time to time made her. She had got a good deal of useful publicity out of her dignified attitude. But Julia did not envy the film-stars; they came and went; she stayed. When it was possible she went to see the performance of actresses who played leading parts on the London stage. She was generous in her praise of them and her praise was sincere. Sometimes she honestly thought them so very good that she could not understand why people made so much fuss over her. She was much too intelligent not to know in what estimation the public held her, but she was modest about herself. It always surprised her when people raved over something she had done that came to her so naturally that she had never thought it possible to do anything else. The critics admitted her variety. They praised especially her capacity for insinuating herself into a part. She was not aware that she deliberately observed people, but when she came to study a new part vague recollections surged up in her from she knew not where, and she found that she knew things about the character she was to represent that she had had no inkling of. It helped her to think of someone she knew or even someone she had seen in the street or at a party; she combined with this recollection her own personality, and thus built up a character founded on fact but enriched with her experience, her knowledge of technique and her amazing magnetism. People thought that she only acted during the two or three hours she was on the stage; they did not know that the character she was playing dwelt in the back of her mind all day long, when she was talking to others with all the appearance of attention, or in whatever business she was engaged. It often seemed to her that she was two persons; the actress, the popular favourite, the best-dressed woman in London, and that was a shadow; and the woman she was playing at night, and that was the substance.

"Damned if I know what genius is," she said to herself. "But I know this, I'd give all I have to be eighteen."

But she knew that wasn't true. If she were given the chance to go back again would she take it? No. Not really. It was not the popularity, the celebrity if you like, that she cared for, nor the hold she had over audiences, the real love they bore her, it was certainly not the money this had brought her; it was the power she felt in herself, her mastery over the medium, that thrilled her. She could step into a part, not a very good one perhaps, with silly words to say, and by her personality, by the dexterity which she had at her finger-tips, infuse it with life. There was no one who could do what she could with a part. Sometimes she felt like God.

"And besides," she chuckled, "Tom wouldn't be born."

After all it was very natural that he should like to play about with Roger. They belonged to the same generation. It was the first day of his holiday, she must let him enjoy himself; there was a whole fortnight more. He would soon get sick of being all the time with a boy of seventeen. Roger was sweet, but he was dull; she wasn't going to let maternal affection blind her to that. She must be very careful not to show that she was in the least put out. From the beginning she had made up her mind that she would never make any claim on Tom; it would be fatal if he felt that he owed something to her.

"Michael, why don't you let that flat in the mews to Tom? Now that he's passed his exam and is a chartered accountant he can't go on living in a bed-sitting-room."

"That's not a bad idea. I'll suggest it to him."

"It would save an agent's fees. We could help him to furnish it. We've got a lot of stuff stored away. We might just as well let him use it as have it moulder away in the attics."

Tom and Roger came back to eat an enormous tea and then played tennis till the light failed. After dinner they played dominoes. Julia gave a beautiful performance of a still young mother fondly watching her son and his boy friend. She went to bed early. Presently they too went upstairs. Their rooms were just over hers. She heard Roger go into Tom's room. They began talking, her windows and theirs were open, and she heard their voices in animated conversation. She wondered with exasperation what they found to say to one another. She had never found either of them very talkative. After a while Michael's voice interrupted them.

"Now then, you kids, you go to bed. You can go on talking to-morrow."

She heard them laugh.

"All right, Daddy," cried Roger.

"A pair of damned chatterboxes, that's what you are."

She heard Roger's voice again.

"Well, good-night, old boy."

And Tom's hearty answer: "So long, old man."

"Idiots!" she said to herself crossly.

Next morning while she was having her breakfast Michael came into Julia's room.

"The boys have gone off to play golf at Huntercombe. They want to play a couple of rounds and they asked if they need come back to lunch. I told them that was quite all right."

"I don't know that I particularly like the idea of Tom treating the house as if it was a hotel."

"Oh, my dear, they're only a couple of kids. Let them have all the fun they can get, I say."

She would not see Tom at all that day, for she had to start for London between five and six in order to get to the theatre in good time. It was all very well for Michael to be so damned good-natured about it. She was hurt. She felt a little inclined to cry. He must be entirely indifferent to her, it was Tom she was thinking of now; and she had made up her mind that to-day was going to be quite different from the day before. She had awakened determined to be tolerant and to take things as they came, but she hadn't been prepared for a smack in the face like this.

"Have the papers come yet?" she asked sulkily.

She drove up to town with rage in her heart.

The following day was not much better. The boys did not go off to play golf, but they played tennis. Their incessant activity profoundly irritated Julia. Tom in shorts, with his bare legs, and a cricket shirt, really did not look more than sixteen. Bathing as they did three or four times a day he could not get his hair to stay down, and the moment it was dry it spread over his head in unruly curls. It made him look younger than ever, but oh, so charming. Julia's heart was wrung. And it seemed to her that his demeanour had strangely changed; in the constant companionship of Roger he had shed the young man about town who was so careful of his dress, so particular about wearing the right thing, and was become again a sloppy little schoolboy. He never gave a hint, no glance even betrayed, that he was her lover; he treated her as if she were no more than Roger's mother. In every remark he made, in his mischievousness, in his polite little ways, he made her feel that she belonged to an older generation. His behaviour had nothing of the chivalrous courtesy a young man might show to a fascinating woman; it was the tolerant kindness he might display to a maiden aunt.

Julia was irritated that Tom should docilely follow the lead of a boy so much younger than himself. It indicated lack of character. But she did not blame him; she blamed Roger. Roger's selfishness revolted her. It was all very well to say he was young. His indifference to anyone's pleasure but his own showed a vile disposition. He was tactless and inconsiderate. He acted as though the house, the servants, his father and mother were there for his particular convenience. She would often have been rather sharp with him, but that she did not dare before Tom assume the rôle of the correcting mother. And when you reproved Roger he had a maddening way of looking deeply hurt, like a stricken hind, which made you feel that you had been unkind and unjust. She could look like that too, it was an expression of the eyes that he had inherited from her; she had used it over and over again on the stage with moving effect, and she knew it need not mean very much, but when she saw it in him it shattered her. The mere thought of it now made her feel tenderly towards him. And that sudden change of feeling showed her the truth: she was jealous of Roger, madly jealous. The realisation gave her something of a shock; she did not know whether to laugh or to be ashamed. She reflected a moment.

"Well, I'll cook his goose all right."

She was not going to let the following Sunday pass like the last. Thank God, Tom was a snob. "A woman attracts men by her charm and holds them by their vices," she murmured and wondered whether she had invented the aphorism or remembered it from some play she had once acted in.

She gave instructions for some telephoning to be done. She got the Dennorants to come for the week-end. Charles Tamerley was staying at Henley and accepted an invitation to come over for Sunday and bring his host, Sir Mayhew Bryanston, who was Chancellor of the Exchequer. To amuse him and the Dennorants, because she knew that the upper classes do not want to meet one another in what they think is Bohemia, but artists of one sort or another, she asked Archie Dexter, her leading man, and his pretty wife who acted under her maiden name of Grace Hardwill. She felt pretty sure that with a marquess and marchioness to hover round and a cabinet minister to be impressed by, Tom would not go off to play golf with Roger or spend the afternoon in a punt. In such a party Roger would sink into his proper place of a school-boy that no one took any notice of, and Tom would see how brilliant she could be when she took the trouble. In the antici-pation of her triumph she managed to bear the intervening days with fortitude. She saw little of Roger and Tom. On her matinée days she did not see them at all. If they were not playing some game they were careering about the country in Roger's car.

Julia drove the Dennorants down after the play. Roger had gone to bed, but Michael and Tom were waiting up to have supper with them. It was a very good supper. The servants had gone to bed too and they helped themselves. Julia noticed the shy eager-ness with which Tom saw that the Dennorants had everything they wanted, and his alacrity to jump up if he could be of service. His civility was somewhat officious. The Dennorants were an un-assuming young couple to whom it had never occurred that their rank could impress anyone, and George Dennorant was a little embarrassed when Tom took away his dirty plate and handed him a dish to help himself to the next course.

"No golf for Roger to-morrow, I think," said Julia to herself.

They stayed up talking and laughing till three in the morning, and when Tom said good-night to her his eyes were shining; but whether from love or champagne she did not know. He pressed her hand.

"What a lovely party," he said.

It was late when Julia, dressed in organdie, looking her best, came down into the garden. She saw Roger in a long chair with a book.

"Reading?" she said, lifting her really beautiful eyebrows. "Why aren't you playing golf?"

Roger looked a trifle sulky.

"Tom said it was too hot."

"Oh?" she smiled charmingly. "I was afraid you thought you ought to stay and entertain my guests. There are going to be so many people, we could easily have managed without you. Where are the others?"

"I don't know. Tom's making chichi with Cecily Dennorant."

"She's very pretty, you know."

"It looks to me as though it's going to be a crashing bore to-day."

"I hope Tom won't find it so," she said, as though she were seriously concerned.

Roger remained silent.

The day passed exactly as she had hoped. It was true that she saw little of Tom, but Roger saw less. Tom made a great hit with the Dennorants; he explained to them how they could get out of paying as much income tax as they did. He listened respectfully to the Chancellor while he discoursed on the stage and to Archie Dexter while he gave his views on the political situation. Julia was at the top of her form. Archie Dexter had a quick wit, a fund of stage stories and a wonderful gift for telling them; between the two of them they kept the table during luncheon laughing uproariously; and after tea, when the tennis players were tired of playing tennis, Julia was persuaded (not much against her will) to do her imitations of Gladys Cooper, Constance Collier and Gertie Lawrence. But Julia did not forget that Charles Tamerley was her devoted, unrewarded lover, and she took care to have a little stroll alone with him in the gloaming. With him she sought to be neither gay nor brilliant, she was tender and wistful. Her heart ached, notwithstanding the scintillating performance she had given during the day; and it was with almost complete sincerity that with sighs, sad looks and broken sentences she made him understand that her life was hollow and despite the long continued success of her career she could not but feel that she had missed something. Sometimes she thought of the villa at Sorrento on the bay of Naples. A beautiful dream. Happiness might have been hers for the asking, perhaps; she had been a fool; after all what were the triumphs of the stage but illusion? Pagliacci. People never realised how true that was: *Vesti la giubba* and all that sort of thing. She was desperately lonely. Of course there was no need to tell Charles that her heart ached not for lost opportunities, but because a young man seemed to prefer playing golf with her son to making love to her.

But then Julia and Archie Dexter got together. After dinner when they were all sitting in the drawing-room, without warning, starting with a few words of natural conversation they burst, as though they were lovers, into a jealous quarrel. For a moment the rest did not realise it was a joke till their mutual accusations became so outrageous and indecent that they were consumed with laughter. Then they played an extempore scene of an intoxicated gentleman picking up a French tart in Jermyn Street. After that, with intense seriousness, while their little audience shook with laughter, they did Mrs. Alving in *Ghosts* trying to seduce Pastor Manders. They finished with a performance that they had given often enough before at theatrical parties to enable them to do it with effect. This was a Chekov play in English, but in moments of passion breaking into something that sounded exactly like Russian. Julia exercised all her great gift for tragedy, but underlined it with a farcical emphasis, so that the effect was incredibly funny. She put into her performance the real anguish of her heart, and with her lively sense of the ridiculous made a mock of it. The audience rolled about in their chairs; they held their sides; they groaned in an agony of laughter. Perhaps Julia had never acted better. She was acting for Tom and for him alone.

"I've seen Bernhardt and Réjane," said the Chancellor; "I've seen Duse and Ellen Terry and Mrs. Kendal. *Nunc Dimittis.*"

Julia, radiant, sank back into a chair and swallowed at a draught a glass of champagne.

"If I haven't cooked Roger's goose I'll eat my hat," she thought.

But for all that the two lads had gone off to play golf when she came downstairs next morning. Michael had taken the Dennorants up to town. Julia was tired. She found it an effort to be bright and chatty when Tom and Roger came in to lunch. In the afternoon the three of them went on the river, but Julia had the feeling that they took her, not because they much wanted to, but because they could not help it. She stifled a sigh when she reflected how much she had looked forward to Tom's holiday. Now she was counting the days that must pass till it ended. She drew a deep breath of relief when she got into the car to go to London. She was not angry with Tom, but deeply hurt; she was exasperated with herself because she had so lost control over her feelings. But when she got into the theatre she felt that she shook off the obsession of him like a bad dream from which one awoke; there, in her dressing-room, she regained possession of herself and the affairs of the common round of daily life faded to insignificance. Nothing really mattered when she had within her grasp this possibility of freedom.

Thus the week went by. Michael, Roger and Tom enjoyed themselves. They bathed, they played tennis, they played golf, they lounged about on the river. There were only four days more. There were only three days more.

("I can stick it out now. It'll be different when we're back in London again. I musn't show how miserable I am. I must pretend it's all right.")

"A snip having this spell of fine weather," said Michael. "Tom's been a success, hasn't he? Pity he can't stay another week."

"Yes, a terrible pity."

"I think he's a nice friend for Roger to have. A thoroughly normal, clean-minded English boy."

"Oh, thoroughly." ("Bloody fool, bloody fool.")

"To see the way they eat is a fair treat."

"Yes, they seem to have enjoyed their food." ("My God, I wish it could have choked them.")

Tom was to go up to town by an early train on Monday morning. The Dexters, who had a house at Bourne End, had asked them all to lunch on Sunday. They were to go down in the launch. Now that Tom's holiday was nearly over, Julia was glad that she had never by so much as a lifted eyebrow betrayed her irritation. She was certain that he had no notion how deeply he had wounded her. After all she must be tolerant, he was only a boy, and if you must cross your t's, she was old enough to be his mother. It was a bore that she had a thing about him, but there it was, she couldn't help it; she had told herself from the beginning that she must never let him feel that she had any claims on him. No one was coming to dinner on Sunday. She would have liked to have Tom to herself on his last evening; that was impossible, but at all events they could go for a stroll by themselves in the garden.

"I wonder if he's noticed that he hasn't kissed me since he came here?"

They might go out in the punt. It would be heavenly to lie in his arms for a few minutes; it would make up for everything.

The Dexters' party was theatrical. Grace Hardwill, Archie's wife, played in musical comedy, and there was a bevy of pretty girls who danced in the piece in which she was then appearing. Julia acted with great naturalness the part of a leading lady who put on no frills. She was charming to the young ladies, with their waved platinum hair, who earned three pounds a week in the chorus. A good many of the guests had brought kodaks and she submitted with affability to being photographed. She applauded enthusiastically when Grace Hardwill sang her famous song to the accompaniment of the composer. She laughed as heartily as anyone when the comic woman did an imitation of her in one of her best-known parts. It was all very gay, rather rowdy, and agreeably light-hearted. Julia enjoyed herself, but when it was seven o'clock was not sorry to go. She was thanking her hosts effusively for the pleasant party when Roger came up to her.

"I say, Mum, there's a whole crowd going on to Maidenhead to dine and dance, and they want Tom and me to go too. You don't mind, do you?"

The blood rushed to her cheeks. She could not help answering rather sharply.

"How are you to get back?"

"Oh, that'll be all right. We'll get someone to drop us."

She looked at him helplessly. She could not think what to say.

"It's going to be a tremendous lark. Tom's crazy to go."

Her heart sank. It was with the greatest difficulty that she managed not to make a scene. But she controlled herself.

"All right, darling. But don't be too late. Remember that Tom's got to rise with the lark."

Tom had come up and heard the last words.

"You're sure you don't mind?" he asked.

"Of course not. I hope you'll have a grand time."

She smiled brightly at him, but her eyes were steely with hatred.

"I'm just as glad those two kids have gone off," said Michael when they got into the launch. "We haven't had an evening to ourselves for ever so long."

She clenched her hands in order to prevent herself from telling him to hold his silly tongue. She was in a black rage. This was the last straw. Tom had neglected her for a fortnight, he had not even treated her with civility, and she had been angelic. There wasn't a woman in the world who would have shown such patience. Any other woman would have told him that if he couldn't behave with common decency he'd better get out. Selfish, stupid and common, that's what he was. She almost wished he wasn't going to-morrow so that she could have the pleasure of turning him out bag and baggage. And to dare to treat her like that, a twopenny half-penny little man in the City; poets, cabinet ministers, peers of the realm would be only too glad to break the most important engagements to have the chance of dining with her, and he threw her over to go and dance with a pack of peroxide blondes who couldn't act for nuts. That showed what a fool he was. You would have thought he'd have some gratitude. Why, the very clothes he had on she'd paid for. That cigarette-case he was so proud of, hadn't she given him that? And the ring he wore. My God, she'd get even with him. Yes, and she knew how she could do it. She knew where he was most sensitive and how she could most cruelly wound him. That would get him on the raw. She felt a faint sensation of relief as she turned the scheme over in her mind. She was impatient to carry out her part of it at once, and they had no sooner got home than she went up to her room. She got four single pounds out of her bag and a ten-shilling note. She wrote a brief letter.

Dear Tom,

I'm enclosing the money for your tips as I shan't see you in the morning. Give three pounds to the butler, a pound to the maid who's been valeting you, and ten shillings to the chauffeur.

Julia.

She sent for Evie and gave instructions that the letter should be given to Tom by the maid who awoke him. When she went down to dinner she felt much better. She carried on an animated conversation with Michael while they dined and afterwards they played six-pack bezique. If she had racked her brains for a week she couldn't have thought of anything that would humiliate Tom more bitterly.

But when she went to bed she could not sleep. She was waiting for Roger and Tom to come home. A notion came to her that made her restless. Perhaps Tom would realise that he had behaved rottenly, if he gave it a moment's thought he must see how unhappy he was making her; it might be that he would be sorry and when he came in, after he had said good-night to Roger, he would creep down to her room. If he did that she would forgive everything. The letter was probably in the butler's pantry; she could easily slip down and get it back. At last a car drove up. She turned on her light to look at the time. It was three. She heard the two young men go upstairs and to their respective rooms. She waited. She put on the light by her bedside so that when he opened the door he should be able to see. She would pretend she was sleeping and then as he crept forward on tiptoe slowly open her eyes and smile at him. She waited. In the silent night she heard him get into bed and switch off the light. She stared straight in front of her for a minute, then with a shrug of the shoulders opened a drawer by her bedside and from a little bottle took a couple of sleeping-tablets.

"If I don't sleep I shall go mad."

CHAPTER XV

JULIA did not wake till after eleven. Among her letters was one that had not come by post. She recognised Tom's neat, commercial hand and tore it open. It contained nothing but the four pounds and the ten-shilling note. She felt slightly sick. She did not quite know what she had expected him to reply to her condescending letter and the humiliating present. It had not occurred to her that he would return it. She was troubled, she had wanted to hurt his feelings, but she had a fear now that she had gone too far.

"Anyhow I hope he tipped the servants," she muttered to reassure herself. She shrugged her shoulders. "He'll come round. It won't hurt him to discover that I'm not all milk and honey."

But she remained thoughtful throughout the day. When she got to the theatre a parcel was waiting for her. As soon as she looked at the address she knew what it contained. Evie asked if she should open it.

"No."

But the moment she was alone she opened it herself. There were the cuff-links and the waistcoat buttons, the pearl studs, the wrist-watch and the cigarette-case of which Tom was so proud. All the presents she had ever given him. But no letter. Not a word of explanation. Her heart sank and she noticed that she was trembling.

"What a damned fool I was! Why didn't I keep my temper?"

Her heart now beat painfully. She couldn't go on the stage with that anguish gnawing at her vitals, she would give a frightful performance; at whatever cost she must speak to him. There was a telephone in his house and an extension to his room. She rang him. Fortunately he was in.

"Tom."

"Yes?"

He had paused for a moment before answering and his voice was peevish.

"What does this mean? Why have you sent me all those things?"

"Did you get the notes this morning?"

"Yes. I couldn't make head or tail of it. Have I offended you?"

"Oh no," he answered. "I like being treated like a kept boy. I like having it thrown in my face that even my tips have to be given me. I thought it rather strange that you didn't send me the money for a third-class ticket back to London."

Although Julia was in a pitiable state of anxiety, so that she could hardly get the words out of her mouth, she almost smiled at his fatuous irony. He was a silly little thing.

"But you can't imagine that I wanted to hurt your feelings. You surely know me well enough to know that's the last thing I should do."

"That only makes it worse." ("Damn and curse," thought

Julia.) "I ought never to have let you make me those presents. I should never have let you lend me money."

"I don't know what you mean. It's all some horrible misunderstanding. Come and fetch me after the play and we'll have it out. I know I can explain."

"I'm going to dinner with my people and I shall sleep at home."

"To-morrow then."

"I'm engaged to-morrow."

"I must see you, Tom. We've been too much to one another to part like this. You can't condemn me unheard. It's so unjust to punish me for no fault of mine."

"I think it's much better that we shouldn't meet again."

Julia was growing desperate.

"But I love you, Tom. I love you. Let me see you once more and then, if you're still angry with me, we'll call it a day."

There was a long pause before he answered.

"All right. I'll come after the matinée on Wednesday."

"Don't think unkindly of me, Tom."

She put down the receiver. At all events he was coming. She wrapped up again the things he had returned to her, and hid them away where she was pretty sure Evie would not see them. She undressed, put on her old pink dressing-gown and began to make-up. She was out of humour: this was the first time she had ever told him that she loved him. It vexed her that she had been forced to humiliate herself by begging him to come and see her. Till then it had always been he who sought her company. She was not pleased to think that the situation between them now was openly reversed.

Julia gave a very poor performance at the matinée on Wednesday. The heat wave had affected business and the house was apathetic. Julia was indifferent. With that sickness of apprehension gnawing at her heart she could not care how the play went. ("What the hell do they want to come to the theatre for on a day like this anyway?") She was glad when it was over.

"I'm expecting Mr. Fennell," she told Evie. "While here's here I don't want to be disturbed."

Evie did not answer. Julia gave her a glance and saw that she was looking grim.

("To hell with her. What do I care what she thinks!")

He ought to have been there by now. It was after five. He was bound to come; after all, he'd promised, hadn't he? She put on a dressing-gown, not the one she made up in, but a man's dressing-gown, in plum-coloured silk. Evie took an interminable time to put things straight.

"For God's sake don't fuss, Evie. Leave me alone."

Evie did not speak. She went on methodically arranging the various objects on the dressing-table exactly as Julia always wanted them.

"Why the devil don't you answer when I speak to you?"

Evie turned round and looked at her. She thoughtfully rubbed her finger along her nostrils.

"Great actress you may be . . ."

"Get the hell out of here."

After taking off her stage make-up Julia had done nothing to her face except put the very faintest shading of blue under her eyes. She had a smooth, pale skin and without rouge on her cheeks or red on her lips she looked wan. The man's dressing-gown gave an effect at once helpless, fragile and gallant. Her heart was beating painfully and she was very anxious, but looking at herself in the glass she murmured: Mimi in the last act of *Bohème*. Almost without meaning to she coughed once or twice con-sumptively. She turned off the bright lights on her dressing-table and lay down on the sofa. Presently there was a knock on the door and Evie announced Mr. Fennell. Julia held out a white, thin hand.

"I'm lying down. I'm afraid I'm not very well. Find yourself a chair. It's nice of you to come."

"I'm sorry. What's the matter?"

"Oh, nothing." She forced a smile to her ashy lips. "I haven't been sleeping very well the last two or three nights."

She turned her beautiful eyes on him and for a while gazed at him in silence. His expression was sullen, but she had a notion that he was frightened.

"I'm waiting for you to tell me what you've got against me," she said at last in a low voice.

It trembled a little, she noticed, but quite naturally. ("Christ, I believe I'm frightened too.")

"There's no object in going back to that. The only thing I wanted to say to you was this: I'm afraid I can't pay you the two hundred pounds I owe you right away, I simply haven't got it, but I'll pay you by degrees. I hate having to ask you to give me time, but I can't help myself."

She sat up on the sofa and put both her hands to her breaking heart.

"I don't understand. I've lain awake for two whole nights turning it all over in my mind. I thought I should go mad. I've been trying to understand. I can't. I can't."

("What play did I say that in?")

"Oh yes, you can, you understand perfectly. You were angry with me and you wanted to get back on me. And you did. You got back on me all right. You couldn't have shown your contempt for me more clearly."

"But why should I want to get back on you? Why should I be angry with you?"

"Because I went to Maidenhead with Roger to that party and you wanted me to come home."

"But I told you to go. I said I hoped you'd have a good time."

"I know you did, but your eyes were blazing with passion. I didn't want to go, but Roger was keen on it. I told him I thought we ought to come back and dine with you and Michael, but he said you'd be glad to have us off your hands, and I didn't like to make a song and dance about it. And when I saw you were in a rage it was too late to get out of it."

"I wasn't in a rage. I can't think how you got such an idea in your head. It was so natural that you should want to go to the party. You can't think I'm such a beast as to grudge you a little fun in your fortnight's holiday. My poor lamb, my only fear was that you would be bored. I so wanted you to have a good time."

"Then why did you send me that money and write me that letter? It was so insulting."

Julia's voice faltered. Her jaw began to tremble and the loss of control over her muscles was strangely moving. Tom looked away uneasily.

"I couldn't bear to think of your having to throw away your good money on tips. I know that you're not terribly rich and I knew you'd spent a lot on green fees. I hate women who go about with young men and let them pay for everything. It's so inconsiderate. I treated you just as I'd have treated Roger. I never thought it would hurt your feelings."

"Will you swear that?"

"Of course I will. My God, is it possible that after all these months you don't know me better than that? If what you think were true, what a mean, cruel, despicable woman I should be, what a cad, what a heartless, vulgar beast! Is that what you think I am?"

A poser.

"Anyhow it doesn't matter. I ought never to have accepted valuable presents from you and allowed you to lend me money. It's put me in a rotten position. Why I thought you despised me is that I can't help feeling that you've got a right to. The fact is I can't afford to run around with people who are so much richer than I am. I was a fool to think I could. It's been fun and I've had a grand time, but now I'm through. I'm not going to see you any more."

She gave a deep sigh.

"You don't care two hoots for me. That's what that means."

"That's not fair."

"You're everything in the world to me. You know that. I'm so lonely and your friendship meant a great deal to me. I'm surrounded by hangers-on and parasites and I knew you were disinterested. I felt I could rely on you. I so loved being with you. You were the only person in the world with whom I could be entirely myself. Don't you know what a pleasure it was to me to help you a little? It wasn't for your sake I made you little presents, it was for my own; it made me so happy to see you using the things I'd given you. If you'd cared for me at all they wouldn't have humiliated you, you'd have been touched to owe me something."

She turned her eyes on him once more. She could always cry easily, and she was really so miserable now that she did not have to make even a small effort. He had never seen her cry before. She could cry, without sobbing, her wonderful dark eyes wide open, with a face that was almost rigid. Great heavy tears ran down it. And her quietness, the immobility of the tragic body, were terribly moving. She hadn't cried like that since she cried in *The Stricken Heart*. Christ, how that play had shattered her. She was not looking at Tom, she was looking straight in front of her; she was really distracted with grief, but, what was it? another self within her knew what she was doing, a self that shared in her unhappiness and yet watched its expression. She felt him go white. She felt a sudden anguish wring his heartstrings, she felt that his flesh and blood could not support the intolerable pain of hers.

"Julia."

His voice was broken. She slowly turned her liquid eyes on

him. It was not a woman crying that he saw, it was all the woe of human kind, it was the immeasurable, the inconsolable grief that is the lot of man. He threw himself down on his knees and took her in his arms. He was shattered.

"Dearest, dearest."

For a minute she did not move. It was as if she did not know that he was there. He kissed her streaming eyes and with his mouth sought hers. She gave it to him as though she were power-less, as though, scarcely conscious of what was befalling her, she had no will left. With a scarcely perceptible movement she pressed her body to his and gradually her arms found their way round his neck. She lay in his arms, not exactly inert, but as though all the strength, all the vitality, had gone out of her. In his mouth he tasted the saltness of her tears. At last, exhausted, clinging to him with soft arms she sank back on the sofa. His lips clung to hers.

You would never have thought had you seen her a quarter of an hour later, so quietly gay, flushed a little, that so short a while before she had passed through such a tempest of weeping. They each had a whisky and soda and a cigarette and looked at one another with fond eyes.

"He's a sweet little thing," she thought.

It occurred to her that she would give him a treat.

"The Duke and Duchess of Rickaby are coming to the play to-night and we're going to have supper at the Savoy. I suppose you wouldn't come, would you? I want a man badly to make a fourth."

"If you'd like me to, of course I will."

The heightened colour on his cheeks told her how excited he was to meet such distinguished persons. She did not tell him that the Rickabys would go anywhere for a free meal. Tom took back the presents that he had returned to her rather shyly, but he took them. When he had gone she sat down at the dressing-table and had a good look at herself.

"How lucky I am that I can cry without my eyelids swelling," she said. She massaged them a little. "All the same, what mugs men are."

She was happy. Everything would be all right now. She had got him back. But somewhere, at the back of her mind or in the bottom of her heart, was a feeling of ever so slight contempt for Tom because he was such a simple fool.

CHAPTER XVI

THEIR quarrel, destroying in some strange way the barrier between them, brought them closer together. Tom offered less resistance than she had expected when she mooted once more the question of the flat. It looked as though, after their reconciliation, having taken back her presents and consented to forget the loan, he had put aside his moral scruples. They had a lot of fun furnishing it. The chauffeur's wife kept it clean for him and cooked his breakfast. Julia had a key and would sometimes let herself in and sit by herself in the little sitting-room till he came back from his office. They supped together two or three times a week and danced, then drove back to the flat in a taxi. Julia enjoyed a happy autumn. The play they put on was a success. She felt alert and young. Roger was coming home at Christmas, but only for a fortnight, and was then going to Vienna. Julia expected him to monopolise Tom and she was determined not to mind. Youth naturally appealed to youth and she told herself that there was no reason for her to feel anxious if for a few days the two of them were so wrapped up in one another that Tom had no thought for her. She held him now. He was proud to be her lover, it gave him confidence in himself, and he was pleased to be on familiar terms with a large number of more or less distinguished persons whom after all he only knew through her. He was anxious now to join a good club and Julia was preparing the ground. Charles had never refused her anything, and with tact she was certain that she could wheedle him into proposing Tom for one of those to which he belonged. It was a new and delicious sensation for Tom to have money to spend; she encouraged him to be extravagant; she had a notion that he would get used to living in a certain way and then would realise that he could not do without her.

"Of course it can't last," she told herself," but when it comes to an end it will have been a wonderful experience for him. It'll really have made a man of him."

But though she told herself that it could not last she did not see really why it shouldn't. As the years went by and he grew older there wouldn't be any particular difference between them. He would no longer be so very young in ten or fifteen years and she would be just the same age as she was now. They were very comfortable together. Men were creatures of habit; that gave women such a hold on them. She did not feel a day older than he, and she was convinced that the disparity in their ages had never even occurred to him. It was true that on this point she had once had a moment's disquietude. She was lying on his bed. He was standing at the dressing-table, in his shirt-sleeves, brushing his hair. She was stark naked and she lay in the position of a Venus by Titian that she remembered to have seen in a country house at which she had stayed. She felt that she made really a lovely picture, and in complete awareness of the charming sight she offered, held the pose. She was happy and satisfied.

"This is romance," she thought, and a light, quick smile hovered over her lips.

He caught sight of her in the mirror, turned round and without a word, twitched the sheet over her. Though she smiled at him affectionately, it gave her quite a turn. Was he afraid that she would catch cold or was it that his English modesty was shocked at her nakedness? Or could it be that, his boyish lust satisfied, he was a trifle disgusted at the sight of her ageing body? When she got home she again took all her clothes off and examined herself in the looking-glass. She determined not to spare herself. She looked at her neck, there was no sign of age there, especially when she held her chin up; and her breasts were small and firm; they might have been a girl's. Her belly was flat, her hips were small, there was a very small roll of fat there, like a long sausage, but everyone had that, and anyhow Miss Phillips could have a go at it. No one could say that her legs weren't good, they were long and slim and comely; she passed her hands over her body, her skin was as soft as velvet and there wasn't a blemish on it. Of course there were a few wrinkles under her eyes, but you had to peer to see them; they said there was an operation now by which you could get rid of them, it might be worth while to inquire into that; it was lucky that her hair had retained its colour; however well hair was dyed, to dye hardened the face; hers remained a rich, deep brown. Her teeth were all right too.

"Prudishness, that's all it was."

She had a moment's recollection of the Spaniard with the beard in the wagon-lit and she smiled roguishly at herself in the glass.

"No damned modesty about him."

But all the same from that day on she took care to act up to Tom's standards of decency.

Julia's reputation was so good that she felt she need not hesitate to show herself with Tom in public places. It was a new experience for her to go to night clubs, she enjoyed it, and though no one could have been better aware than she that she could go nowhere without being stared at, it never entered her head that such a change in her habits must excite comment. With twenty years of fidelity behind her, for of course she did not count the Spaniard, an accident that might happen to any woman, Julia was confident that no one would imagine for a moment that she was having an affair with a boy young enough to be her son. It never occurred to her that perhaps Tom was not always so discreet as he might have been. It never occurred to her that the look in her eyes when they danced together betrayed her. She looked upon her position as so privileged that it never occurred to her that people at last were beginning to gossip.

When this gossip reached the ears of Dolly de Vries she laughed. At Julia's request she had invited Tom to parties and once or twice had him down for a week-end in the country, but she had never paid any attention to him. He seemed a nice little thing, a useful escort for Julia when Michael was busy, but perfectly insignificant. He was one of those persons who everywhere pass unnoticed, and even after you had met him you could not remember what he was like. He was the extra man you invited to dinner to make an odd number even. Julia talked of him gaily as "me boy friend" or as "my young man"; she could hardly have been so cool about it, so open, if there were anything in it. Besides, Dolly knew very well that the only two men there had ever been in Julia's life were Michael and Charles Tamerley. But it was funny of Julia, after taking so much care of herself for years, suddenly to start going to night clubs three or four times a week. Dolly had seen little of her of late and indeed had been somewhat piqued by her neglect. She had many friends in theatrical circles and she began to make enquiries. She did not at all like what she heard. She did not know what to think. One thing was evident, Julia couldn't know what was being said about her, and someone must tell her. Not she; she hadn't the courage. Even after all these years she was a little frightened of Julia. Julia was a very good-tempered woman, and though her language was often brusque it was hard to ruffle her; but there was something about her that prevented you from taking liberties with her; you had a feeling that if once you went too far you would regret it. But something must be done. Dolly turned the matter over in her mind for a

F.A.A. 1 O

fortnight, anxiously; she tried to put her own wounded feelings aside and look at it only from the point of view of Julia's career, and at last she came to the conclusion that Michael must speak to her. She had never liked Michael, but after all he was Julia's husband and it was her duty to tell him at least enough to make him put a stop to whatever was going on.

She rang Michael up and made an appointment with him at the theatre. Michael liked Dolly as little as she liked him, though for other reasons, and when he heard that she wanted to see him he swore. He was annoyed that he had never been able to induce her to sell out her shares in the management, and he resented whatever suggestions she made as an unwarrantable interference. But when she was shown into his office he greeted her with cordiality. He kissed her on both cheeks.

"Sit down and make yourself comfy. Come to see that the old firm's still raking in dividends for you?"

Dolly de Vries was now a woman of sixty. She was very fat, and her face, with its large nose and heavy red lips, seemed larger than life. There was a slightly masculine touch in her black satin dress, but she wore a double string of pearls round her neck, a diamond brooch at her waist and another in her hat. Her short hair was dyed a rich copper. Her lips and her finger-nails were bright red. Her voice was loud and deep, but when she got excited the words were apt to tumble over one another and a slight Cockney accent revealed itself.

"Michael, I'm upset about Julia."

Michael, always the perfect gentleman, slightly raised his eyebrows and compressed his thin lips. He was not prepared to discuss his wife even with Dolly.

"I think she's doing a great deal too much. I don't know what's come over her. All these parties she's going to now. These night clubs and things. After all, she's not a young woman any more; she'll just wear herself out."

"Oh, nonsense. She's as strong as a horse and she's in the best of health. She's looking younger than she has for years. You're not going to grudge her a bit of fun when her day's work is over. The part she's playing just now doesn't take it out of her; I'm very glad that she should want to go out and amuse herself. It only shows how much vitality she has."

"She never cared for that sort of thing before. It seems so strange that she should suddenly take to dancing till two in the morning in the horrible atmosphere of those places."

"It's the only exercise she gets. I can't expect her to put on shorts and come for a run with me in the park."

"I think you ought to know that people are beginning to talk. It's doing her reputation a lot of harm."

"What the devil d'you mean by that?"

"Well, it's absurd that at her age she should make herself so conspicuous with a young boy."

He looked at her for a moment without understanding, and when he caught what she meant he laughed loud.

"Tom? Don't be such a fool, Dolly."

"I'm not a fool. I know what I'm talking about. When anyone's as well known as Julia and she's always about with the same man naturally people talk."

"But Tom's just as much my friend as hers. You know very well that I can't take Julia out dancing. I have to get up every morning at eight to get my exercise in before my day's work. Hang it all, I do know something about human nature after thirty years on the stage. Tom's a very good type of clean honest English boy and he's by way of being a gentleman. I dare say he admires Julia, boys of that age often think they're in love with women older than themselves, well, it won't do him any harm, it'll do him good; but to think Julia could possibly give him a thought—my poor Dolly, you make me laugh."

"He's boring, he's dull, he's common and he's a snob."

"Well, if you think he's all that, doesn't it strike you as rather strange that Julia should be so wrapped up in him as you seem to think?"

"Only a woman knows what a woman can do."

"That's not a bad line, Dolly. We shall have you writing a play next. Now let's get this straight. Can you look me in the face and tell me that you really think Julia is having an affair with Tom?"

She looked him in the face. Her eyes were anguished. For though at first she had only laughed at what was being said about Julia she had not been able altogether to suppress the doubts that soon assailed her; she remembered a dozen little incidents that at the time had escaped her notice, but when considered in cold blood looked terribly suspicious. She had suffered such torture as she had never thought it possible to endure. Proof? She had no proof; she only had an intuition that she could not mistrust; she wanted to say yes, the impulse to do so was almost uncontrollable;

she controlled it. She could not give Julia away. The fool might go and tell her and Julia would never speak to her again. He might have Julia watched and catch her out. No one could tell what might happen if she told the truth.

"No, I don't."

Her eyes filled with tears and began to roll down her massive cheeks. Michael saw her misery. He thought her ridiculous, but he realised that she was suffering and in the kindness of his heart sought to console her.

"I was sure you didn't really. You know how fond Julia is of you; you mustn't be jealous, you know, if she has other friends."

"God knows I don't grudge her anything," she sobbed. "She's been so different to me lately. She's been so cold. I've been such a loyal friend to her, Michael."

"Yes, dear, I know you have."

"Had I but served my God with half the zeal I served my King . . ."

"Oh, come now, it's not so bad as that. You know, I'm not the sort of chap to talk about his wife to other people. I always think that's such frightfully bad form. But, you know, honestly you don't know the first thing about Julia. Sex doesn't mean a thing to her. When we were first married it was different, and I don't mind telling you after all these years that she made life a bit difficult for me. I don't say she was a nymphomaniac or anything like that, but she was inclined to be rather tiresome sometimes. Bed's all very well in its way, but there are other things in life. But after Roger was born she changed completely. Having a baby settled her. All those instincts went into her acting. You've read Freud, Dolly; what does he call it when that happens?"

"Oh, Michael, what do I care about Freud?"

"Sublimation. That's it. I often think that's what's made her such a great actress. Acting's a whole-time job and if you want to be really good you've got to give your whole self to it. I'm so impatient with the public who think actors and actresses lead a devil of a life. We haven't got the time for that sort of nonsense."

What Michael was saying made her so angry that she recovered her self-control.

"But, Michael, it may be that you and I know that there's nothing wrong with Julia's going about all the time with that miserable little pip-squeak. It's so bad for her reputation. After all, one of your great assets has been your exemplary married life.

Everyone has looked up to you. The public has loved to think of you as such a devoted and united couple."

"And so we are, damn it."

Dolly was growing impatient.

"But I tell you people are talking. You can't be so stupid as not to see that they're bound to. I mean, if Julia had had one flagrant affair after another, nobody would take any notice, but after the life she's led for so many years suddenly to break out like this— naturally everybody starts chattering. It's so bad for business."

Michael gave her a swift glance. He smiled a little.

"I see what you mean, Dolly. I dare say there's something in what you say and in the circumstances I feel that you have a perfect right to say it. You were awfully good to us when we started and I should hate to see you let down now. I'll tell you what, I'll buy you out."

"Buy me out?"

Dolly straightened herself and her face, a moment ago rumpled and discomposed, hardened. She was seized with indignation. He went on suavely.

"I see your point. If Julia's gadding about all night it must tell on her performances. That's obvious. She's got a funny sort of public, a lot of old ladies come to our matinées because they think she's such a sweet good woman. I don't mind admitting that if she gets herself unpleasantly talked about it might have some effect on the takings. I know Julia well enough to know that she wouldn't put up with any interference with her liberty of action. I'm her husband and I've got to put up with it. But you're in a different position altogether. I shouldn't blame you if you wanted to get out while the going was good."

Dolly was alert now. She was far from a fool and when it came to business was a match for Michael. She was angry, but her anger gave her self-control.

"I should have thought after all these years, Michael, that you knew me better than that. I thought it my duty to warn you, but I'm prepared to take the rough with the smooth. I'm not the woman to desert a sinking ship. I dare say I can afford to lose my money better than you can."

It gave her a great deal of satisfaction to see the disappointment that was clearly expressed on Michael's face. She knew how much money meant to him and she had a hope that what she had said would rankle. He pulled himself together quickly.

"Well, think it over, Dolly."

She gathered up her bag and they parted with mutual expressions of affection and good will.

"Silly old bitch," he said when the door was closed behind her.

"Pompous old ass," she hissed as she went down in the lift.

But when she got into her magnificent and very expensive car and drove back to Montagu Square she could not hold back the heavy, painful tears that filled her eyes. She felt old, lonely, unhappy, and desperately jealous.

CHAPTER XVII

MICHAEL flattered himself on his sense of humour. On the Sunday evening that followed his conversation with Dolly he strolled into Julia's room while she was dressing. They were going to the pictures after an early dinner.

"Who's coming to-night besides Charles?" he asked her.

"I couldn't find another woman. I've asked Tom."

"Good! I wanted to see him."

He chuckled at the thought of the joke he had up his sleeve. Julia was looking forward to the evening. At the cinema she would arrange the seating so that Tom sat next to her and he would hold her hand while she chatted in undertones to Charles on the other side of her. Dear Charles, it was nice of him to have loved her so long and so devotedly; she would go out of her way to be very sweet to him. Charles and Tom arrived together. Tom was wearing his new dinner-jacket for the first time and he and Julia exchanged a little private glance, of satisfaction on his part and of compliment on hers.

"Well, young feller," said Michael heartily, rubbing his hands, "do you know what I hear about you? I hear that you're compromising my wife."

Tom gave him a startled look and went scarlet. The habit of flushing mortified him horribly, but he could not break himself of it.

"Oh, my dear," cried Julia gaily, "how marvellous! I've been trying to get someone to compromise me all my life. Who told you, Michael?"

"A little bird," he said archly.

"Well, Tom, if Michael divorces me you'll have to marry me, you know."

Charles smiled with his gentle, rather melancholy eyes.

"What have you been doing, Tom?" he asked.

Charles was gravely, Michael boisterously, diverted by the young man's obvious embarrassment. Julia, though she seemed to share their amusement, was alert and watchful.

"Well, it appears that the young rip has been taking Julia to night clubs when she ought to have been in bed and asleep."

Julia crowed with delight.

"Shall we deny it, Tom, or shall we brazen it out?"

"Well, I'll tell you what I said to the little bird," Michael broke in. "I said to her, as long as Julia doesn't want me to go to night clubs with her . . ."

Julia ceased to listen to what he said. Dolly, she thought, and oddly enough she described her to herself in exactly the words Michael had used a couple of days before. Dinner was announced and their bright talk turned to other things. But though Julia took part in it with gaiety, though she appeared to be giving her guests all her attention and even listened with a show of appreciation to one of Michael's theatrical stories that she had heard twenty times before, she was privately holding an animated conversation with Dolly. Dolly cowered before her while she told her exactly what she thought of her.

"You old cow," she said to her. "How dare you interfere with my private concerns? No, don't speak. Don't try to excuse yourself. I know exactly what you said to Michael. It was unpardonable. I thought you were a friend of mine. I thought I could rely on you. Well, that finishes it. I'll never speak to you again. Never. Never. D'you think I'm impressed by your rotten old money? Oh, it's no good saying you didn't mean it. Where would you be except for me, I should like to know. Any distinction you've got, the only importance you have in the world, is that you happen to know me. Who's made your parties go all these years? D'you think that people came to them to see you? They came to see me. Never again. Never."

It was in point of fact a monologue rather than a conversation.

Later on, at the cinema, she sat next to Tom as she had intended and held his hand, but it seemed to her singularly unresponsive. Like a fish's fin. She suspected that he was thinking uncomfortably of what Michael had said. She wished that she had had an opportunity of a few words with him so that she might have told him not to worry. After all no one could have carried off the incident with more brilliance than she had. Aplomb; that was the word. She wondered what it was exactly that Dolly had told Michael. She had better find out. It would not do to ask Michael, that would look as though she attached importance to it; she must find out from Dolly herself. It would be much wiser not to have a row with her. Julia smiled as she thought of the scene she would have with Dolly. She would be sweetness itself, she would wheedle it all out of her, and never give her an inkling that she was angry. It was curious that it should send a cold shiver down her back to think that people were talking about her. After all if she couldn't do what she liked, who could? Her private life was nobody's business. All the same one couldn't deny that it wouldn't be very nice if people were laughing at her. She wondered what Michael would do if he found out the truth. He couldn't very well divorce her and continue to manage for her. If he had any sense he'd shut his eyes. But Michael was funny in some ways; every now and then he would get up on his hind legs and start doing his colonel stuff. He was quite capable of saying all of a sudden that damn it all, he must behave like a gentleman. Men were such fools; there wasn't one of them who wouldn't cut off his nose to spite his face. Of course it wouldn't really matter very much to her. She could go and act in America for a year till the scandal had died down and then go into management with somebody else. But it would be a bore. And then there was Roger to consider; he'd feel it, poor lamb; he'd be humiliated, naturally; it was no good shutting one's eyes to the fact, at her age she'd look a perfect fool being divorced on account of a boy of three-and-twenty. Of course she wouldn't be such a fool as to marry Tom. Would Charles marry her? She turned and in the half-light looked at his distinguished profile. He had been madly in love with her for years; he was one of those chivalrous idiots that a woman could turn round her little finger; perhaps he wouldn't mind being co-respondent instead of Tom. That might be a very good way out. Lady Charles Tamerley. It sounded all right. Perhaps she *had* been a little imprudent. She had always been very careful when she went to Tom's flat, but it might be that one of the chauffeurs in the mews had seen her go in or come out and had thought things. That class of people had such filthy minds. As far as the night clubs were concerned, she'd have been only too glad to go with Tom to quiet little places where no one would see them, but he didn't like that. He loved a crowd, he wanted to see smart people, and be seen. He liked to show her off.

"Damn," she said to herself. "Damn, damn."

Julia didn't enjoy her evening at the cinema as much as she had expected.

CHAPTER XVIII

NEXT day Julia got Dolly on her private number.

"Darling, it seems ages since I've seen you. What have you been doing with yourself all this time?"

"Nothing very much."

Dolly's voice sounded cold.

"Now listen, Roger's coming home to-morrow. You know he's leaving Eton for good. I'm sending the car for him early and I want you to come to lunch. Not a party; only you and me, Michael and Roger."

"I'm lunching out to-morrow."

In twenty years Dolly had never been engaged when Julia wanted her to do something with her. The voice at the other end of the telephone was hostile.

"Dolly, how can you be so unkind? Roger'll be terribly disappointed. His first day at home; besides, I want to see you. I haven't seen you for ages and I miss you terribly. Can't you break your engagement, just for this once, darling, and we'll have a good old gossip after lunch, just you and me?"

No one could be more persuasive than Julia when she liked, no one could put more tenderness into her voice, nor a more irresistible appeal. There was a moment's pause and Julia knew that Dolly was struggling with her wounded feelings.

"All right, darling, I'll manage."

"Darling." But when she rang off Julia through clenched teeth muttered: "The old cow."

Dolly came. Roger listened politely while she told him that he had grown and with his grave smile answered her suitably when she said the sort of things she thought proper to a boy of his age.

Julia was puzzled by him. Without talking much he listened, apparently with attention, to what the rest of them were saying, but she had an odd feeling that he was occupied with thoughts of his own. He seemed to observe them with a detached curiosity like that with which he might have observed animals in a zoo. It was faintly disquieting. When the opportunity presented itself she delivered the little bit of dialogue she had prepared for Dolly's benefit.

"Oh, Roger darling, you know your wretched father's busy to-night. I've got a couple of seats for the second house at the Palladium and Tom wants you to dine with him at the Café Royal."

"Oh!" He paused for a second. "All right."

She turned to Dolly.

"It's so nice for Roger to have somebody like Tom to go about with. They're great friends, you know."

Michael gave Dolly a glance. There was a twinkle in his eyes. He spoke.

"Tom's a very decent sort of boy. He won't let Roger get into any mischief."

"I should have thought Roger would prefer to go about with his Eton friends," said Dolly.

"Old cow," thought Julia. "Old cow."

But when luncheon was over she asked her to come up to her room.

"I'll get into bed and you can talk to me while I'm resting. A good old girls' gossip, that's what I want."

She put her arm affectionately round Dolly's vast waist and led her upstairs. For a while they spoke of indifferent things, clothes and servants, make-up and scandal; then Julia, leaning on her elbow, looked at Dolly with confiding eyes.

"Dolly, there's something I want to talk to you about. I want advice and you're the only person in the world whose advice I would take. I know I can trust you."

"Of course, darling."

"It appears that people are saying rather disagreeable things about me. Someone's been to Michael and told him that there's a lot of gossip about me and poor Tom Fennell."

Though her eyes still wore the charming and appealing look that she knew Dolly found irresistible, she watched her closely for a start or for some change in her expression. She saw nothing.

"Who told Michael?"

"I don't know. He won't say. You know what he is when he starts being a perfect gentleman."

She wondered if she only imagined that Dolly's features at this slightly relaxed.

"I want the truth, Dolly."

"I'm so glad you've asked me, darling. You know how I hate to interfere in other people's business and if you hadn't brought the matter up yourself nothing would have induced me to mention it."

"My dear, if I don't know that you're a loyal friend, who does?"

Dolly slipped off her shoes and settled down massively in her chair. Julia never took her eyes off her.

"You know how malicious people are. You've always led such a quiet, regular life. You've gone out so little, and then only with Michael or Charles Tamerley. He's different; of course everyone knows he's adored you for ages. It seems so funny that all of a sudden you should run around all over the place with a clerk in the firm that does your accounts."

"He isn't exactly that. His father has bought him a share in the firm and he's a junior partner."

"Yes, he gets four hundred a year."

"How d'you know?" asked Julia quickly.

This time she was certain that Dolly was disconcerted.

"You persuaded me to go to his firm about my income tax. One of the head partners told me. It seems a little strange that on that he should be able to have a flat, dress the way he does and take people to night clubs."

"For all I know, his father may make him an allowance."

"His father's a solicitor in the North of London. You know very well that if he's bought him a partnership he isn't making him an allowance as well."

"Surely you don't imagine that I'm keeping him," said Julia, with a ringing laugh.

"I don't imagine anything, darling. Other people do."

Julia liked neither the words Dolly spoke nor the way she said them. But she gave no sign of her uneasiness.

"It's too absurd. He's Roger's friend much more than mine. Of course I've been about with him. I felt I was getting too set. I'm tired of just going to the theatre and taking care of myself. It's

no life. After all if I don't enjoy myself a little now I never shall.
I'm getting on, you know, Dolly, it's no good denying it. You
know what Michael is; of course he's sweet, but he is a bore."

"No more a bore than he's ever been," said Dolly acidly.

"I should have thought I was the last person anyone would
dream would have an affair with a boy twenty years younger than
myself."

"Twenty-five," corrected Dolly. "I should have thought so
too. Unfortunately he's not very discreet."

"What do you mean by that?"

"Well, he's told Avice Crichton that he'll get her a part in your
next play."

"Who the devil is Avice Crichton?"

"Oh, she's a young actress I know. She's as pretty as a picture."

"He's only a silly kid. I suppose he thinks he can get round
Michael. You know what Michael is with his little bits."

"He says he can get you to do anything he wants. He says you
just eat out of his hand."

It was lucky for Julia that she was a good actress. For a second
her heart stood still. How could he say a thing like that? The fool.
The blasted fool. But recovering herself at once she laughed
lightly.

"What nonsense! I don't believe a word of it."

"He's a very commonplace, rather vulgar young man. It's not
surprising if all the fuss you've made of him has turned his
head."

Julia, smiling good-naturedly, looked at her with ingenuous
eyes.

"But, darling, *you* don't think he's my lover, do you?"

"If I don't, I'm the only person who doesn't."

"And do you?"

For a minute Dolly did not answer. They looked at one another
steadily, their hearts were black with hatred; but Julia still smiled.

"If you give me your solemn word of honour that he isn't, of
course I'll believe you."

Julia dropped her voice to a low, grave note. It had a true ring of
sincerity:

"I've never told you a lie yet, Dolly, and I'm too old to begin
now. I give you my solemn word of honour that Tom has never
been anything more to me than just a friend."

"You take a great weight off my mind."

Julia knew that Dolly did not believe her and Dolly was aware that Julia knew it. She went on.

"But in that case, for your own sake, Julia dear, do be sensible. Don't go about with this young man any more. Drop him."

"Oh, I couldn't do that. That would be an admission that people were right in what they thought. After all, my conscience is clear. I can afford to hold my head high. I should despise myself if I allowed my behaviour to be influenced by malicious gossip."

Dolly slipped her feet back into her shoes and getting her lipstick out of her bag did her lips.

"Well, dear, you're old enough to know your own mind."

They parted coldly.

But one or two of Dolly's remarks had been somewhat of a shock to Julia. They rankled. It was disconcerting that gossip had so nearly reached the truth. But did it matter? Plenty of women had lovers and who bothered? And an actress. No one expected an actress to be a pattern of propriety.

"It's my damned virtue. That's at the bottom of the trouble."

She had acquired the reputation of a perfectly virtuous woman, whom the tongue of scandal could not touch, and now it looked as though her reputation was a prison that she had built round herself. But there was worse. What had Tom meant by saying that she ate out of his hand? That deeply affronted her. Silly little fool. How dare he? She didn't know what to do about it either. She would have liked to tax him with it. What was the good? He would deny it. The only thing was to say nothing; it had all gone too far now, she must accept everything. It was no good not facing the truth: he didn't love her, he was her lover because it gratified his self-esteem, because it brought him various things he cared for and because in his own eyes at least it gave him a sort of position.

"If I had any sense I'd chuck him." She gave an angry laugh. "It's easy to say that. I love him."

The strange thing was that when she looked into her heart it was not Julia Lambert the woman who resented the affront, she didn't care for herself, it was the affront to Julia Lambert the actress that stung her. She had often felt that her talent—genius the critics called it, but that was a very grand word, her gift, if you like—was not really herself, not even part of her, but something outside that used her, Julia Lambert the woman, in order to express itself. It was a strange, immaterial personality that seemed to descend upon her and it did things through her that she did not know she was capable of doing. She was an ordinary, prettyish, ageing woman. Her gift had neither age nor form. It was a spirit that played on her body as the violinist plays on his violin. It was the slight to that that galled her.

She tried to sleep. She was so accustomed to sleeping in the afternoon that she could always drop off the moment she composed herself, but on this occasion she turned restlessly from side to side and sleep would not come. At last she looked at the clock. Tom often got back from his office soon after five. She yearned for him; in his arms was peace, when she was with him nothing else mattered. She dialled his number.

"Hulloa? Yes. Who is it?"

She held the receiver to her ear, panic-stricken. It was Roger's voice. She hung up.

CHAPTER XIX

Nor did Julia sleep well that night. She was awake when she heard Roger come in, and turning on her light she saw that it was four. She frowned. He came clattering down the stone stairs next morning just when she was beginning to think of getting up.

"Can I come in, Mummy?"

"Come in."

He was still in his pyjamas and dressing-gown. She smiled at him because he looked so fresh and young.

"You were very late last night."

"No, not very. I was in by one."

"Liar. I looked at my clock. It was four."

"All right. It was four then," he agreed cheerfully.

"What on earth were you doing?"

"We went on to some place after the show and had supper. We danced."

"Who with?"

"A couple of girls we picked up. Tom knew them before."

"What were their names?"

"One was called Jill and one was called Joan. I don't know what their other names were. Joan's on the stage. She asked me if I couldn't get her an understudy in your next play."

At all events neither of them was Avice Crichton. That name had been in her thoughts ever since Dolly had mentioned it.

"But those places aren't open till four."

"No, we went back to Tom's flat. Tom made me promise I wouldn't tell you. He said you'd be furious."

"Oh, my dear, it takes a great deal more than that to make me furious. I promise you I won't say a word."

"If anyone's to blame I am. I went to see Tom yesterday afternoon and we arranged it then. All this stuff about love that one hears about in plays and reads in novels. I'm nearly eighteen. I thought I ought to see for myself what it was all about."

Julia sat up in bed and looked at Roger with wide, enquiring eyes.

"Roger, what *do* you mean?"

He was composed and serious.

"Tom said he knew a couple of girls who were all right. He's had them both himself. They live together and so we phoned and asked them to meet us after the show. He told them I was a virgin and they'd better toss up for me. When we got back to the flat he took Jill into the bedroom and left me the sitting-room and Joan."

For the moment she did not think of Tom, she was so disturbed at what Roger was saying.

"I don't think it's so much really. I don't see it's anything to make all that fuss about."

She could not speak. The tears filled her eyes and ran quickly down her face.

"Mummy, what's the matter? Why are you crying?"

"But you're a little boy."

He came over to her and sitting on the side of her bed took her in his arms.

"Darling, don't cry. I wouldn't have told you if I'd thought it was going to upset you. After all, it had to happen sooner or later."

"But so soon. So soon. It makes me feel so old."

"Not you, darling. Age cannot wither her, nor custom stale her infinite variety."

She giggled through her tears.

"You fool, Roger, d'you think Cleopatra would have liked what that silly old donkey said of her? You might have waited a little longer."

"It's just as well I didn't. I know all about it now. To tell you the truth I think it's rather disgusting."

She sighed deeply. It was a comfort to feel him holding her so tenderly. But she felt terribly sorry for herself.

"You're not angry with me, darling?" he asked.

"Angry? No. But if it had to come I wish it hadn't been quite so matter-of-fact. You talk as though it had just been a rather curious experiment."

"I suppose it was in a way."

She gave him a little smile.

"And you really think that was love?"

"Well, it's what most people mean by it, isn't it?"

"No, they don't, they mean pain and anguish, shame, ecstasy, heaven and hell; they mean the sense of living more intensely, and unutterable boredom; they mean freedom and slavery; they mean peace and unrest."

Something in the stillness with which he listened to her made her give him a glance through her eyelashes. There was a curious expression in his eyes. She did not know what it meant. It was as though he were gravely listening to a sound that came from a long way off.

"It doesn't sound as though it were much fun," he murmured.

She took his smooth face in her hands and kissed his lips.

"I'm a fool, aren't I? You see, I still see you as a little baby boy that I'm holding in my arms."

A twinkle shone in his eyes.

"What are you grinning at, you ape?"

"It made a damned good photograph, didn't it?"

She could not but laugh.

"You pig. You filthy pig."

"I say, about the understudy, is there any chance for Joan?"

"Tell her to come and see me one day."

But when Roger left her she sighed. She was depressed. She felt very lonely. Her life had always been so full and so exciting that she had never had the time to busy herself much with Roger. She got in a state, of course, when he had whooping-cough or measles, but he was for the most part in robust health, and then he occupied a pleasant place in the background of her consciousness. But she had always felt that he was there to be attended to when she was inclined and she had often thought it would be nice when he was old enough really to share her interests. It came to her as a shock now to realise that, without ever having really possessed him, she had lost him. Her lips tightened when she thought of the girl who had taken him from her.

"An understudy. My foot."

Her pain absorbed her so that she could not feel the grief she might have felt from her discovery of Tom's perfidy. She had always known in her bones that he was unfaithful to her. At his age, with his wanton temperament, with herself tied down by her performances at the theatre, by all manner of engagements which her position forced upon her, it was plain that he had ample opportunity to gratify his inclinations. She had shut her eyes. All she asked was that she should not know. This was the first time that an actual fact had been thrust upon her notice.

"I must just put up with it," she sighed. Thoughts wandered through her mind. "It's like lying and not knowing you're lying, that's what's fatal; I suppose it's better to be a fool and know it than a fool and not know it."

CHAPTER XX

Tom went to Eastbourne with his family for Christmas. Julia had two performances on Boxing Day, so the Gosselyns stayed in town; they went to a large party at the Savoy that Dolly de Vries gave to see the New Year in; and a few days later Roger set off for Vienna. While he was in London Julia saw little of Tom. She did not ask Roger what they did when they tore about the town together, she did not want to know, she steeled herself not to think and distracted her mind by going to as many parties as she could. And there was always her acting; when once she got into the theatre her anguish, her humiliation, her jealousy were allayed. It gave her a sense of triumphant power to find, as it were in her pot of grease-paint, another personality that could be touched by no human griefs. With that refuge always at hand she could support anything.

On the day that Roger left, Tom rang her up from his office.

"Are you doing anything to-night? What about going out on the binge?"

"No, I'm busy."

It was not true, but the words slipped out of her mouth independent of her will.

"Oh, are you? Well, what about to-morrow?"

If he had expressed disappointment, if he had asked her to cut the date he supposed she had, she might have had strength to break with him then and there. His casualness defeated her.

"To-morrow's all right."

"O.K. I'll fetch you at the theatre after the show. Bye-bye."

Julia was ready and waiting when he was shown into her dressing-room. She was strangely nervous. His face lit up when he saw her, and when Evie went out of the room for a moment he caught her in his arms and warmly kissed her on the lips.

"I feel all the better for that," he laughed.

You would never have thought, to look at him, so young, fresh and ingenuous, in such high spirits, that he was capable of giving her so much pain. You would never have thought that he was so deceitful. It was quite plain that he had not noticed that for more than a fortnight he had hardly seen her.

("Oh, God, if I could only tell him to go to hell.")

But she looked at him with a gay smile in her lovely eyes.

"Where are we going?"

"I've got a table at Quag's. They've got a new turn there, an American conjurer, who's grand."

She talked with vivacity all through supper. She told him about the various parties she had been to, and the theatrical functions she had not been able to get out of, so that it seemed only on account of her engagements that they had not met. It disconcerted her to perceive that he took it as perfectly natural. He was glad to see her, that was plain, he was interested in what she had been doing and in the people she had seen, but it was plain also that he had not missed her. To see what he would say she told him that she had had an offer to take the play in which she was acting to New York. She told him the terms that had been suggested.

"They're marvellous," he said, his eyes glittering. "What a snip! You can't lose and you may make a packet."

"The only thing is, I don't much care for leaving London."

"Why on earth not? I should have thought you'd jump at it. The play's had a good long run, for all you know it'll be pretty well through by Easter, and if you want to make a stab at America you couldn't have a better vehicle."

"I don't see why it shouldn't run through the summer. Besides, I don't like strangers very much. I'm fond of my friends."

"I think that's silly. Your friends'll get along without you all right. And you'll have a grand time in New York."

Her gay laugh was very convincing.

"One would think you were terribly anxious to get rid of me."

"Of course I should miss you like hell. But it would only be for a few months. If I had a chance like that I'd jump at it."

But when they had finished supper and the commissionaire had called up a taxi for them he gave the address of the flat as if it were an understood thing that they should go back to it. In the taxi he put his arm round her waist and kissed her, and later, when she lay in his arms, in the little single bed, she felt that all the pain she had suffered during that last fortnight was not too great a price to pay for the happy peace that filled her heart.

Julia continued to go to the smart supper places and to night clubs with Tom. If people wanted to think he was her lover, let them; she was past caring. But it happened more than once that he was engaged when she wanted him to go somewhere with her. It had spread around among Julia's grander friends that Tom was very clever at helping one with one's income-tax returns. The Dennorants had asked him down to the country for a week-end, and here he had met a number of persons who were glad to take advantage of his technical knowledge. He began to get invitations from people whom Julia did not know. Acquaintances would mention him to her.

"You know Tom Fennell, don't you? He's very clever, isn't he? I hear he's saved the Gillians hundreds of pounds on their income tax."

Julia was none too pleased. It was through her that he had got asked to parties that he wanted to go to. It began to look as if in this respect he could do without her. He was pleasant and un-assuming, very well-dressed now, and with a fresh, clean look that was engaging; he was able to save people money; Julia knew the world which he was so anxious to get into well enough to realise that he would soon establish himself in it. She had no very high opinion of the morals of the women he would meet there and she could name more than one person of title who would be glad to snap him up. Julia's comfort was that they were all as mean as cat's meat. Dolly had said he was only earning four hundred a year; he certainly couldn't live in those circles on that.

Julia had with decision turned down the American offer before ever she mentioned it to Tom; their play was playing to very good business. But one of those inexplicable slumps that occasionally affect the theatre now swept over London and the takings suddenly dropped. It looked as though they would not be able to carry on long after Easter. They had a new play on which they set great hopes. It was called *Nowadays*, and the intention had been to produce it early in the autumn. It had a great part for Julia and the advantage of one that well suited Michael. It was the sort of play that might easily run a year. Michael did not much like the idea of producing it in May, with the summer coming on, but there seemed no help for it and he began looking about for a cast.

One afternoon, during the interval at a matinée, Evie brought a note in to Julia. She was surprised to see Roger's handwriting.

Dear Mother,
    This is to introduce to you Miss Joan Denver who I talked to you about. She's awfully keen on getting in the Siddons Theatre and would be quite satisfied with an understudy however small.

Your affectionate son,
Roger.

Julia smiled at the formal way in which he wrote; she was tickled because he was so grown up as to try to get jobs for his girl friends. Then she suddenly remembered who Joan Denver was. Joan and Jill. She was the girl who had seduced poor Roger. Her face went grim. But she was curious to see her.

"Is George there?" George was the doorkeeper. Evie nodded and opened the door.

"George."

He came in.

"Is the lady who brought this letter here now?"

"Yes, miss."

"Tell her I'll see her after the play."

She wore in the last act an evening dress with a train; it was a very grand dress and showed her beautiful figure to advantage. She wore diamonds in her dark hair and diamond bracelets on her arms. She looked, as indeed the part required, majestic. She received Joan Denver the moment she had taken her last call. Julia could in the twinkling of an eye leap from her part into private life, but now without an effort she continued to play the imperious, aloof, stately and well-bred woman of the play.

"I've kept you waiting so long I thought I wouldn't keep you till I'd got changed."

Her cordial smile was the smile of a queen; her graciousness kept you at a respectful distance. In a glance she had taken in the young girl who entered her dressing-room. She was young, with a pretty little face and a snub nose, a good deal made-up and not very well made-up.

"Her legs are too short," thought Julia. "Very second-rate."

She had evidently put on her best clothes and the same glance had told Julia all about them.

("Shaftesbury Avenue. Off the nail.")

The poor thing was at the moment frightfully nervous. Julia made her sit down and offered her a cigarette.

"There are matches by your side."

She saw her hands tremble when she tried to strike one. It broke and she rubbed a second three times against the box before she could get it to light.

("If Roger could only see her now! Cheap rouge, cheap lipstick, and scared out of her wits. Gay little thing, he thought she was.")

"Have you been on the stage long, Miss—— I'm so sorry I've forgotten your name."

"Joan Denver." Her throat was dry and she could hardly speak. Her cigarette went out and she held it helplessly. She answered Julia's question. "Two years."

"How old are you?"

"Nineteen."

("That's a lie. You're twenty-two if you're a day.") "You know my son, don't you?"

"Yes."

"He's just left Eton. He's gone to Vienna to learn German. Of course he's very young, but his father and I thought it would be good for him to spend a few months abroad before going up to Cambridge. And what parts have you played? Your cigarette's gone out. Won't you have another?"

"Oh, it's all right, thanks. I've been playing on tour. But I'm frightfully anxious to be in town." Despair gave her courage and she uttered the speech she had evidently prepared. "I've got the most tremendous admiration for you, Miss Lambert. I always say you're the greatest actress on the stage. I've learnt more from you than I did all the years I was at the R.A.D.A. My greatest ambition is to be in your theatre, Miss Lambert, and if you could see your way to giving me a little something, I know it would be the most wonderful chance a girl could have."

"Will you take off your hat?"

Joan Denver took the cheap little hat off her head and with a quick gesture shook out her close-cropped curls.

"What pretty hair you have," said Julia.

Still with that slightly imperious, but infinitely cordial smile, the smile that a queen in royal procession bestows on her subjects, Julia gazed at her. She did not speak. She remembered Jane Taitbout's maxim: Don't pause unless it's necessary, but then pause as long as you can. She could almost hear the girl's heart beating and she felt her shrinking in her ready-made clothes, shrinking in her skin.

"What made you think of asking my son to give you a letter to me?"

Joan grew red under her make-up and she swallowed before she answered.

"I met him at a friend's house and I told him how much I admired you and he said he thought perhaps you'd have something for me in your next play."

"I'm just turning over the parts in my mind."

"I wasn't thinking of a part. If I could have an understudy—I mean, that would give me a chance of attending rehearsals and studying your technique. That's an education in itself. Everyone agrees about that."

("Silly little fool, trying to flatter me. As if I didn't know that. And why the hell should I educate her?") "It's very sweet of you to put it like that. I'm only a very ordinary person really. The public is so kind, so very kind. You're a pretty little thing. And young. Youth is so beautiful. Our policy has always been to give the younger people a chance. After all we can't go on for ever, and we look upon it as a duty we owe the public to train up actors and actresses to take our place when the time comes."

Julia said these words so simply, in her beautifully modulated voice, that Joan Denver's heart was warmed. She'd got round the old girl and the understudy was as good as hers. Tom Fennell had said that if she played her cards well with Roger it might easily lead to something.

"Oh, that won't be for a long while yet, Miss Lambert," she said, her eyes, her pretty dark eyes, glowing.

("You're right there, my girl, dead right. I bet I could play you off the stage when I was seventy.")

"I must think it over. I hardly know yet what understudies we shall want in our next play."

"I hear there's some talk of Avice Crichton for the girl's part. I thought perhaps I could understudy her."

Avice Crichton. No flicker of the eyes showed that the name meant anything to Julia.

"My husband has mentioned her, but nothing is settled yet. I don't know her at all. Is she clever?"

"I think so. I was at the Academy with her."

"And pretty as a picture, they tell me." Rising to her feet to show that the audience was at an end, Julia put off her royalty. She changed her tone and became on a sudden the jolly, good-natured actress who would do a good turn to anyone if she could. "Well, dear, leave me your name and address and if there's anything doing I'll let you know."

"You won't forget me, Miss Lambert?"

"No, dear, I promise you I won't. It's been so nice to see you. You have a very sweet personality. You'll find your way out, won't you? Good-bye."

"A fat chance she's got of ever setting foot in this theatre," said Julia to herself when she was gone. "Dirty little bitch to seduce my son. Poor lamb. It's a shame, that's what it is; women like that oughtn't to be allowed."

She looked at herself in the glass as she slipped out of her beautiful gown. Her eyes were hard and her lips had a sardonic curl. She addressed her reflection.

"And I may tell you this, old girl: there's one person who isn't going to play in *Nowadays* and that's Miss Avice Crichton."

CHAPTER XXI

But a week or so later Michael mentioned her.

"I say, have you ever heard of a girl called Avice Crichton?"

"Never."

"I'm told she's rather good. A lady and all that sort of

thing. Her father's in the army. I was wondering if she'd do for Honor."

"How did you hear about her?"

"Through Tom. He knows her, he says she's clever. She's playing in a Sunday night show. Next Sunday, in point of fact. He says he thinks it might be worth while to go and have a look-see."

"Well, why don't you?"

"I was going down to Sandwich to play golf. Would it bore you awfully to go? I expect the play's rotten, but you'd be able to tell if it was worth while letting her read the part. Tom'll go with you."

Julia's heart was beating nineteen to the dozen.

"Of course I'll go."

She phoned to Tom and asked him to come round and have a snack before they went to the theatre. He arrived before she was ready.

"Am I late or were you early?" she said, when she came into the drawing-room.

She saw that he had been waiting impatiently. He was nervous and eager.

"They're going to ring up sharp at eight," he said. "I hate getting to a play after it's begun."

His agitation told her all she wanted to know. She lingered a little over the cocktails.

"What is the name of this actress we're going to see to-night?" she asked.

"Avice Crichton. I'm awfully anxious to know what you think about her. I think she's a find. She knows you're coming to-night. She's frightfully nervous, but I told her she needn't be. You know what these Sunday night plays are; scratch rehearsals and all that; I said you'd quite understand and you'd make allowances."

All through dinner he kept looking at his watch. Julia acted the woman of the world. She talked of one thing and another and noticed that he listened with distraction. As soon as he could he brought the conversation back to Avice Crichton.

"Of course I haven't said anything to her about it, but I believe she'd be all right for Honor." He had read *Nowadays*, as he read, before they were produced, all Julia's plays. "She looks the part all right, I'm sure of that. She's had a struggle and of course it would be a wonderful chance for her. She admires you tremendously and she's terribly anxious to get into a play with you."

"That's understandable. It means the chance of a year's run and a lot of managers seeing her."

"She's the right colour, she's very fair; she'd be a good contrast to you."

"What with platinum and peroxide there's no lack of blondes on the stage."

"But hers is natural."

"Is it? I had a long letter from Roger this morning. He seems to be having quite a good time in Vienna."

Tom's interest subsided. He looked at his watch. When the coffee came Julia said it was undrinkable. She said she must have some more made.

"Oh, Julia, it isn't worth while. We shall be awfully late."

"I don't suppose it matters if we miss the first few minutes."

His voice was anguished.

"I promised we wouldn't be late. She's got a very good scene almost at the beginning."

"I'm sorry, but I can't go without my coffee."

While they waited for it she maintained a bright flow of conversation. He scarcely answered. He looked anxiously at the door. And when the coffee came she drank it with maddening deliberation. By the time they got in the car he was in a state of cold fury and he stared silently in front of him with a sulky pout on his mouth. Julia was not dissatisfied with herself. They reached the theatre two minutes before the curtain rose and as Julia appeared there was a burst of clapping from the audience. Julia, apologising to the people she disturbed, threaded her way to her seat in the middle of the stalls. Her faint smile acknowledged the applause that greeted her beautifully-timed entrance, but her downcast eyes modestly disclaimed that it could have any connection with her.

The curtain went up and after a short scene two girls came in, one very pretty and young, the other much older and plain. In a minute Julia turned to Tom and whispered:

"Which is Avice Crichton, the young one or the old one?"

"The young one."

"Oh, of course, you said she was fair, didn't you?"

She gave his face a glance. He had lost his sulky look; a happy smile played on his lips. Julia turned her attention to the stage. Avice Crichton was very pretty, no one could deny that, with lovely golden hair, fine blue eyes and a little straight nose; but it was a type that Julia did not care for.

"Insipid," she said to herself. "Chorus-girly."

She watched her performance for a few minutes. She watched intently; then she leant back in her stall with a little sigh.

"She can't act for toffee," she decided.

When the curtain fell Tom turned to her eagerly. He had completely got over his bad temper.

"What do you think of her?"

"She's as pretty as a picture."

"I know that. But her acting. Don't you think she's good?"

"Yes, clever."

"I wish you'd come round and tell her that yourself. It would buck her up tremendously."

"I?"

He did not realise what he was asking her to do. It was un-heard-of that she, Julia Lambert, should go behind and con-gratulate a small-part actress.

"I promised I'd take you round after the second act. Be a sport, Julia. It'll please her so much."

("The fool. The blasted fool. All right, I'll go through with it.") "Of course if you think it'll mean anything to her, I'll come with pleasure."

After the second act they went through the iron door and Tom led her to Avice Crichton's dressing-room. She was sharing it with the plain girl with whom she had made her first entrance. Tom effected the introductions. She held out a limp hand in a slightly affected manner.

"I'm so glad to meet you, Miss Lambert. Excuse this dressing-room, won't you? But it was no good trying to make it look nice just for one night."

She was not in the least nervous. Indeed, she seemed self-assured.

("Hard as nails. And with an eye to the main chance. Doing the colonel's daughter on me.")

"It's awfully nice of you to come round. I'm afraid it's not much of a play, but when one's starting like I am one has to put up with what one can get. I was rather doubtful about it when they sent it me to read, but I took a fancy to the part."

"You play it charmingly," said Julia.

"It's awfully nice of you to say so. I wish we could have had a few more rehearsals. I particularly wanted to show *you* what I could do."

"Well, you know, I've been connected with the profession a good many years. I always think, if one has talent one can't help showing it. Don't you?"

"I know what you mean. Of course I want a lot more experience, I know that, but it's only a chance I want really. I know I can act. If I could only get a part that I could really get my teeth into."

She waited a little in order to let Julia say that she had in her new play just the part that would suit her, but Julia continued to look at her smilingly. Julia was grimly amused to find herself treated like a curate's wife to whom the squire's lady was being very kind.

"Have you been on the stage long?" she said at last. "It seems funny I should never have heard of you."

"Well, I was in revue for a while, but I felt I was just wasting my time. I was out on tour all last season. I don't want to leave London again if I can help it."

"The theatrical profession's terribly overcrowded," said Julia.

"Oh, I know. It seems almost hopeless unless you've got influence or something. I hear you're putting a new play on soon."

"Yes."

Julia continued to smile with an almost intolerable sweetness.

"If there's a part for me in it, I'd most awfully like to play with you. I'm so sorry Mr. Gosselyn couldn't come to-night."

"I'll tell him about you."

"D'you really think there's a chance for me?" Through her self-assurance, through the country-house manner she assumed in order to impress Julia, there pierced an anxious eagerness. "If you'd put in a word for me it would help so much."

Julia gave her a reflective look.

"I take my husband's advice more often than he takes mine," she smiled.

When they left the dressing-room so that Avice Crichton might change for the third act, Julia caught the questioning glance she gave Tom as she said good-bye to him. Julia was conscious, though she saw no movement, that he slightly shook his head. Her sensibility at that moment was extraordinarily acute and she translated the mute dialogue into words.

"Coming to supper afterwards?"

"No, damn it, I can't, I've got to see her home."

Julia listened to the third act grimly. That was in order since the play was serious. When it was over and a pale shattered author had made a halting speech, Tom asked her where she would like to go for supper.

"Let's go home and talk," she said. "If you're hungry I'm sure we can find you something to eat in the kitchen."

"D'you mean to Stanhope Place?"

"Yes."

"All right."

She felt his relief that she did not want to go back to the flat. He was silent in the car and she knew that it irked him to have to come back with her. She guessed that someone was giving a supper party to which Avice Crichton was going and he wanted to be there. The house was dark and empty when they reached it. The servants were in bed. Julia suggested that they should go down to the basement and forage.

"I don't want anything to eat unless you do," he said. "I'll just have a whisky and soda and go to bed. I've got a very heavy day to-morrow at the office."

"All right. Bring it up to the drawing-room. I'll go and turn on the lights."

When he came up she was doing her face in front of a mirror and she continued till he had poured out the whisky and sat down. Then she turned round. He looked very young, and incredibly charming, in his beautiful clothes, sitting there in the big arm-chair, and all the bitterness she had felt that evening, all the devouring jealousy of the last few days, were dissipated on a sudden by the intensity of her passion. She sat down on the arm of his chair and caressingly passed her hand over his hair. He drew back with an angry gesture.

"Don't do that," he said. "I do hate having my hair mussed about."

It was like a knife in her heart. He had never spoken to her in that tone before. But she laughed lightly and getting up took the whisky he had poured out for her and sat down in a chair opposite him. The movement he had made, the words he had spoken, were instinctive and he was a trifle abashed. He avoided her glance and his face once more bore a sulky look. The moment was decisive. For a while they were silent. Julia's heart beat painfully, but at last she forced herself to speak.

"Tell me," she said, smiling, "have you been to bed with Avice Crichton?"

"Of course not," he cried.

"Why not? She's pretty."

"She's not that sort of girl. I respect her."

Julia let none of her feelings appear on her face. Her manner was wonderfully casual; she might have been talking of the fall of empires or the death of kings.

"D'you know what I should have said? I should have said you were madly in love with her." He still avoided her eyes. "Are you engaged to her by any chance?"

"No."

He looked at her now, but the eyes that met Julia's were hostile.

"Have you asked her to marry you?"

"How could I? A damned rotter like me."

He spoke so passionately that Julia was astonished.

"What *are* you talking about?"

"Oh what's the good of beating about the bush? How could I ask a decent girl to marry me? I'm nothing but a kept boy and, God knows, you have good reason to know it."

"Don't be so silly. What a fuss to make over a few little presents I've given you."

"I oughtn't to have taken them. I knew all the time it was wrong. It all came so gradually that I didn't realise what was happening till I was in it up to my neck. I couldn't afford to lead the life you made me lead; I was absolutely up against it. I had to take money from you."

"Why not? After all, I'm a very rich woman."

"Damn your money."

He was holding a glass in his hands and yielding to a sudden impulse, he flung it into the fireplace. It shattered.

"You needn't break up the happy home," said Julia ironically.

"I'm sorry. I didn't mean to do that." He sank back into his chair and turned his head away. "I'm so ashamed of myself. It's not very nice to have lost one's self-respect."

Julia hesitated. She did not quite know what to say.

"It seemed only natural to help you when you were in a hole. It was a pleasure to me."

"I know, you were wonderfully tactful about it. You almost persuaded me that I was doing you a service when you paid my debts. You made it easy for me to behave like a cad."

"I'm sorry you should feel like that about it."

She spoke rather tartly. She was beginning to feel a trifle irritated.

"There's nothing for you to be sorry about. You wanted me and you bought me. If I was such a skunk as to let myself be bought that was no business of yours."

"How long have you been feeling like this?"

"From the beginning."

"That isn't true."

She knew that what had awakened his conscience was the love that had seized him for a girl who he believed was pure. The poor fool! Didn't he know that Avice Crichton would go to bed with an assistant stage manager if she thought it would get her a part?

"If you're in love with Avice Crichton why don't you tell me so?" He looked at her miserably, but did not answer. "Are you afraid it'll crab her chances of getting a part in the new play? You ought to know me well enough by now to know that I would never let sentiment interfere with business."

He could hardly believe his ears.

"What do you mean by that?"

"I think she's rather a find. I'm going to tell Michael that I think she'll do very well."

"Oh, Julia, you are a brick. I never knew what a wonderful woman you were."

"You should have asked me and I'd have told you."

He gave a sigh of relief.

"My dear, I'm so terribly fond of you."

"I know, and I'm terribly fond of you. You're great fun to go about with and you're always so well turned out, you're a credit to any woman. I've liked going to bed with you and I've a sort of notion you've liked going to bed with me. But let's face it, I've never been in love with you any more than you've been in love with me. I knew it couldn't last. Sooner or later you were bound to fall in love and that would end it. And you have fallen in love, haven't you?"

"Yes."

She was determined to make him say it, but when he did the pang it gave her was dreadful. Nothwithstanding, she smiled good-humouredly.

"We've had some very jolly times together, but don't you think the moment has come to call it a day?"

She spoke so naturally, almost jestingly, that no one could have guessed that the pain at her heart seemed past bearing. She waited for his answer with sickening dread.

"I'm awfully sorry, Julia; I must regain my self-respect." He looked at her with troubled eyes. "You aren't angry with me?"

"Because you've transferred your volatile affections from me to Avice Crichton?" Her eyes danced with mischievous laughter. "My dear, of course not. After all they stay in the profession."

"I'm very grateful to you for all you've done for me. I don't want you to think I'm not."

"Oh, my pet, don't talk such nonsense. I've done nothing for you." She got up. "Now you really must go. You've got a heavy day at the office to-morrow and I'm dog-tired."

It was a load off his mind. But he wasn't quite happy for all that, he was puzzled by her tone, which was so friendly and yet at the same time faintly ironical; he felt a trifle let down. He went up to her to kiss her good-night. She hesitated for the fraction of a second, then with a friendly smile gave him first one cheek and then the other.

"You'll find your way out, won't you?" She put her hand to her mouth to hide an elaborate yawn. "Oh, I'm so sleepy."

The moment he had gone she turned out the lights and went to the window. She peered cautiously through the curtains. She heard him slam the front door and saw him come out. He looked right and left. She guessed at once that he was looking for a taxi. There was none in sight and he started to walk in the direction of the Park. She knew that he was going to join Avice Crichton at the supper party and tell her the glad news. Julia sank into a chair. She had acted, she had acted marvellously, and now she felt all in. Tears, tears that nobody could see, rolled down her cheeks. She was miserably unhappy. There was only one thing that enabled her to bear her wretchedness, and that was the icy contempt that she could not but feel for the silly boy who could prefer to her a small-part actress who didn't even begin to know how to act. It was grotesque. She couldn't use her hands; why, she didn't even know how to walk across the stage.

"If I had any sense of humour I'd just laugh my head off," she cried. "It's the most priceless joke I've ever heard."

She wondered what Tom would do now. The rent of the flat

would be falling due on quarter-day. A lot of the things in it belonged to her. He wouldn't much like going back to his bed-sitting-room in Tavistock Square. She thought of the friends he had made through her. He'd been clever with them. They found him useful and he'd keep them. But it wouldn't be so easy for him to take Avice about. She was a hard, mercenary little thing, Julia was sure of that, she wouldn't be much inclined to bother about him when his money flowed less freely. The fool to be taken in by her pretence of virtue! Julia knew the type. It was quite obvious, she was only using Tom to get a part at the Siddons and the moment she got it she would give him the air. Julia started when this notion crossed her mind. She had promised Tom that Avice should have the part in *Nowadays* because it fell into the scene she was playing, but she had attached no importance to her promise. Michael was always there to put his foot down.

"By God, she shall have the part," she said out loud. She chuckled maliciously. "Heaven knows, I'm a good-natured woman, but there are limits to everything."

It would be a satisfaction to turn the tables on Tom and Avice Crichton. She sat on, in the darkness, grimly thinking how she would do it. But every now and then she started to cry again, for from the depths of her subconscious surged up recollections that were horribly painful. Recollections of Tom's slim, youthful body against hers, his warm nakedness and the peculiar feel of his lips, his smile, at once shy and roguish, and the smell of his curly hair.

"If I hadn't been a fool I'd have said nothing. I ought to know him by now. It's only an infatuation. He'd have got over it and then he'd have come hungrily back to me."

Now she was nearly dead with fatigue. She got up and went to bed. She took a sleeping-draught.

CHAPTER XXII

BUT she woke early next morning, at six, and began to think of Tom. She repeated to herself all she had said to him and all he had said to her. She was harassed and unhappy. Her only consolation was that she had carried the rupture through with so careless a gaiety that he could not guess how miserable he had made her.

She spent a wretched day, unable to think of anything else, and angry with herself because she could not put Tom out of her mind. It would not have been so bad if she could have confided her grief to a friend. She wanted someone to console her, someone to tell her that Tom was not worth troubling about and to assure her that he had treated her shamefully. As a rule she took her troubles to Charles or to Dolly. Of course Charles would give her all the sympathy she needed, but it would be a terrible blow to him; after all, he had loved her to distraction for twenty years, and it would be cruel to tell him that she had given to a very ordinary young man what he would gladly have sacrificed ten years of his life for. She was his ideal and it would be heartless on her part to shatter it. It certainly did her good at that moment to be assured that Charles Tamerley, so distinguished, so cultured, so elegant, loved her with an imperishable devotion. Of course Dolly would be delighted if she confided in her. They had not seen much of one another lately, but Julia knew that she had only to call up and Dolly would come running. Even though she more than suspected the truth already, she'd be shocked and jealous when Julia made a clean breast of it, but she'd be so thankful that everything was over, she'd forgive. It would be a comfort to both of them to tear Tom limb from limb. Of course it wouldn't be very nice to admit that Tom had chucked her, and Dolly was so shrewd, she would never get away with the lie that she had chucked him. She wanted to have a good cry with somebody, and there didn't seem to be any reason for it if she had made the break herself. It would be a score for Dolly, and however sympathetic she was it was asking too much of human nature to expect that she would be altogether sorry that Julia had been taken down a peg or two. Dolly had always worshipped her. She wasn't going to give her a peep at her feet of clay.

"It almost looks as if the only person I can go to is Michael," she giggled. "But I suppose it wouldn't do."

She knew exactly what he would say.

"My dear girl, I'm really not the sort of feller you ought to come to with a story like that. Damn it all, you put me in a very awkward position. I flatter myself I'm pretty broad-minded, I may be an actor, but when all's said and done I am a gentleman, and well, I mean, I mean it's such damned bad form."

Michael did not get home till the afternoon, and when he came into her room she was resting. He told her about his week-end and the result of his matches. He had played very well, some of his recoveries had been marvellous, and he described them in detail.

"By the way, what about that girl you saw last night, is she any good?"

"I really think she is, you know. She's very pretty. You're sure to fall for her."

"Oh, my dear, at my time of life. Can she act?"

"She's inexperienced of course, but I think she's got it in her."

"Oh well, I'd better have her up and give her the once-over. How can I get hold of her?"

"Tom's got her address."

"I'll phone him right away."

He took off the receiver and dialled Tom's number. Tom was in and Michael wrote down the address on a pad.

The conversation went on.

"Oh, my dear old chap, I'm sorry to hear that. What rotten luck!"

"What's the matter?" asked Julia.

He motioned her to be quiet.

"Oh, well, I don't want to be hard on you. Don't you worry. I'm sure we can come to some arrangement that will be satisfactory to you." He put his hand over the receiver and turned to Julia. "Shall I ask him to dinner next Sunday?"

"If you like."

"Julia says, will you come and dine on Sunday? Oh, I'm sorry. Well, so long, old man."

He put down the receiver.

"He's got a date. Is the young ruffian having an affair with this girl?"

"He assures me not. He respects her. She's a colonel's daughter."

"Oh, she's a lady."

"I don't know that that follows," said Julia acidly. "What were you talking to him about?"

"He says they've cut his salary. Bad times. He wants to give up the flat." Julia's heart gave a sudden sickening beat. "I've told him not to worry. I'll let him stay there rent-free till times improve."

"I don't know why you should do that. After all, it was a purely business arrangement."

"It seems rather tough luck on a young chap like that. And you know he's very useful to us; if we want an extra man we can always call upon him, and it's convenient having him round the corner when I want someone to play golf with me. It's only twenty-five pounds a quarter."

"You're the last person I should expect to see indulge in indiscriminate generosity."

"Oh, don't you be afraid, if I lose on the swings I'll get back on the roundabouts."

The masseuse came in and put an end to the conversation. Julia was thankful that it would soon be time to go down to the theatre and so put an end for a while to the misery of that long day; when she got back she would take a sleeping-draught again and so get some hours of forgetfulness. She had a notion that in a few days the worst of her pain would be over; the important thing was to get through them as best she could. She must distract her mind. When she left for the theatre she told the butler to ring up Charles Tamerley and see if she could lunch with him at the Ritz next day.

He was extraordinarily nice at luncheon. His look, his manner bespoke the different world he lived in, and she felt a sudden abhorrence for the circle in which on Tom's account she had moved during the last year. He spoke of politics, of art, of books; and peace entered into her soul. Tom had been an obsession and she saw now that it had been hurtful; but she would escape from it. Her spirits rose. She did not want to be alone, she knew that even though she went home after luncheon she would not sleep, so she asked Charles if he would take her to the National Gallery. She could give him no greater pleasure; he liked to talk about pictures and he talked of them well. It took them back to the old days when she had made her first success in London and they used to spend so many afternoons together, walking in the park or sauntering through museums. The day after that she had a matinée and the next a luncheon-party, but when they separated they arranged to lunch again together on the Friday and go to the Tate.

A few days later Michael told her that he had engaged Avice Crichton.

"She has the looks for the part, there's no doubt about that, and she'll be a good contrast to you. I'm taking her acting on the strength of what you said."

Next morning they rang through from the basement to say that

Mr. Fennell was on the telephone. It seemed to her that her heart stopped beating.

"Put him through."

"Julia, I wanted to tell you, Michael has engaged Avice."

"Yes, I know."

"He told her he was engaging her on what you'd told him. You are a brick."

Julia, her heart now beating nineteen to the dozen, made an effort to control her voice.

"Oh, don't talk such nonsense," she answered gaily. "I told you it would be all right."

"I'm awfully glad it's fixed up. She's accepted the part on what I've told her about it. Ordinarily she won't take anything unless she's read the play."

It was just as well he could not see Julia's face when she heard him say this. She would have liked to answer tartly that it was not their habit when they engaged small-part actresses to let them read the play, but instead she said mildly:

"Well, I think she'll like it, don't you? It's quite a good part."

"And you know, she'll play it for all it's worth. I believe she'll make a sensation."

Julia took a long breath.

"It'll be wonderful, won't it? I mean, it may make her."

"Yes, I've told her that. I say, when am I going to see you again?"

"I'll phone you, shall I? It's such a bore, I'm terribly full of engagements for the next few days."

"You're not going to drop me just because . . ."

She gave a low, rather hoarse chuckle, that chuckle which so delighted audiences.

"Don't be so silly. Oh lord, there's my bath running. I must go and have it. Good-bye, my sweet."

She put down the receiver. The sound of his voice! The pain in her heart was unendurable. Sitting up in her bed she rocked to and fro in an agony.

"What shall I do? What shall I do?"

She had thought she was getting over it, and now that brief, silly conversation had shown her that she loved him as much as ever. She wanted him. She missed him every minute of the day. She could not do without him.

"I shall never get over it," she moaned.

Once again the theatre was her only refuge. By an ironic chance the great scene of the play in which she was then acting, the scene to which the play owed its success, showed the parting of two lovers. It was true that they parted from a sense of duty; and Julia, in the play, sacrificed her love, her hopes of happiness, all that she held dear, to an ideal of uprightness. It was a scene that had appealed to her from the beginning. She was wonderfully moving in it. She put into it now all the agony of her spirit; it was no longer the broken heart of a character that she portrayed but her own. In ordinary life she tried to stifle a passion that she knew very well was ridiculous, a love that was unworthy of the woman she was, and she steeled herself to think as little as possible of the wretched boy who had wrought such havoc with her; but when she came to this scene she let herself go. She gave free rein to her anguish. She was hopeless with her own loss, and the love she poured out on the man who was playing opposite to her was the love she still felt, the passionate, devouring love, for Tom. The prospect of the empty life that confronted the woman of the play was the prospect of her own empty life. There was at least that solace, she felt she had never played so magnificently.

"My God, it's almost worth while to suffer so frightfully to give such a performance."

She had never put more of herself into a part.

One night a week or two later when she came into her dressing-room at the end of the play, exhausted by all the emotion she had displayed, but triumphant after innumerable curtain calls, she found Michael sitting there.

"Hulloa? You haven't been in front, have you?"

"Yes."

"But you were in front two or three days ago."

"Yes, I've sat through the play for the last four nights."

She started to undress. He got up from his chair and began to walk up and down. She gave him a glance and saw that he was frowning slightly.

"What's the matter?"

"That's what I want to know."

She gave a start. The thought flashed through her mind that he had once more heard something about Tom.

"Why the devil isn't Evie here?" she asked.

"I told her to go out. I've got something to say to you, Julia. It's no good your flying in a temper. You've just got to listen."

A cold shiver ran down her spine.

"Well, what is it?"

"I heard something was up and I thought I'd better see for myself. At first I thought it was just an accident. That's why I didn't say anything till I was quite sure. What's wrong with you, Julia?"

"With me?"

"Yes. Why are you giving such a lousy performance?"

"Me?" That was the last thing she expected to hear him say. She faced him with blazing eyes. "You damned fool, I've never acted better in my life."

"Nonsense. You're acting like hell."

Of course it was a relief that he was talking about her acting, but what he was saying was so ridiculous that, angry as she was, she had to laugh.

"You blasted idiot, you don't know what you're talking about. Why, what I don't know about acting isn't worth knowing. Everything you know about it I've taught you. If you're even a tolerable actor it's due to me. After all, the proof of the pudding's in the eating. D'you know how many curtain calls I got to-night? The play's never gone better in all its run."

"I know all about that. The public are a lot of jackasses. If you yell and scream and throw yourself about you'll always get a lot of damned fools to shout themselves silly. Just barn-storming, that's what you've been doing the last four nights. It was false from beginning to end."

"False? But I felt every word of it."

"I don't care what you felt, you weren't acting it. Your performance was a mess. You were exaggerating; you were over-acting, you didn't carry conviction for a moment. It was about as rotten a piece of ham acting as I've ever seen in my life."

"You bloody swine, how dare you talk to me like that? It's you the ham."

With her open hand she gave him a great swinging blow on the face. He smiled.

"You can hit me, you can swear at me, you can yell your head off, but the fact remains that your acting's gone all to hell. I'm not going to start rehearsing *Nowadays* with you acting like that."

"Find someone who can act the part better than I can, then."

"Don't be silly, Julia. I may not be a very good actor myself, I never thought I was, but I know good acting from bad. And what's more there's nothing about *you* I don't know. I'm going to put up the notices on Saturday and then I want you to go abroad. We'll make *Nowadays* our autumn production."

The quiet, decisive way in which he spoke calmed her. It was true that when it came to acting Michael knew everything there was to know about her.

"Is it true that I'm acting badly?"

"Rottenly."

She thought it over. She knew exactly what had happened. She had let her emotion run away with her; she had been feeling, not acting. Again a cold shiver ran down her spine. This was serious. It was all very fine to have a broken heart, but if it was going to interfere with her acting . . . no, no, no. That was quite another pair of shoes. Her acting was more important than any love affair in the world.

"I'll try and pull myself together."

"It's no good trying to force oneself. You're tired out. It's my fault, I ought to have insisted on your taking a holiday long ago. What you want is a good rest."

"What about the theatre?"

"If I can't let it, I'll revive some play that I can play in. There's *Hearts are Trumps*. You always hated your part in that."

"Everyone says the season's going to be wonderful. You can't expect much of a revival with me out of the cast; you won't make a penny."

"I don't care a hang about that. The only thing that matters is your health."

"Oh, Christ, don't be so magnanimous," she cried. "I can't bear it."

Suddenly she burst into a storm of weeping.

"Darling!"

He took her in his arms and sat her down on the sofa with himself beside her. She clung to him desperately.

"You're so good to me, Michael, and I hate myself. I'm a beast, I'm a slut, I'm just a bloody bitch. I'm rotten through and through."

"All that may be," he smiled, "but the fact remains that you're a very great actress."

"I don't know how you can have the patience you have with me. I've treated you foully. You've been too wonderful and I've sacrificed you heartlessly."

"Now, dear, don't say a lot of things that you'll regret later. I shall only bring them up against you another time."

His tenderness melted her and she reproached herself bitterly because for years she had found him so boring.

"Thank God, I've got you. What should I do without you?"

"You haven't got to do without me."

He held her close and though she sobbed still she began to feel comforted.

"I'm sorry I was so beastly to you just now."

"Oh, my dear."

"Do you really think I'm a ham actress?"

"Darling, Duse couldn't hold a candle to you."

"Do you honestly think that? Give me your hanky. You never saw Sarah Bernhardt, did you?"

"No, never."

"She ranted like the devil."

They sat together for a little while, in silence, and Julia grew calmer in spirit. Her heart was filled with a great love for Michael.

"You're still the best-looking man in England," she murmured at last. "No one will ever persuade me to the contrary."

She felt that he drew in his belly and thrust out his chin, and it seemed to her rather sweet and touching.

"You're quite right. I'm tired out. I feel low and miserable. I feel all empty inside. The only thing is to go away."

CHAPTER XXIII

AFTER Julia had made up her mind to that she was glad. The prospect of getting away from the misery that tormented her at once made it easier to bear. The notices were put up; Michael collected his cast for the revival and started rehearsals. It amused Julia to sit idly in a stall and watch the actress who had been engaged rehearse the part which she had played herself some years before. She had never lost the thrill it gave her when she first went on the stage to sit in the darkened playhouse, under dust-sheets, and see the characters grow in the actors' hands. Merely to be inside a theatre rested her; nowhere was she so happy. Watching the rehearsals she was able to relax so that when at night she had her own performance to give she felt fresh. She realised that all Michael had said was true. She took hold of herself. Thrusting her private emotion into the background and thus getting the character under control, she managed once more to play with her accustomed virtuosity. Her acting ceased to be a means by which she gave release to her feelings and was again the manifestation of her creative instinct. She got a quiet exhilaration out of thus recovering mastery over her medium. It gave her a sense of power and of liberation.

But the triumphant effort she made took it out of her, and when she was not in the theatre she felt listless and discouraged. She lost her exuberant vitality. A new humility overcame her. She had a feeling that her day was done. She sighed as she told herself that nobody wanted her any more. Michael suggested that she should go to Vienna to be near Roger, and she would have liked that, but she shook her head.

"I should only cramp his style."

She was afraid he would find her a bore. He was enjoying himself and she would only be in the way. She could not bear the thought that he would find it an irksome duty to take her here and there and occasionally have luncheon or dinner with her. It was only natural that he should have more fun with the friends of his own age that he had made. She decided to go and stay with her mother. Mrs. Lambert—Madame de Lambert, as Michael insisted on calling her—had lived for many years now with her sister, Madame Falloux, at St. Malo. She spent a few days every year in London with Julia, but this year had not been well enough to come. She was an old lady, well over seventy, and Julia knew that it would be a great joy for her to have her daughter on a long visit. Who cared about an English actress in Vienna? She wouldn't be anyone there. In St. Malo she would be something of a figure, and it would be fun for the two old women to be able to show her off to their friends.

"*Ma fille, la plus grande actrice d'Angleterre*," and all that sort of thing.

Poor old girls, they couldn't live much longer and they led drab, monotonous lives. Of course it would be fearfully boring for her, but it would be a treat for them. Julia had a feeling that perhaps in the course of her brilliant and triumphant career she had a trifle neglected her mother. She could make up for it now. She would lay herself out to be charming. Her tenderness for Michael and her ever-present sense of having been for years unjust to him filled her with contrition. She felt that she had been selfish and overbearing, and she wanted to atone for all that. She was eager to sacrifice herself, and so wrote to her mother to announce her imminent arrival.

She managed in the most natural way in the world to see nothing of Tom till her last day in London. The play had closed the night before and she was starting for St. Malo in the evening. Tom came in about six o'clock to say good-bye to her. Michael was there, Dolly, Charles Tamerley and one or two others, so that there was no chance of their being left even for a moment by themselves. Julia found no difficulty in talking to him naturally. To see him gave her not the anguish she had feared but no more than a dull heartache. They had kept the date and place of her departure secret, that is to say, the Press representative of the theatre had only rung up a very few newspapers, so that when Julia and Michael reached the station there were not more than half a dozen reporters and three cameramen. Julia said a few gracious words to them, and Michael a few more, then the Press representative took the reporters aside and gave them a succinct account of Julia's plans. Meanwhile Julia and Michael posed while the cameramen to the glare of flashes photographed them arm-in-arm, exchanging a final kiss, and at last Julia, half out of the carriage window, giving her hand to Michael who stood on the platform.

"What a nuisance these people are," she said. "One simply cannot escape them."

"I can't imagine how they knew you were going."

The little crowd that had assembled when they realised that something was going on stood at a respectful distance. The Press representative came up and told Michael he thought he'd given the reporters enough for a column. The train steamed out.

Julia had refused to take Evie with her. She had a feeling that in order to regain her serenity she must cut herself off completely for a time from her old life. Evie in that French household would be out of place. For Madame Falloux, Julia's Aunt Carrie, married as a girl to a Frenchman, now as an old, old lady spoke French more easily than English. She had been a widow for many years and her only son had been killed in the war. She lived in a tall, narrow stone house on a hill, and when you crossed its threshold from the cobbled street you entered upon the peace of a by-gone age. Nothing had been changed for half a century. The drawing-room was furnished with a Louis XV suite under covers, and the covers were only taken off once a month to give the silk underneath a delicate brushing. The crystal chandelier was shrouded in muslin so that the flies should not spot it. In front of the chimney-piece was a fire-screen of peacocks' feathers artfully arranged and protected by glass. Though the room was never used Aunt Carrie dusted it herself every day. The dining-room was panelled and here too the chairs were under dust-covers. On the sideboard was a silver epergne, a silver coffee-pot, a silver teapot and a silver tray. Aunt Carrie and Julia's mother, Mrs. Lambert, lived in the morning-room, a long narrow room, with Empire furniture. On the walls in oval frames were oil portraits of Aunt Carrie and her deceased husband, of his father and mother, and a pastel of the dead son as a child. Here they had their work-boxes, here they read their papers, the Catholic *La Croix*, the *Revue des Deux Mondes* and the local daily, and here they played dominoes in the evening. Except on Thursday evenings when the Abbé and the Commandant La Garde, a retired naval officer, came to dinner, they had their meals there; but when Julia arrived they decided that it would be more convenient to eat in the dining-room.

Aunt Carrie still wore mourning for her husband and her son. It was seldom warm enough for her to leave off the little black tricot that she crocheted herself. Mrs. Lambert wore black too, but when Monsieur l'Abbé and the Commandant came to dinner she put over her shoulders a white lace shawl that Julia had given her. After dinner they played plafond for two sous a hundred. Mrs. Lambert, because she had lived for so many years in Jersey and still went to London, knew all about the great world, and she said that a game called contract was much played, but the Commandant said it was all very well for Americans, but he was content to stick to plafond, and the Abbé said that for his part he thought it a pity that whist had been abandoned. But there, men were never satisfied with what they had; they wanted change, change, change, all the time.

Every Christmas Julia gave her mother and her aunt expensive presents, but they never used them. They showed them to their friends with pride, these wonderful things that came from London, and then wrapped them up in tissue paper and put them away in cupboards. Julia had offered her mother a car, but she refused it. For the little they went out, they could go on foot; a chauffeur would steal their petrol, if he had his meals out it would be ruinous and if he had them in it would upset Annette. Annette was cook, housekeeper and housemaid. She had been with Aunt Carrie for five-and-thirty years. Her niece was there to do the rough work, but Angèle was young, she wasn't forty yet, and it would hardly do to have a man constantly about the house.

They put Julia in the same room she had had as a girl when she was living with Aunt Carrie for her education. It gave her a peculiar, heart-rending sensation, indeed for a little it made her quite emotional. But she fell into the life very easily. Aunt Carrie had become a Catholic on her marriage and Mrs. Lambert, when on losing her husband she settled down in St. Malo, having received instructions from the Abbé, in due course took the same step. The two old ladies were very devout. They went to Mass every morning and to High Mass on Sundays. Otherwise they seldom went out. When they did it was to pay a ceremonious call on some old lady who had had a bereavement in the family or one of whose grandchildren was become engaged. They read their papers, and their magazine, did a great deal of sewing for charitable purposes, played dominoes and listened to the radio that Julia had given them. Though the Abbé and the Commandant had dined with them every Thursday for many years they were always in a flutter when Thursday came. The Commandant, with the sailor's downrightness that they expected of him, did not hesitate to say so if something was not cooked to his liking, and even the Abbé, though a saint, had his likes and dislikes. For instance, he was very fond of sole normande, but he insisted on its being cooked with the best butter, and with butter at the price it was since the war that was very expensive. Every Thursday morning Aunt Carrie took the cellar key from the place where she had hidden it and herself fetched a bottle of claret from the cellar. She and her sister finished what was left of it by the end of the week.

They made a great fuss of Julia. They dosed her with tisanes, and were anxious that she should not sit in anything that might be thought a draught. Indeed a great part of their lives was devoted to avoiding draughts. They made her lie on sofas and were solicitous that she should cover her feet. They reasoned with her about the clothes she wore. Those silk stockings that were so thin you could see through them; and what did she wear next to her skin? Aunt Carrie would not have been surprised to learn that she wore nothing but a chemise.

"She doesn't even wear that," said Mrs. Lambert.

"What does she wear then?"

"Panties," said Julia.

"And a *soutien-gorge*, I suppose."

"Certainly not," cried Julia tartly.

"Then, my niece, under your dress you are naked?"

"Practically."

"*C'est de la folie*," said Aunt Carrie.

"*C'est vraiment pas raisonnable, ma fille*," said Mrs. Lambert.

"And without being a prude," added Aunt Carrie, "I must say that it is hardly decent."

Julia showed them her clothes, and on the first Thursday after her arrival they discussed what she should wear for dinner. Aunt Carrie and Mrs. Lambert grew rather sharp with one another. Mrs. Lambert thought that since her daughter had evening dresses with her she ought to wear one, but Aunt Carrie considered it quite unnecessary.

"When I used to come and visit you in Jersey, my dear, and gentlemen were coming to dinner, I remember you would put on a tea-gown."

"Of course a tea-gown would be very suitable."

They looked at Julia hopefully. She shook her head.

"I would sooner wear a shroud."

Aunt Carrie wore a high-necked dress of heavy black silk, with a string of jet, and Mrs. Lambert a similar one, but with her lace shawl and a paste necklace. The Commandant, a sturdy little man with a much-wrinkled face, white hair cut *en brosse* and an imposing moustache dyed a deep black, was very gallant, and though well past seventy pressed Julia's foot under the table during dinner. On the way out he seized the opportunity to pinch her bottom.

"Sex appeal," Julia murmured to herself as with dignity she followed the two old ladies into the parlour.

They made a fuss of her, not because she was a great actress, but because she was in poor health and needed rest. Julia to her great amazement soon discovered that to them her celebrity was an embarrassment rather than an asset. Far from wanting to show her off, they did not offer to take her with them to pay calls. Aunt Carrie had brought the habit of afternoon tea with her from Jersey, and had never abandoned it. One day, soon after Julia's arrival, when they had invited some ladies to tea, Mrs. Lambert at luncheon thus addressed her daughter.

"My dear, we have some very good friends at St. Malo, but of course they still look upon us as foreigners, even after all these years, and we don't like to do anything that seems at all eccentric. Naturally we don't want you to tell a lie, but unless you are forced to mention it, your Aunt Carrie thinks it would be better if you did not tell anyone that you are an actress."

Julia was taken aback, but, her sense of humour prevailing, she felt inclined to laugh.

"If one of the friends we are expecting this afternoon happens to ask you what your husband is, it wouldn't be untrue, would it? to say that he was in business."

"Not at all," said Julia, permitting herself to smile.

"Of course, we know that English actresses are not like French ones," Aunt Carrie added kindly. "It's almost an understood thing for a French actress to have a lover."

"Dear, dear," said Julia.

Her life in London, with its excitements, its triumphs and its pains, began to seem very far away. She found herself able soon to consider Tom and her feeling for him with a tranquil mind. She realised that her vanity had been more wounded than her heart. The days passed monotonously. Soon the only thing that recalled London to her was the arrival on Monday of the Sunday papers. She got a batch of them and spent the whole day reading them. Then she was a trifle restless. She walked on the ramparts and looked at the islands that dotted the bay. The grey sky made her sick for the grey sky of England. But by Tuesday morning she had sunk back once more into the calmness of the provincial life. She read a good deal, novels, English and French, that she bought at the local bookshop, and her favourite Verlaine. There was a tender melancholy in his verses that seemed to fit the grey Breton town, the sad old stone houses and the quietness of those steep and tortuous streets. The peaceful habits of the two old ladies, the routine of their uneventful existence and their quiet gossip, excited her compassion. Nothing had happened to them for years, nothing now would ever happen to them till they died, and then how little would their lives have signified. The strange thing was that they were content. They knew neither malice nor envy. They had achieved the aloofness from the common ties of men that Julia felt in herself when she stood at the footlights bowing to the applause of an enthusiastic audience. Sometimes she had thought that aloofness her most precious possession. In her it was born of pride; in them of humility. In both cases it brought one precious thing, liberty of spirit; but with them it was more secure.

Michael wrote to her once a week, brisk, businesslike letters in which he told her what the takings were at the Siddons and the preparations he was making for the next production; but Charles Tamerley wrote to her every day. He told her the gossip of the town, he talked in his charming, cultivated way of the pictures he saw and the books he read. He was tenderly allusive and playfully erudite. He philosophised without pedantry. He told her that he adored her. They were the most beautiful love letters Julia had ever received, and for the sake of posterity she made up her mind to keep them. One day perhaps someone would publish them and people would go to the National Portrait Gallery and look at her portrait, the one McEvoy had painted, and sigh when they thought of the sad, romantic love-story of which she had been the heroine.

Charles had been wonderful to her during the first two weeks of her bereavement, she did not know what she would have done without him. He had always been at her beck and call. His conversation, by taking her into a different world, had soothed her nerves. Her soul had been muddied, and in his distinction of spirit she had washed herself clean. It had rested her wonderfully to wander about the galleries with him and look at pictures. She had good reason to be grateful to him. She thought of all the years he had loved her. He had waited for her now for more than twenty years. She had not been very kind to him. It would have given him so much happiness to possess her and really it would not have hurt her. She wondered why she had resisted him so long. Perhaps because he was so faithful, because his devotion was so humble, perhaps only because she wanted to preserve in his mind the ideal that he had of her. It was stupid really and she had been selfish. It occurred to her with exultation that she could at last reward him for all his tenderness, his patience and his selflessness. She had not lost the sense of unworthiness which Michael's great kindness had aroused in her, and she was remorseful still because she had been for so long impatient of him. The desire for self-sacrifice with which she left England burnt still in her breast with an eager flame. She felt that Charles was a worthy object for its exercise. She laughed a little, kindly and compassionately, as she thought of his amazement when he understood what she intended; for a moment he would hardly be able to believe it, and then what rapture, then what ecstasy! The love that he had held banked up for so many years would burst its sluices like a great torrent and in a flood o'erwhelm her. Her heart swelled at the thought of his infinite gratitude. But still he could hardly believe in his good fortune; and when it was all over and she lay in his arms she would nestle up to him and whisper tenderly:

"Was it worth waiting for?"

"Like Helen, you make me immortal with a kiss."

It was wonderful to be able to give so much happiness to a human being.

"I'll write to him just before I leave St. Malo," she decided.

The spring passed into summer, and at the end of July it was time for Julia to go to Paris and see about her clothes. Michael wanted to open with the new play early in September, and rehearsals were to start in August. She had brought the play with her to St. Malo, intending to study her part, but the circumstances in which she lived had made it impossible. She had all the leisure she needed, but in that grey, austere and yet snug little town, in the constant company of those two old ladies whose interests were confined to the parish church and their household affairs, though it was a good play, she could take but little interest in it.

"It's high time I was getting back," she said. "It would be hell if I really came to the conclusion that the theatre wasn't worth the fuss and bother they make about it."

She said good-bye to her mother and to Aunt Carrie. They had been very kind to her, but she had an inkling that they would not be sorry when her departure allowed them to return to the life she had interrupted. They were a little relieved besides to know that now there was no more danger of some eccentricity, such as you must always run the risk of with an actress, which might arouse the unfavourable comment of the ladies of St. Malo.

She arrived in Paris in the afternoon, and when she was shown into her suite at the Ritz, she gave a sigh of satisfaction. It was a treat to get back to luxury. Three or four people had sent her flowers. She had a bath and changed. Charley Deverill, who always made her clothes for her, an old friend, called to take her to dinner in the Bois.

"I had a wonderful time," she told him, "and of course it was a grand treat for those old girls to have me there, but I have a feeling that if I'd stayed a day longer I should have been bored."

To drive up the Champs Elysées on that lovely evening filled her with exhilaration. It was good to smell once more the smell of petrol. The cars, the taxis, the hooting of horns, the chestnut trees, the street lights, the crowd on the pavement and the crowd sitting outside the cafés; it was an enchantment. And when they got to the Château de Madrid, so gay, so civilised and so expensive, it was grand to see once more well-dressed women, decently made-up, and tanned men in dinner-jackets.

"I feel like a queen returning from exile."

Julia spent several happy days choosing her clothes and having the first fittings. She enjoyed every moment of them. But she was a woman of character, and when she had come to a decision she adhered to it; before leaving for London she wrote a note to Charles. He had been to Goodwood and Cowes and was spending twenty-four hours in London on his way to Salzburg.

Charles dear,
    How wonderful that I shall see you so soon. Of course I am free on Wednesday. Shall we dine together and do you love me still?
Your Julia.

As she stuck down the envelope she murmured: *Bis dat qui cito dat.* It was a Latin tag that Michael always quoted when, asked to subscribe to a charity, he sent by return of post exactly half what was expected of him.

CHAPTER XXIV

On Wednesday morning Julia had her face massaged and her hair waved. She could not make up her mind whether to wear for dinner a dress of flowered organdie, very pretty and spring-like with its suggestion of Botticelli's Primavera, or one of white satin beautifully cut to show off her slim young figure, and virginal; but while she was having her bath she decided on the white satin: it indicated rather delicately that the sacrifice she intended was in the nature of an expiation for her long ingratitude to Michael. She wore no jewels but a string of pearls and a diamond bracelet; besides her wedding-ring only one square-cut diamond. She would have liked to put on a slight brown tan, it looked open-air-girl and suited her, but reflecting on what lay before her she refrained. She could not very well, like the actor who painted himself black all over to play Othello, tan her whole body. Always a punctual woman, she came downstairs as the front door was being opened for Charles. She greeted him with a look into which she put tenderness, a roguish charm and intimacy. Charles now wore his thinning grey hair rather long, and with advancing years his intellectual, distinguished features had sagged a little; he was slightly bowed and his clothes looked as though they needed pressing.

"Strange world we live in," thought Julia. "Actors do their damnedest to look like gentlemen and gentlemen do all they can to look like actors."

There was no doubt that she was making a proper effect on him. He gave her the perfect opening.

"Why are you looking so lovely to-night?" he asked.

"Because I'm looking forward to dining with you."

With her beautiful, expressive eyes she looked deep into his. She parted her lips in the manner that she found so seductive in Romney's portraits of Lady Hamilton.

They dined at the Savoy. The head-waiter gave them a table on the gangway so that they were admirably in view. Though everyone was supposed to be out of town the grill-room was well filled. Julia bowed and smiled to various friends of whom she caught sight. Charles had much to tell her; she listened to him with flattering interest.

"You are the best company in the world, Charles," she told him.

They had come late, they dined well, and by the time Charles had finished his brandy people were already beginning to come in for supper.

"Good gracious, are the theatres out already?" he said, glancing at his watch. "How quickly the time flies when I'm with you. D'you imagine they want to get rid of us?"

"I don't feel a bit like going to bed."

"I suppose Michael will be getting home presently?"

"I suppose so."

"Why don't you come back to my house and have a talk?"

That was what she called taking a cue.

"I'd love it," she answered, putting into her tone the slight blush which she felt would have well become her cheek.

They got into his car and drove to Hill Street. He took her into his study. It was on the ground floor and looked on a tiny garden. The french windows were wide open. They sat down on a sofa.

"Put out some of the lights and let the night into the room," said Julia. She quoted from *The Merchant of Venice*: " 'In such a night as this, when the sweet wind did gently kiss the trees . . .' "

Charles switched off everything but one shaded lamp, and when he sat down again she nestled up to him. He put his arm round her waist and she rested her head on his shoulder.

"This is heaven," she murmured.

"I've missed you terribly all these months."

"Did you get into mischief?"

"Well, I bought an Ingres drawing and paid a lot of money for it. I must show it you before you go."

"Don't forget. Where have you put it?"

She had wondered from the moment she got into the house whether the seduction would take place in the study or upstairs.

"In my bedroom," he answered.

"That's much more comfortable really," she reflected.

She laughed in her sleeve as she thought of poor old Charles devising a simple little trick like that to get her into his bedroom. What mugs men were! Shy, that was what was the matter with them. A sudden pang shot through her heart as she thought of Tom. Damn Tom. Charles really was very sweet and she was determined to reward him at last for his long devotion.

"You've been a wonderful friend to me, Charles," she said in her low, rather husky voice. She turned a little so that her face was very near his, her lips, again like Lady Hamilton's, slightly open. "I'm afraid I haven't always been very kind to you."

She looked so deliciously yielding, a ripe peach waiting to be picked, that it seemed inevitable that he should kiss her. Then she would twine her soft white arms round his neck. But he only smiled.

"You musn't say that. You've been always divine."

("He's afraid, poor lamb.") "I don't think anyone has ever been so much in love with me as you were."

He gave her a little squeeze.

"I am still. You know that. There's never been any woman but you in my life."

Since, however, he did not take the proffered lips she slightly turned. She looked reflectively at the electric fire. Pity it was unlit. The scene wanted a fire.

"How different everything would have been if we'd bolted that
time. Heigh-ho."

She never quite knew what heigh-ho meant, but they used it a
lot on the stage, and said with a sigh it always sounded very sad.

"England would have lost its greatest actress. I know now how
dreadfully selfish it was of me ever to propose it."

"Success isn't everything. I sometimes wonder whether to
gratify my silly little ambition I didn't miss the greatest thing in the
world. After all, love is the only thing that matters." And now
she looked at him again with eyes more beautiful than ever in their
melting tenderness. "D'you know, I think that now, if I had my
time over again, I'd say take me."

She slid her hand down to take his. He gave it a graceful
pressure.

"Oh, my dear."

"I've so often thought of that dream villa of ours. Olive trees
and oleanders and the blue sea. Peace. Sometimes I'm appalled
by the dullness and vulgarity of my life. What you offered was
beauty. It's too late now, I know; I didn't know then how much I
cared for you, I never dreamt that as the years went on you would
mean more and more to me."

"It's heavenly to hear you say that, my sweet. It makes up for so
much."

"I'd do anything in the world for you, Charles. I've been
selfish. I've ruined your life, I didn't know what I was doing."

Her voice was low and tremulous and she threw back her head
so that her neck was like a white column. Her *décolleté* showed
part of her small firm breasts and with her hands she pressed them
forward a little.

"You mustn't say that, you mustn't think that," he answered
gently. "You've been perfect always. I wouldn't have had you
otherwise. Oh, my dear, life is so short and love is so transitory.
The tragedy of life is that sometimes we get what we want. Now
that I look back on our long past together I know that you were
wiser than I. 'What leaf-fringed legend haunts about thy shape?'
Don't you remember how it goes? 'Never, never canst thou kiss,
though winning near the goal—yet, do not grieve; she cannot fade,
though thou hast not thy bliss. For ever wilt thou love, and she be
fair!' "

("Idiotic.") "Such lovely lines," she sighed. "Perhaps you're
right. Heigh-ho."

He went on quoting. That was a trick of his that Julia had always found somewhat tiresome.

> " 'Ah, happy, happy boughs! that cannot shed
> Your leaves, nor ever bid the Spring adieu;
> And, happy melodist, unwearied,
> For ever piping songs for ever new! . . .' "

It gave Julia an opportunity to think. She stared in the unlit fire, her gaze intent, as though she were entranced by the exquisite beauty of those words. It was quite obvious that he just hadn't understood. It could hardly be wondered at. She had been deaf to his passionate entreaties for twenty years, and it was very natural if he had given up his quest as hopeless. It was like Mount Everest; if those hardy mountaineers who had tried for so long in vain to reach the summit finally found an easy flight of steps that led to it, they simply would not believe their eyes: they would think there was a catch in it. Julia felt that she must make herself a little plainer; she must, as it were, reach out a helping hand to the weary pilgrim.

"It's getting dreadfully late," she said softly. "Show me your new drawing and then I must go home."

He rose and she gave him both her hands so that he should help her up from the sofa. They went upstairs. His pyjamas and dressing-gown were neatly arranged on a chair.

"How well you single men do yourselves. Such a cosy, friendly bedroom."

He took the framed drawing off the wall and brought it over for her to look at under the light. It was a portrait in pencil of a stoutish woman in a bonnet and a low-necked dress with puffed sleeves. Julia thought her plain and the dress ridiculous.

"Isn't it ravishing?" she cried.

"I knew you'd like it. A good drawing, isn't it?"

"Amazing."

He put the little picture back on its nail. When he turned round again she was standing near the bed with her hands behind her back, a little like a Circassian slave introduced by the chief eunuch to the inspection of the Grand Vizier; there was a hint of modest withdrawal in her bearing, a delicious timidity, and at the same time the virgin's anticipation that she was about to enter into her kingdom. Julia gave a sigh that was ever so slightly voluptuous.

"My dear, it's been such a wonderful evening. I've never felt so close to you before."

She slowly raised her hands from behind her back and with the exquisite timing that came so naturally to her moved them forwards, stretching out her arms, and held them palms upward as though there rested on them, invisibly, a lordly dish, and on the dish lay her proffered heart. Her beautiful eyes were tender and yielding and on her lips played a smile of shy surrender.

She saw Charles's smile freeze on his face. He had understood all right.

("Christ, he doesn't want me. It was all a bluff.") The revelation for a moment staggered her. ("God, how am I going to get out of it? What a bloody fool I must look.")

She very nearly lost her poise. She had to think like lightning. He was standing there, looking at her with an embarrassment that he tried hard to conceal. Julia was panic-stricken. She could not think what to do with those hands that held the lordly dish; God knows, they were small, but at the moment they felt like legs of mutton hanging there. Nor did she know what to say. Every second made her posture and the situation more intolerable.

("The skunk, the dirty skunk. Codding me all these years.")

She did the only thing possible. She continued the gesture. Counting so that she should not go too fast, she drew her hands towards one another, till she could clasp them, and then throwing back her head, raised them, very slowly, to one side of her neck. The attitude she reached was as lovely as the other, and it was the attitude that suggested to her what she had to say. Her deep rich voice trembled a little with emotion.

"I'm so glad when I look back to think that we have nothing to reproach ourselves with. The bitterness of life is not death, the bitterness of life is that love dies. (She'd heard something like that said in a play.) If we'd been lovers you'd have grown tired of me long ago, and what should we have now to look back on but regret for our own weakness? What was that line of Shelley's that you said just now about fading?"

"Keats," he corrected. "'She cannot fade though thou hast not thy bliss'."

"That's it. Go on."

She was playing for time.

"'For ever wilt thou love, and she be fair.'"

She threw her arms wide in a great open gesture and tossed her curly head. She'd got it.

"It's true, isn't it? 'For ever wilt thou love and I be fair.' What fools we should have been if for a few moments' madness we had thrown away the wonderful happiness our friendship has brought us. We have nothing to be ashamed of. We're clean. We can walk with our heads held high and look the whole world in the face."

She instinctively felt that this was an exit line, and suiting her movements to the words, with head held high, backed to the door and flung it open. Her power was such that she carried the feeling of the scene all the way down the stairs with her. Then she let it fall and with the utmost simplicity turned to Charles, who had followed her.

"My cloak."

"The car is there," he said as he wrapped it round her. "I'll drive you home."

"No, let me go alone. I want to stamp this hour on my heart. Kiss me before I go."

She held up her lips to him. He kissed them. But she broke away from him, with a stifled sob, and tearing open the door ran to the waiting car.

When she got home and stood in her own bedroom she gave a great whoof of relief.

"The bloody fool. Fancy me being taken in like that. Thank God, I got out of it all right. He's such an ass, I don't suppose he began to see what I was getting at." But that frozen smile disconcerted her. "He may have suspected, he couldn't have been certain, and afterwards he must have been pretty sure he'd made a mistake. My God, the rot I talked. It seemed to go down all right, I must say. Lucky I caught on when I did. In another minute I'd have had me dress off. That wouldn't have been so damned easy to laugh away."

Julia began to titter. The situation was mortifying of course, he had made a damned fool of her, but if you had any sense of humour you could hardly help seeing that there was a funny side to it. She was sorry that there was nobody to whom she could tell it; even if it was against herself it would make a good story. What she couldn't get over was that she had fallen for the comedy of undying passion that he had played all those years; for of course it was just a pose; he liked to see himself as the constant adorer, and the last thing he wanted, apparently, was to have his constancy rewarded.

"Bluffed me, he did, completely bluffed me."

But an idea occurred to Julia and she ceased to smile. When a woman's amorous advances are declined by a man she is apt to draw one of two conclusions: one is that he is homosexual and the other is that he is impotent. Julia reflectively lit a cigarette. She asked herself if Charles had used his devotion to her as a cover to distract attention from his real inclinations. But she shook her head. If he had been homosexual she would surely have had some hint of it; after all, in society since the war they talked of practically nothing else. Of course it was quite possible he was impotent. She reckoned out his age. Poor Charles. She smiled again. And if that were the case it was he, not she, who had been placed in an embarrassing and even ridiculous position. He must have been scared stiff, poor lamb. Obviously it wasn't the sort of thing a man liked to tell a woman, especially if he were madly in love with her; the more she thought of it the more probable she considered the explanation. She began to feel very sorry for him, almost maternal in fact.

"I know what I'll do," she said, as she began to undress, "I'll send him a huge bunch of white lilies to-morrow."

CHAPTER XXV

Julia lay awake next morning for some time before she rang her bell. She thought. When she reflected on her adventure of the previous night she could not but be pleased that she had shown so much presence of mind. It was hardly true to say that she had snatched victory from defeat, but looking upon it as a strategic retreat her conduct had been masterly. She was notwithstanding ill at ease. There might be yet another explanation for Charles's singular behaviour. It was possible that he did not desire her because she was not desirable. The notion had crossed her mind in the night, and though she had at once dismissed it as highly improbable, there was no denying it, at that hour of the morning it had a nasty look. She rang. As a rule, since Michael often came in while Julia had breakfast, Evie when she had drawn the curtains handed her a mirror and a comb, her powder and lipstick. On this occasion, instead of running the comb rapidly through her hair and giving her face a perfunctory dab with the puff, Julia took some trouble. She painted her lips with care and put on some rouge; she arranged her hair.

"Speaking without passion or prejudice," she said, still looking at herself in the glass, when Evie placed the breakfast tray on her bed, "would you say I was by way of being a good-looking woman, Evie?"

"I must know what I'm letting myself in for before answering that question."

"You old bitch," said Julia.

"You're no beauty, you know."

"No great actress ever has been."

"When you're all dolled up posh like you was last night, and got the light be'ind you, I've seen worse, you know."

("Fat lot of good it did me last night.") "What I want to say is, if I really set my mind on getting off with a man, d'you think I could?"

"Knowing what men are, I wouldn't be surprised. Who d'you want to get off with now?"

"Nobody. I was only talking generally."

Evie sniffed and drew her forefinger along her nostrils.

"Don't sniff like that. If your nose wants blowing, blow it."

Julia ate her boiled egg slowly. She was busy with her thoughts. She looked at Evie. Funny-looking old thing of course, but one never knew.

"Tell me, Evie, do men ever try to pick you up in the street?"

"Me? I'd like to see 'em try."

"So would I, to tell you the truth. Women are always telling me how men follow them in the street and if they stop and look in at a shop window come up and try to catch their eye. Sometimes they have an awful bother getting rid of them."

"Disgusting, I call it."

"I don't know about that. It's rather flattering. You know, it's a most extraordinary thing, no one ever follows me in the street. I don't remember a man ever having tried to pick me up."

"Oh well, you walk along Edgware Road one evening. You'll get picked up all right."

"I shouldn't know what to do if I was."

"Call a policeman," said Evie grimly.

"I know a girl who was looking in a shop window in Bond

Street, a hat shop, and a man came up and asked her if she'd like a hat. I'd love one, she said, and they went in and she chose one and gave her name and address, he paid for it on the nail, and then she said: Thank you so much, and walked out while he was waiting for the change."

"That's what she told you." Evie's sniff was sceptical. She gave Julia a puzzled look. "What's the idea?"

"Oh, nothing. I was only wondering why in point of fact I never have been accosted by a man. It's not as if I had no sex appeal."

But had she? She made up her mind to put the matter to the test.

That afternoon, when she had had her sleep, she got up, made up a little more than usual, and without calling Evie put on a dress that was neither plain nor obviously expensive and a red straw hat with a wide brim.

"I don't want to look like a tart," she said as she looked at herself in the glass. "On the other hand I don't want to look too respectable."

She tiptoed down the stairs so that no one should hear her and closed the door softly behind her. She was a trifle nervous, but pleasantly excited; she felt that she was doing something rather shocking. She walked through Connaught Square into the Edgware Road. It was about five o'clock. There was a dense line of buses, taxis and lorries; bicyclists dangerously threaded their way through the traffic. The pavements were thronged. She sauntered slowly north. At first she walked with her eyes straight in front of her, looking neither to the right nor to the left, but soon realised that this was useless. She must look at people if she wanted them to look at her. Two or three times when she saw half a dozen persons gazing at a shop window she paused and gazed too, but none of them took any notice of her. She strolled on. People passed her in one direction and another. They seemed in a hurry. No one paid any attention to her. When she saw a man alone coming towards her she gave him a bold stare, but he passed on with a blank face. It occurred to her that her expression was too severe, and she let a slight smile hover on her lips. Two or three men thought she was smiling at them and quickly averted their gaze. She looked back as one of them passed her and he looked back too, but catching her eye he hurried on. She felt a trifle snubbed and decided not to look round again. She walked on and on. She had always heard that the London crowd was the best behaved in the world, but really its behaviour on this occasion was unconscionable.

"This couldn't happen to one in the streets of Paris, Rome or Berlin," she reflected.

She decided to go as far as the Marylebone Road, and then turn back. It would be too humiliating to have to go home without being once accosted. She was walking so slowly that passers-by sometimes jostled her. This irritated her.

"I ought to have tried Oxford Street," she said. "That fool Evie. The Edgware Road's obviously a wash-out."

Suddenly her heart gave an exultant leap. She had caught a young man's eye and she was sure that there was a gleam in it. He passed, and she had all she could do not to turn round. She started, for in a moment he passed her again, he had retraced his steps, and this time he gave her a stare. She shot him a glance and then modestly lowered her eyes. He fell back and she was conscious that he was following her. It was all right. She stopped to look into a shop window and he stopped too. She knew how to behave now. She pretended to be absorbed in the goods that were displayed, but just before she moved on gave him a quick flash of her faintly-smiling eyes. He was rather short, he looked like a clerk or a shop-walker, he wore a grey suit and a brown soft hat. He was not the man she would have chosen to be picked up by, but there it was, he was evidently trying to pick her up. She forgot that she was beginning to feel tired. She did not know what would happen next. Of course she wasn't going to let the thing go too far, but she was curious to see what his next step would be. She wondered what he would say to her. She was excited and pleased; it was a weight off her mind. She walked on slowly and she knew he was close behind her. She stopped at another shop window, and this time when he stopped he was close beside her. Her heart began to beat wildly. It was really beginning to look like an adventure.

"I wonder if he'll ask me to go to a hotel with him. I don't suppose he could afford that. A cinema. That's it. It would be rather fun."

She looked him full in the face now and very nearly smiled. He took off his hat.

"Miss Lambert, isn't it?"

She almost jumped out of her skin. She was indeed so taken aback that she had not the presence of mind to deny it.

"I thought I recognised you the moment I saw you, that's why I turned back, to make sure, see, and I said to meself, if that's not Julia Lambert I'm Ramsay MacDonald. Then you stopped to look in that shop window and that give me the chance to 'ave a good look at you. What made me 'esitate was seeing you in the Edgware Road. It seems so funny, if you know what I mean."

It was much funnier than he imagined. Anyhow it didn't matter if he knew who she was. She ought to have guessed that she couldn't go far in London without being recognised. He had a Cockney accent and a pasty face, but she gave him a jolly, friendly smile. He mustn't think she was putting on airs.

"Excuse me talking to you, not 'aving been introduced and all that, but I couldn't miss the opportunity. Will you oblige me with your autograph?"

Julia caught her breath. It couldn't be that this was why he had followed her for ten minutes. He must have thought that up as an excuse for speaking to her. Well, she would play up.

"I shall be delighted. But I can't very well give it you in the street. People would stare so."

"That's right. Look here, I was just going along to 'ave my tea. There's a Lyons at the next corner. Why don't you come in and 'ave a cup too?"

She was getting on. When they'd had tea he'd probably suggest going to the pictures.

"All right," she said.

They walked along till they came to the shop and took their places at a small table.

"Two teas, please, miss," he ordered. "Anything to eat?" And when Julia declined: "Scone and butter for one, miss."

Julia was able now to have a good look at him. Though stocky and short he had good features, his black hair was plastered down on his head and he had fine eyes, but his teeth were poor and his pale skin gave him an unhealthy look. There was a sort of impudence in his manner that Julia did not much like, but then, as she sensibly reflected, you could hardly expect the modesty of the violet in a young man who picked you up in the Edgware Road.

"Before we go any further let's 'ave this autograph, eh? Do it now, that's my motto."

He took a fountain-pen from his pocket and from a bulging pocket-book a large card.

"One of our trade cards," he said. "That'll do O.K."

Julia thought it silly to carry the subterfuge to this length, but she good-humouredly signed her name on the back of the card.

"Do you collect autographs?" she asked him with a subtle smile.

"Me? Noa. I think it's a lot of tommy-rot. My young lady does. She's got Charlie Chaplin and Douglas Fairbanks and I don't know what all. Show you 'er photo if you like."

From his pocket-book he extracted a snapshot of a rather pert-looking young woman showing all her teeth in a cinema smile.

"Pretty," said Julia.

"And how. We're going to the pictures to-night. She will be surprised when I give her your autograph. The first thing I said to meself when I knew it was you was, I'll get Julia Lambert's autograph for Gwen or die in the attempt. We're going to get married in August, when I 'ave my 'oliday, you know; we're going to the Isle of Wight for the 'oneymoon. I shall 'ave a rare lot of fun with 'er over this. She won't believe me when I tell her you an' me 'ad tea together, she'll think I'm kidding, and then I'll show 'er the autograph, see?"

Julia listened to him politely, but the smile had left her face.

"I'm afraid I shall have to go in a minute," she said. "I'm late already."

"I 'aven't got too much time meself. You see, meeting my young lady, I want to get away from the shop on the tick."

The check had been put on the table when the girl brought their tea, and when they got up Julia took a shilling out of her bag.

"What are you doing that for? You don't think I'm going to let you pay. I invited you."

"That's very kind of you."

"But I'll tell you what you can do, let me bring my young lady to see you in your dressing-room one day. Just shake 'ands with her, see? It would mean a rare lot to her. Why, she'd go on talking about it the rest of her life."

Julia's manner had been for some minutes growing stiffer and now, though gracious still, it was almost haughty.

"I'm so sorry, but we never allow strangers behind."

"Oh, sorry. You don't mind my asking though, do you? I mean, it's not as if it was for meself."

"Not at all. I quite understand."

She signalled to a cab crawling along the kerb and gave her hand to the young man.

"Good-bye, Miss Lambert. So long, good luck and all that sort of thing. And thanks for the autograph."

Julia sat in the corner of the taxi raging.

"Vulgar little beast. Him and his young lady. The nerve of asking if he could bring her to see ME."

When she got home she went upstairs to her room. She snatched her hat off her head and flung it angrily on the bed. She strode over to the looking-glass and stared at herself.

"Old, old, old," she muttered. "There are no two ways about it; I'm entirely devoid of sex appeal. You wouldn't believe it, would you? You'd say it was preposterous. What other explanation is there? I walk from one end of the Edgware Road to the other and God knows I'd dressed the part perfectly, and not a man pays the smallest attention to me except a bloody little shop-assistant who wants my autograph for his young lady. It's absurd. A lot of sexless bastards. I don't know what's coming to the English. The British Empire!"

The last words she said with a scorn that would have withered a whole front bench of cabinet ministers. She began to gesticulate.

"It's ridiculous to suppose that I could have got to my position if I hadn't got sex appeal. What do people come to see an actress for? Because they want to go to bed with her. Do you mean to tell me that I could fill a theatre for three months with a rotten play if I hadn't got sex appeal? What is sex appeal anyway?"

She paused, looking at herself reflectively.

"Surely I can act sex appeal. I can act anything."

She began to think of the actresses who notoriously had it, of one especially, Lydia Mayne, whom one always engaged when one wanted a vamp. She was not much of an actress, but in certain parts she was wonderfully effective. Julia was a great mimic, and now she began to do an imitation of Lydia Mayne. Her eyelids drooped sensually over her eyes as Lydia's did and her body writhed sinuously in her dress. She got into her eyes the provoking indecency of Lydia's glance and into her serpentine gestures that invitation which was Lydia's speciality. She began to speak in Lydia's voice, with the lazy drawl that made every remark she uttered sound faintly obscene.

"Oh, my dear man, I've heard that sort of thing so often. I don't want to make trouble between you and your wife. Why won't men leave me alone?"

It was a cruel caricature that Julia gave. It was quite ruthless. It amused her so much that she burst out laughing.

"Well, there's one thing, I may not have any sex appeal, but after seeing my imitation there aren't many people who'd think Lydia had either."

It made her feel much better.

CHAPTER XXVI

REHEARSALS began and distracted Julia's troubled mind. The revival that Michael put on when she went abroad had done neither very well nor very badly, but rather than close the theatre he was keeping it in the bill till *Nowadays* was ready. Because he was acting two matinées a week, and the weather was hot, he determined that they should take rehearsals easy. They had a month before them.

Though Julia had been on the stage so long she had never lost the thrill she got out of rehearsing, and the first rehearsal still made her almost sick with excitement. It was the beginning of a new adventure. She did not feel like a leading lady then, she felt as gay and eager as if she were a girl playing her first small part. But at the same time she had a delicious sense of her own powers. Once more she had the chance to exercise them.

At eleven o'clock she stepped on to the stage. The cast stood about idly. She kissed and shook hands with the artists she knew and Michael with urbanity introduced to her those she did not. She greeted Avice Crichton with cordiality. She told her how pretty she was and how much she liked her hat; she told her about the lovely frocks she had chosen for her in Paris.

"Have you seen Tom lately?" she asked.

"No, I haven't. He's away on his holiday."

"Oh, yes. He's a nice little thing, isn't he?"

"Sweet."

The two women smiled into one another's eyes. Julia watched her when she read her part and listened to her intonations. She smiled grimly. It was exactly what she had expected. Avice was one of those actresses who were quite sure of themselves from the first rehearsal. She didn't know what was coming to her. Tom meant nothing to Julia any more, but she had a score to settle with Avice and she wasn't going to forget it. The slut!

The play was a modern version of *The Second Mrs. Tanqueray*, but with the change of manners of this generation it had been treated from the standpoint of comedy. Some of the old characters were introduced, and Aubrey Tanqueray, now a very old man, appeared in the second act. After Paula's death he had married for the third time. Mrs. Cortelyou had undertaken to compensate him for his unfortunate experience with his second wife, and she was now a cantankerous and insolent old lady. Ellean, his daughter, and Hugh Ardale had agreed to let bygones be bygones, for Paula's tragic death had seemed to wipe out the recollection of his lapse into extra-conjugal relations; and they had married. He was now a retired brigadier-general who played golf and deplored the decline of the British Empire—"Gad, sir, I'd stand those damned socialists against a wall and shoot 'em if I had my way"; whereas Ellean, by this time an elderly woman, after a prudish youth had become gay, modern and plain-spoken. The character that Michael played was called Robert Humphreys, and like the Aubrey of Pinero's play he was a widower with an only daughter; he had been a consul in China for many years, and having come into money had retired and was settling on the estate, near where the Tanquerays still lived, which a cousin had left him. His daughter, Honor (this was the part for which Avice Crichton had been engaged), was studying medicine with the intention of practising in India. Alone in London, and friendless after so many years abroad, he had picked up a well-known woman of the town called Mrs. Marten. Mrs. Marten belonged to the same class as Paula, but she was less exclusive; she "did" the summer and the winter season at Cannes and in the intervals lived in a flat in Albemarle Street where she entertained the officers of His Majesty's Brigade. She played a good game of bridge and an even better game of golf. The part well suited Julia.

The author followed the lines of the old play closely. Honor announced to her father that she was abandoning her medical studies and until her marriage wished to live with him, for she had just become engaged to Ellean's son, a young guardsman. Somewhat disconcerted, Robert Humphreys broke to her his intention of marrying Mrs. Marten. Honor took the information with composure.

"Of course you know she's a tart, don't you?" she said coolly.

He, much embarrassed, spoke of the unhappy life she had led and how he wanted to make up to her for all she had suffered.

"Oh, don't talk such rot," she answered. "It's grand work if you can get it."

Ellean's son had been one of Mrs. Marten's numerous lovers just as Ellean's husband had been one of Paula Tanqueray's. When Robert Humphreys brought his wife down to his home in the country and this fact was discovered, they decided that Honor must be informed. To their consternation Honor did not turn a hair. She knew already.

"I was as pleased as Punch when I found out," she told her step-mother. "You see, darling, you can tell me if he's all right in bed."

This was Avice Crichton's best scene, it lasted a full ten minutes, and Michael had realised from the beginning that it was effective and important. Avice's cold, matter-of-fact prettiness had been exactly what he had thought would be so telling in the circumstances. But after half a dozen rehearsals he began to think that that was all she had to give. He talked it over with Julia.

"How d'you think Avice is shaping?"

"It's early days to tell yet."

"I'm not happy about her. You said she could act. I've seen no sign of it yet."

"It's a cast-iron part. She can't really go wrong in it."

"You know just as well as I do that there's no such thing as a cast-iron part. However good a part is, it has to be acted for all it's worth. I'm not sure if it wouldn't be better to kick her out and get somebody else."

"That wouldn't be so easy. I think you ought to give her a chance."

"She's so awkward, her gestures are so meaningless."

Julia reflected. She had her reasons for wishing to keep Avice in the cast. She knew her well enough to be sure that if she were dismissed she would tell Tom that it was because Julia was jealous of her. He loved her and would believe anything she said. He might even think that Julia had put this affront on her in revenge for his desertion. No, no, she must stay. She must play the part, and fail; and Tom must see with his own eyes what a bad actress she was. They both of them thought the play would make her. Fools. It would kill her.

"You know how clever you are, Michael, I'm sure you can train her if you're willing to take a little trouble."

"But that's just it, she doesn't seem able to take direction. I show her exactly how to say a line and then she goes and says it in her own way. You wouldn't believe it, but sometimes I can hardly help thinking she's under the delusion that she knows better than I do."

"You make her nervous. When you tell her to do something she's in such a dither she doesn't know what she's up to."

"Good lord, no one could be more easy than I am. I've never even been sharp with her."

Julia gave him an affectionate smile.

"Are you going to pretend that you really don't know what's the matter with her?"

"No, what?"

He looked at her with a blank face.

"Come off it, darling. Haven't you noticed that she's madly in love with you?"

"With me? But I thought she was practically engaged to Tom. Nonsense. You're always fancying things like that."

"But it's quite obvious. After all she isn't the first who's fallen for your fatal beauty, and I don't suppose she'll be the last."

"Heaven knows, I don't want to queer poor Tom's pitch."

"It's not your fault, is it?"

"What d'you want me to do about it then?"

"Well, I think you ought to be nice to her. She's very young, you know, poor thing. What she wants is a helping hand. If you took her alone a few times and went through the part with her I believe you could do wonders. Why don't you take her out to lunch one day and have a talk to her?"

She saw the gleam in Michael's eyes as he considered the proposition and the shadow of a smile that was outlined on his lips.

"Of course the great thing is to get the play as well acted as we can."

"I know it'll be a bore for you, but, honestly, for the sake of the play I think it'll be worth while."

"You know that I would never do anything to upset you, Julia. I mean, I'd much sooner fire the girl and get someone else in her place."

"I think that would be such a mistake. I'm convinced that if you'll only take enough trouble with her she'll give a very good performance."

He walked up and down the room once or twice. He seemed to be considering the matter from every side.

"Well, I suppose it's my job to get the best performance I can out of every member of my cast. In every case you have to find out which is the best method of approach."

He threw out his chin and drew in his belly. He straightened his back. Julia knew that Avice Crichton would hold the part, and next day at rehearsal he took her aside and had a long talk with her. She knew by his manner exactly what he was saying and, watching them out of the corner of her eye, presently she saw Avice nod and smile. He had asked her to lunch with him. With a contented mind Julia went on studying her part.

CHAPTER XXVII

THEY had been rehearsing for a fortnight when Roger arrived from Austria. He had been spending a few weeks on a Carinthian lake, and after a day or two in London was to go and stay with friends in Scotland. Since Michael had to dine early to go to the theatre Julia went to meet him by herself. When she was dressing, Evie, sniffing as usual, told her that she was taking as much pains to make herself look nice as if she were going to meet a young man. She wanted Roger to be proud of her, and certainly she looked very young and pretty in her summer frock as she strolled up and down the platform. You would have thought, but wrongly, that she was perfectly unconscious of the attention she attracted. Roger, after a month in the sun, was very brown, but he was still rather spotty and he seemed thinner than when he had left London at the New Year. She hugged him with exuberant affection. He smiled slightly.

They were to dine by themselves. Julia asked him if he would like to go to a play afterwards or to the pictures, but he said he preferred to stay at home.

"That'll be much nicer," she answered, "and we'll just talk."

There was indeed a subject that Michael had invited her to discuss with Roger when the opportunity arose. Now that he was going to Cambridge so soon he ought to make up his mind what he wanted to do. Michael was afraid that he would drift through his time there and then go into a broker's office or even on the stage. Thinking that Julia had more tact than he, and more influence with the boy, he had urged her to put before him the advantages of the Foreign Office and the brilliant possibilities of the Bar. Julia thought it would be strange if in the course of two or three hours' conversation she could not find a way to lead to this important topic. At dinner she tried to get him to talk about Vienna. But he was reticent.

"Oh, I just did the usual things, you know. I saw the sights and worked hard at my German. I knocked about in beer places. I went to the opera a good deal."

She wondered if he had had any love affairs.

"Anyhow, you haven't come back engaged to a Viennese maiden," she said, thinking to draw him out.

He gave her a reflective, but faintly amused look. You might almost have thought that he had seen what she was driving at. It was strange; though he was her own son she did not feel quite at home with him.

"No," he answered, "I was too busy to bother with that sort of thing."

"I suppose you went to all the theatres."

"I went two or three times."

"Did you see anything that would be any use to me?"

"You know, I never thought about that."

His answer might have seemed a little ungracious but that it was accompanied by a smile, and his smile was very sweet. Julia wondered again how it was that he had inherited so little of Michael's beauty and of her charm. His red hair was nice, but his pale lashes gave his face a sort of empty look. Heaven only knew where with such a father and such a mother he had got his rather lumpy figure. He was eighteen now; it was time he fined down. He seemed a trifle apathetic; he had none of her sparkling vitality; she could picture the vividness with which she would have narrated her experiences if she had just spent six months in Vienna. Why, already she had made a story about her stay at St. Malo with Aunt Carrie and her mother that made people roar with laughter. They all said it was as good as a play, and her own impression was that it was much better than most. She told it to Roger now. He listened with his slow, quiet smile; but she had an uneasy feeling that he did not think it quite so funny as she did. She sighed in her heart. Poor lamb, he could have no sense of humour. Then he made some remark that led her to speak of *Nowadays*. She told him its story, and explained what she was doing with her part; she talked to him of the cast and described the sets. At the end of dinner it suddenly struck her that she had been talking entirely of herself and her own interests. She did not know how she had been led to do this, and the suspicion flashed across her mind that Roger had guided the conversation in that direction so that it should be diverted from him and his affairs. But she put it aside. He really wasn't intelligent enough for that. It was later, when they sat in the drawing-room listening to the radio and smoking, that Julia found the chance to slip in, apparently in the most casual fashion, the question she had prepared.

"Have you made up your mind what you're going to be yet?"

"No. Is there any hurry?"

"You know how ignorant I am about everything. Your father says that if you're going to be a barrister you ought to work at law when you go to Cambridge. On the other hand, if you fancy the Foreign Office you should take up modern languages."

He looked at her for so long, with that queer, reflective air of his, that Julia had some difficulty in holding her light, playful and yet affectionate expression.

"If I believed in God I'd be a priest," he said at last.

"A priest?"

Julia could hardly believe her ears. She had a feeling of acute discomfort. But his answer sank into her mind and in a flash she saw him as a cardinal, inhabiting a beautiful palazzo in Rome, filled with wonderful pictures, and surrounded by obsequious prelates; and then again as a saint, in a mitre and vestments heavily embroidered with gold, with benevolent gestures distributing bread to the poor. She saw herself in a brocaded dress and a string of pearls. The mother of the Borgias.

"That was all right in the sixteenth century," she said. "It's too late in the day for that."

"Much."

"I can't think what put such an idea in your head." He did not answer, so that she had to speak again. "Aren't you happy?"

"Quite," he smiled.

"What is it you want?"

Once again he gave her his disconcerting stare. It was hard to know if he was serious, for his eyes faintly shimmered with amusement.

"Reality."

"What *do* you mean?"

"You see, I've lived all my life in an atmosphere of make-believe.

I want to get down to brass tacks. You and Father are all right breathing this air, it's the only air you know and you think it's the air of heaven. It stifles me."

Julia listened to him attentively, trying to understand what he meant.

"We're actors, and successful ones. That's why we've been able to surround you with every luxury since you were born. You could count on the fingers of one hand the actors who've sent their son to Eton."

"I'm very grateful for all you've done for me."

"Then what are you reproaching us for?"

"I'm not reproaching you. You've done everything you could for me. Unfortunately for me you've taken away my belief in everything."

"We've never interfered with your beliefs. I know we're not religious people, we're actors, and after eight performances a week one wants one's Sundays to oneself. I naturally expected they'd see to all that at school."

He hesitated a little before he spoke again. One might have thought that he had to make a slight effort over himself to continue.

"When I was just a kid—I was fourteen—I was standing one night in the wings watching you act. It must have been a pretty good scene, you said the things you had to say so sincerely, and what you were saying was so moving, I couldn't help crying. I was all worked up. I don't know how to say it quite, I was uplifted; I felt terribly sorry for you, I felt a bloody little hero; I felt I'd never do anything again that was beastly or underhand. And then you had to come to the back of the stage, near where I was standing, the tears were streaming down your face; you stood with your back to the audience and in your ordinary voice you said to the stage manager: What the bloody hell is that electrician doing with the lights? I told him to leave out the blue. And then in the same breath you turned round and faced the audience with a great cry of anguish and went on with the scene."

"But, darling, that was acting. If an actress felt the emotions she represented she'd tear herself to pieces. I remember the scene well. It used to bring down the house. I've never heard such applause in my life."

"I suppose I was a fool to be taken in by it. I believed you meant what you said. When I saw that it was all pretence it smashed something. I've never believed in you since. I'd been made a fool of once; I made up my mind that I wouldn't ever be made a fool of again."

She gave him her delightful and disarming smile.

"Darling, I think you're talking nonsense."

"Of course you do. You don't know the difference between truth and make-believe. You never stop acting. It's second nature to you. You act when there's a party here. You act to the servants, you act to Father, you act to me. To me you act the part of the fond, indulgent, celebrated mother. You don't exist, you're only the innumerable parts you've played. I've often wondered if there was ever a you or if you were never anything more than a vehicle for all these other people that you've pretended to be. When I've seen you go into an empty room I've sometimes wanted to open the door suddenly, but I've been afraid to in case I found nobody there."

She looked up at him quickly. She shivered, for what he said gave her an eerie sensation. She listened to him attentively, with a certain anxiety, for he was so serious that she felt he was expressing something that had burdened him for years. She had never in his whole life heard him talk so much.

"D'you think I'm only sham?"

"Not quite. Because sham is all you are. Sham is your truth. Just as margarine is butter to people who don't know what butter is."

She had a vague feeling of guilt. The Queen in *Hamlet*: "And let me wring your heart; for so I shall, if it be made of penetrable stuff." Her thoughts wandered.

("I wonder if I'm too old to play Hamlet. Siddons and Sarah Bernhardt played him. I've got better legs than any of the men I've seen in the part. I'll ask Charles what he thinks. Of course there's that bloody blank verse. Stupid of him not to write it in prose. Of course I might do it in French at the Française. God, what a stunt that would be.")

She saw herself in a black doublet, with long silk hose. "Alas, poor Yorick." But she bethought herself.

"You can hardly say that your father doesn't exist. Why, he's been playing himself for the last twenty years." ("Michael could play the King, not in French of course, but if we decided to have a shot at it in London.")

"Poor Father, I suppose he's good at his job, but he's not very intelligent, is he? He's so busy being the handsomest man in England."

"I don't think it's very nice of you to speak of your father like that."

"Have I told you anything you don't know?" he asked coolly.

Julia wanted to smile, but would not allow the look of somewhat pained dignity to leave her face.

"It's our weakness, not our strength, that endears us to those who love us," she replied.

"In what play did you say that?"

She repressed a gesture of annoyance. The words had come naturally to her lips, but as she said them she remembered that they were out of a play. Little brute! But they came in very appositely.

"You're hard," she said plaintively. She was beginning to feel more and more like Hamlet's mother. "Don't you love me?"

"I might if I could find you. But where are you? If one stripped you of your exhibitionism, if one took your technique away from you, if one peeled you as one peels an onion of skin after skin of pretence and insincerity, of tags of old parts and shreds of faked emotions, would one come upon a soul at last?" He looked at her with his grave sad eyes and then he smiled a little. "I like you all right."

"Do you believe I love you?"

"In your way."

Julia's face was suddenly discomposed.

"If you only knew the agony I suffered when you were ill! I don't know what I should have done if you'd died!"

"You would have given a beautiful performance of a bereaved mother at the bier of her only child."

"Not nearly such a good performance as if I'd had the opportunity of rehearsing it a few times," Julia answered tartly. "You see, what you don't understand is that acting isn't nature; it's art, and art is something you create. Real grief is ugly; the business of the actor is to represent it not only with truth but with beauty. If I were really dying as I've died in half a dozen plays, d'you think I'd care whether my gestures were graceful and my faltering words distinct enough to carry to the last row of the gallery? If it's a sham it's no more a sham than a sonata of Beethoven's, and I'm no more of a sham than the pianist who plays it. It's cruel to say that I'm not fond of you. I'm devoted to you. You've been the only thing in my life."

"No. You were fond of me when I was a kid and you could

have me photographed with you. It made a lovely picture and it was fine publicity. But since then you haven't bothered much about me. I've bored you rather than otherwise. You were always glad to see me, but you were thankful that I went my own way and didn't want to take up your time. I don't blame you; you hadn't got time in your life for anyone but yourself."

Julia was beginning to grow a trifle impatient. He was getting too near the truth for her comfort.

"You forget that young things are rather boring."

"Crashing, I should think," he smiled. "But then why do you pretend that you can't bear to let me out of your sight? That's just acting too."

"You make me very unhappy. You make me feel as if I hadn't done my duty to you."

"But you have. You've been a very good mother. You've done something for which I shall always be grateful to you, you've left me alone."

"I don't understand what you want."

"I told you. Reality."

"But where are you going to find it?"

"I don't know. Perhaps it doesn't exist. I'm young still; I'm ignorant. I thought perhaps that at Cambridge, meeting people and reading books, I might discover where to look for it. If they say it only exists in God, I'm done."

Julia was disturbed. What he said had not really penetrated to her understanding, his words were lines and the important thing was not what they meant, but whether they "got over", but she was sensitive to the emotion she felt in him. Of course he was only eighteen, and it would be silly to take him too seriously, she couldn't help thinking he'd got all that from somebody else, and that there was a good deal of pose in it. Did anyone have ideas of his own and did anyone not pose just a wee, wee bit? But of course it might be that at the moment he felt everything he said, and it wouldn't be very nice of her to make light of it.

"Of course I see what you mean," she said. "My greatest wish in the world is that you should be happy. I'll manage your father, and you can do as you like. You must seek your own salvation, I see that. But I think you ought to make sure that all these ideas of yours aren't just morbid. Perhaps you were too much alone in Vienna and I dare say you read too much. Of course your father and I belong to a different generation and I don't suppose we can help you. Why don't you talk it over with someone more of your own age? Tom, for instance."

"Tom? A poor little snob. His only ambition in life is to be a gentleman, and he hasn't the sense to see that the more he tries the more hopeless it is."

"I thought you liked him so much. Why, at Taplow last summer you just lived in his pocket."

"I didn't dislike him. I made use of him. He could tell me a lot of things that I wanted to know. But I thought him an insignificant, silly little thing."

Julia remembered how insanely jealous she had been of their friendship. It made her angry to think of all the agony she had wasted.

"You've dropped him, haven't you?" he asked suddenly.

She was startled.

"I suppose I have more or less."

"I think it's very wise of you. He wasn't up to your mark."

He looked at her with his calm, reflective eyes, and on a sudden Julia had a sickening fear that he knew that Tom had been her lover. It was impossible, she told herself, it was only her guilty conscience that made her think so; at Taplow there had been nothing; it was incredible that any of the horrid gossip had reached his ears; and yet there was something in his expression that made her certain that he knew. She was ashamed.

"I only asked him to come down to Taplow because I thought it would be nice for you to have a boy of that age to play around with."

"It was."

There was in his eyes a faint twinkle of amusement. She felt desperate. She would have liked to ask him what he was grinning at, but dared not; for she knew; he was not angry with her, she could have borne that, he was merely diverted. She was bitterly hurt. She would have cried, but that he would only laugh. And what could she say to him? He believed nothing she said. Acting! For once she was at a loss how to cope with a situation. She was up against something that she did not know, something mysterious and rather frightening. Could that be reality? At that moment they heard a car drive up.

"There's your father," she exclaimed.

What a relief! The scene was intolerable, and she was thankful that his arrival must end it. In a moment Michael, very hearty, with his chin thrust out and his belly pulled in, looking for all his fifty-odd years incredibly handsome, burst into the room and, in his manly way, thrust out his hand to greet, after a six months' absence, his only begotten son.

CHAPTER XXVIII

THREE days later Roger went up to Scotland. By the exercise of some ingenuity Julia had managed that they should not again spend any length of time alone together. When they happened to be by themselves for a few minutes they talked of indifferent things. Julia was not really sorry to see him go. She could not dismiss from her mind the curious conversation she had had with him. There was one point in particular that unaccountably worried her: this was his suggestion that if she went into an empty room and someone suddenly opened the door there would be nobody there. It made her feel very uncomfortable.

"I never set out to be a raving beauty, but the one thing no one has ever denied me is personality. It's absurd to pretend that because I can play a hundred different parts in a hundred different ways I haven't got an individuality of my own. I can do that because I'm a bloody good actress."

She tried to think what happened to her when she went alone into an empty room.

"But I never am alone, even in an empty room. There's always Michael, or Evie, or Charles, or the public; not in the flesh, of course, but in the spirit, as it were. I must speak to Charles about Roger."

Unfortunately he was away. But he was coming back for the dress-rehearsal and the first night; he had not missed these occasions for twenty years, and they had always had supper together after the dress-rehearsal. Michael would remain in the theatre, busy with the lights and so on, so that they would be alone. They would be able to have a good talk.

She studied her part. Julia did not deliberately create the character she was going to act by observation; she had a knack of getting into the shoes of the woman she had to portray so that she thought with her mind and felt with her senses. Her intuition suggested to her a hundred small touches that afterwards amazed people by their verisimilitude; but when they asked her where she had got them she could not say. Now she wanted to show the courageous yet uneasy breeziness of the Mrs. Marten who played golf and could talk to a man like one good chap to another and yet, essentially a respectable, middle-class woman, hankered for the security of the marriage state.

Michael never liked to have a crowd at a dress-rehearsal, and this time, anxious to keep the secret of the play till the first night, he had admitted besides Charles only the people, photographers and dressmakers, whose presence was necessary. Julia spared herself. She had no intention of giving all she had to give till the first night. It was enough if her performance was adequate. Under Michael's businesslike direction everything went off without a hitch, and by ten o'clock Julia and Charles were sitting in the Grill Room of the Savoy. The first thing she asked him was what he thought of Avice Crichton.

"Not at all bad and wonderfully pretty. She really looked lovely in that second-act dress."

"I'm not going to wear the dress I wore in the second act. Charley Deverill has made me another."

He did not see the slightly humorous glance she gave him, and if he had would not have guessed what it meant. Michael, having taken Julia's advice, had gone to a good deal of trouble with Avice. He had rehearsed her by herself upstairs in his private room and had given her every intonation and every gesture. He had also, Julia had good reason to believe, lunched with her several times and taken her out to supper. The result of all this was that she was playing the part uncommonly well. Michael rubbed his hands.

"I'm very pleased with her. I think she'll make quite a hit. I've half a mind to give her a contract."

"I wouldn't," said Julia. "Not till after the first night. You can never really tell how a performance is going to pan out till you've got an audience."

"She's a nice girl and a perfect lady."

"A nice girl, I suppose, because she's madly in love with you, and a perfect lady because she's resisting your advances till she's got a contract."

"Oh, my dear, don't be so silly. Why, I'm old enough to be her father."

But he smiled complacently. She knew very well that his love-making went no farther than holding hands and a kiss or two in a taxi, but she knew also that it flattered him to imagine that she suspected him capable of infidelity.

But now Julia, having satisfied her appetite with proper regard for her figure, attacked the subject which was on her mind.

"Charles dear, I want to talk to you about Roger."

"Oh yes, he came back the other day, didn't he? How is he?"

"My dear, a most terrible thing has happened. He's come back a fearful prig and I don't know what to do about it."

She gave him her version of the conversation. She left out one or two things that it seemed inconvenient to mention, but what she told was on the whole accurate.

"The tragic thing is that he has absolutely no sense of humour," she finished.

"After all he's only eighteen."

"You could have knocked me down with a feather when he said all those things to me. I felt just like Balaam when his ass broke into light conversation."

She gave him a gay look, but he did not even smile. He did not seem to think her remark as funny as she did.

"I can't imagine where he got his ideas. It's absurd to think that he could have thought out all that nonsense for himself."

"Are you sure that boys of that age don't think more than we older people imagine? It's a sort of puberty of the spirit and its results are often strange."

"It seems so deceitful of Roger to have harboured thoughts like those all these years and never breathed a word about them. He might have been accusing me." She gave a chuckle. "To tell you the truth, when Roger was talking to me I felt just like Hamlet's mother." Then with hardly a break: "I wonder if I'm too old to play Hamlet?"

"Gertrude isn't a very good part, is it?"

Julia broke into a laugh of frank amusement.

"Don't be idiotic, Charles. I wouldn't play the Queen. I'd play Hamlet."

"D'you think it's suited to a woman?"

"Mrs. Siddons played it and so did Sarah Bernhardt. It would set a seal on my career, if you know what I mean. Of course there's the difficulty of the blank verse."

"I have heard actors speak it so that it was indistinguishable from prose," he answered.

"Yes, but that's not quite the same, is it?"

"Were you nice to Roger?"

She was surprised at his going back to that subject so suddenly, but she returned to it with a smile.

"Oh, charming."

"It's hard not to be impatient with the absurdity of the young; they tell us that two and two make four as though it had never occurred to us, and they're disappointed if we can't share their surprise when they have just discovered that a hen lays an egg. There's a lot of nonsense in their ranting and raving, but it's not all nonsense. One ought to sympathise with them; one ought to do one's best to understand. One has to remember how much has to be forgotten and how much has to be learnt when for the first time one faces life. It's not very easy to give up one's ideals, and the brute facts of every day are bitter pills to swallow. The spiritual conflicts of adolescence can be very severe and one can do so little to resolve them."

"But you don't really think there's anything in all this stuff of Roger's? I believe it's all a lot of communist nonsense that he's learnt in Vienna. I wish we'd never sent him there."

"You may be right. It may be that in a year or two he'll lose sight of the clouds of glory and accept the chain. It may be that he'll find what he's looking for, if not in God, then in art."

"I should hate him to be an actor, if that's what you mean."

"No, I don't think he'll fancy that."

"And of course he can't be a playwright, he hasn't a sense of humour."

"I dare say he'll be quite content to go into the Foreign Office. It would be an asset to him there."

"What would you advise me to do?"

"Nothing. Let him be. That's probably the greatest kindness you can do him."

"But I can't help being worried about him."

"You needn't be. Be hopeful. You thought you'd only given birth to an ugly duckling; perhaps he's going to turn into a white-winged swan."

Charles was not giving Julia what she wanted. She had expected him to be more sympathetic.

"I suppose he's getting old, poor dear," she reflected. "He's losing his grip of things. He must have been impotent for years; I wonder it never struck me before."

She asked what the time was.

"I think I ought to go. I must get a long night's rest."

Julia slept well and when she awoke had at once a feeling of exultation. To-night was the first night. It gave her a little thrill of pleasure to recollect that people had already been assembling at the pit and gallery doors when she left the theatre after the dress-rehearsal, and now at ten in the morning there was probably already a long queue.

"Lucky it's a fine day for them, poor brutes."

In bygone years she had been intolerably nervous before a first night. She had felt slightly sick all day and as the hours passed got into such a state that she almost thought she would have to leave the stage. But by now, after having passed through the ordeal so many times, she had acquired a certain nonchalance. Throughout the early part of the day she felt only happy and mildly excited; it was not till late in the afternoon that she began to feel ill at ease. She grew silent and wanted to be left alone. She also grew irritable, and Michael, having learnt from experience, took care to keep out of her way. Her hands and feet got cold and by the time she reached the theatre they were like lumps of ice. But still the apprehension that filled her was not unpleasant.

Julia had nothing to do that morning but go down to the Siddons for a word-rehearsal at noon, so she lay in bed till late. Michael did not come back to luncheon, having last things to do to the sets, and she ate alone. Then she went to bed and for an hour slept soundly. Her intention was to rest all the afternoon; Miss Phillips was coming at six to give her a light massage, and by seven she wanted to be at the theatre. But when she awoke she felt so much refreshed that it irked her to stay in bed, so she made up her mind to get up and go for a walk. It was a fine, sunny day. Liking the town better than the country and streets more than trees, she did not go into the Park, but sauntered round the neighbouring squares, deserted at that time of year, idly looking at the houses, and thought how much she preferred her own to any of them. She felt at ease and light-hearted. Then she thought it time to go home. She had just reached the corner of Stanhope Place when she heard her name called in a voice that she could not but recognise.

"Julia."

She turned round and Tom, his face all smiles, caught her up. She had not seen him since her return from France. He was very smart in a neat grey suit and a brown hat. He was tanned by the sun.

"I thought you were away."

"I came back on Monday. I didn't ring up because I knew you were busy with the final rehearsals. I'm coming to-night; Michael gave me a stall."

"Oh, I'm glad."

It was plain that he was delighted to see her. His face was eager and his eyes shone. She was pleased to discover that the sight of him excited no emotion in her. She wondered as they went on talking what there was in him that had ever so deeply affected her.

"What on earth are you wandering about like this for?"

"I've been for a stroll. I was just going in to tea."

"Come and have tea with me."

His flat was just round the corner. Indeed he had caught sight of her just as he was going down the mews to get to it.

"How is it you're back so early?"

"Oh, there's nothing much on at the office just now. You know, one of our partners died a couple of months ago, and I'm getting a bigger share. It means I shall be able to keep on the flat after all. Michael was jolly decent about it, he said I could stay on rent-free till things got better. I hated the idea of turning out. Do come. I'd love to make you a cup of tea."

He rattled on so vivaciously that Julia was amused. You would never have thought, to listen to him, that there had ever been anything between them. He seemed perfectly unembarrassed.

"All right. But I can only stay a minute."

"O.K."

They turned into the mews and she preceded him up the narrow staircase.

"You toddle along to the sitting-room and I'll put the water on to boil."

She went in and sat down. She looked round the room that had been the scene of so many emotions for her. Nothing was changed. Her photograph stood in its old place, but on the chimney-piece was a large photograph also of Avice Crichton. On it was written: For Tom from Avice. Julia took everything in. The room might have been a set in which she had once acted; it was vaguely familiar, but no longer meant anything to her. The love that had consumed her then, the jealousy she had stifled, the ecstasy of surrender, it had no more reality than one of the innumerable parts she had played in the past. She relished her indifference. Tom came in, with the tea-cloth she had given him, and neatly set out the tea-service which she had also given him. She did not know why the thought of his casually using still all her little presents made her inclined to laugh. Then he came in with the tea and they drank it sitting side by side on the sofa. He told her more about his improved circumstances. In his pleasant, friendly way he acknowledged that it was owing to the work that through her he had been able to bring the firm that he had secured a larger share in the profits. He told her of the holiday from which he had just returned. It was quite clear to Julia that he had no inkling how much he had made her suffer. That too made her now inclined to laugh.

"I hear you're going to have an enormous success to-night."

"It would be nice, wouldn't it?"

"Avice says that both you and Michael have been awfully good to her. Take care she doesn't romp away with the play."

He said it chaffingly, but Julia wondered whether Avice had told him that this was what she expected to do.

"Are you engaged to her?"

"No. She wants her freedom. She says an engagement would interfere with her career."

"With her what?" The words slipped out of Julia's mouth before she could stop them, but she immediately recovered herself. "Yes, I see what she means of course."

"Naturally, I don't want to stand in her way. I mean, supposing after to-night she got a big offer for America I can quite see that she ought to be perfectly free to accept."

Her career! Julia smiled quietly to herself.

"You know, I do think you're a brick, the way you've behaved to her."

"Why?"

"Oh well, you know what women are!"

As he said this he slipped his arm round her waist and kissed her. She laughed outright.

"What an absurd little thing you are."

"How about a bit of love?"

"Don't be so silly."

"What is there silly about it? Don't you think we've been divorced long enough?"

"I'm all for irrevocable divorce. And what about Avice?"

"Oh, she's different. Come on."

"Has it slipped your memory that I've got a first night to-night?"

"There's plenty of time."

He put both arms round her and kissed her softly. She looked at him with mocking eyes. Suddenly she made up her mind.

"All right."

They got up and went into the bedroom. She took off her hat and slipped out of her dress. He held her in his arms as he had held her so often before. He kissed her closed eyes and the little breasts of which she was so proud. She gave him her body to do what he wanted with, but her spirit held aloof. She returned his kisses out of amiability, but she caught herself thinking of the part she was going to play that night. She seemed to be two persons, the mistress in her lover's embrace, and the actress who already saw in her mind's eye the vast vague dark audience and heard the shouts of applause as she stepped on to the stage. When, a little later, they lay side by side, he with his arm round her neck, she forgot about him so completely that she was quite surprised when he broke a long silence.

"Don't you care for me any more?"

She gave him a little hug.

"Of course, darling. I dote on you."

"You're so strange to-day."

She realised that he was disappointed. Poor little thing, she didn't want to hurt his feelings. He was very sweet really.

"With the first night before me I'm not really myself to-day. You mustn't mind."

When she came to the conclusion, quite definitely now, that she no longer cared two straws for him she could not help feeling a great pity for him. She stroked his cheek gently.

"Sweetie pie." ("I wonder if Michael remembered to have tea sent along to the queues. It doesn't cost much and they do appreciate it so enormously.") "You know, I really must get up. Miss Phillips is coming at six. Evie will be in a state, she won't be able to think what's happened to me."

She chattered brightly while she dressed. She was conscious, although she did not look at him, that Tom was vaguely uneasy. She put her hat on, then she took his face in both her hands and gave him a friendly kiss.

"Good-bye, my lamb. Have a good time to-night."

"Best of luck."

He smiled with some awkwardness. She perceived that he did not quite know what to make of her. Julia slipped out of the flat, and if she had not been England's leading actress, and a woman of hard on fifty, she would have hopped on one leg all the way down Stanhope Place till she got to her house. She was as pleased as Punch. She let herself in with her latchkey and closed the front door behind her.

"I dare say there's something in what Roger said. Love isn't worth all the fuss they make about it."

CHAPTER XXIX

FOUR hours later it was all over. The play went well from the beginning; the audience, notwithstanding the season a fashionable one, were pleased after the holidays to find themselves once more in a playhouse, and were ready to be amused. It was an auspicious beginning for the theatrical season. There had been great applause after each act and at the end a dozen curtains calls; Julia took two by herself, and even she was startled by the warmth of her reception. She had made the little halting speech, prepared beforehand, which the occasion demanded. There had been a final call of the entire company and then the orchestra had struck up the National Anthem. Julia, pleased, excited and happy, went to her dressing-room. She had never felt more sure of herself. She had never acted with greater brilliance, variety and resource. The play ended with a long tirade in which Julia, as the retired harlot, castigated the flippancy, the uselessness, the immorality of the idle set into which her marriage had brought her. It was two pages long, and there was not another actress in England who could have held the attention of the audience while she delivered it. With her exquisite timing, with the modulation of her beautiful voice, with her command of the gamut of emotions, she had succeeded by a miracle of technique in making it a thrilling, almost spectacular climax to the play. A violent action could not have been more exciting nor an unexpected dénouement more surprising. The whole cast had been excellent with the exception of Avice Crichton. Julia hummed in an undertone as she went into her dressing-room.

Michael followed her in almost at once.

"It looks like a winner all right." He threw his arms round her and kissed her. "By God, what a performance you gave."

"You weren't so bad yourself, dear."

"That's the sort of part I can play on my head," he answered carelessly, modest as usual about his own acting. "Did you hear them during your long speech? That ought to knock the critics."

"Oh, you know what they are. They'll give all their attention to the blasted play and then three lines at the end to me."

"You're the greatest actress in the world, darling, but, by God, you're a bitch."

Julia opened her eyes very wide in an expression of the most naïve surprise.

"Michael, what do you mean?"

"Don't look so innocent. You know perfectly well. Do you think you can cod an old trouper like me?"

He was looking at her with twinkling eyes, and it was very difficult for her not to burst out laughing.

"I am as innocent as a babe unborn."

"Come off it. If anyone ever deliberately killed a performance you killed Avice's. I couldn't be angry with you, it was so beautifully done."

Now Julia simply could not conceal the little smile that curled her lips. Praise is always grateful to the artist. Avice's one big scene was in the second act. It was with Julia, and Michael had rehearsed it so as to give it all to the girl. This was indeed what the play demanded and Julia, as always, had in rehearsals accepted his direction. To bring out the colour of her blue eyes and to emphasise her fair hair they had dressed Avice in pale blue. To contrast with this Julia had chosen a dress of an agreeable yellow. This she had worn at the dress rehearsal. But she had ordered another dress at the same time, of sparkling silver, and to the surprise of Michael and the consternation of Avice it was in this that she made her entrance in the second act. Its brilliance, the way it took the light, attracted the attention of the audience. Avice's blue looked drab by comparison. When they reached the important scene they were to have together Julia produced, as a conjurer produces a rabbit from his hat, a large handkerchief of scarlet chiffon and with this she played. She waved it, she spread it out as though to look at it, she screwed it up, she wiped her brow with it, she delicately blew her nose. The audience, fascinated, could not take their eyes away from the red rag. And she moved up stage so that Avice to speak to her had to turn her back on the audience, and when they were sitting on a sofa together she took her hand, in an impulsive way that seemed to the public exquisitely natural, and sitting well back herself forced Avice to turn her profile to the house. Julia had noticed early in rehearsals that in profile Avice had a sheep-like look. The author had given Avice lines to say that had so much amused the cast at the first rehearsal that they had all burst out laughing. Before the audience had quite realised how funny they were Julia had cut in with her reply, and the audience anxious to hear it suppressed their laughter. The scene which was devised to be extremely amusing took on a sardonic colour, and the character Avice played acquired a certain odiousness. Avice in her inexperience, not getting the laughs she had expected, was rattled; her voice grew hard and her gestures awkward. Julia took the scene away from her and played it with miraculous virtuosity. But her final stroke was accidental. Avice had a long speech to deliver, and Julia nervously screwed her red handkerchief into a ball; the action almost automatically suggested an expression; she looked at Avice with troubled eyes and two heavy tears rolled down her cheeks. You felt the shame with which the girl's flippancy affected her, and you saw her pain because her poor little ideals of uprightness, her hankering for goodness, were so brutally mocked. The episode lasted no more than a minute, but in that minute, by those tears and by the anguish of her look, Julia laid bare the sordid misery of the woman's life. That was the end of Avice.

"And I was such a damned fool, I thought of giving her a contract," said Michael.

"Why don't you?"

"When you've got your knife into her? Not on your life. You're a naughty little thing to be so jealous. You don't really think she means anything to me, do you? You ought to know by now that you're the only woman in the world for me."

Michael thought that Julia had played this trick on account of the rather violent flirtation he had been having with Avice, and though, of course, it was hard luck on Avice, he could not help being a trifle flattered.

"You old donkey," smiled Julia, knowing exactly what he was thinking and tickled to death at his mistake. "After all, you are the handsomest man in London."

"All that's as it may be. But I don't know what the author'll say. He's a conceited little ape and it's not a bit the scene he wrote."

"Oh, leave him to me. I'll fix him."

There was a knock at the door and it was the author himself who came in. With a cry of delight, Julia went up to him, threw her arms round his neck and kissed him on both cheeks.

"Are you pleased?"

"It looks like a success," he answered, but a trifle coldly.

"My dear, it'll run for a year." She placed her hands on his shoulders and looked him full in the face. "But you're a wicked, wicked man."

"I?"

"You almost ruined my performance. When I came to that bit in the second act and suddenly saw what it meant I nearly broke down. You knew what was in that scene, you're the author; why did you let us rehearse it all the time as if there was no more in it than appeared on the surface? We're only actors, how can you expect us to—to fathom your subtlety? It's the best scene in your play and I almost bungled it. No one in the world could have written it but you. Your play's brilliant, but in that scene there's more than brilliance, there's genius."

The author flushed. Julia looked at him with veneration. He felt shy and happy and proud.

("In twenty-four hours the mug'll think he really meant the scene to go like that.")

Michael beamed.

"Come along to my dressing-room and have a whisky and soda. I'm sure you need a drink after all that emotion."

They went out as Tom came in. Tom's face was red with excitement.

"My dear, it was grand. You were simply wonderful. Gosh, what a performance!"

"Did you like it? Avice was good, wasn't she?"

"No, rotten."

"My dear, what do you mean? I thought she was charming."

"You simply wiped the floor with her. She didn't even look pretty in the second act."

Avice's career!

"I say, what are you doing afterwards?"

"Dolly's giving a party for us."

"Can't you cut it and come along to supper with me? I'm madly in love with you."

"Oh, what nonsense. How can I let Dolly down?"

"Oh, do."

His eyes were eager. She could see that he desired her as he had never done before, and she rejoiced in her triumph. But she shook her head firmly. There was a sound in the corridor of a crowd of people talking, and they both knew that a troop of friends were forcing their way down the narrow passage to congratulate her.

"Damn all these people. God, how I want to kiss you. I'll ring you up in the morning."

The door burst open and Dolly, fat, perspiring and bubbling over with enthusiasm, swept in at the head of a throng that packed the dressing-room to suffocation. Julia submitted to being kissed by all and sundry. Among others were three or four well-known actresses, and they were prodigal of their praise. Julia gave a beautiful performance of unaffected modesty. The corridor was packed now with people who wanted to get at least a glimpse of her. Dolly had to fight her way out.

"Try not to be too late," she said to Julia. "It's going to be a heavenly party."

"I'll come as soon as ever I can."

At last the crowd was got rid of and Julia, having undressed, began to take off her make-up. Michael came in, wearing a dressing-gown.

"I say, Julia, you'll have to go to Dolly's party by yourself. I've got to see the libraries and I can't manage it. I'm going to sting them."

"Oh, all right."

"They're waiting for me now. See you in the morning."

He went out and she was left alone with Evie. The dress she had arranged to wear for Dolly's party was placed over a chair. Julia smeared her face with cleansing cream.

"Evie, Mr. Fennell will be ringing up to-morrow. Will you say I'm out."

Evie looked in the mirror and caught Julia's eyes.

"And if he rings up again?"

"I don't want to hurt his feelings, poor lamb, but I have a notion I shall be very much engaged for some time now."

Evie sniffed loudly, and with that rather disgusting habit of hers drew her forefinger across the bottom of her nose.

"I understand," she said dryly.

"I always said you weren't such a fool as you looked." Julia went on with her face. "What's that dress doing on that chair?"

"That? That's the dress you said you'd wear for the party."

"Put it away. I can't go to the party without Mr. Gosselyn."

"Since when?"

"Shut up, you old hag. Phone through and say that I've got a bad headache and had to go home to bed, but Mr. Gosselyn will come if he possibly can."

"The party's being given special for you. You can't let the poor old gal down like that!"

Julia stamped her feet.

"I don't want to go to a party. I won't go to a party."

"There's nothing for you to eat at home."

"I don't want to go home. I'll go and have supper at a restaurant."

"Who with?"

"By myself."

Evie gave her a puzzled glance.

"The play's a success, isn't it?"

"Yes. Everything's a success. I feel on the top of the world. I feel like a million dollars. I want to be alone and enjoy myself. Ring up the Berkeley and tell them to keep a table for one in the little room. They'll know what I mean."

"What's the matter with you?"

"I shall never in all my life have another moment like this. I'm not going to share it with anyone."

When Julia had got her face clean she left it. She neither painted her lips nor rouged her cheeks. She put on again the brown coat and skirt in which she had come to the theatre and the same hat. It was a felt hat with a brim, and this she pulled down over one eye so that it should hide as much of her face as possible. When she was ready she looked at herself in the glass.

"I look like a working dressmaker whose husband's left her, and who can blame him? I don't believe a soul would recognise me."

Evie had had the telephoning done from the stage-door, and when she came back Julia asked her if there were many people waiting for her there.

"About three 'undred I should say."

"Damn." She had a sudden desire to see nobody and be seen by nobody. She wanted just for one hour to be obscure. "Tell the fireman to let me out at the front and I'll take a taxi, and then as soon as I've got out let the crowd know there's no use in their waiting."

"God only knows what I 'ave to put up with," said Evie darkly.

"You old cow."

Julia took Evie's face in her hands and kissed her raddled cheeks; then slipped out of her dressing-room, on to the stage and through the iron door into the darkened auditorium.

Julia's simple disguise was evidently adequate, for when she came into the little room at the Berkeley of which she was peculiarly fond, the head-waiter did not immediately know her.

"Have you got a corner that you can squeeze me into?" she asked diffidently.

Her voice and a second glance told him who she was.

"Your favourite table is waiting for you, Miss Lambert. The message said you would be alone?" Julia nodded and he led her to a table in the corner of the room. "I hear you've had a big success to-night, Miss Lambert." How quickly good news travelled. "What can I order?"

The head-waiter was surprised that Julia should be having supper by herself, but the only emotion that it was his business to show clients was gratification at seeing them.

"I'm very tired, Angelo."

"A little caviare to begin with, madame, or some oysters?"

"Oysters, Angelo, but fat ones."

"I will choose them myself, Miss Lambert, and to follow?"

Julia gave a long sigh, for now she could, with a free conscience, order what she had had in mind ever since the end of the second act. She felt she deserved a treat to celebrate her triumph, and for once she meant to throw prudence to the winds.

"Grilled steak and onions, Angelo, fried potatoes, and a bottle of Bass. Give it me in a silver tankard."

She probably hadn't eaten fried potatoes for ten years. But what an occasion it was! By a happy chance on this day she had confirmed her hold on the public by a performance that she could only describe as scintillating, she had settled an old score, by one ingenious device disposing of Avice and making Tom see what a fool he had been, and best of all had proved to herself beyond all question that she was free from the irksome bonds that had oppressed her. Her thought flickered for an instant round Avice.

"Silly little thing to try to put a spoke in my wheel. I'll let her have her laughs to-morrow."

The oysters came and she ate them with enjoyment. She ate two pieces of brown bread and butter with the delicious sense of imperilling her immortal soul, and she took a long drink from the silver tankard.

"Beer, glorious beer," she murmured.

She could see Michael's long face if he knew what she was doing. Poor Michael who imagined she had killed Avice's scene because she thought he was too attentive to that foolish little blonde. Really, it was pitiful how stupid men were. They said women were vain; why, they were modest violets in comparison with men. She could not but laugh when she thought of Tom. He had wanted her that afternoon, he had wanted her still more that night. It was wonderful to think that he meant no more to her than a stage-hand. It gave one a grand feeling of confidence to be heart-whole.

The room in which she sat was connected by three archways with the big dining-room where they supped and danced; amid the crowd doubtless were a certain number who had been to the play. How surprised they would be if they knew that the quiet little woman in the corner of the adjoining room, her face half hidden by a felt hat, was Julia Lambert. It gave her a pleasant sense of independence to sit there unknown and unnoticed. They were acting a play for her and she was the audience. She caught brief glimpses of them as they passed the archway, young men and young women, young men and women not so young, men with bald heads and men with fat bellies, old harridans clinging desperately to their painted semblance of youth. Some were in love, and some were jealous, and some were indifferent.

Her steak arrived. It was cooked exactly as she liked it, and the onions were crisp and brown. She ate the fried potatoes delicately, with her fingers, savouring each one as though it were the passing moment that she would bid delay.

"What is love beside steak and onions?" she asked. It was enchanting to be alone and allow her mind to wander. She thought once more of Tom and spiritually shrugged a humorous shoulder. "It was an amusing experience."

It would certainly be useful to her one of these days. The sight of the dancers seen through the archway was so much like a scene in a play that she was reminded of a notion that she had first had in St. Malo. The agony that she had suffered when Tom deserted her recalled to her memory Racine's *Phèdre*, which she had studied as a girl with old Jane Taitbout. She read the play again. The torments that afflicted Theseus' queen were the torments that afflicted her, and she could not but think that there was a striking similarity in their situations. That was a part she could act; she knew what it felt like to be turned down by a young man one had a fancy for. Gosh, what a performance she could give! She knew why in the spring she had acted so badly that Michael had preferred to close down; it was because she was feeling the emotions she portrayed. That was no good. You had to have had the emotions, but you could only play them when you had got over them. She remembered that Charles had once said to her that the origin of poetry was emotion recollected in tranquillity. She didn't know anything about poetry, but it was certainly true about acting.

"Clever of poor old Charles to get hold of an original idea like that. It shows how wrong it is to judge people hastily. One thinks the aristocracy are a bunch of nit-wits, and then one of them suddenly comes out with something like that that's so damned good it takes your breath away."

There was no reason why she should not get some dramatist to do a translation of Racine's play for her, not in blank verse, of course, but in prose, or, if he insisted on verse, in short lines with rhymes at not too frequent intervals. She could manage that, and effectively. It was a good idea, there was no doubt about it, and she knew the clothes she would wear, not those flowing draperies in which Sarah swathed herself, but the short Greek tunic that she had seen on a bas-relief when she went to the British Museum with Charles.

"How funny things are! You go to those museums and galleries and think what a damned bore they are and then, when you least expect it, you find that something you've seen comes in useful. It shows art and all that isn't really waste of time."

Of course she had the legs for a tunic, but could one be tragic in one? This she thought about seriously for two or three minutes. When she was eating out her heart for the indifferent Hippolytus (and she giggled when she thought of Tom, in his Savile Row clothes, masquerading as a young Greek hunter) could she really get her effects without abundant draperies? The difficulty excited her. But then a thought crossed her mind that for a moment dashed her spirits.

"It's all very well, but where are the dramatists? Sarah had her Sardou, Duse her D'Annunzio. But who have I got? 'The Queen of Scots hath a bonnie bairn and I am but a barren stock.' "

She did not, however, let this melancholy reflection disturb her serenity for long. Her elation was indeed such that she felt capable of creating dramatists from the vast inane as Deucalion created men from the stones of the field.

"What nonsense that was that Roger talked the other day, and poor Charles, who seemed to take it seriously. He's a silly little prig, that's all." She indicated a gesture towards the dance room. The lights had been lowered, and from where she sat it looked more than ever like a scene in a play. "All the world's a stage, and all the men and women merely players. But there's the illusion, through that archway; it's we, the actors, who are the reality. That's the answer to Roger. They are our raw material. We are the meaning of their lives. We take their silly little emotions and turn them into art, out of them we create beauty, and their significance is that they form the audience we must have to fulfil ourselves. They are the instruments on which we play, and what is an instrument without somebody to play on it?"

The notion exhilarated her, and for a moment or two she savoured it with satisfaction. Her brain seemed miraculously lucid.

"Roger says we don't exist. Why, it's only we who do exist. They are the shadows and we give them substance. We are the symbols of all this confused, aimless struggling that they call life, and it's only the symbol which is real. They say acting is only make-believe. That make-believe is the only reality."

Thus Julia out of her own head framed anew the Platonic theory of ideas. It filled her with exultation. She felt a sudden wave of friendliness for that immense anonymous public who had being only to give her opportunity to express herself. Aloof on her mountain top she considered the innumerable activities of men. She had a wonderful sense of freedom from all earthly ties, and it was such an ecstasy that nothing in comparison with it had any value. She felt like a spirit in heaven.

The head-waiter came up to her with an ingratiating smile.

"Everything all right, Miss Lambert?"

"Lovely. You know, it's strange how people differ. Mrs. Siddons was a rare one for chops; I'm not a bit like her in that; I'm a rare one for steaks."

THE MOON AND SIXPENCE

The Moon and Sixpence

CHAPTER I

I CONFESS that when first I made acquaintance with Charles Strickland I never for a moment discerned that there was in him anything out of the ordinary. Yet now few will be found to deny his greatness. I do not speak of that greatness which is achieved by the fortunate politician or the successful soldier; that is a quality which belongs to the place he occupies rather than to the man; and a change of circumstances reduces it to very discreet proportions. The Prime Minister out of office is seen, too often, to have been but a pompous rhetorician, and the General without an army is but the tame hero of a market town. The greatness of Charles Strickland was authentic. It may be that you do not like his art, but at all events you can hardly refuse it the tribute of your interest. He disturbs and arrests. The time has passed when he was an object of ridicule, and it is no longer a mark of eccentricity to defend or of perversity to extol him. His faults are accepted as the necessary complement to his merits. It is still possible to discuss his place in art, and the adulation of his admirers is perhaps no less capricious than the disparagement of his detractors; but one thing can never be doubtful, and that is that he had genius. To my mind the most interesting thing in art is the personality of the artist; and if that is singular, I am willing to excuse a thousand faults. I suppose Velasquez was a better painter than El Greco, but custom stales one's admiration for him: the Cretan, sensual and tragic, proffers the mystery of his soul like a standing sacrifice. The artist, painter, poet, or musician, by his decoration, sublime or beautiful, satisfies the aesthetic sense; but that is akin to the sexual instinct, and shares its barbarity: he lays before you also the greater gift of himself. To pursue his secret has something of the fascination of a detective story. It is a riddle which shares with the universe the merit of having no answer. The most insignificant of Strickland's works suggests a personality which is strange, tormented, and complex; and it is this surely which prevents even those who do not like his pictures from being indifferent to them;

it is this which has excited so curious an interest in his life and character.

It was not till four years after Strickland's death that Maurice Huret wrote that article in the *Mercure de France* which rescued the unknown painter from oblivion and blazed the trail which succeeding writers, with more or less docility, have followed. For a long time no critic has enjoyed in France a more incontestable authority, and it was impossible not to be impressed by the claims he made; they seemed extravagant; but later judgments have confirmed his estimate, and the reputation of Charles Strickland is now firmly established on the lines which he laid down. The rise of this reputation is one of the most romantic incidents in the history of art. But I do not propose to deal with Charles Strickland's work except in so far as it touches upon his character. I cannot agree with the painters who claim superciliously that the layman can understand nothing of painting, and that he can best show his appreciation of their works by silence and a cheque-book. It is a grotesque misapprehension which sees in art no more than a craft comprehensible perfectly only to the craftsman; art is a manifestation of emotion, and emotion speaks a language that all may understand. But I will allow that the critic who has not a practical knowledge of technique is seldom able to say anything on the subject of real value, and my ignorance of painting is extreme. Fortunately, there is no need for me to risk the adventure, since my friend Mr. Edward Leggatt, an able writer as well as an admirable painter, has exhaustively discussed Charles Strickland's work in a little book* which is a charming example of a style, for the most part, less happily cultivated in England than in France.

Maurice Huret in his famous article gave an outline of Charles Strickland's life which was well calculated to whet the appetites of the inquiring. With his disinterested passion for art, he had a real desire to call the attention of the wise to a talent which was in the highest degree original; but he was too good a journalist to be unaware that the "human interest" would enable him more easily to effect his purpose. And when such as had come in contact with Strickland in the past, writers who had known him in London, painters who had met him in the cafés of Montmartre, discovered to their amazement that where they had seen but an unsuccessful artist, like another, authentic genius had rubbed shoulders with

* "A Modern Artist: Notes on the Work of Charles Strickland," by Edward Leggatt, A.R.H.A. Martin Secker, 1917.

them, there began to appear in the magazines of France and America a succession of articles, the reminiscences of one, the appreciation of another, which added to Strickland's notoriety, and fed without satisfying the curiosity of the public. The subject was grateful, and the industrious Weitbrecht-Rotholz in his imposing monograph* has been able to give a remarkable list of authorities.

The faculty for myth is innate in the human race. It seizes with avidity upon any incidents, surprising or mysterious, in the career of those who have at all distinguished themselves from their fellows, and invents a legend to which it then attaches a fanatical belief. It is the protest of romance against the commonplace of life. The incidents of the legend become the hero's surest passport to immortality. The ironic philosopher reflects with a smile that Sir Walter Raleigh is more safely enshrined in the memory of mankind because he set his cloak for the Virgin Queen to walk on than because he carried the English name to undiscovered countries. Charles Strickland lived obscurely. He made enemies rather than friends. It is not strange, then, that those who wrote of him should have eked out their scanty recollections with a lively fancy, and it is evident that there was enough in the little that was known of him to give opportunity to the romantic scribe; there was much in his life which was strange and terrible, in his character something outrageous, and in his fate not a little that was pathetic. In due course a legend arose of such circumstantiality that the wise historian would hesitate to attack it.

But a wise historian is precisely what the Rev. Robert Strickland is not. He wrote his biography† avowedly to "remove certain misconceptions which had gained currency" in regard to the later part of his father's life, and which had "caused considerable pain to persons still living". It is obvious that there was much in the commonly received account of Strickland's life to embarrass a respectable family. I have read this work with a good deal of amusement, and upon this I congratulate myself, since it is colourless and dull. Mr. Strickland has drawn the portrait of an excellent husband and father, a man of kindly temper, industrious habits, and moral disposition. The modern clergyman has

---

* "Karl Strickland: sein Leben und seine Kunst," by Hugo Weitbrecht-Rotholz, Ph.D. Schwingel und Hanisch. Leipzig, 1914.
† "Strickland: The Man and His Work," by his son, Robert Strickland. Wm. Heinemann, 1913.

acquired in his study of the science which I believe is called exegesis an astonishing facility for explaining things away, but the subtlety with which the Rev. Robert Strickland has "interpreted" all the facts in his father's life which a dutiful son might find it inconvenient to remember must surely lead him in the fullness of time to the highest dignities of the Church. I see already his muscular calves encased in the gaiters episcopal. It was a hazardous though maybe a gallant thing to do, since it is probable that the legend commonly received has had no small share in the growth of Strickland's reputation; for there are many who have been attracted to his art by the detestation in which they held his character or the compassion with which they regarded his death; and the son's well-meaning efforts threw a singular chill upon the father's admirers. It is due to no accident that when one of his most important works, *The Woman of Samaria*,* was sold at Christie's shortly after the discussion which followed the publication of Mr. Strickland's biography, it fetched £235 less than it had done nine months before, when it was bought by the distinguished collector whose sudden death had brought it once more under the hammer. Perhaps Charles Strickland's power and originality would scarcely have sufficed to turn the scale if the remarkable mythopœic faculty of mankind had not brushed aside with impatience a story which disappointed all its craving for the extraordinary. And presently Dr. Weitbrecht-Rotholz produced the work which finally set at rest the misgivings of all lovers of art.

Dr. Weitbrecht-Rotholz belongs to that school of historians which believes that human nature is not only about as bad as it can be, but a great deal worse; and certainly the reader is safer of entertainment in their hands than in those of the writers who take a malicious pleasure in representing the great figures of romance as patterns of the domestic virtues. For my part, I should be sorry to think that there was nothing between Antony and Cleopatra but an economic situation; and it will require a great deal more evidence than is ever likely to be available, thank God, to persuade me that Tiberius was as blameless a monarch as King George V. Dr. Weitbrecht-Rotholz has dealt in such terms with the Rev. Robert Strickland's innocent biography that it is difficult to avoid feeling a certain sympathy for the unlucky parson. His decent

* This was described in Christie's catalogue as follows: "A nude woman, a native of the Society Islands, is lying on the ground beside a brook. Behind is a tropical landscape with palm-trees, bananas, etc. 60 in. × 48 in."

reticence is branded as hypocrisy, his circumlocutions are roundly called lies, and his silence is vilified as treachery. And on the strength of peccadillos, reprehensible in an author but excusable in a son, the Anglo-Saxon race is accused of prudishness, humbug, pretentiousness, deceit, cunning, and bad cooking. Personally I think it was rash of Mr. Strickland, in refuting the account which had gained belief of a certain "unpleasantness" between his father and mother, to state that Charles Strickland in a letter written from Paris had described her as "an excellent woman", since Dr. Weitbrecht-Rotholz was able to print the letter in facsimile, and it appears that the passage referred to ran in fact as follows: *God damn my wife. She is an excellent woman. I wish she was in hell.* It is not thus that the Church in its great days dealt with evidence that was unwelcome.

Dr. Weitbrecht-Rotholz was an enthusiastic admirer of Charles Strickland, and there was no danger that he would whitewash him. He had an unerring eye for the despicable motive in actions that had all the appearance of innocence. He was a psychopathologist as well as a student of art, and the subconscious had few secrets from him. No mystic ever saw deeper meaning in common things. The mystic sees the ineffable and the psychopathologist the unspeakable. There is a singular fascination in watching the eagerness with which the learned author ferrets out every circumstance which may throw discredit on his hero. His heart warms to him when he can bring forward some example of cruelty or meanness, and he exults like an inquisitor at the *auto-da-fé* of an heretic when with some forgotten story he can confound the filial piety of the Rev. Robert Strickland. His industry has been amazing. Nothing has been too small to escape him, and you may be sure that if Charles Strickland left a laundry bill unpaid it will be given you *in extenso*, and if he forbore to return a borrowed half-crown no detail of the transaction will be omitted.

CHAPTER II

WHEN so much has been written about Charles Strickland, it may seem unnecessary that I should write more. A painter's monument is his work. It is true I knew him more intimately than most: I met him first before ever he became a painter, and I saw him not infrequently during the difficult years he spent in Paris; but I do not suppose I should ever have set down my recollections if the hazards of the war had not taken me to Tahiti. There, as is notorious, he spent the last years of his life; and there I came across persons who were familiar with him. I find myself in a position to throw light on just that part of his tragic career which has remained most obscure. If they who believe in Strickland's greatness are right, the personal narratives of such as knew him in the flesh can hardly be superfluous. What would we not give for the reminiscences of someone who had been as intimately acquainted with El Greco as I was with Strickland?

But I seek refuge in no such excuses. I forget who it was that recommended men for their souls' good to do each day two things they disliked: it was a wise man, and it is a precept that I have followed scrupulously; for every day I have got up and I have gone to bed. But there is in my nature a strain of asceticism, and I have subjected my flesh each week to a more severe mortification. I have never failed to read the Literary Supplement of *The Times*. It is a salutary discipline to consider the vast number of books that are written, the fair hopes with which their authors see them published, and the fate which awaits them. What chance is there that any book will make its way among that multitude? And the successful books are but the successes of a season. Heaven knows what pains the author has been at, what bitter experiences he has endured and what heartache suffered, to give some chance reader a few hours' relaxation or to while away the tedium of a journey. And if I may judge from the reviews, many of these books are well and carefully written; much thought has gone to their composition; to some even has been given the anxious labour of a lifetime. The moral I draw is that the writer should seek his reward in the pleasure of his work and in release from the burden of his thought; and, indifferent to aught else, care nothing for praise or censure, failure or success.

Now the war has come, bringing with it a new attitude. Youth has turned to gods we of an earlier day knew not, and it is possible to see already the direction in which those who come after us will move. The younger generation, conscious of strength and tumultuous, have done with knocking at the door; they have burst in and seated themselves in our seats. The air is noisy with their shouts. Of their elders some, by imitating the antics of youth, strive to persuade themselves that their day is not yet over; they shout with the lustiest, but the war-cry sounds hollow in their mouth; they are like poor wantons attempting with pencil, paint and powder, with shrill gaiety, to recover the illusion of their spring. The wiser go their way with a decent grace. In their chastened smile is an indulgent mockery. They remember that they too trod down a sated generation, with just such clamour and with just such scorn, and they foresee that these brave torch-bearers will presently yield their place also. There is no last word. The new evangel was old when Nineveh reared her greatness to the sky. These gallant words which seemed so novel to those that speak them were said in accents scarcely changed a hundred times before. The pendulum swings backwards and forwards. The circle is ever travelled anew.

Sometimes a man survives a considerable time from an era in which he had his place into one which is strange to him, and then the curious are offered one of the most singular spectacles in the human comedy. Who now, for example, thinks of George Crabbe? He was a famous poet in his day, and the world re-cognised his genius with a unanimity which the greater complexity of modern life has rendered infrequent. He had learnt his craft at the school of Alexander Pope, and he wrote moral stories in rhymed couplets. Then came the French Revolution and the Napoleonic Wars, and the poets sang new songs. Mr. Crabbe continued to write moral stories in rhymed couplets. I think he must have read the verse of these young men who were making so great a stir in the world, and I fancy he found it poor stuff. Of course, much of it was. But the odes of Keats and of Words-worth, a poem or two by Coleridge, a few more by Shelley, discovered vast realms of the spirit that none had explored before. Mr. Crabbe was as dead as mutton, but Mr. Crabbe continued to write moral stories in rhymed couplets. I have read desultorily the writings of the younger generation. It may be that among them a more fervid Keats, a more ethereal Shelley, has already published numbers the world will willingly remember. I cannot tell. I admire their polish—their youth is already so accomplished that it seems absurd to speak of promise—I marvel at the felicity of their style; but with all their copiousness (their vocabulary suggests that they fingered Roget's *Thesaurus* in their cradles) they say nothing to me; to my mind they know too much and feel too obviously; I cannot stomach the heartiness with which they slap me on the back or the emotion with which they hurl themselves on my bosom; their passion seems to me a little anæmic and their dreams a trifle dull. I do not like them. I am on the shelf. I will continue to write moral stories in rhymed couplets. But I should be thrice a fool if I did it for aught but my own entertainment.

CHAPTER III

But all this is by the way.

I was very young when I wrote my first book. By a lucky chance it excited attention, and various persons sought my acquaintance.

It is not without melancholy that I wander among my re-collections of the world of letters in London when first, bashful but eager, I was introduced to it. It is long since I frequented it, and if the novels that describe its present singularities are accurate, much in it is now changed. The venue is different. Chelsea and Bloomsbury have taken the place of Hampstead, Notting Hill Gate, and High Street, Kensington. Then it was a distinction to be under forty, but now to be more than twenty-five is absurd. I think in those days we were a little shy of our emotions, and the fear of ridicule tempered the more obvious forms of pretentiousness. I do not believe that there was in that genteel Bohemia an intensive culture of chastity, but I do not remember so crude a promiscuity as seems to be practised in the present day. We did not think it hypocritical to draw over our vagaries the curtain of a decent silence. The spade was not invariably called a bloody shovel. Woman had not yet altogether come into her own.

I lived near Victoria Station, and I recall long excursions by bus to the hospitable houses of the literary. In my timidity I wandered up and down the street while I screwed up my courage to ring the bell; and then, sick with apprehension, was ushered into an airless room full of people. I was introduced to this celebrated person after that one, and the kind words they said about my book made me excessively uncomfortable. I felt they expected me to say clever things, and I never could think of any till after the party was over. I tried to conceal my embarrassment by handing round cups of tea and rather ill-cut bread-and-butter. I wanted no one to take notice of me, so that I could observe these famous creatures at my ease and listen to the clever things they said.

I have a recollection of large, unbending women with great noses and rapacious eyes, who wore their clothes as though they were armour; and of little, mouse-like spinsters, with soft voices and a shrewd glance. I never ceased to be fascinated by their persistence in eating buttered toast with their gloves on, and I observed with admiration the unconcern with which they wiped their fingers on their chair when they thought no one was looking. It must have been bad for the furniture, but I suppose the hostess took her revenge on the furniture of her friends when, in turn, she visited them. Some of them were dressed fashionably, and they said they couldn't for the life of them see why you should be dowdy just because you had written a novel; if you had a neat figure you might as well make the most of it, and a smart shoe on a small foot had never prevented an editor from taking your "stuff". But others thought this frivolous, and they wore "art fabrics" and barbaric jewellery. The men were seldom eccentric in appearance. They tried to look as little like authors as possible. They wished to be taken for men of the world, and could have passed anywhere for the managing clerks of a City firm. They always seemed a little tired. I had never known writers before, and I found them very strange, but I do not think they ever seemed to me quite real.

I remember that I thought their conversation brilliant, and I used to listen with astonishment to the stinging humour with which they would tear a brother-author to pieces the moment that his back was turned. The artist has this advantage over the rest of the world, that his friends offer not only their appearance and their character to his satire, but also their work. I despaired of ever expressing myself with such aptness or with such fluency. In those days conversation was still cultivated as an art; a neat repartee was more highly valued than the crackling of thorns under a pot; and the epigram, not yet a mechanical appliance by which the dull may achieve a semblance of wit, gave sprightliness to the small talk of the urbane. It is sad that I can remember nothing of all this scintillation. But I think the conversation never settled down so comfortably as when it turned to the details of the trade which was the other side of the art we practised. When we had done discussing the merits of the latest book, it was natural to wonder how many copies had been sold, what advance the author had received, and how much he was likely to make out of it. Then we would speak of this publisher and of that, comparing the generosity of one with the meanness of another; we would argue whether it was better to go to one who gave handsome royalties or to another who "pushed" a book for all it was worth. Some advertised badly and some well. Some were modern and some were old-fashioned. Then we would talk of agents and the offers they had obtained for us; of editors and the sort of contributions they welcomed, how much they paid a thousand, and whether they paid promptly or otherwise. To me it was all very romantic. It gave me an intimate sense of being a member of some mystic brotherhood.

CHAPTER IV

No one was kinder to me at that time than Rose Waterford. She combined a masculine intelligence with a feminine perversity, and the novels she wrote were original and disconcerting. It was at her house one day that I met Charles Strickland's wife. Miss Waterford was giving a tea-party, and her small room was more than usually full. Everyone seemed to be talking, and I, sitting in silence, felt awkward; but I was too shy to break into any of the groups that seemed absorbed in their own affairs. Miss Waterford was a good hostess, and seeing my embarrassment came up to me.

"I want you to talk to Mrs. Strickland," she said. "She's raving about your book."

"What does she do?" I asked.

I was conscious of my ignorance, and if Mrs. Strickland was a well-known writer I thought it as well to ascertain the fact before I spoke to her.

Rose Waterford cast down her eyes demurely to give greater effect to her reply.

"She gives luncheon-parties. You've only got to roar a little, and she'll ask you."

Rose Waterford was a cynic. She looked upon life as an opportunity for writing novels and the public as her raw material. Now and then she invited members of it to her house if they showed an appreciation of her talent and entertained with proper lavishness. She held their weakness for lions in good-humoured contempt, but played to them her part of the distinguished woman of letters with decorum.

I was led up to Mrs. Strickland, and for ten minutes we talked together. I noticed nothing about her except that she had a pleasant voice. She had a flat in Westminster, overlooking the

unfinished cathedral, and because we lived in the same neighbourhood we felt friendly disposed to one another. The Army and
Navy Stores are a bond of union between all who dwell between
the river and St. James's Park. Mrs. Strickland asked me for my
address, and a few days later I received an invitation to luncheon.

My engagements were few, and I was glad to accept. When I
arrived, a little late, because in my fear of being too early I had
walked three times round the cathedral, I found the party already
complete. Miss Waterford was there and Mrs. Jay, Richard
Twining and George Road. We were all writers. It was a fine day,
early in spring, and we were in a good humour. We talked about a
hundred things. Miss Waterford, torn between the æstheticism of
her early youth, when she used to go to parties in sage green,
holding a daffodil, and the flippancy of her maturer years, which
tended to high heels and Paris frocks, wore a new hat. It put her in
high spirits. I had never heard her more malicious about our
common friends. Mrs. Jay, aware that impropriety is the soul of
wit, made observations in tones hardly above a whisper that might
well have tinged the snowy table-cloth with a rosy hue. Richard
Twining bubbled over with quaint absurdities, and George Road,
conscious that he need not exhibit a brilliancy which was almost a
byword, opened his mouth only to put food into it. Mrs. Strickland did not talk much, but she had a pleasant gift for keeping the
conversation general; and when there was a pause she threw in just
the right remark to set it going once more. She was a woman of
thirty-seven, rather tall, and plump, without being fat; she was not
pretty, but her face was pleasing, chiefly, perhaps, on account of
her kind brown eyes. Her skin was rather sallow. Her dark hair
was elaborately dressed. She was the only woman of the three
whose face was free of make-up, and by contrast with the others
she seemed simple and unaffected.

The dining-room was in the good taste of the period. It was
very severe. There was a high dado of white wood and a green
paper on which were etchings of Whistler in neat black frames.
The green curtains, with their peacock design, hung in straight
lines, and the green carpet, in the pattern of which pale rabbits
frolicked among leafy trees, suggested the influence of William
Morris. There was blue delf on the chimney-piece. At that time
there must have been five hundred dining-rooms in London
decorated in exactly the same manner. It was chaste, artistic, and
dull.

When we left I walked away with Miss Waterford, and the fine day and her new hat persuaded us to saunter through the Park.

"That was a very nice party," I said.

"Did you think the food was good? I told her that if she wanted writers she must feed them well."

"Admirable advice," I answered. "But why does she want them?"

Miss Waterford shrugged her shoulders.

"She finds them amusing. She wants to be in the movement. I fancy she's rather simple, poor dear, and she thinks we're all wonderful. After all, it pleases her to ask us to luncheon, and it doesn't hurt us. I like her for it."

Looking back, I think that Mrs. Strickland was the most harmless of all the lion-hunters that pursue their quarry from the rarefied heights of Hampstead to the nethermost studios of Cheyne Walk. She had led a very quiet youth in the country, and the books that came down from Mudie's Library brought with them not only their own romance, but the romance of London. She had a real passion for reading (rare in her kind, who for the most part are more interested in the author than in his book, in the painter than in his pictures), and she invented a world of the imagination in which she lived with a freedom she never acquired in the world of every day. When she came to know writers it was like adventuring upon a stage which till then she had only known from the other side of the footlights. She saw them dramatically, and really seemed herself to live a larger life because she entertained them and visited them in their fastnesses. She accepted the rules with which they played the game of life as valid for them, but never for a moment thought of regulating her own conduct in accordance with them. Their moral eccentricities, like their oddities of dress, their wild theories and paradoxes, were an entertainment which amused her, but had not the slightest influence on her convictions.

"Is there a Mr. Strickland?" I asked.

"Oh yes; he's something in the city. I believe he's a stockbroker. He's very dull."

"Are they good friends?"

"They adore one another. You'll meet him if you dine there. But she doesn't often have people to dinner. He's very quiet. He's not in the least interested in literature or the arts."

"Why do nice women marry dull men?"

"Because intelligent men won't marry nice women."

I could not think of any retort to this, so I asked if Mrs. Strickland had children.

"Yes; she has a boy and a girl. They're both at school."

The subject was exhausted, and we began to talk of other things.

CHAPTER V

DURING the summer I met Mrs. Strickland not infrequently. I went now and then to pleasant little luncheons at her flat, and to rather more formidable tea-parties. We took a fancy to one another. I was very young, and perhaps she liked the idea of guiding my virgin steps on the hard road of letters; while for me it was pleasant to have someone I could go to with my small troubles, certain of an attentive ear and reasonable counsel. Mrs. Strickland had the gift of sympathy. It is a charming faculty, but one often abused by those who are conscious of its possession: for there is something ghoulish in the avidity with which they will pounce upon the misfortune of their friends so that they may exercise their dexterity. It gushes forth like an oil-well, and the sympathetic pour out their sympathy with an abandon that is sometimes embarrassing to their victims. There are bosoms on which so many tears have been shed that I cannot bedew them with mine. Mrs. Strickland used her advantage with tact. You felt that you obliged her by accepting her sympathy. When, in the enthusiasm of my youth, I remarked on this to Rose Waterford, she said:

"Milk is very nice, especially with a drop of brandy in it, but the domestic cow is only too glad to be rid of it. A swollen udder is very uncomfortable."

Rose Waterford had a blistering tongue. No one could say such bitter things; on the other hand, no one could do more charming ones.

There was another thing I liked in Mrs. Strickland. She managed her surroundings with elegance. Her flat was always neat and cheerful, gay with flowers, and the chintzes in the drawing-room, notwithstanding their severe design, were bright and pretty. The meals in the artistic little dining-room were pleasant; the table looked nice, the two maids were trim and comely, the food was well cooked. It was impossible not to see that Mrs. Strickland was an excellent housekeeper. And you felt sure that she was an admirable mother. There were photographs in the drawing-room of her son and daughter. The son—his name was Robert—was a boy of sixteen at Rugby; and you saw him in flannels and a cricket cap, and again in a tail-coat and a stand-up collar. He had his mother's candid brow and fine, reflective eyes. He looked clean, healthy, and normal.

"I don't know that he's very clever," she said one day, when I was looking at the photograph, "but I know he's good. He has a charming character."

The daughter was fourteen. Her hair, thick and dark like her mother's, fell over her shoulders in fine profusion, and she had the same kindly expression and sedate, untroubled eyes.

"They're both of them the image of you," I said.

"Yes; I think they are more like me than their father."

"Why have you never let me meet him?" I asked.

"Would you like to?"

She smiled, her smile was really very sweet, and she blushed a little; it was singular that a woman of that age should flush so readily. Perhaps her naïveté was her greatest charm.

"You know, he's not at all literary," she said. "He's a perfect philistine."

She said this not disparagingly, but affectionately rather, as though, by acknowledging the worst about him, she wished to protect him from the aspersions of her friends.

"He's on the Stock Exchange, and he's a typical broker. I think he'd bore you to death."

"Does he bore you?" I asked.

"You see, I happen to be his wife. I'm very fond of him."

She smiled to cover her shyness, and I fancied she had a fear that I would make the sort of gibe that such a confession could hardly have failed to elicit from Rose Waterford. She hesitated a little. Her eyes grew tender.

"He doesn't pretend to be a genius. He doesn't even make much money on the Stock Exchange. But he's awfully good and kind."

"I think I should like him very much."

"I'll ask you to dine with us quietly some time, but mind, you come at your own risk; don't blame me if you have a very dull evening."

CHAPTER VI

BUT when at last I met Charles Strickland, it was under circumstances which allowed me to do no more than just make his acquaintance. One morning Mrs. Strickland sent me round a note to say that she was giving a dinner-party that evening, and one of her guests had failed her. She asked me to stop the gap. She wrote:

It's only decent to warn you that you will be bored to extinction. It was a thoroughly dull party from the beginning, but if you will come I shall be uncommonly grateful. And you and I can have a little chat by ourselves.

It was only neighbourly to accept.

When Mrs. Strickland introduced me to her husband, he gave me a rather indifferent hand to shake. Turning to him gaily, she attempted a small jest.

"I asked him to show him that I really had a husband. I think he was beginning to doubt it."

Strickland gave the polite little laugh with which people acknowledge a facetiousness in which they see nothing funny, but did not speak. New arrivals claimed my host's attention, and I was left to myself. When at last we were all assembled, waiting for dinner to be announced, I reflected, while I chatted with the woman I had been asked to "take in", that civilised man practises a strange ingenuity in wasting on tedious exercises the brief span of his life. It was the kind of party which makes you wonder why the hostess has troubled to bid her guests, and why the guests have troubled to come. There were ten people. They met with indifference, and would part with relief. It was, of course, a purely social function. The Stricklands "owed" dinners to a number of persons, whom they took no interest in, and so had asked them; these persons had accepted. Why? To avoid the tedium of dining tête-à-tête, to give their servants a rest, because there was no reason to refuse, because they were "owed" a dinner.

The dining-room was inconveniently crowded. There was a K.C. and his wife, a Government official and his wife, Mrs. Strickland's sister and her husband, Colonel MacAndrew, and the wife of a Member of Parliament. It was because the Member of

Parliament found that he could not leave the House that I had been invited. The respectability of the party was portentous. The women were too nice to be well dressed, and too sure of their position to be amusing. The men were solid. There was about all of them an air of well-satisfied prosperity.

Everyone talked a little louder than natural in an instinctive desire to make the party go, and there was a great deal of noise in the room. But there was no general conversation. Each one talked to his neighbour; to his neighbour on the right during the soup, fish and entrée; to his neighbour on the left during the roast, sweet, and savoury. They talked of the political situation and of golf, of their children and the latest play, of the pictures at the Royal Academy, of the weather and their plans for the holidays. There was never a pause, and the noise grew louder. Mrs. Strickland might congratulate herself that her party was a success. Her husband played his part with decorum. Perhaps he did not talk very much, and I fancied there was toward the end a look of fatigue in the faces of the women on either side of him. They were finding him too heavy. Once or twice Mrs. Strickland's eyes rested on him somewhat anxiously.

At last she rose and shepherded the ladies out of the room. Strickland shut the door behind her, and, moving to the other end of the table, took his place between the K.C. and the Government official. He passed round the port again and handed us cigars. The K.C. remarked on the excellence of the wine, and Strickland told us where he got it. We began to chat about vintages and tobacco. The K.C. told us of a case he was engaged in, and the colonel talked about polo. I had nothing to say and so sat silent, trying politely to show interest in the conversation; and because I thought no one was in the least concerned with me, examined Strickland at my ease. He was bigger than I expected; I do not know why I had imagined him slender and of insignificant appearance; in point of fact, he was broad and heavy, with large hands and feet, and he wore his evening clothes clumsily. He gave you somewhat the idea of a coachman dressed up for the occasion. He was a man of forty, not good-looking, and yet not ugly, for his features were rather good; but they were all a little larger than life-size, and the effect was ungainly. He was clean-shaven, and his large face looked uncomfortably naked. His hair was reddish, cut very short, and his eyes were small, blue or grey. He looked commonplace. I no longer wondered that Mrs. Strickland felt a certain embarrassment about him; he was scarcely a credit to a woman who wanted to make herself a position in the world of art and letters. It was obvious that he had no social gifts, but these a man can do without; he had no eccentricity even, to take him out of the common run; he was just a good, dull, honest, plain man. One would admire his excellent qualities but avoid his company. He was null. He was probably a worthy member of society, a good husband and father, an honest broker, but there was no reason to waste one's time over him.

CHAPTER VII

THE season was drawing to its dusty end, and everyone I knew was arranging to go away. Mrs. Strickland was taking her family to the coast of Norfolk, so that the children might have the sea and her husband golf. We said good-bye to one another, and arranged to meet in the autumn. But on my last day in town, coming out of the Stores, I met her with her son and daughter; like myself, she had been making her final purchases before leaving London, and we were both hot and tired. I proposed that we should all go and eat ices in the Park.

I think Mrs. Strickland was glad to show me her children, and she accepted my invitation with alacrity. They were even more attractive than their photographs had suggested, and she was right to be proud of them. I was young enough for them not to feel shy, and they chattered merrily about one thing and another. They were extraordinarily nice, healthy young children. It was very agreeable under the trees.

When in an hour they crowded into a cab to go home, I strolled idly to my club. I was perhaps a little lonely, and it was with a touch of envy that I thought of the pleasant family life of which I had had a glimpse. They seemed devoted to one another. They had little private jokes of their own which, unintelligible to the outsider, amused them enormously. Perhaps Charles Strickland was dull, judged by a standard that demanded above all things verbal scintillation; but his intelligence was adequate to his surroundings, and that is a passport, not only to reasonable success, but still more to happiness. Mrs. Strickland was a charming woman, and she loved him. I pictured their lives, troubled by no untoward adventure, honest, decent, and, by reason of those two upstanding, pleasant children, so obviously destined to carry on the normal traditions of their race and station, not without significance. They would grow old insensibly; they would see their son and daughter come to years of reason, marry in due course—the one a pretty girl, future mother of healthy children; the other a handsome, manly fellow, obviously a soldier; and at last, prosperous in their dignified retirement, beloved by their descendants, after a happy, not unuseful life, in the fullness of their age they would sink into the grave.

That must be the story of innumerable couples, and the pattern of life it offers has a homely grace. It reminds you of a placid rivulet, meandering smoothly through green pastures and shaded by pleasant trees, till at last it falls into the vasty sea; but the sea is so calm, so silent, so indifferent, that you are troubled suddenly by a vague uneasiness. Perhaps it is only a kink in my nature, strong in me even in those days, that I felt in such an existence, the share of the great majority, something amiss. I recognised its social value, I saw its ordered happiness, but a fever in my blood asked for a wilder course. There seemed to me something alarming in such easy delights. In my heart was a desire to live more danger-ously. I was not unprepared for jagged rocks and treacherous shoals if I could only have change—change and the excitement of the unforeseen.

CHAPTER VIII

On reading over what I have written of the Stricklands, I am conscious that they must seem shadowy. I have been able to invest them with none of those characteristics which make the persons of a book exist with a real life of their own; and, wonder-ing if the fault is mine, I rack my brains to remember idiosyncrasies which might lend them vividness. I feel that by dwelling on some trick of speech or some queer habit I should be able to give them a significance peculiar to themselves. As they stand they are like the figures in an old tapestry; they do not separate themselves from the background, and at a distance seem to lose their pattern, so that you have little but a pleasing piece of colour. My only excuse is that the impression they made on me was no other.

There was just that shadowiness about them which you find in people whose lives are part of the social organism, so that they exist in it and by it only. They are like cells in the body, essential, but, so long as they remain healthy, engulfed in the momentous whole. The Stricklands were an average family in the middle class. A pleasant, hospitable woman, with a harmless craze for the small lions of literary society; a rather dull man, doing his duty in that state of life in which a merciful Providence had placed him; two nice-looking, healthy children. Nothing could be more ordinary. I do not know that there was anything about them to excite the attention of the curious.

When I reflect on all that happened later, I ask myself if I was thick-witted not to see that there was in Charles Strickland at least something out of the common. Perhaps. I think that I have gathered in the years that intervene between then and now a fair knowledge of mankind, but even if when I first met the Stricklands I had the experience which I have now, I do not believe that I should have judged them differently. But because I have learnt that man is incalculable, I should not at this time of day be so surprised by the news that reached me when in the early autumn I returned to London.

I had not been back twenty-four hours before I ran across Rose Waterford in Jermyn Street.

"You look very gay and sprightly," I said. "What's the matter with you?"

She smiled, and her eyes shone with a malice I knew already. It meant that she had heard some scandal about one of her friends, and the instinct of the literary woman was all alert.

"You did meet Charles Strickland, didn't you?"

Not only her face, but her whole body, gave a sense of alacrity. I nodded. I wondered if the poor devil had been hammered on the Stock Exchange or run over by an omnibus.

"Isn't it dreadful? He's run away from his wife."

Miss Waterford certainly felt that she could not do her subject justice on the kerb of Jermyn Street, and so, like an artist, flung the bare fact at me and declared that she knew no details. I could not do her the injustice of supposing that so trifling a circumstance would have prevented her from giving them, but she was obstinate.

"I tell you I know nothing," she said, in reply to my agitated questions, and then, with an airy shrug of the shoulders: "I believe that a young person in a City tea-shop has left her situation."

She flashed a smile at me, and, protesting an engagement with her dentist, jauntily walked on. I was more interested than distressed. In those days my experience of life at first hand was small, and it excited me to come upon an incident among people I knew of the same sort as I had read in books. I confess that time has now accustomed me to incidents of their character among my acquaintance. But I was also a little shocked. Strickland was certainly forty, and I thought it disgusting that a man of his age should concern himself with affairs of the heart. With the superciliousness of extreme youth, I put thirty-five as the utmost limit at which a man might fall in love without making a fool of himself. And this news was slightly disconcerting to me personally, because I had written from the country to Mrs. Strickland, announcing my return, and had added that unless I heard from her to the contrary, I would come on a certain day to drink a dish of tea with her. This was the very day, and I had received no word from Mrs. Strickland. Did she want to see me or did she not? It was likely enough that in the agitation of the moment my note has escaped her memory. Perhaps I should be wiser not to go. On the other hand, she might wish to keep the affair quiet, and it might be highly indiscreet on my part to give any sign that this strange news had reached me. I was torn between the fear of hurting a nice woman's feelings and the fear of being in the way. I felt she must be suffering, and I did not want to see a pain which I could not help; but in my heart was a desire, that I felt a little ashamed of, to see how she was taking it. I did not know what to do.

Finally it occurred to me that I would call as though nothing had happened, and send a message in by the maid asking Mrs. Strickland if it was convenient for her to see me. This would give her the opportunity to send me away. But I was overwhelmed with embarrassment when I said to the maid the phrase I had prepared, and while I waited for the answer in a dark passage I had to call up all my strength of mind not to bolt. The maid came back. Her manner suggested to my excited fancy a complete knowledge of the domestic calamity.

"Will you come this way, sir?" she said.

I followed her into the drawing-room. The blinds were partly drawn to darken the room, and Mrs. Strickland was sitting with her back to the light. Her brother-in-law, Colonel MacAndrew, stood in front of the fireplace, warming his back at an unlit fire. To myself my entrance seemed excessively awkward. I imagined that my arrival had taken them by surprise, and Mrs. Strickland had let me come in only because she had forgotten to put me off. I fancied that the colonel resented the interruption.

"I wasn't quite sure if you expected me," I said, trying to seem unconcerned.

"Of course I did. Anne will bring the tea in a minute."

Even in the darkened room, I could not help seeing that Mrs. Strickland's face was all swollen with tears. Her skin, never very good, was earthy.

"You remember my brother-in-law, don't you? You met at dinner here, just before the holidays."

We shook hands. I felt so shy that I could think of nothing to say, but Mrs. Strickland came to my rescue. She asked me what I had been doing with myself during the summer, and with this help I managed to make some conversation till tea was brought in. The colonel asked for a whisky-and-soda.

"You'd better have one too, Amy," he said.

"No; I prefer tea."

This was the first suggestion that anything untoward had happened. I took no notice, and did my best to engage Mrs. Strickland in talk. The colonel, still standing in front of the fire-place, uttered no word. I wondered how soon I could decently take my leave, and I asked myself why on earth Mrs. Strickland had allowed me to come. There were no flowers, and various knick-knacks, put away during the summer, had not been replaced; there was something cheerless and stiff about the room which had always seemed so friendly; it gave you an odd feeling, as though someone were lying dead on the other side of the wall. I finished tea.

"Will you have a cigarette?" asked Mrs. Strickland.

She looked about for the box, but it was not to be seen.

"I'm afraid there are none."

Suddenly she burst into tears, and hurried from the room.

I was startled. I suppose now that the lack of cigarettes, brought as a rule by her husband, forced him back upon her recollection, and the new feeling that the small comforts she was used to were missing gave her a sudden pang. She realised that the old life was gone and done with. It was impossible to keep up our social pretences any longer.

"I dare say you'd like me to go," I said to the colonel, getting up.

"I suppose you've heard that blackguard has deserted her," he cried explosively.

I hesitated.

"You know how people gossip," I answered. "I was vaguely told that something was wrong."

"He's bolted. He's gone off to Paris with a woman. He's left Amy without a penny."

"I'm awfully sorry," I said, not knowing what else to say.

The colonel gulped down his whisky. He was a tall, lean man of fifty, with a drooping moustache and grey hair. He had pale blue eyes and a weak mouth. I remembered from my previous meeting with him that he had a foolish face, and was proud of the fact that for ten years before he left the army he had played polo three days a week.

"I don't suppose Mrs. Strickland wants to be bothered with me just now," I said. "Will you tell her how sorry I am? If there's anything I can do, I shall be delighted to do it."

He took no notice of me.

"I don't know what's to become of her. And then there are the children. Are they going to live on air? Seventeen years."

"What about seventeen years?"

"They've been married," he snapped. "I never liked him. Of course he was my brother-in-law, and I made the best of it. Did you think him a gentleman? She ought never to have married him."

"Is it absolutely final?"

"There's only one thing for her to do, and that's to divorce him. That's what I was telling her when you came in. 'Fire in with your petition, my dear Amy,' I said. 'You owe it to yourself and you owe it to the children.' He'd better not let me catch sight of him. I'd thrash him within an inch of his life."

I could not help thinking that Colonel MacAndrew might have some difficulty in doing this, since Strickland had struck me as a hefty fellow, but I did not say anything. It is always distressing when outraged morality does not possess the strength of arm to administer direct chastisement on the sinner. I was making up my mind to another attempt at going when Mrs. Strickland came back. She had dried her eyes and powdered her nose.

"I'm sorry I broke down," she said. "I'm glad you didn't go away."

She sat down. I did not at all know what to say. I felt a certain shyness at referring to matters which were no concern of mine. I did not then know the besetting sin of woman, the passion to discuss her private affairs with anyone who is willing to listen. Mrs. Strickland seemed to make an effort over herself.

"Are people talking about it?" she asked.

I was taken aback by her assumption that I knew all about her domestic misfortune.

"I've only just come back. The only person I've seen is Rose Waterford."

Mrs. Strickland clasped her hands.

"Tell me exactly what she said." And when I hesitated, she insisted. "I particularly want to know."

"You know the way people talk. She's not very reliable, is she? She said your husband had left you."

"Is that all?"

I did not choose to repeat Rose Waterford's parting reference to a girl from a tea-shop. I lied.

"She didn't say anything about his going with anyone?"

"No."

"That's all I wanted to know."

I was a little puzzled, but at all events I understood that I might now take my leave. When I shook hands with Mrs. Strickland I told her that if I could be of any use to her I should be very glad. She smiled wanly.

"Thank you so much. I don't know that anybody can do anything for me."

Too shy to express my sympathy, I turned to say good-bye to the colonel. He did not take my hand.

"I'm just coming. If you're walking up Victoria Street, I'll come along with you."

"All right," I said. "Come on."

CHAPTER IX

"This is a terrible thing," he said, the moment we got out into the street.

I realised that he had come away with me in order to discuss once more what he had been already discussing for hours with his sister-in-law.

"We don't know who the woman is, you know," he said. "All we know is that the blackguard's gone to Paris."

"I thought they got on so well."

"So they did. Why, just before you came in Amy said they'd never had a quarrel in the whole of their married life. You know Amy. There never was a better woman in the world."

Since these confidences were thrust on me, I saw no harm in asking a few questions.

"But do you mean to say she suspected nothing?"

"Nothing. He spent August with her and the children in Norfolk. He was just the same as he'd always been. We went down for two or three days, my wife and I, and I played golf with them. He came back to town in September to let his partner go away, and Amy stayed on in the country. They'd taken a house for six weeks, and at the end of her tenancy she wrote to tell him on which day she was arriving in London. He answered from Paris. He said he'd made up his mind not to live with her any more."

"What explanation did he give?"

"My dear fellow, he gave no explanation. I've seen the letter. It wasn't more than ten lines."

"But that's extraordinary."

We happened then to cross the street, and the traffic prevented us from speaking. What Colonel MacAndrew had told me seemed very improbable, and I suspected that Mrs. Strickland, for reasons of her own, had concealed from him some part of the facts. It was clear that a man after seventeen years of wedlock did not leave his wife without certain occurrences which must have led her to suspect that all was not well with their married life. The colonel caught me up.

"Of course, there was no explanation he could give except that he'd gone off with a woman. I suppose he thought she could find that out for herself. That's the sort of chap he was."

"What is Mrs. Strickland going to do?"

"Well, the first thing is to get our proofs. I'm going over to Paris myself."

"And what about his business?"

"That's where he's been so artful. He's been drawing in his horns for the last year."

"Did he tell his partner he was leaving?"

"Not a word."

Colonel MacAndrew had a very sketchy knowledge of business matters, and I had none at all, so I did not quite understand under what conditions Strickland had left his affairs. I gathered that the deserted partner was very angry and threatened proceedings. It appeared that when everything was settled he would be four or five hundred pounds out of pocket.

"It's lucky the furniture in the flat is in Amy's name. She'll have that at all events."

"Did you mean it when you said she wouldn't have a bob?"

"Of course I did. She's got two or three hundred pounds and the furniture."

"But how is she going to live?"

"God knows."

The affair seemed to grow more complicated, and the colonel, with his expletives and his indignation, confused rather than informed me. I was glad that, catching sight of the clock at the Army and Navy Stores, he remembered an engagement to play cards at his club, and so left me to cut across St. James's Park.

CHAPTER X

A DAY or two later Mrs. Strickland sent me round a note asking if I could go and see her that evening after dinner. I found her alone. Her black dress, simple to austerity, suggested her bereaved condition, and I was innocently astonished that notwithstanding a real emotion she was able to dress the part she had to play according to her notions of seemliness.

"You said that if I wanted you to do anything you wouldn't mind doing it," she remarked.

"It was quite true."

"Will you go over to Paris and see Charlie?"

"I?"

I was taken aback. I reflected that I had only seen him once. I did not know what she wanted me to do.

"Fred is set on going." Fred was Colonel MacAndrew. "But I'm sure he's not the man to go. He'll only make things worse. I don't know who else to ask."

Her voice trembled a little, and I felt a brute even to hesitate.

"But I've not spoken ten words to your husband. He doesn't know me. He'll probably just tell me to go to the devil."

"That wouldn't hurt you," said Mrs. Strickland, smiling.

"What is it exactly you want me to do?"

She did not answer directly.

"I think it's rather an advantage that he doesn't know you. You see, he never really liked Fred; he thought him a fool; he didn't understand soldiers. Fred would fly into a passion, and there'd be a quarrel, and things would be worse instead of better. If you said you came on my behalf, he couldn't refuse to listen to you."

"I haven't known you very long," I answered. "I don't see how anyone can be expected to tackle a case like this unless he knows all the details. I don't want to pry into what doesn't concern me. Why don't you go and see him yourself?"

"You forget he isn't alone."

I held my tongue. I saw myself calling on Charles Strickland and sending in my card; I saw him come into the room, holding it between finger and thumb:

"To what do I owe this honour?"

"I've come to see you about your wife."

"Really. When you are a little older you will doubtless learn the advantage of minding your own business. If you will be so good as to turn your head slightly to the left, you will see the door. I wish you good-afternoon."

I foresaw that it would be difficult to make my exit with dignity and I wished to goodness that I had not returned to London till Mrs. Strickland had composed her difficulties. I stole a glance at her. She was immersed in thought. Presently she looked up at me, sighed deeply, and smiled.

"It was all so unexpected," she said. "We'd been married seventeen years. I never dreamed that Charlie was the sort of man to get infatuated with anyone. We always got on well together. Of course, I had a great many interests that he didn't share."

"Have you found out who"—I did not quite know how to express myself—"who the person, who it is he's gone away with?"

"No. No one seems to have an idea. It's so strange. Generally when a man falls in love with someone people see them about together, lunching or something, and her friends always come and tell the wife. I had no warning—nothing. His letter came like a thunderbolt. I thought he was perfectly happy."

She began to cry, poor thing, and I felt very sorry for her. But in a little while she grew calmer.

"It's no good making a fool of myself," she said, drying her eyes. "The only thing is to decide what is the best thing to do."

She went on, talking somewhat at random, now of the recent past, then of their first meeting and their marriage; but presently I began to form a fairly coherent picture of their lives; and it seemed to me that my surmises had not been incorrect. Mrs. Strickland was the daughter of an Indian Civilian, who on his retirement had settled in the depths of the country, but it was his habit every August to take his family to Eastbourne for change of air; and it was here, when she was twenty, that she met Charles Strickland. He was twenty-three. They played tennis together, walked on the front together, listened together to the nigger minstrels; and she had made up her mind to accept him a week before he proposed to her. They lived in London, first in Hampstead, and then, as he grew more prosperous, in town. Two children were born to them.

"He always seemed very fond of them. Even if he was tired of me, I wonder that he had the heart to leave them. It's all so incredible. Even now I can hardly believe it's true."

At last she showed me the letter he had written. I was curious to see it, but had not ventured to ask for it.

My dear Amy,

I think you will find everything all right in the flat. I have given Anne your instructions, and dinner will be ready for you and the children when you come. I shall not be there to meet you. I have made up my mind to live apart from you, and I am going to Paris in the morning. I shall post this letter on my arrival. I shall not come back. My decision is irrevocable.

Yours always,
Charles Strickland.

"Not a word of explanation or regret. Don't you think it's inhuman?"

"It's a very strange letter under the circumstances," I replied.

"There's only one explanation, and that is that he's not himself. I don't know who this woman is who's got hold of him, but she's made him into another man. It's evidently been going on a long time."

"What makes you think that?"

"Fred found that out. My husband said he went to the club three or four nights a week to play bridge. Fred knows one of the members, and said something about Charles being a great bridge-player. The man was surprised. He said he'd never even seen Charles in the card-room. It's quite clear now that when I thought Charles was at his club he was with her."

I was silent for a moment. Then I thought of the children.

"It must have been very difficult to explain to Robert," I said.

"Oh, I never said a word to either of them. You see, we only came up to town the day before they had to go back to school. I had the presence of mind to say that their father had been called away on business."

It could not have been very easy to be bright and careless with that sudden secret in her heart, nor to give her attention to all the things that needed doing to get her children comfortably packed off. Mrs. Strickland's voice broke again.

"And what is to happen to them, poor darlings? How are we going to live?"

She struggled for self-control, and I saw her hands clench and unclench spasmodically. It was dreadfully painful.

"Of course I'll go over to Paris if you think I can do any good, but you must tell me exactly what you want me to do."

"I want him to come back."

"I understand from Colonel MacAndrew that you'd made up your mind to divorce him."

"I'll never divorce him," she answered with a sudden violence. "Tell him that from me. He'll never be able to marry that woman. I'm as obstinate as he is, and I'll never divorce him. I have to think of my children."

I think she added this to explain her attitude to me, but I thought it was due to a very natural jealousy rather than to maternal solicitude.

"Are you in love with him still?"

"I don't know. I want him to come back. If he'll do that we'll let bygones be bygones. After all, we've been married for seventeen years. I'm a broad-minded woman. I wouldn't have minded what he did as long as I knew nothing about it. He must know that his infatuation won't last. If he'll come back now everything can be smoothed over, and no one will know anything about it."

It chilled me a little that Mrs. Strickland should be concerned with gossip, for I did not know then how great a part is played in women's life by the opinion of others. It throws a shadow of insincerity over their most deeply felt emotions.

It was known where Strickland was staying. His partner in a violent letter, sent to his bank, had taunted him with hiding his whereabouts; and Strickland, in a cynical and humorous reply, had told his partner exactly where to find him. He was apparently living in an hotel.

"I've never heard of it," said Mrs. Strickland. "But Fred knows it well. He says it's very expensive."

She flushed darkly. I imagined that she saw her husband installed in a luxurious suite of rooms, dining at one smart restaurant after another, and she pictured his days spent at race meetings and his evenings at the play.

"It can't go on at his age," she said. "After all, he's forty. I could understand it in a young man, but I think it's horrible in a man of his years, with children who are nearly grown up. His health will never stand it."

Anger struggled in her breast with misery.

"Tell him our home cries out for him. Everything is just the same, and yet everything is different. I can't live without him. I'd sooner kill myself. Talk to him about the past, and all we've gone through together. What am I to say to the children when they ask for him? His room is exactly as it was when he left it. It's waiting for him. We're all waiting for him."

Now she told me exactly what I should say. She gave me elaborate answers to every possible observation of his.

"You will do everything you can for me?" she said pitifully. "Tell him what a state I'm in."

I saw that she wished me to appeal to his sympathies by every means in my power. She was weeping freely. I was extraordinarily touched. I felt indignant at Strickland's cold cruelty, and I promised to do all I could to bring him back. I agreed to go over on the next day but one, and to stay in Paris till I had achieved something. Then, as it was growing late and we were both exhausted by so much emotion, I left her.

CHAPTER XI

DURING the journey I thought over my errand with misgiving. Now that I was free from the spectacle of Mrs. Strickland's distress I could consider the matter more calmly. I was puzzled by the contradictions that I saw in her behaviour. She was very unhappy, but to excite my sympathy she was able to make a show of her unhappiness. It was evident that she had been prepared to weep, for she had provided herself with a sufficiency of handker-chiefs; I admired her forethought, but in retrospect it made her tears perhaps less moving. I could not decide whether she desired the return of her husband because she loved him, or because she dreaded the tongue of scandal; and I was perturbed by the suspicion that the anguish of love contemned was alloyed in her broken heart with the pangs, sordid to my young mind, of wounded vanity. I had not yet learnt how contradictory is human nature; I did not know how much pose there is in the sincere, how much baseness in the noble, nor how much goodness in the reprobate.

But there was something of an adventure in my trip, and my spirits rose as I approached Paris. I saw myself, too, from the dramatic standpoint, and I was pleased with the rôle of the trusted friend bringing back the errant husband to his forgiving wife. I made up my mind to see Strickland the following evening, for I felt instinctively that the hour must be chosen with delicacy. An appeal to the emotions is little likely to be effectual before luncheon. My own thoughts were then constantly occupied with love, but I never could imagine connubial bliss till after tea.

I enquired at my hotel for that in which Charles Strickland was living. It was called the Hôtel des Belges. But the concierge, somewhat to my surprise, had never heard of it. I had understood Mrs. Strickland that it was a large and sumptuous place at the back of the Rue de Rivoli. We looked it out in the directory. The only hotel of that name was in the Rue des Moines. The quarter was not fashionable; it was not even respectable. I shook my head.

"I'm sure that's not it," I said.

The concierge shrugged his shoulders. There was no other hotel of that name in Paris. It occurred to me that Strickland had concealed his address, after all. In giving his partner the one I knew he was perhaps playing a trick on him. I do not know why I had an inkling that it would appeal to Strickland's sense of humour to bring a furious stockbroker over to Paris on a fool's errand to an ill-famed house in a mean street. Still, I thought I had better go and see. Next day about six o'clock I took a cab to the Rue des Moines, but dismissed it at the corner, since I preferred to walk to the hotel and look at it before I went in. It was a street of small shops subservient to the needs of poor people, and about the middle of it, on the left as I walked down, was the Hôtel des Belges. My own hotel was modest enough, but it was magnificent in comparison with this. It was a tall, shabby building, that cannot have been painted for years, and it had so bedraggled an air that the houses on each side of it looked neat and clean. The dirty windows were all shut. It was not here that Charles Strickland lived in guilty splendour with the unknown charmer for whose sake he had abandoned honour and duty. I was vexed, for I felt that I had been made a fool of, and I nearly turned away without making an enquiry. I went in only to be able to tell Mrs. Strickland that I had done my best.

The door was at the side of a shop. It stood open, and just within was a sign: *Bureau au premier*. I walked up narrow stairs, and on the landing found a sort of box, glassed in, within which were a desk and a couple of chairs. There was a bench outside, on which it might be presumed the night porter passed uneasy nights. There was no one about, but under an electric bell was written *Garçon*. I rang, and presently a waiter appeared. He was a young man with furtive eyes and a sullen look. He was in shirt-sleeves and carpet slippers.

I do not know why I made my enquiry as casual as possible.

"Does Mr. Strickland live here by any chance?" I asked.

"Number thirty-two. On the sixth floor."

I was so surprised that for a moment I did not answer.

"Is he in?"

The waiter looked at a board in the *bureau*.

"He hasn't left his key. Go up and you'll see."

I thought it as well to put one more question.

"*Madame est là?*"

"*Monsieur est seul.*"

The waiter looked at me suspiciously as I made my way upstairs. They were dark and airless. There was a foul and musty smell. Three flights up a woman in a dressing-gown, with touzled hair, opened a door and looked at me silently as I passed. At length I reached the sixth floor, and knocked at the door numbered thirty-two. There was a sound within, and the door was partly opened. Charles Strickland stood before me. He uttered not a word. He evidently did not know me.

I told him my name. I tried my best to assume an airy manner.

"You don't remember me. I had the pleasure of dining with you last July."

"Come in," he said cheerily. "I'm delighted to see you. Take a pew."

I entered. It was a very small room, overcrowded with furniture of the style which the French know as Louis Philippe. There was a large wooden bedstead on which was a billowing red eiderdown, and there was a large wardrobe, a round table, a very small washstand, and two stuffed chairs covered with red rep. Everything was dirty and shabby. There was no sign of the abandoned luxury that Colonel MacAndrew had so confidently described. Strickland threw on the floor the clothes that burdened one of the chairs, and I sat down on it.

"What can I do for you?" he asked.

In that small room he seemed even bigger than I remembered him. He wore an old Norfolk jacket, and he had not shaved for several days. When last I saw him he was spruce enough, but he looked ill at ease: now, untidy and ill-kempt, he looked perfectly at home. I did not know how he would take the remark I had prepared.

"I've come to see you on behalf of your wife."

"I was just going out to have a drink before dinner. You'd better come too. Do you like absinthe?"

"I can drink it."

"Come on, then."

He put on a bowler hat much in need of brushing.

"We might dine together. You owe me a dinner, you know."

"Certainly. Are you alone?"

I flattered myself that I had got in that important question very naturally.

"Oh yes. In point of fact I've not spoken to a soul for three days. My French isn't exactly brilliant."

I wondered as I preceded him downstairs what had happened to the little lady in the tea-shop. Had they quarrelled already, or was his infatuation passed? It seemed hardly likely if, as appeared, he had been taking steps for a year to make his desperate plunge. We walked to the Avenue de Clichy, and sat down at one of the tables on the pavement of a large café.

CHAPTER XII

THE Avenue de Clichy was crowded at that hour, and a lively fancy might see in the passers-by the personages of many a sordid romance. There were clerks and shop-girls; old fellows who might have stepped out of the pages of Honoré de Balzac; members male and female, of the professions which make their profit of the frailties of mankind. There is in the streets of the poorer quarters of Paris a thronging vitality which excites the blood and prepares the soul for the unexpected.

"Do you know Paris well?" I asked.

"No. We came on our honeymoon. I haven't been since."

"How on earth did you find out your hotel?"

"It was recommended to me. I wanted something cheap."

The absinthe came, and with due solemnity we dropped water over the melting sugar.

"I thought I'd better tell you at once why I had come to see you," I said, not without embarrassment.

His eyes twinkled.

"I thought somebody would come along sooner or later. I've had a lot of letters from Amy."

"Then you know pretty well what I've got to say."

"I've not read them."

I lit a cigarette to give myself a moment's time. I did not quite know how to set about my mission. The eloquent phrases I had arranged, pathetic or indignant, seemed out of place on the Avenue de Clichy. Suddenly he gave a chuckle.

"Beastly job for you this, isn't it?"

"Oh, I don't know," I answered.

"Well, look here, you get it over, and then we'll have a jolly evening."

I hesitated.

"Has it occurred to you that your wife is frightfully unhappy?"

"She'll get over it."

I cannot describe the extraordinary callousness with which he made this reply. It disconcerted me, but I did my best not to

F.A.A.   1 S

show it. I adopted the tone used by my Uncle Henry, a clergyman, when he was asking one of his relatives for a subscription to the Additional Curates Society.

"You don't mind my talking to you frankly?"

He shook his head, smiling.

"Has she deserved that you should treat her like this?"

"No."

"Have you any complaint to make against her?"

"None."

"Then, isn't it monstrous to leave her in this fashion, after seventeen years of married life, without a fault to find with her?"

"Monstrous."

I glanced at him with surprise. His cordial agreement with all I said cut the ground from under my feet. It made my position complicated, not to say ludicrous. I was prepared to be persuasive, touching, and hortatory, admonitory and expostulating, if need be vituperative even, indignant and sarcastic; but what the devil does a mentor do when the sinner makes no bones about confessing his sin? I had no experience, since my own practice has always been to deny everything.

"What, then?" asked Strickland.

I tried to curl my lip.

"Well, if you acknowledge that, there doesn't seem much more to be said."

"I don't think there is."

I felt that I was not carrying out my embassy with any great skill. I was distinctly nettled.

"Hang it all, one can't leave a woman without a bob."

"Why not?"

"How is she going to live?"

"I've supported her for seventeen years. Why shouldn't she support herself for a change?"

"She can't."

"Let her try."

Of course there were many things I might have answered to this. I might have spoken of the economic position of woman, of the contract, tacit and overt, which a man accepts by his marriage, and of much else; but I felt that there was only one point which really signified.

"Don't you care for her any more?"

"Not a bit," he replied.

The matter was immensely serious for all the parties concerned, but there was in the manner of his answers such a cheerful effrontery that I had to bite my lips in order not to laugh. I reminded myself that his behaviour was abominable. I worked myself up into a state of moral indignation.

"Damn it all, there are your children to think of. They've never done you any harm. They didn't ask to be brought into the world. If you chuck everything like this, they'll be thrown on the streets."

"They've had a good many years of comfort. It's much more than the majority of children have. Besides, somebody will look after them. When it comes to the point, the MacAndrews will pay for their schooling."

"But aren't you fond of them? They're such awfully nice kids. Do you mean to say you don't want to have anything more to do with them?"

"I liked them all right when they were kids, but now they're growing up I haven't got any particular feeling for them."

"It's just inhuman."

"I dare say."

"You don't seem in the least ashamed."

"I'm not."

I tried another tack.

"Everyone will think you a perfect swine."

"Let them."

"Won't it mean anything to you to know that people loathe and despise you?"

"No."

His brief answer was so scornful that it made my question, natural though it was, seem absurd. I reflected for a minute or two.

"I wonder if one can live quite comfortably when one's conscious of the disapproval of one's fellows? Are you sure it won't begin to worry you? Everyone has some sort of conscience, and sooner or later it will find you out. Supposing your wife died, wouldn't you be tortured by remorse?"

He did not answer, and I waited for some time for him to speak. At last I had to break the silence myself.

"What have you to say to that?"

"Only that you're a damned fool."

"At all events, you can be forced to support your wife and children," I retorted, somewhat piqued. "I suppose the law has some protection to offer them."

"Can the law get blood out of a stone? I haven't any money. I've got about a hundred pounds."

I began to be more puzzled than before. It was true that his hotel pointed to the most straitened circumstances.

"What are you going to do when you've spent that?"

"Earn some."

He was perfectly cool, and his eyes kept that mocking smile which made all I said seem rather foolish. I paused for a little while to consider what I had better say next. But it was he who spoke first.

"Why doesn't Amy marry again? She's comparatively young, and she's not unattractive. I can recommend her as an excellent wife. If she wants to divorce me I don't mind giving her the necessary grounds."

Now it was my turn to smile. He was very cunning, but it was evidently this that he was aiming at. He had some reason to conceal the fact that he had run away with a woman, and he was using every precaution to hide her whereabouts. I answered with decision.

"Your wife says that nothing you can do will ever induce her to divorce you. She's quite made up her mind. You can put any possibility of that definitely out of your head."

He looked at me with an astonishment that was certainly not feigned. The smile abandoned his lips, and he spoke quite seriously.

"But, my dear fellow, I don't care. It doesn't matter a twopenny damn to me one way or the other."

I laughed.

"Oh, come now; you musn't think us such fools as all that. We happen to know that you came away with a woman."

He gave a little start, and then suddenly burst into a shout of laughter. He laughed so uproariously that the people sitting near us looked round, and some of them began to laugh too.

"I don't see anything very amusing in that."

"Poor Amy," he grinned.

Then his face grew bitterly scornful.

"What poor minds women have got! Love. It's always love. They think a man leaves them only because he wants others. Do you think I should be such a fool as to do what I've done for a woman?"

"Do you mean to say you didn't leave your wife for another woman?"

"Of course not."

"On your word of honour?"

I don't know why I asked for that. It was very ingenuous of me.

"On my word of honour."

"Then, what in God's name have you left her for?"

"I want to paint."

I looked at him for quite a long time. I did not understand. I thought he was mad. It must be remembered that I was very young, and I looked upon him as a middle-aged man. I forgot everything but my own amazement.

"But you're forty."

"That's what made me think it was high time to begin."

"Have you ever painted?"

"I rather wanted to be a painter when I was a boy, but my father made me go into business because he said there was no money in art. I began to paint a bit a year ago. For the last year I've been going to some classes at night."

"Was that where you went when Mrs. Strickland thought you were playing bridge at your club?"

"That's it."

"Why didn't you tell her?"

"I preferred to keep it to myself."

"Can you paint?"

"Not yet. But I shall. That's why I've come over here. I couldn't get what I wanted in London. Perhaps I can here."

"Do you think it's likely that a man will do any good when he starts at your age? Most men begin painting at eighteen."

"I can learn quicker than I could when I was eighteen."

"What makes you think you have any talent?"

He did not answer for a minute. His gaze rested on the passing throng, but I do not think he saw it. His answer was no answer.

"I've got to paint."

"Aren't you taking an awful chance?"

He looked at me then. His eyes had something strange in them, so that I felt rather uncomfortable.

"How old are you? Twenty-three?"

It seemed to me that the question was beside the point. It was natural that I should take chances; but he was a man whose youth was past, a stockbroker with a position of respectability, a wife and two children. A course that would have been natural for me was absurd for him. I wished to be quite fair.

"Of course a miracle may happen, and you may be a great painter, but you must confess the chances are a million to one against it. It'll be an awful sell if at the end you have to acknowledge you've made a hash of it."

"I've got to paint," he repeated.

"Supposing you're never anything more than third-rate, do you think it will have been worth while to give up everything? After all, in any other walk of life it doesn't matter if you're not very good: you can get along quite comfortably if you're just adequate; but it's different with an artist."

"You blasted fool," he said.

"I don't see why, unless it's folly to say the obvious."

"I tell you I've got to paint. I can't help myself. When a man falls into the water it doesn't matter how he swims, well or badly: he's got to get out or else he'll drown."

There was real passion in his voice, and in spite of myself I was impressed. I seemed to feel in him some vehement power that was struggling within him; it gave me the sensation of something very strong, overmastering, that held him, as it were, against his will. I could not understand. He seemed really to be possessed of a devil, and I felt that it might suddenly turn and rend him. Yet he looked ordinary enough. My eyes, resting on him curiously, caused him no embarrassment. I wondered what a stranger would have taken him to be, sitting there in his old Norfolk jacket and his unbrushed bowler; his trousers were baggy, his hands were not clean; and his face, with the red stubble of the unshaved chin, the little eyes, and the large, aggressive nose, was uncouth and coarse. His mouth was large, his lips were heavy and sensual. No; I could not have placed him.

"You won't go back to your wife?" I said at last.

"Never."

"She's willing to forget everything that's happened and start afresh. She'll never make you a single reproach."

"She can go to hell."

"You don't care if people think you an utter blackguard? You don't care if she and your children have to beg their bread?"

"Not a damn."

I was silent for a moment in order to give greater force to my next remark. I spoke as deliberately as I could.

"You are a most unmitigated cad."

"Now that you've got that off your chest, let's go and have dinner."

CHAPTER XIII

I DARE say it would have been more seemly to decline this proposal. I think perhaps I should have made a show of the indignation I really felt, and I am sure that Colonel MacAndrew at least would have thought well of me if I had been able to report my stout refusal to sit at the same table with a man of such character. But the fear of not being able to carry it through effectively has always made me shy of assuming the moral attitude; and in this case the certainty that my sentiments would be lost on Strickland made it peculiarly embarrassing to utter them. Only the poet or the saint can water an asphalt pavement in the confident anticipation that lilies will reward his labour.

I paid for what we had drunk, and we made our way to a cheap restaurant, crowded and gay, where we dined with pleasure. I had the appetite of youth and he of a hardened conscience. Then we went to a tavern to have coffee and liqueurs.

I had said all I had to say on the subject that had brought me to Paris, and though I felt it in a manner treacherous to Mrs. Strickland not to pursue it, I could not struggle against his indifference. It requires the feminine temperament to repeat the same thing three times with unabated zest. I solaced myself by thinking that it would be useful for me to find out what I could about Strickland's state of mind. It also interested me much more. But this was not an easy thing to do, for Strickland was not a fluent talker. He seemed to express himself with difficulty, as though words were not the medium with which his mind worked; and you had to guess the intentions of his soul by hackneyed phrases, slang, and vague, unfinished gestures. But though he said nothing of any consequence, there was something in his personality which prevented him from being dull. Perhaps it was sincerity. He did not seem to care much about the Paris he was now seeing for the first time (I did not count the visit with his wife), and he accepted sights which must have been strange to him without any sense of astonishment. I have been to Paris a hundred times, and it never fails to give me a thrill of excitement; I can never walk its streets without feeling myself on the verge of adventure. Strickland remained placid. Looking back, I think now that he was blind to everything but to some disturbing vision in his soul.

One rather absurd incident took place. There were a number of harlots in the tavern: some were sitting with men, others by themselves; and presently I noticed that one of these was looking at us. When she caught Strickland's eye she smiled. I do not think he saw her. In a little while she went out, but in a minute returned and, passing our table, very politely asked us to buy her something to drink. She sat down and I began to chat with her; but it was plain that her interest was in Strickland. I explained that he knew no more than two words of French. She tried to talk to him, partly by signs, partly in pidgin French, which, for some reason, she thought would be more comprehensible to him, and she had half a dozen phrases of English. She made me translate what she could only express in her own tongue, and eagerly asked for the meaning of his replies. He was quite good-tempered, a little amused, but his indifference was obvious.

"I think you've made a conquest," I laughed.

"I'm not flattered."

In his place I should have been more embarrassed and less calm. She had laughing eyes and a most charming mouth. She was young. I wondered what she found so attractive in Strickland. She made no secret of her desires, and I was bidden to translate.

"She wants you to go home with her."

"I'm not taking any," he replied.

I put his answer as pleasantly as I could. It seemed to me a little ungracious to decline an invitation of that sort, and I ascribed his refusal to lack of money.

"But I like him," she said. "Tell him it's for love."

When I translated this, Strickland shrugged his shoulders impatiently.

"Tell her to go to hell," he said.

His manner made his answer quite plain, and the girl threw back her head with a sudden gesture. Perhaps she reddened under her paint. She rose to her feet.

"*Monsieur n'est pas poli*," she said.

She walked out of the inn. I was slightly vexed.

"There wasn't any need to insult her that I can see," I said. "After all, it was rather a compliment she was paying you."

"That sort of thing makes me sick," he said roughly.

I looked at him curiously. There was real distaste in his face, and yet it was the face of a coarse and sensual man. I suppose the girl had been attracted by a certain brutality in it.

"I could have got all the women I wanted in London. I didn't come here for that."

CHAPTER XIV

DURING the journey back to England I thought much of Strickland. I tried to set in order what I had to tell his wife. It was unsatisfactory, and I could not imagine that she would be content with me; I was not content with myself. Strickland perplexed me. I could not understand his motives. When I had asked him what first gave him the idea of being a painter, he was unable or unwilling to tell me. I could make nothing of it. I tried to persuade myself that an obscure feeling of revolt had been gradually coming to a head in his slow mind, but to challenge this was the undoubted fact that he had never shown any impatience with the monotony of his life. If, seized by an intolerable boredom, he had determined to be a painter merely to break with irksome ties, it would have been comprehensible, and commonplace; but commonplace is precisely what I felt he was not. At last, because I was romantic, I devised an explanation which I acknowledge to be far-fetched, but which was the only one that in any way satisfied me. It was this: I asked myself whether there was not in his soul some deep-rooted instinct of creation, which the circumstances of his life had obscured, but which grew relentlessly, as a cancer may grow in the living tissues, till at last it took possession of his whole being and forced him irresistibly to action. The cuckoo lays its egg in the strange bird's nest, and when the young one is hatched it shoulders its foster-brothers out and breaks at last the nest that has sheltered it.

But how strange it was that the creative instinct should seize upon this dull stockbroker, to his own ruin, perhaps, and to the misfortune of such as were dependent on him; and yet no stranger than the way in which the spirit of God has seized men, powerful and rich, pursuing them with stubborn vigilance till at last, conquered, they have abandoned the joy of the world and the love of women for the painful austerities of the cloister. Conversion may come under many shapes, and it may be brought about in many ways. With some men it needs a cataclysm, as a stone may be broken to fragments by the fury of a torrent; but with some it comes gradually, as a stone may be worn away by the ceaseless fall of a drop of water. Strickland had the directness of the fanatic and the ferocity of the apostle.

But to my practical mind it remained to be seen whether the passion which obsessed him would be justified of its works. When I asked him what his brother-students at the night classes he had attended in London thought of his painting, he answered with a grin:

"They thought it a joke."

"Have you begun to go to a studio here?"

"Yes. The blighter came round this morning—the master, you know; when he saw my drawing he just raised his eyebrows and walked on."

Strickland chuckled. He did not seem discouraged. He was independent of the opinion of his fellows.

And it was just that which had most disconcerted me in my dealings with him. When people say they do not care what others think of them, for the most part they deceive themselves. Generally they mean only that they will do as they choose, in the confidence that no one will know their vagaries; and at the utmost only that they are willing to act contrary to the opinion of the majority because they are supported by the approval of their neighbours. It is not difficult to be unconventional in the eyes of the world when your unconventionality is but the convention of your set. It affords you then an inordinate amount of self-esteem. You have the self-satisfaction of courage without the inconvenience of danger. But the desire for approbation is perhaps the most deeply seated instinct of civilised man. No one runs so hurriedly to the cover of respectability as the unconventional woman who has exposed herself to the slings and arrows of outraged propriety. I do not believe the people who tell me they do not care a row of pins for the opinion of their fellows. It is the bravado of ignorance. They mean only that they do not fear reproaches for peccadillos which they are convinced none will discover.

But here was a man who sincerely did not mind what people thought of him, and so convention had no hold on him; he was like a wrestler whose body is oiled; you could not get a grip on him; it gave him a freedom which was an outrage. I remember saying to him:

"Look here, if everyone acted like you, the world couldn't go on."

"That's a damned silly thing to say. Everyone doesn't want to act like me. The great majority are perfectly content to do the ordinary thing."

And once I sought to be satirical.

"You evidently don't believe in the maxim: Act so that every one of your actions is capable of being made into a universal rule."

"I never heard it before, but it's rotten nonsense."

"Well, it was Kant who said it."

"I don't care; it's rotten nonsense."

Nor with such a man could you expect the appeal to conscience to be effective. You might as well ask for a reflection without a mirror. I take it that conscience is the guardian in the individual of the rules which the community has evolved for its own preservation. It is the policeman in all our hearts, set there to watch that we do not break its laws. It is the spy seated in the central stronghold of the ego. Man's desire for the approval of his fellows is so strong, his dread of their censure so violent, that himself has brought his enemy within his gates; and it keeps watch over him, vigilant always in the interests of its master to crush any half-formed desire to break away from the herd. It will force him to place the good of society before his own. It is the very strong link that attaches the individual to the whole. And man, subservient to interests he has persuaded himself are greater than his own, makes himself a slave to his taskmaster. He sits him in a seat of honour. At last, like a courtier fawning on the royal stick that is laid about his shoulders, he prides himself on the sensitiveness of his conscience. Then he has no words hard enough for the man who does not recognise its sway; for, a member of society now, he realises accurately enough that against him he is powerless. When I saw that Strickland was really indifferent to the blame his conduct must excite, I could only draw back in horror as from a monster of hardly human shape.

The last words he said to me when I bade him good-night were:

"Tell Amy it's no good coming after me. Anyhow, I shall change my hotel, so she wouldn't be able to find me."

"My own impression is that she's well rid of you," I said.

"My dear fellow, I only hope you'll be able to make her see it. But women are very unintelligent."

CHAPTER XV

WHEN I reached London I found waiting for me an urgent request that I should go to Mrs. Strickland's as soon after dinner as I could. I found her with Colonel MacAndrew and his wife. Mrs. Strickland's sister was older than she, not unlike her, but more faded; and she had the efficient air, as though she carried the British Empire in her pocket, which the wives of senior officers acquire from the consciousness of belonging to a superior caste. Her manner was brisk, and her good breeding scarcely concealed her conviction that if you were not a soldier you might as well be a counter-jumper. She hated the Guards, whom she thought conceited, and she could not trust herself to speak of their ladies, who were so remiss in calling. Her gown was dowdy and expensive.

Mrs. Strickland was plainly nervous.

"Well, tell us your news," she said.

"I saw your husband. I'm afraid he's quite made up his mind not to return." I paused a little. "He wants to paint."

"What do you mean?" cried Mrs. Strickland, with the utmost astonishment.

"Did you never know that he was keen on that sort of thing?"

"He must be as mad as a hatter," exclaimed the colonel.

Mrs. Strickland frowned a little. She was searching among her recollections.

"I remember before we were married he used to potter about with a paint-box. But you never saw such daubs. We used to chaff him. He had absolutely no gift for anything like that."

"Of course it's only an excuse," said Mrs. MacAndrew.

Mrs. Strickland pondered deeply for some time. It was quite clear that she could not make head or tail of my announcement. She had put some order into the drawing-room by now, her house-wifely instincts having got the better of her dismay; and it no longer bore that deserted look, like a furnished house long to let, which I had noticed on my first visit after the catastrophe. But now that I had seen Strickland in Paris it was difficult to imagine him in those surroundings. I thought it could hardly have failed to strike them that there was something incongruous in him.

"But if he wanted to be an artist, why didn't he say so?" asked Mrs. Strickland at last. "I should have thought I was the last person to be unsympathetic to—to aspirations of that kind."

Mrs. MacAndrew tightened her lips. I imagine that she had never looked with approval on her sister's leaning towards persons who cultivated the arts. She spoke of "culchaw" derisively.

Mrs. Strickland continued:

"After all, if he had any talent I should be the first to encourage it. I wouldn't have minded sacrifices. I'd much rather be married to a painter than to a stockbroker. If it weren't for the children, I wouldn't mind anything. I could be just as happy in a shabby studio in Chelsea as in this flat."

"My dear, I have no patience with you," cried Mrs. Mac-Andrew. "You don't mean to say you believe a word of this nonsense?"

"But I think it's true," I put in mildly.

She looked at me with good-humoured contempt.

"A man doesn't throw up his business and leave his wife and children at the age of forty to become a painter unless there's a woman in it. I suppose he met one of your—artistic friends, and she's turned his head."

A spot of colour rose suddenly to Mrs. Strickland's pale cheeks.

"What is she like?"

I hesitated a little. I knew that I had a bombshell.

"There isn't a woman."

Colonel MacAndrew and his wife uttered expressions of incredulity, and Mrs. Strickland sprang to her feet.

"Do you mean to say you never saw her?"

"There's no one to see. He's quite alone."

"That's preposterous," cried Mrs. MacAndrew.

"I knew I ought to have gone over myself," said the colonel. "You can bet your boots I'd have rooted her out fast enough."

"I wish you had gone over," I replied, somewhat tartly. "You'd have seen that every one of your suppositions was wrong. He's not at a smart hotel. He's living in one tiny room in the most squalid way. If he's left his home, it's not to live a gay life. He's got hardly any money."

"Do you think he's done something that we don't know about, and is lying doggo on account of the police?"

The suggestion sent a ray of hope in all their breasts, but I would have nothing to do with it.

"If that were so, he would hardly have been such a fool as to give his partner his address," I retorted acidly. "Anyhow, there's one thing I'm positive of, he didn't go away with anyone. He's not in love. Nothing is farther from his thoughts."

There was a pause while they reflected over my words.

"Well, if what you say is true," said Mrs. MacAndrew at last, "things aren't so bad as I thought."

Mrs. Strickland glanced at her, but said nothing. She was very pale now, and her fine brow was dark and lowering. I could not understand the expression of her face. Mrs. MacAndrew continued:

"If it's just a whim, he'll get over it."

"Why don't you go over to him, Amy?" hazarded the colonel. "There's no reason why you shouldn't live with him in Paris for a year. We'll look after the children. I dare say he'd got stale. Sooner or later he'll be quite ready to come back to London, and no great harm will have been done."

"I wouldn't do that," said Mrs. MacAndrew. "I'd give him all the rope he wants. He'll come back with his tail between his legs and settle down again quite comfortably." Mrs. MacAndrew looked at her sister coolly. "Perhaps you weren't very wise with him sometimes. Men are queer creatures, and one has to know how to manage them."

Mrs. MacAndrew shared the common opinion of her sex that a man is always a brute to leave a woman who is attached to him, but that a woman is much to blame if he does. *Le cœur a ses raisons que la raison ne connaît pas.*

Mrs. Strickland looked slowly from one to another of us.

"He'll never come back," she said.

"Oh, my dear, remember what we've just heard. He's been used to comfort and to having someone to look after him. How long do you think it'll be before he gets tired of a scrubby room in a scrubby hotel? Besides, he hasn't any money. He must come back."

"As long as I thought he'd run away with some woman I thought there was a chance. I don't believe that sort of thing ever answers. He'd have got sick to death of her in three months. But if he hasn't gone because he's in love, then it's finished."

"Oh, I think that's awfully subtle," said the colonel, putting into the word all the contempt he felt for a quality so alien to the traditions of his calling. "Don't you believe it. He'll come back, and, as Dorothy says, I dare say he'll be none the worse for having had a bit of a fling."

"But I don't want him back," she said.

"Amy!"

It was anger that had seized Mrs. Strickland, and her pallor was the pallor of a cold and sudden rage. She spoke quickly now, with little gasps.

"I could have forgiven it if he'd fallen desperately in love with someone and gone off with her. I should have thought that natural. I shouldn't really have blamed him. I should have thought he was led away. Men are so weak, and women are so unscrupulous. But this is different. I hate him. I'll never forgive him now."

Colonel MacAndrew and his wife began to talk to her together. They were astonished. They told her she was mad. They could not understand. Mrs. Strickland turned desperately to me.

"Don't *you* see?" she cried.

"I'm not sure. Do you mean that you could have forgiven him if he'd left you for a woman, but not if he's left you for an idea? You think you're a match for the one, but against the other you're helpless?"

Mrs. Strickland gave me a look in which I read no great friend-liness, but did not answer. Perhaps I had struck home. She went on in a low and trembling voice:

"I never knew it was possible to hate anyone as much as I hate him. Do you know, I've been comforting myself by thinking that however long it lasted he'd want me at the end? I knew when he was dying he'd send for me, and I was ready to go; I'd have nursed him like a mother, and at the last I'd have told him that it didn't matter, I'd loved him always, and I forgave him everything."

I have always been a little disconcerted by the passion women have for behaving beautifully at the death-bed of those they love. Sometimes it seems as if they grudge the longevity which postpones their chance of an effective scene.

"But now—now it's finished. I'm as indifferent to him as if he were a stranger. I should like him to die miserable, poor, and starving, without a friend. I hope he'll rot with some loathsome disease. I've done with him."

I thought it as well then to say what Strickland had suggested.

"If you want to divorce him, he's quite willing to do whatever is necessary to make it possible."

"Why should I give him his freedom?"

"I don't think he wants it. He merely thought it might be more convenient to you."

Mrs. Strickland shrugged her shoulders impatiently. I think I was a little disappointed in her. I expected then people to be more of a piece than I do now, and I was distressed to find so much vindictiveness in so charming a creature. I did not realise how motley are the qualities that go to make up a human being. Now I am well aware that pettiness and grandeur, malice and charity, hatred and love, can find place side by side in the same human heart.

I wondered if there was anything I could say that would ease the sense of bitter humiliation which at present tormented Mrs. Strickland. I thought I would try.

"You know, I'm not sure that your husband is quite responsible for his actions. I do not think he is himself. He seems to me to be possessed by some power which is using him for its own ends, and in whose hold he is as helpless as a fly in a spider's web. It's as though someone had cast a spell over him. I'm reminded of those strange stories one sometimes hears of another personality entering into a man and driving out the old one. The soul lives unstably in the body, and is capable of mysterious transformations. In the old days they would say Charles Strickland had a devil."

Mrs. MacAndrew smoothed down the lap of her gown, and gold bangles fell over her wrists.

"All that seems to me very far-fetched," she said acidly. "I don't deny that perhaps Amy took her husband a little too much for granted. If she hadn't been so busy with her own affairs, I can't believe that she wouldn't have suspected something was the matter. I don't think that Alec could have something on his mind for a year or more without my having a pretty shrewd idea of it."

The colonel stared into vacancy, and I wondered whether anyone could be quite so innocent of guile as he looked.

"But that doesn't prevent the fact that Charles Strickland is a heartless beast." She looked at me severely. "I can tell you why he left his wife—from pure selfishness and nothing else whatever."

"That is certainly the simplest explanation," I said. But I thought it explained nothing. When, saying I was tired, I rose to go, Mrs. Strickland made no attempt to detain me.

CHAPTER XVI

WHAT followed showed that Mrs. Strickland was a woman of character. Whatever anguish she suffered she concealed. She saw shrewdly that the world is quickly bored by the recital of misfortune, and willingly avoids the sight of distress. Whenever she went out—and compassion for her misadventure made her friends eager to entertain her—she bore a demeanour that was perfect. She was brave, but not too obviously; cheerful, but not brazenly; and she seemed more anxious to listen to the troubles of others than to discuss her own. Whenever she spoke of her husband it was with pity. Her attitude toward him at first perplexed me. One day she said to me:

"You know, I'm convinced you were mistaken about Charles being alone. From what I've been able to gather from certain sources that I can't tell you, I know that he didn't leave England by himself."

"In that case he has a positive genius for covering up his tracks."

She looked away and slightly coloured.

"What I mean is, if anyone talks to you about it, please don't contradict it if they say he eloped with somebody."

"Of course not."

She changed the conversation as though it were a matter to which she attached no importance. I discovered presently that a peculiar story was circulating among her friends. They said that Charles Strickland had become infatuated with a French dancer, whom he had first seen in the ballet at the Empire, and had accompanied her to Paris. I could not find out how this had arisen, but, singularly enough, it created much sympathy for Mrs. Strickland, and at the same time gave her not a little prestige. This was not without its use in the calling which she had decided to follow. Colonel MacAndrew had not exaggerated when he said she would be penniless, and it was necessary for her to earn her living as quickly as she could. She made up her mind to profit by her acquaintance with so many writers and without loss of time began to learn shorthand and typewriting. Her education made it likely that she would be a typist more efficient than the average, and her story made her claims appealing. Her friends promised to send her work, and took care to recommend her to all theirs.

The MacAndrews, who were childless and in easy circumstances, arranged to undertake the care of the children, and Mrs. Strickland had only herself to provide for. She let her flat and sold her furniture. She settled in two tiny rooms in Westminster, and faced the world anew. She was so efficient that it was certain she would make a success of the adventure.

CHAPTER XVII

It was about five years after this that I decided to live in Paris for a while. I was growing stale in London. I was tired of doing much the same thing every day. My friends pursued their course with uneventfulness; they had no longer any surprises for me, and when I met them I knew pretty well what they would say; even their love affairs had a tedious banality. We were like tram-cars running on their lines from terminus to terminus, and it was possible to calculate within small limits the number of passengers they would carry. Life was ordered too pleasantly. I was seized with panic. I gave up my small apartment, sold my few belongings, and resolved to start afresh.

I called on Mrs. Strickland before I left. I had not seen her for some time, and I noticed changes in her; it was not only that she was older, thinner, and more lined; I think her character had altered. She had made a success of her business, and now had an office in Chancery Lane; she did little typing herself, but spent her time correcting the work of the four girls she employed. She had had the idea of giving it a certain daintiness, and she made much use of blue and red inks; she bound the copy in coarse paper, that looked vaguely like watered silk, in various pale colours; and she had acquired a reputation for neatness and accuracy. She was making money. But she could not get over the idea that to earn her living was somewhat undignified, and she was inclined to remind you that she was a lady by birth. She could not help bringing into her conversation the names of people she knew which would satisfy you that she had not sunk in the social scale. She was a little ashamed of her courage and business capacity, but delighted that she was going to dine the next night with a K.C. who lived in South Kensington. She was pleased to be able to tell you that her son was at Cambridge, and it was with a little laugh that she spoke of the rush of dances to which her daughter, just out, was invited. I suppose I said a very stupid thing.

"Is she going into your business?" I asked.

"Oh no; I wouldn't let her do that," Mrs. Strickland answered. "She's so pretty. I'm sure she'll marry well."

"I should have thought it would be a help to you."

"Several people have suggested that she should go on the stage, but of course I couldn't consent to that. I know all the chief dramatists, and I could get her a part to-morrow, but I shouldn't like her to mix with all sorts of people."

I was a little chilled by Mrs. Strickland's exclusiveness.

"Do you ever hear of your husband?"

"No; I haven't heard a word. He may be dead for all I know."

"I may run across him in Paris. Would you like me to let you know about him?"

She hesitated a minute.

"If he's in any real want I'm prepared to help him a little. I'd send you a certain sum of money, and you could give it him gradually, as he needed it."

"That's very good of you," I said.

But I knew it was not kindness that prompted the offer. It is not true that suffering ennobles the character; happiness does that sometimes, but suffering, for the most part, makes men petty and vindictive.

CHAPTER XVIII

In point of fact, I met Strickland before I had been a fortnight in Paris.

I quickly found myself a tiny apartment on the fifth floor of a house in the Rue des Dames, and for a couple of hundred francs bought at a second-hand dealer's enough furniture to make it habitable. I arranged with the concierge to make my coffee in the morning and to keep the place clean. Then I went to see my friend Dirk Stroeve.

Dirk Stroeve was one of those persons whom, according to your character, you cannot think of without derisive laughter or an embarrassed shrug of the shoulders. Nature had made him a buffoon. He was a painter, but a very bad one, whom I had met in

Rome, and I still remembered his pictures. He had a genuine
enthusiasm for the commonplace. His soul palpitating with love
of art, he painted the models who hung about the stairway of
Bernini in the Piazza di Spagna, undaunted by their obvious
picturesqueness; and his studio was full of canvases on which were
portrayed moustachioed, large-eyed peasants in peaked hats,
urchins in becoming rags, and women in bright petticoats.
Sometimes they lounged at the steps of a church, and sometimes
dallied among cypresses against a cloudless sky; sometimes they
made love by a Renaissance well-head, and sometimes they
wandered through the Campagna by the side of an ox-wagon.
They were carefully drawn and carefully painted. A photograph
could not have been more exact. One of the painters at the Villa
Medici had called him *Le Maître de la Boîte à Chocolats*. To look at
his pictures you would have thought that Monet, Manet, and the
rest of the Impressionists had never been.

"I don't pretend to be a great painter," he said. "I'm not a
Michel Angelo, no, but I have something. I sell. I bring romance
into the homes of all sorts of people. Do you know, they buy my
pictures not only in Holland, but in Norway and Sweden and
Denmark? It's mostly merchants who buy them, and rich tradesmen. You can't imagine what the winters are like in those
countries, so long and dark and cold. They like to think that Italy is
like my pictures. That's what they expect. That's what I expected
Italy to be before I came here."

And I think that was the vision that had remained with him
always, dazzling his eyes so that he could not see the truth; and
notwithstanding the brutality of fact, he continued to see with the
eyes of the spirit an Italy of romantic brigands and picturesque
ruins. It was an ideal that he painted—a poor one, common, and
shop-soiled, but still it was an ideal; and it gave his character a
definite charm.

It was because I felt this that Dirk Stroeve was not to me, as to
others, merely an object of ridicule. His fellow-painters made no
secret of their contempt for his work, but he earned a fair amount
of money, and they did not hesitate to make free use of his purse.
He was generous, and the needy, laughing at him because he
believed so naïvely their stories of distress, borrowed from him
with effrontery. He was very emotional, yet his feeling, so easily
aroused, had in it something absurd, so that you accepted his
kindness, but felt no gratitude. To take money from him was like

robbing a child, and you despised him because he was so foolish. I imagine that a pickpocket, proud of his light fingers, must feel a sort of indignation with the careless woman who leaves in a cab a vanity-bag with all her jewels in it. Nature had made him a butt, but had denied him insensibility. He writhed under the jokes, practical and otherwise, which were perpetually made at his expense, and yet never ceased, it seemed wilfully, to expose himself to them. He was constantly wounded, and yet his good-nature was such that he could not bear malice: the viper might sting him, but he never learned by experience, and had no sooner recovered from his pain than he tenderly placed it once more in his bosom. His life was a tragedy written in the terms of knock-about farce. Because I did not laugh at him he was grateful to me, and he used to pour into my sympathetic ear the long list of his troubles. The saddest thing about them was that they were grotesque, and the more pathetic they were, the more you wanted to laugh.

But though so bad a painter, he had a very delicate feeling for art, and to go with him to picture galleries was a rare treat. His enthusiasm was sincere and his criticism acute. He was catholic. He had not only a true appreciation of the old masters, but sympathy with the moderns. He was quick to discover talent, and his praise was generous. I think I have never known a man whose judgment was surer. And he was better educated than most painters. He was not, like most of them, ignorant of kindred arts, and his taste for music and literature gave depth and variety to his comprehension of painting. To a young man like myself his advice and guidance were of incomparable value.

When I left Rome I corresponded with him, and about once in two months received from him long letters in queer English, which brought before me vividly his spluttering, enthusiastic, gesticulating conversation. Some time before I went to Paris he had married an Englishwoman, and was now settled in a studio in Montmartre. I had not seen him for four years, and had never met his wife.

CHAPTER XIX

I HAD not announced my arrival to Stroeve, and when I rang the bell of his studio, on opening the door himself, for a moment he did not know me. Then he gave a cry of delighted surprise and drew me in. It was charming to be welcomed with so much eagerness. His wife was seated near the stove at her sewing, and she rose as I came in. He introduced me.

"Don't you remember?" he said to her. "I've talked to you about him often." And then to me: "But why didn't you let me know you were coming? How long have you been here? How long are you going to stay? Why didn't you come an hour earlier, and we would have dined together?"

He bombarded me with questions. He sat me down in a chair, patting me as though I were a cushion, pressed cigars upon me, cakes, wine. He could not leave me alone. He was heart-broken because he had no whisky, wanted to make coffee for me, racked his brain for something he could possibly do for me, and beamed and laughed, and in the exuberance of his delight sweated at every pore.

"You haven't changed," I said, smiling, as I looked at him.

He had the same absurd appearance that I remembered. He was a fat little man, with short legs, young still—he could not have been more than thirty—but prematurely bald. His face was perfectly round, and he had a very high colour, a white skin, red cheeks, and red lips. His eyes were blue and round, too, he wore large gold-rimmed spectacles, and his eyebrows were so fair you could not see them. He reminded you of those jolly, fat merchants that Rubens painted.

When I told him that I meant to live in Paris for a while, and had taken an apartment, he reproached me bitterly for not having let him know. He would have found me an apartment himself, and lent me furniture—did I really mean that I had gone to the expense of buying it?—and he would have helped me to move in. He really looked upon it as unfriendly that I had not given him the opportunity of making himself useful to me. Meanwhile, Mrs. Stroeve sat quietly, mending her stockings, without talking, and she listened to all he said with a quiet smile on her lips.

"So, you see, I'm married," he said suddenly; "what do you think of my wife?"

He beamed at her, and settled his spectacles on the bridge of his nose. The sweat made them constantly slip down.

"What on earth do you expect me to say to that?" I laughed.

"Really, Dirk," put in Mrs. Stroeve, smiling.

"But isn't she wonderful? I tell you, my boy, lose no time; get married as soon as ever you can. I'm the happiest man alive. Look at her sitting there. Doesn't she make a picture? Chardin, eh? I've seen all the most beautiful women in the world; I've never seen anyone more beautiful than Madame Dirk Stroeve."

"If you don't be quiet, Dirk, I shall go away."

"*Mon petit choux*," he said.

She flushed a little, embarrassed by the passion in his tone. His letters had told me that he was very much in love with his wife, and I saw that he could hardly take his eyes off her. I could not tell if she loved him. Poor pantaloon, he was not an object to excite love, but the smile in her eyes was affectionate, and it was possible that her reserve concealed a very deep feeling. She was not the ravishing creature that his love-sick fancy saw, but she had a grave comeliness. She was rather tall, and her grey dress, simple and quite well-cut, did not hide the fact that her figure was beautiful. It was a figure that might have appealed more to the sculptor than to the costumier. Her hair, brown and abundant, was plainly done, her face was very pale, and her features were good without being distinguished. She had quiet grey eyes. She just missed being beautiful, and in missing it was not even pretty. But when Stroeve spoke of Chardin it was not without reason, and she reminded me curiously of that pleasant housewife in her mob-cap and apron whom the great painter has immortalised. I could imagine her sedately busy among her pots and pans, making a ritual of her household duties, so that they acquired a moral significance; I did not suppose that she was clever or could ever be amusing, but there was something in her grave intentness which excited my interest. Her reserve was not without mystery. I wondered why she had married Dirk Stroeve. Though she was English, I could not exactly place her, and it was not obvious from what rank in society she sprang, what had been her upbringing, or how she had lived before her marriage. She was very silent, but when she spoke it was with a pleasant voice, and her manners were natural.

I asked Stroeve if he was working.

"Working? I'm painting better than I've ever painted before."

We sat in the studio, and he waved his hand to an unfinished picture on an easel. I gave a little start. He was painting a group of Italian peasants, in the costume of the Campagna, lounging on the steps of a Roman church.

"Is that what you're doing now?" I asked.

"Yes. I can get my models here just as well as in Rome."

"Don't you think it's very beautiful?" said Mrs. Stroeve.

"This foolish wife of mine thinks I'm a great artist," said he.

His apologetic laugh did not disguise the pleasure that he felt. His eyes lingered on the picture. It was strange that his critical sense, so accurate and unconventional when he dealt with the work of others, should be satisfied in himself with what was hackneyed and vulgar beyond belief.

"Show him some more of your pictures," she said.

"Shall I?"

Though he had suffered so much from the ridicule of his friends, Dirk Stroeve, eager for praise and naïvely self-satisfied, could never resist displaying his work. He brought out a picture of two curly-headed Italian urchins playing marbles.

"Aren't they sweet?" said Mrs. Stroeve.

And then he showed me more. I discovered that in Paris he had been painting just the same stale, obviously picturesque things that he had painted for years in Rome. It was all false, insincere, shoddy; and yet no one was more honest, sincere, and frank than Dirk Stroeve. Who could resolve the contradiction?

I do not know what put it into my head to ask:

"I say, have you by any chance run across a painter called Charles Strickland?"

"You don't mean to say you know him?" cried Stroeve.

"Beast," said his wife.

Stroeve laughed.

"*Ma pauvre chérie.*" He went over to her and kissed both her hands. "She doesn't like him. How strange that you should know Strickland!"

"I don't like bad manners," said Mrs. Stroeve.

Dirk, laughing still, turned to me to explain.

"You see, I asked him to come here one day and look at my pictures. Well, he came, and I showed him everything I had." Stroeve hesitated a moment with embarrassment. I do not know why he had begun the story against himself; he felt an awkwardness at finishing it. "He looked at—at my pictures, and he didn't say anything. I thought he was reserving his judgment till the end. And at last I said: 'There, that's the lot!' He said: 'I came to ask you to lend me twenty francs.'"

"And Dirk actually gave it him," said his wife indignantly.

"I was so taken aback. I didn't like to refuse. He put the

money in his pocket, just nodded, said 'Thanks', and walked out."

Dirk Stroeve, telling the story, had such a look of blank astonishment on his round, foolish face that it was almost impossible not to laugh.

"I shouldn't have minded if he'd said my pictures were bad, but he said nothing—nothing."

"And you *will* tell the story, Dirk," said his wife.

It was lamentable that one was more amused by the ridiculous figure cut by the Dutchman than outraged by Strickland's brutal treatment of him.

"I hope I shall never see him again," said Mrs. Stroeve.

Stroeve smiled and shrugged his shoulders. He had already recovered his good humour.

"The fact remains that he's a great artist, a very great artist."

"Strickland?" I exclaimed. "It can't be the same man."

"A big fellow with a red beard. Charles Strickland. An Englishman."

"He had no beard when I knew him, but if he has grown one it might well be red. The man I'm thinking of only began painting five years ago."

"That's it. He's a great artist."

"Impossible."

"Have I ever been mistaken?" Dirk asked me. "I tell you he has genius. I'm convinced of it. In a hundred years if you and I are remembered at all, it will be because we knew Charles Strickland."

I was astonished, and at the same time I was very much excited. I remembered suddenly my last talk with him.

"Where can one see his work?" I asked. "Is he having any success? Where is he living?"

"No; he has no success. I don't think he's ever sold a picture. When you speak to men about him they only laugh. But I *know* he's a great artist. After all, they laughed at Manet. Corot never sold a picture. I don't know where he lives, but I can take you to see him. He goes to a café in the Avenue de Clichy at seven o'clock every evening. If you like we'll go there to-morrow."

"I'm not sure if he'll wish to see me. I think I may remind him of a time he prefers to forget. But I'll come all the same. Is there any chance of seeing any of his pictures?"

"Not from him. He won't show you a thing. There's a little dealer I know who has two or three. But you mustn't go without me, you wouldn't understand. I must show them to you myself."

"Dirk, you make me impatient," said Mrs. Stroeve. "How can you talk like that about his pictures when he treated you as he did?" She turned to me. "Do you know, when some Dutch people came here to buy Dirk's pictures he tried to persuade them to buy Strickland's? He insisted on bringing them here to show."

"What did *you* think of them?" I asked her, smiling.

"They were awful."

"Ah, sweetheart, you don't understand."

"Well, your Dutch people were furious with you. They thought you were having a joke with them."

Dirk Stroeve took off his spectacles and wiped them. His flushed face was shining with excitement.

"Why should you think that beauty, which is the most precious thing in the world, lies like a stone on the beach for the careless passer-by to pick up idly? Beauty is something wonderful and strange that the artist fashions out of the chaos of the world in the torment of his soul. And when he has made it, it is not given to all to know it. To recognise it you must repeat the adventure of the artist. It is a melody that he sings to you, and to hear it again in your own heart you want knowledge and sensitiveness and imagination."

"Why did I always think your pictures beautiful, Dirk? I admired them the very first time I saw them."

Stroeve's lips trembled a little.

"Go to bed, my precious. I will walk a few steps with our friend, and then I will come back."

CHAPTER XX

DIRK STROEVE agreed to fetch me on the following evening and take me to the café at which Strickland was most likely to be found. I was interested to learn that it was the same as that at which Strickland and I had drunk absinthe when I had gone over to Paris to see him. The fact that he had never changed suggested a sluggishness of habit which seemed to me characteristic.

"There he is," said Stroeve, as we reached the café.

Though it was October, the evening was warm, and the tables on the pavement were crowded. I ran my eyes over them, but did not see Strickland.

"Look. Over there, in the corner. He's playing chess."

I noticed a man bending over a chess-board, but could see only a large felt hat and a red beard. We threaded our way among the tables till we came to him.

"Strickland."

He looked up.

"Hulloa, fatty. What do you want?"

"I've brought an old friend to see you."

Strickland gave me a glance, and evidently did not recognise me. He resumed his scrutiny of the chess-board.

"Sit down, and don't make a noise," he said.

He moved a piece and straightway became absorbed in the game. Poor Stroeve gave me a troubled look, but I was not disconcerted by so little. I ordered something to drink, and waited quietly till Strickland had finished. I welcomed the opportunity to examine him at my ease. I certainly should never have known him. In the first place his red beard, ragged and untrimmed, hid much of his face, and his hair was long; but the most surprising change in him was his extreme thinness. It made his great nose protrude more arrogantly; it emphasised his cheek-bones; it made his eyes seem larger. There were deep hollows at his temples. His body was cadaverous. He wore the same suit that I had seen him in five years before; it was torn and stained, threadbare, and it hung upon him loosely, as though it had been made for someone else. I noticed his hands, dirty, with long nails; they were merely bone and sinew, large and strong; but I had forgotten that they were so shapely. He gave me an extraordinary impression as he sat there, his attention riveted on his game—an impression of great strength; and I could not understand why it was that his emaciation somehow made it more striking.

Presently, after moving, he leaned back and gazed with a curious abstraction at his antagonist. This was a fat, bearded Frenchman. The Frenchman considered the position, then broke suddenly into jovial expletives, and with an impatient gesture, gathering up the pieces, flung them into their box. He cursed Strickland freely, then, calling for the waiter, paid for the drinks, and left. Stroeve drew his chair closer to the table.

"Now I suppose we can talk," he said.

Strickland's eyes rested on him, and there was in them a malicious expression. I felt sure he was seeking for some gibe, could think of none, and so was forced to silence.

"I've brought an old friend to see you," repeated Stroeve, beaming cheerfully.

Strickland looked at me thoughtfully for nearly a minute. I did not speak.

"I've never seen him in my life," he said.

I do not know why he said this, for I felt certain I had caught a gleam of recognition in his eyes. I was not so easily abashed as I had been some years earlier.

"I saw your wife the other day," I said. "I felt sure you'd like to have the latest news of her."

He gave a short laugh. His eyes twinkled.

"We had a jolly evening together," he said. "How long ago is it?"

"Five years."

He called for another absinthe. Stroeve, with voluble tongue, explained how he and I had met, and by what an accident we discovered that we both knew Strickland. I do not know if Strickland listened. He glanced at me once or twice reflectively, but for the most part seemed occupied with his own thoughts; and certainly without Stroeve's babble the conversation would have been difficult. In half an hour the Dutchman, looking at his watch, announced that he must go. He asked whether I would come too. I thought, alone, I might get something out of Strickland, and so answered that I would stay.

When the fat man had left I said:

"Dirk Stroeve thinks you're a great artist."

"What the hell do you suppose I care?"

"Will you let me see your pictures?"

"Why should I?"

"I might feel inclined to buy one."

"I might not feel inclined to sell one."

"Are you making a good living?" I asked, smiling. He chuckled.

"Do I look it?"

"You look half starved."

"I am half starved."

"Then come and let's have a bit of dinner."

"Why do you ask me?"

"Not out of charity," I answered coolly. "I don't really care a twopenny damn if you starve or not."

His eyes lit up again.

"Come on, then," he said, getting up. "I'd like a decent meal."

CHAPTER XXI

I LET him take me to a restaurant of his choice, but on the way I bought a paper. When we had ordered our dinner, I propped it against a bottle of St. Galmier and began to read. We ate in silence. I felt him looking at me now and again, but I took no notice. I meant to force him to conversation.

"Is there anything in the paper?" he said, as we approached the end of our silent meal.

I fancied there was in his tone a slight note of exasperation.

"I always like to read the *feuilleton* on the drama," I said.

I folded the paper and put it down beside me.

"I've enjoyed my dinner," he remarked.

"I think we might have our coffee here, don't you?"

"Yes."

We lit our cigars. I smoked in silence. I noticed that now and then his eyes rested on me with a faint smile of amusement. I waited patiently.

"What have you been up to since I saw you last?" he asked at length.

I had not very much to say. It was a record of hard work and of little adventure; of experiments in this direction and in that; of the gradual acquisition of the knowledge of books and of men. I took care to ask Strickland nothing about his own doings. I showed not the least interest in him, and at last I was rewarded. He began to talk of himself. But with his poor gift of expression he gave but indications of what he had gone through, and I had to fill up the gaps with my own imagination. It was tantalising to get no more than hints into a character that interested me so much. It was like making one's way through a mutilated manuscript. I received the impression of a life which was a bitter struggle against every sort of difficulty; but I realised that much which would have seemed horrible to most people did not in the least affect him. Strickland was distinguished from most Englishmen by his perfect in-difference to comfort; it did not irk him to live always in one shabby room; he had no need to be surrounded by beautiful things. I do not suppose he had ever noticed how dingy was the paper on the wall of the room in which on my first visit I found him. He did not want arm-chairs to sit in; he really felt more at his ease on a kitchen chair. He ate with appetite, but was indifferent to what he ate; to him it was only food that he devoured to still the pangs of hunger; and when no food was to be had he seemed capable of doing without it. I learned that for six months he had lived on a loaf of bread and a bottle of milk a day. He was a sensual man, and yet was indifferent to sensual things. He looked upon privation as no hardship. There was something impressive in the manner in which he lived a life wholly of the spirit.

When the small sum of money which he brought with him from London came to an end he suffered from no dismay. He sold no pictures; I think he made little attempt to sell any; he set about finding some way to make a bit of money. He told me with grim humour of the time he had spent acting as guide to Cockneys who wanted to see the night side of life in Paris; it was an occupation that appealed to his sardonic temper; and somehow or other he had acquired a wide acquaintance with the more disreputable quarters of the city. He told me of the long hours he spent walking about the Boulevard de la Madeleine on the look-out for Englishmen, preferably the worse for liquor, who desired to see things which the law forbade. When in luck he was able to make a tidy sum; but the shabbiness of his clothes at last frightened the sightseers, and he could not find people adventurous enough to trust themselves to him. Then he happened on a job to translate the advertisements of patent medicines which were sent broadcast to the medical profession in England. During a strike he had been employed as a house-painter.

Meanwhile he had never ceased to work at his art; but, soon tiring of the studios, entirely by himself. He had never been so poor that he could not buy canvas and paint, and really he needed nothing else. So far as I could make out, he painted with great difficulty, and in his unwillingness to accept help from anyone lost much time in finding out for himself the solution of technical problems which preceding generations had already worked out one by one. He was aiming at something, I knew not what, and perhaps he hardly knew himself; and I got again more strongly the impression of a man possessed. He did not seem quite sane. It seemed to me that he would not show his pictures because he was really not interested in them. He lived in a dream, and the reality meant nothing to him. I had the feeling that he worked on a canvas with all the force of his violent personality, oblivious of everything in his effort to get what he saw with the mind's eye; and then, having finished, not the picture perhaps, for I had an idea that he seldom brought anything to completion, but the passion that fired him, he lost all care for it. He was never satisfied with what he had done; it seemed to him of no consequence compared with the vision that obsessed his mind.

"Why don't you ever send your work to exhibitions?" I asked. "I should have thought you'd like to know what people thought about it."

"Would you?"

I cannot describe the unmeasurable contempt he put into the two words.

"Don't you want fame? It's something that most artists haven't been indifferent to."

"Children. How can you care for the opinion of the crowd, when you don't care twopence for the opinion of the individual?"

"We're not all reasonable beings," I laughed.

"Who makes fame? Critics, writers, stockbrokers, women."

"Wouldn't it give you a rather pleasant sensation to think of people you didn't know and had never seen receiving emotions, subtle and passionate, from the work of your hands? Everyone likes power. I can't imagine a more wonderful exercise of it than to move the souls of men to pity or terror."

"Melodrama."

"Why do you mind if you paint well or badly?"

"I don't. I only want to paint what I see."

"I wonder if I could write on a desert island, with the certainty that no eyes but mine would ever see what I had written."

Strickland did not speak for a long time, but his eyes shone strangely, as though he saw something that kindled his soul to ecstasy.

"Sometimes I've thought of an island lost in a boundless sea, where I could live in some hidden valley, among strange trees, in silence. There I think I could find what I want."

He did not express himself quite like this. He used gestures instead of adjectives, and he halted. I have put into my own words what I think he wanted to say.

"Looking back on the last five years, do you think it was worth it?" I asked.

He looked at me, and I saw that he did not know what I meant. I explained.

"You gave up a comfortable home and a life as happy as the average. You were fairly prosperous. You seem to have had a rotten time in Paris. If you had your time over again would you do what you did?"

"Rather."

"Do you know that you haven't asked anything about your wife and children? Do you ever think of them?"

"No."

"I wish you weren't so damned monosyllabic. Have you never had a moment's regret for all the unhappiness you caused them?"

His lips broke into a smile, and he shook his head.

"I should have thought sometimes you couldn't help thinking of the past. I don't mean the past of seven or eight years ago, but further back still, when you first met your wife, and loved her, and married her. Don't you remember the joy with which you first took her in your arms?"

"I don't think of the past. The only thing that matters is the everlasting present."

I thought for a moment over this reply. It was obscure, perhaps, but I thought that I saw dimly his meaning.

"Are you happy?" I asked.

"Yes."

I was silent. I looked at him reflectively. He held my stare, and presently a sardonic twinkle lit up his eyes.

"I'm afraid you disapprove of me?"

"Nonsense," I answered promptly; "I don't disapprove of the boa-constrictor; on the contrary, I'm interested in his mental process."

"It's a purely professional interest you take in me?"

"Purely."

"It's only right that you shouldn't disapprove of me. You have a despicable character."

"Perhaps that's why you feel at home with me," I retorted.

He smiled dryly, but said nothing. I wish I knew how to describe his smile. I do not know that it was attractive, but it lit up his face, changing the expression, which was generally sombre, and gave it a look of not ill-natured malice. It was a slow smile, starting and sometimes ending in the eyes; it was very sensual, neither cruel nor kindly, but suggested rather the inhuman glee of the satyr. It was his smile that made me ask him:

"Haven't you been in love since you came to Paris?"

"I haven't got time for that sort of nonsense. Life isn't long enough for love and art."

"Your appearance doesn't suggest the anchorite."

"All that business fills me with disgust."

"Human nature is a nuisance, isn't it?" I said.

"Why are you sniggering at me?"

"Because I don't believe you."

"Then you're a damned fool."

I paused, and I looked at him searchingly.

"What's the good of trying to humbug me?" I said.

"I don't know what you mean."

I smiled.

"Let me tell you. I imagine that for months the matter never comes into your head, and you're able to persuade yourself that you've finished with it for good and all. You rejoice in your freedom, and you feel that at last you can call your soul your own. You seem to walk with your head among the stars. And then, all of a sudden you can't stand it any more, and you notice that all the time your feet have been walking in the mud. And you want to roll yourself in it. And you find some woman, coarse and low and vulgar, some beastly creature in whom all the horror of sex is blatant, and you fall upon her like a wild animal. You drink till you're blind with rage."

He stared at me without the slightest movement. I held his eyes with mine. I spoke very slowly.

"I'll tell you what must seem strange, that when it's over you feel so extraordinarily pure. You feel like a disembodied spirit, immaterial; and you seem to be able to touch beauty as though it were a palpable thing; and you feel an intimate communion with the breeze, and with the trees breaking into leaf, and with the iridescence of the river. You feel like God. Can you explain that to me?"

He kept his eyes fixed on mine till I had finished, and then he turned away. There was on his face a strange look, and I thought that so might a man look when he had died under the torture. He was silent. I knew that our conversation was ended.

CHAPTER XXII

I settled down in Paris and began to write a play. I led a very regular life, working in the morning, and in the afternoon lounging

F.A.A.   1 T

about the gardens of the Luxembourg or sauntering through the streets. I spent long hours in the Louvre, the most friendly of all galleries and the most convenient for meditation; or idled on the quays, fingering second-hand books that I never meant to buy. I read a page here and there, and made acquaintance with a great many authors whom I was content to know thus desultorily. In the evenings I went to see my friends. I looked in often on the Stroeves, and sometimes shared their modest fare. Dirk Stroeve flattered himself on his skill in cooking Italian dishes, and I confess that his *spaghetti* were very much better than his pictures. It was a dinner for a king when he brought in a huge dish of it, succulent with tomatoes, and we ate it together with the good household bread and a bottle of red wine. I grew more intimate with Blanche Stroeve, and I think, because I was English and she knew few English people, she was glad to see me. She was pleasant and simple, but she remained always rather silent, and, I knew not why, gave me the impression that she was concealing something. But I thought that was perhaps no more than a natural reserve accentuated by the verbose frankness of her husband. Dirk never concealed anything. He discussed the most intimate matters with a complete lack of self-consciousness. Sometimes he embarrassed his wife, and the only time I saw her put out of countenance was when he insisted on telling me that he had taken a purge, and went into somewhat realistic details on the subject. The perfect seriousness with which he narrated his misfortunes convulsed me with laughter, and this added to Mrs. Stroeve's irritation.

"You seem to like making a fool of yourself," she said.

His round eyes grew rounder still, and his brow puckered in dismay as he saw that she was angry.

"Sweetheart, have I vexed you? I'll never take another. It was only because I was bilious. I lead a sedentary life. I don't take enough exercise. For three days I hadn't . . ."

"For goodness' sake, hold your tongue," she interrupted, tears of annoyance in her eyes.

His face fell, and he pouted his lips like a scolded child. He gave me a look of appeal, so that I might put things right, but, unable to control myself, I shook with helpless laughter.

We went one day to the picture-dealer in whose shop Stroeve thought he could show me at least two or three of Strickland's pictures, but when we arrived were told that Strickland himself had taken them away. The dealer did not know why.

"But don't imagine to yourself that I make myself bad blood on that account. I took them to oblige Monsieur Stroeve, and I said I would sell them if I could. But really——" He shrugged his shoulders. "I'm interested in the young men, but *voyons*, you yourself, Monsieur Stroeve, you don't think there's any talent there."

"I give you my word of honour, there's no one painting to-day in whose talent I am more convinced. Take my word for it, you are missing a good affair. Some day those pictures will be worth more than all you have in your shop. Remember Monet, who could not get anyone to buy his pictures for a hundred francs. What are they worth now?"

"True. But there were a hundred as good painters as Monet who couldn't sell their pictures at that time, and their pictures are worth nothing still. How can one tell? Is merit enough to bring success? Don't believe it. *Du reste*, it has still to be proved that this friend of yours has merit. No one claims it for him but Monsieur Stroeve."

"And how, then, will you recognise merit?" asked Dirk, red in the face with anger.

"There is only one way—by success."

"Philistine!" cried Dirk.

"But think of the great artists of the past—Raphael, Michel Angelo, Ingres, Delacroix—they were all successful."

"Let us go," said Stroeve to me, "or I shall kill this man."

CHAPTER XXIII

I saw Strickland not infrequently, and now and then played chess with him. He was of uncertain temper. Sometimes he would sit silent and abstracted, taking no notice of anyone; and at others, when he was in a good humour, he would talk in his own halting way. He never said a clever thing, but he had a vein of brutal sarcasm which was not ineffective, and he always said exactly what he thought. He was indifferent to the susceptibilities of others, and when he wounded them was amused. He was constantly offending Dirk Stroeve so bitterly that he flung away, vowing he would never speak to him again; but there was a solid force in Strickland that attracted the fat Dutchman against his will, so that he came back, fawning like a clumsy dog, though he knew that his only greeting would be the blow he dreaded.

I do not know why Strickland put up with me. Our relations were peculiar. One day he asked me to lend him fifty francs.

"I wouldn't dream of it," I replied.

"Why not?"

"It wouldn't amuse me."

"I'm frightfully hard up, you know."

"I don't care."

"You don't care if I starve?"

"Why on earth should I?" I asked in my turn.

He looked at me for a minute or two, pulling his untidy beard. I smiled at him.

"What are you amused at?" he said, with a gleam of anger in his eyes.

"You're so simple. You recognise no obligations. No one is under any obligation to you."

"Wouldn't it make you uncomfortable if I went and hanged myself because I'd been turned out of my room as I couldn't pay the rent?"

"Not a bit."

He chuckled.

"You're bragging. If I really did you'd be overwhelmed with remorse."

"Try it, and we'll see," I retorted.

A smile flickered in his eyes, and he stirred his absinthe in silence.

"Would you like to play chess?" I asked.

"I don't mind."

We set up the pieces, and when the board was ready he considered it with a comfortable eye. There is a sense of satisfaction in looking at your men all ready for the fray.

"Did you really think I'd lend you money?" I asked.

"I didn't see why you shouldn't."

"You surprise me."

"Why?"

"It's disappointing to find that at heart you are sentimental. I should have liked you better if you hadn't made that ingenuous appeal to my sympathies."

"I should have despised you if you'd been moved by it," he answered.

"That's better," I laughed.

We began to play. We were both absorbed in the game. When it was finished I said to him:

"Look here, if you're hard up, let me see your pictures. If there's anything I like I'll buy it."

"Go to hell," he answered.

He got up and was about to go away. I stopped him.

"You haven't paid for your absinthe," I said, smiling.

He cursed me, flung down the money, and left.

I did not see him for several days after that, but one evening, when I was sitting in the café, reading a paper, he came up and sat beside me.

"You haven't hanged yourself after all," I remarked.

"No. I've got a commission. I'm painting the portrait of a retired plumber for two hundred francs."*

"How did you manage that?"

"The woman where I get my bread recommended me. He'd told her he was looking out for someone to paint him. I've got to give her twenty francs."

"What's he like?"

"Splendid. He's got a great red face like a leg of mutton, and on his right cheek there's an enormous mole with long hairs growing out of it."

Strickland was in a good humour, and when Dirk Stroeve came up and sat down with us he attacked him with ferocious banter. He showed a skill I should never have credited him with in finding the places where the unhappy Dutchman was most sensitive. Strickland employed not the rapier of sarcasm but the bludgeon of invective. The attack was so unprovoked that Stroeve, taken unawares, was defenceless. He reminded you of a frightened sheep running aimlessly hither and thither. He was startled and amazed. At last the tears ran from his eyes. And the worst of it was that, though you hated Strickland, and the exhibition was horrible, it was impossible not to laugh. Dirk Stroeve was one of those unlucky persons whose most sincere emotions are ridiculous.

But after all when I look back upon that winter in Paris, my pleasantest recollection is of Dirk Stroeve. There was something very charming in his little household. He and his wife made a

* This picture, formerly in the possession of a wealthy manufacturer at Lille, who fled from that city on the approach of the Germans, is now in the National Gallery at Stockholm. The Swede is adept at the gentle pastime of fishing in troubled waters.

picture which the imagination gratefully dwelt upon, and the simplicity of his love for her had a deliberate grace. He remained absurd, but the sincerity of his passion excited one's sympathy. I could understand how his wife must feel for him, and I was glad that her affection was so tender. If she had any sense of humour, it must amuse her that he should place her on a pedestal and worship her with such an honest idolatry, but even while she laughed she must have been pleased and touched. He was the constant lover, and though she grew old, losing her rounded lines and her fair comeliness, to him she would certainly never alter. To him she would always be the loveliest woman in the world. There was a pleasing grace in the orderliness of their lives. They had but the studio, a bedroom, and a tiny kitchen. Mrs. Stroeve did all the housework herself; and while Dirk painted bad pictures, she went marketing, cooked the luncheon, sewed, occupied herself like a busy ant all the day; and in the evening sat in the studio, sewing again, while Dirk played music which I am sure was far beyond her comprehension. He played with taste, but with more feeling than was always justified, and into his music poured all his honest, sentimental, exuberant soul.

Their life in its own way was an idyl, and it managed to achieve a singular beauty. The absurdity that clung to everything connected with Dirk Stroeve gave it a curious note, like an unresolved discord, but made it somehow more modern, more human; like a rough joke thrown into a serious scene, it heightened the poignancy which all beauty has.

CHAPTER XXIV

SHORTLY before Christmas Dirk Stroeve came to ask me to spend the holiday with him. He had a characteristic sentimentality about the day and wanted to pass it among his friends with suitable ceremonies. Neither of us had seen Strickland for two or three weeks—I because I had been busy with friends who were spending a little while in Paris, and Stroeve because, having quarrelled with him more violently than usual, he had made up his mind to have nothing more to do with him. Strickland was impossible, and he swore never to speak to him again. But the season touched him with gentle feeling, and he hated the thought of Strickland spending Christmas Day by himself; he ascribed his own emotions to him, and could not bear that on an occasion given up to good-fellowship the lonely painter should be abandoned to his own melancholy. Stroeve had set up a Christmas tree in his studio, and I suspected that we should both find absurd little presents hanging on its festive branches; but he was shy about seeing Strickland again; it was a little humiliating to forgive so easily insults so outrageous, and he wished me to be present at the reconciliation on which he was determined.

We walked together down the Avenue de Clichy, but Strickland was not in the café. It was too cold to sit outside, and we took our places on leather benches within. It was hot and stuffy, and the air was grey with smoke. Strickland did not come, but presently we saw the French painter who occasionally played chess with him. I had formed a casual acquaintance with him, and he sat down at our table. Stroeve asked him if he had seen Strickland.

"He's ill," he said. "Didn't you know?"

"Seriously?"

"Very, I understand."

Stroeve's face grew white.

"Why didn't he write and tell me? How stupid of me to quarrel with him! We must go to him at once. He can have no one to look after him. Where does he live?"

"I have no idea," said the Frenchman.

We discovered that none of us knew how to find him. Stroeve grew more and more distressed.

"He might die, and not a soul would know anything about it. It's dreadful. I can't bear the thought. We must find him at once."

I tried to make Stroeve understand that it was absurd to hunt vaguely about Paris. We must first think of some plan.

"Yes, but all this time he may be dying, and when we get there it may be too late to do anything."

"Sit still and let us think," I said impatiently.

The only address I knew was the Hôtel des Belges, but Strickland had long left that, and they would have no recollection of him. With that queer idea of his to keep his whereabouts secret, it was unlikely that, on leaving, he had said where he was going. Besides, it was more than five years ago. I felt pretty sure that he had not moved far. If he continued to frequent the same café as when he had stayed at the hotel, it was probably because it was the most convenient. Suddenly I remembered that he had got his commission to paint a portrait through the baker from whom he bought his bread, and it struck me that there one might find his address. I called for a directory and looked out the bakers. There were five in the immediate neighbourhood, and the only thing was to go to all of them. Stroeve accompanied me unwillingly. His own plan was to run up and down the streets that led out of the Avenue de Clichy and ask at every house if Strickland lived there. My commonplace scheme was, after all, effective, for in the second shop we asked at the woman behind the counter acknowledged that she knew him. She was not certain where he lived, but it was in one of the three houses opposite. Luck favoured us, and in the first we tried the concierge told us that we should find him on the top floor.

"It appears that he's ill," said Stroeve.

"It may be," answered the concierge indifferently. *"En effet*, I have not seen him for several days."

Stroeve ran up the stairs ahead of me, and when I reached the top floor I found him talking to a workman in his shirt-sleeves who had opened a door at which Stroeve had knocked. He pointed to another door. He believed that the person who lived there was a painter. He had not seen him for a week. Stroeve made as though he were about to knock, and then turned to me with a gesture of helplessness. I saw that he was panic-stricken.

"Supposing he's dead?"

"Not he," I said.

I knocked. There was no answer. I tried the handle, and found the door unlocked. I walked in, and Stroeve followed me. The room was in darkness. I could only see that it was an attic, with a sloping roof; and a faint glimmer, no more than a less profound obscurity, came from a skylight.

"Strickland," I called.

There was no answer. It was really rather mysterious, and it seemed to me that Stroeve, standing just behind, was trembling in his shoes. For a moment I hesitated to strike a light. I dimly perceived a bed in the corner, and I wondered whether the light would disclose lying on it a dead body.

"Haven't you got a match, you fool?"

Strickland's voice, coming out of the darkness, harshly, made me start.

Stroeve cried out:

"Oh, my God, I thought you were dead."

I struck a match, and looked about for a candle. I had a rapid glimpse of a tiny apartment, half room, half studio, in which was nothing but a bed, canvases with their faces to the wall, an easel, a table, and a chair. There was no carpet on the floor. There was no fireplace. On the table, crowded with paints, palette-knives, and litter of all kinds, was the end of a candle. I lit it. Strickland was lying in the bed, uncomfortably because it was too small for him, and he had put all his clothes over him for warmth. It was obvious at a glance that he was in a high fever. Stroeve, his voice cracking with emotion, went up to him.

"Oh, my poor friend, what is the matter with you? I had no idea you were ill. Why didn't you let me know? You must know I'd have done anything in the world for you. Were you thinking of what I said? I didn't mean it. I was wrong. It was stupid of me to take offence."

"Go to hell," said Strickland.

"Now, be reasonable. Let me make you comfortable. Haven't you anyone to look after you?"

He looked round the squalid attic in dismay. He tried to arrange the bed-clothes. Strickland, breathing laboriously, kept an angry silence. He gave me a resentful glance. I stood quite quietly, looking at him.

"If you want to do something for me, you can get me some milk," he said at last. "I haven't been able to get out for two days."

There was an empty bottle by the side of the bed, which had contained milk, and in a piece of newspaper a few crumbs.

"What have you been having?" I asked.

"Nothing."

"For how long?" cried Stroeve. "Do you mean to say you've had nothing to eat or drink for two days? It's horrible."

"I've had water."

His eyes dwelt for a moment on a large can within reach of an outstretched arm.

"I'll go immediately," said Stroeve. "Is there anything you fancy?"

I suggested that he should get a thermometer, and a few grapes, and some bread. Stroeve, glad to make himself useful, clattered down the stairs.

"Damned fool," muttered Strickland.

I felt his pulse. It was beating quickly and feebly. I asked him one or two questions, but he would not answer, and when I pressed him he turned his face irritably to the wall. The only thing was to wait in silence. In ten minutes Stroeve, panting, came back. Besides what I had suggested, he brought candles, and meat-juice, and a spirit-lamp. He was a practical little fellow, and without delay set about making bread-and-milk. I took Strickland's temperature. It was a hundred and four. He was obviously very ill.

CHAPTER XXV

PRESENTLY we left him. Dirk was going home to dinner, and I proposed to find a doctor and bring him to see Strickland; but when we got down into the street, fresh after the stuffy attic, the Dutchman begged me to go immediately to his studio. He had something in mind which he would not tell me, but he insisted that it was very necessary for me to accompany him. Since I did not think a doctor could at the moment do any more than we had done, I consented. We found Blanche Stroeve laying the table for dinner. Dirk went up to her, and took both her hands.

"Dear one, I want you to do something for me," he said.

She looked at him with the grave cheerfulness which was one of her charms. His red face was shining with sweat, and he had a look of comic agitation, but there was in his round, surprised eyes an eager light.

"Strickland is very ill. He may be dying. He is alone in a filthy attic, and there is not a soul to look after him. I want you to let me bring him here."

She withdrew her hands quickly, I had never seen her make so rapid a movement, and her cheeks flushed.

"Oh no."

"Oh, my dear one, don't refuse. I couldn't bear to leave him where he is. I shouldn't sleep a wink for thinking of him."

"I have no objection to your nursing him."

Her voice was cold and distant.

"But he'll die."

"Let him."

Stroeve gave a little gasp. He wiped his face. He turned to me for support, but I did not know what to say.

"He's a great artist."

"What do I care? I hate him."

"Oh, my love, my precious, you don't mean that. I beseech you to let me bring him here. We can make him comfortable. Perhaps we can save him. He shall be no trouble to you. I will do everything. We'll make him up a bed in the studio. We can't let him die like a dog. It would be inhuman."

"Why can't he go to a hospital?"

"A hospital! He needs the care of loving hands. He must be treated with infinite tact."

I was surprised to see how moved she was. She went on laying the table, but her hands trembled.

"I have no patience with you. Do you think if you were ill he would stir a finger to help you?"

"But what does that matter? I should have you to nurse me. It wouldn't be necessary. And besides, I'm different; I'm not of any importance."

"You have no more spirit than a mongrel cur. You lie down on the ground and ask people to trample on you."

Stroeve gave a little laugh. He thought he understood the reason of his wife's attitude.

"Oh, my poor dear, you're thinking of that day he came here to look at my pictures. What does it matter if he didn't think them any good? It was stupid of me to show them to him. I dare say they're not very good."

He looked round the studio ruefully. On the easel was a half-finished picture of a smiling Italian peasant, holding a bunch of grapes over the head of a dark-eyed girl.

"Even if he didn't like them he should have been civil. He needn't have insulted you. He showed that he despised you, and you lick his hand. Oh, I hate him."

"Dear child, he has genius. You don't think I believe that I have it. I wish I had; but I know it when I see it, and I honour it with all my heart. It's the most wonderful thing in the world. It's a great burden to its possessors. We should be very tolerant with them, and very patient."

I stood apart, somewhat embarrassed by the domestic scene, and wondered why Stroeve had insisted on my coming with him. I saw that his wife was on the verge of tears.

"But it's not only because he's a genius that I ask you to let me bring him here; it's because he's a human being, and he is ill and poor."

"I will never have him in my house—never."

Stroeve turned to me.

"Tell her that it's a matter of life and death. It's impossible to leave him in that wretched hole."

"It's quite obvious that it would be much easier to nurse him here," I said, "but of course it would be very inconvenient. I have an idea that someone will have to be with him day and night."

"My love, it's not you who would shirk a little trouble."

"If he comes here, I shall go," said Mrs. Stroeve violently.

"I don't recognise you. You're so good and kind."

"Oh, for goodness' sake, let me be. You drive me to distraction."

Then at last the tears came. She sank into a chair, and buried her face in her hands. Her shoulders shook convulsively. In a moment Dirk was on his knees beside her, with his arms round her, kissing her, calling her all sorts of pet names, and the facile tears ran down his own cheeks. Presently she released herself and dried her tears.

"Leave me alone," she said, not unkindly; and then to me, trying to smile: "What must you think of me?"

Stroeve, looking at her with perplexity, hesitated. His forehead was all puckered and his red mouth set in a pout. He reminded me oddly of an agitated guinea-pig.

"Then it's No, darling?" he said at last.

She gave a gesture of lassitude. She was exhausted.

"The studio is yours. Everything belongs to you. If you want to bring him here, how can I prevent you?"

A sudden smile flashed across his round face.

"Then you consent? I knew you would. Oh, my precious."

Suddenly she pulled herself together. She looked at him with haggard eyes. She clasped her hands over her heart as though its beating were intolerable.

"Oh, Dirk, I've never since we met asked you to do anything for me."

"You know there's nothing in the world that I wouldn't do for you."

"I beg you not to let Strickland come here. Anyone else you like. Bring a thief, a drunkard, any outcast off the streets, and I promise you I'll do everything I can for them gladly. But I beseech you not to bring Strickland here."

"But why?"

"I'm frightened of him. I don't know why, but there's something in him that terrifies me. He'll do us some great harm. I know it. I feel it. If you bring him here it can only end badly."

"But how unreasonable!"

"No, no. I know I'm right. Something terrible will happen to us."

"Because we do a good action?"

She was panting now, and in her face was a terror which was inexplicable. I do not know what she thought. I felt that she was possessed by some shapeless dread which robbed her of all self-control. As a rule she was so calm; her agitation now was amazing. Stroeve looked at her for a while with puzzled consternation.

"You are my wife; you are dearer to me than anyone in the world. No one shall come here without your entire consent."

She closed her eyes for a moment, and I thought she was going to faint. I was a little impatient with her; I had not suspected that she was so neurotic a woman. Then I heard Stroeve's voice again. It seemed to break oddly on the silence.

"Haven't you been in bitter distress once when a helping hand was held out to you? You know how much it means. Wouldn't you like to do someone a good turn when you have the chance?"

The words were ordinary enough, and to my mind there was in them something so hortatory that I almost smiled. I was astonished at the effect they had on Blanche Stroeve. She started a little, and gave her husband a long look. His eyes were fixed on the ground. I did not know why he seemed embarrassed. A faint colour came into her cheeks, and then her face became white—more than white, ghastly; you felt that the blood had shrunk away from the whole surface of her body; and even her hands were pale. A shiver passed through her. The silence of the studio seemed to gather body, so that it became an almost palpable presence. I was bewildered.

"Bring Strickland here, Dirk. I'll do my best for him."

"My precious," he smiled.

He wanted to take her in his arms, but she avoided him.

"Don't be affectionate before strangers, Dirk," she said. "It makes me feel such a fool."

Her manner was quite normal again, and no one could have told that so shortly before she had been shaken by such a great emotion.

CHAPTER XXVI

NEXT day we moved Strickland. It needed a good deal of firmness and still more patience to induce him to come, but he was really too ill to offer any effective resistance to Stroeve's entreaties and to my determination. We dressed him, while he feebly cursed us, got him downstairs, into a cab, and eventually to Stroeve's studio. He was so exhausted by the time we arrived that he allowed us to put him to bed without a word. He was ill for six weeks. At one time it looked as though he could not live more than a few hours, and I am convinced that it was only through the Dutchman's doggedness that he pulled through. I have never known a more difficult patient. It was not that he was exacting and querulous; on the contrary, he never complained, he asked for nothing, he was perfectly silent; but he seemed to resent the care that was taken of him; he received all enquiries about his feelings or his needs with a gibe, a sneer, or an oath. I found him detestable, and as soon as he was out of danger I had no hesitation in telling him so.

"Go to hell," he answered briefly.

Dirk Stroeve, giving up his work entirely, nursed Strickland with tenderness and sympathy. He was dexterous to make him comfortable, and he exercised a cunning of which I should never have thought him capable to induce him to take the medicines prescribed by the doctor. Nothing was too much trouble for him. Though his means were adequate to the needs of himself and his wife, he certainly had no money to waste; but now he was wantonly extravagant in the purchase of delicacies, out of season and dear, which might tempt Strickland's capricious appetite. I shall never forget the tactful patience with which he persuaded him to take nourishment. He was never put out by Strickland's rudeness; if it was merely sullen, he appeared not to notice it; if it was aggressive, he only chuckled. When Strickland, recovering somewhat, was in a good humour and amused himself by laughing at him, he deliberately did absurd things to excite his ridicule. Then he would give me little happy glances, so that I might notice in how much better form the patient was. Stroeve was sublime.

But it was Blanche who most surprised me. She proved herself not only a capable but a devoted nurse. There was nothing in her to remind you that she had so vehemently struggled against her husband's wish to bring Strickland to the studio. She insisted on doing her share of the offices needful to the sick. She arranged his bed so that it was possible to change the sheet without disturbing him. She washed him. When I remarked on her competence, she told me with that pleasant little smile of hers that for a while she had worked in a hospital. She gave no sign that she hated Strickland so desperately. She did not speak to him much, but she was quick to forestall his wants. For a fortnight it was necessary that someone should stay with him all night, and she took turns at watching with her husband. I wondered what she thought during the long darkness as she sat by the bedside. Strickland was a weird figure as he lay there, thinner than ever, with his ragged red beard and his eyes staring feverishly into vacancy; his illness seemed to have made them larger, and they had an unnatural brightness.

"Does he ever talk to you in the night?" I asked her once.

"Never."

"Do you dislike him as much as you did?"

"More, if anything."

She looked at me with her calm grey eyes. Her expression was so placid, it was hard to believe that she was capable of the violent emotion I had witnessed.

"Has he ever thanked you for what you do for him?"

"No," she smiled.

"He's inhuman."

"He's abominable."

Stroeve was, of course, delighted with her. He could not do enough to show his gratitude for the whole-hearted devotion with which she had accepted the burden he laid on her. But he was a little puzzled by the behaviour of Blanche and Strickland toward one another.

"Do you know, I've seen them sit there for hours together without saying a word?"

On one occasion, when Strickland was so much better that in a day or two he was to get up, I sat with them in the studio. Dirk and I were talking. Mrs. Stroeve sewed, and I thought I recognised the shirt she was mending as Strickland's. He lay on his back; he did not speak. Once I saw that his eyes were fixed on Blanche Stroeve, and there was in them a curious irony. Feeling their gaze, she raised her own, and for a moment they stared at one another. I could not quite understand her expression. Her eyes had in them a strange perplexity, and perhaps—but why?—alarm.

In a moment Strickland looked away and idly surveyed the ceiling, but she continued to stare at him, and now her look was quite inexplicable.

In a few days Strickland began to get up. He was nothing but skin and bone. His clothes hung upon him like rags on a scarecrow. With his untidy beard and long hair, his features, always a little larger than life, now emphasised by illness, he had an extraordinary aspect; but it was so odd that it was not quite ugly. There was something monumental in his ugliness. I do not know how to express precisely the impression he made upon me. It was not exactly spirituality that was obvious, though the screen of the flesh seemed almost transparent, because there was in his face an outrageous sensuality; but, though it sounds nonsense, it seemed as though his sensuality were curiously spiritual. There was in him something primitive. He seemed to partake of those obscure forces of nature which the Greeks personified in shapes part human and part beast, the satyr and the faun. I thought of Marsyas, whom the god flayed because he had dared to rival him in song. Strickland seemed to bear in his heart strange harmonies and unadventured patterns, and I foresaw for him an end of torture and despair. I had again the feeling that he was possessed of a devil; but you could not say that it was a devil of evil, for it was a primitive force that existed before good and ill.

He was still too weak to paint, and he sat in the studio, silent, occupied with God knows what dreams, or reading. The books he liked were queer; sometimes I would find him poring over the poems of Mallarmé, and he read them as a child reads, forming the words with his lips, and I wondered what strange emotion he got from those subtle cadences and obscure phrases; and again I found him absorbed in the detective novels of Gaboriau. I amused myself by thinking that in his choice of books he showed pleasantly the irreconcilable sides of his fantastic nature. It was singular to notice that even in the weak state of his body he had no thought for its comfort. Stroeve liked his ease, and in his studio were a couple of heavily upholstered arm-chairs and a large divan. Strickland would not go near them, not from any affectation of stoicism, for I found him seated on a three-legged stool when I went into the studio one day and he was alone, but because he did not like them. For choice he sat on a kitchen chair without arms. It often exasperated me to see him. I never knew a man so entirely indifferent to his surroundings.

CHAPTER XXVII

Two or three weeks passed. One morning, having come to a pause in my work, I thought I would give myself a holiday, and I went to the Louvre. I wandered about, looking at the pictures I knew so well, and let my fancy play idly with the emotions they suggested. I sauntered into the long gallery, and there suddenly saw Stroeve. I smiled, for his appearance, so rotund and yet so startled, could never fail to excite a smile, and then as I came nearer I noticed that he seemed singularly disconsolate. He looked woebegone and yet ridiculous, like a man who has fallen into the water with all his clothes on, and, being rescued from death, frightened still, feels that he only looks a fool. Turning round, he stared at me, but I perceived that he did not see me. His round blue eyes looked harassed behind his glasses.

"Stroeve," I said.

He gave a little start, and then smiled, but his smile was rueful.

"Why are you idling in this disgraceful fashion?" I asked gaily.

"It's a long time since I was at the Louvre. I thought I'd come and see if they had anything new."

"But you told me you had to get a picture finished this week."

"Strickland's painting in my studio."

"Well?"

"I suggested it myself. He's not strong enough to go back to his own place yet. I thought we could both paint there. Lots of fellows in the Quarter share a studio. I thought it would be fun. I've always thought it would be jolly to have someone to talk to when one was tired of work."

He said all this slowly, detaching statement from statement with a little awkward silence, and he kept his kind, foolish eyes fixed on mine. They were full of tears.

"I don't think I understand," I said.

"Strickland can't work with anyone else in the studio."

"Damn it all, it's your studio. That's his look-out."

He looked at me pitifully. His lips were trembling.

"What happened?" I asked, rather sharply.

He hesitated and flushed. He glanced unhappily at one of the pictures on the wall.

"He wouldn't let me go on painting. He told me to get out."

"But why didn't you tell him to go to hell?"

"He turned me out. I couldn't very well struggle with him. He threw my hat after me, and locked the door."

I was furious with Strickland, and was indignant with myself, because Dirk Stroeve cut such an absurd figure that I felt inclined to laugh.

"But what did your wife say?"

"She'd gone out to do the marketing."

"Is he going to let her in?"

"I don't know."

I gazed at Stroeve with perplexity. He stood like a schoolboy with whom a master is finding fault.

"Shall I get rid of Strickland for you?" I asked.

He gave a little start, and his shining face grew very red.

"No. You'd better not do anything."

He nodded to me and walked away. It was clear that for some reason he did not want to discuss the matter. I did not understand.

CHAPTER XXVIII

THE explanation came a week later. It was about ten o'clock at night; I had been dining by myself at a restaurant and, having returned to my small apartment, was sitting in my parlour, reading. I heard the cracked tinkling of the bell, and, going into the corridor, opened the door. Stroeve stood before me.

"Can I come in?" he asked.

In the dimness of the landing I could not see him very well, but there was something in his voice that surprised me. I knew he was of abstemious habit or I should have thought he had been drinking. I led the way into my sitting-room and asked him to sit down.

"Thank God I've found you," he said.

"What's the matter?" I asked in astonishment at his vehemence.

I was able now to see him well. As a rule he was neat in his person, but now his clothes were in disorder. He looked suddenly bedraggled. I was convinced he had been drinking, and I smiled. I was on the point of chaffing him on his state.

"I didn't know where to go," he burst out. "I came here earlier, but you weren't in."

"I dined late," I said.

I changed my mind: it was not liquor that had driven him to this obvious desperation. His face, usually so rosy, was now strangely mottled. His hands trembled.

"Has anything happened?" I asked.

"My wife has left me."

He could hardly get the words out. He gave a little gasp, and the tears began to trickle down his round cheeks. I did not know what to say. My first thought was that she had come to the end of her forbearance with his infatuation for Strickland, and, goaded by the latter's cynical behaviour, had insisted that he should be turned out. I knew her capable of temper, for all the calmness of her manner; and if Stroeve still refused, she might easily have flung out of the studio with vows never to return. But the little man was so distressed that I could not smile.

"My dear fellow, don't be unhappy. She'll come back. You mustn't take very seriously what women say when they're in a passion.

"You don't understand. She's in love with Strickland."

"What!" I was startled at this, but the idea had no sooner taken possession of me than I saw it was absurd.

"How can you be so silly? You don't mean to say you're jealous of Strickland?" I almost laughed. "You know very well that she can't bear the sight of him."

"You don't understand," he moaned.

"You're an hysterical ass," I said a little impatiently. "Let me give you a whisky-and-soda, and you'll feel better."

I supposed that for some reason or other—and Heaven knows what ingenuity men exercise to torment themselves—Dirk had got it into his head that his wife cared for Strickland, and with his genius for blundering he might quite well have offended her so that, to anger him, perhaps, she had taken pains to foster his suspicion.

"Look here," I said, "let's go back to your studio. If you've made a fool of yourself you must eat humble pie. Your wife doesn't strike me as the sort of woman to bear malice."

"How can I go back to the studio?" he said wearily. "They're there. I've left it to them."

"Then it's not your wife who's left you; it's you who've left your wife."

"For God's sake don't talk to me like that."

Still I could not take him seriously. I did not for a moment believe what he had told me. But he was in very real distress.

"Well, you've come here to talk to me about it. You'd better tell me the whole story."

"This afternoon I couldn't stand it any more. I went to Strickland and told him I thought he was quite well enough to go back to his own place. I wanted the studio myself."

"No one but Strickland would have needed telling," I said. "What did he say?"

"He laughed a little; you know how he laughs, not as though he were amused, but as though you were a damned fool, and said he'd go at once. He began to put his things together. You remember I fetched from his room what I thought he needed, and he asked Blanche for a piece of paper and some string to make a parcel."

Stroeve stopped, gasping, and I thought he was going to faint. This was not at all the story I had expected him to tell me.

"She was very pale, but she brought the paper and the string. He didn't say anything. He made the parcel and he whistled a tune. He took no notice of either of us. His eyes had an ironic smile in them. My heart was like lead. I was afraid something was going to happen, and I wished I hadn't spoken. He looked round for his hat. Then she spoke:

" 'I'm going with Strickland, Dirk,' she said. 'I can't live with you any more.'

"I tried to speak, but the words wouldn't come. Strickland didn't say anything. He went on whistling as though it had nothing to do with him."

Stroeve stopped again and mopped his face. I kept quite still. I believed him now, and I was astounded. But all the same I could not understand.

Then he told me, in a trembling voice, with the tears pouring down his cheeks, how he had gone up to her, trying to take her in his arms, but she had drawn away and begged him not to touch her. He implored her not to leave him. He told her how passionately he loved her, and reminded her of all the devotion he had lavished upon her. He spoke to her of the happiness of their life. He was not angry with her. He did not reproach her.

"Please let me go quietly, Dirk," she said at last. "Don't you understand that I love Strickland? Where he goes I shall go."

"But you must know that he'll never make you happy. For

your own sake don't go. You don't know what you've got to look forward to."

"It's your fault. You insisted on his coming here."

He turned to Strickland.

"Have mercy on her," he implored him. "You can't let her do anything so mad."

"She can do as she chooses," said Strickland. "She's not forced to come."

"My choice is made," she said, in a dull voice.

Strickland's injurious calm robbed Stroeve of the rest of his self-control. Blind rage seized him, and without knowing what he was doing he flung himself on Strickland. Strickland was taken by surprise and he staggered, but he was very strong, even after his illness, and in a moment, he did not exactly know how, Stroeve found himself on the floor.

"You funny little man," said Strickland.

Stroeve picked himself up. He noticed that his wife had remained perfectly still, and to be made ridiculous before her increased his humiliation. His spectacles had tumbled off in the struggle, and he could not immediately see them. She picked them up and silently handed them to him. He seemed suddenly to realise his unhappiness, and though he knew he was making himself still more absurd, he began to cry. He hid his face in his hands. The others watched him without a word. They did not move from where they stood.

"Oh, my dear," he groaned at last, "how can you be so cruel?"

"I can't help myself, Dirk," she answered.

"I've worshipped you as no woman was ever worshipped before. If in anything I did I displeased you, why didn't you tell me, and I'd have changed. I've done everything I could for you."

She did not answer. Her face was set, and he saw that he was only boring her. She put on a coat and her hat. She moved towards the door, and he saw that in a moment she would be gone. He went up to her quickly and fell on his knees before her, seizing her hands: he abandoned all self-respect.

"Oh, don't go, my darling. I can't live without you; I shall kill myself. If I've done anything to offend you I beg you to forgive me. Give me another chance. I'll try harder still to make you happy."

"Get up, Dirk. You're making yourself a perfect fool."

He staggered to his feet, but still he would not let her go.

"Where are you going?" he said hastily. "You don't know what Strickland's place is like. You can't live there. It would be awful."

"If I don't care, I don't see why you should."

"Stay a minute longer. I must speak. After all, you can't grudge me that."

"What is the good? I've made up my mind. Nothing that you can say will make me alter it."

He gulped, and put his hand to his heart to ease its painful beating.

"I'm not going to ask you to change your mind, but I want you to listen to me for a minute. It's the last thing I shall ever ask you. Don't refuse me that."

She paused, looking at him with those reflective eyes of hers, which now were so indifferent to him. She came back into the studio and leaned against the table.

"Well?"

Stroeve made a great effort to collect himself.

"You must be a little reasonable. You can't live on air, you know. Strickland hasn't got a penny."

"I know."

"You'll suffer the most awful privations. You know why he took so long to get well. He was half starved."

"I can earn money for him."

"How?"

"I don't know. I shall find a way."

A horrible thought passed through the Dutchman's mind, and he shuddered.

"I think you must be mad. I don't know what has come over you."

She shrugged her shoulders.

"Now may I go?"

"Wait one second longer."

He looked round his studio wearily; he had loved it because her presence had made it gay and home-like; he shut his eyes for an instant; then he gave her a long look as though to impress on his mind the picture of her. He got up and took his hat.

"No; I'll go."

"You?"

She was startled. She did not know what he meant.

"I can't bear to think of you living in that horrible, filthy attic. After all, this is your home just as much as mine. You'll be comfortable here. You'll be spared at least the worst privations."

He went to the drawer in which he kept his money and took out several bank-notes.

"I would like to give you half what I've got here."

He put them on the table. Neither Strickland nor his wife spoke. Then he recollected something else.

"Will you pack up my clothes and leave them with the concierge? I'll come and fetch them to-morrow." He tried to smile. "Good-bye, my dear. I'm grateful for all the happiness you gave me in the past."

He walked out and closed the door behind him. With my mind's eye I saw Strickland throw his hat on a table, and, sitting down, begin to smoke a cigarette.

CHAPTER XXIX

I KEPT silence for a little while, thinking of what Stroeve had told me. I could not stomach his weakness, and he saw my disapproval.

"You know as well as I do how Strickland lived," he said tremulously. "I couldn't let her live in those circumstances—I simply couldn't."

"That's your business," I answered.

"What would *you* have done?" he asked.

"She went with her eyes open. If she had to put up with certain inconveniences it was her own look-out."

"Yes; but, you see, you don't love her."

"Do you love her still?"

"Oh, more than ever. Strickland isn't the man to make a woman happy. It can't last. I want her to know that I shall never fail her."

"Does that mean that you're prepared to take her back?"

"I shouldn't hesitate. Why, she'll want me more than ever then. When she's alone and humiliated and broken it would be dreadful if she had nowhere to go."

He seemed to bear no resentment. I suppose it was commonplace in me that I felt slightly outraged at his lack of spirit. Perhaps he guessed what was in my mind, for he said:

"I couldn't expect her to love me as I loved her. I'm a buffoon.

I'm not the sort of man that women love. I've always known that. I can't blame her if she's fallen in love with Strickland."

"You certainly have less vanity than any man I've ever known," I said.

"I love her so much better than myself. It seems to me that when vanity comes into love it can only be because really you love yourself best. After all, it constantly happens that a man when he's married falls in love with somebody else; when he gets over it he returns to his wife, and she takes him back, and everyone thinks it very natural. Why should it be different with women?"

"I dare say that's logical," I smiled, "but most men are made differently, and they can't."

But while I talked to Stroeve I was puzzling over the suddenness of the whole affair. I could not imagine that he had had no warning. I remembered the curious look I had seen in Blanche Stroeve's eyes; perhaps its explanation was that she was growing dimly conscious of a feeling in her heart that surprised and alarmed her.

"Did you have no suspicion before to-day that there was anything between them?" I asked.

He did not answer for a while. There was a pencil on the table, and unconsciously he drew a head on the blotting-paper.

"Please say so, if you hate my asking you questions," I said.

"It eases me to talk. Oh, if you knew the frightful anguish in my heart." He threw the pencil down. "Yes, I've known it for a fortnight. I knew it before she did."

"Why on earth didn't you send Strickland packing?"

"I couldn't believe it. It seemed so improbable. She couldn't bear the sight of him. It was more than improbable; it was incredible. I thought it was merely jealousy. You see, I've always been jealous, but I trained myself never to show it; I was jealous of every man she knew; I was jealous of you. I knew she didn't love me as I loved her. That was only natural, wasn't it? But she allowed me to love her, and that was enough to make me happy. I forced myself to go out for hours together in order to leave them by themselves; I wanted to punish myself for suspicions which were unworthy of me; and when I came back I found they didn't want me—not Strickland, he didn't care if I was there or not, but Blanche. She shuddered when I went to kiss her. When at last I was certain, I didn't know what to do; I knew they'd only laugh at me if I made a scene. I thought if I held my tongue and pretended not to see, everything would come right. I made up my mind to get him away quietly, without quarrelling. Oh, if you only knew what I've suffered."

Then he told me again of his asking Strickland to go. He chose his moment carefully, and tried to make his request sound casual; but he could not master the trembling of his voice, and he felt himself that into words that he wished to seem jovial and friendly there crept the bitterness of his jealousy. He had not expected Strickland to take him up on the spot and make his preparations to go there and then; above all, he had not expected his wife's decision to go with him. I saw that now he wished with all his heart that he had held his tongue. He preferred the anguish of jealousy to the anguish of separation.

"I wanted to kill him, and I only made a fool of myself."

He was silent for a long time, and then he said what I knew was in his mind.

"If I'd only waited, perhaps it would have gone all right. I shouldn't have been so impatient. Oh, poor child, what have I driven her to?"

I shrugged my shoulders, but did not speak. I had no sympathy for Blanche Stroeve, but knew that it would only pain poor Dirk if I told him exactly what I thought of her.

He had reached the stage of exhaustion when he could not stop talking. He went over again every word of the scene. Now something occurred to him that he had not told me before; now he discussed what he ought to have said instead of what he did say; then he lamented his blindness. He regretted that he had done this, and blamed himself that he had omitted the other. It grew later and later, and at last I was as tired as he.

"What are you going to do now?" I said finally.

"What can I do? I shall wait till she sends for me."

"Why don't you go away for a bit?"

"No, no; I must be at hand when she wants me."

For the present he seemed quite lost. He had made no plans. When I suggested that he should go to bed he said he could not sleep; he wanted to go out and walk the streets till day. He was evidently in no state to be left alone. I persuaded him to stay the night with me, and I put him into my own bed. I had a divan in my sitting-room, and could very well sleep on that. He was by now so worn out that he could not resist my firmness. I gave him a sufficient dose of veronal to insure his unconsciousness for several hours. I thought that was the best service I could render him.

CHAPTER XXX

But the bed I made up for myself was sufficiently uncomfortable to give me a wakeful night, and I thought a good deal of what the unlucky Dutchman had told me. I was not so much puzzled by Blanche Stroeve's action, for I saw in that merely the result of a physical appeal. I do not suppose she had ever really cared for her husband, and what I had taken for love was no more than the feminine response to caresses and comfort which in the minds of most women passes for it. It is a passive feeling capable of being roused for any object, as the vine can grow on any tree; and the wisdom of the world recognises its strength when it urges a girl to marry the man who wants her with the assurance that love will follow. It is an emotion made up of the satisfaction in security, pride of property, the pleasure of being desired, the gratification of a household, and it is only by an amiable vanity that women ascribe to it spiritual value. It is an emotion which is defenceless against passion. I suspected that Blanche Stroeve's violent dislike of Strickland had in it from the beginning a vague element of sexual attraction. Who am I that I should seek to unravel the mysterious intricacies of sex? Perhaps Stroeve's passion excited without satisfying that part of her nature, and she hated Strickland because she felt in him the power to give her what she needed. I think she was quite sincere when she struggled against her husband's desire to bring him into the studio; I think she was frightened of him, though she knew not why; and I remembered how she had foreseen disaster. I think in some curious way the horror which she felt for him was a transference of the horror which she felt for herself because he so strangely troubled her. His appearance was wild and uncouth; there was aloofness in his eyes and sensuality in his mouth; he was big and strong; he gave the impression of untamed passion; and perhaps she felt in him, too, that sinister element which had made me think of those wild beings of the world's early history when matter, retaining its early connection with the earth, seemed to possess yet a spirit of its own.

If he affected her at all, it was inevitable that she should love or hate him. She hated him.

And then I fancy that the daily intimacy with the sick man moved her strangely. She raised his head to give him food, and it was heavy against her hand; when she had fed him she wiped his sensual mouth and his red beard. She washed his limbs; they were covered with thick hair; and when she dried his hands, even in his weakness they were strong and sinewy. His fingers were long; they were the capable, fashioning fingers of the artist; and I know not what troubling thoughts they excited in her. He slept very quietly, without a movement, so that he might have been dead, and he was like some wild creature of the woods, resting after a long chase; and she wondered what fancies passed through his dreams. Did he dream of the nymph flying through the woods of Greece with the satyr in hot pursuit? She fled, swift of foot and desperate, but he gained on her step by step, till she felt his hot breath on her cheek; and still she fled silently, and silently he pursued, and when at last he seized her was it terror that thrilled her heart or was it ecstasy?

Blanche Stroeve was in the cruel grip of appetite. Perhaps she hated Strickland still, but she hungered for him, and everything that had made up her life till then became of no account. She ceased to be a woman, complex, kind and petulant, considerate and thoughtless; she was a Mænad. She was desire.

But perhaps this is very fanciful; and it may be that she was merely bored with her husband and went to Strickland out of a callous curiosity. She may have had no particular feeling for him, but succumbed to his wish from propinquity or idleness, to find then that she was powerless in a snare of her own contriving. How did I know what were the thoughts and emotions behind that placid brow and those cool grey eyes?

But if one could be certain of nothing in dealing with creatures so incalculable as human beings, there were explanations of Blanche Stroeve's behaviour which were at all events plausible. On the other hand, I did not understand Strickland at all. I racked my brain, but could in no way account for an action so contrary to my conception of him. It was not strange that he should so heartlessly have betrayed his friends' confidence, nor that he hesitated not at all to gratify a whim at the cost of another's misery. That was in his character. He was a man without any conception of gratitude. He had no compassion. The emotions common to most of us simply did not exist in him, and it was as absurd to blame him for not feeling them as for blaming the tiger because he is fierce and cruel. But it was the whim I could not understand.

I could not believe that Strickland had fallen in love with Blanche Stroeve. I did not believe him capable of love. That is an emotion in which tenderness is an essential part, but Strickland had no tenderness either for himself or for others; there is in love a sense of weakness, a desire to protect, an eagerness to do good and to give pleasure—if not unselfishness, at all events a selfishness which marvellously conceals itself; it has in it a certain diffidence. These were not traits which I could imagine in Strickland. Love is absorbing; it takes the lover out of himself; the most clear-sighted, though he may know, cannot realise that his love will cease; it gives body to what he knows is illusion, and, knowing it is nothing else, he loves it better than reality. It makes a man a little more than himself, and at the same time a little less. He ceases to be himself. He is no longer an individual, but a thing, an instrument to some purpose foreign to his ego. Love is never quite devoid of sentimentality, and Strickland was the least inclined to that infirmity of any man I have known. I could not believe that he would ever suffer that possession of himself which love is; he could never endure a foreign yoke. I believed him capable of uprooting from his heart, though it might be with agony, so that he was left battered and ensanguined, anything that came between himself and that uncomprehended craving that urged him constantly to he knew not what. If I have succeeded at all in giving the complicated impression that Strickland made on me, it will not seem outrageous to say that I felt he was at once too great and too small for love.

But I suppose that everyone's conception of the passion is formed on his own idiosyncrasies, and it is different with every different person. A man like Strickland would love in a manner peculiar to himself. It was vain to seek the analysis of his emotion.

CHAPTER XXXI

NEXT day, though I pressed him to remain, Stroeve left me. I offered to fetch his things from the studio, but he insisted on going himself; I think he hoped they had not thought of getting them together, so that he would have an opportunity of seeing his wife again and perhaps inducing her to come back to him. But he found his traps awaiting for him in the porter's lodge, and the concierge told him that Blanche had gone out. I do not think he resisted the temptation of giving her an account of his troubles. I found that he was telling them to everyone he knew; he expected sympathy, but only excited ridicule.

He bore himself most unbecomingly. Knowing at what time his wife did her shopping, one day, unable any longer to bear not seeing her, he waylaid her in the street. She would not speak to him, but he insisted on speaking to her. He spluttered out words of apology for any wrong he had committed toward her; he told her he loved her devotedly and begged her to return to him. She would not answer; she walked hurriedly, with averted face. I imagined him with his fat little legs trying to keep up with her. Panting a little in his haste, he told her how miserable he was; he besought her to have mercy on him; he promised, if she would forgive him, to do everything she wanted. He offered to take her for a journey. He told her that Strickland would soon tire of her. When he repeated to me the whole sordid little scene I was outraged. He had shown neither sense nor dignity. He had omitted nothing that could make his wife despise him. There is no cruelty greater than a woman's to a man who loves her and whom she does not love; she has no kindness then, no tolerance even, she has only an insane irritation. Blanche Stroeve stopped suddenly, and as hard as she could slapped her husband's face. She took advantage of his confusion to escape, and ran up the stairs to the studio. No word had passed her lips.

When he told me this he put his hand to his cheek as though he still felt the smart of the blow, and in his eyes was a pain that was heartrending and an amazement that was ludicrous. He looked like an overblown schoolboy, and though I felt so sorry for him, I could hardly help laughing.

Then he took to walking along the street which she must pass through to get to the shops, and he would stand at the corner, on the other side, as she went along. He dared not speak to her again, but sought to put into his round eyes the appeal that was in his heart. I suppose he had some idea that the sight of his misery would touch her. She never made the smallest sign that she saw him. She never even changed the hour of her errands or sought an alternative route. I have an idea that there was some cruelty in her indifference. Perhaps she got enjoyment out of the torture she inflicted. I wondered why she hated him so much.

I begged Stroeve to behave more wisely. His want of spirit was exasperating.

"You're doing no good at all by going on like this," I said. "I think you'd have been wiser if you'd hit her over the head with a stick. She wouldn't have despised you as she does now."

I suggested that he should go home for a while. He had often spoken to me of the silent town, somewhere up in the north of Holland, where his parents still lived. They were poor people. His father was a carpenter, and they dwelt in a little old red-brick house, neat and clean, by the side of a sluggish canal. The streets were wide and empty; for two hundred years the place had been dying, but the houses had the homely stateliness of their time. Rich merchants, sending their wares to the distant Indies, had lived in them calm and prosperous lives, and in their decent decay they kept still an aroma of their splendid past. You could wander along the canal till you came to broad green fields, with windmills here and there, in which cattle, black and white, grazed lazily. I thought that among those surroundings, with their recollections of his boyhood, Dirk Stroeve would forget his unhappiness. But he would not go.

"I must be here when she needs me," he repeated. "It would be dreadful if something terrible happened and I were not at hand."

"What do you think is going to happen?" I asked.

"I don't know. But I'm afraid."

I shrugged my shoulders.

For all his pain, Dirk Stroeve remained a ridiculous object. He might have excited sympathy if he had grown worn and thin. He did nothing of the kind. He remained fat, and his round, red cheeks shone like ripe apples. He had great neatness of person, and he continued to wear his spruce black coat and his bowler hat, always a little too small for him, in a dapper, jaunty manner. He was getting something of a paunch, and sorrow had no effect on it. He looked more than ever like a prosperous bagman. It is hard that a man's exterior should tally so little sometimes with his soul. Dirk Stroeve had the passion of Romeo in the body of Sir Toby Belch. He had a sweet and generous nature, and yet was always blundering; a real feeling for what was beautiful and the capacity to create only what was commonplace; a peculiar delicacy of sentiment and gross manners. He could exercise tact when dealing with the affairs of others, but none when dealing with his own. What a cruel practical joke old Nature played when she flung so many contradictory elements together, and left the man face to face with the perplexing callousness of the universe.

CHAPTER XXXII

I DID not see Strickland for several weeks. I was disgusted with him, and if I had had an opportunity should have been glad to tell him so, but I saw no object in seeking him out for the purpose. I am a little shy of any assumption of moral indignation; there is always in it an element of self-satisfaction which makes it awkward to anyone who has a sense of humour. It requires a very lively passion to steel me to my own ridicule. There was a sardonic sincerity in Strickland which made me sensitive to anything that might suggest a pose.

But one evening when I was passing along the Avenue de Clichy in front of the café which Strickland frequented and which I now avoided, I ran straight into him. He was accompanied by Blanche Stroeve, and they were just going to Strickland's favourite corner.

"Where the devil have you been all this time?" said he. "I thought you must be away."

His cordiality was proof that he knew I had no wish to speak to him. He was not a man with whom it was worth while wasting politeness.

"No," I said; "I haven't been away."

"Why haven't you been here?"

"There are more cafés in Paris than one, at which to trifle away an idle hour."

Blanche then held out her hand and bade me good-evening. I do not know why I had expected her to be somehow changed; she wore the same grey dress that she wore so often, neat and becoming, and her brow was as candid, her eyes as untroubled, as when I had been used to see her occupied with her household duties in the studio.

"Come and have a game of chess," said Strickland.

I do not know why at the moment I could think of no excuse. I followed them rather sulkily to the table at which Strickland always sat, and he called for the board and the chessmen. They both took the situation so much as a matter of course that I felt it absurd to do otherwise. Mrs. Stroeve watched the game with inscrutable face. She was silent, but she had always been silent. I looked at her mouth for an expression that could give me a clue to what she felt; I watched her eyes for some tell-tale flash, some hint of dismay or bitterness; I scanned her brow for any passing line that might indicate a settling emotion. Her face was a mask that told nothing. Her hands lay on her lap motionless, one in the other loosely clasped. I knew from what I had heard that she was a woman of violent passions; and that injurious blow that she had given Dirk, the man who had loved her so devotedly, betrayed a sudden temper and a horrid cruelty. She had abandoned the safe shelter of her husband's protection and the comfortable ease of a well-provided establishment for what she could not but see was an extreme hazard. It showed an eagerness for adventure, a readiness for the hand-to-mouth, which the care she took of her home and her love of good housewifery made not a little remarkable. She must be a woman of complicated character, and there was something dramatic in the contrast of that with her demure appearance.

I was excited by the encounter, and my fancy worked busily while I sought to concentrate myself on the game I was playing. I always tried my best to beat Strickland, because he was a player who despised the opponent he vanquished; his exultation in victory made defeat more difficult to bear. On the other hand, if he was beaten he took it with complete good-humour. He was a bad winner and a good loser. Those who think that man betrays his character nowhere more clearly than when he is playing a game might on this draw subtle inferences.

When he had finished I called the waiter to pay for the drinks, and left them. The meeting had been devoid of incident. No word had been said to give me anything to think about and any surmises I might make were unwarranted. I was intrigued. I could not tell how they were getting on. I would have given much to be a disembodied spirit so that I could see them in the privacy of the studio and hear what they talked about. I had not the smallest indication on which to let my imagination work.

CHAPTER XXXIII

Two or three days later Dirk Stroeve called on me.

"I hear you've seen Blanche," he said.

"How on earth did you find out?"

"I was told by someone who saw you sitting with them. Why didn't you tell me?"

"I thought it would only pain you."

"What do I care if it does? You must know that I want to hear the smallest thing about her."

I waited for him to ask me questions.

"What does she look like?" he said.

"Absolutely unchanged."

"Does she seem happy?"

I shrugged my shoulders.

"How can I tell? We were in a café; we were playing chess; I had no opportunity to speak to her."

"Oh, but couldn't you tell by her face?"

I shook my head. I could only repeat that by no word, by no hinted gesture, had she given an indication of her feelings. He must know better than I how great were her powers of self-control. He clasped his hands emotionally.

"Oh, I'm so frightened. I know something is going to happen, something terrible, and I can do nothing to stop it."

"What sort of thing?" I asked.

"Oh, I don't know," he moaned, seizing his head with his hands. "I foresee some terrible catastrophe."

Stroeve had always been excitable, but now he was beside himself; there was no reasoning with him. I thought it probable enough that Blanche Stroeve would not continue to find life with Strickland tolerable, but one of the falsest of proverbs is that you must lie on the bed that you have made. The experience of life shows that people are constantly doing things which must lead to disaster, and yet by some chance manage to evade the result of their folly. When Blanche quarrelled with Strickland she had only to leave him, and her husband was waiting humbly to forgive and forget. I was not prepared to feel any great sympathy for her.

"You see, you don't love her," said Stroeve.

"After all, there's nothing to prove that she is unhappy. For all we know they may have settled down into a most domestic couple."

Stroeve gave me a look with his woeful eyes.

"Of course it doesn't much matter to you, but to me it's so serious, so intensely serious."

I was sorry if I had seemed impatient or flippant.

"Will you do something for me?" asked Stroeve.

"Willingly."

"Will you write to Blanche for me?"

"Why can't you write yourself?"

"I've written over and over again. I didn't expect her to answer. I don't think she reads the letters."

"You make no account of feminine curiosity. Do you think she could resist?"

"She could—mine."

I looked at him quickly. He lowered his eyes. That answer of his seemed to me strangely humiliating. He was conscious that she regarded him with an indifference so profound that the sight of his handwriting would have not the slightest effect on her.

"Do you really believe that she'll ever come back to you?" I asked.

"I want her to know that if the worst comes to the worst she can count on me. That's what I want you to tell her."

I took a sheet of paper.

"What is it exactly you wish me to say?"

This is what I wrote:

Dear Mrs. Stroeve,

Dirk wishes me to tell you that if at any time you want him he will be grateful for the opportunity of being of service to you. He has no ill-feeling towards you on account of anything that has happened. His love for you is unaltered. You will always find him at the following address.

CHAPTER XXXIV

But though I was no less convinced than Stroeve that the connection between Strickland and Blanche would end disastrously, I did not expect the issue to take the tragic form it did. The summer came, breathless and sultry, and even at night there was no coolness to rest one's jaded nerves. The sun-baked streets seemed to give back the heat that had beat down on them during the day, and the passers-by dragged their feet along them wearily. I had not seen Strickland for weeks. Occupied with other things, I had ceased to think of him and his affairs. Dirk, with his vain lamentations, had begun to bore me, and I avoided his society. It was a sordid business, and I was not inclined to trouble myself with it further.

One morning I was working. I sat in my pyjamas. My thoughts wandered, and I thought of the sunny beaches of Brittany and the freshness of the sea. By my side was the empty bowl in which the concierge had brought me my *café au lait* and the fragment of *croissant* which I had not had appetite enough to eat. I heard the concierge in the next room emptying my bath. There was a tinkle at my bell, and I left her to open the door. In a moment I heard Stroeve's voice asking if I was in. Without moving, I shouted to him to come in. He entered the room quickly, and came up to the table at which I sat.

"She's killed herself," he said hoarsely.

"What do you mean?" I cried, startled.

He made movements with his lips as though he were speaking, but no sound issued from them. He gibbered like an idiot. My heart thumped against my ribs, and, I do not know why, I flew into a temper.

"For God's sake, collect yourself, man," I said. "What on earth are you talking about?"

He made despairing gestures with his hands, but still no words came from his mouth. He might have been struck dumb. I do not know what came over me; I took him by the shoulders and shook him. Looking back, I am vexed that I made such a fool of myself; I suppose the last restless nights had shaken my nerves more than I knew.

"Let me sit down," he gasped at length.

I filled a glass with St. Galmier and gave it to him to drink. I held it to his mouth as though he were a child. He gulped down a mouthful, and some of it was spilt on his shirt-front.

"Who's killed herself?"

I do not know why I asked, for I knew whom he meant. He made an effort to collect himself.

"They had a row last night. He went away."

"Is she dead?"

"No; they've taken her to the hospital."

"Then what are you talking about?" I cried impatiently. "Why did you say she'd killed herself?"

"Don't be cross with me. I can't tell you anything if you talk to me like that."

I clenched my hands, seeking to control my irritation. I attempted a smile.

"I'm sorry. Take your time. Don't hurry, there's a good fellow."

His round blue eyes behind the spectacles were ghastly with terror. The magnifying-glasses he wore distorted them.

"When the concierge went up this morning to take a letter she could get no answer to her ring. She heard someone groaning. The door wasn't locked, and she went in. Blanche was lying on the bed. She'd been frightfully sick. There was a bottle of oxalic acid on the table."

Stroeve hid his face in his hands and swayed backwards and forwards, groaning.

"Was she conscious?"

"Yes. Oh, if you knew how she's suffering! I can't bear it. I can't bear it."

His voice rose to a shriek.

"Damn it all, you haven't got to bear it," I cried impatiently. "She's got to bear it."

"How can you be so cruel!"

"What have you done?"

"They sent for a doctor and for me, and they told the police. I'd given the concierge twenty francs, and told her to send for me if anything happened."

He paused a minute, and I saw that what he had to tell me was very hard to say.

"When I went she wouldn't speak to me. She told them to send me away. I swore that I forgave her everything, but she wouldn't listen. She tried to beat her head against the wall. The doctor told me that I mustn't remain with her. She kept on saying, 'Send him away!' I went, and waited in the studio. And when the ambulance came and they put her on a stretcher, they made me go in the kitchen so that she shouldn't know I was there."

While I dressed—for Stroeve wished me to go at once with him to the hospital—he told me that he had arranged for his wife to have a private room, so that she might at least be spared the sordid promiscuity of a ward. On our way he explained to me why he desired my presence; if she still refused to see him, perhaps she would see me. He begged me to repeat to her that he loved her still; he would reproach her for nothing, but desired only to help her; he made no claim on her, and on her recovery would not seek to induce her to return to him; she would be perfectly free.

But when we arrived at the hospital, a gaunt, cheerless building, the mere sight of which was enough to make one's heart sick, and after being directed from this official to that, up endless stairs and through long, bare corridors, found the doctor in charge of the case, we were told that the patient was too ill to see anyone that day. The doctor was a little bearded man in white, with an off-hand manner. He evidently looked upon a case as a case, and anxious relatives as a nuisance which must be treated with firmness. Moreover, to him the affair was commonplace; it was just an hysterical woman who had quarrelled with her lover and taken poison; it was constantly happening. At first he thought that Dirk was the cause of the disaster, and he was needlessly brusque with him. When I explained that he was the husband, anxious to forgive, the doctor looked at him suddenly, with curious, searching eyes. I seemed to see in them a hint of mockery; it was true that Stroeve had the head of the husband who is deceived. The doctor faintly shrugged his shoulders.

"There is no immediate danger," he said, in answer to our questioning. "One doesn't know how much she took. It may be that she will get off with a fright. Women are constantly trying to commit suicide for love, but generally they take care not to succeed. It's generally a gesture to arouse pity or terror in their lover."

There was in his tone a frigid contempt. It was obvious that to him Blanche Stroeve was only a unit to be added to the statistical list of attempted suicides in the city of Paris during the current year. He was busy, and could waste no more time on us. He told us that if we came at a certain hour next day, should Blanche be better, it might be possible for her husband to see her.

CHAPTER XXXV

I scarcely know how we got through that day. Stroeve could not bear to be alone, and I exhausted myself in efforts to distract him.

I took him to the Louvre, and he pretended to look at pictures, but I saw that his thoughts were constantly with his wife. I forced him to eat, and after luncheon I induced him to lie down, but he could not sleep. He accepted willingly my invitation to remain for a few days in my apartment. I gave him books to read, but after a page or two he would put the book down and stare miserably into space. During the evening we played innumerable games of piquet, and bravely, not to disappoint my efforts, he tried to appear interested. Finally I gave him a draught, and he sank into uneasy slumber.

When we went again to the hospital we saw a nursing sister. She told us that Blanche seemed a little better, and she went in to ask if she would see her husband. We heard voices in the room in which she lay, and presently the nurse returned to say that the patient refused to see anyone. We told her that if she refused to see Dirk the nurse was to ask if she would see me, but this she refused also. Dirk's lips trembled.

"I dare not insist," said the nurse. "She is too ill. Perhaps in a day or two she may change her mind."

"Is there anyone else she wants to see?" asked Dirk, in a voice so low it was almost a whisper.

"She says she only wants to be left in peace."

Dirk's hands moved strangely, as though they had nothing to do with his body, with a movement of their own.

"Will you tell her that if there is anyone else she wishes to see I will bring him? I only want her to be happy."

The nurse looked at him with her calm, kind eyes, which had seen all the horror and pain of the world, and yet, filled with the vision of a world without sin, remained serene.

"I will tell her when she is a little calmer."

Dirk, filled with compassion, begged her to take the message at once.

"It may cure her. I beseech you to ask her now."

With a faint smile of pity, the nurse went back into the room. We heard her low voice, and then, in a voice I did not recognise, the answer:

"No No. No."

The nurse came out again and shook her head.

"Was that she who spoke then?" I asked. "Her voice sounded so strange."

"It appears that her vocal cords have been burnt by the acid."

Dirk gave a low cry of distress. I asked him to go on and wait for me at the entrance, for I wanted to say something to the nurse. He did not ask what it was, but went silently. He seemed to have lost all power of will; he was like an obedient child.

"Has she told you why she did it?" I asked.

"No. She won't speak. She lies on her back quite quietly. She doesn't move for hours at a time. But she cries always. Her pillow is all wet. She's too weak to use a handkerchief, and the tears just run down her face."

It gave me a sudden wrench of the heart-strings. I could have killed Strickland then, and I knew that my voice was trembling when I bade the nurse good-bye.

I found Dirk waiting for me on the steps. He seemed to see nothing, and did not notice that I had joined him till I touched him on the arm. We walked along in silence, I tried to imagine what had happened to drive the poor creature to that dreadful step. I presumed that Strickland knew what had happened, for someone must have been to see him from the police, and he must have made his statement. I did not know where he was. I supposed he had gone back to the shabby attic which served him as a studio. It was curious that she should not wish to see him. Perhaps she refused to have him sent for because she knew he would refuse to come. I wondered what an abyss of cruelty she must have looked into that in horror she refused to live.

CHAPTER XXXVI

THE next week was dreadful. Stroeve went twice a day to the hospital to enquire after his wife, who still declined to see him; and came away at first relieved and hopeful because he was told that she seemed to be growing better, and then in despair because, the complication which the doctor had feared having ensued, recovery was impossible. The nurse was pitiful to his distress, but she had little to say that could console him. The poor woman lay quite still, refusing to speak, with her eyes intent, as though she watched for the coming of death. It could now be only a question of a day or two; and when, late one evening, Stroeve came to see me I knew it was to tell me that she was dead. He was absolutely exhausted. His volubility had left him at last, and he sank down wearily on my sofa. I felt that no words of condolence availed, and I let him lie there quietly. I feared he would think it heartless if I read, so I sat by the window, smoking a pipe, till he felt inclined to speak.

"You've been very kind to me," he said at last. "Everyone's been very kind."

"Nonsense," I said, a little embarrassed.

"At the hospital they told me I might wait. They gave me a chair, and I sat outside the door. When she became unconscious they said I might go in. Her mouth and chin were all burnt by the acid. It was awful to see her lovely skin all wounded. She died very peacefully, so that I didn't know she was dead till the sister told me."

He was too tired to weep. He lay on his back limply, as though all the strength had gone out of his limbs, and presently I saw that he had fallen asleep. It was the first natural sleep he had had for a week. Nature, sometimes so cruel, is sometimes merciful. I covered him and turned down the light. In the morning when I awoke he was still asleep. He had not moved. His gold-rimmed spectacles were still on his nose.

CHAPTER XXXVII

THE circumstances of Blanche Stroeve's death necessitated all manner of dreadful formalities, but at last we were allowed to bury her. Dirk and I alone followed the hearse to the cemetery. We went at a foot-pace, but on the way back we trotted, and there was something to my mind singularly horrible in the way the driver of the hearse whipped up his horses. It seemed to dismiss the dead with a shrug of the shoulders. Now and then I caught sight of the swaying hearse in front of us, and our own driver urged his pair so that we might not remain behind. I felt in myself, too, the desire to get the whole thing out of my mind. I was beginning to be bored with a tragedy that did not really concern me, and pretending to myself that I spoke in order to distract Stroeve, I turned with relief to other subjects.

"Don't you think you'd better go away for a bit?" I said. "There can be no object in your staying in Paris now."

He did not answer, but I went on ruthlessly:

"Have you made any plans for the immediate future?"

"No."

"You must try and gather together the threads again. Why don't you go down to Italy and start working?"

Again he made no reply, but the driver of our carriage came to my rescue. Slackening his pace for a moment, he leaned over and spoke. I could not hear what he said, so I put my head out of the window; he wanted to know where we wished to be set down. I told him to wait a minute.

"You'd better come and have lunch with me," I said to Dirk. "I'll tell him to drop us in the Place Pigalle."

"I'd rather not. I want to go to the studio."

I hesitated a moment.

"Would you like me to come with you?" I asked then.

"No; I should prefer to be alone."

"All right."

I gave the driver the necessary direction, and in renewed silence we drove on. Dirk had not been to the studio since the wretched morning on which they had taken Blanche to the hospital. I was glad he did not want me to accompany him, and when I left him at the door I walked away with relief. I took a new pleasure in the streets of Paris, and I looked with smiling eyes at the people who hurried to and fro. The day was fine and sunny, and I felt in myself a more acute delight in life. I could not help it; I put Stroeve and his sorrows out of my mind. I wanted to enjoy.

CHAPTER XXXVIII

I DID not see him again for nearly a week. Then he fetched me soon after seven one evening and took me out to dinner. He was dressed in the deepest mourning, and on his bowler was a broad black band. He had even a black border to his handkerchief. His garb of woe suggested that he had lost in one catastrophe every relation he had in the world, even to cousins by marriage twice removed. His plumpness and his red, fat cheeks made his mourning not a little incongruous. It was cruel that his extreme unhappiness should have in it something of buffoonery.

He told me he had made up his mind to go away, though not to Italy, as I had suggested, but to Holland.

"I'm starting to-morrow. This is perhaps the last time we shall ever meet."

I made an appropriate rejoinder, and he smiled wanly.

"I haven't been home for five years. I think I'd forgotten it all; I seemed to have come so far away from my father's house that I was shy at the idea of revisiting it; but now I feel it's my only refuge."

He was sore and bruised, and his thoughts went back to the tenderness of his mother's love. The ridicule he had endured for years seemed now to weigh him down, and the final blow of Blanche's treachery had robbed him of the resiliency which had made him take it so gaily. He could no longer laugh with those who laughed at him. He was an outcast. He told me of his childhood in the tidy brick house, and of his mother's passionate orderliness. Her kitchen was a miracle of clean brightness. Everything was always in its place, and nowhere could you see a speck of dust. Cleanliness, indeed, was a mania with her. I saw a neat little old woman, with cheeks like apples, toiling away from morning to night, through the long years, to keep her house trim and spruce. His father was a spare old man, his hands gnarled after the work of a lifetime, silent and upright; in the evening he read the paper aloud, while his wife and daughter (now married to the captain of a fishing smack), unwilling to lose a moment, bent over their sewing. Nothing ever happened in that little town, left behind by the advance of civilisation, and one year followed the next till death came, like a friend, to give rest to those who had laboured so diligently.

"My father wished me to become a carpenter like himself. For five generations we've carried on the same trade, from father to son. Perhaps that is the wisdom of life, to tread in your father's steps, and look neither to the right nor to the left. When I was a little boy I said I would marry the daughter of the harness-maker who lived next door. She was a little girl with blue eyes and a flaxen pigtail. She would have kept my house like a new pin, and I should have had a son to carry on the business after me."

Stroeve sighed a little and was silent. His thoughts dwelt among pictures of what might have been, and the safety of the life he had refused filled him with longing.

"The world is hard and cruel. We are here none knows why, and we go none knows whither. We must be very humble. We must see the beauty of quietness. We must go through life so inconspicuously that Fate does not notice us. And let us seek the

love of simple, ignorant people. Their ignorance is better than all
our knowledge. Let us be silent, content in our little corner, meek
and gentle like them. That is the wisdom of life."

To me it was his broken spirit that expressed itself, and I
rebelled against his renunciation. But I kept my own counsel.

"What made you think of being a painter?" I asked.

He shrugged his shoulders.

"It happened that I had a knack for drawing. I got prizes for it at
school. My poor mother was very proud of my gift, and she gave
me a box of water-colours as a present. She showed my sketches
to the pastor and the doctor and the judge. And they sent me to
Amsterdam to try for a scholarship, and I won it. Poor soul, she
was so proud; and though it nearly broke her heart to part from
me, she smiled, and would not show me her grief. She was pleased
that her son should be an artist. They pinched and saved so that I
should have enough to live on, and when my first picture was
exhibited they came to Amsterdam to see it, my father and mother
and my sister, and my mother cried when she looked at it." His
kind eyes glistened. "And now on every wall of the old house
there is one of my pictures in a beautiful gold frame."

He glowed with happy pride. I thought of those cold scenes of
his, with their picturesque peasants and cypresses and olive trees.
They must look queer in their garish frames on the walls of the
peasant house.

"The dear soul thought she was doing a wonderful thing for me
when she made me an artist, but perhaps, after all, it would have
been better for me if my father's will had prevailed and I were now
but an honest carpenter."

"Now that you know what art can offer, would you change your
life? Would you have missed all the delight it has given you?"

"Art is the greatest thing in the world," he answered, after a
pause.

He looked at me for a minute reflectively; he seemed to hesitate;
then he said:

"Did you know that I had been to see Strickland?"

"You?"

I was astonished. I should have thought he could not bear to
set eyes on him. Stroeve smiled faintly.

"You know already that I have no proper pride."

"What do you mean by that?"

He told me a singular story.

CHAPTER XXXIX

WHEN I left him, after we had buried poor Blanche, Stroeve walked into the house with a heavy heart. Something impelled him to go to the studio, some obscure desire for self-torture, and yet he dreaded the anguish that he foresaw. He dragged himself up the stairs; his feet seemed unwilling to carry him; and outside the door he lingered for a long time, trying to summon up courage to go in. He felt horribly sick. He had an impulse to run down the stairs after me and beg me to go in with him; he had a feeling that there was somebody in the studio. He remembered how often he had waited for a minute or two on the landing to get his breath after the ascent, and how absurdly his impatience to see Blanche had taken it away again. To see her was a delight that never staled, and even though he had not been out an hour he was as excited at the prospect as if they had been parted for a month. Suddenly he could not believe that she was dead. What had happened could only be a dream, a frightful dream; and when he turned the key and opened the door, he would see her bending slightly over the table in the gracious attitude of the woman in Chardin's *Benedicite*, which always seemed to him so exquisite. Hurriedly he took the key out of his pocket, opened, and walked in.

The apartment had no look of desertion. His wife's tidiness was one of the traits which had so much pleased him; his own upbringing had given him a tender sympathy for the delight in orderliness; and when he had seen her instinctive desire to put each thing in its appointed place it had given him a little warm feeling in his heart. The bedroom looked as though she had just left it: the brushes were neatly placed on the toilet-table, one on each side of the comb; someone had smoothed down the bed on which she had spent her last night in the studio; and her night-dress in a little case lay on the pillow. It was impossible to believe that she would never come into that room again.

But he felt thirsty, and went into the kitchen to get himself some water. Here, too, was order. On a rack were the plates that she had used for dinner on the night of her quarrel with Strickland, and they had been carefully washed. The knives and forks were put away in a drawer. Under a cover were the remains of a piece of cheese, and in a tin box was a crust of bread. She had done her marketing from day to day, buying only what was strictly needful, so that nothing was left over from one day to the next. Stroeve knew from the enquiries made by the police that Strickland had walked out of the house immediately after dinner, and the fact that Blanche had washed up the things as usual gave him a little thrill of horror. Her methodicalness made her suicide more deliberate. Her self-possession was frightening. A sudden pang seized him, and his knees felt so weak that he almost fell. He went back into the bedroom and threw himself on the bed. He cried out her name:

"Blanche. Blanche."

The thought of her suffering was intolerable. He had a sudden vision of her standing in the kitchen—it was hardly larger than a cupboard—washing the plates and glasses, the forks and spoons, giving the knives a rapid polish on the knife-board; and then putting everything away, giving the sink a scrub, and hanging the dish-cloth up to dry—it was there still, a grey, torn rag; then looking round to see that everything was clean and nice. He saw her roll down her sleeves and remove her apron—the apron hung on a peg behind the door—and take the bottle of oxalic acid and go with it into the bedroom.

The agony of it drove him up from the bed and out of the room. He went into the studio. It was dark, for the curtains had been drawn over the great window, and he pulled them quickly back; but a sob broke from him as with a rapid glance he took in the place where he had been so happy. Nothing was changed here, either. Strickland was indifferent to his surroundings, and he had lived in the other's studio without thinking of altering a thing. It was deliberately artistic. It represented Stroeve's idea of the proper environment for an artist. There were bits of old brocade on the walls, and the piano was covered with a piece of silk, beautiful and tarnished; in one corner was a copy of the *Venus of Milo*, and in another of the *Venus of the Medici*. Here and there was an Italian cabinet surmounted with delf, and here and there a bas-relief. In a handsome gold frame was a copy of Velasquez' *Innocent X.*, that Stroeve had made in Rome, and placed so as to make the most of their decorative effect were a number of Stroeve's pictures, all in splendid frames. Stroeve had always been very proud of his taste. He had never lost his appreciation for the romantic atmosphere of a studio, and though now the sight of it was like a stab in his heart, without thinking what he was at, he changed slightly the position of a Louis XV table which was one of his treasures. Suddenly he caught sight of a canvas with its face to the wall. It was a much larger one than he himself was in the habit of using, and he wondered what it did there. He went over to it and leaned it towards him so that he could see the painting. It was a nude. His heart began to beat quickly, for he guessed at once that it was one of Strickland's pictures. He flung it back against the wall angrily—what did he mean by leaving it there?—but his movement caused it to fall, face downwards, on the ground. No matter whose the picture, he could not leave it there in the dust, and he raised it; but then curiosity got the better of him. He thought he would like to have a proper look at it, so he brought it along and set it on the easel. Then he stood back in order to see it at his ease.

He gave a gasp. It was the picture of a woman lying on a sofa, with one arm beneath her head and the other along her body; one knee was raised, and the other leg was stretched out. The pose was classic. Stroeve's head swam. It was Blanche. Grief and jealousy and rage seized him, and he cried out hoarsely; he was inarticulate; he clenched his fists and raised them threateningly at an invisible enemy. He screamed at the top of his voice. He was beside himself. He could not bear it. That was too much. He looked round wildly for some instrument; he wanted to hack the picture to pieces; it should not exist another minute. He could see nothing that would serve his purpose; he rummaged about his painting things; somehow he could not find a thing; he was frantic. At last he came upon what he sought, a large scraper, and he pounced on it with a cry of triumph. He seized it as though it were a dagger, and ran to the picture.

As Stroeve told me this he became as excited as when the incident occurred, and he took hold of a dinner-knife on the table between us, and brandished it. He lifted his arm as though to strike, and then, opening his hand, let it fall with a clatter to the ground. He looked at me with a tremulous smile. He did not speak.

"Fire away," I said.

"I don't know what happened to me. I was just going to make a great hole in the picture, I had my arm all ready for the blow, when suddenly I seemed to see it."

"See what?"

"The picture. It was a work of art. I couldn't touch it. I was afraid."

Stroeve was silent again, and he stared at me with his mouth open and his round blue eyes starting out of his head.

"It was a great, a wonderful picture. I was seized with awe. I had nearly committed a dreadful crime. I moved a little to see it better, and my foot knocked against the scraper. I shuddered."

I really felt something of the emotion that had caught him. I was strangely impressed. It was as though I were suddenly transported into a world in which the values were changed. I stood by, at a loss, like a stranger in a land where the reactions of man to familiar things are all different from those he has known. Stroeve tried to talk to me about the picture, but he was incoherent, and I had to guess at what he meant. Strickland had burst the bonds that hitherto had held him. He had found, not himself, as the phrase goes, but a new soul with unsuspected powers. It was not only the bold simplification of the drawing which showed so rich and so singular a personality; it was not only the painting, though the flesh was painted with a passionate sensuality which had in it something miraculous; it was not only the solidity, so that you felt extraordinarily the weight of the body; there was also a spirituality, troubling and new, which led the imagination along unsuspected ways, and suggested dim empty spaces, lit only by the eternal stars, where the soul, all naked, adventured fearful to the discovery of new mysteries.

If I am rhetorical it is because Stroeve was rhetorical. (Do we not know that man in moments of emotion expresses himself naturally in the terms of a novelette?) Stroeve was trying to express a feeling which he had never known before, and he did not know how to put it into common terms. He was like the mystic seeking to describe the ineffable. But one fact he made clear to me: people talk of beauty lightly and, having no feeling for words, they use that one carelessly, so that it loses its force; and the thing it stands for, sharing its name with a hundred trivial objects, is deprived of dignity. They call beautiful a dress, a dog, a sermon; and when they are face to face with Beauty cannot recognise it. The false emphasis with which they try to deck their worthless thoughts blunts their susceptibilities. Like the charlatan who counterfeits a spiritual force he has sometimes felt, they lose the power they have abused. But Stroeve, the unconquerable buffoon, had a love and an understanding of beauty which were as honest and sincere as was his own sincere and honest soul. It meant to him what God means to the believer, and when he saw it he was afraid.

"What did you say to Strickland when you saw him?"

"I asked him to come with me to Holland."

I was dumbfounded. I could only look at Stroeve in stupid amazement.

"We both loved Blanche. There would have been room for him in my mother's house. I think the company of poor, simple people would have done his soul a great good. I think he might have learnt from them something that would be very useful to him."

"What did he say?"

"He smiled a little. I suppose he thought me very silly. He said he had other fish to fry."

I could have wished that Strickland had used some other phrase to indicate his refusal.

"He gave me the picture of Blanche."

I wondered why Strickland had done that. But I made no remark, and for some time we kept silence.

"What have you done with all your things?" I said at last.

"I got a Jew in, and he gave me a round sum for the lot. I'm taking my pictures home with me. Beside them I own nothing in the world now but a box of clothes and a few books."

"I'm glad you're going home," I said.

I felt that his chance was to put all the past behind him. I hoped that the grief which now seemed intolerable would be softened by the lapse of time, and a merciful forgetfulness would help him to take up once more the burden of life. He was young still, and in a few years he would look back on all his misery with a sadness in which there would be something not unpleasurable. Sooner or later he would marry some honest soul in Holland, and I felt sure he would be happy. I smiled at the thought of the vast number of bad pictures he would paint before he died.

Next day I saw him off for Amsterdam.

CHAPTER XL

FOR the next month, occupied with my own affairs, I saw no one connected with this lamentable business, and my mind ceased to be occupied with it. But one day, when I was walking along, bent on some errand, I passed Charles Strickland. The sight of him brought back to me all the horror which I was not unwilling to forget, and I felt in me a sudden repulsion for the cause of it. Nodding, for it would have been childish to cut him, I walked on quickly; but in a minute I felt a hand on my shoulder.

"You're in a great hurry," he said cordially.

It was characteristic of him to display geniality with anyone who showed a disinclination to meet him, and the coolness of my greeting can have left him in little doubt of that.

"I am," I answered briefly.

"I'll walk along with you," he said.

"Why?" I asked.

"For the pleasure of your society."

I did not answer, and he walked by my side silently. We continued thus for perhaps a quarter of a mile. I began to feel a little ridiculous. At last we passed a stationer's, and it occurred to me that I might as well buy some paper. It would be an excuse to be rid of him.

"I'm going in here," I said. "Good-bye."

"I'll wait for you."

I shrugged my shoulders, and went into the shop. I reflected that French paper was bad, and that, foiled of my purpose, I need not burden myself with a purchase that I did not need. I asked for something I knew could not be provided, and in a minute came out into the street.

"Did you get what you wanted?" he asked.

"No."

We walked on in silence, and then came to a place where several streets met. I stopped at the kerb.

"Which way do you go?" I enquired.

"Your way," he smiled.

"I'm going home."

"I'll come along with you and smoke a pipe."

"You might wait for an invitation," I retorted frigidly.

"I would if I thought there was any chance of getting one."

"Do you see that wall in front of you?" I said, pointing.

"Yes."

"In that case I should have thought you could see also that I don't want your company."

"I vaguely suspected it, I confess."

I could not help a chuckle. It is one of the defects of my

character that I cannot altogether dislike anyone who makes me laugh. But I pulled myself together.

"I think you're detestable. You're the most loathsome beast that it's ever been my misfortune to meet. Why do you seek the society of someone who hates and despises you?"

"My dear fellow, what the hell do you suppose I care what you think of me?"

"Damn it all," I said, more violently because I had an inkling my motive was none too creditable, "I don't want to know you."

"Are you afraid I shall corrupt you?"

His tone made me feel not a little ridiculous. I knew that he was looking at me sideways, with a sardonic smile.

"I suppose you are hard up," I remarked insolently.

"I should be a damned fool if I thought I had any chance of borrowing money from you."

"You've come down in the world if you can bring yourself to flatter."

He grinned.

"You'll never really dislike me so long as I give you the opportunity to get off a good thing now and then."

I had to bite my lip to prevent myself from laughing. What he said had a hateful truth in it, and another defect of my character is that I enjoy the company of those, however depraved, who can give me a Roland for my Oliver. I began to feel that my abhorrence for Strickland could only be sustained by an effort on my part. I recognised my moral weakness, but saw that my disapprobation had in it already something of a pose; and I knew that if I felt it, his own keen instinct had discovered it too. He was certainly laughing at me up his sleeve. I left him the last word, and sought refuge in a shrug of the shoulders and taciturnity.

CHAPTER XLI

WE arrived at the house in which I lived. I would not ask him to come in with me, but walked up the stairs without a word. He followed me and entered the apartment on my heels. He had not been in it before, but he never gave a glance at the room I had been at pains to make pleasing to the eye. There was a tin of tobacco on the table, and, taking out his pipe, he filled it. He sat down on the only chair that had no arms and tilted himself on the back legs.

"If you're going to make yourself at home, why don't you sit in an arm-chair?" I asked irritably.

"Why are you concerned about my comfort?"

"I'm not," I retorted, "but only about my own. It makes me uncomfortable to see someone sit on an uncomfortable chair."

He chuckled, but did not move. He smoked on in silence, taking no further notice of me, and apparently was absorbed in thought. I wondered why he had come.

Until long habit has blunted the sensibility, there is something disconcerting to the writer in the instinct which causes him to take an interest in the singularities of human nature so absorbing that his moral sense is powerless against it. He recognises in himself an artistic satisfaction in the contemplation of evil which a little startles him; but sincerity forces him to confess that the disapproval he feels for certain actions is not nearly so strong as his curiosity in their reasons. The character of a scoundrel, logical and complete, has a fascination for his creator which is an outrage to law and order. I expect that Shakespeare devised Iago with a gusto which he never knew when, weaving moonbeams with his fancy, he imagined Desdemona. It may be that in his rogues the writer gratifies instincts deep-rooted in him, which the manners and customs of a civilised world have forced back to the mysterious recesses of the subconscious. In giving to the character of his invention flesh and bones he is giving life to that part of himself which finds no other means of expression. His satisfaction is a sense of liberation.

The writer is more concerned to know than to judge.

There was in my soul a perfectly genuine horror of Strickland, and side by side with it a cold curiosity to discover his motives. I was puzzled by him, and I was eager to see how he regarded the tragedy he had caused in the lives of people who had used him with so much kindness. I applied the scalpel boldly.

"Stroeve told me that picture you painted of his wife was the best thing you've ever done."

Strickland took his pipe out of his mouth, and a smile lit up his eyes.

"It was great fun to do."

"Why did you give it him?"

"I'd finished it. It wasn't any good to me."

"Do you know that Stroeve nearly destroyed it?"

"It wasn't altogether satisfactory."

He was quiet for a moment or two, then he took his pipe out of his mouth again, and chuckled.

"Do you know that the little man came to see me?"

"Weren't you rather touched by what he had to say?"

"No; I thought it damned silly and sentimental."

"I suppose it escaped your memory that you'd ruined his life?" I remarked.

He rubbed his bearded chin reflectively.

"He's a very bad painter."

"But a very good man."

"And an excellent cook," Strickland added derisively.

His callousness was inhuman, and in my indignation I was not inclined to mince my words.

"As a mere matter of curiosity I wish you'd tell me, have you felt the smallest twinge of remorse for Blanche Stroeve's death?"

I watched his face for some change of expression, but it remained impassive.

"Why should I?" he asked.

"Let me put the facts before you. You were dying, and Dirk Stroeve took you into his own house. He nursed you like a mother. He sacrificed his time and his comfort and his money for you. He snatched you from the jaws of death."

Strickland shrugged his shoulders.

"The absurd little man enjoys doing things for other people. That's his life."

"Granting that you owed him no gratitude, were you obliged to go out of your way to take his wife from him? Until you came on the scene they were happy. Why couldn't you leave them alone?"

"What makes you think they were happy?"

"It was evident."

"You are a discerning fellow. Do you think she could ever have forgiven him for what he did for her?"

"What do you mean by that?"

"Don't you know why he married her?"

I shook my head.

"She was a governess in the family of some Roman prince, and the son of the house seduced her. She thought he was going to marry her. They turned her out into the street neck and crop.

She was going to have a baby, and she tried to commit suicide. Stroeve found her and married her."

"It was just like him. I never knew anyone with so compassionate a heart."

I had often wondered why that ill-assorted pair had married, but just that explanation had never occurred to me. That was perhaps the cause of the peculiar quality of Dirk's love for his wife. I had noticed in it something more than passion. I remembered also how I had always fancied that her reserve concealed I knew not what; but now I saw in it more than the desire to hide a shameful secret. Her tranquillity was like the sullen calm that broods over an island which has been swept by a hurricane. Her cheefulness was the cheerfulness of despair. Strickland interrupted my reflections with an observation the profound cynicism of which startled me.

"A woman can forgive a man for the harm he does her," he said, "but she can never forgive him for the sacrifice he makes on her account."

"It must be reassuring to you to know that you certainly run no risk of incurring the resentment of the women you come in contact with," I retorted.

A slight smile broke on his lips.

"You are always prepared to sacrifice your principles for a repartee," he answered.

"What happened to the child?"

"Oh, it was still-born, three or four months after they were married."

Then I came to the question which had seemed to me most puzzling.

"Will you tell me why you bothered about Blanche Stroeve at all?"

He did not answer for so long that I nearly repeated it.

"How do I know?" he said at last. "She couldn't bear the sight of me. It amused me."

"I see."

He gave a sudden flash of anger.

"Damn it all, I wanted her."

But he recovered his temper immediately, and looked at me with a smile.

"At first she was horrified."

"Did you tell her?"

"There wasn't any need. She knew. I never said a word. She was frightened. At last I took her."

I do not know what there was in the way he told me this that extraordinarily suggested the violence of his desire. It was disconcerting and rather horrible. His life was strangely divorced from material things, and it was as though his body at times wreaked a fearful revenge on his spirit. The satyr in him suddenly took possession, and he was powerless in the grip of an instinct which had all the strength of the primitive forces of nature. It was an obsession so complete that there was no room in his soul for prudence or gratitude.

"But why did you want to take her away with you?" I asked.

"I didn't," he answered, frowning. "When she said she was coming I was nearly as surprised as Stroeve. I told her that when I'd had enough of her she'd have to go, and she said she'd risk that." He paused a little. "She had a wonderful body, and I wanted to paint a nude. When I'd finished my picture I took no more interest in her."

"And she loved you with all her heart."

He sprang to his feet and walked up and down the small room.

"I don't want love. I haven't time for it. It's weakness. I am a man, and sometimes I want a woman. When I've satisfied my passion I'm ready for other things. I can't overcome my desire, but I hate it; it imprisons my spirit; I look forward to the time when I shall be free from all desire and can give myself without hindrance to my work. Because women can do nothing except love, they've given it a ridiculous importance. They want to persuade us that it's the whole of life. It's an insignificant part. I know lust. That's normal and healthy. Love is a disease. Women are the instruments of my pleasure; I have no patience with their claim to be helpmates, partners, companions."

I had never heard Strickland speak so much at one time. He spoke with a passion of indignation. But neither here nor elsewhere do I pretend to give his exact words; his vocabulary was small, and he had no gift for framing sentences, so that one had to piece his meaning together out of interjections, the expression of his face, gestures and hackneyed phrases.

"You should have lived at a time when women were chattels and men the masters of slaves," I said.

"It just happens that I am a completely normal man."

I could not help laughing at this remark, made in all seriousness;

but he went on, walking up and down the room like a caged beast, intent on expressing what he felt but found such difficulty in putting coherently.

"When a woman loves you she's not satisfied until she possesses your soul. Because she's weak she has a rage for domination, and nothing less will satisfy her. She has a small mind, and she resents the abstract which she is unable to grasp. She is occupied with material things, and she is jealous of the ideal. The soul of man wanders through the uttermost regions of the universe, and she seeks to imprison it in the circle of her account book. Do you remember my wife? I saw Blanche little by little trying all her tricks. With infinite patience she prepared to snare me and bind me. She wanted to bring me down to her level; she cared nothing for me, she only wanted me to be hers. She was willing to do everything in the world for me except the one thing I wanted: to leave me alone."

I was silent for a while.

"What did you expect her to do when you left her?"

"She could have gone back to Stroeve," he said irritably. "He was ready to take her."

"You're inhuman," I answered. "It's as useless to talk to you about these things as to describe colours to a man who was born blind."

He stopped in front of my chair, and stood looking down at me with an expression in which I read a contemptuous amazement.

"Do you really care a twopenny damn if Blanche Stroeve is alive or dead?"

I thought over his question, for I wanted to answer it truthfully, at all events to my soul.

"It may be a lack of sympathy in myself if it does not make any great difference to me that she is dead. Life had a great deal to offer her. I think it's terrible that she should have been deprived of it in that cruel way, and I am ashamed because I do not really care."

"You have not the courage of your convictions. Life has no value. Blanche Stroeve didn't commit suicide because I left her, but because she was a foolish and unbalanced woman. But we've talked about her quite enough; she was an entirely unimportant person. Come, and I'll show you my pictures."

He spoke as though I were a child that needed to be distracted. I was sore, but not with him so much as with myself. I thought of the happy life that pair had led in the cosy studio in Montmartre, Stroeve and his wife, their simplicity, kindness, and hospitality; it seemed to me cruel that it should have been broken to pieces by a ruthless chance; but the cruellest thing of all was that in fact it made no great difference. The world went on, and no one was a penny the worse for all that wretchedness. I had an idea that Dirk, a man of greater emotional reactions than depth of feeling, would soon forget; and Blanche's life, begun with who knows what bright hopes and what dreams, might just as well have never been lived. It all seemed useless and inane.

Strickland had found his hat, and stood looking at me.

"Are you coming?"

"Why do you seek my acquaintance?" I asked him. "You know that I hate and despise you."

He chuckled good-humouredly.

"Your only quarrel with me really is that I don't care a two-penny damn what you think about me."

I felt my cheeks grow red with sudden anger. It was impossible to make him understand that one might be outraged by his callous selfishness. I longed to pierce his armour of complete indifference. I knew also that in the end there was truth in what he said. Unconsciously, perhaps, we treasure the power we have over people by their regard for our opinion of them, and we hate those upon whom we have no such influence. I suppose it is the bitterest wound to human pride. But I would not let him see that I was put out.

"Is it possible for any man to disregard others entirely?" I said, though more to myself than to him. "You're dependent on others for everything in existence. It's a preposterous attempt to try to live only for yourself and by yourself. Sooner or later you'll be ill and tired and old, and then you'll crawl back into the herd. Won't you be ashamed when you feel in your heart the desire for comfort and sympathy? You're trying an impossible thing. Sooner or later the human being in you will yearn for the common bonds of humanity.

"Come and look at my pictures."

"Have you ever thought of death?"

"Why should I? It doesn't matter."

I stared at him. He stood before me, motionless, with a mocking smile in his eyes; but for all that, for a moment I had an inkling of a fiery, tortured spirit, aiming at something greater than could be conceived by anything that was bound up with the flesh. I had a fleeting glimpse of a pursuit of the ineffable. I looked at the man before me in his shabby clothes, with his great nose and shining eyes, his red beard and untidy hair; and I had a strange sensation that it was only an envelope, and I was in the presence of a disembodied spirit.

"Let us go and look at your pictures," I said.

CHAPTER XLII

I DID not know why Strickland had suddenly offered to show them to me. I welcomed the opportunity. A man's work reveals him. In social intercourse he gives you the surface that he wishes the world to accept, and you can only gain a true knowledge of him by inferences from little actions, of which he is unconscious, and from fleeting expressions, which cross his face unknown to him. Sometimes people carry to such perfection the mask they have assumed that in due course they actually become the person they seem. But in his book or his picture the real man delivers himself defenceless. His pretentiousness will only expose his vacuity. The lath painted to look like iron is seen to be but a lath. No affectation of peculiarity can conceal a commonplace mind. To the acute observer no one can produce the most casual work without disclosing the innermost secrets of his soul.

As I walked up the endless stairs of the house in which Strickland lived, I confess that I was a little excited. It seemed to me that I was on the threshold of a surprising adventure. I looked about the room with curiosity. It was even smaller and more bare than I remembered it. I wondered what those friends of mine would say who demanded vast studios, and vowed they could not work unless all the conditions were to their liking.

"You'd better stand there," he said, pointing to a spot from which, presumably, he fancied I could see to best advantage what he had to show me.

"You don't want me to talk, I suppose," I said.

"No, blast you; I want you to hold your tongue."

He placed a picture on the easel, and let me look at it for a minute or two; then took it down and put another in its place. I think he showed me about thirty canvases. It was the result of the six years during which he had been painting. He had never sold a picture. The canvases were of different sizes. The smaller were pictures of still-life and the largest were landscapes. There were about half a dozen portraits.

"That is the lot," he said at last.

I wish I could say that I recognised at once their beauty and their great originality. Now that I have seen many of them again and the rest are familiar to me in reproductions, I am astonished that at first sight I was bitterly disappointed. I felt nothing of the peculiar thrill which it is the property of art to give. The impression that Strickland's pictures gave me was disconcerting; and the fact remains, always to reproach me, that I never even thought of buying any. I missed a wonderful chance. Most of them have found their way into museums, and the rest are the treasured possessions of wealthy amateurs. I try to find excuses for myself. I think that my taste is good, but I am conscious that it has no originality. I know very little about painting, and I wander along trails that others have blazed for me. At that time I had the greatest admiration for the Impressionists. I longed to possess a Sisley and a Degas, and I worshipped Manet. His *Olympia* seemed to me the greatest picture of modern times, and *Le Déjeuner sur l'Herbe* moved me profoundly. These works seemed to me the last word in painting.

I will not describe the pictures that Strickland showed me. Descriptions of pictures are always dull, and, these, besides, are familiar to all who take an interest in such things. Now that his influence has so enormously affected modern painting, now that others have charted the country which he was among the first to explore, Strickland's pictures, seen for the first time, would find the mind more prepared for them; but it must be remembered that I had never seen anything of the sort. First of all I was taken aback by what seemed to me the clumsiness of his technique. Accustomed to the drawing of the old masters, and convinced that Ingres was the greatest draughtsman of recent times, I thought that Strickland drew very badly. I knew nothing of the simplification at which he aimed. I remember a still-life of oranges on a plate, and I was bothered because the plate was not round and the oranges were lop-sided. The portraits were a little larger than life-size, and this gave them an ungainly look. To my eyes the faces looked like caricatures. They were painted in a way that was entirely new to me. The landscapes puzzled me even more. There

were two or three pictures of the forest of Fontainebleau and
several of streets in Paris: my first feeling was that they might have
been painted by a drunken cab-driver. I was perfectly bewildered.
The colour seemed to me extraordinarily crude. It passed through
my mind that the whole thing was a stupendous, incomprehensible
farce. Now that I look back I am more than ever impressed by
Stroeve's acuteness. He saw from the first that here was a revolution in art, and he recognised in its beginnings the genius
which now all the world allows.

But if I was puzzled and disconcerted, I was not unimpressed.
Even I, in my colossal ignorance, could not but feel that here,
trying to express itself, was real power. I was excited and interested. I felt that these pictures had something to say to me that
was very important for me to know, but I could not tell what it
was. They seemed to me ugly, but they suggested without
disclosing a secret of momentous significance. They were strangely
tantalising. They gave me an emotion that I could not analyse.
They said something that words were powerless to utter. I fancy
that Strickland saw vaguely some spiritual meaning in material
things that was so strange that he could only suggest it with halting
symbols. It was as though he found in the chaos of the universe a
new pattern, and were attempting clumsily, with anguish of soul,
to set it down. I saw a tormented spirit striving for the release of
expression.

I turned to him.

"I wonder if you haven't mistaken your medium," I said.

"What the hell do you mean?"

"I think you're trying to say something, I don't quite know
what it is, but I'm not sure that the best way of saying it is by
means of painting."

When I imagined that on seeing his pictures I should get a clue
to the understanding of his strange character I was mistaken. They
merely increased the astonishment with which he filled me. I was
more at sea than ever. The only thing that seemed clear to me—
and perhaps even this was fanciful—was that he was passionately
striving for liberation from some power that held him. But what
the power was and what line the liberation would take remained
obscure. Each one of us is alone in the world. He is shut in a
tower of brass, and can communicate with his fellows only by
signs, and the signs have no common value, so that their sense is
vague and uncertain. We seek pitifully to convey to others the

treasures of our heart, but they have not the power to accept them
and so we go, lonely, side by side but not together, unable to know
our fellows and unknown by them. We are like people living in a
country whose language they know so little that, with all manner
of beautiful and profound things to say, they are condemned to the
banalities of the conversation manual. Their brain is seething with
ideas, and they can only tell you that the umbrella of the gardener's
aunt is in the house.

The final impression I received was of a prodigious effort to
express some state of the soul, and in this effort, I fancied, must be
sought the explanation of what so utterly perplexed me. It was
evident that colours and forms had a significance for Strickland
that was peculiar to himself. He was under an intolerable necessity
to convey something that he felt, and he created them with that
intention alone. He did not hesitate to simplify or to distort if he
could get nearer to that unknown thing he sought. Facts were
nothing to him, for beneath the mass of irrelevant incidents he
looked for something significant to himself. It was as though he
had become aware of the soul of the universe and were compelled
to express it. Though these pictures confused and puzzled me, I
could not be unmoved by the emotion that was patent in them;
and, I knew not why, I felt in myself a feeling that with regard to
Strickland was the last I had ever expected to experience. I felt an
overwhelming compassion.

"I think I know now why you surrendered to your feeling for
Blanche Stroeve," I said to him.

"Why?"

"I think your courage failed. The weakness of your body
communicated itself to your soul. I do not know what infinite
yearning possesses you, so that you are driven to a perilous, lonely
search for some goal where you expect to find a final release from
the spirit that torments you. I see you as the eternal pilgrim to
some shrine that perhaps does not exist. I do not know to what
inscrutable Nirvana you aim. Do you know yourself? Perhaps it is
Truth and Freedom that you seek, and for a moment you thought
that you might find release in Love. I think your tired soul sought
rest in a womans arms, and when you found no rest there you
hated her. You had no pity for her, because you have no pity for
yourself. And you killed her out of fear, because you trembled
still at the danger you had barely escaped."

He smiled dryly and pulled his beard.

"You are a dreadful sentimentalist, my poor friend."

A week later I heard by chance that Strickland had gone to Marseilles. I never saw him again.

CHAPTER XLIII

LOOKING back, I realise that what I have written about Charles Strickland must seem very unsatisfactory. I have given incidents that came to my knowledge, but they remain obscure because I do not know the reasons that led to them. The strangest, Strickland's determination to become a painter, seems to be arbitrary; and though it must have had causes in the circumstances of his life, I am ignorant of them. From his own conversation I was able to glean nothing. If I were writing a novel, rather than narrating such facts as I know of a curious personality, I should have invented much to account for this change of heart. I think I should have shown a strong vocation in boyhood, crushed by the will of his father or sacrificed to the necessity of earning a living, I should have pictured him impatient of the restraints of life; and in the struggle between his passion for art and the duties of his station I could have aroused sympathy for him. I should so have made him a more imposing figure. Perhaps it would have been possible to see in him a new Prometheus. There was here, maybe, the opportunity for a modern version of the hero who for the good of mankind exposes himself to the agonies of the damned. It is always a moving subject.

On the other hand, I might have found his motives in the influence of the married relation. There are a dozen ways in which this might be managed. A latent gift might reveal itself on acquaintance with the painters and writers whose society his wife sought; or domestic incompatibility might turn him upon himself; a love affair might fan into bright flame a fire which I could have shown smouldering dimly in his heart. I think then I should have drawn Mrs. Strickland quite differently. I should have abandoned the facts and made her a nagging, tiresome woman, or else a bigoted one with no sympathy for the claims of the spirit. I should have made Strickland's marriage a long torment from which escape was the only possible issue. I think I should have emphasised his patience with the unsuitable mate, and the compassion which made him unwilling to throw off the yoke that oppressed him. I should certainly have eliminated the children.

An effective story might also have been made by bringing him into contact with some old painter whom the pressure of want or the desire for commercial success had made false to the genius of his youth, and who, seeing in Strickland the possibilities which himself had wasted, influenced him to forsake all and follow the divine tyranny of art. I think there would have been something ironic in the picture of the successful old man, rich and honoured, living in another the life which he, though knowing it was the better part, had not had the strength to pursue.

The facts are much duller. Strickland, a boy fresh from school, went into a broker's office without any feeling of distaste. Until he married he led the ordinary life of his fellows, gambling mildly on the Exchange, interested to the extent of a sovereign or two on the result of the Derby or the Oxford and Cambridge Race. I think he boxed a little in his spare time. On his chimney-piece he had photographs of Mrs. Langtry and Mary Anderson. He read *Punch* and the *Sporting Times*. He went to dances in Hampstead.

It matters less that for so long I should have lost sight of him. The years during which he was struggling to acquire proficiency in a difficult art were monotonous, and I do not know that there was anything significant in the shifts to which he was put to earn enough money to keep him. An account of them would be an account of the things he had seen happen to other people. I do not think they had any effect on his own character. He must have acquired experiences which would form abundant material for a picaresque novel of modern Paris, but he remained aloof, and judging from his conversation there was nothing in those years that had made a particular impression on him. Perhaps when he went to Paris he was too old to fall a victim to the glamour of his environment. Strange as it may seem, he always appeared to me not only practical, but immensely matter-of-fact. I suppose his life during this period was romantic, but he certainly saw no romance in it. It may be that in order to realise the romance of life you must have something of the actor in you; and, capable of standing outside yourself, you must be able to watch your actions with an interest at once detached and absorbed. But no one was more single-minded than Strickland. I never knew anyone who was less self-conscious. But it is unfortunate that I can give no description of the arduous steps by which he reached such mastery over his art as he ever acquired; for if I could show him undaunted by failure, by an unceasing effort of courage holding despair at bay, doggedly persistent in the face of self-doubt, which is the artist's bitterest enemy, I might excite some sympathy for a personality which, I am all too conscious, must appear singularly devoid of charm. But I have nothing to go on. I never once saw Strickland at work, nor do I know that anyone else did. He kept the secret of his struggles to himself. If in the loneliness of his studio he wrestled desperately with the Angel of the Lord he never allowed a soul to divine his anguish.

When I come to his connection with Blanche Stroeve I am exasperated by the fragmentariness of the facts at my disposal. To give my story coherence I should describe the progress of their tragic union, but I know nothing of the three months during which they lived together. I do not know how they got on or what they talked about. After all, there are twenty-four hours in the day, and the summits of emotion can only be reached at rare intervals. I can only imagine how they passed the rest of the time. While the light lasted and so long as Blanche's strength endured, I suppose that Strickland painted, and it must have irritated her when she saw him absorbed in his work. As a mistress she did not then exist for him, but only as a model; and then there were long hours in which they lived side by side in silence. It must have frightened her. When Strickland suggested that in her surrender to him there was a sense of triumph over Dirk Stroeve, because he had come to her help in her extremity, he opened the door to many a dark conjecture. I hope it was not true. It seems to me rather horrible. But who can fathom the subtleties of the human heart? Certainly not those who expect from it only decorous sentiments and normal emotions. When Blanche saw that, notwithstanding his moments of passion, Strickland remained aloof, she must have been filled with dismay, and even in those moments I surmise that she realised that to him she was not an individual, but an instrument of pleasure; he was a stranger still, and she tried to bind him to herself with pathetic arts. She strove to ensnare him with comfort and would not see that comfort meant nothing to him. She was at pains to get him the things to eat that he liked, and would not see that he was indifferent to food. She was afraid to leave him alone. She pursued him with attentions, and when his passion was dormant sought to excite it, for then at least she had the illusion of holding him. Perhaps she knew with her intelligence that the chains she forged only aroused his instinct of destruction, as the plate-glass window makes your fingers itch for half a brick; but her heart, incapable of reason, made her continue on a course she knew was fatal. She must have been very unhappy. But the blindness of love led her to believe what she wanted to be true, and her love was so great that it seemed impossible to her that it should not in return awake an equal love.

But my study of Strickland's character suffers from a graver defect than my ignorance of many facts. Because they were obvious and striking, I have written of his relations to women; and yet they were but an insignificant part of his life. It is an irony that they should so tragically have affected others. His real life consisted of dreams and of tremendously hard work.

Here lies the unreality of fiction. For in men, as a rule, love is but an episode which takes its place among the other affairs of the day, and the emphasis laid on it in novels gives it an importance which is untrue to life. There are few men to whom it is the most important thing in the world, and they are not very interesting ones; even women, with whom the subject is of paramount interest, have a contempt for them. They are flattered and excited by them, but have an uneasy feeling that they are poor creatures. But even during the brief intervals in which they are in love, men do other things which distract their mind: the trades by which they earn their living engage their attention; they are absorbed in sport; they can interest themselves in art. For the most part, they keep their various activities in various compartments, and they can pursue one to the temporary exclusion of the other. They have a faculty of concentration on that which occupies them at the moment, and it irks them if one encroaches on the other. As lovers, the difference between men and women is that women can love all day long, but men only at times.

With Strickland the sexual appetite took a very small place. It was unimportant. It was irksome. His soul aimed elsewhither. He had violent passions, and on occasion desire seized his body so that he was driven to an orgy of lust, but he hated the instincts that robbed him of his self-possession. I think, even, he hated the inevitable partner in his debauchery. When he had regained command over himself, he shuddered at the sight of the woman he had enjoyed. His thoughts floated then serenely in the empyrean, and he felt toward her the horror that perhaps the painted butterfly, hovering about the flowers, feels to the filthy chrysalis from which it has triumphantly emerged. I suppose that art is a manifestation of the sexual instinct. It is the same emotion which is excited in the human heart by the sight of a lovely woman, the Bay of Naples under the yellow moon, and the *Entombment* of Titian. It is possible that Strickland hated the normal release of sex because it seemed to him brutal by comparison with the satisfaction of artistic creation. It seems strange even to myself, when I have described a man who was cruel, selfish, brutal and sensual, to say that he was a great idealist. The fact remains.

He lived more poorly than an artisan. He worked harder. He cared nothing for those things which with most people make life gracious and beautiful. He was indifferent to money. He cared nothing about fame. You cannot praise him because he resisted the temptation to make any of those compromises with the world which most of us yield to. He had no such temptation. It never entered his head that compromise was possible. He lived in Paris more lonely than an anchorite in the deserts of Thebes. He asked nothing from his fellows except that they should leave him alone. He was single-hearted in his aim, and to pursue it he was willing to sacrifice not only himself—many can do that—but others. He had a vision.

Strickland was an odious man, but I still think he was a great one.

CHAPTER XLIV

A CERTAIN importance attaches to the views on art of painters, and this is the natural place for me to set down what I know of Strickland's opinions of the great artists of the past. I am afraid I have very little worth noting. Strickland was not a conversationalist, and he had no gift for putting what he had to say in the striking phrase that the listener remembers. He had no wit. His humour, as will be seen if I have in any way succeeded in reproducing the manner of his conversation, was sardonic. His repartee was rude. He made one laugh sometimes by speaking the truth, but this is a form of humour which gains its force only by its unusualness; it would cease to amuse if it were commonly practised.

Strickland was not, I should say, a man of great intelligence, and his views on painting were by no means out of the ordinary. I never heard him speak of those whose work had a certain analogy with his own—of Cézanne, for instance, or of Van Gogh; and I doubt very much if he had ever seen their pictures. He was not greatly interested in the Impressionists. Their technique impressed him, but I fancy that he thought their attitude commonplace. When Stroeve was holding forth at length on the excellence of Monet, he said: "I prefer Winterhalter." But I dare say he said it to annoy, and if he did he certainly succeeded.

I am disappointed that I cannot report any extravagances in his opinions on the old masters. There is so much in his character which is strange that I feel it would complete the picture if his views were outrageous. I feel the need to ascribe to him fantastic theories about his predecessors, and it is with a certain sense of disillusion that I confess he thought about them pretty much as does everybody else. I do not believe he knew El Greco. He had a great but somewhat impatient admiration for Velasquez. Chardin delighted him, and Rembrandt moved him to ecstasy. He described the impression that Rembrandt made on him with a coarseness I cannot repeat. The only painter that interested him who was at all unexpected was Brueghel the Elder. I knew very little about him at that time, and Strickland had no power to explain himself. I remember what he said about him because it was so unsatisfactory.

"He's all right," said Strickland. "I bet he found it hell to paint."

When later, in Vienna, I saw several of Peter Brueghel's pictures, I thought I understood why he had attracted Strickland's attention. Here, too, was a man with a vision of the world peculiar to himself. I made somewhat copious notes at the time, intending to write something about him, but I have lost them, and have now only the recollection of an emotion. He seemed to see his fellow-creatures grotesquely, and he was angry with them because they were grotesque; life was a confusion of ridiculous, sordid happenings, a fit subject for laughter, and yet it made him sorrowful to laugh. Brueghel gave me the impression of a man striving to express in one medium feelings more appropriate to expression in another, and it may be that it was the obscure consciousness of this that excited Strickland's sympathy. Perhaps both were trying to put down in paint ideas which were more suitable to literature.

Strickland at this time must have been nearly forty-seven.

CHAPTER XLV

I HAVE said already that but for the hazard of a journey to Tahiti I should doubtless never have written this book. It is thither that after many wanderings Charles Strickland came, and it is there that he painted the pictures on which his fame most securely rests. I suppose no artist achieves completely the realisation of the dream that obsesses him, and Strickland, harassed incessantly by his struggle with technique, managed, perhaps, less than others to express the vision that he saw with his mind's eye; but in Tahiti the circumstances were favourable to him; he found in his surroundings the accidents necessary for his inspiration to become effective, and his later pictures give at least a suggestion of what he sought. They offer the imagination something new and strange. It is as though in this far country his spirit, that had wandered disembodied, seeking a tenement, at last was able to clothe itself in flesh. To use the hackneyed phrase, here he found himself.

It would seem natural that my visit to this remote island should immediately revive my interest in Strickland, but the work I was engaged in occupied my attention to the exclusion of whatever was irrelevant, and it was not till I had been there some days that I even remembered his connection with it. After all, I had not seen him for fifteen years, and it was nine since he died. But I think my arrival at Tahiti would have driven out of my head matters of much more immediate importance to me, and even after a week I found it not easy to order myself soberly. I remember that on my first morning I awoke early, and when I came on to the terrace of the hotel no one was stirring. I wandered round to the kitchen, but it was locked, and on a bench outside it a native boy was sleeping. There seemed no chance of breakfast for some time, so I sauntered down to the water-front. The Chinamen were already busy in their shops. The sky had still the pallor of dawn, and there was a ghostly silence on the lagoon. Ten miles away the island of Murea, like some high fastness of the Holy Grail, guarded its mystery.

I did not altogether believe my eyes. The days that had passed since I left Wellington seemed extraordinary and unusual. Wellington is trim and neat and English; it reminds you of a seaport town on the South Coast. And for three days afterwards the sea was stormy. Grey clouds chased one another across the sky. Then the wind dropped, and the sea was calm and blue. The

Pacific is more desolate than other seas; its spaces seem more vast, and the most ordinary journey upon it has somehow the feeling of an adventure. The air you breathe is an elixir which prepares you for the unexpected. Nor is it vouchsafed to man in the flesh to know aught that more nearly suggests the approach to the golden realms of fancy than the approach to Tahiti. Murea, the sister isle, comes into view in rocky splendour, rising from the desert sea mysteriously, like the unsubstantial fabric of a magic wand. With its jagged outline it is like a Montserrat of the Pacific, and you may imagine that there Polynesian knights guard with strange rites mysteries unholy for men to know. The beauty of the island is unveiled as diminishing distance shows you in distincter shape its lovely peaks, but it keeps its secret as you sail by, and, darkly inviolable, seems to fold itself together in a stony, inaccessible grimness. It would not surprise you if, as you came near seeking for an opening in the reef, it vanished suddenly from your view, and nothing met your gaze but the blue loneliness of the Pacific.

Tahiti is a lofty green island, with deep folds of a darker green, in which you divine silent valleys; there is mystery in their sombre depths, down which murmur and plash cool streams, and you feel that in those umbrageous places life from immemorial times has been led according to immemorial ways. Even here is something sad and terrible. But the impression is fleeting, and serves only to give a greater acuteness to the enjoyment of the moment. It is like the sadness which you may see in the jester's eyes when a merry company is laughing at his sallies; his lips smile and his jokes are gayer because in the communion of laughter he finds himself more intolerably alone. For Tahiti is smiling and friendly; it is like a lovely woman graciously prodigal of her charm and beauty; and nothing can be more conciliatory than the entrance into the harbour at Papeete. The schooners moored to the quay are trim and neat, the little town along the bay is white and urbane, and the flamboyants, scarlet against the blue sky, flaunt their colour like a cry of passion. They are sensual with an unashamed violence that leaves you breathless. And the crowd that throngs the wharf as the steamer draws alongside is gay and debonair; it is a noisy, cheerful, gesticulating crowd. It is a sea of brown faces. You have an impression of coloured movement against the flaming blue of the sky. Everything is done with a great deal of bustle, the unloading of the baggage, the examination of the customs; and everyone seems to smile at you. It is very hot. The colour dazzles you.

CHAPTER XLVI

I HAD not been in Tahiti long before I met Captain Nichols. He came in one morning when I was having breakfast on the terrace of the hotel and introduced himself. He had heard that I was interested in Charles Strickland, and announced that he was come to have a talk about him. They are as fond of gossip in Tahiti as in an English village, and one or two enquiries I had made for pictures by Strickland had been quickly spread. I asked the stranger if he had breakfasted.

"Yes; I have my coffee early," he answered, "but I don't mind having a drop of whisky."

I called the Chinese boy.

"You don't think it's too early?" said the captain.

"You and your liver must decide that between you," I replied.

"I'm practically a teetotaller," he said, as he poured himself out a good half-tumbler of "Canadian Club".

When he smiled he showed broken and discoloured teeth. He was a very lean man, of no more than average height, with grey hair cut short and a stubby grey moustache. He had not shaved for a couple of days. His face was deeply lined, burned brown by long exposure to the sun, and he had a pair of small blue eyes which were astonishingly shifty. They moved quickly, following my smallest gesture, and they gave him the look of a very thorough rogue. But at the moment he was all heartiness and good-fellowship. He was dressed in a bedraggled suit of khaki, and his hands would have been all the better for a wash.

"I knew Strickland well," he said, as he leaned back in his chair and lit the cigar I had offered him. "It's through me he came out to the islands."

"Where did you meet him?" I asked.

"In Marseilles."

"What were you doing there?"

He gave me an ingratiating smile.

"Well, I guess I was on the beach."

My friend's appearance suggested that he was now in the same predicament, and I prepared myself to cultivate an agreeable acquaintance. The society of beachcombers always repays the small pains you need be at to enjoy it. They are easy of approach and affable in conversation. They seldom put on airs, and the offer of a drink is a sure way to their hearts. You need no laborious steps to enter upon familiarity with them, and you can earn not only their confidence but their gratitude by turning an attentive ear to their discourse. They look upon conversation as the great pleasure of life, thereby proving the excellence of their civilisation, and for the most part they are entertaining talkers. The extent of their experience is pleasantly balanced by the fertility of their imagination. It cannot be said that they are without guile, but they have a tolerant respect for the law, when the law is supported by strength. It is hazardous to play poker with them, but their ingenuity adds a peculiar excitement to the best game in the world. I came to know Captain Nichols very well before I left Tahiti, and I am the richer for his acquaintance. I do not consider that the cigars and whisky he consumed at my expense (he always refused cocktails, since he was practically a teetotaller), and the few dollars, borrowed with a civil air of conferring a favour upon me, that passed from my pocket to his, were in any way equivalent to the entertainment he afforded me. I remained his debtor. I should be sorry if my conscience, insisting on a rigid attention to the matter in hand, forced me to dismiss him in a couple of lines.

I do not know why Captain Nichols first left England. It was a matter upon which he was reticent, and with persons of his kidney a direct question is never very discreet. He hinted at undeserved misfortune, and there is no doubt that he looked upon himself as the victim of injustice. My fancy played with the various forms of fraud and violence, and I agreed with him sympathetically when he remarked that the authorities in the old country were so damned technical. But it was nice to see that any unpleasantness he had endured in his native land had not impaired his ardent patriotism. He frequently declared that England was the finest country in the world, sir, and he felt a lively superiority over Americans, Colonials, Dagos, Dutchmen, and Kanakas.

But I do not think he was a happy man. He suffered from dyspepsia, and he might often be seen sucking a tablet of pepsin; in the morning his appetite was poor; but this affliction alone would hardly have impaired his spirits. He had a greater cause of discontent with life than this. Eight years before he had rashly married a wife. There are men whom a merciful Providence has undoubtedly ordained to a single life, but who from wilfulness or through circumstances they could not cope with have flown in the face of its decrees. There is no object more deserving of pity than the married bachelor. Of such was Captain Nichols. I met his wife. She was a woman of twenty-eight, I should think, though of a type whose age is always doubtful; for she cannot have looked different when she was twenty, and at forty would look no older. She gave me an impression of extraordinary tightness. Her plain face with its narrow lips was tight, her skin was stretched tightly over her bones, her smile was tight, her hair was tight, her clothes were tight, and the white drill she wore had all the effect of black bombazine. I could not imagine why Captain Nichols had married her, and having married her why he had not deserted her. Perhaps he had, often, and his melancholy arose from the fact that he could never succeed. However far he went and in howsoever secret a place he hid himself, I felt sure that Mrs. Nichols, inexorable as fate and remorseless as conscience, would presently rejoin him. He could as little escape her as the cause can escape the effect.

The rogue, like the artist and perhaps the gentleman, belongs to no class. He is not embarrassed by the *sans gêne* of the hobo, nor put out of countenance by the etiquette of the prince. But Mrs. Nichols belonged to the well-defined class, of late become vocal, which is known as the lower-middle. Her father, in fact, was a policeman. I am certain that he was an efficient one. I do not know what her hold was on the captain, but I do not think it was love. I never heard her speak, but it may be that in private she had a copious conversation. At any rate, Captain Nichols was frightened to death of her. Sometimes, sitting with me on the terrace of the hotel, he would become conscious that she was walking in the road outside. She did not call him; she gave no sign that she was aware of his existence; she merely walked up and down composedly. Then a strange uneasiness would seize the captain; he would look at his watch and sigh.

"Well, I must be off," he said.

Neither wit nor whisky could detain him then. Yet he was a man who had faced undaunted hurricane and typhoon, and would not have hesitated to fight a dozen unarmed niggers with nothing but a revolver to help him. Sometimes, Mrs. Nichols would send her daughter, a pale-faced, sullen child of seven, to the hotel.

"Mother wants you," she said, in a whining tone.

"Very well, my dear," said Captain Nichols.

He rose to his feet at once, and accompanied his daughter along the road. I suppose it was a very pretty example of the triumph of spirit over matter, and so my digression has at least the advantage of a moral.

CHAPTER XLVII

I HAVE tried to put some connection into the various things Captain Nichols told me about Strickland, and I here set them down in the best order I can. They made one another's acquaintance during the latter part of the winter following my last meeting with Strickland in Paris. How he had passed the intervening months I do not know, but life must have been very hard, for Captain Nichols saw him first in the Asile de Nuit. There was a strike at Marseilles at the time, and Strickland, having come to the end of his resources, had apparently found it impossible to earn the small sum he needed to keep body and soul together.

The Asile de Nuit is a large stone building where pauper and vagabond may get a bed for a week, provided their papers are in order and they can persuade the friars in charge that they are working-men. Captain Nichols noticed Strickland for his size and his singular appearance among the crowd that waited for the doors to open; they waited listlessly, some walking to and fro, some leaning against the wall, and others seated on the kerb with their feet in the gutter; and when they filed into the office he heard the monk who read his papers address him in English. But he did not have a chance to speak to him, since, as he entered the common-room, a monk came in with a huge Bible in his arms, mounted a pulpit which was at the end of the room, and began the service which the wretched outcasts had to endure as the price of their lodging. He and Strickland were assigned to different rooms and when, thrown out of bed at five in the morning by a stalwart monk, he had made his bed and washed his face, Strickland had already disappeared. Captain Nichols wandered about the streets for an hour of bitter cold, and then made his way to the Place Victor Gélu, where the sailormen are wont to congregate. Dozing against the pedestal of a statue he saw Strickland again. He gave him a kick to awaken him.

"Come and have breakfast, mate," he said.

"Go to hell," answered Strickland.

I recognised my friend's limited vocabulary, and I prepared to regard Captain Nichols as a trustworthy witness.

"Busted?" asked the captain.

"Blast you," answered Strickland.

"Come along with me. I'll get you some breakfast."

After a moment's hesitation, Strickland scrambled to his feet, and together they went to the Bouchée de Pain, where the hungry are given a wedge of bread, which they must eat there and then, for it is forbidden to take it away; and then to the Cuillère de Soupe, where for a week, at eleven and four, you may get a bowl of thin, salt soup. The two buildings are placed far apart, so that only the starving should be tempted to make use of them. So they had breakfast, and so began the queer companionship of Charles Strickland and Captain Nichols.

They must have spent something like four months at Marseilles in one another's society. Their career was devoid of adventure, if by adventure you mean unexpected or thrilling incident, for their days were occupied in the pursuit of enough money to get a night's lodging and such food as would stay the pangs of hunger. But I wish I could give here the pictures, coloured and racy, which Captain Nichols's vivid narrative offered to the imagination. His account of their discoveries in the low life of a seaport town would have made a charming book, and in the various characters that came their way the student might easily have found matter for a very complete dictionary of rogues. But I must content myself with a few paragraphs. I received the impression of a life intense and brutal, savage, multi-coloured, and vivacious. It made the Marseilles that I knew, gesticulating and sunny, with its comfortable hotels and its restaurants crowded with the well-to-do, tame and commonplace. I envied men who had seen with their own eyes the sights that Captain Nichols described.

When the doors of the Asile de Nuit were closed to them, Strickland and Captain Nichols sought the hospitality of Tough Bill. This was the master of a sailors' boarding-house, a huge mulatto with a heavy fist, who gave the stranded mariner food and shelter till he found him a berth. They lived with him a month, sleeping with a dozen others, Swedes, negroes, Brazilians, on the floor of the two bare rooms in his house which he assigned to his charges; and every day they went with him to the Place Victor Gélu, whither came ships' captains in search of a man. He was married to an American woman, obese and slatternly, fallen to this pass by heaven knows what process of degradation, and every day the boarders took it in turns to help her with the housework. Captain Nichols looked upon it as a smart piece of work on Strickland's part that he had got out of this by painting a portrait of Tough Bill. Tough Bill not only paid for the canvas, colours, and brushes, but gave Strickland a pound of smuggled tobacco into the bargain. For all I know, this picture may still adorn the parlour of the tumble-down little house somewhere near the Quai de la Joliette, and I suppose it could now be sold for fifteen hundred pounds. Strickland's idea was to ship on some vessel bound for Australia or New Zealand, and from there make his way to Samoa or Tahiti. I do not know how he had come upon the notion of going to the South Seas, though I remember that his imagination had long been haunted by an island, all green and sunny, encircled by a sea more blue than is found in Northern latitudes. I suppose that he clung to Captain Nichols because he was acquainted with those parts, and it was Captain Nichols who persuaded him that he would be more comfortable in Tahiti.

"You see, Tahiti's French," he explained to me. "And the French aren't so damned technical."

I thought I saw his point.

Strickland had no papers, but that was not a matter to disconcert Tough Bill when he saw a profit (he took the first month's wages of the sailor for whom he found a berth), and he provided Strickland with those of an English stoker who had providentially died on his hands. But both Captain Nichols and Strickland were bound East, and it chanced that the only opportunities for signing on were with ships sailing West. Twice Strickland refused a berth on tramps sailing for the United States, and once on a collier going to Newcastle. Tough Bill had no patience with an obstinacy which could only result in loss to himself, and on the last occasion he flung both Strickland and Captain Nichols out of his house without more ado. They found themselves once more adrift.

Tough Bill's fare was seldom extravagant, and you rose from his table almost as hungry as you sat down, but for some days they had good reason to regret it. They learned what hunger was. The Cuillère de Soupe and the Asile de Nuit were both closed to them, and their only sustenance was the wedge of bread which the Bouchée de Pain provided. They slept where they could, sometimes in an empty truck on a siding near the station, sometimes in a cart behind a warehouse; but it was bitterly cold, and after an hour or two of uneasy dozing they would tramp the streets again. What they felt the lack of most bitterly was tobacco, and Captain Nichols, for his part, could not do without it; he took to hunting the "Can o' Beer" for cigarette-ends and the butt-ends of cigars which the promenaders of the night before had thrown away.

"I've tasted worse smoking mixtures in a pipe," he added, with a philosophic shrug of his shoulders, as he took a couple of cigars from the case I offered him, putting one in his mouth and the other in his pocket.

Now and then they made a bit of money. Sometimes a mail steamer would come in, and Captain Nichols, having scraped acquaintance with the time-keeper, would succeed in getting the pair of them a job as stevedores. When it was an English boat, they would dodge into the forecastle and get a hearty breakfast from the crew. They took the risk of running against one of the ship's officers and being hustled down the gangway with the toe of a boot to speed their going.

"There's no harm in a kick in the hindquarters when your belly's full," said Captain Nichols, "and personally I never take it in bad part. An officer's got to think about discipline."

I had a lively picture of Captain Nichols flying headlong down a narrow gangway before the uplifted foot of an angry mate and, like a true Englishman, rejoicing in the spirit of the Mercantile Marine.

There were often odd jobs to be got about the fish-market. Once they each earned a franc by loading trucks with innumerable boxes of oranges that had been dumped down on the quay. One day they had a stroke of luck: one of the boarding-masters got a contract to paint a tramp that had come in from Madagascar round the Cape of Good Hope, and they spent several days on a plank hanging over the side, covering the rusty hull with paint. It was a situation that must have appealed to Strickland's sardonic humour. I asked Captain Nichols how he bore himself during these hardships.

"Never knew him say a cross word," answered the captain. "He'd be a bit surly sometimes, but when we hadn't had a bite since morning, and we hadn't even got the price of a lie-down at the Chink's, he'd be as lively as a cricket."

I was not surprised at this. Strickland was just the man to rise superior to circumstances, when they were such as to occasion despondency in most; but whether this was due to equanimity of soul or to contradictoriness it would be difficult to say.

The Chink's Head was a name the beachcombers gave to a wretched inn off the Rue Bouterie, kept by a one-eyed Chinaman, where for six sous you could sleep in a cot and for three on the floor. Here they made friends with others in as desperate condition as themselves, and when they were penniless and the night was bitter cold, they were glad to borrow from anyone who had earned a stray franc during the day the price of a roof over their heads. They were not niggardly, these tramps, and he who had money did not hesitate to share it among the rest. They belonged to all the countries in the world, but this was no bar to good-fellowship; for they felt themselves freemen of a country whose frontiers include them all, the great country of Cockaigne.

"But I guess Strickland was an ugly customer when he was roused," said Captain Nichols, reflectively. "One day we ran into Tough Bill in the Place, and he asked Charlie for the papers he'd given him.

" 'You'd better come and take them if you want them,' says Charlie.

"He was a powerful fellow, Tough Bill, but he didn't quite like the look of Charlie, so he began cursing him. He called him pretty near every name he could lay hands on, and when Tough Bill began cursing it was worth listening to him. Well, Charlie stuck it for a bit, then he stepped forward and he just said: 'Get out, you bloody swine.' It wasn't so much what he said, but the way he said it. Tough Bill never spoke another word; you could see him go yellow, and he walked away as if he'd remembered he had a date."

Strickland, according to Captain Nichols, did not use exactly the words I have given, but since this book is meant for family reading I have thought it better, at the expense of truth, to put into his mouth expressions familiar to the domestic circle.

Now, Tough Bill was not the man to put up with humiliation at the hands of a common sailor. His power depended on his prestige, and first one, then another, of the sailors who lived in his house told them that he had sworn to do Strickland in.

One night Captain Nichols and Strickland were sitting in one of the bars of the Rue Bouterie. The Rue Bouterie is a narrow street of one-storeyed houses, each house consisting of but one room; they are like the booths in a crowded fair or the cages of animals in a circus. At every door you see a woman. Some lean lazily against the side-posts, humming to themselves or calling to the passer-by in a raucous voice, and some listlessly read. They are French, Italian, Spanish, Japanese, coloured; some are fat and some are thin; and under the thick paint on their faces, the heavy smears on their eyebrows, and the scarlet of their lips you see the lines of age and the scars of dissipation. Some wear black shifts and flesh-coloured stockings; some with curly hair, dyed yellow, are dressed like little girls in short muslin frocks. Through the open door you see a red-tiled floor, a large wooden bed, and on a deal table a ewer and a basin. A motley crowd saunters along the street—Lascars off a P. & O., blond Northmen from a Swedish barque, Japanese from a man-of-war, English sailors, Spaniards, pleasant-looking fellows from a French cruiser, negroes off an American tramp. By day it is merely sordid, but at night, lit only by the lamps in the little huts, the street has a sinister beauty. The hideous lust that pervades the air is oppressive and horrible, and yet there is something mysterious in the sight which haunts and troubles you. You feel I know not what primitive force which repels and yet fascinates you. Here all the decencies of civilisation are swept away, and you feel that men are face to face with a sombre reality. There is an atmosphere that is at once intense and tragic.

In the bar in which Strickland and Nichols sat a mechanical piano was loudly grinding out dance music. Round the room people were sitting at tables, here half a dozen sailors uproariously drunk, there a group of soldiers; and in the middle, crowded together, couples were dancing. Bearded sailors with brown faces and large horny hands clasped their partners in a tight embrace. The women wore nothing but a shift. Now and then two sailors would get up and dance together. The noise was deafening. People were singing, shouting, laughing; and when a man gave a long kiss to the girl sitting on his knees, cat-calls from the English sailors increased the din. The air was heavy with the dust beaten up by the heavy boots of the men, and grey with smoke. It was very hot. Behind the bar was seated a woman nursing her baby. The waiter, an undersized youth with a flat, spotty face, hurried to and fro carrying a tray laden with glasses of beer.

In a little while Tough Bill, accompanied by two huge negroes, came in, and it was easy to see that he was already three parts drunk. He was looking for trouble. He lurched against a table at which three soldiers were sitting and knocked over a glass of beer.

There was an angry altercation, and the owner of the bar stepped forward and ordered Tough Bill to go. He was a hefty fellow, in the habit of standing no nonsense from his customers, and Tough Bill hesitated. The landlord was not a man he cared to tackle, for the police were on his side, and with an oath he turned on his heel. Suddenly he caught sight of Strickland. He rolled up to him. He did not speak. He gathered the spittle in his mouth and spat full in Strickland's face. Strickland seized his glass and flung it at him. The dancers stopped suddenly still. There was an instant of complete silence, but when Tough Bill threw himself on Strickland the lust of battle seized them all, and in a moment there was a confused scrummage. Tables were overturned, glasses crashed to the ground. There was a hellish row. The women scattered to the door and behind the bar. Passers-by surged in from the street. You heard curses in every tongue, the sound of blows, cries; and in the middle of the room a dozen men were fighting with all their might. On a sudden the police rushed in, and everyone who could made for the door. When the bar was more or less cleared, Tough Bill was lying insensible on the floor with a great gash in his head. Captain Nichols dragged Strickland, bleeding from a wound in his arm, his clothes in rags, into the street. His own face was covered with blood from a blow on the nose.

"I guess you'd better get out of Marseilles before Tough Bill comes out of hospital," he said to Strickland, when they had got back to the Chink's Head and were cleaning themselves.

"This beats cock-fighting," said Strickland.

I could see his sardonic smile.

Captain Nichols was anxious. He knew Tough Bill's vindictiveness. Strickland had downed the mulatto twice, and the mulatto, sober, was a man to be reckoned with. He would bide his time stealthily. He would be in no hurry, but one night Strickland would get a knife-thrust in his back, and in a day or two the corpse of a nameless beachcomber would be fished out of the dirty water of the harbour. Nichols went next evening to Tough Bill's house and made enquiries. He was in hospital still, but his wife, who had been to see him, said he was swearing hard to kill Strickland when they let him out.

A week passed.

"That's what I always say," reflected Captain Nichols, "when you hurt a man, hurt him bad. It gives you a bit of time to look about and think what you'll do next."

Then Strickland had a bit of luck. A ship bound for Australia had sent to the Sailors' Home for a stoker in place of one who had thrown himself overboard off Gibraltar in an attack of delirium tremens.

"You double down to the harbour, my lad," said the captain to Strickland, "and sign on. You've got your papers."

Strickland set off at once, and that was the last Captain Nichols saw of him. The ship was only in port for six hours, and in the evening Captain Nichols watched the vanishing smoke from her funnels as she ploughed East through the wintry sea.

I have narrated all this as best I could, because I like the contrast of these episodes with the life that I had seen Strickland live in Ashley Gardens when he was occupied with stocks and shares; but I am aware that Captain Nichols was an outrageous liar, and I dare say there is not a word of truth in anything he told me. I should not be surprised to learn that he had never seen Strickland in his life, and owed his knowledge of Marseilles to the pages of a magazine.

CHAPTER XLVIII

IT is here that I purposed to end my book. My first idea was to begin it with the account of Strickland's last years in Tahiti and with his horrible death, and then to go back and relate what I knew of his beginnings. This I meant to do, not from wilfulness, but because I wished to leave Strickland setting out with I know not what fancies in his lonely soul for the unknown islands which fired his imagination. I liked the picture of him, starting at the age of forty-seven, when most men have already settled comfortably in a groove, for a new world. I saw him, the sea grey under the mistral and foam-flecked, watching the vanishing coast of France, which he was destined never to see again; and I thought there was something gallant in his bearing and dauntless in his soul. I wished so to end on a note of hope. It seemed to emphasise the unconquerable spirit of man. But I could not manage it. Somehow I could not get into my story, and after trying once or twice I had to give it up; I started from the beginning in the usual way, and made up my mind I could only tell what I knew of Strickland's life in the order in which I learnt the facts.

Those that I have now are fragmentary. I am in the position of a biologist who from a single bone must reconstruct not only the appearance of an extinct animal, but its habits. Strickland made no particular impression on the people who came in contact with him in Tahiti. To them he was no more than a beachcomber in constant need of money, remarkable only for the peculiarity that he painted pictures which seemed to them absurd; and it was not till he had been dead for some years, and agents came from the dealers in Paris and Berlin to look for any pictures which might still remain on the island, that they had any idea that among them had dwelt a man of consequence. They remembered then that they could have bought for a song canvases which now were worth large sums, and they could not forgive themselves for the opportunity which had escaped them. There was a Jewish trader called Cohen who had come by one of Strickland's pictures in a singular way. He was a little old Frenchman, with soft kind eyes and a pleasant smile, half trader and half seaman, who owned a cutter in which he wandered boldly among the Paumotus and the Marquesas, taking out trade goods and bringing back copra, shell, and pearls. I went to see him because I was told he had a large black pearl which he was willing to sell cheaply, and when I discovered that it was beyond my means I began to talk to him about Strickland. He had known him well.

"You see, I was interested in him because he was a painter," he told me. "We don't get many painters in the islands, and I was sorry for him because he was such a bad one. I gave him his first job. I had a plantation on the peninsula, and I wanted a white overseer. You never get any work out of the natives unless you have a white man over them. I said to him: 'You'll have plenty of time for painting, and you can earn a bit of money.' I knew he was starving, but I offered him good wages."

"I can't imagine that he was a very satisfactory overseer," I said, smiling.

"I made allowances. I have always had a sympathy for artists. It is in our blood, you know. But he only remained a few months. When he had enough money to buy paints and canvases he left me. The place had got hold of him by then, and he wanted to get away into the bush. But I continued to see him now and then. He would turn up in Papeete every few months and stay a little while; he'd get money out of someone or other and then disappear again. It was on one of these visits that he came to me and asked for the loan of two hundred francs. He looked as if he hadn't had a meal for a week, and I hadn't the heart to refuse him. Of course, I never expected to see my money again. Well, a year later he came to see me once more, and he brought a picture with him. He did not mention the money he owed me, but he said: 'Here is a picture of your plantation that I've painted for you.' I looked at it. I did not know what to say, but of course I thanked him, and when he had gone away I showed it to my wife."

"What was it like?" I asked.

"Do not ask me. I could not make head or tail of it. I never saw such a thing in my life. 'What shall we do with it?' I said to my wife. 'We can never hang it up,' she said. 'People would laugh at us.' So she took it into an attic and put it away with all sorts of rubbish, for my wife can never throw anything away. It is her mania. Then, imagine to yourself, just before the war my brother wrote to me from Paris, and said: 'Do you know anything about an English painter who lived in Tahiti? It appears that he was a genius, and his pictures fetch large prices. See if you can lay your hands on anything and send it to me. There's money to be made.' So I said to my wife: 'What about that picture that Strickland gave me? Is it possible that it is still in the attic?' 'Without doubt,' she answered, 'for you know that I never throw anything away. It is my mania.' We went up to the attic, and there, among I know not what rubbish that had been gathered during the thirty years we have inhabited that house, was the picture. I looked at it again, and I said: 'Who would have thought that the overseer of my plantation on the peninsula, to whom I lent two hundred francs, had genius? Do you see anything in the picture?' 'No,' she said, 'it does not resemble the plantation and I have never seen coconuts with blue leaves; but they are mad in Paris, and it may be that your brother will be able to sell it for the two hundred francs you lent Strickland.' Well, we packed it up and we sent it to my brother. And at last I received a letter from him. What do you think he said? 'I received your picture,' he said, 'and I confess I thought it was a joke that you had played on me. I would not have given the cost of postage for the picture. I was half afraid to show it to the gentleman who had spoken to me about it. Imagine my surprise when he said it was a masterpiece, and offered me thirty thousand francs. I dare say he would have paid more, but frankly I was so taken aback that I lost my head; I accepted the offer before I was able to collect myself.' "

Then Monsieur Cohen said an admirable thing.

"I wish that poor Strickland had been still alive. I wonder what he would have said when I gave him twenty-nine thousand eight hundred francs for his picture."

CHAPTER XLIX

I LIVED at the Hôtel de la Fleur, and Mrs. Johnson, the proprietress, had a sad story to tell of lost opportunity. After Strickland's death certain of his effects were sold by auction in the market-place at Papeete, and she went to it herself because there was among the truck an American stove she wanted. She paid twenty-seven francs for it.

"There were a dozen pictures," she told me, "but they were unframed, and nobody wanted them. Some of them sold for as much as ten francs, but mostly they went for five or six. Just think, if I had bought them I should be a rich woman now."

But Tiaré Johnson would never under any circumstances have been rich. She could not keep money. The daughter of a native and an English sea-captain settled in Tahiti, when I knew her she was a woman of fifty, who looked older, and of enormous proportions. Tall and extremely stout, she would have been of imposing presence if the great good-nature of her face had not made it impossible for her to express anything but kindliness. Her arms were like legs of mutton, her breasts like giant cabbages; her face, broad and fleshy, gave you an impression of almost indecent nakedness, and vast chin succeeded to vast chin. I do not know how many of them there were. They fell away voluminously into the capaciousness of her bosom. She was dressed usually in a pink Mother Hubbard, and she wore all day long a large straw hat. But when she let down her hair, which she did now and then, for she was vain of it, you saw that it was long and dark and curly; and her eyes had remained young and vivacious. Her laughter was the most catching I ever heard; it would begin, a low peal in her throat, and would grow louder and louder till her whole vast body shook. She loved three things—a joke, a glass of wine, and a handsome man. To have known her is a privilege.

She was the best cook on the island, and she adored good food. From morning till night you saw her sitting on a low chair in the kitchen, surrounded by a Chinese cook and two or three native girls, giving her orders, chatting sociably with all and sundry, and tasting the savoury messes she devised. When she wished to do honour to a friend she cooked the dinner with her own hands. Hospitality was a passion with her, and there was no one on the island who need go without a dinner when there was anything to eat at the Hôtel de la Fleur. She never turned her customers out of her house because they did not pay their bills. She always hoped they would pay when they could. There was one man there who had fallen on adversity, and to him she had given board and lodging for several months. When the Chinese laundryman refused to wash for him without payment she had sent his things to be washed with hers. She could not allow the poor fellow to go about in a dirty shirt, she said, and since he was a man, and men must smoke, she gave him a franc a day for cigarettes. She used him with the same affability as those of her clients who paid their bills once a week.

Age and obesity had made her inapt for love, but she took a keen interest in the amatory affairs of the young. She looked upon venery as the natural occupation for men and women, and was ever ready with precept and example from her own wide experience.

"I was not fifteen when my father found that I had a lover," she said. "He was third mate on the *Tropic Bird*. A good-looking boy."

She sighed a little. They say a woman always remembers her first lover with affection; but perhaps she does not always remember him.

"My father was a sensible man."

"What did he do?" I asked.

"He thrashed me within an inch of my life, and then he made me marry Captain Johnson. I did not mind. He was older, of course, but he was good-looking too."

Tiaré—her father had called her by the name of the white, scented flower which, they tell you, if you have once smelt, will always draw you back to Tahiti in the end, however far you may have roamed—Tiaré remembered Strickland very well.

"He used to come here sometimes, and I used to see him walking about Papeete. I was sorry for him, he was so thin, and he never had any money. When I heard he was in town, I used to send a boy to find him and make him come to dinner with me. I got him a job once or twice, but he couldn't stick to anything. After a little while he wanted to get back to the bush, and one morning he would be gone."

Strickland reached Tahiti about six months after he left Marseilles. He worked his passage on a sailing vessel that was making the trip from Auckland to San Francisco, and he arrived with a box of paints, an easel, and a dozen canvases. He had a few pounds in his pocket, for he had found work in Sydney, and he took a small room in a native house outside the town. I think the moment he reached Tahiti he felt himself at home. Tiaré told me that he said to her once:

"I'd been scrubbing the deck, and all at once a chap said to me: 'Why, there it is.' And I looked up and I saw the outline of the island. I knew right away that there was the place I'd been looking for all my life. Then we came near, and I seemed to recognise it. Sometimes when I walk about it all seems familiar. I could swear I've lived here before."

"Sometimes it takes them like that," said Tiaré. "I've known men come on shore for a few hours while their ship was taking in cargo, and never go back. And I've known men who came here to be in an office for a year, and they cursed the place, and when they went away they took their dying oath they'd hang themselves before they came back again, and in six months you'd see them land once more, and they'd tell you they couldn't live anywhere else."

CHAPTER L

I HAVE an idea that some men are born out of their due place. Accident has cast them amid certain surroundings, but they have always a nostalgia for a home they know not. They are strangers in their birthplace, and the leafy lanes they have known from childhood, or the populous streets in which they have played, remain but a place of passage. They may spend their whole lives aliens among their kindred and remain aloof among the only scenes they have ever known. Perhaps it is this sense of strangeness that sends men far and wide in the search for something permanent, to which they may attach themselves. Perhaps some deep-rooted atavism urges the wanderer back to lands which his ancestors left in the dim beginnings of history. Sometimes a man hits upon a place to which he mysteriously feels that he belongs.

Here is the home he sought, and he will settle amid scenes that he has never seen before, among men he has never known, as though they were familiar to him from his birth. Here at last he finds rest.

I told Tiaré the story of a man I had known at St. Thomas's Hospital. He was a Jew named Abraham, a blond, rather stout young man, shy and very unassuming; but he had remarkable gifts. He entered the hospital with a scholarship and during the five years of the curriculum gained every prize that was open to him. He was made house-physician and house-surgeon. His brilliance was allowed by all. Finally he was elected to a position on the staff, and his career was assured. So far as human things can be predicted, it was certain that he would rise to the greatest heights in his profession. Honours and wealth awaited him. Before he entered upon his new duties he wished to take a holiday, and, having no private means, he went as surgeon on a tramp steamer to the Levant. It did not generally carry a doctor, but one of the senior surgeons at the hospital knew a director of the line, and Abraham was taken as a favour.

In a few weeks the authorities received his resignation of the coveted position on the staff. It created profound astonishment, and wild rumours were current. Whenever a man does anything unexpected, his fellows ascribe it to the most discreditable motives. But there was a man ready to step into Abraham's shoes, and Abraham was forgotten. Nothing more was heard of him. He vanished.

It was perhaps ten years later that one morning on board ship, about to land at Alexandria, I was bidden to line up with the other passengers for the doctor's examination. The doctor was a stout man in shabby clothes, and when he took off his hat I noticed that he was very bald. I had an idea that I had seen him before. Suddenly I remembered.

"Abraham," I said.

He turned to me with a puzzled look, and then, recognising me, seized my hand. After expressions of surprise on either side, hearing that I meant to spend the night in Alexandria, he asked me to dine with him at the English Club. When we met again I declared my astonishment at finding him there. It was a very modest position that he occupied, and there was about him an air of straitened circumstance. Then he told me his story. When he set out on his holiday in the Mediterranean he had every intention of returning to London and his appointment at St. Thomas's. One morning the tramp docked at Alexandria, and from the deck he looked at the city, white in the sunlight, and the crowd on the wharf; he saw the natives in their shabby gabardines, the blacks from the Soudan, the noisy throng of Greeks and Italians, the grave Turks in tarbooshes, the sunshine and the blue sky; and something happened to him. He could not describe it. It was like a thunder-clap, he said, and then, dissatisfied with this, he said it was like a revelation. Something seemed to twist his heart, and suddenly he felt an exultation, a sense of wonderful freedom. He felt himself at home, and he made up his mind there and then, in a minute, that he would live the rest of his life in Alexandria. He had no great difficulty in leaving the ship, and in twenty-four hours, with all his belongings, he was on shore.

"The captain must have thought you as mad as a hatter," I smiled.

"I didn't care what anybody thought. It wasn't I that acted, but something stronger within me. I thought I would go to a little Greek hotel, while I looked about, and I felt I knew where to find one. And do you know, I walked straight there, and when I saw it I recognised it at once."

"Had you been to Alexandria before?"

"No; I'd never been out of England in my life."

Presently he entered the Government service, and there he had been ever since.

"Have you never regretted it?"

"Never, not for a minute. I earn just enough to live upon, and I'm satisfied. I ask nothing more than to remain as I am till I die. I've had a wonderful life."

I left Alexandria next day, and I forgot about Abraham till a little while ago, when I was dining with another old friend in the profession, Alec Carmichael, who was in England on short leave. I ran across him in the street and congratulated him on the knighthood with which his eminent services during the war had been rewarded. We arranged to spend an evening together for old time's sake, and when I agreed to dine with him he proposed that he should ask nobody else, so that we could chat without interruption. He had a beautiful old house in Queen Anne Street, and being a man of taste he had furnished it admirably. On the walls of the dining-room I saw a charming Bellotto, and there was a pair of Zoffanys that I envied. When his wife, a tall, lovely creature in cloth of gold, had left us, I remarked laughingly on the change in his present circumstances from those when we had both been medical students. We had looked upon it then as an extravagance to dine in a shabby Italian restaurant in the Westminster Bridge Road. Now Alec Carmichael was on the staff of half a dozen hospitals. I should think he earned ten thousand a year, and his knighthood was but the first of the honours which must inevitably fall to his lot.

"I've done pretty well," he said, "but the strange thing is that I owe it all to one piece of luck."

"What do you mean by that?"

"Well, do you remember Abraham? He was the man who had the future. When we were students he beat me all along the line. He got the prizes and the scholarships that I went in for. I always played second fiddle to him. If he'd kept on he'd be in the position I'm in now. That man had a genius for surgery. No one had a look-in with him. When he was appointed Registrar at Thomas's I hadn't a chance of getting on the staff. I should have had to become a G.P., and you know what likelihood there is for a G.P. ever to get out of the common rut. But Abraham fell out, and I got the job. That gave me my opportunity."

"I dare say that's true."

"It was just luck. I suppose there was some kink in Abraham. Poor devil, he's gone to the dogs altogether. He's got some twopenny-halfpenny job in the medical at Alexandria—sanitary officer or something like that. I'm told he lives with an ugly old Greek woman and has half a dozen scrofulous kids. The fact is, I suppose, that it's not enough to have brains. The thing that counts is character. Abraham hadn't got character."

Character? I should have thought it needed a good deal of character to throw up a career after half an hour's meditation, because you saw in another way of living a more intense significance. And it required still more character never to regret the sudden step. But I said nothing, and Alec Carmichael proceeded reflectively:

"Of course it would be hypocritical for me to pretend that I regret what Abraham did. After all, I've scored by it." He puffed luxuriously at the long Corona he was smoking. "But if I weren't personally concerned I should be sorry at the waste. It seems a rotten thing that a man should make such a hash of life."

I wondered if Abraham really had made a hash of life. Is to do what you most want, to live under the conditions that please you, in peace with yourself, to make a hash of life; and is it success to be an eminent surgeon with ten thousand a year and a beautiful wife? I suppose it depends on what meaning you attach to life, the claim which you acknowledge to society, and the claim of the individual. But again I held my tongue, for who am I to argue with a knight?

CHAPTER LI

TIARÉ, when I told her this story, praised my prudence, and for a few minutes we worked in silence, for we were shelling peas. Then her eyes, always alert for the affairs of her kitchen, fell on some action of the Chinese cook which aroused her violent disapproval. She turned on him with a torrent of abuse. The Chink was not backward to defend himself, and a very lively quarrel ensued. They spoke in the native language, of which I had learnt but half a dozen words, and it sounded as though the world would shortly come to an end; but presently peace was restored and Tiaré gave the cook a cigarette. They both smoked comfortably.

"Do you know, it was I who found him his wife?" said Tiaré suddenly, with a smile that spread all over her immense face.

"The cook?"

"No, Strickland."

"But he had one already."

"That is what he said, but I told him she was in England, and England is at the other end of the world."

"True," I replied.

"He would come to Papeete every two or three months, when he wanted paints or tobacco or money, and then he would wander about like a lost dog. I was sorry for him. I had a girl here then called Ata to do the rooms; she was some sort of a relation of mine, and her father and mother were dead, so I had her to live with me. Strickland used to come here now and then to have a square meal or to play chess with one of the boys. I noticed that she looked at him when he came, and I asked her if she liked him. She said she liked him well enough. You know what these girls are; they're always pleased to go with a white man."

"Was she a native?" I asked.

"Yes; she hadn't a drop of white blood in her. Well, after I'd talked to her I sent for Strickland, and I said to him: 'Strickland, it's time for you to settle down. A man of your age shouldn't go playing about with the girls down at the front. They're bad lots, and you'll come to no good with them. You've got no money, and you can never keep a job for more than a month or two. No one will employ you now. You say you can always live in the bush with one or other of the natives, and they're glad to have you because you're a white man, but it's not decent for a white man. Now, listen to me, Strickland.' "

Tiaré mingled French with English in her conversation, for she used both languages with equal facility. She spoke them with a singing accent which was not unpleasing. You felt that a bird would speak in these tones if it could speak English.

" 'Now, what do you say to marrying Ata? She's a good girl and she's only seventeen. She's never been promiscuous like some of these girls—a captain or a first mate, yes, but she's never been touched by a native. *Elle se respecte, vois-tu?* The purser of the *Oahu* told me last journey that he hadn't met a nicer girl in the islands. It's time she settled down too, and besides, the captains and the first mates like a change now and then. I don't keep my girls too long. She has a bit of property down by Taravao, just before you come to the peninsula, and with copra at the price it is now you could live quite comfortably. There's a house, and you'd have all the time you wanted for your painting. What do you say to that?' "

Tiaré paused to take breath.

"It was then he told me of his wife in England. 'My poor Strickland,' I said to him, 'they've all got a wife somewhere; that is generally why they come to the islands. Ata is a sensible girl, and she doesn't expect any ceremony before the Mayor. She's a Protestant, and you know they don't look upon these things like the Catholics.'

"Then he said: 'But what does Ata say to it?' 'It appears that she has a *béguin* for you,' I said. 'She's willing if you are. Shall I call her?' He chuckled in a funny, dry way he had, and I called her. She knew what I was talking about, the hussy, and I saw her out of the corner of my eyes listening with all her ears, while she pretended to iron a blouse that she had been washing for me. She came. She was laughing, but I could see that she was a little shy, and Strickland looked at her without speaking."

"Was she pretty?" I asked.

"Not bad. But you must have seen pictures of her. He painted her over and over again, sometimes with a *pareo* on and sometimes with nothing at all. Yes, she was pretty enough. And she knew how to cook. I taught her myself. I saw Strickland was thinking of it, so I said to him: 'I've given her good wages and she's saved them, and the captains and the first mates she's known have given her a little something now and then. She's saved several hundred francs.'

"He pulled his great red beard and smiled.

" 'Well, Ata,' he said, 'do you fancy me for a husband?'

"She did not say anything, but just giggled.

" 'But I tell you, my poor Strickland, the girl has a *béguin* for you,' I said.

" 'I shall beat you,' he said, looking at her.

" 'How else should I know you loved me?' she answered."

Tiaré broke off her narrative and addressed herself to me reflectively.

"My first husband, Captain Johnson, used to thrash me regularly. He was a man. He was handsome, six foot three, and when he was drunk there was no holding him. I would be black and blue all over for days at a time. Oh, I cried when he died. I thought I should never get over it. But it wasn't till I married George Rainey that I knew what I'd lost. You can never tell what a man is like till you live with him. I've never been so deceived in a man as I was in George Rainey. He was a fine, upstanding fellow too. He was nearly as tall as Captain Johnson, and he looked strong enough. But it was all on the surface. He never drank. He never raised his hand to me. He might have been a missionary. I made love with the officers of every ship that touched at the island, and George Rainey never saw anything. At last I was disgusted with him, and I got a divorce. What was the good of a husband like that? It's a terrible thing the way some men treat women."

I condoled with Tiaré, and remarked feelingly that men were deceivers ever, then asked her to go on with her story of Strickland.

" 'Well,' I said to him, 'there's no hurry about it. Take your time and think it over. Ata has a very nice room in the annexe. Live with her for a month, and see how you like her. You can have your meals here. And at the end of a month, if you decide you want to marry her, you can just go and settle down on her property.'

"Well, he agreed to that. Ata continued to do the housework, and I gave him his meals as I said I would. I taught Ata how to make one or two dishes I knew he was fond of. He did not paint much. He wandered about the hills and bathed in the stream. And he sat about the front looking at the lagoon, and at sunset he would go down and look at Murea. He used to go fishing on the reef. He loved to moon about the harbour talking to the natives. He was a nice quiet fellow. And every evening after dinner he would go down to the annexe with Ata. I saw he was longing to get away to the bush, and at the end of the month I asked him what he intended to do. He said if Ata was willing to go, he was willing to go with her. So I gave them a wedding dinner. I cooked it with my own hands. I gave them a pea soup and lobster *à la portugaise*, and a curry, and a coconut salad—you've never had one of my coconut salads, have you? I must make you one before you go—and then I made them an ice. We had all the champagne we could drink and liqueurs to follow. Oh, I'd made up my mind to do things well. And afterwards we danced in the drawing-room. I was not so fat then, and I always loved dancing."

The drawing-room at the Hôtel de la Fleur was a small room, with a cottage piano, and a suite of mahogany furniture, covered in stamped velvet, neatly arranged round the walls. On round tables were photograph albums, and on the walls enlarged photographs of Tiaré and her first husband, Captain Johnson. Still, though Tiaré was old and fat, on occasion we rolled back the Brussels carpet, brought in the maids and one or two friends of Tiaré's, and danced, though now to the wheezy music of a gramophone. On the veranda the air was scented with the heavy perfume of the tiaré, and overhead the Southern Cross shone in a cloudless sky.

Tiaré smiled indulgently as she remembered the gaiety of a time long passed.

"We kept it up till three, and when we went to bed I don't think anyone was very sober. I had told them they could have my trap to take them as far as the road went, because after that they had a long walk. Ata's property was right away in a fold of the mountain. They started at dawn, and the boy I sent with them didn't come back till next day.

"Yes, that's how Strickland was married."

CHAPTER LII

I SUPPOSE the next three years were the happiest of Strickland's life. Ata's house stood about eight kilometres from the road that runs round the island, and you went to it along a winding pathway shaded by the luxuriant trees of the tropics. It was a bungalow of unpainted wood, consisting of two small rooms, and outside was a small shed that served as a kitchen. There was no furniture except the mats they used as beds and a rocking-chair, which stood on the veranda. Bananas with their great ragged leaves, like the tattered habiliments of an empress in adversity, grew close up to the house. There was a tree just behind which bore alligator-pears, and all about were the coconuts which gave the land its revenue. Ata's father had planted crotons round his property, and they grew in coloured profusion, gay and brilliant; they fenced the land with flame. A mango grew in front of the house, and at the edge of the clearing were two flamboyants, twin trees, that challenged the gold of the coconuts with their scarlet flowers.

Here Strickland lived, coming seldom to Papeete, on the produce of the land. There was a little stream that ran not far away, in which he bathed, and down this on occasion would come a shoal of fish. Then the natives would assemble with spears, and with much shouting would transfix the great startled things as they hurried down to the sea. Sometimes Strickland would go down to the reef, and come back with a basket of small, coloured fish that Ata would fry in coconut oil, or with a lobster; and sometimes she would make a savoury dish of the great land-crabs that scuttled away under your feet. Up the mountain were wild-orange trees, and now and then Ata would go with two or three women from the village and return laden with the green, sweet, luscious fruit. Then the coconuts would be ripe for picking, and her cousins (like all the natives, Ata had a host of relatives) would swarm up the trees and throw down the big ripe nuts. They split them open and put them in the sun to dry. Then they cut out the copra and put it into sacks, and the women would carry it down to the trader at the village by the lagoon, and he would give in exchange for it rice and soap and tinned meat and a little money. Sometimes there would be a feast in the neighbourhood, and a pig would be killed. Then they would go and eat themselves sick, and dance, and sing hymns.

But the house was a long way from the village, and the Tahitians are lazy. They love to travel and they love to gossip, but they do not care to walk, and for weeks at a time Strickland and Ata lived alone. He painted and he read, and in the evening, when it was dark, they sat together on the veranda, smoking and looking at the night. Then Ata had a baby, and the old woman who came up to help her through her trouble stayed on. Presently the grand-daughter of the old woman came to stay with her, and then a youth appeared—none quite knew wherefrom or to whom he belonged—but he settled down with them in a happy-go-lucky way, and they all lived together.

CHAPTER LIII

"*Tenez, voilà le Capitaine Brunot,*" said Tiaré, one day when I was fitting together what she could tell me of Strickland. "He knew Strickland well; he visited him at his house."

I saw a middle-aged Frenchman with a big black beard, streaked with grey, a sunburned face, and large, shining eyes. He was dressed in a neat suit of ducks. I had noticed him at luncheon, and Ah Lin, the Chinese boy, told me he had come from the Paumotus on the boat that had that day arrived. Tiaré introduced me to him, and he handed me his card, a large card on which was printed *René Brunot,* and underneath, *Capitaine au Long Cours.* We were sitting on a little veranda outside the kitchen, and Tiaré was cutting out a dress that she was making for one of the girls about the house. He sat down with us.

"Yes; I knew Strickland well," he said. "I am very fond of chess, and he was always glad of a game. I come to Tahiti three or four times a year for my business, and when he was at Papeete he would come here and we would play. When he married"— Captain Brunot smiled and shrugged his shoulders—"*enfin*, when he went to live with the girl that Tiaré gave him, he asked me to go and see him. I was one of the guests at the wedding feast." He looked at Tiaré, and they both laughed. "He did not come much to Papeete after that, and about a year later it chanced that I had to go to that part of the island for I forget what business, and when I had finished it I said to myself: '*Voyons*, why should I not go and see that poor Strickland?' I asked one or two natives if they knew anything about him, and I discovered that he lived not more than five kilometres from where I was. So I went. I shall never forget the impression my visit made on me. I live on an atoll, a low island, it is a strip of land surrounding a lagoon, and its beauty is the beauty of the sea and sky, and the varied colour of the lagoon, and the grace of the coconut trees; but the place where Strickland lived had the beauty of the Garden of Eden. Ah, I wish I could make you see the enchantment of that spot, a corner hidden away from all the world, with the blue sky overhead and the rich, luxuriant trees. It was a feast of colour. And it was fragrant and cool. Words cannot describe that paradise. And here he lived, unmindful of the world and by the world forgotten. I suppose to European eyes it would have seemed astonishingly sordid. The house was dilapidated and none too clean. When I approached I saw three or four natives lying on the veranda. You know how natives love to herd together. There was a young man lying full length, smoking a cigarette, and he wore nothing but a *pareo*."

The *pareo* is a long strip of trade cotton, red or blue, stamped with a white pattern. It is worn round the waist and hangs to the knees.

"A girl of fifteen, perhaps, was plaiting pandanus-leaf to make a hat, and an old woman was sitting on her haunches smoking a pipe. Then I saw Ata. She was suckling a new-born child, and another child, stark naked, was playing at her feet. When she saw me she called out to Strickland, and he came to the door. He, too, wore nothing but a *pareo*. He was an extraordinary figure, with his red beard and matted hair, and his great hairy chest. His feet were horny and scarred, so that I knew he went always bare-foot. He had gone native with a vengeance. He seemed pleased to see me, and told Ata to kill a chicken for our dinner. He took me into the house to show me the picture he was at work on when I came in. In one corner of the room was the bed, and in the middle was an easel with the canvas upon it. Because I was sorry for him, I had bought a couple of his pictures for small sums, and I had sent others to friends of mine in France. And though I had bought them out of compassion, after living with them I began to like them. Indeed, I found a strange beauty in them. Everyone thought I was mad, but it turns out that I was right. I was his first admirer in the islands."

He smiled maliciously at Tiaré, and with lamentations she told us again the story of how at the sale of Strickland's effects she had neglected the pictures, but bought an American stove for twenty-seven francs.

"Have you the pictures still?" I asked.

"Yes; I am keeping them till my daughter is of marriageable age, and then I shall sell them. They will be her *dot*."

Then he went on with the account of his visit to Strickland.

"I shall never forget the evening I spent with him. I had not intended to stay more than an hour, but he insisted that I should spend the night. I hesitated, for I confess I did not much like the look of the mats on which he proposed that I should sleep; but I shrugged my shoulders. When I was building my house in the Paumotus I had slept out for weeks on a harder bed than that, with nothing to shelter me but wild shrubs; and as for vermin, my tough skin should be proof against their malice.

"We went down to the stream to bathe while Ata was preparing the dinner, and after we had eaten it we sat on the veranda. We smoked and chatted. The young man had a concertina, and he played the tunes popular on the music-halls a dozen years before. They sounded strangely in the tropical night thousands of miles from civilisation. I asked Strickland if it did not irk him to live in that promiscuity. No, he said; he liked to have his models under his hand. Presently, after loud yawning, the natives went away to sleep, and Strickland and I were left alone. I cannot describe to you the intense silence of the night. On my island in the Paumotus there is never at night the complete stillness that there was here. There is the rustle of the myriad animals on the beach, all the little shelled things that crawl about ceaselessly, and there is the noisy scurrying of the land-crabs. Now and then in the lagoon you hear the leaping of a fish, and sometimes a hurried noisy splashing as a brown shark sends all the other fish scampering for their lives. And above all, ceaseless like time, is the dull roar of the breakers on the reef. But here there was not a sound, and the air was scented with the white flowers of the night. It was a night so beautiful that your soul seemed hardly able to bear the prison of the body. You felt that it was ready to be wafted away on the immaterial air, and death bore all the aspect of a beloved friend."

Tiaré sighed.

"Ah, I wish I were fifteen again."

Then she caught sight of a cat trying to get at a dish of prawns on the kitchen table, and with a dexterous gesture and a lively volley of abuse flung a book at its scampering tail.

"I asked him if he was happy with Ata.

" 'She leaves me alone,' he said. 'She cooks my food and looks after her babies. She does what I tell her. She gives me what I want from a woman.'

" 'And do you never regret Europe? Do you not yearn sometimes for the light of the streets in Paris or London, the companionship of your friends and equals, *que sais-je?* for theatres and newspapers, and the rumble of omnibuses on the cobbled pavements?'

"For a long time he was silent. Then he said:

" 'I shall stay here till I die.'

" 'But are you never bored or lonely?' I asked.

"He chuckled.

" '*Mon pauvre ami,*' he said. 'It is evident that you do not know what it is to be an artist.' "

Capitaine Brunot turned to me with a gentle smile, and there was a wonderful look in his dark, kind eyes.

"He did me an injustice, for I too know what it is to have dreams. I have my visions too. In my way I also am an artist."

We were all silent for a while, and Tiaré fished out of her capacious pocket a handful of cigarettes. She handed one to each of us, and we all three smoked. At last she said:

"Since *ce monsieur* is interested in Strickland, why do you not take him to see Dr. Coutras? He can tell him something about his illness and death."

"*Volontiers,*" said the captain, looking at me.

I thanked him, and he looked at his watch.

"It is past six o'clock. We should find him at home if you care to come now."

I got up without further ado, and we walked along the road that led to the doctor's house. He lived out of the town, but the Hôtel de la Fleur was on the edge of it, and we were quickly in the country. The broad road was shaded by pepper-trees, and on each side were the plantations, coconut and vanilla. The pirate birds were screeching among the leaves of the palms. We came to a stone bridge over a shallow river, and we stopped for a few minutes to see the native boys bathing. They chased one another with shrill cries and laughter, and their bodies, brown and wet, gleamed in the sunlight.

CHAPTER LIV

As we walked along I reflected on a circumstance which all that I had lately heard about Strickland forced on my attention. Here, on this remote island, he seemed to have aroused none of the detestation with which he was regarded at home, but compassion rather; and his vagaries were accepted with tolerance. To these people, native and European, he was a queer fish, and they took him for granted; the world was full of odd persons, who did odd things; and perhaps they knew that a man is not what he wants to be, but what he must be. In England and France he was the square peg in the round hole, but here the holes were any sort of shape, and no sort of peg was quite amiss. I do not think he was any gentler here, less selfish or less brutal, but the circumstances were more favourable. If he had spent his life amid these surroundings he might have passed for no worse a man than another. He received here what he neither expected nor wanted among his own people—sympathy.

I tried to tell Captain Brunot something of the astonishment with which this filled me, and for a little while he did not answer.

"It is not strange that I, at all events, should have had sympathy for him," he said at last, "for, though perhaps neither of us knew it, we were both aiming at the same thing."

"What on earth can it be that two people so dissimilar as you and Strickland could aim at?" I asked, smiling.

"Beauty."

"A large order," I murmured.

"Do you know how men can be so obsessed by love that they are deaf and blind to everything else in the world? They are as little their own masters as the slaves chained to the benches of a galley. The passion that held Strickland in bondage was no less tyrannical than love."

"How strange that you should say that!" I answered. "For long ago I had the idea that he was possessed of a devil."

"And the passion that held Strickland was a passion to create beauty. It gave him no peace. It urged him hither and thither. He was eternally a pilgrim, haunted by a divine nostalgia, and the demon within him was ruthless. There are men whose desire for truth is so great that to attain it they will shatter the very foundation of their world. Of such was Strickland, only beauty

F.A.A. 1 Y

with him took the place of truth. I could only feel for him profound compassion."

"That is strange also. A man whom he had deeply wronged told me that he felt a great pity for him." I was silent for a moment. "I wonder if there you have found the explanation of a character which has always seemed to me inexplicable. How did you hit on it?"

He turned to me with a smile.

"Did I not tell you that I, too, in my way was an artist? I realised in myself the same desire as animated him. But whereas his medium was paint, mine has been life."

Then Captain Brunot told me a story which I must repeat, since, if only by way of contrast, it adds something to my impression of Strickland. It has also to my mind a beauty of its own.

Captain Brunot was a Breton, and had been in the French Navy. He left it on his marriage, and settled down on a small property he had near Quimper to live for the rest of his days in peace; but the failure of an attorney left him suddenly penniless, and neither he nor his wife was willing to live in penury where they had enjoyed consideration. During his seafaring days he had cruised the South Seas, and he determined now to seek his fortune there. He spent some months in Papeete to make his plans and gain experience; then, on money borrowed from a friend in France, he bought an island in the Paumotus. It was a ring of land round a deep lagoon, uninhabited, and covered only with scrub and wild guava. With the intrepid woman who was his wife, and a few natives, he landed there, and set about building a house, and clearing the scrub so that he could plant coconuts. That was twenty years before, and now what had been a barren island was a garden.

"It was hard and anxious work at first, and we worked strenuously, both of us. Every day I was up at dawn, clearing, planting, working on my house, and at night when I threw myself on my bed it was to sleep like a log till morning. My wife worked as hard as I did. Then children were born to us, first a son and then a daughter. My wife and I have taught them all they know. We had a piano sent out from France, and she has taught them to play and to speak English, and I have taught them Latin and mathematics, and we read history together. They can sail a boat. They can swim as well as the natives. There is nothing about the land of which they are ignorant. Our trees have prospered, and there is shell on my reef. I have come to Tahiti now to buy a schooner. I can get enough shell to make it worth while to fish for it, and, who knows? I may find pearls. I have made something where there was nothing. I too have made beauty. Ah, you do not know what it is to look at those tall, healthy trees and think that every one I planted myself."

"Let me ask you the question that you asked Strickland. Do you never regret France and your old home in Brittany?"

"Some day, when my daughter is married and my son has a wife and is able to take my place on the island, we shall go back and finish our days in the old house in which I was born."

"You will look back on a happy life," I said.

"*Évidemment*, it is not exciting on my island, and we are very far from the world—imagine, it takes me four days to come to Tahiti —but we are happy there. It is given to few men to attempt a work and to achieve it. Our life is simple and innocent. We are untouched by ambition, and what pride we have is due only to our contemplation of the work of our hands. Malice cannot touch us, nor envy attack. Ah, *mon cher monsieur*, they talk of the blessedness of labour, and it is a meaningless phrase, but to me it has the most intense significance. I am a happy man."

"I am sure you deserve to be," I smiled.

"I wish I could think so. I do not know how I have deserved to have a wife who was the perfect friend and helpmate, the perfect mistress and the perfect mother."

I reflected for a while on the life that the captain suggested to my imagination.

"It is obvious that to lead such an existence and make so great a success of it, you must both have needed a strong will and a determined character."

"Perhaps; but without one other factor we could have achieved nothing."

"And what was that?"

He stopped, somewhat dramatically, and stretched out his arm.

"Belief in God. Without that we should have been lost."

Then we arrived at the house of Dr. Coutras.

CHAPTER LV

DR. COUTRAS was an old Frenchman of great stature and exceeding bulk. His body was shaped like a huge duck's egg; and his eyes, sharp, blue, and good-natured, rested now and then with self-satisfaction on his enormous paunch. His complexion was florid and his hair white. He was a man to attract immediate sympathy. He received us in a room that might have been in a house in a provincial town in France, and the one or two Polynesian curios had an odd look. He took my hand in both of his—they were huge—and gave me a hearty look, in which, however, was great shrewdness. When he shook hands with Capitaine Brunot he enquired politely after *Madame et les enfants*. For some minutes there was an exchange of courtesies and some local gossip about the island, the prospects of the copra and the vanilla crop; then we came to the object of my visit.

I shall not tell what Dr. Coutras related to me in his words, but in my own, for I cannot hope to give at second hand any impression of his vivacious delivery. He had a deep, resonant voice, fitted to his massive frame, and a keen sense of the dramatic. To listen to him was, as the phrase goes, as good as a play; and much better than most.

It appears that Dr. Coutras had gone one day to Taravao in order to see an old chiefess, who was ill, and he gave a vivid picture of the obese old lady, lying in a huge bed, smoking cigarettes, and surrounded by a crowd of dark-skinned retainers. When he had seen her he was taken into another room and given dinner—raw fish, fried bananas, and chicken—*que sais-je?* the typical dinner of the *indigène*—and while he was eating it he saw a young girl being driven away from the door in tears. He thought nothing of it, but when he went out to get into his trap and drive home, he saw her again, standing a little way off; she looked at him with a woebegone air, and tears streamed down her cheeks. He asked someone what was wrong with her, and was told that she had come down from the hills to ask him to visit a white man who was sick. They had told her that the doctor could not be disturbed. He called her, and himself asked what she wanted. She told him that Ata had sent her, she who used to be at the Hôtel de la Fleur, and that the Red One was ill. She thrust into his hand a crumpled piece of newspaper, and when he opened it he found in it a hundred-franc note.

"Who is the Red One?" he asked of one of the bystanders.

He was told that that was what they called the Englishman, a painter, who lived with Ata up in the valley seven kilometres from where they were. He recognised Strickland by the description. But it was necessary to walk. It was impossible for him to go; that was why they had sent the girl away.

"I confess," said the doctor, turning to me, "that I hesitated. I did not relish fourteen kilometres over a bad pathway, and there was no chance that I could get back to Papeete that night. Besides, Strickland was not sympathetic to me. He was an idle, useless scoundrel, who preferred to live with a native woman rather than work for his living like the rest of us. *Mon Dieu*, how was I to know that one day the world would come to the conclusion that he had genius? I asked the girl if he was not well enough to have come down to see me. I asked her what she thought was the matter with him. She would not answer. I pressed her, angrily perhaps, but she looked down on the ground and began to cry. Then I shrugged my shoulders; after all, perhaps it was my duty to go, and in a very bad temper I bade her lead the way."

His temper was certainly no better when he arrived, perspiring freely and thirsty. Ata was on the look-out for him, and came a little way along the path to meet him.

"Before I see anyone give me something to drink or I shall die of thirst," he cried out. "*Pour l'amour de Dieu*, get me a coconut."

She called out, and a boy came running along. He swarmed up a tree, and presently threw down a ripe nut. Ata pierced a hole in it, and the doctor took a long, refreshing draught. Then he rolled himself a cigarette and felt in a better humour.

"Now, where is the Red One?" he asked.

"He is in the house, painting. I have not told him you were coming. Go in and see him."

"But what does he complain of? If he is well enough to paint, he is well enough to have come down to Taravao and save me this confounded walk. I presume my time is no less valuable than his."

Ata did not speak, but with the boy followed him to the house. The girl who had brought him was by this time sitting on the veranda, and here was lying an old woman, with her back to the wall, making native cigarettes. Ata pointed to the door. The doctor, wondering irritably why they behaved so strangely, entered, and there found Strickland cleaning his palette. There was a picture on the easel. Strickland, clad only in a *pareo*, was standing with his back to the door, but he turned round when he heard the sound of boots. He gave the doctor a look of vexation. He was surprised to see him, and resented the intrusion. But the doctor gave a gasp, he was rooted to the floor, and he stared with all his eyes. This was not what he expected. He was seized with horror.

"You enter without ceremony," said Strickland. "What can I do for you?"

The doctor recovered himself, but it required quite an effort for him to find his voice. All his irritation was gone, and he felt—*eh bien, oui, je ne le nie pas*—he felt an overwhelming pity.

"I am Dr. Coutras. I was down at Taravao to see the chiefess, and Ata sent for me to see you."

"She's a damned fool. I have had a few aches and pains lately and a little fever, but that's nothing; it will pass off. Next time anyone went to Papeete I was going to send for some quinine."

"Look at yourself in the glass."

Strickland gave him a glance, smiled, and went over to a cheap mirror in a little wooden frame, that hung on the wall.

"Well?"

"Do you not see a strange change in your face? Do you not see the thickening of your features and a look—how shall I describe it?—the books call it lion-faced. *Mon pauvre ami*, must I tell you that you have a terrible disease?"

"I?"

"When you look at yourself in the glass you see the typical appearance of the leper."

"You are jesting," said Strickland.

"I wish to God I were."

"Do you intend to tell me that I have leprosy?"

"Unfortunately, there can be no doubt about it."

Dr. Coutras had delivered sentence of death on many men, and he could never overcome the horror with which it filled him. He felt always the furious hatred that must seize a man condemned when he compared himself with the doctor, sane and healthy, who had the inestimable privilege of life. Strickland looked at him in silence. Nothing of emotion could be seen on his face, disfigured already by the loathsome disease.

"Do they know?" he asked at last, pointing to the persons on the veranda, now sitting in unusual, unaccountable silence.

"These natives know the signs so well," said the doctor. "They were afraid to tell you."

Strickland stepped to the door and looked out. There must have been something terrible in his face, for suddenly they all burst out into loud cries and lamentation. They lifted up their voices and they wept. Strickland did not speak. After looking at them for a moment, he came back into the room.

"How long do you think I can last?"

"Who knows? Sometimes the disease continues for twenty years. It is a mercy when it runs its course quickly."

Strickland went to his easel and looked reflectively at the picture that stood on it.

"You have had a long journey. It is fitting that the bearer of important tidings should be rewarded. Take this picture. It means nothing to you now, but it may be that one day you will be glad to have it."

Dr. Coutras protested that he needed no payment for his journey; he had already given back to Ata the hundred-franc note, but Strickland insisted that he should take the picture. Then together they went out on the veranda. The natives were sobbing violently.

"Be quiet, woman. Dry thy tears," said Strickland, addressing Ata. "There is no great harm. I shall leave thee very soon."

"They are not going to take thee away?" she cried.

At that time there was no rigid sequestration on the islands, and lepers, if they chose, were allowed to go free.

"I shall go up into the mountain," said Strickland.

Then Ata stood up and faced him.

"Let the others go if they choose, but I will not leave thee. Thou art my man and I am thy woman. If thou leavest me I shall hang myself on the tree that is behind the house. I swear it by God."

There was something immensely forcible in the way she spoke. She was no longer the meek, soft native girl, but a determined woman. She was extraordinarily transformed.

"Why shouldst thou stay with me? Thou canst go back to Papeete, and thou wilt soon find another white man. The old woman can take care of thy children, and Tiaré will be glad to have thee back."

"Thou art my man and I am thy woman. Whither thou goest I will go too."

For a moment Strickland's fortitude was shaken, and a tear

filled each of his eyes and trickled slowly down his cheeks. Then he gave the sardonic smile which was usual with him.

"Women are strange little beasts," he said to Dr. Coutras. "You can treat them like dogs, you can beat them till your arm aches, and still they love you." He shrugged his shoulders. "Of course, it is one of the most absurd illusions of Christianity that they have souls."

"What is it that thou art saying to the doctor?" asked Ata suspiciously. "Thou wilt not go?"

"If it please thee I will stay, poor child."

Ata flung herself on her knees before him, and clasped his legs with her arms and kissed them. Strickland looked at Dr. Coutras with a faint smile.

"In the end they get you, and you are helpless in their hands. White or brown, they are all the same."

Dr. Coutras felt that it was absurd to offer expressions of regret in so terrible a disaster, and he took his leave. Strickland told Tané, the boy, to lead him to the village. Dr. Coutras paused for a moment, and then he addressed himself to me.

"I did not like him, I have told you he was not sympathetic to me, but as I walked slowly down to Taravao I could not prevent an unwilling admiration for the stoical courage which enabled him to bear perhaps the most dreadful of human afflictions. When Tané left me I told him I would send some medicine that might be of service; but my hope was small that Strickland would consent to take it, and even smaller that, if he did, it would do him good. I gave the boy a message for Ata that I would come whenever she sent for me. Life is hard, and Nature takes sometimes a terrible delight in torturing her children. It was with a heavy heart that I drove back to my comfortable home in Papeete."

For a long time none of us spoke.

"But Ata did not send for me," the doctor went on, at last, "and it chanced that I did not go to that part of the island for a long time. I had no news of Strickland. Once or twice I heard that Ata had been to Papeete to buy painting materials, but I did not happen to see her. More than two years passed before I went to Taravao again, and then it was once more to see the old chiefess. I asked them whether they had heard anything of Strickland. By now it was known everywhere that he had leprosy. First Tané, the boy, had left the house, and then, a little time afterwards, the old woman and her grandchild. Strickland and Ata were left alone with their babies. No one went near the plantation, for, as you know, the natives have a very lively horror of the disease, and in the old days when it was discovered the sufferer was killed; but sometimes when the village boys were scrambling about the hills, they would catch sight of the white man, with his great red beard, wandering about. They fled in terror. Sometimes Ata would come down to the village at night and arouse the trader, so that he might sell her various things of which she stood in need. She knew that the natives looked upon her with the same horrified aversion as they looked upon Strickland, and she kept out of their way. Once some women, venturing nearer than usual to the plantation, saw her washing clothes in the brook, and they threw stones at her. After that the trader was told to give her the message that if she used the brook again men would come and burn down her house."

"Brutes," I said.

"*Mais non, mon cher monsieur*, men are always the same. Fear makes them cruel. . . . I decided to see Strickland, and when I had finished with the chiefess asked for a boy to show me the way. But none would accompany me, and I was forced to find it alone."

When Dr. Coutras arrived at the plantation he was seized with a feeling of uneasiness. Though he was hot from walking, he shivered. There was something hostile in the air which made him hesitate, and he felt that invisible forces barred his way. Unseen hands seemed to draw him back. No one would go near now to gather the coconuts, and they lay rotting on the ground. Everywhere was desolation. The bush was encroaching, and it looked as though very soon the primeval forest would regain possession of that strip of land which had been snatched from it at the cost of so much labour. He had the sensation that here was the abode of pain. As he approached the house he was struck by the unearthly silence, and at first he thought it was deserted. Then he saw Ata. She was sitting on her haunches in the lean-to that served her as kitchen, watching some mess cooking in a pot. Near her a small boy was playing silently in the dirt. She did not smile when she saw him.

"I have come to see Strickland," he said.

"I will go and tell him."

She went to the house, ascended the few steps that led to the veranda, and entered. Dr. Coutras followed her, but waited outside in obedience to her gesture. As she opened the door he smelt the sickly sweet smell which makes the neighbourhood of the leper nauseous. He heard her speak, and then he heard Strickland's answer, but he did not recognise the voice. It had become hoarse and indistinct. Dr. Coutras raised his eyebrows. He judged that the disease had already attacked the vocal cords. Then Ata came out again.

"He will not see you. You must go away."

Dr. Coutras insisted, but she would not let him pass. Dr. Coutras shrugged his shoulders, and after a moment's reflection turned away. She walked with him. He felt that she too wanted to be rid of him.

"Is there nothing I can do at all?" he asked.

"You can send him some paints," she said. "There is nothing else he wants."

"Can he paint still?"

"He is painting the walls of the house."

"This is a terrible life for you, my poor child."

Then at last she smiled, and there was in her eyes a look of superhuman love. Dr. Coutras was startled by it, and amazed. And he was awed. He found nothing to say.

"He is my man," she said.

"Where is your other child?" he asked. "When I was here last you had two."

"Yes; it died. We buried it under the mango."

When Ata had gone with him a little way she said she must turn back. Dr. Coutras surmised she was afraid to go farther in case she met any of the people from the village. He told her again that if she wanted him she had only to send and he would come at once.

CHAPTER LVI

THEN two years more went by, or perhaps three, for time passes imperceptibly in Tahiti, and it is hard to keep count of it; but at last a message was brought to Dr. Coutras that Strickland was dying. Ata had waylaid the cart that took the mail into Papeete, and besought the man who drove it to go at once to the doctor. But the doctor was out when the summons came, and it was evening when he received it. It was impossible to start at so late an

hour, and so it was not till next day soon after dawn that he set out.
He arrived at Taravao, and for the last time tramped the seven
kilometres that led to Ata's house. The path was overgrown, and
it was clear that for years now it had remained all but untrodden.
It was not easy to find the way. Sometimes he had to stumble
along the bed of the stream, and sometimes he had to push
through shrubs, dense and thorny; often he was obliged to climb
over rocks in order to avoid the hornet-nests that hung on the
trees over his head. The silence was intense.

It was with a sigh of relief that at last he came upon the little unpainted house, extraordinarily bedraggled now, and unkempt; but
here too was the same intolerable silence. He walked up, and a
little boy, playing unconcernedly in the sunshine, started at his
approach and fled quickly away: to him the stranger was the
enemy. Dr. Coutras had a sense that the child was stealthily
watching him from behind a tree. The door was wide open. He
called out, but no one answered. He stepped in. He knocked at a
door, but again there was no answer. He turned the handle and
entered. The stench that assailed him turned him horribly sick.
He put his handkerchief to his nose and forced himself to go in.
The light was dim, and after the brilliant sunshine for a while he
could see nothing. Then he gave a start. He could not make out
where he was. He seemed on a sudden to have entered a magic
world. He had a vague impression of a great primeval forest and of
naked people walking beneath the trees. Then he saw that there
were paintings on the walls.

"*Mon Dieu*, I hope the sun hasn't affected me," he muttered.

A slight movement attracted his attention, and he saw that Ata
was lying on the floor, sobbing quietly.

"Ata," he called. "Ata."

She took no notice. Again the beastly stench almost made him
faint, and he lit a cheroot. His eyes grew accustomed to the darkness, and now he was seized by an overwhelming sensation as he
stared at the painted walls. He knew nothing of pictures, but
there was something about these that extraordinarily affected him.
From floor to ceiling the walls were covered with a strange and
elaborate composition. It was indescribably wonderful and
mysterious. It took his breath away. It filled him with an emotion
which he could not understand nor analyse. He felt the awe and
the delight which a man might feel who watched the beginning of a
world. It was tremendous, sensual, passionate; and yet there was

something horrible there too, something which made him afraid. It was the work of a man who had delved into the hidden depths of nature and had discovered secrets which were beautiful and fearful too. It was the work of a man who knew things which it is unholy for men to know. There was something primeval there and terrible. It was not human. It brought to his mind vague recollections of black magic. It was beautiful and obscene.

"*Mon Dieu,* this is genius."

The words were wrung from him, and he did not know he had spoken.

Then his eyes fell on the bed of mats in the corner, and he went up, and he saw the dreadful, mutilated, ghastly object which had been Strickland. He was dead. Dr. Coutras made an effort of will and bent over that battered horror. Then he started violently, and terror blazed in his heart, for he felt that someone was behind him. It was Ata. He had not heard her get up. She was standing at his elbow, looking at what he looked at.

"Good Heavens, my nerves are all distraught," he said. "You nearly frightened me out of my wits."

He looked again at the poor dead thing that had been man, and then he started back in dismay.

"But he was blind."

"Yes; he has been blind for nearly a year."

CHAPTER LVII

AT that moment we were interrupted by the appearance of Madame Coutras, who had been paying visits. She came in, like a ship in full sail, an imposing creature, tall and stout, with an ample bust and an obesity girthed in alarmingly by straight-fronted corsets. She had a bold hooked nose and three chins. She held herself upright. She had not yielded for an instant to the enervating charm of the tropics, but contrariwise was more active, more worldly, more decided than anyone in a temperate clime would have thought it possible to be. She was evidently a copious talker, and now poured forth a breathless stream of anecdote and comment. She made the conversation we had just had seem far away and unreal.

Presently Dr. Coutras turned to me.

"I still have in my *bureau* the picture that Strickland gave me," he said. "Would you like to see it?"

"Willingly."

We got up, and he led me on to the veranda which surrounded his house. We paused to look at the gay flowers that rioted in his garden.

"For a long time I could not get out of my head the recollection of the extraordinary decoration with which Strickland had covered the walls of his house," he said reflectively.

I had been thinking of it too. It seemed to me that here Strickland had finally put the whole expression of himself. Working silently, knowing that it was his last chance, I fancied that here he must have said all that he knew of life and all that he divined. And I fancied that perhaps here he had at last found peace. The demon which possessed him was exorcised at last, and with the completion of the work, for which all his life had been a painful preparation, rest descended on his remote and tortured soul. He was willing to die, for he had fulfilled his purpose.

"What was the subject?" I asked.

"I scarcely know. It was strange and fantastic. It was a vision of the beginnings of the world, the Garden of Eden, with Adam and Eve—*que sais-je?*—it was a hymn to the beauty of the human form, male and female, and the praise of Nature, sublime, indifferent, lovely, and cruel. It gave you an awful sense of the infinity of space and of the endlessness of time. Because he painted the trees I see about me every day, the coconuts, the banyans, the flamboyants, the alligator-pears, I have seen them ever since differently, as though there were in them a spirit and a mystery which I am ever on the point of seizing and which for ever escapes me. The colours were the colours familiar to me, and yet they were different. They had a significance which was all their own. And those nude men and women. They were on the earth, and yet apart from it. They seemed to possess something of the clay of which they were created, and at the same time something divine. You saw man in the nakedness of his primeval instincts, and you were afraid, for you saw yourself."

Dr. Coutras shrugged his shoulders and smiled.

"You will laugh at me. I am a materialist, and I am a gross, fat man—Falstaff, eh?—the lyrical mode does not become me. I make myself ridiculous. But I have never seen painting which made so deep an impression upon me. *Tenez*, I had just the same feeling as when I went to the Sistine Chapel in Rome. There too I was awed by the greatness of the man who had painted that ceiling. It was genius, and it was stupendous and overwhelming. I felt small and insignificant. But you are prepared for the greatness of Michel Angelo. Nothing had prepared me for the immense surprise of these pictures in a native hut, far away from civilisation, in a fold of the mountain above Taravao. And Michel Angelo is sane and healthy. Those great works of his have the calm of the sublime; but here, notwithstanding beauty, was something troubling. I do not know what it was. It made me uneasy. It gave me the impression you get when you are sitting next door to a room that you know is empty, but in which, you know not why, you have a dreadful consciousness that notwithstanding there is someone. You scold yourself; you know it is only your nerves—and yet, and yet. . . . In a little while it is impossible to resist the terror that seizes you, and you are helpless in the clutch of an unseen horror. Yes; I confess I was not altogether sorry when I heard that those strange masterpieces had been destroyed."

"Destroyed?" I cried.

"*Mais oui*; did you not know?"

"How should I know? It is true I had never heard of this work; but I thought perhaps it had fallen into the hands of a private owner. Even now there is no certain list of Strickland's paintings."

"When he grew blind he would sit hour after hour in those two rooms that he had painted, looking at his works with sightless eyes, and seeing, perhaps, more than he had ever seen in his life before. Ata told me that he never complained of his fate, he never lost courage. To the end his mind remained serene and undisturbed. But he made her promise that when she had buried him—did I tell you that I dug his grave with my own hands, for none of the natives would approach the infected house, and we buried him, she and I, sewn up in three *pareos* joined together, under the mango tree—he made her promise that she would set fire to the house and not leave it till it was burned to the ground and not a stick remained."

I did not speak for a while, for I was thinking. Then I said:

"He remained the same to the end, then."

"Do you understand? I must tell you that I thought it my duty to dissuade her."

"Even after what you have just said?"

"Yes; for I knew that here was a work of genius, and I did not think we had the right to deprive the world of it. But Ata would not listen to me. She had promised. I would not stay to witness the barbarous deed, and it was only afterwards that I heard what she had done. She poured paraffin on the dry floors and on the pandanus-mats, and then she set fire. In a little while nothing remained but smouldering embers, and a great masterpiece existed no longer.

"I think Strickland knew it was a masterpiece. He had achieved what he wanted. His life was complete. He had made a world and saw that it was good. Then, in pride and contempt, he destroyed it.

"But I must show you my picture," said Dr. Coutras, moving on.

"What happened to Ata and the child?"

"They went to the Marquesas. She had relations there. I have heard that the boy works on one of Cameron's schooners. They say he is very like his father in appearance."

At the door that led from the veranda to the doctor's consulting-room, he paused and smiled.

"It is a fruit-piece. You would think it not a very suitable picture for a doctor's consulting-room, but my wife will not have it in the drawing-room. She says it is frankly obscene."

"A fruit-piece!" I exclaimed in surprise.

We entered the room, and my eyes fell at once on the picture. I looked at it for a long time.

It was a pile of mangoes, bananas, oranges, and I know not what; and at first sight it was an innocent picture enough. It would have been passed in an exhibition of the Post-Impressionists by a careless person as an excellent but not very remarkable example of the school; but perhaps afterwards it would come back to his recollection, and he would wonder why. I do not think then he could ever entirely forget it.

The colours were so strange that words can hardly tell what a troubling emotion they gave. There were sombre blues, opaque like a delicately carved bowl in lapis lazuli, and yet with a quivering lustre that suggested the palpitation of mysterious life; there were purples, horrible like raw and putrid flesh, and yet with a glowing, sensual passion that called up vague memories of the Roman Empire of Heliogabalus; there were reds, shrill like the berries of holly—one thought of Christmas in England, and the snow, the good cheer, and the pleasure of children—and yet by some magic softened till they had the swooning tenderness of a dove's breast; there were deep yellows that died with an unnatural passion into a green as fragrant as the spring and as pure as the sparkling water of a mountain brook. Who can tell what anguished fancy made these fruits? They belonged to a Polynesian garden of the Hesperides. There was something strangely alive in them, as though they were created in a stage of the earth's dark history when things were not irrevocably fixed to their forms. They were extravagantly luxurious. They were heavy with tropical odours. They seemed to possess a sombre passion of their own. It was enchanted fruit, to taste which might open the gateway to God knows what secrets of the soul and to mysterious palaces of the imagination. They were sullen with unawaited dangers, and to eat them might turn a man to beast or god. All that was healthy and natural, all that clung to happy relationships and the simple joys of simple men, shrunk from them in dismay; and yet a fearful attraction was in them, and, like the fruit on the Tree of the Knowledge of Good and Evil, they were terrible with the possibilities of the Unknown.

At last I turned away. I felt that Strickland had kept his secret to the grave.

"*Voyons, René, mon ami,*" came the loud, cheerful voice of Madame Coutras, "what are you doing all this time? Here are the *apéritifs*. Ask *Monsieur* if he will not drink a little glass of Quinquina Dubonnet."

"*Volontiers, Madame,*" I said, going out on to the veranda.

The spell was broken.

CHAPTER LVIII

THE time came for my departure from Tahiti. According to the gracious custom of the island, presents were given me by the persons with whom I had been thrown in contact—baskets made of the leaves of the coconut tree, mats of pandanus, fans; and Tiaré gave me three little pearls and three jars of guava jelly made with her own plump hands. When the mail-boat, stopping for twenty-four hours on its way from Wellington to San Francisco, blew the whistle that warned the passengers to get on board, Tiaré clasped me to her vast bosom, so that I seemed to sink into a billowy sea, and pressed her red lips to mine. Tears glistened in her eyes. And when we steamed slowly out of the lagoon, making our way gingerly through the opening in the reef, and then steered for the open sea, a certain melancholy fell upon me. The breeze was laden still with the pleasant odours of the land. Tahiti is very far away, and I knew that I should never see it again. A chapter of my life was closed, and I felt a little nearer to inevitable death.

Not much more than a month later I was in London; and after I had arranged certain matters which claimed my immediate attention, thinking Mrs. Strickland might like to hear what I knew of her husband's last years, I wrote to her. I had not seen her since long before the war, and I had to look out her address in the telephone book. She made an appointment, and I went to the trim little house on Campden Hill which she now inhabited. She was by this time a woman of hard on sixty, but she bore her years well, and no one would have taken her for more than fifty. Her face, thin and not much lined, was of the sort that ages gracefully, so that you thought in youth she must have been a much handsomer woman than in fact she was. Her hair, not yet very grey, was becomingly arranged, and her black gown was modish. I remembered having heard that her sister, Mrs. MacAndrew, outliving her husband but a couple of years, had left money to Mrs. Strickland; and by the look of the house and the trim maid who opened the door I judged that it was a sum adequate to keep the widow in modest comfort.

When I was ushered into the drawing-room I found that Mrs. Strickland had a visitor, and when I discovered who he was, I guessed that I had been asked to come at just that time not without intention. The caller was Mr. Van Busche Taylor, an American, and Mrs. Strickland gave me particulars with a charming smile of apology to him.

"You know, we English are so dreadfully ignorant. You must forgive me if it's necessary to explain." Then she turned to me. "Mr. Van Busche Taylor is the distinguished American critic. If you haven't read his book your education has been shamefully neglected, and you must repair the omission at once. He's writing something about dear Charlie, and he's come to ask me if I can help him."

Mr. Van Busche Taylor was a very thin man with a large, bald head, bony and shining; and under the great dome of his skull his face, yellow, with deep lines in it, looked very small. He was quiet and exceedingly polite. He spoke with the accent of New England, and there was about his demeanour a bloodless frigidity which made me ask myself why on earth he was busying himself with Charles Strickland. I had been slightly tickled at the gentleness which Mrs. Strickland put into her mention of her husband's name, and while the pair conversed I took stock of the room in which we sat. Mrs. Strickland had moved with the times. Gone were the Morris papers and gone the severe cretonnes, gone were the Arundel prints that had adorned the walls of her drawing-room in Ashley Gardens; the room blazed with fantastic colour, and I wondered if she knew that those varied hues, which fashion had imposed upon her, were due to the dreams of a poor painter in a South Sea island. She gave me the answer herself.

"What wonderful cushions you have," said Mr. Van Busche Taylor.

"Do you like them?" she said, smiling. "Bakst, you know."

And yet on the walls were coloured reproductions of several of Strickland's best pictures, due to the enterprise of a publisher in Berlin.

"You're looking at my pictures," she said, following my eyes. "Of course, the originals are out of my reach, but it's a comfort to have these. The publisher sent them to me himself. They're a great consolation to me."

"They must be very pleasant to live with," said Mr. Van Busche Taylor.

"Yes; they're so essentially decorative."

"That is one of my profoundest convictions," said Mr. Van Busche Taylor. "Great art is always decorative."

Their eyes rested on a nude woman suckling a baby, while a girl was kneeling by their side holding out a flower to the indifferent child. Looking over them was a wrinkled, scraggy hag. It was Strickland's version of the Holy Family. I suspected that for the figures had sat his household above Taravao, and the woman and the baby were Ata and his first son. I asked myself if Mrs. Strickland had any inkling of the facts.

The conversation proceeded, and I marvelled at the tact with which Mr. Van Busche Taylor avoided all subjects that might have been in the least embarrassing, and at the ingenuity with which Mrs. Strickland, without saying a word that was untrue, insinuated that her relations with her husband had always been perfect. At last Mr. Van Busche Taylor rose to go. Holding his hostess's hand, he made her a graceful, though perhaps too elaborate, speech of thanks, and left us.

"I hope he didn't bore you," she said, when the door closed behind him. "Of course it's a nuisance sometimes, but I feel it's only right to give people any information I can about Charlie. There's a certain responsibility about having been the wife of a genius."

She looked at me with those pleasant eyes of hers, which had remained as candid and as sympathetic as they had been more than twenty years before. I wondered if she was making a fool of me.

"Of course you've given up your business?" I said.

"Oh yes," she answered airily. "I ran it more by way of a hobby than for any other reason, and my children persuaded me to sell it. They thought I was overtaxing my strength."

I saw that Mrs. Strickland had forgotten that she had ever done anything so disgraceful as to work for her living. She had the true instinct of the nice woman that it is only really decent for her to live on other people's money.

"They're here now," she said. "I thought they'd like to hear what you had to say about their father. You remember Robert, don't you? I'm glad to say he's been recommended for the Military Cross."

She went to the door and called them. There entered a tall man in khaki, with the parson's collar, handsome in a somewhat heavy fashion, but with the frank eyes that I remembered in him as a boy. He was followed by his sister. She must have been the same age as was her mother when first I knew her, and she was very like her. She too gave one the impression that as a girl she must have been prettier than indeed she was.

"I suppose you don't remember them in the least," said Mrs. Strickland, proud and smiling. "My daughter is now Mrs. Ronaldson. Her husband's a major in the Gunners."

"He's by way of being a pukka soldier, you know," said Mrs. Ronaldson gaily. "That's why he's only a major."

I remembered my anticipation long ago that she would marry a soldier. It was inevitable. She had all the graces of the soldier's wife. She was civil and affable, but she could hardly conceal her intimate conviction that she was not quite as others were. Robert was breezy.

"It's a bit of luck that I should be in London when you turned up," he said. "I've only got three days' leave."

"He's dying to get back," said his mother.

"Well, I don't mind confessing it, I have a rattling good time at the front. I've made a lot of good pals. It's a first-rate life. Of course war's terrible, and all that sort of thing; but it does bring out the best qualities in a man, there's no denying that."

Then I told them what I had learnt about Charles Strickland in Tahiti. I thought it unnecessary to say anything of Ata and her boy, but for the rest I was as accurate as I could be. When I had narrated his lamentable death I ceased. For a minute or two we were all silent. Then Robert Strickland struck a match and lit a cigarette.

"The mills of God grind slowly, but they grind exceeding small," he said, somewhat impressively.

Mrs. Strickland and Mrs. Ronaldson looked down with a slightly pious expression which indicated, I felt sure, that they thought the quotation was from Holy Writ. Indeed, I was unconvinced that Robert Strickland did not share their illusion. I do not know why I suddenly thought of Strickland's son by Ata. They had told me he was a merry, light-hearted youth. I saw him, with my mind's eye, on the schooner on which he worked, wearing nothing but a pair of dungarees; and at night, when the boat sailed along easily before a light breeze, and the sailors were gathered on the upper deck, while the captain and the supercargo lolled in deck-chairs, smoking their pipes, I saw him dance with another lad, dance wildly, to the wheezy music of the concertina. Above was the blue sky, and the stars, and all about the desert of the Pacific Ocean.

A quotation from the Bible came to my lips, but I held my tongue, for I know that clergymen think it a little blasphemous when the laity poach upon their preserves. My Uncle Harry, for twenty-seven years Vicar of Whitstable, was on these occasions in the habit of saying that the devil could always quote scripture to his purpose. He remembered the days when you could get thirteen Royal Natives for a shilling.

THE NARROW CORNER

*Short therefore, is man's life, and
narrow is the corner of the earth
wherein he dwells.*

The Narrow Corner

CHAPTER I

All this happened a good many years ago.

CHAPTER II

DR. SAUNDERS yawned. It was nine o'clock in the morning. The day lay before him and he had nothing in the world to do. He had already seen a few patients. There was no doctor on the island and on his arrival such as had anything the matter with them seized the opportunity to consult him. But the place was not unhealthy and the ailments he was asked to cure were chronic, and he could do little; or they were trifling, and responded quickly to simple remedies. Dr. Saunders had practised for fifteen years in Fu-chou and had acquired a great reputation among the Chinese for his skill in dealing with the ills that affect the eye, and it was to remove a cataract for a rich Chinese merchant that he had come to Takana. This was an island in the Malay Archipelago, a long way down, and the distance from Fu-chou was so great that at first he had refused to go. But the Chinese, Kim Ching by name, was himself a native of that city and two of his sons lived there. He was well-acquainted with Dr. Saunders, and on his periodical visits to Fu-chou had consulted him on his failing sight. He had heard how the doctor, by what looked like a miracle, had caused the blind to see, and when in due course he found himself in such a state that he could only tell day from night, he was prepared to trust no one else to perform the operation which he was assured would restore his sight. Dr. Saunders had advised him to come to Fu-chou when certain symptoms appeared, but he had delayed, fearing the surgeon's knife, and when at last he could no longer distinguish one object from another the long journey made him nervous and he bade his sons persuade the doctor to come to him.

1

Kim Ching had started life as a coolie, but by hard work and courage, aided by good luck, cunning and unscrupulousness, he had amassed a large fortune. At this time, a man of seventy, he owned large plantations on several islands; his own schooners fished for pearl, and he traded extensively in all the products of the Archipelago. His sons, themselves middle-aged men, went to see Dr. Saunders. They were his friends and patients. Two or three times a year they invited him to a grand dinner, when they gave him bird's-nest soup, shark fins, bêche de mer and many other delicacies; singing girls engaged at a high price entertained the company with their performances; and everyone got tight. The Chinese liked Dr. Saunders. He spoke the dialect of Fu-chou with fluency. He lived, not like the other foreigners in the settlement, but in the heart of the Chinese city; he stayed there year in and year out and they had become accustomed to him. They knew that he smoked opium, though with moderation, and they knew what else there was to be known about him. He seemed to them a sensible man. It did not displease them that the foreigners in the community turned a cold shoulder on him. He never went to the club but to read the papers when the mail came in, and was never invited to dinner by them; they had their own English doctor and called in Dr. Saunders only when he was away on leave. But when they had anything the matter with their eyes they put their disapproval in their pockets and came down for treatment to the shabby little Chinese house over the river where Dr. Saunders dwelt happily amid the stenches of a native city. They looked about them with distaste as they sat in what was both the doctor's consulting-room and parlour. It was furnished in the Chinese style but for a roll-top desk and a couple of rocking-chairs much the worse for wear. On the discoloured walls Chinese scrolls, presented by grateful patients, contrasted oddly with the sheet of cardboard on which were printed in different sizes and combinations the letters of the alphabet. It always seemed to them that there hung about the house faintly the acrid scent of opium.

But this the sons of Kim Ching did not notice, and if they had it would not have incommoded them. After the usual compliments had passed and Dr. Saunders had offered them cigarettes from a green tin, they set forth their business. Their father had bidden them say that now, too old and too blind to make the journey to Fu-chou, he desired Dr. Saunders to come to Takana and perform the operation which he had said two years before would be necessary. What would be his fee? The doctor shook his head. He had a large practice in Fu-chou and it was out of the question for him to absent himself for any length of time. He saw no reason why Kim Ching should not come there; he could come on one of his own schooners. If that did not suit him he could get a surgeon from Macassar who was perfectly competent to perform the operation. The sons of Kim Ching, talking very volubly, explained that their father knew that there was no one who could do the miracles that Dr. Saunders could, and he was determined that no one else should touch him. He was prepared to double the sum that the doctor reckoned he could earn at Fu-chou during the period he would be away. Dr. Saunders continued to shake his head. Then the two brothers looked at one another and the elder took out from an inner pocket a large and shabby wallet of black leather bulging with the notes of the Chartered Bank. He spread them out before the doctor, a thousand dollars, two thousand dollars; the doctor smiled and his sharp, bright eyes twinkled; the Chinese continued to spread out the notes; the two brothers were smiling too, ingratiatingly, but they keenly watched the doctor's face and presently they were conscious of a change in his expression. He did not move. His eyes kept their tolerant good-humour, but they felt in their bones that his interest was aroused. Kim Ching's elder son paused and looked inquiringly into his face.

"I can't leave all my patients for three solid months," said the doctor. "Let Kim Ching get one of the Dutch doctors from Macassar or Amboyna. There's a fellow at Amboyna who's quite all right."

The Chinese did not reply. He put more notes on the table. They were hundred-dollar bills and he arranged them in little packets of ten. The wallet bulged less. He laid the packets side by side and at last there were ten of them.

"Stop," said the doctor. "That'll do."

CHAPTER III

It was a complicated journey. From Fu-chou he went on a Chinese vessel to Manila in the Philippines, and from there, after waiting a few days, by cargo boat to Macassar. Thence he took passage on the Dutch ship that ran every other month to Merauke in New

Guinea, stopping at a great many places on the way, and thus at last landed at Takana. He travelled with a Chinese boy who acted as his servant, gave anæsthetics when required and made his pipes when he smoked opium. Dr. Saunders performed a successful operation on Kim Ching, and now there was nothing for him to do but sit and twiddle his thumbs till the Dutch ship called on her way back from Merauke. The island was fairly large, but it was isolated and the Dutch Régisseur visited it only at intervals. The Government was represented by a half-caste Javanese, who spoke no English, and a few policemen. The town consisted of a single street of shops. Two or three were owned by Arabs from Baghdad, but the rest by Chinese. There was a small rest-house about ten minutes' walk from the town which the Régisseur inhabited on his periodical visits, and here Dr. Saunders had installed himself. The path that led to it ran on through plantations for three miles, and then was lost in the virgin jungle.

When the Dutch ship came in, there was a certain animation. The captain, one or two of the officers and the chief engineer came ashore, and the passengers if there were any, and they sat in Kim Ching's store and drank beer, but they never stayed for more than three hours and when they got back into their boat and rowed away the little town went to sleep again. It was in the doorway of this store that Dr. Saunders sat now. There was a rattan awning that protected it from the sun, but in the street the sun beat down with a harsh glare. A mangy dog sniffed about some offal over which a swarm of flies was buzzing and looked for something to eat. Two or three chickens scratched about in the roadway and one, squatting, ruffled her feathers in the dust. Outside the shop opposite a naked Chinese child with a distended belly was trying to make a sand castle out of the dust in the road. Flies flew about him, settling on him, but he did not mind them, and intent on his game did not try to brush them away. Then a native passed, with nothing on but a discoloured sarong, and he carried two baskets of sugar-cane suspended to each end of a pole balanced on one shoulder. With his shuffling feet he kicked up the dust as he walked. Inside the store a clerk, hunched over a table, was busy with brush and ink writing some document in Chinese characters. A coolie sitting on the floor was rolling cigarettes and smoking them one after the other. No one came in to buy. Dr. Saunders asked for a bottle of beer. The clerk left his writing and going to the back of the store took a bottle out of a pail of

5

water and brought it along with a glass to the doctor. It was pleasantly cool.

Time hung somewhat heavily on the doctor's hands, but he was not discontented. He was able to amuse himself with little things, and the mangy dog, the thin chickens, the pot-bellied child all diverted him. He drank his bottle of beer slowly.

CHAPTER IV

HE looked up. He gave a cry of surprise. For there, strolling towards him, down the middle of the dusty road, were two white men. No ship was in and he wondered where they had come from. They walked idly, looking to right and left of them, like strangers visiting the island for the first time. They were shabbily dressed in trousers and singlets. Their topis were grimy. They came up, saw him sitting in the open shop and stopped. One of them addressed him.

"Is this Kim Ching's?"

"Yes."

"Is he here?"

"No, he's sick."

"Bad luck. I suppose we can get a drink."

"Surely."

The speaker turned to his companion.

"Come on in."

They entered.

"What'll you have?" asked Dr. Saunders.

"A bottle of beer for me."

"Same here," said the other.

The doctor gave the order to the coolie. He brought bottles of beer and chairs for the strangers to sit on. One of them was middle-aged, with a sallow, lined face, white hair and a scrub of white moustache. He was of the middle height, spare, and when he spoke he showed hideously decayed teeth. His eyes were cunning and restless. They were small and pale and set somewhat close together, which gave him a foxy look, but his manner was ingratiating.

"Where have you come from?" asked the doctor.

"We just come in on a lugger. From Thursday Island."

"A goodish way. Have fine weather?"

"Couldn't want better. A nice breeze and no sea to speak of. Nichols's my name. Captain Nichols. Maybe you've 'eard of me."

"I can't say I have."

"I been sailin' these seas for thirty years. There's not an island in the Archipelago I ain't put in at one time or another. I'm pretty well known around 'ere. Kim Ching knows me. Known me for twenty years."

"I'm a stranger myself," said the doctor.

Captain Nichols looked at him, and though his face was open and his expression cordial, you had a feeling that there was suspicion in his glance.

"I seem to know your face," he said. "I could swear I seen you somewhere."

Dr. Saunders smiled but did not volunteer any information about himself. Captain Nichols screwed up his eyes in the effort to remember where he had run across the little man. He scanned his face with attention. The doctor was short, only just over five foot six, and slight, but with something of a paunch. His hands were soft and podgy, but they were small, with tapering fingers, and if he had been vain it was possible to suppose that once upon a time he had been not a little pleased with them. They had still a sort of well-bred elegance. He was very ugly, with a snub nose and a large mouth; and when he laughed, which he did often, you saw big, yellow, uneven teeth. Under his bushy grey eyebrows his green eyes gleamed bright, amusing and clever. He was not very closely shaved and his skin was blotchy; he had a high colour which over the cheek-bones spread into a purple flush. It suggested some long-standing affection of the heart. His hair must once have been thick and black and coarse, but now it was nearly white and on the crown very thin. But his ugliness, far from being repellent, was attractive. When he laughed his skin puckered round the eyes, giving his face infinite vivacity, and his expression was charged with an extreme but not ill-natured malice. You would have taken him then for a buffoon, but for the shrewdness that gleamed from his shining eyes. His intelligence was obvious. And though merry and bright, fond of a joke and amused both at his own and at others', you had an impression that even in the abandon of laughter he never quite gave himself away. He seemed to be on his guard. For all his chattiness and however hearty his manner, you were conscious (if you were observant and did not allow yourself to be taken in by his superficial frankness) that those merry, laughing eyes were watching, weighing, judging and forming an opinion. He was not a man to take things at their face value.

Since the doctor did not speak Captain Nichols went on:

"This is Fred Blake," he said, with a gesture of his thumb towards his companion.

Dr. Saunders nodded.

"Makin' a long stay?" continued the captain.

"I'm waiting for the Dutch packet."

"North or south?"

"North."

"What did you say your name was?"

"I didn't mention it. Saunders."

"I've knocked about too long in the Indian Ocean to ask questions," said the captain, with his ingratiating laugh. "Ask no questions and you won't be told no lies. Saunders? I've known a lot of chaps as answered to that name, but whether it was theirs or not by rights nobody knew but theirselves. What's the matter with old Kim Ching? Fine old sport. I was lookin' forward to 'avin' a bit of a chin-wag with 'im."

"His eyes went back on him. He's had cataract."

Captain Nichols sat up and held out his hand.

"Doc Saunders. I knew I'd seen your face. Fu-chou. I was up there seven years ago."

The doctor took the proffered hand. Captain Nichols turned to his friend.

"Everyone knows Doc Saunders. Best doctor in the Far East. Eyes. That's his line. I 'ad a pal once, everyone said 'e'd go blind, nothing could stop it, 'e went to see the doc and in a month 'e could see as well as you or me. The Chinks just swear by him. Doc Saunders. Well, this is a joyful surprise. I thought you never left Fu-chou from one year's end to the other."

"Well, I have now."

"It's a bit of luck for me, this. You're the very man I wanted to meet." Captain Nichols leaned forward and his cunning eyes fixed the doctor with an intensity in which there was something very like menace. "I suffer from dyspepsia something awful."

"Oh, Christ!" muttered Fred Blake.

It was the first time he had spoken since they sat down and Dr.

Saunders turned to look at him. He slouched in his chair, gnawing
his fingers, in an attitude that suggested boredom and ill-humour.
He was a tall young man, slight but wiry, with curly, dark brown
hair and large blue eyes. He did not look more than twenty. In
his dirty singlet and dungarees he looked loutish, an unlicked cub,
thought the doctor, and there was a surliness in his expression that
was somewhat disagreeable; but he had a straight nose and a well-
formed mouth.

"Leave off bitin' your nails, Fred," said the captain. "Disgustin'
'abit, I call it."

"You and your dyspepsia," retorted the young man, with a
chuckle.

When he smiled you saw that he had exquisite teeth. They were
very white, small and of a perfect shape; they were so unexpected a
grace in that sombre face, their beauty was so dazzling, that you
were taken aback. His sulky smile had great sweetness.

"You can laugh because you don't know what it is," said
Captain Nichols. "I'm a martyr to it. Don't say I'm not careful
what I eat. I've tried everything. Nothin' does me any good. This
beer now. Do you think I shan't suffer for it? You know just as
well as I do that I shall."

"Go on. Tell the doctor all about it," said Blake.

Captain Nichols asked nothing better. He proceeded to narrate
the history of his malady. He described his symptoms with a
scientific accuracy. There was not a revolting detail that he
omitted to mention. He enumerated the doctors he had consulted
and the patent remedies he had tried. Dr. Saunders listened in
silence, an expression of sympathetic interest on his face, and
occasionally nodded his head.

"If there's anyone as can do anythin' for me it's you, Doc," said
the captain earnestly. "They don't 'ave to tell me you're clever, I
can see that for meself."

"I can't work miracles. You can't expect anyone to do much in
a minute for a chronic condition like yours."

"No, I don't ask that, but you can prescribe for me, can't you?
There's nothin' I won't try. What I'd like you to do is to make a
thorough examination of me, see?"

"How long are you staying here?"

"Our time's our own."

"But we're pushing off as soon as we've got what we want," said
Blake.

A quick look passed between the two men. Dr. Saunders noticed it. He did not know why he had an impression that there was something strange in it.

"What made you put in here?" he asked.

Fred Blake's face once more grew sullen, and when the doctor put his question he threw him a glance. Dr. Saunders read suspicion in it and perhaps fear. He wondered. It was the captain who replied.

"I've known Kim Ching donkey's years. We wanted some stores, and we thought it wouldn't do us any 'arm to fill up our tank."

"Are you trading?"

"In a manner of speakin'. If anythin' comes along we ain't goin' to miss a chance. Who would?"

"What cargo are you carrying?"

"A bit of everything."

Captain Nichols smiled genially, showing his decayed, discoloured teeth, and he looked strangely shifty and dishonest. It occurred to Dr. Saunders that perhaps they were smuggling opium.

"You're not going to Macassar by any chance?"

"We might be."

"What's that paper?" said Fred Blake suddenly, pointing to one that lay on the counter.

"Oh, that's three weeks old. We brought it down in the ship I came on."

"Have they got any Australian papers here?"

"No."

Dr. Saunders chuckled at the notion.

"Is there any Australian news in that paper?"

"It's Dutch. I don't know Dutch. In any case, you'd have had later news than that on Thursday Island."

Blake frowned a little. The captain grinned craftily.

"This ain't exactly the hub of the universe, Fred," he sniggered.

"Don't you ever have any English papers here at all?" asked Blake.

"Now and then a stray copy of the Hong-Kong paper finds its way here or a *Straits Times*, but they're a month old."

"Don't they ever get any news?"

"Only what the Dutch ship brings."

"Haven't they got a cable or a wireless?"

"No."

"If a man wanted to keep out of the way of the police I should think he'd be pretty safe here," said Captain Nichols.

"For some time, anyway," agreed the doctor.

"Have another bottle of beer, Doc?" asked Blake.

"No, I don't think I will. I'm going back to the rest-house. If you two fellows would like to come and dine there to-night, I can get you some sort of a meal."

He addressed himself to Blake because he had a feeling that his impulse would be to refuse, but it was Captain Nichols who answered.

"That'd be fine. A change from the lugger."

"You don't want to be bothered with us," said Blake.

"No bother. I'll meet you here about six. We'll have a few drinks and then go up."

The doctor rose, nodded and left.

CHAPTER V

BUT he did not go immediately to the rest-house. The invitation he had so cordially given to these strangers was due to no sudden urge of hospitality, but to a notion that had come into his head while he was talking to them. Now that he had left Fu-chou and his practice, he was in no hurry to get back, and he had made up his mind to make a trip to Java, his first holiday for many years, before he returned to work. It occurred to him that if they would give him a passage on the lugger, if not to Macassar, at least to one of the more frequented islands, he could then find a steamer to take him in the direction he wished to go. He had been resigned to spending another three weeks or so on Takana when it seemed impossible to get away; but Kim Ching needed his services no longer, and now that a chance offered he was seized with an immense eagerness to profit by it. The thought of staying where he was for so long with nothing to do suddenly became intolerable to him. He walked down the broad street—it was less than half a mile long—till he came to the sea. There was no quay. Coconuts grew to the water's edge, and among them were the huts of the natives of the island. Children were playing about and gaunt pigs rooted among the piles. There was a straight line of silver beach

with a few prahus and dug-outs drawn up on it. The coral sand
glistened under the fiery sun, and even with shoes on it was hot
under the soles of your feet. Hideous crabs scuttled out of your
way as you walked. One of the prahus lay bottom up and three
dark-skinned Malays in sarongs were working on it. A reef a few
hundred yards out formed a lagoon, and in this the water was clear
and deep. A small crowd of boys were romping in the shallow.
One of Kim Ching's schooners lay at anchor and not far from it
was the strangers' lugger. She was very shabby beside Kim Ching's
trim craft and badly needed a coat of paint. She seemed very small
to rove the trackless ocean, and Dr. Saunders had a moment's
hesitation. He looked up at the sky. It was cloudless. No wind
stirred the leaves of the coconut trees. Drawn up on the beach was
a squat little dinghy, and he supposed it was in this that the two
men had rowed ashore. He could see no crew on the lugger.

Having had a good look, he turned back and strolled along to
the rest-house. He changed into the Chinese trousers and silk
tunic in which from long habit he felt most at ease, and taking a
book went out to sit on the veranda. Fruit trees grew round about
the rest-house, and opposite, on the other side of the path, was a
handsome grove of coconuts. They rose, very tall and straight, in
their regular lines, and the bright sun, piercing the leaves, splashed
the ground with a fantastic pattern of yellow light. Behind him, in
the cook-house, the boy was preparing tiffin.

Dr. Saunders was not a great reader. He seldom opened a novel.
Interested in character, he liked books that displayed the oddities
of human nature, and he had read over and over again Pepys and
Boswell's Johnson, Florio's Montaigne and Hazlitt's essays. He
liked old travel books, and he could peruse with pleasure the
accounts in Hakluyt of countries he had never been to. He had at
home a considerable library of the books written about China by
the early missionaries. He read neither for information nor to
improve his mind, but sought in books occasion for reverie. He
read with a sense of humour peculiar to himself, and was able to
get out of the narratives of missionary enterprise an amount of
demure fun which would have much surprised the authors. He
was a quiet man, of an agreeable discourse, but not one to force his
conversation on you, and he could enjoy his little joke without
feeling a desire to impart it to another.

He held in his hand now a volume of Père Huc's travels, but he
read with divided attention. His thoughts were occupied with the

two strangers who had so unexpectedly appeared on the island. Dr. Saunders had known so many thousands of people in his Eastern life that he had no difficulty in placing Captain Nichols. He was a bad hat. By his accent he was English, and if he had knocked about the China seas for so many years it was likely that he had got into some trouble in England. Dishonesty was stamped on his mean and crafty features. He could not have prospered greatly if he was no more now than skipper of this shabby little lugger, and Dr. Saunders let a sigh, an ironical sigh, fall on the still air as he reflected how seldom it was that the crook received an adequate return for his labours. But of course the probability was that Captain Nichols preferred dirty work to clean. He was the sort of man who was willing to put his hand to anything. You would not trust him out of your sight. You could rely on him for nothing but to do you down. He had said he knew Kim Ching. It was probable that he was more often out of a job than in one, and he would have been glad enough to take employment under a Chinese owner. He was the kind of fellow you would engage if you had something shady to do, and it might very well be that at one time he had been skipper of one of Kim Ching's schooners. The conclusion Dr. Saunders arrived at was that he rather liked Captain Nichols. He was taken by the skipper's genial friendliness; it gave a pleasant savour to his roguery, and the dyspepsia he suffered from added a comic note that pleased. The doctor was glad that he would see him again that evening.

Dr. Saunders took an interest in his fellows that was not quite scientific and not quite human. He wanted to receive entertainment from them. He regarded them dispassionately and it gave him just the same amusement to unravel the intricacies of the individual as a mathematician might find in the solution of a problem. He made no use of the knowledge he obtained. The satisfaction he got from it was æsthetic, and if to know and judge men gave him a subtle sense of superiority he was unconscious of it. He had fewer prejudices than most men. The sense of disapproval was left out of him. Many people are indulgent to the vices they practise, and have small patience with those they have no mind to; some, broader-minded, can accept them all in a comprehensive toleration, a toleration, however, that is more often theoretical than practical; but few can suffer manners different from their own without distaste. It is seldom that a man is shocked by the thought that someone has seduced another's wife, and it may be that he preserves his equanimity when he knows that another has cheated at cards or forged a cheque (though this is not easy when you are yourself the victim), but it is hard for him to make a bosom friend of one who drops his aitches and almost impossible if he scoops up gravy with his knife. Dr. Saunders lacked this sensitiveness. Unpleasant table manners affected him as little as a purulent ulcer. Right and wrong were no more to him than good weather and bad weather. He took them as they came. He judged but he did not condemn. He laughed.

He was very easy to get on with. He was much liked. But he had no friends. He was an agreeable companion, but neither sought intimacy nor gave it. There was no one in the world to whom he was not at heart indifferent. He was self-sufficient. His happiness depended not on persons but on himself. He was selfish, but since he was at the same time shrewd and disinterested, few knew it and none was inconvenienced by it. Because he wanted nothing, he was never in anybody's way. Money meant little to him, and he never much minded whether patients paid him or not. They thought him philanthropic. Since time was as unimportant to him as cash, he was just as willing to doctor them as not. It amused him to see their ailments yield to treatment, and he continued to find entertainment in human nature. He confounded persons and patients. Each was like another page in an interminable book, and that there were so many repetitions oddly added to the interest. It was curious to see how all these people, white, yellow and brown, responded to the critical situations of humanity, but the sight neither touched his heart nor troubled his nerves. Death was, after all, the greatest event in every man's life, and he never ceased to find interest in the way he faced it. It was with a little thrill that he sought to pierce into a man's consciousness, looking through the eyes, frightened, defiant, sullen or resigned, into the soul confronted for the first time with the knowledge that its race was run, but the thrill was merely one of curiosity. His sensibility was unaffected. He felt neither sorrow nor pity. He only faintly wondered how it was that what was so important to one could matter so little to another. And yet his manner was full of sympathy. He knew exactly what to say to alleviate the terror or pain of the moment, and he left no one but fortified, consoled and encouraged. It was a game that he played, and it gave him satisfaction to play it well. He had great natural kindliness, but it was a kindliness of instinct, which betokened no interest in the recipient:

he would come to the rescue if you were in a fix, but if there was no getting you out of it would not bother about you further. He did not like to kill living things, and he would neither shoot nor fish. He went so far, for no reason other than that he felt that every creature had a right to life, that he preferred to brush away a mosquito or a fly than to swat it. Perhaps he was an intensely logical man. It could not be denied that he led a good life (if at least you did not confine goodness to conformity with your own sensual inclinations), for he was charitable and kindly, and he devoted his energies to the alleviation of pain, but if motive counts for righteousness, then he deserved no praise; for he was influenced in his actions neither by love, pity, nor charity.

CHAPTER VI

DR. SAUNDERS sat down to tiffin and having finished went into the bedroom and threw himself on his bed. But it was very hot and he could not sleep. He wondered what the connection was between Captain Nichols and Fred Blake. Notwithstanding his grimy dungarees, the young man did not give the impression of being a sailor; the doctor did not quite know why, and for want of a better reason surmised that it was because he had not got the sea in his eyes. He was hard to place. He spoke with something of an Australian accent, but he was evidently not a rough-neck, and he might have had some education: his manners seemed quite good. Perhaps his people had a business of sorts in Sydney, and he was used to a comfortable home and decent surroundings. But why he was sailing these lonely seas on a pearling lugger with a scoundrel like Captain Nichols was mysterious. Of course the pair of them might be in partnership, but what traffic they were engaged in remained to be seen. Dr. Saunders was inclined to believe that it was not a very honest one, and, whatever it was, that Fred Blake would get the thin end of the stick.

Though Dr. Saunders was stark naked, the sweat poured off him. Between his legs was a Dutch wife. This is the bolster which they use in those parts for coolness' sake, and many grow so accustomed to it that even in temperate climes they cannot sleep without it; but it was strange to the doctor and it irked him. He threw it aside and rolled over on his back. In the garden round the rest-house, in the coconut grove opposite, a myriad insects were making noise and the insistent din, which generally fell unheard on ears benumbed, now throbbed on his nerves with a racket to awake the dead. He gave up the attempt to sleep and, wrapping a sarong round him, went out again on to the veranda. It was as hot there as within and as airless. He was weary. His mind was restless, but it worked perversely, and thoughts jerked through his brain like the misfirings of a defective carburettor. He tried to cool himself with a bath, but it brought no refreshment to his spirit. It remained hot, listless and uneasy. The veranda was intolerable, and he threw himself once more on his bed. The air under the mosquito curtains seemed to stand still. He could not read, he could not think, he could not rest. The hours were leaden-footed.

He was aroused at last by a voice on the steps, and going out he found there a messenger from Kim Ching, who asked him to go and see him. The doctor had paid his patient a professional visit that morning, and there was nothing much more he could do for him, but he put on his clothes and sallied forth. Kim Ching had heard of the lugger's arrival, and was curious to know what the strangers wanted. He had been told that the doctor had spent an hour with them that morning. He did not much care for un-known persons to come to the island, so much of which belonged to him. Captain Nichols had sent a message asking to see him, but the Chinese had replied that he was too sick to receive anyone. The captain claimed acquaintance with him, but Kim Ching had no recollection of him. An accurate description of the man had already reached him, and the doctor's account added nothing to help him. It appeared that they were staying two or three days.

"They told me they were sailing at dawn," said Dr. Saunders. He reflected for a moment. "Perhaps they changed their plans when I told them there was no cable or wireless on the island."

"They've got nothing in the lugger but ballast," said Kim Ching. "Stones."

"No cargo at all?"

"Nothing."

"Opium?"

Kim Ching shook his head. The doctor smiled.

"Perhaps it's just a pleasure trip. The skipper's got stomach trouble. He wants me to do something for him."

Kim Ching gave an exclamation. That gave him the clue. He remembered. He had had Captain Nichols on one of his schooners, eight or ten years before, and had fired him. There had been some dispute, but Kim Ching did not go into any detail.

"He's a bad man," said Kim Ching. "I could have had him put in prison."

Dr. Saunders guessed that the transaction, whatever it was, had been far from straight, and it might well be that Captain Nichols, knowing Kim Ching would not venture to prosecute, had taken more than his fair share of the profits. There was an ugly look in the Chinaman's face. He knew all about Captain Nichols now. He had lost his certificate, there had been some trouble with an insurance company, and since then he had been glad to take employment with owners who were not particular about such things. He had been a heavy drinker till his stomach went back on him. He picked up a living as best he could. He was often on the beach. But he was a first-rate seaman, and he got jobs. He did not keep them long, because it was impossible for him to go straight.

"You tell him he more better get out of here pletty damn quick," said Kim Ching, to finish, breaking into English.

CHAPTER VII

NIGHT had fallen when Dr. Saunders sauntered down once more to Kim Ching's store. Nichols and Blake were sitting there drinking beer. He took them up to the rest-house. The sailor was full of small talk, of a facetious nature, but Fred remained sullen and silent. Dr. Saunders was conscious that he came against his will. When he entered the living-room of the bungalow he gave a quick, suspicious look round as though he awaited he did not quite know what, and when the house ghekko gave its sudden harsh cry he started suddenly.

"It's only a lizard," said Dr. Saunders.

"It made me jump."

Dr. Saunders called Ah Kay, his boy, and told him to bring the whisky and some glasses.

"I daren't drink it," said the skipper. "It's poison to me. How would you like never to be able to eat a thing or drink a thing, without knowin' you was goin' to suffer for it?"

"Let me see what I can do for you," said Dr. Saunders.

He went to his medicine chest and mixed something in a glass. He gave it to the captain and told him to swallow it.

"Maybe that'll help you to eat your dinner in comfort."

He poured out whisky for himself and Fred Blake and turned on the gramophone. The young man listened to the record and his expression grew more alert; when it was finished he put on another himself and, slightly swaying to the rhythm, stood looking at the instrument. He stole one or two glances at the doctor, but the doctor pretended not to notice him. Captain Nichols, his shifty eyes never still, carried on the conversation. It consisted chiefly of enquiries about this man and that in Fu-chou, Shanghai and Hong-Kong, and descriptions of the drunken parties he had been on in those parts. Ah Kay brought in the dinner and they sat down.

"I enjoy my food," said the captain. "Not fallals, mind you. I like it good and I like it simple. Not a big eater. I never been that. A cut off the joint and a couple of veges, with a bit of cheese to finish up with, and I'm satisfied. You couldn't eat anything simpler than that, could you? And then twenty minutes after—as regular as clockwork—agony. I tell you life ain't worth livin' when you suffer like what I do. D'you ever know old George Vaughan? One of the best. He was on one of the Jardine boats, used to go up to Amoy, he 'ad dyspepsia so bad he 'anged himself. I shouldn't be surprised if I didn't, too, one of these days."

Ah Kay was not a bad cook, and Fred Blake did full justice to the dinner.

"This is a treat after what we've had to eat on the lugger."

"Most of it comes out of a tin, but the boy flavours it up. The Chinese are natural-born cooks."

"It's the best dinner I've had for five weeks."

Dr. Saunders remembered that they had said they had come from Thursday Island. With the fine weather they admitted that could not have taken them more than a week.

"What sort of a place is Thursday Island?" he asked.

It was the captain who answered.

"Hell of a place. Nothin' but goats. The wind blows six months one way and then it blows six months the other. Gets on your nerves."

Captain Nichols spoke with a twinkle in his eyes as though he saw what was at the back of the doctor's simple question and was amused at the easy way he tackled it.

"Do you live there?" Dr. Saunders asked the young man, a guileless smile on his lips.

"No, Brisbane," he answered abruptly.

"Fred's got a bit of capital," said Captain Nichols, "and 'e thought he'd like to 'ave a look-see on the chance 'e might find somethin' in these parts 'e'd like to invest it in. My idea, that was. You see, I know all these islands inside out, and what I say is, there's a rare lot of chances for a young fellow with a bit of capital. That's what I'd do if I 'ad a bit of capital, buy a plantation in one of these islands."

"Do a bit of pearl fishing, too," said Blake.

"You can get all the labour you want. Native labour's the only thing. Then you sit back and let other people work for you. Fine life, too. Grand thing for a young fellow."

The skipper's shifty eyes, for a moment still, were fixed on Dr. Saunders's bland face, and it was not hard to see that he was watching the effect of what he was saying. The doctor felt that they had concocted the story between them that afternoon. And when the skipper saw that Dr. Saunders did not swallow it, he grinned cheerfully. It was as if he took so much delight in lying that it would have spoilt it for him if you had accepted it as the truth.

"That's why we put in 'ere," he went on. "There's not much about these islands that old Kim Ching don't know, and it struck me we might do business with 'im. I told the boy in the store to tell the old fellow I was 'ere."

"I know. He told me."

"You seen 'im, then? Did 'e say anythin' about me?"

"Yes, he said you'd better get out of here pretty damn quick."

"Why, what's 'e got against me?"

"He didn't say."

"We 'ad a bit of a disagreement, I know that, but that was donkey's years ago. There's no sense in 'oldin' a thing up against a fellow all that while. Forgive and forget, I say."

Captain Nichols had the unusual trait that he could play a mean trick on a man without bearing him any ill-feeling afterwards, and he could not understand that the injured party might continue to harbour malice. Dr. Saunders noticed the idiosyncrasy with amused detachment.

"My impression is that Kim Ching has a good memory," he said.

They talked of one thing and another.

"Do you know," said the captain suddenly, "I don't believe I'm goin' to 'ave dyspepsia to-night. Say, what was that stuff you give me?"

"A little preparation that I've found useful in chronic cases like yours."

"I wish you'd give me some more of it."

"It mightn't do you any good next time. What you want is treatment."

"Do you think you could cure me?"

The doctor saw his opportunity coming.

"I don't know about that. If I could watch you for a few days and try one or two things, I might be able to do something for you."

"I've got a good mind to stay on 'ere for a bit and let you see. We're in no 'urry."

"What about Kim Ching?"

"What can 'e do?"

"Come off it," said Fred Blake. "We don't want to get into any trouble here. We're sailing to-morrow."

"It's all right for you to talk. You don't suffer like what I do. Look 'ere, I'll tell you what I'll do, I'll go and see the old devil to-morrow and find out what 'e's got against me."

"We're sailing to-morrow," repeated the other.

"We're sailin' when I say we sail."

The two men looked at one another for an instant. The skipper smiled with his usual foxy geniality, but Fred Blake frowned with sullen anger. Dr. Saunders interrupted the quarrel that was in the air.

"I don't suppose you know Chinamen as well as I do, Captain, but you must know something about them. If they've got their knife into you they're not going to let you off for the asking."

The skipper thumped his fist on the table.

"Well, it was only a matter of a couple of 'undred quid. Old Kim's as rich as be damned. What difference can that make to 'im? He's an old crook, anyway."

"Have you never noticed that nothing hurts the feelings of a crook so much as to have another crook do the dirty on him?"

Captain Nichols wore a moody scowl. His little greenish eyes, set too close together, seemed to converge as he shot a bitter glance into space. He looked a very ugly customer. But at the doctor's remark he threw back his head and laughed.

"That's a good one. I like you, Doc, you don't mind what you say, do you? Well, it takes all sorts to make a world. Keep your eyes skinned and let the devil take the 'indmost, that's what I say. And when you see a chance of makin' a bit you're a fool if you don't take it. Of course everyone makes a mistake now and again. But you can't always tell beforehand 'ow things are goin' to turn out."

"If the doctor gives you some more of that stuff and tells you what to do, you'll be all right," said Blake.

He had recovered his temper.

"No, I won't do that," said Dr. Saunders. "But I'll tell you what: I'm fed up with this God-forsaken island and I want to get out; if you'll give me a passage on the lugger to Timor or Macassar or Surabaya, you shall have all the treatment you want."

"That's an idea," said Captain Nichols.

"A damned rotten one," cried the other.

"Why?"

"We can't carry passengers."

"We can sign 'im on."

"There's no accommodation."

"I guess the doctor ain't particular."

"Not a bit. I'll bring my own food and drink. I'll get a lot of canned stuff at Kim Ching's, and he's got plenty of beer."

"Nothing doing," said Blake.

"Look 'ere, young feller-me-lad, who gives orders on this boat, you or me?"

"Well, if it comes down to brass tacks, I do."

"Put that out of your 'ead at once, my lad. I'm skipper and what I say goes."

"Whose boat is it?"

"You know very well whose boat it is."

Dr. Saunders watched them curiously. His bright, quick eyes missed nothing. The captain had lost all his geniality and his face was mottled with red. The youth bore a look of thunder. His fists were clenched and his head thrust forward.

"I won't have him on the boat, and that's that," he cried.

"Oh, come on," said the doctor, "it's not going to hurt you. It'll only be for five or six days. Be a sport. If you won't take me I shall have to stay here God knows how long."

"That's your look-out."

"What have you got against me?"

"That's my business."

Dr. Saunders gave him a questioning glance. Blake was not only angry, he was nervous. His handsome, sullen face was pale. It was curious that he should be so disinclined to let him come on the lugger. In these seas people made no bones about that sort of thing. Kim Ching had said they carried no cargo, but it might be the sort of cargo that did not take up much space and was easily hidden. Neither morphine nor cocaine took up a great deal of room, and there was a lot of money to be made if you could take them to the right places.

"You'd be doing me a great favour," he said gently.

"I'm sorry; I don't want to seem a rotten sport, but me and Nichols are here on business, and we can't go out of our way to land a passenger in some place we don't want to go to."

"I've known the doctor for twenty years," said Nichols. "He's all right."

"You never set eyes on him till this morning."

"I know all about 'im." The captain grinned, showing his broken, discoloured little teeth, and Dr. Saunders reflected that he should have them out. "And if what I 'ear is true 'e ain't got much on any of us."

He gave the doctor a shrewd look. It was interesting to see the hardness behind his genial smile. The doctor bore the glance without flinching. You could not have told if the shaft had gone home or if he had no notion of what the skipper was talking.

"I don't bother myself much with other people's concerns," he smiled.

"Live and let live, I say," said the captain, with the amiable toleration of the scamp.

"When I say no, I mean no," answered the young man obstinately.

"Oh, you make me tired," said Nichols. "There ain't nothin' to be scared about."

"Who says I'm scared?"

"I do."

"I've got nothing to be scared about."

They flung the short sentences at one another quickly. Their exasperation was increasing. Dr. Saunders wondered what the secret was that lay between them. It had evidently more to do with Fred Blake than with Nichols. For once the rascal had nothing on his conscience. He reflected that Captain Nichols was not the sort of man who would make it easy for anyone whose secret he knew. He could not exactly tell why, but he had an impression that, whatever it was, Captain Nichols did not know but only suspected it. The doctor, however, was very anxious to get on the lugger, and he did not mean to give up the project before he need. It amused him to exercise a certain astuteness to gain his end.

"Look here, I don't want to cause a quarrel between you two. If Blake doesn't want me, let's say no more about it."

"But I want you," retorted the skipper. "It's a chance in a million for me. If there's a man alive as can put my digestion right, it is you, and d'you think I'm goin' to miss an opportunity like that? Not 'alf."

"You think too much about your digestion," said Blake. "That's my belief. If you just ate what you wanted to and didn't bother, you'd be all right."

"Oh, should I? I suppose you know more about me digestive apparatus than what I do. I suppose you know when a bit of dry toast sits on me stomach like a ton of lead. I suppose you'll say it's all fancy next."

"Well, if you ask me, I think fancy's got a damned sight more to do with it than you think."

"You son of a bitch."

"Who are you calling a son of a bitch?"

"I'm calling you a son of a bitch."

"Oh, shut up," said the doctor.

Captain Nichols gave a loud belch.

"Now the bastard's brought it on again. It's three months if it's a day that I was able to sit down after supper and feel comfortable, and now he's brought it on again. An upset like this is the death of me. Flies to me stomach at once. I'm a bundle of nerves. Always 'ave been. I thought I was goin' to 'ave a pleasant evenin' for once, and now he's gone and ruined it. I've got dyspepsia somethin' cruel."

"I'm sorry to hear that," said the doctor.

"They all say the same thing; they all say: Captain, you're a bundle of nerves. Delicate? You're more delicate than a child."

Dr. Saunders was gravely sympathetic.

"It's as I suspected, you want watching; your stomach wants educating. If I'd been coming with you on the lugger I should have made it my business to teach your digestive juices to function in a proper manner. I don't say I could have effected a cure in six or seven days, but I could have put you on the way."

"But who says you're not comin' on the lugger?"

"Blake does, and from what I gather he's the boss."

"Oh, do you? Well, you're mistaken. I'm skipper, and what I say goes. Get your kit packed and come on board to-morrow mornin'. I'll sign you on as a member of the crew."

"You'll do nothing of the sort," said Blake, jumping to his feet. "I've got as much say as you have, and I say he's not coming. I won't have anyone on the lugger, and that's that."

"Oh, won't you? And what'll you say if I run her straight up to B.N.B.? British territory, young feller-me-lad."

"You take care an accident doesn't happen to you."

"D'you think I'm scared of you? D'you think I've knocked about all over the world since before you was born without knowin' 'ow to take care of meself? Stick a knife in me back, would you? And who's goin' to sail the boat? You and them four black niggers? You make me laugh. Why, you don't know one end of the boat from the other."

Blake clenched his hands again. The two men glared at one another, but in the captain's eyes was a mocking sneer. He knew that when it came to a show-down he held the cards. A little sigh escaped the other.

"Where d'you want to go?" he asked the doctor.

"Any Dutch island where I can get a ship that'll take me on my way."

"All right, come on, then. Anyway, it'll be better than being cooped up alone with that all the time."

He gave the skipper a glance of impotent hatred. Captain Nichols laughed good-naturedly.

"That's true, it'll be company for you, me boy. We're getting off about ten to-morrow. That suit you?"

"Suit me A1," said the doctor.

CHAPTER VIII

His guests left early and Dr. Saunders, taking his book, lay down in a long, rattan chair. He glanced at his watch. It was a little after nine. It was his habit to smoke half a dozen pipes of an evening. He liked to begin at ten. He waited for this moment, not with *malaise*, but with a little tremor of anticipation which was pleasant, and he would not cut this short by advancing the hour of his indulgence.

He called Ah Kay and told him that they were sailing in the morning on the strangers' lugger. The boy nodded. He, too, was glad to get away. Dr. Saunders had engaged him when he was thirteen, and now he was nineteen. He was a slim, comely youth with large black eyes and a skin as smooth as a girl's. His hair, coal-black and cut very short, fitted his head like a close cap. His oval face was of the colour of old ivory. He was quick to smile, and then he showed two rows of the most exquisite teeth possible, small and white and regular. In his short Chinese trousers of white cotton and the tight jacket without a collar he had a languorous elegance that was strangely touching. He moved silently and his gestures had the deliberate grace of a cat. Dr. Saunders sometimes flattered himself with the thought that Ah Kay regarded him with affection.

At ten, closing his book, he called:

"Ah Kay!"

The boy came in and Dr. Saunders watched him placidly as he took from a table the little tray on which were the oil lamp, the needle, the pipe and the round tin of opium. The boy put it down on the floor by the doctor, and himself squatting on his haunches lit the lamp. He held the needle in the flame, and with the warm end extracted a sufficiency from the tin of opium; with deft fingers he made it into a ball and delicately cooked it over the little yellow flame. Dr. Saunders watched it sizzle and swell. The boy withdrew it from the flame, kneaded the pellet again and cooked it once more; he inserted it into the pipe and handed it to his master. The doctor took it and with the strong quick pull of the practised smoker inhaled the sweet-tasting smoke. He held it for a minute in his lungs and then slowly exhaled it. He handed the pipe back. The boy scraped it out and put it on the tray. He warmed the needle again and began to cook another pellet. The doctor smoked a second pipe and a third. The boy rose from the floor and went into the cook-house. He came back with a little pot of jasmine tea and poured it into a Chinese bowl. The fragrance for an instant overpowered the acrid odour of the drug. The doctor lay back in his long chair, his head against a cushion and looked at the ceiling. They did not speak. It was very silent in the compound, and the only sound that broke the stillness was the sharp cry of a ghekko. The doctor watched it as it stood still on the ceiling, a little yellow beast that looked like a prehistoric monster in miniature, and occasionally made a rapid dart as a fly or a moth caught its attention. Ah Kay lit himself a cigarette, and taking an odd, stringed instrument, something like a banjo, amused himself by playing softly. The thin notes straggled along the air, disconnected sounds they seemed, and if now and then you heard the beginning of a melody, it was not completed and your ear was deceived; it was a slow and plaintive music, as incoherent as the varied scents of flowers, and it seemed to offer you but indications, a hint here and there, the suggestion of a rhythm, with which to create in your own soul a more subtle music than ears could hear. Now and then a sharp discord, like the scratching of a pencil on a slate, assaulted the nerves with a sudden shock. It gave the soul the same delicious tremor as startles the body when in the heat you plunge into an ice-cold pool. The boy sat on the floor in an attitude of unaffected beauty and meditatively plucked the strings of his lute. Dr. Saunders wondered what vague emotions touched him. His melancholy face was impassive. He seemed to be looking into his memory for melodies heard in some long past existence.

Presently the boy looked up, a rapid, charming smile suddenly lighting up his features, and asked his master if he was ready. The doctor nodded. Ah Kay put down his lute and relit the little lamp. He prepared another pipe. The doctor smoked it and two more besides. This was his limit. He smoked regularly, but with moderation. Then he lay back and surrendered himself to his thoughts. Ah Kay now made himself a couple of pipes, and having smoked them put out the lamp. He lay down on a mat with a wooden rest under his neck and presently fell asleep.

But the doctor, exquisitely at peace, considered the riddle of existence. His body rested in the long chair so comfortably that he was not conscious of it except in so far as an obscure sense of well-being in it added to his spiritual relief. In this condition of freedom his soul could look down upon his flesh with the affectionate tolerance with which you might regard a friend who bored you but whose love was grateful to you. His mind was extraordinarily alert, but in its activity there was no restlessness and no anxiety; it moved with an assurance of power, as you might imagine a great physicist would move among his symbols, and his lucidity had the absolute delight of pure beauty. It was an end in itself. He was lord of space and time. There was no problem that he could not solve if he chose; everything was clear, everything was exquisitely simple; but it seemed foolish to resolve the difficulties of being when there was so delicate a pleasure in knowing that you could completely do so whensoever you chose.

CHAPTER IX

DR. SAUNDERS was an early riser. The dawn had but just broken when he went out on his veranda and called Ah Kay. The boy brought his breakfast, the little delicate bananas known as lady's fingers, the inevitable fried eggs, toast and tea. The doctor ate with good appetite. There was little packing to do. Ah Kay's scanty wardrobe went into a brown-paper parcel and the doctor's into a Chinese portmanteau of pale pigskin. The medical stores and the surgical appliances were kept in a tin box of moderate size. Three or four natives were waiting at the foot of the steps that led up to the veranda, patients who wanted to consult the doctor, and he had them up one by one while he ate his breakfast. He told them he was leaving that morning. Then he walked over to Kim Ching's house. It stood in a plantation of coconut trees. It was an imposing bungalow, the largest on the island, with bits and pieces of architecture to give it style, but its pretentiousness contrasted oddly with a sordid environment. It had no garden and the ground round about it, littered with empty tins of preserved foodstuff and fragments of packing-cases, was untended. Chickens, ducks, dogs and pigs wandered about trying to find something to eat among the refuse. It was furnished in the European style, with sideboards of fumed oak, American rockers of the kind you used to see in Middle-Western hotels and occasional tables upholstered in plush. On the walls were enlarged photographs in massive gold frames of Kim Ching and the many members of his family.

Kim Ching was tall and stout, of a dignified presence, and he wore white ducks and a watch-chain of massive gold. He was much pleased with the result of his operation; he could see as he had never expected to, but all the same he would have liked to keep Dr. Saunders on the island a little longer.

"You damn fool to go on that lugger," he said when the doctor told him he was sailing with Captain Nichols. "You velly

comfortable here. Why you no wait? Take it easy an' enjoy
youself. Much more better you wait for Dutch boat. Nichols velly
bad man."

"You're not a velly good man yourself, Kim Ching."

The trader, showing a row of expensive gold teeth, greeted this
sally with a slow, fat smile in which there was no hint of disagreement. He liked the doctor and was grateful to him. When he saw
that there was no persuading him to stay, he ceased to urge it. Dr.
Saunders gave him his final instructions and took leave of him.
Kim Ching accompanied him to the door and they parted. The
doctor went down to the village and bought provisions for the
journey, a bag of rice, a bunch of bananas, canned goods, whisky
and beer; he told the coolie to take them down to the beach and
wait for him, and returned to the rest-house. Ah Kay was ready
and one of that morning's patients, willing to earn a trifle, was
waiting to carry the luggage. When they came to the beach one of
Kim Ching's sons was there to see him off, and he had brought at
his father's instructions a roll of Chinese silk as a parting present
and a little square packet wrapped in white paper with Chinese
characters on it, the contents of which Dr. Saunders guessed.

"Chandu?"

"My father say velly good stuff. P'laps you not have plenty for
journey."

There was no sign of life on the lugger, and the dinghy was not to
be seen on the beach. Dr. Saunders shouted, but his voice was
thin and throaty and did not carry. Ah Kay and Kim Ching's son
tried to make someone hear, but in vain, so they put the luggage
and the stores into a dug-out and a native paddled the doctor and
Ah Kay out. When they came up Dr. Saunders shouted again:

"Captain Nichols."

Fred Blake appeared.

"Oh, it's you. Nichols has gone ashore to get water."

"I didn't see him."

Blake said nothing more. The doctor climbed on board,
followed by Ah Kay, and the native handed them up their kit and
the provisions.

"Where shall I put my stuff?"

"There's the cabin," said Blake, pointing.

The doctor went down the companion. The cabin was aft. It
was so low that you could not stand upright in it, far from spacious,
and the main mast went through it. The ceiling was blackened

where a smoking lamp hung. There were small portholes with wooden shutters. The mattresses of Nichols and Fred Blake were lengthways, and the only place for himself that the doctor could see was at the foot of the companion. He went on deck again and told Ah Kay to take down his sleeping mat and his portmanteau.

"The stores had better go in the hold," he said to Fred.

"Fat chance there is for them there. We keep ours in the cabin. Tell your boy he'll find a place under the boards. They're loose."

The doctor looked about him. He knew nothing of the sea. Except on occasion on the Min River, he had never been on anything but a steamer. The lugger looked very small for so long a voyage. It was a little more than fifty feet long. He would have liked to ask Blake several things, but he had gone forward. It was plain that though he had consented to the doctor's coming it was against his will. He was sulking. There were a couple of old canvas chairs on deck, and in one of them the doctor sat down.

In a little while a blackfellow, wearing nothing but a dingy *pareo*, came along. He was of solid build and his crisp curly hair was very grey.

"Captain coming," he said.

Dr. Saunders looked in the direction in which he pointed, and saw the dinghy advancing towards them. Captain Nichols was steering and two blackfellows were rowing. They came alongside and the skipper called out:

"Utan, Tom, give a hand with the casks."

Another blackfellow came up from the hold. The crew consisted of these four, Torres Straits islanders, tall, strong men with fine figures. Captain Nichols climbed on board and shook hands with the doctor.

"Settled in all right, Doc? Not much of the ocean grey'ound about the *Fenton*, but as good a sea-boat as anyone can want. She'll stand anything."

He gave the dirty, unkempt little craft a sweeping glance in which there was the satisfaction of the workman with the tools he knew how to handle.

"Well, we'll be gettin' off."

He gave his orders sharply. Mainsail and foresail were hoisted, the anchor weighed, and they slipped out of the lagoon. There was not a cloud in the sky, and the sun beat down on the shining sea. The monsoon was blowing, but with no great force, and there was a slight swell. Two or three gulls flew round them in wide circles.

Now and then a flying-fish pierced the surface of the water, made a long dart over it and dived down with a tiny splash. Dr. Saunders read, smoked cigarettes, and when he was tired of reading looked at the sea and the green islands they passed. After a while the skipper handed over the wheel to one of the crew and came and sat down by him.

"We'll anchor at Badu to-night," he said. "That's about forty-five miles. It looks all right in the Sailing Directions. There's an anchorage there."

"What is it?"

"Oh, just an uninhabited island. We generally anchor for the night."

"Blake doesn't seem any more pleased to have me on board," said the doctor.

"We 'ad a bit of an argument last night."

"What's the trouble?"

"He's only a kid."

Dr. Saunders knew that he must earn his passage, and he knew also that when a man has told you all his symptoms he will have gained confidence and will tell you a great deal more besides. He began to ask the skipper questions about his health. There was nothing on which he was prepared to talk at greater length. The doctor took him down into the cabin, made him lie down, and carefully examined him. When they went on deck again the grey-haired blackfellow, Tom Obu by name, who was cook and steward, was bringing aft their dinner.

"Come on, Fred," called the skipper.

They sat down.

"This smells good," said Nichols, as Tom Obu took the lid off the saucepan. "Somethin' new, Tom?"

"I shouldn't be surprised if my boy hadn't lent a hand," said the doctor.

"I think I can eat this," said the skipper as he took a mouthful of a mess of rice and meat that he ladled on to his plate. "What do you think of this, Fred? Seems to me we're goin' to do ourselves O.K. with the doc on board."

"It's better than Tom's cooking, I'll say that for it."

They ate with hearty appetite. The captain lit his pipe.

"If I don't 'ave a pain after this I'll say you're a wonder, Doc."

"You won't have a pain."

"What beats me is 'ow a fellow like you come to settle in

a place like Fu-chou. You could make a fortune in Sydney."

"I'm all right in Fu-chou. I like China."

"Yep? Studied in England, didn't you?"

"Yes."

"I've 'eard tell you was a specialist, 'ad a big practice in London, and I don't know what all."

"You mustn't believe all you hear."

"Seems funny your chuckin' everything and settlin' in a lousy Chinese city. You must 'ave been makin' a packet in London."

The skipper looked at him with his little shifty blue eyes and his grinning face was quick with malice. But the doctor bore his scrutiny blandly. He smiled, showing those large discoloured teeth of his, his eyes shrewd and alert, but gave no sign of embarrassment.

"Ever go back to England?"

"No. Why should I? My home's in Fu-chou."

"I don't blame you. England's finished, if you ask me. Too many rules and regulations for my taste. Why can't they leave a fellow alone? that's what I'd like to know. Not on the register, are you?"

He shot the question out suddenly as though he wished to take the doctor by surprise. But he had met someone who was a match for him.

"Don't say you haven't confidence in me, Captain. You must believe in your doctor. He can't do much for you if you don't."

"Believe in you? Why, if I didn't believe in you you wouldn't be 'ere." Captain Nichols grew deadly serious; this was something that concerned himself. "I know there's no one as is a patch on you anywheres between Bombay and Sydney, and if the truth was only told I shouldn't be surprised if you'd 'ave to go a long way in London before you could find anyone as could 'old a candle to you. I know you've taken every degree a fellow can take. I've 'eard tell as 'ow if you'd stayed in London you'd be a baronet by now."

"I don't mind telling you that I've got more degrees than are any use to me," the doctor laughed.

"Funny you shouldn't be in the book. What's it called? The *Medical Directory*."

"What makes you think I'm not?" murmured the doctor, smiling but wary.

"Fellow I knew in Sydney looked you up. Talkin' about you, 'e was, to another doctor, pal of 'is, and sayin' you was such a marvel and all that, and out of curiosity they 'ad a look-see."

"Perhaps your friend looked in the wrong edition."

Captain Nichols chuckled slyly.

"Perhaps he did. I never thought of that."

"Anyhow, I've never seen the inside of a gaol, Captain."

The skipper gave a little start. He repressed it at once, but he changed colour. Dr. Saunders had made a shot in the dark and his eyes twinkled. The skipper laughed.

"That's a good one. No more 'ave I, Doc, but don't you forget there's many a man's gone to gaol for no fault of 'is own and there's many a man as might 'ave gone there if he 'adn't thought a change of air would suit him."

They looked at one another and chuckled.

"What's there to laugh about?" said Fred Blake.

CHAPTER X

TOWARD evening they sighted the island where Captain Nichols designed to pass the night, a cone covered to its summit with trees so that it looked like a hill in a picture by Piero della Francesca, and sailing round it they came to the anchorage they had read of in the Sailing Directions. It was a well-sheltered cove and the water was so clear that as you looked over the side you saw on the ocean floor the fantastic efflorescence of the coral. You saw the fish swimming, like natives of the forest threading their familiar way through the jungle. Not a little to their surprise they found a schooner anchored there.

"What's that?" asked Fred Blake.

His eyes were anxious, and indeed it was strange to enter upon that silent cove, protected by the green hill, in the still cool of the evening and see there a sailing vessel. She lay, sails furled, and because the spot was so solitary her presence was vaguely sinister. Captain Nichols looked at her through his glasses.

"She's a pearler. Port Darwin. I don't know what she's doin' 'ere. There's a lot of 'em round by the Aru Islands."

They saw the crew, a white man among them, watching them, and presently a boat was lowered.

"They're comin' over," said the skipper.

By the time they were anchored, the dinghy had rowed up and Captain Nichols exchanged shouts of greeting with the captain of the schooner. He came on board, an Australian, and told them that his Japanese diver was sick and he was on his way to one of the Dutch islands where he could get a doctor.

"We got a doctor on board," said Captain Nichols. "We're givin' 'im a passage."

The Australian asked Dr. Saunders if he would come along and see his sick man, and after they had given him a cup of tea, for he refused a drink, the doctor got into the dinghy.

"Have you got any Australian papers?" asked Fred.

"I've got a *Bulletin*. It's a month old."

"Never mind. It'll be new to us."

"You're welcome to it. I'll send it back by the doctor."

It did not take Dr. Saunders long to discover that the diver was suffering from a severe attack of dysentery. He was very ill. He gave him a hypodermic injection, and told the captain there was nothing to do but keep him quiet.

"Damn these Japs, they've got no constitution. I shan't get any more work out of him for some time then?"

"If ever," said the doctor.

They shook hands and he got into the dinghy again. The black-fellow pushed off.

"Here, wait a bit. I forgot to give you that paper."

The Australian dived into the cabin and in a minute came out again with a *Sydney Bulletin*. He threw it into the dinghy.

Captain Nichols and Fred were playing cribbage when the doctor climbed back on to the *Fenton*. The sun was setting and the smooth sea was lucid with pale and various colour, blue, green, salmon-pink and milky purple, and it was like the subtle and tender colour of silence.

"Fixed 'im up all right?" enquired the skipper indifferently.

"He's pretty bad."

"Is that the paper?" Fred asked.

He took it out of the doctor's hand, and strolled forwards.

"Play cribbage?" said Nichols.

"No, I don't."

"Me and Fred play it every night. Luck of the devil 'e 'as. I shouldn't like to tell you 'ow much money 'e's won off me. It can't go on. It must turn soon." He called out: "Come on, Fred."

"Half a mo."

The skipper shrugged his shoulders.

"No manners. Anxious to see a paper, wasn't 'e?"

"And a month old one at that," answered the doctor. "How long is it since you left Thursday Island?"

"We never went near Thursday Island."

"Oh!"

"What about a spot? D'you think it'd do me any 'arm?"

"I don't think so."

The skipper shouted for Tom Obu, and the blackfellow brought them a couple of glasses and some water. Nichols fetched the whisky. The sun set and the night crept softly over the still water. The only sound that broke the silence was the leap now and then of a fish. Tom Obu brought a hurricane lamp and placed it on the deck-house, and going below lit the smoking oil-lamp in the cabin.

"I wonder what our young friend is readin' all this time."

"In the dark?"

"Maybe 'e's thinkin' of what 'e 'as read."

But when at last Fred joined them and sat down to finish the interrupted game, it seemed to Dr. Saunders, in the uncertain light, that he was very pale. He had not brought the paper with him and the doctor went forward to get it. He could not see it. He called Ah Kay and told him to look for it. Standing in the darkness he watched the players.

"Fifteen two. Fifteen four. Fifteen six. Fifteen eight and six are fourteen. And one for his nob seventeen."

"God, what luck you 'ave."

The skipper was a bad loser. His face was set and hard. His shifty eyes glanced at each card he turned up with a sneering look. But the other played with a smile on his lips. The light of the hurricane lamp cut his profile out of the darkness, and it was astonishingly fine. His long lashes cast a little shadow on his cheeks. Just then he was more than a handsome young man; he had a tragic beauty that was very moving. Ah Kay came and said he could not find the paper.

"Where did you leave that *Bulletin*, Fred?" asked the doctor. "My boy can't find it."

"Isn't it there?"

"No, we've both looked."

"How the hell should I know where it is? Two for his heels."

"Throw it overboard when you done with it?" asked the captain.

"Me? Why should I throw it overboard?"

"Well, if you didn't it must be somewhere about," said the doctor.

"That's another game to you," the skipper growled. "I never see anyone 'old such cards."

CHAPTER XI

IT was between one and two in the morning. Dr. Saunders sat in a deck-chair. The skipper was asleep in the cabin and Fred had taken his mattress forrard. It was very still. The stars were so bright that the shape of the island was very distinctly outlined against the night. Distance is less an affair of space than of time and though they had gone but five-and-forty miles it seemed to the doctor that Takana was very far away. London was at the other end of the world. He had a fleeting vision of Piccadilly Circus, with its bright lights, the crowd of buses, cars and taxis, and the crowd that surged when the theatres disgorged their audiences. There was a part that in his day they called the Front, the street on the north side that led from Shaftesbury Avenue to the Charing Cross Road, where from eleven to twelve people walked up and down in a serried throng. That was before the war. There was a sense of adventure in the air. Eyes met and then. . . . The doctor smiled. He did not regret the past; he regretted nothing. Then his wandering thoughts hovered over the bridge at Fu-chou, the bridge over the Min River, from which you saw the fishermen in the barges below fishing with cormorants; rickshaws crossed the bridge, and coolies bearing heavy loads, and the innumerable Chinese walked to and fro. On the right bank as you looked downstream was the Chinese City with its crowded houses and its temples. The schooner showed no light and the doctor only saw it in the darkness because he knew that it was there. All was silent on board. But in the hold where the pearl shell was piled, on one of the wooden bunks along the side, lay the dying diver. The doctor attached small value to human life. Who, that had lived so long amid those teeming Chinese where it was held so cheap, could have much feeling about it? He was a Japanese, the diver, and probably a Buddhist. Transmigration? Look at the sea: wave follows wave, it is not the same wave, yet one causes another and transmits its form and movement. So the beings travelling through the world are not the same to-day and to-morrow, nor in one life the same as in another; and yet it is the urge and the form of the previous lives that determine the character of those that follow. A reasonable belief but an incredible. But was it any more incredible than that so much striving, such a variety of accidents, so many miraculous hazards should have combined, through the long æons of time, to produce from the primeval slime at long last this man who, by means of Flexner's bacillus, was aimlessly snuffed out? Dr. Saunders thought it odd, but natural, senseless certainly, but he had long made himself at home in the futility of things. Of course the spirit was a difficulty. Did that cease to exist when the matter which was its instrument dissolved? In that lovely night, his thoughts flowing without purpose, like birds, sea-gulls, wheeling over the sea, rising and falling as the wind took them, he could not but keep an open mind.

There was the sound of shuffling steps on the companion and the skipper appeared. The stripe of his pyjamas was bold enough to tell against the darkness.

"Captain?"

"It's me. I thought I'd come up for a breath of air." He sank into the chair by the doctor's side. "Had your smoke?"

"Yes."

"I've never took to it meself. I've known a good many as did, though. Never seemed to do 'em much 'arm. Settles the stomach, they say. One fellow I knew went all to pieces. Skipper of one of Butterfield's boats on the Yang-tze at one time. Good position and everything. They thought a rare lot of 'im. Sent him 'ome once to get cured, but 'e took to it again the moment 'e come back. Ended up as a tout for a fantan 'ouse. Used to 'ang about the docks at Shanghai and cadge 'alf-dollars.''

They were silent for a while. Captain Nichols sucked a briar pipe.

"Seen anythin' of Fred?"

"He's sleeping on deck."

"Funny thing about that paper. He didn't want you and me to read somethin'."

"What d'you suppose he did with it?"

"Dropped it overboard."

"What's it all about?"

The skipper gave a low chuckle.

"Believe me, or believe me not, I don't know any more than you do."

"I've lived in the East long enough to know that it's better to mind my own business."

But the skipper was inclined to be confidential. His digestion was not troubling him and after three or four hours of good sleep he felt very wide awake.

"There's somethin' fishy about it, I know that, but I'm like you, Doc, I'm all for mindin' me own business. Ask no questions an' you'll be told no lies. That's what I say, an' if you get a chance of makin' a bit of money, take it quick." The skipper gave his pipe a pull. "You won't let this go any further, will you?"

"Not on your life."

"Well, it's like this. I was in Sydney. I 'adn't 'ad a job for the best part of two years. And not for the want of tryin', mind you. Just bad luck. First-rate seaman I am and got a lot of experience. Steam or sail, I don't mind what it is. You'd think they'd jump at me. But no. I'm a married man too. Things got so bad my old woman 'ad to go into service, I didn't 'alf like it, I can tell you, but there, I just 'ad to lump it. I 'ad a roof over me 'ead and three meals a day, she give me that all right, but when it come to lettin' me 'ave 'alf a dollar to go to the pictures and get one or two drinks, no, sir. An' nag. Never been married, 'ave you?"

"No."

"Well, I don't blame you. They're near, you know. Women can't bear partin' with their money. I been married twenty years, and it's been nag, nag, nag all the time. Very superior woman, my missus, that's what begun the trouble, she thought she demeaned 'erself by marryin' me. Her father was a big draper up in Liverpool, and she never let me forget it. She blamed me because I couldn't get a job. Said I liked bein' on the beach. Lazy, idle loafer she called me and she said she was fair sick of workin' 'erself to the bone to give me board and lodgin' and if I didn't get a billet soon I could just get out and shift for meself. I give you my word, sometimes I just 'ad to 'old on to meself like grim death not to give her a sock on the jaw, lady though she was, and no one knows that better than what I do. D'you know Sydney?"

"No, I've never been there."

"Well, one night I was just standin' around in a bar down by the

'arbour I used to go to sometimes. I 'adn't 'ad a drink all day, and
I was just parched; my dyspepsia was somethin' awful, and I was
feelin' pretty low. I 'adn't got a penny in me pocket, me what's
commanded more ships than you can count on the fingers of your
two 'ands, and I couldn't go 'ome. I knew the missus'd start on
me, and she'd give me a bit of cold mutton for me supper, though
she knows it's the death of me, and she'd go on and on, always the
lady, if you know what I mean, but just nasty, cuttin' and superior-
like, never raisin' her voice, but not a minute's peace. An' if I was
to lose me temper and tell 'er to go to hell, she'd just draw 'erself
up and say: 'None of your foul language 'ere, Captain, *if* you
please. I may 'ave married a common sailor, but I will be treated
like a lady.' ''

Captain Nichols lowered his voice and leant over in a very
confidential manner.

"Now this is quite *infra dig.*, you know what I mean, just
between you and me: you don't know where you are with women.
They don't behave like 'uman beings. Would you believe it, I've
run away from 'er four times. You would think a woman'd see
what you meant after that, wouldn't you?"

"You would."

"But no. Every time she's followed me. Of course, once she
knew where I'd gone, and it was easy, but the others she didn't
know any more than the man in the moon. I'd 'ave bet every
penny I 'ad in the world that she wouldn't find me. Like lookin'
for a needle in a bundle of 'ay, it was. An' then one day she'd walk
up, quite cool, as if she seen me the day before, and not a 'ow-
d'you-do or a fancy seein' you or anythin' like that, but: 'You
want a shave if you ask me, Captain,' or: 'Them trousers of yours is
a disgrace, Captain.' . . . I don't care who it is, it's the kind of
thing to break anyone's nerve."

Captain Nichols was silent and his eyes swept the empty sea. In
that lucid night you saw quite clearly the thin sharp line of the
horizon.

"This time I been an' gone an' done the trick, and I 'ave got
away from 'er. She don't know where I am and she can't find out,
but I give you my word I wouldn't be surprised if she was to come
rowin' over that sea in a dinghy, all neat and tidy, she's always the
lady to look at, I will say that for 'er, and come on board and just
say to me: 'What's that nasty, filthy tobacco you're smokin',
Captain? You know, I can't abide anythin' but Player's Navy Cut.'

It's me **nerves.** That's what's at the bottom of my dyspepsia, if the truth was only known. I remember, once I went to see a doctor in Singapore as 'ad been very strongly recommended to me and 'e wrote a lot of stuff in a book, you know 'ow doctors do, and he put a cross down. Well, I didn't 'alf like the look of that, so I said to 'im: 'I say, Doctor,' I says, 'what's that cross mean?' 'Oh,' he says, 'I always put a cross when I 'ave reason to suspect domestic unpleasantness.' 'Oh, I see,' I says; 'well, you've 'it the nail on the 'ead, Doctor; I bear a cross all right.' Clever fellow 'e was, but 'e never done my dyspepsia much good."

"Socrates suffered from the same sort of affliction, Captain, but I never heard that it affected his digestion."

"Who was 'e?"

"An honest man."

"Much good it did 'im, I lay."

"In point of fact, it didn't."

"You've got to take things as you find 'em, I say, and if you're too particular you won't get anywhere."

Dr. Saunders laughed in his heart. It appealed to his sense of humour to think of this mean and unscrupulous blackguard in abject terror of his wife. It was the triumph of spirit over matter. He wondered what she looked like.

"I was tellin' you about Fred Blake," the skipper continued, after a pause to relight his pipe. "Well, as I was sayin', I was in that bar. I said good-evenin' to one or two chaps, cordial like, you know, and they said good-evenin' to me and looked the other way. You could see them just sayin' to theirselves: There's that bum again, cadgin' around for drinks; 'e ain't goin' to get one out of me. You can't wonder I was feelin' pretty low. Humiliating, that's what it was, for a man as 'ad been in a good position like what I 'ave. It's terrible 'ow near a fellow can be with 'is money when he knows you ain't got none. The boss give me a dirty look and I 'alf thought he was going to ask me what I'd 'ave, and then when I said I'd wait a bit, 'e'd say, well, I'd better wait outside. I began talkin' to one or two chaps I didn't know, but they wasn't what you'd call cordial. I cracked a joke or two, but I couldn't get 'em laughin', and they made it pretty plain that I was buttin' in. And then I saw a fellow come in I knew. Big bully of a chap. What they call a larrikin in Australia. Name of Ryan. You 'ad to keep in with 'im. He 'ad something to do with politics. Always 'ad plenty of money. He lent me five bob once. Well, I didn't think 'e'd want to see me, so I pretended I didn't recognise 'im and just went on talkin'. But I was watchin' 'im out of the corner of me eye. He looked round and then 'e come right up to me.

" 'Good-evenin', Captain,' he says, very friendly like. 'How's the world been treatin' you these days?'

" 'Rotten,' I says.

" 'Still lookin' for a job?'

" 'Yes,' I says.

" 'What'll you 'ave?' he says.

"I 'ad a beer and 'e 'ad a beer. It pretty near saved my life. But you know, I'm not much of a one for believin' in miracles. I wanted that beer pretty bad, but I knew just as well as I know I'm talkin' to you that Ryan wasn't givin' it me for nothin'. He's one of them 'earties, you know; slaps you on the back and laughs at your jokes as though he'd fair bust, and it's ' 'Ullo, where 'ave you been 'idin' yourself?' and, 'My missus is a grand little woman and you should see my kiddies,' and all that; and then all the time 'e's watchin' you and 'is eyes look right through you. It takes in the mugs. 'Good old Ryan,' they say; 'one of the best.' There are no flies on me, Doc. You don't catch me so easy as that. And while I was drinkin' my beer I said to myself: 'Now, then, old boy, you keep your eyes skinned. He wants something.' But of course I didn't let on. I told 'im a yarn or two and 'e just laughed 'is 'ead off.

" 'You're a caution, Captain,' 'e said; 'great old sport, that's what you are. Finish your beer and we'll 'ave another. I could listen to you talkin' all night.'

"Well, I finished my beer and I saw 'e was goin' to order another.

" 'Look 'ere, Bill,' he says: well, my name's Tom, but I didn't say nothing. I saw 'e was tryin' to be friendly. 'Look 'ere, Bill,' he says, 'there's too many people round 'ere, one simply can't 'ear oneself talk, and you never know who's listenin' to what you say. I'll tell you what we'll do.' He called the boss. 'Look 'ere, George, come 'ere a minute.' And up he comes with a run. 'Look 'ere, George, me and my friend we want to 'ave a little quiet yarn about old times. What about that room of yours?'

" 'My office? All right. You can go in there if you want to, and welcome.'

" 'That's the ticket. And you bring us a couple of beers.'

"Well, we walks round and we goes into the office, and George brings us a couple of beers 'imself. In person; gives me a nod, 'e does. And George goes out. Ryan shut the door after 'im and 'e looked at the window to see it was shut all right. Said 'e couldn't stand a draught at any price. I didn't know what 'e was after, and I thought I'd better get straight with 'im at once.

" 'Look 'ere, Ryan,' I says; 'I'm sorry about that five bob you lent me. It's been on me mind ever since, but the truth is I've 'ad all I can do just to keep body and soul together.'

" 'Forget it,' he says. 'What's five bob? I know you're all right. You're a fine feller, Bill. What's the good of 'avin' money if you can't lend it to a pal when 'e's down on his luck?'

" 'Well, I'd do the same by you, Ryan,' says I, takin' my cue from 'im. To listen to us you'd 'ave thought us a pair of brothers."

Captain Nichols chuckled as he recalled the scene they had played. He took an artist's delight in his own rascality.

" 'Chin, chin,' says I.

"We both 'ad a drink of beer. 'Now look 'ere, Bill,' says 'e, wipin' 'is mouth with the back of 'is 'and, 'I been makin' enquiries about you. Good seaman and all that, ain't you?' 'None better,' says I. 'If you ain't 'ad a job for some time I reckon it's more by bad luck than bad management.' 'That's right,' says I. 'Now I'm going to give you a surprise, Bill,' says 'e. 'I'm going to offer you a job meself.' 'I'll take it,' says I. 'No matter what it is.' 'That's the spirit,' says 'e. 'I knew I could count on you.'

" 'Well, what is it?' I ask 'im.

"He give me a look, and though 'e was smilin' at me as if I was his long lost brother and 'e loved me like anything, 'e was lookin' at me pretty 'ard. It was no jokin' matter, I could see that.

" 'Can you keep your mouth shut?' 'e asks me.

" 'Like a clam,' says I.

" 'That's good,' says 'e. 'Now what d'you say to takin' a tidy little pearling lugger, you know, one of them ketches they 'ave at Thursday Island and Port Darwin, and cruisin' about the islands for a few months?'

" 'Sounds all right to me,' I says.

" 'Well, that's the job.'

" 'Tradin'?' I says.

" 'No, just pleasure.'

Captain Nichols sniggered.

"I nearly laughed outright when 'e said that, but one 'as to be careful, lot of people 'ave no sense of humour, so I just looked as grave as a judge. He give me another look and I could see 'e could be an ugly customer if you put 'is back up.

" 'I'll tell you 'ow it is,' 'e says. 'Young fellow I know been workin' too 'ard. His dad's an old pal of mine, and I'm doin' this to please 'im, see? He's a man in a very good position. Got a lot of influence in one way and another.'

"He 'ad another drink of beer. I kep' me eyes on 'im, but I never said a word. Not a syllable.

" 'The old man's in a rare state. Only kid, you know. Well, I know what it is with me own kids. If one of 'em gets a pain in 'is big toe, I'm upset for the day.'

" 'You don't 'ave to tell me,' I says. 'I got a daughter meself.'

" 'Only child?' he says.

"I nodded.

" 'Grand thing, children,' he says. 'Nothin' like 'em to bring 'appiness in a man's life.'

" 'You're right there,' I says.

" 'Always delicate, this boy's been,' 'e says, shakin' 'is 'ead. 'Got a touch of the lungs. The doctors say the best thing 'e can do is to 'ave a cruise on a sailin' ship. Well, 'is dad didn't 'alf like the idea of 'is takin' a passage on any old ship and 'e 'eard of this 'ere ketch and 'e bought her. You see, like that, you're not tied down and you can go anywhere. Nice easy life, that's what 'e wants the boy to 'ave; I mean, you don't 'ave to 'urry. You choose your own weather an' when you get to some island what looks like you could stay there for a bit, why, you just stay. There's dozens of them islands up between Australia and China, they tell me.'

" 'Thousands,' says I.

" 'An' the boy's got to be kep' quiet. Essential, that is. His dad wants you to keep away from where there's a lot of people.'

" 'That's all right,' says I, lookin' as innocent as a new-born babe. 'And 'ow long for?'

" 'I don't exactly know,' says he. 'Depends on the boy's 'ealth. Two or three months, maybe, or maybe a year.'

" 'I see,' says I; 'and what do I get out of it?'

" 'Two 'undred quid when your passenger comes on board, and two 'undred quid when you comes back.'

" 'Make it five 'undred down and I'm game,' says I. He never says a thing, but 'e give me a dirty look. And 'e just shoved his jaw out at me. My word, 'e looked a beauty. If there's one thing I got it's tact. He could make things pretty unpleasant for me if 'e wanted to. I knew that, and I 'ad a feeling that if I didn't take care 'e would want to. So I just shrugged me shoulders, careless like, and laughed. 'Oh, well, I don't care about the money,' I says. 'Money means nothin' to me, never 'as. If it 'ad I'd be one of the richest men in Australia to-day. I'll take what you say. Anythin' to oblige a friend.'

" 'Good old Bill,' says 'e.

" 'Where's the ketch now?' says I. 'I'd like to go and 'ave a look at her.'

" 'Oh, she's all right. Friend of mine just brought her down from Thursday Island to sell 'er. She's in grand shape. She ain't in Sydney. She's up the coast a few miles.'

" 'What about a crew?'

" 'Niggers from Torres Straits. They brought 'er down. All you've got to do is to get on board and sail away.'

" 'When would you want me to sail?'

" 'Now.'

" 'Now?' says I, surprised. 'Not to-night?'

" 'Yes, to-night. I got a car waitin' down the street. I'll drive you over to where she's lying.'

" 'What's the 'urry?' I says, smiling, but giving 'im a look as much as to say I thought it damned fishy.

" 'The boy's dad's a big business man. Always does things like that.'

" 'Politician?' says I.

"I was beginning to put two and two together, so to speak.

" 'My aunt,' says Ryan.

" 'But I'm a married man,' says I. 'If I just go off like this without sayin' so much as a word to nobody, my old woman'll be makin' enquiries all over the place. She'll want to know where I am and when she can't find nobody to tell her she'll go to the police.'

"He looked at me pretty sharp when I said this. I knew he didn't 'alf like the idea of 'er goin' to the police.

" 'It'll look funny, a master mariner disappearin' like this. I mean, it ain't like as if I was a blackfellow or a Kanaka. Of course I don't know if there's anyone 'as reason to be inquisitive. There's a lot of nosey-parkers about, especially just now with the election comin' on.'

"I couldn't 'elp thinkin' I got a good one in there, about the election, but 'e didn't let on a thing. His great ugly face might 'a' been a blank wall.

" 'I'll go and see 'er meself,' 'e said.

"I 'ad me own game to play, too, and I wasn't goin' to let a chance like this pass me by.

" 'Tell 'er the first mate of a steamer broke his neck just as she was going out and they took me on and I didn't 'ave time to go 'ome and she'll 'ear from me next from Cape Town.'

" 'That's the ticket,' says 'e.

" 'An' if she kicks up a racket give 'er a passage to Cape Town and a five-pound note. That's not askin' much.'

"He laughed then, honest, and 'e said 'e'd do it.

"He finished 'is beer and I finished mine.

" 'Now then,' says 'e, 'if you're ready we'll be startin'.' He looked at 'is watch. 'You meet me at the corner of Market Street in 'alf an hour. I'll drive by in my car and you just jump in. You go out first. No need for you to go out by the bar. There's a door at the end of the passage. You take that and you'll find yourself in the street.'

" 'O.K.,' says I, and I takes me 'at.

" 'There's just one thing I'd like to say to you,' 'e says, as I was going. 'An' this refers to now and later. If you don't want a knife in your back or a bullet in your guts you better not try no monkey tricks. See?'

"He said it quite pleasant, but I'm no fool, and I knew 'e meant it.

" 'Don't you 'ave no fear,' says I. 'When a chap treats me like a gentleman, I behave like one.' Then very casual like: 'Young feller on board, I suppose?'

" 'No, 'e ain't. Comin' on board later.'

"I walked out and I got into the street. I walked along to where he said. It was only a matter of two 'undred yards. I thought to meself if 'e wanted me to wait there for 'alf an hour it was because he 'ad to go and see someone and say what 'ad 'appened. I couldn't 'elp wonderin' what the police'd say if I told 'em somethin' funny was up and it'd be worth their while to follow the car and 'ave a look at this ketch. But I thought p'raps it wouldn't be worth *my* while. It's all very well to do a public duty, and I don't mind bein' in well with the cops any more than anyone else does, but it wouldn't do me much good if I got a knife in me belly for me pains. And there was no four 'undred quid to be got out of them. P'raps it's just as well I didn't try any 'anky-panky on with Ryan, because I see a chap on the other side of the street, standin' in the shadow as if 'e didn't want no one to see 'im, and it looked to me

F.A.A.   1-2A

as if 'e was watchin' me. I walked over to 'ave a look at 'im and 'e walked away when he saw me comin', then I walked back again and he come and stood just where 'e was before. Funny. It was all damned funny. The thing what grizzled me was that Ryan 'adn't shown more confidence in me. If you're goin' to trust a man, trust 'im, that's what I say. I want you to understand I didn't mind its bein' funny. I seen a lot of funny things in my day and I take 'em as they come."

Dr. Saunders smiled. He began to understand Captain Nichols. He was a man who found the daily round of honest life a trifle humdrum. He needed a spice of crookedness to counteract the depression his dyspepsia caused him. His blood ran faster, he felt better in health, his vitality was heightened when his fingers dabbled in crime. The alertness he must then exercise to protect himself from harm took his mind off the processes of his lamentable digestion. If Dr. Saunders was somewhat lacking in sympathy, he made up for it by being uncommonly tolerant. He thought it no business of his to praise or condemn. He was able to recognise that one was a saint and another a villain, but his consideration of both was fraught with the same cool detachment.

"I couldn't 'elp laughin' as I thought of meself standin' there," continued the skipper, "and startin' off on a cruise without so much as a change of clothes, me shavin' tackle or a toothbrush. You wouldn't find many men as'd be prepared to do that and not give a tinker's cuss."

"You wouldn't," said the doctor.

"And then I thought of the face my old woman'd make when Ryan told 'er I'd sailed. I can just see 'er toddlin' off to Cape Town by the next ship. She'll never find me no more. This time I 'ave got away from her. And who'd 'ave thought it'd come like that just when I was thinkin' I couldn't stand another day of it. If it wasn't Providence, I don't know what it was."

"It's ways are always said to be inscrutable."

"Don't I know it? Brought up a Baptist, I was. 'Not a sparrow shall fall——' you know 'ow it goes. I seen it come true over and over again. And then after I'd been waitin' there a bit, a good 'alf hour, a car come along and stops just by me. 'Jump in,' says Ryan, and off we go. The roads are terrible bad round Sydney and we was bumpin' up and down like a cork in the water. Pretty fast he drove.

" 'What about stores and all that?' I says to Ryan.

" 'It's all on board,' 'e says. 'You got enough to last you three months.'

"I didn't know where 'e was goin'. Dark night and I couldn't see a thing; it must 'ave been gettin' on for midnight.

" 'Here we are,' 'e says, and stops. 'Get out.'

"I got out and 'e got out after me. He turns off 'is lights. I knew we was pretty near the sea, but I couldn't see a yard in front of me. He 'ad an electric torch.

" 'You follow me,' 'e says, 'an' look where you're goin'.'

"We walked a bit. A sort of pathway there was. I'm pretty nimble on me feet, but I nearly come arse over tip two or three times. 'Nice thing if I break my bloody leg goin' down 'ere,' I says to meself. I wasn't 'alf glad when we come to the bottom and I felt the beach under me feet. You could see the water, but you couldn't see nothin' else. Ryan give a whistle. Someone on the water shouted, but low, if you know what I mean, and Ryan flashed his torch to show where we was. Then I 'eard oars splashin' and in a minute or two a couple of blackfellows rowed up in the dinghy. Ryan and me, we got in, and they pushed off. If I'd 'ad twenty quid on me I wouldn't 'ave given much for my chances of ever seein' Australia no more. Australia felix, by gum. We rowed for about ten minutes, I should say, and then we come alongside the ketch.

" 'What d'you think of 'er?' asks Ryan, when we got on board.

" 'Can't see much,' says I. 'Tell you more in the morning.'

" 'In the morning you got to be well out to sea,' says Ryan.

" 'When's this poor invalid boy comin'?' says I.

" 'Pretty soon now,' says Ryan. 'You go down into the cabin and light the lamp and 'ave a look round. We'll 'ave a bottle of beer. Here's a box of matches.'

" 'Suits me,' I says, and down I goes.

"I couldn't see much, but I knew the way about by instinct. And I didn't go down so quick I couldn't 'ave a look behind me. I twigged he was up to somethin'. I see 'im give three or four flashes with the torch. ' 'Ullo,' I says to meself, 'someone's watchin',' but if it was ashore or on sea, I couldn't say. Then Ryan comes down and I 'ad a look round. He fished out a bottle of beer for 'isself and a bottle of beer for me.

" 'The moon'll be gettin' up soon,' he says. 'There's a nice little breeze.'

" 'Startin' right away, are we?' I says.

" 'Sooner the better, after the boy's come on board, and just keep goin', see?'

" 'Look 'ere, Ryan,' I says, 'I ain't got so much as a safety razor with me.'

" 'Grow a beard then, Bill,' he answers. 'The orders is, no landin' anywhere till you get to New Guinea. If you want to go ashore at Merauke, you can.'

" 'Dutch, ain't it?' He nods. 'Look here, Ryan,' I says. 'You know I wasn't born yesterday. I can't 'elp thinkin', can I? What's the good, why don't you come out with it straight and tell me what it's all about?'

" 'Bill, old boy,' 'e says very friendly like, 'you drink your beer and don't you ask no questions. I know I can't 'elp you thinkin', but you just believe what you're told or I swear to God I'll gouge your bloody eyes out meself.'

" 'Well, that's straight enough,' says I, laughing.

" 'Here's luck,' says 'e.

"He took a swig of beer and so did I.

" 'Plenty of it?' I asked.

" 'Enough to last you. I know you're not a soaker. I wouldn't 'ave given you the job if I 'adn't known that.'

" 'No,' I says, 'I like me little drop of beer, but I know when I've 'ad enough. What about the money?'

" 'I got it 'ere,' 'e says. 'I'll give it you before I get off.'

"Well, we sat talkin' of one thing and another. I ask 'im what crew there was and a lot like that, and he ask me if I'd 'ave a job gettin' out at night and I says, no, I could sail the boat with me eyes shut, and then suddenly I 'eard something. I got sharp ears, I 'ave, and there ain't much goin' on that I miss that way.

" 'There's a boat comin',' I says.

" 'And about time, too,' 'e says. 'I got to get back to my missus and the kids to-night.'

" 'Better go on deck, 'adn't we?' I says.

" 'No necessity at all,' 'e says.

" 'All right,' I says.

"We just sat there listenin'. Sounded like a dinghy. She come up and give a bump on the side. Then someone come on board. He come down the companion. All dressed up he was, blue serge suit, collar and tie, brown shoes. Not like what 'e is now.

" 'This is Fred,' says Ryan, givin' me a look.

" 'Fred Blake,' says the young fellow.

" 'This is Captain Nichols. First-rate seaman. He's all right.'

"The kid give me a look and I give 'im one. He didn't look exactly what you'd call delicate, I must say, picture of 'ealth, I'd 'ave said. Bit jumpy. If you'd asked me I'd 'ave said he was scared.

" 'Bad luck your crockin' up like this,' I says, very affable like. 'The sea air'll pull you together, believe me. Nothin' like a cruise to build up a young fellow's constitution.'

"I never see anyone go so red as 'e done when I said that. Ryan looked at 'im an' 'e looked at me and laughed. Then 'e says 'e'd tip over the dibs and be gettin' off. He 'ad it in his belt and 'e took it off and paid it over to me, two 'undred golden sovereigns. I 'adn't seen gold in donkey's years. Only the banks 'ad it. Seemed to me that whoever it was wanted to get this 'ere boy out of the way, 'e must be pretty high up.

" 'Throw in the belt, Ryan,' I says. 'I can't leave a lot of money like that lyin' about.'

" 'All right,' says 'e, 'take the belt. Well, good luck.' And before I could say a word he was out of the cabin and 'e'd popped over the side and the boat was movin' away. They wasn't takin' no chances of my seein' who was in it."

"And what happened then?"

"Well, I put the money back in the belt and strapped it round me."

"Devil of a weight, isn't it?"

"When we come to Merauke we bought a couple of boxes and I've hid mine away so as nobody knows where it is. But if things go on like they are, I'll be able to carry all what's left without so much as feelin' it."

"What d'you mean by that?"

"Well, we sailed all the way up the coast, inside the Bank, of course, fine weather and all that, nice breeze, and I said to the kid: 'What about a game of cribbage?' Had to pass the time somehow, you know, and I knew 'e'd got a good bit of money. I didn't see why I shouldn't 'ave some of it. I've played cribbage all me life, and I thought I got a soft thing on. I believe the devil's in them cards. D'you know, I 'aven't 'ad a winnin' day since we left Sydney. I've lost a matter of seventy pounds, I 'ave. And it's not as if 'e could play. It's the devil's own luck he's got."

"Perhaps he plays better than you think."

"Don't you believe it. What I don't know about cribbage ain't worth knowin'. D'you think I'd 'ave took him on if I 'adn't known that? No, it's luck, and luck can't go on for ever. It's bound to change and then I'll get back all I've lost and all he's got besides. It's aggravatin', of course, but I ain't worryin'."

"Has he told you anything about himself?"

"Not a thing. But I've put two and two together and I got a pretty shrewd idea what's at the bottom of it."

"Oh!"

"There's politics at the bottom of it or I'll eat my 'at. If there 'adn't been Ryan wouldn't 'ave been mixed up in it. The Government's pretty rocky in New South Wales. They're 'angin' on by their teeth. If there was a scandal they'd go out to-morrow. There'll 'ave to be an election soon, anyway. They think they'll get in again, but my belief is it's a toss-up and I guess they know they can't take a risk. I shouldn't be surprised if Fred wasn't the son of somebody pretty important."

"Premier, or somebody like that, you mean? Is there one of the Ministers called Blake?"

"Blake's no more 'is name than it is mine. It's one of the Ministers all right, and Fred's 'is son or 'is nephew; and whatever it is, if it come out, he'd lose 'is seat, and my opinion is they all thought it better Fred should be out of the way for a few months."

"And what d'you think it is he did?"

"Murder, if you ask me."

"He's only a kid."

"Old enough to 'ang."

CHAPTER XII

"Hulloa, what's that?" said the skipper. "There's a boat comin'."

His hearing was indeed acute, for Dr. Saunders heard nothing. The captain peered into the darkness. He put his hand on the doctor's arm and, getting up noiselessly, slipped down into the cabin. In a moment he came up again and the doctor saw that he carried a revolver.

"No 'arm bein' on the safe side," he said.

Now the doctor discerned the faint grating of oars turning in rusty rowlocks.

"It's the schooner's dinghy," he said.

"I know it is. But I don't know what they want. Pretty late to pay a social call."

The two men waited in silence and listened to the approaching sound. Presently, they not only heard the splash of the water, but saw the vague outline of the boat, a little black mass against the black sea.

"Hullo, there," cried Nichols suddenly. "Boat ahoy."

"That you, Captain?" a voice travelled over the water.

"Yes, it's me. What d'you want?"

He stood at the gunwale, the revolver in his hand, hanging from the end of his loose arm. The Australian rowed on.

"Wait till I come on board," he said.

"Pretty late, ain't it?" cried Nichols.

The Australian told the man who was rowing to stop.

"Wake up the doctor, will you? I don't half like the look of my Jap. Seems to me he's sinking."

"The doctor's 'ere. Come to the side."

The dinghy came on and Captain Nichols, leaning over, saw that the Australian was alone with a blackfellow.

"D'you want me to come over?" asked Dr. Saunders.

"Sorry to trouble you, Doc, but I think he's pretty bad."

"I'll come. Wait till I get my things."

He stumbled down the companion and picked up a satchel in which he had what was necessary for emergencies. He climbed over the side and let himself down into the dinghy. The blackfellow rowed off quickly.

"You know what it is," said the Australian, "you can't get a diver for the asking, not a Jap, and they're the only ones worth having. There isn't one in the Arus out of a job now, and if I lose this chap it's going to queer my pitch good and proper. I mean, I shall have to go all the way to Yokohama, and then the chances are I shall have to hang around for a month before I get what I want."

The diver was lying on one of the lower bunks in the crew's quarters. The air was fetid and the heat fearful. Two black-fellows were asleep and one of them, lying on his back, breathed stertorously. A third, sitting on his haunches on the floor by the

sick man's side, was staring at him with eyes that had no meaning.
A hurricane lamp hanging from a beam gave a dim light. The
diver was in a state of collapse. He was conscious, but when the
doctor went up to him there was no change in the expression of
the coal-black Oriental eyes. One might have thought that they
gazed already at Eternity and could not be distracted by a transitory
object. Dr. Saunders felt his pulse and put his hand on the clammy
forehead. He gave him a hypodermic injection. He stood by the
side of the bunk and looked reflectively at the recumbent form.

"Let's go up and get a little air," he said presently. "Tell this
man to come and tell us if there's any change."

"Is he for it?" asked the Australian, when they got on deck.

"Looks like it."

"God, I do have bad luck."

The doctor chuckled. The Australian asked him to sit down.
The night was as still as death. In the calm water the stars from
their vast distances looked at themselves. The two men were
silent. Some say that if you believe a thing with sufficient force it
becomes true. For that Jap, lying there, dying there, painlessly, it
was not the end, but the turning over of a page; he knew, as
certainly as he knew that the sun in a few hours would rise, that he
was but slipping from one life to another. Karma, the deeds of this
as of all the other lives he had passed, would be somehow continued; and perhaps, in his exhaustion, the only emotion that
remained to him was curiosity, anxious it might be or amused, to
know in what condition he would be reborn. Dr. Saunders dozed
off. He was awakened by a black man's hand on his shoulder.

"Come quick."

The dawn was breaking. It was not yet day, but the light of the
stars had dwindled and the sky was ghostly. He went below. The
diver was sinking fast. His eyes were open still, but his pulse was
imperceptible and his body had the coldness of death. Suddenly
there was a little rattle, not loud, but deprecating and conciliatory,
like the manners of the Japanese, and he was dead. The two
sleepers had wakened and one sat on the edge of his bunk, his
black naked legs dangling, while the other, as though he wanted to
shut away from him what was happening so close, sat crouched
on the floor with his back to the dying man, and held his head in
his hands.

When the doctor went back on deck, and told the captain, he
shrugged his shoulders.

"No physique, these Japs," he said.

Dawn now was stealing over the water, and the first rays of the sun touched its stillness with cool and delicate colours.

"Well, I'll be getting back to the *Fenton*," said the doctor. "I know the captain wants to sail soon after it's light."

"You'd better have some breakfast before you go. You must be pretty peckish."

"Well, I could do with a cup of tea."

"I'll tell you what. I've got some eggs, I was keeping them for the Jap, but he won't want 'em now, let's have some bacon and eggs."

He shouted for the cook.

"I just fancy a plate of bacon and eggs," he said, rubbing his hands. "They ought to be pretty fresh still."

Presently the cook brought them, piping hot, with tea and biscuits.

"God, they smell good," said the Australian. "Funny thing, you know, I never get tired of bacon and eggs. When I'm at home I have them every day. Sometimes my wife gives me something else for a change, but there's nothing I like 'alf so much."

But when the blackfellow was rowing Dr. Saunders back to the *Fenton*, it struck him that death was a funnier thing even than that the schooner's captain should like bacon and eggs for breakfast. The flat sea was shining like polished steel. Its colours were pale and delicate like the colours in the boudoir of an eighteenth-century marquise. It seemed very odd to the doctor that men should die. There was something absurd in the notion that this pearl diver, the heir of innumerable generations, the result of a complicated process of evolution that had lasted since the planet was formed, here and now, because of a succession of accidents that confounded the imagination, should be brought to death on this lost and uninhabited spot.

Captain Nichols was shaving when the doctor reached the side and he gave him a hand to help him on board.

"Well, what's the news?"

"Oh, he's dead."

"I thought as much. What's bein' done about buryin' 'im?"

"I don't know, I didn't ask. I suppose they'll just throw him overboard."

"Like a dog?"

"Why not?"

The skipper gave signs of an agitation that not a little surprised Dr. Saunders.

"That won't do at all. Not on a British vessel. He must be buried in the proper way. I mean, he must 'ave a proper service and all that."

"He was a Buddhist or Shintoist or something like that, you know."

"I can't 'elp that. I been at sea, man and boy, for more than thirty years, and when a chap dies on a British ship he must 'ave a British funeral. Death levels all men, Doc, you ought to know that, and at a time like this we can't 'old it up against a fellow that he's a Jap, or a nigger, or a dago, or anything. Hi, you men, lower a boat and look sharp about it. I'll go over to the schooner meself. When I see you didn't come back all this time I said to meself that this was going to 'appen. That's why I was shavin' when you come alongside."

"What are you going to do?"

"I'm goin' to talk to the skipper of that there schooner. We must do what's right. Give that Jap a send-off in style. I've always made a point of that on every vessel I've commanded. Makes a rare good impression on the crew. Then they know what to expect if anything 'appens to them."

The dinghy was lowered and the skipper rowed away. Fred Blake came aft. With his tousled hair, his clear skin and blue eyes, his springtime radiance, he looked like a young Bacchus in a Venetian picture. The doctor, tired after a night of little sleep, felt a moment's envy of his insolent youth.

"How's the patient, Doctor?"

"Dead."

"Some fellows have all the luck, don't they?"

Dr. Saunders gave him a sharp look, but did not speak.

In a little while, they saw the dinghy coming back from the schooner, but without Captain Nichols. The man called Utan spoke English well. He brought them a message that they were all to go over.

"What the hell for?" asked Blake.

"Come on," said the doctor.

The two white men climbed over the side and the remaining two members of the crew.

"Captain say everybody. China boy, too."

"Jump in, Ah Kay," said the doctor to his servant, who was sitting on deck, unconcerned, sewing a button on a pair of trousers.

Ah Kay put down his work and with his friendly little smile stepped down on light feet into the dinghy. They rowed over to the schooner. When they climbed up the ladder, they found Captain Nichols and the Australian waiting for them.

"Captain Atkinson agrees with me that we ought to do the right thing by this poor Jap," said Nichols, "and as he 'asn't the experience what I 'ave, 'e's asked me to conduct the ceremony in proper style."

"That's right," said the Australian.

"It isn't my place, I know that. When you 'ave a death at sea it's the captain's place to read the service, but 'e don't 'appen to 'ave a prayer-book on board and 'e don't know what to do any more than a canary with a rumpsteak. Am I right, Captain?"

The Australian nodded gravely.

"But I thought you were a Baptist," said the doctor.

"Ordinarily, I am," said Nichols. "But when it comes to funerals and that-like I always 'ave used the prayer-book and I always shall use the prayer-book. Now, Captain, as soon as your party's ready we'll assemble the men and get on with the job."

The Australian walked forrard and in a minute or two rejoined them.

"Looks to me as if they was just putting in the last stitches," he said.

"A stitch in time saves nine," said Captain Nichols, somewhat to the doctor's perplexity.

"What d'you say to a little drink while we're waiting?"

"Not yet, Captain. We'll 'ave that afterwards. Business before pleasure."

Then a man came along.

"All finished, boss," he said.

"That's fine," said Nichols. "Come on, chaps."

He was alert. He held himself erect. His little foxy eyes were twinkling with pleasant anticipation. The doctor observed with demure amusement his air of subdued gaiety. It was plain that he enjoyed the situation. They marched aft. The crews of the two boats, blackfellows all of them, were standing about, some with pipes in their mouths, one or two with the fag-end of a cigarette sticking to their thick lips. On the deck lay a bundle in what looked to the doctor like a copra sack. It was very small. You could hardly believe that it contained what had once been a man.

"Are you all 'ere?" asked Captain Nichols, looking round. "No smokin', please. Respect for the dead."

They put away their pipes, and spat out the ends of their cigarettes.

"Stand round now. You near me, Captain. I'm only doin' this to oblige, you understand, and I don't want you to think I don't know it's your place and not mine. Now then, are you all ready?"

Captain Nichols's recollection of the burial service was somewhat sketchy. He began with a prayer that owed much to his invention, but which he delivered with unction. Its language was florid. He ended with a resounding amen.

"Now we'll sing a 'ymn." He looked at the blackfellows. "You've all been to missionary schools and I want you to put your guts in it. Let 'em 'ear you right away to Macassar. Come on, all of you. Onward Christian Soldiers, onwards as to war."

He burst out singing in a throaty, tuneless strain, but with fervour, and he had hardly started before the crews of the two boats joined in. They sang lustily with rich deep voices and the sound travelled over the peaceful sea. It was a hymn they had all learnt in their native islands, and they knew every word of it; but in their unfamiliar speech, with its queer intonations, it gathered a strange mystery so that it seemed not like a Christian hymn but like the barbaric, rhythmical shouting of a savage multitude. It rang with fantastic sounds, the beating of drums and the clang of curious instruments, and it suggested the night and dark ceremonies by the water's edge and the dripping of blood in human sacrifice. Ah Kay, very clean in his neat white dress, stood a little apart from the black men in an attitude of negligent grace, and in his lovely liquid eyes was a look of a slightly scornful astonishment. They ended the first verse and without prompting from Captain Nichols sang the second. But when they started on the third he clapped his hands sharply.

"Now then, that's enough," he cried. "This ain't a bloody concert. We don't want to stay 'ere all night."

They stopped suddenly and he looked round with severity. The doctor's eyes fell on that small bundle in the copra sack that lay on deck in the middle of the circle. He did not know why, but he thought of the little boy the dead diver once had been, with his yellow face and sloe-black eyes, who played in the streets of a

Japanese town and was taken by his mother in her pretty Japanese dress, with pins in her elaborately done hair and clogs on her feet, to see the cherry blossom when it was in flower and, on holidays, to the temple, where he was given a cake; and perhaps once, dressed all in white, with an ashen wand in his hand, he had gone with all his family on pilgrimage and watched the sun rise from the summit of Fuji Yama, the sacred mountain.

"Now I'm going to say another prayer and when I come to the words, 'we therefore commend 'is body to the deep,' and mind you watch out for them, I don't want a hitch or anythin' like that, you just catch 'old of 'im and pop 'im over, see? Better detail two men to do that, Captain."

"You, Bob. And Jo."

The two men stepped forward and made to seize the body.

"Not yet, you damned fools," cried Captain Nichols. "Let me get the words out of me mouth, blast you." And then, without stopping to take breath, he burst into prayer. He went on till he could evidently think of nothing more to say, and then, raising his voice a little: "Forasmuch as it 'as pleased Almighty God of 'is great mercy to take unto 'isself the soul of our dear brother 'ere departed: We therefore commend his body to the deep . . ." He gave the two men a severe look, but they were staring at him with open mouths. "Now then, don't be all night about it. Pop the bleeder over, blast you."

With a start they leapt at the little bundle that lay on deck and flung it overboard. It plunged into the water with hardly a splash. Captain Nichols went on with a little satisfied smile on his face:

"To be turned into corruption, lookin' for the resurrection of the body when the sea shall give up its dead. Now, dearly beloved brethren, we'll all say the Lord's Prayer, and no mumblin', please. God wants to 'ear and I want to 'ear. Our Father which art in 'eaven . . ."

He repeated it to the crew in a loud voice and all but Ah Kay said it with him.

"Now, men, that's about all," he continued, but in the same unctuous voice: "I'm glad to 'ave 'ad the opportunity to conduct this sad ceremony in the proper way. In the midst of life we are in death, and accidents will 'appen in the best regulated families. I want you to know that if you're taken to the bourne from which no one ever comes back, so long as you're on a British ship and under the British flag, you can be sure of 'avin' a decent funeral and bein' buried like a faithful son of our Lord Jesus Christ. Under ordinary circumstances I should now call upon you to give three cheers for your captain, Captain Atkinson, but this is a sad occasion upon which we are gathered together and our thoughts are too deep for tears, so I will ask you to give 'im three cheers in your 'earts. And now to God the Father, God the Son and God the 'oly Ghost. A-a-men."

Captain Nichols turned aside with the manner of a man descending from the pulpit and held out his hand to the captain of the schooner. The Australian wrung it warmly.

"By God, you done that first-rate," he said.

"Practice," said Captain Nichols modestly.

"Now, boys, what about a tiddly?"

"That's the idea," said Captain Nichols. He turned to his crew. "You fellers get back to the Fenton and, Tom, you come back and fetch us."

The four men shambled along the deck. Captain Atkinson brought up from the cabin a bottle of whisky and some glasses.

"A parson couldn't have done it better," he said, raising his glass to Captain Nichols.

"It's just a matter of feelin'. You 'ave to 'ave the feelin'. I mean, when I was conductin' that service I didn't think it was only a dirty little Jap, it was just the same to me as if it been you or Fred or the doctor. That's Christianity, that is."

CHAPTER XIII

THE monsoon was blowing hard and when they left the shelter of the land they found a heavy sea. The doctor was ignorant of sailing vessels and to his unaccustomed eyes it seemed formidable. Captain Nichols had the water-cask aft lashed down. The waves, crested with white, looked very large and in that small craft one was very near the water. Now and then a heavy sea struck them and a cloud of spoon-drift swept along the deck. They were passing islands and as they passed each one the doctor asked himself if he could swim so far if they were capsized. He was nervous. It exasperated him. He knew there was no need. Two of the black-fellows were sitting on the hatch tying rope together to make a fishing line, and, intent on their job, never so much as gave the sea a glance. The water was muddy and there were reefs all around them. The skipper ordered one of the men to stand on the jib-boom and keep a look-out. The blackfellow guided the skipper with a gesture of one arm or the other. The sun shone and the sky was bright blue, but high above them white clouds raced with a swift and even motion. The doctor tried to read, but he had to duck constantly to avoid the spray when a sea broke over them. Presently there was a dull scraping and he clutched the gunwale. They had struck a reef. They bumped over and were again in deep water. Nichols shouted a curse at the look-out man for not being more careful. They struck another reef and again bumped off.

"We'd better get out of this," said the skipper.

He altered his course and made for the open sea. The ketch rolled heavily and righted herself each time with a peevish jerk. Dr. Saunders was wet through.

"Why don't you go down into the cabin?" the skipper shouted.

"I prefer being on deck."

"No danger, you know."

"Is it going to get any worse?"

"I shouldn't wonder. Looks to me as if it was blowin' up a bit."

The doctor, looking over the stern, watched a heavy sea charge down upon them, and he expected the next wave to crash before the ketch had time to recover, but with an agility that was almost human she avoided it just in time and triumphantly rode on. He was not comfortable. He was not happy. Fred Blake came up to him.

"Grand, isn't it? Exhilarating having a bit of a blow like this."

His curling hair was all blown about in the wind and his eyes were shining. He was enjoying himself. The doctor shrugged his shoulders, but did not answer. He looked at a great billow, with overhanging, breaking crest, that came rolling towards them, as though it were not the unconscious result of natural forces, but had a malignant purpose. Nearer and nearer it came and it seemed as though it must inevitably overwhelm them. The frail craft could never withstand that monstrous mountain of water.

"Look out," shouted the skipper.

He kept the lugger dead before it. Dr. Saunders instinctively clung to the mast. It struck them and it seemed that a wall of water poured over them. The deck was swimming.

"That was a whopper," shouted Fred.

"I needed a bath," said the skipper.

They both laughed. But the doctor was sick with fear. He wished with all his heart that he had stayed safely on the island of Takana till the steamer called. How stupid it was to risk his life rather than endure two or three weeks of boredom! He swore to himself that if he escaped this time nothing would induce him again to do anything so absurd. He did not attempt to read any more. He could not see through his spectacles splashed with water, and his book was drenched. He watched the waves that swept on. The islands now were dim in the distance.

"Enjoyin' it, Doc?" shouted the skipper.

The lugger was tossing about like a cork. Dr. Saunders tried to force a smile to his lips.

"Fine thing to blow the cobwebs away," the skipper added.

The doctor had never seen him in better spirits. He was alert. He seemed to enjoy his own competence. It was no figure of speech to say that he was in his element. Fear? He knew nothing of it, that vulgar, cheating, shifty man; there was nothing decent in him, he knew nothing of whatever gave dignity to man, or beauty, and you had only to know him for twenty-four hours to be certain that if there were two ways of doing a thing, a straight one and a crooked, he would choose the crooked one. In that low and squalid mind there was but one motive, the desire to get the better of his fellow men by foul means; it was not even a passion of evil, in which after all there might be a sinister grandeur, it was a puckish malice that found satisfaction in besting another. And yet here, in this tiny vessel in that vast desert of angry waves, without possibility of succour if catastrophe befell them, he was at ease, strong in his knowledge of the sea, proud, self-assured and happy. He seemed to take pleasure in his mastery of the little boat he managed with such confident skill; it was in his hands like a horse in a horseman's when he knows every trick and habit it has, every whim and every capacity; he watched the waves with a smile in his foxy little eyes, and he nodded with self-satisfaction as they thundered by. It almost seemed to the doctor that to him they too were living things that he found a cynical amusement in getting the better of.

Dr. Saunders flinched as he watched the huge waves race after them and clinging to the mast he swayed away from the sea as the lugger heeled over; and then, as though his weight could make all the difference, swayed back as she rolled. He knew he was pale, and he felt his face stiff. He wondered if there would be any chance of getting into one of the two dinghies if the boat foundered. There wouldn't be much chance for them if they did. They were a hundred miles away from any inhabited spot and out of the line of traffic. If anything happened the only thing was to let oneself drown quickly. It was not death he minded, but dying, and he wondered if it would be very unpleasant while he swallowed the water and choked, and, notwithstanding his will, desperately struggled.

Then the cook lurched along the deck bearing their dinner. A heavy sea had swamped out the hold, and he had not been able to light a fire, so it consisted of a tin of corned beef and cold potatoes.

"Send Utan along to take the helm," the skipper shouted.

The blackfellow took the skipper's place, and the three men gathered round their wretched meal.

"Pretty peckish, I am," said Nichols jovially, as he helped himself. "How's the appetite, Fred?"

"All right."

The lad was soaked to the skin, but his cheeks were bright and his eyes glistened. Dr. Saunders wondered if his air of unconcern was assumed. Frightened, and angry with himself because he was, he gave the skipper a sour look.

"If you can digest this you can digest an ox."

"Bless you, I never 'ave dyspepsia when there's a bit of a gale. Like a tonic to me, it is."

"How long is this blasted wind going to blow?"

"Not likin' it much, Doc?" The skipper chuckled slyly. "It may drop toward sunset or it may blow up a bit."

"Can't we get in the shelter of some island?"

"Better off at sea. These boats, they can stand anythin'. I don't fancy goin' to pieces on a reef."

When they had finished eating, Captain Nichols lit his pipe.

"What about a game of cribbage, Fred?" he said.

"I'm on."

"You're not going to play that damned game now?" cried the doctor.

Captain Nichols gave the sea a sneering glance.

"A little bit of water; that's nothin'. Them niggers, they can steer a boat with anyone."

They went down into the cabin. Dr. Saunders stayed on deck and sullenly watched the sea. The afternoon stretched interminably before him. He wondered what Ah Kay was up to and presently he scrambled forward. Only one of the crew was on deck. The hatch was battened down.

"Where's my boy?" he asked.

The man pointed to the hold.

"Sleeping. Want to go down?"

He raised the hatch, and the doctor clambered down the companion. A lamp was alight. It was dark and noisome. One blackfellow was sitting on the floor, with nothing on but a loin-cloth, mending his trousers; the other and Ah Kay were in their bunks. They were sleeping quietly. But when the doctor lurched up to Ah Kay he woke and gave his master his sweet and friendly smile.

"Feeling all right?"

"Yes."

"Frightened?"

Ah Kay, smiling again, shook his head.

"Go back to sleep," said the doctor.

He climbed up the companion and with difficulty pushed up the hatch. The man on deck helped him, and as he came out on deck a sheet of water hit him in the face. His heart sank. He swore and shook his fist at the angry sea.

"Better get below," said the blackfellow. "Wet up here."

The doctor shook his head. He stood there clinging to a rope. He wanted human companionship. He knew perfectly well that he was the only man on board who was afraid. Even Ah Kay, who knew no more of the sea than he, was unconcerned. There was no danger. They were as safe on the lugger as on dry land, and yet he could not prevent the pang of terror that seized him each time that a following wave caught them up and sent a cloud of spoon-drift hurtling along the deck. The water flowed out of the scuppers in a great rush. He was terrified. It seemed to him that it was only by an effort of will that he did not curl up in a corner and whimper. He had an instinct to appeal for succour to a God he did not believe in, and he had to clench his teeth to prevent his trembling lips from uttering a prayer. The circumstance seemed to him ironical that he, an intelligent man, who looked upon himself as something of a philosopher, should be affected with this craven fear, and he smiled grimly at the absurdity. It was a bit thick, if you came to think of it, that he, with his quick brain, his wide knowledge and reasoned view of life, he who had nothing to lose by death, should tremble while these men, ignorant like the blackfellow by his side, base like the captain or dull like Fred Blake, should remain unperturbed. It just showed what a poor thing the mind was. He felt sick with fright, and he asked himself what it was he was frightened of. Death? He had faced death before. Once indeed he had decided to make an end of himself, but painlessly, and it had needed an odd mixture of courage, cynicism and cold reason to make him go on with a life that seemed to offer nothing desirable. He was glad now that he had had the sense. But he knew that he had no great attachment to life. Sometimes when ill he had felt his hold on it so slight that he looked forward to dissolution not only with resignation but with cheerfulness. Pain? He bore pain pretty well. After all, if you could bear dengue or a bad toothache with serenity, you could bear anything. No, it was not that, it was just some instinct over which he had no control; and he looked curiously, as though it were something outside himself, at the terror that made his throat dry and his knees shake.

"Very odd," he muttered as he made his way aft.

He glanced at his wrist-watch. By God, it was only three. There was something horrible in that clean, wind-swept sky. Its brilliance was heartless. It seemed to have nothing to do with the tempestuous sea; and the sea, so hard and bright a blue, recked nothing of man. Strange, senseless powers that sported with him and destroyed him not from malice, but in wanton amusement.

"Give me the sea from the beach," the doctor muttered to himself grimly.

He went down into the cabin.

"Two for his 'eels at all events," he heard from the skipper.

They were still playing their dreary game.

"How's the weather, Doc?"

"Rotten."

"It'll 'ave to be worse before it's better, like a woman 'avin' a baby. Grand boats these are. Weather a hurricane. I'd rather go to sea in one of these Australian pearlin' luggers than in a transatlantic liner."

"It's your crib," said Fred.

They were playing on the captain's mattress, and the doctor, changing his dripping clothes, flung himself on the other. He could not read in the fitful light of the swaying lamp. He lay and listened to the monotonous terms of the game. They struck the ear with an insistent jar. The cabin creaked and groaned and over his head the wind roared furiously. He was shaken from side to side.

"That was a roll," said Fred.

"Takin' it grand, ain't she? Fifteen two. Fifteen four."

Fred was winning again and the skipper played to a running accompaniment of complaint. Dr. Saunders stiffened his limbs to bear the misery of his fear. The hours passed with frightful slowness. Toward sunset Captain Nichols went on deck.

"Blowin' up a bit," he said, when he came down again. "I'm goin' to 'ave a nap. It don't look to me as if I'd get much sleep to-night."

"Why don't you lay her to?" asked Fred.

"Bring 'er up to the wind with a sea like this runnin'? No, sir. She's all right as long as everythin' 'olds."

He coiled himself up on his mattress and in five minutes was snoring peacefully. Fred went on deck to get a breath of air. The doctor was angry with himself for having been such a fool as to take a passage on this small craft, and he was angry with the captain and with Fred because they were free of the terror that obsessed him. But when the ketch had seemed about to founder a hundred times, and each time righted herself, there stole upon him gradually an unwilling admiration for the gallant little boat. At seven the cook brought them their supper and woke Captain Nichols to eat it. He had been able to make a fire, and they had hot stew and hot tea. Then the three of them went on deck and the skipper took the helm. It was a clear night, with the stars in their myriads twinkling brightly; the sea was rough, and in the darkness the waves looked enormous.

"By God, there's a big 'un," cried Fred.

A huge wall of green water, with a breaking crest, was rushing down on them. It looked as though it must inevitably fall on them, and if it did, the *Fenton*, powerless to rise to it, must be rolled over and over. The skipper glanced round and jammed himself against the wheel. He steered so that the wave should strike them dead aft. Suddenly the stern slewed off the course and there was a crash and a mass of water swept over the quarter. They were blinded. Then the bulwarks rose above the sea. The *Fenton* shook herself like a dog stepping on to dry land and the water poured out of the scuppers.

"Gettin' beyond a joke," bellowed the skipper.

"Any islands near?"

"Yep. If we can keep goin' for a couple of hours we can get under their lee."

"What about reefs?"

"There ain't any marked. Moon'll be out soon. You two chaps better go below."

"I'll stay on deck," said Fred. "Stuffy in the cabin."

"Please yourself. What about you, Doc?"

The doctor hesitated. He hated the look of the angry sea and he was bored with being frightened. He had died so many deaths that he had exhausted his emotion.

"Can I be any use?"

"No more than a snowball in 'ell."

"Remember you carry Cæsar and his fortunes," he shouted in the skipper's ear.

But Captain Nichols, not having had a classical education, did not see the point of the jest. If I perish, I perish, the doctor reflected, and he made up his mind to get all the enjoyment he could out of what might be his last hours on earth. He went forward to fetch Ah Kay. The boy followed him back and came down with him into the cabin.

"Let's try Kim Ching's chandu," said Dr. Saunders. "No need to stint ourselves to-night."

The boy got the lamp and the opium from the valise, and with his accustomed nonchalance started to prepare the pipe. Never had the first long inhalation seemed more delicious. They smoked alternately. Gradually peace descended upon the doctor's soul. His nerves ceased to tingle with the roll of the lugger. Fear left him. After the usual six pipes that the doctor smoked every night Ah Kay lay back as if he had finished.

"Not yet," said Dr. Saunders softly. "For once I'm going the whole hog."

The motion of the boat was not unpleasant. Little by little it seemed to him that he grasped its rhythm. It was only his carcase that was tossed from side to side, his spirit soared in regions far above the storm. He walked in the infinite, but he knew, before Einstein, that it was bounded by his own thought. He knew once more that he had but to stretch his intelligence ever so little to solve a great mystery; and again he did not do it because it gave him more pleasure to know that it was there waiting to be solved. It had agreeably tantalised him so long, it was indelicate, when any moment might be his last, to ravish its secret. He was like a

well-bred man who will not expose his mistress to the humiliation
of knowing that he does not believe her lies. Ah Kay fell asleep,
curled up at the foot of the mattress. Dr. Saunders moved a little
so as not to disturb him. He thought of God and of eternity, and
he laughed softly, in his heart, at the absurdity of life. Scraps of
poetry floated in his memory. It seemed to him that he was dead
already and Captain Nichols, Charon in a tarpaulin, was bearing
him to a strange, sweet place. At last he fell asleep also.

CHAPTER XIV

HE was awakened by the chill of the dawn. He opened his eyes and
saw that the companion hatch was open, and then he was aware of
the skipper and Fred Blake sleeping on their mattresses. They had
come down and left the hatch open on account of the pungent
smell of the opium. Suddenly it occurred to him that the lugger
rolled no longer. He raised himself. He felt a trifle heavy, for he
was unaccustomed to smoke so much, and he thought he would
get into the air. Ah Kay was resting peacefully where he had fallen
asleep. He touched him on the shoulder. The boy opened his
eyes and his lips broke immediately into the slow smile that gave
such beauty to his young face. He stretched himself and yawned.

"Get me some tea," said the doctor.

Ah Kay was on his feet in a minute. The doctor followed him
up the companion. The sun had not yet risen and one pale star
still loitered in the sky, but the night had thinned to a ghostly
grey, and the ketch seemed to float on the surface of a cloud. The
man at the helm in an old coat, with a muffler round his neck and a
battered hat crammed down on his head, gave the doctor a surly
nod. The sea was quite calm. They were passing between two
islands so close together that they might have been sailing down a
canal. There was a very light breeze. The blackfellow at the helm
seemed half asleep. The dawn slid between the low, wooded
islands, gravely, with a deliberate calmness that seemed to conceal
an inward apprehension, and you felt it natural and even inevitable that men should have personified it in a maiden. It had
indeed the shyness and the grace of a young girl, the charming
seriousness, the indifference and the ruthlessness. The sky had the
washed-out colour of an archaic statue. The virgin forests on each

side of them still held the night, but then insensibly the grey of the sea was shot with the soft hues of a pigeon's breast. There was a pause, and with a smile the day broke. Sailing between those uninhabited islands, on that still sea, in a silence that caused you almost to hold your breath, you had a strange and exciting impression of the beginning of the world. There man might never have passed and you had a feeling that what your eyes saw had never been seen before. You had a sensation of primeval freshness, and all the complication of the generations disappeared. A stark simplicity, as bare and severe as a straight line, filled the soul with rapture. Dr. Saunders knew at that moment the ecstasy of the mystic.

Ah Kay brought him a cup of tea, jasmine-scented, and scrambling down from the spiritual altitudes on which for an instant he had floated he made himself comfortable, as in an armchair, in the bliss of a material enjoyment. The air was cool but balmy. He asked for nothing but to go on for ever in that boat sailing on an even keel between green islands.

When he had been sitting there an hour, delighting in his ease, he heard steps on the companion, and Fred Blake came on deck. In his pyjamas, with his tousled hair, he looked very young, and as was natural to his age he had awakened fresh, with all the lines smoothed out of his face, and not puckered and wrinkled and time-worn as sleep had left the doctor.

"Up early, Doctor?" He noticed the empty cup. "I wonder if I can get a cup of tea."

"Ask Ah Kay."

"All right. I'll just get Utan to throw a couple of buckets of water over me."

He went forward and spoke to one of the men. The doctor saw the blackfellow lower a bucket by a rope into the sea, and then Fred Blake stripped his pyjamas and stood on deck naked while the other threw the contents over him. The bucket was lowered again and Fred turned round. He was tall, with square shoulders, a small waist and slender hips; his arms and neck were tanned, but the rest of his body was very white. He dried himself, and putting on his pyjamas again came aft. His eyes were shining and on his lips was the outline of a smile.

"You're a very good-looking young fellow," said the doctor.

Fred gave an indifferent shrug of the shoulders and sank into the next chair.

"We lost a boat in the night. D'you know that?"

"No, I didn't."

"Blew like the devil. We've lost the jib. Just torn to tatters. Nichols wasn't half glad to get into the shelter of the islands, I can tell you. I thought we'd never make it."

"Did you stay up on deck all the time?"

"Yes, I thought if we foundered I'd rather be in the open."

"There wouldn't have been much chance for you."

"No, I know that."

"Weren't you afraid?"

"No. You know, I think if it's coming to you, it'll come. And there's nothing to do about it."

"I was frightened."

"Nichols said you were in the afternoon. He thought it a hell of a joke."

"It's a question of age, you know. The old are much more easily frightened than the young. I couldn't help thinking it rather funny at the time that I, who had so much less to lose than you who've got all your life before you, should dread losing it so much more than you did."

"How could you think if you were as scared as all that?"

"I was scared with my body. That didn't prevent me from thinking with my mind."

"Bit of a character, aren't you, Doctor."

"I don't know about that."

"I'm sorry I was so short with you when you asked if you could have a passage on this boat." He hesitated an instant. "I've been ill, you know, and my nerves are a bit funny. I'm not crazy about people I don't know."

"Oh, that's all right."

"I don't want you to think I'm just a rough-neck." He looked round at the peaceful scene. They had sailed out of the narrow arm between the two islands, and now found themselves in what looked like an inland sea. They were surrounded by low-lying islets, thickly covered with vegetation, and the water was as calm and blue as a Swiss lake. "Bit of a change from last night. Got worse when the moon rose. How you could have slept through it beats me. There was a hell of a racket."

"I smoked."

"Nichols said you were going to when you and the Chink went into the cabin. I wouldn't believe it. But when we came down—huh, it was enough to take the roof of your head off."

"Why wouldn't you believe it?"

"I couldn't imagine that a man like you could degrade himself by doing such a thing."

The doctor chuckled.

"One should be tolerant of other people's vices," he said calmly.

"I've got no cause to blame anybody."

"What else has Nichols said about me?"

"Oh, well." He paused as he saw Ah Kay, as neat as a new pin in his white dress, slim and graceful, come along to fetch the empty cups. "It's no business of mine, anyway. He says you were struck off the rolls for something."

"Removed from the Register is the correct expression," placidly interrupted the doctor.

"And he says he believes you went to gaol. Naturally one can't help wondering when one sees a man with your intelligence, and the reputation you have in the East, settled in a beastly Chinese city."

"What makes you think I'm intelligent?"

"I can see that you're educated. I don't want you to think that I'm just a larrikin. I was studying to be an accountant when my health broke down. This isn't the sort of life I'm used to."

The doctor smiled. No one could have looked more radiantly well than Fred Blake. His broad chest, his athletic build, gave the lie to his tale of tuberculosis.

"Shall I tell you something?"

"Not if you don't want to."

"Oh, not about myself. I don't talk much about myself. I think there's no harm in a doctor being a trifle mysterious. It adds to his patients' belief in him. I was going to give you a reflection based on experience. When some incident has shattered the career you've mapped out for yourself, a folly, a crime or a misfortune, you mustn't think you're down and out. It may be a stroke of luck, and when you look back years after you may say to yourself that you wouldn't for anything in the world exchange the new life disaster has forced upon you for the dull, humdrum existence you would have led if circumstances hadn't intervened."

Fred looked down.

"Why do you say that to me?"

"I thought it might be a useful piece of information."

The young man sighed a little.

"You never know about people, do you? I used to think you were either white or yellow. It seems to me you can't tell what anyone'll do when it comes to the pinch. Of all the rotten skunks I've met I've never met one to beat Nichols. He'd rather go crooked than straight. You can't trust him an inch. We've been together a good while now, and I thought there wasn't much I didn't know about him. He'd do his own brother down if he got the chance. Not a decent thing about him. You should have seen him last night. I don't mind telling you it was a pretty near thing. You'd have been surprised. Calm as a cucumber. My opinion is that he just revelled in it. Once he said to me: 'Said your prayers, Fred? If we don't make the islands before it gets much worse, we shall be feeding the fishes in the morning.' And he grinned all over his ugly face. He kept his head all right. I've done a bit of sailing in Sydney harbour and I give you my word I've never seen a boat handled like he handled this one. I take my hat off to him. If we're here now it's him we owe it to. He's got nerve all right. And if he thought there was twenty pounds to be made without risk by doing us in, you and me, d'you think he'd hesitate? How d'you explain that?"

"Oh, I don't know."

"But don't you think it's funny that a chap who's nothing but a born crook should have all that pluck? I mean, I've always heard that when a man was a wrong 'un he might bluster and bully, but when it comes to a crisis he'd just crumple up. I hate that chap, and, all the same, last night I couldn't help admiring him."

The doctor smiled quietly, but did not answer. He was amused by the lad's ingenuous surprise at the complexity of human nature.

"And he's conceited. We play cribbage all the time, fancies himself at the game. I always beat him, and he will go on."

"He tells me you've been very lucky."

"Lucky in love, unlucky at cards, they say. I've played cards all my life. I've got a knack for it. That's one of the reasons why I went in for being an accountant. I've got that sort of head. It's not luck. You have luck in streaks. I know about cards, and in the long run it's always the fellow who plays best who wins. Nichols thinks he's smart. He hasn't got a dog's chance playing with me."

The conversation dropped and they sat side by side in easy

comfort. After a while Captain Nichols woke and came on deck. In his dirty pyjamas, unwashed, unshaved, with his decayed teeth and general air of having run to seed, he presented an appearance that was almost repulsive. His face, grey in the light of early morning, bore a peevish expression.

"It's come on again, Doc."

"What?"

"My dyspepsia. I 'ad a snack last night before I went to bed. I knew I oughtn't to eat anything just before turnin' in, but I was that 'ungry I just 'ad to, and it's on me chest now somethin' cruel."

"We'll see what we can do about it," smiled the doctor, getting up from his chair.

"You won't be able to do a thing," answered the skipper gloomily. "I know my digestion. After I been through a patch of dirty weather I always 'ave dyspepsia as sure as my name's Nichols. Cruel 'ard, I call it. I mean, you would think after I'd been at the wheel for eight hours I could eat a bit of cold sausage and a slice of cheese without sufferin' for it. Damn it all, a man must eat."

CHAPTER XV

DR. SAUNDERS was to leave them at Kanda-Meira, twin islands in the Kanda Sea, at which vessels of the Royal Netherlands Steam Packet Company called regularly. He thought it unlikely that he would have to wait long before a ship came in bound for some place to which he was not unwilling to go. The gale had forced them out of their course, and for twenty-four hours they were becalmed, so that it was not till the sixth day that, early in the morning, with but just enough wind to fill their sails, they sighted the volcano of Meira. The town was on Kanda. It was nine o'clock before they reached the entrance to the harbour, and the Sailing Directions had warned them that it was difficult. Meira was a tall conical hill covered with jungle almost to its summit, and a plume of dense smoke, like a huge umbrella pine, rose from its crater. The channel between the two islands was narrow and tidal streams were said to run through it with great force. In one place it was barely half a cable wide, and there were shoals in the centre with very little water over them. But Captain Nichols was a fine seaman and knew it. He liked an opportunity to show off. Looking astonishingly disreputable in loud, striped pyjamas, a battered topi on his head, and a week's growth of white beard, he took the *Fenton* in with style.

"Don't look so bad," he said, as the little town was discovered.

There were warehouses to the water's edge and native houses on poles with thatched roofs. Naked children were playing about in the clear water. A Chinese in a broad-brimmed hat was fishing from a dug-out. The harbour was far from crowded: there were only two junks, three or four large prahus, a motor-boat and a derelict schooner. Beyond the town was a hill surmounted by a flagstaff, and from it dangled limply a Dutch flag.

"I wonder if there's a hotel," murmured the doctor.

He and Fred Blake stood on each side of Captain Nichols at the helm.

"Sure to be. Used to be a grand place in the old days. Centre of the spice trade and all that. Nutmegs. Never been 'ere meself, but I been told there's marble palaces and I don't know what all."

There were two piers. One was neat and tidy; the other, of wood, was ramshackle and badly needed a coat of paint. It was shorter than the first.

"The long 'un belongs to the Netherlands Company, I guess," said the skipper. "Let's go to the other."

They reached the side. The mainsail was lowered with a clatter and they tied up.

"Well, Doc, you've arrived. Luggage ready and all that?"

"You're coming ashore, aren't you?"

"What about it, Fred?"

"Yes, come on. I'm sick of being aboard this boat. And we've got to get another dinghy, anyway."

"We'll be wantin' a new jib, too. I'll just go and doll meself up and then I'll join you."

The skipper went down into the cabin. His toilet did not take him long, for it consisted only in changing his pyjamas for a pair of khaki trousers, putting a khaki coat on his bare back and slipping his naked feet into old tennis shoes. They clambered by rickety steps on to the pier and walked along it. There was no one there. They reached the quay and after hesitating for a moment took what looked like the main street. It was empty and silent. They wandered down the middle of the roadway, abreast, and looked about them. It was pleasant to be able to stretch one's legs after those days on the lugger, and a relief to feel under one's feet the solid earth. The bungalows on either side of the road had very high roofs, thatched and pointed, and the roofs, jutting out, were supported by pillars, Doric and Corinthian, so as to form broad verandas. They had an air of ancient opulence, but their white-wash was stained and worn, and the little gardens in front of them were rank with tangled weeds. They came to shops and they all seemed to sell the same sort of things, cottons, sarongs and canned foods. There was no animation. Some of the shops had not even an attendant, as though no purchaser could possibly be expected. The few persons they passed, Malays or Chinese, walked quickly as though they were afraid to awaken the echo. Now and then a whiff of nutmeg assaulted the nostrils. Dr. Saunders stopped a Chinese and asked him where the hotel was. He told them to go straight on, and presently they came to it. They went in. There was no one about, but they sat down at a table on the veranda and thumped on it with their fists. A native woman in a sarong came and looked at them, but vanished when the doctor addressed her. Then appeared a half-caste, buttoning up his stengah-shifter, and Dr. Saunders asked if he could have a room. The man did not understand, and the doctor spoke to him in Chinese. The man answered in Dutch, but when the doctor shook his head, with a smile made signs that they were to wait and ran down the steps. They saw him cross the road.

"Gone to fetch someone, I expect," said the skipper. "Extra-ordinary thing they shouldn't speak English. They give me to understand the place was civilised."

The half-caste returned in a few minutes with a white man, who gave them a curious glance as his companion pointed them out to him, and then as he came up the steps politely raised his topi.

"Good-morning, gentlemen," he said. "Can I be of any service to you? Van Ryk cannot understand what you want."

He spoke English very correctly, but with a foreign accent. He was a young man, in the twenties, very tall, six foot three at least, and broad-shouldered, a powerful fellow, but clumsily built, so that though he gave you an impression of great strength, it was of an ungainly nature. His ducks were neat and clean. A fountain-pen protruded from the pocket of his closely-buttoned tunic.

"We've just come in on a sailing-boat," said the doctor, "and I want to know if I can have a room here till the next steamer comes in."

"Surely. The hotel isn't as full as all that."

He turned to the half-caste and fluently explained what the doctor wanted. After a brief conversation he returned to English.

"Yes, he can give you a nice room. Your board included, it'll come to eight gulden a day. The manager's away at Batavia, but van Ryk's looking after things, and he'll make you comfortable."

"What about a drink?" said the skipper. "Let's 'ave some beer."

"Won't you join us?" asked the doctor politely.

"Thank you very much."

The young man sat down and took off his topi. He had a broad, flat face and a flat nose, with high cheek-bones and rather small black eyes; his smooth skin was sallow, and there was no colour in his cheeks; his hair, cut very short, was coal-black. He was not at all good-looking, but his great ugly face bore an expression of such good-nature that you could not but be somewhat taken by him. His eyes were mild and kindly.

"Dutch?" asked the skipper.

"No, I'm a Dane. Erik Christessen. I represent a Danish company here."

"Been here long?"

"Four years."

"Good God!" cried Fred Blake.

Erik Christessen gave a little laugh, childlike in its simplicity, and his friendly eyes beamed with goodwill.

"It's a fine place. It's the most romantic spot in the East. They wanted to move me, but I begged them to let me stay on."

A boy brought them bottled beer, and the huge Dane before drinking raised his glass.

"Your very good health, gentlemen."

Dr. Saunders did not know why the stranger so very much attracted him. It was not only his cordiality, that was common enough in the East: there was something in his personality that pleased.

"Don't look as if there was much business 'ere," said Captain Nichols.

"The place is dead. We live on our memories. That is what gives the island its character. In the old days, you know, there was so much traffic that sometimes the harbour was full and vessels had to wait outside till the departure of a fleet gave them a chance to enter. I hope you'll stay here long enough to let me show you round. It's lovely. An unsuspected isle in far-off seas."

The doctor pricked up his ears. He recognised it as a quotation, but could not place it.

"What does that come from?"

"That? Oh, 'Pippa Passes'. Browning, you know."

"How does it happen that you've read that?"

"I read a lot. I have plenty of time, you see. I like English poetry best of all. Ah, Shakespeare." He looked at Fred with a soft, gracious glance, a smile on his great mouth, and began to recite:

> " '. . . of one whose hand,
> Like the base Indian, threw a pearl away
> Richer than all his tribe: of one whose subdued eyes,
> Albeit unused to the melting mood,
> Drop tears as fast as the Arabian trees
> Their medicinal gum.' "

It sounded odd in that foreign accent, somewhat gruff and guttural, but what was odder still was that there a young Danish trader should quote Shakespeare to the shifty scoundrel Captain Nichols and to the oafish lad Fred Blake. Dr. Saunders found the situation faintly humorous. The skipper gave him a wink that signified quite clearly that this was a queer fish, but Fred Blake flushed and looked shy. The Dane had no notion that he had done anything to excite surprise. He went on eagerly:

"The old Dutch merchants were so rich here in the great days of the spice trade, they didn't know what to do with their money. There was no cargo for the ships to bring out and so they used to bring marble and use it for their houses. If you're not in a hurry I'll show you mine. It used to belong to one of the perkeniers. And sometimes, in winter, they'd bring a cargo of nothing but ice. Funny, isn't it? That was the greatest luxury they could have. Just think of bringing ice all the way from Holland. It took six months, the journey. And they all had their carriages, and in the cool of the evening the smart thing was to drive along the shore and round and round the square. Someone ought to write about it. It was like a Dutch Arabian Nights Tale. Did you see the Portuguese fort as you came in? I'll take you there this afternoon. If there is anything I can do for you, you must let me know. I shall be very glad."

"I shall get my traps," said the doctor. "These gentlemen have very kindly given me a passage here. I don't want to put them out more than I can help."

Erik Christessen beamed amiably on the other two. "Ah, that is what I like in the East. Everyone is so nice. Nothing is too much trouble. You cannot imagine the kindness I've received at the hands of perfect strangers."

The four of them got up and the Dane told the half-caste manager that Dr. Saunders would be coming along in a little while with his luggage and his boy.

"You should have tiffin here. It is *reistafel* to-day, and they make it very well. I shall be here."

"You two fellows had better have tiffin with me," said the doctor.

"*Reistafel's* death to me," said Captain Nichols. "But I don't mind sittin' and watch you eat it."

Erik Christessen solemnly shook hands with the three of them.

"I'm so very glad to have met you. It's not often we get strangers on the island. And it's always a pleasure to me to meet English gentlemen."

He gave them a bow as they separated at the bottom of the steps.

"Intelligent chap, that," said Captain Nichols when they had walked a little. "Knew we was gentlemen at once."

Dr. Saunders gave him a glance. There was no trace of irony in his expression.

CHAPTER XVI

A COUPLE of hours later, the doctor having settled in, he and his guests off the *Fenton* were sitting on the veranda of the hotel drinking a glass of Schnapps before tiffin.

"The East ain't what it was," said the skipper, shaking his head. "Why, when I was a young chap, at Dutch 'otels there'd be bottles of Schnapps on the table, at tiffin and dinner, and you just 'elped yourself. Free of charge it was. And when you'd finished the bottle you told the boy to bring another."

"Must have come expensive."

"Well, you know, that's the funny thing, it didn't. You very seldom found a chap as took advantage of it. Human nature's like that. Treat a man proper and 'e'll respond wonderfully. I believe in 'uman nature, I always 'ave."

Erik Christessen came up the steps, took off his hat to them and was passing into the hotel.

"Come and have a drink with us," called Fred.

"With pleasure. I'll just go in and wash first."

He went in.

"Hulloa, what's this?" said the skipper, eyeing Fred slyly. "I thought you didn't like strangers?"

"It depends. Seems rather a good sort to me. He never asked us who we were or what we were doing here. Generally everyone's so curious."

"He has naturally good manners," said the doctor.

"What'll you have?" asked Fred when the Dane rejoined them.

"The same as you."

He dropped his ungainly bulk into a chair. They began to chat. He said nothing that was very clever or amusing, but there was a guilelessness in his conversation that made it pleasing. He filled you with confidence. He irradiated well-being. Dr. Saunders did not judge hastily, and he mistrusted his instincts, but this he could not miss and, reflecting upon it, he could ascribe it to nothing but an amazing and delightful sincerity. It was quite obvious that Fred Blake was much taken with the huge Dane. Dr. Saunders had never heard him talk so easily.

"Look here, you'd better know our names," he said after a few minutes. "Mine's Blake, Fred Blake, and the doctor's called Saunders, and this fellow is Captain Nichols."

Somewhat absurdly Erik Christessen got up and shook hands all round.

"I'm very pleased to make your acquaintance," he said. "I hope you're going to stay here a few days."

"Are you still sailing to-morrow?" asked the doctor.

"Nothing to stay for. We saw a dinghy this morning."

They went into the dining-room. It was cool and dim. Punkahs drawn by a small boy fitfully stirred the air. There was one long table, and at one end of it were sitting a Dutchman with a half-caste wife, a stout woman in loose pale draperies, and another Dutchman with a dark enough skin to suggest that he, too, had native blood in him. Erik Christessen exchanged polite greeting with them. They gave the strangers an incurious stare. *Reistafel* was served. They piled their plates with rice and curry, fried eggs, bananas and a dozen strange concoctions that boys kept bringing them. When everything was handed they were faced with a mountain of food. Captain Nichols looked at his with profound distaste.

"This'll be my death," he said solemnly.

"Don't eat it, then," said Fred.

"I must keep up me strength. Where would you be now if I 'adn't 'ad me strength when we struck that bad weather? It's not for my sake I'm eatin' it. It's for yours. I don't take a job unless I know I can do it, and not me worst enemy can say I spare meself."

Gradually the piles of food diminished, and Captain Nichols with stubborn determination cleaned up his plate.

"God, we haven't had a meal like this for weeks," said Fred.

He ate voraciously, with a boy's appetite, and enjoyed his food. They drank beer.

"If I don't suffer for this it'll be a miracle," said the skipper.

They had their coffee on the veranda.

"You'd better have a sleep now," said Erik, "and then when it's cooler I'll come round and show you the sights. Pity you're not staying a bit longer. It's a beautiful walk up the volcano. You can see for miles. The sea and all the islands."

"I don't see why we shouldn't stay till the doctor sails," said Fred.

"Suits me," said the skipper. "After all the 'ardships of life on the ocean wave this is a bit of all right. I'm not sure if a drop of brandy wouldn't settle that *reistafel* now I come to think of it."

"Trading, I suppose?" asked the Dane.

"We're prospectin' for shell," said the skipper. "Got to find some new beds. There's a fortune for anyone who's lucky."

"D'you have any papers here?" asked Blake. "In English, I mean."

"Not London papers. But Frith gets a paper from Australia."

"Frith. Who's Frith?"

"He's an Englishman. He gets a bundle of *Sydney Bulletins* every mail."

Fred went strangely pale, but what the emotion was that blanched his cheek, who could tell?

"D'you think there's a chance of my having a squint at them?"

"Of course. I'll borrow them or I'll take you up there."

"How old's the latest?"

"It oughtn't to be very old. A mail came in four days ago."

CHAPTER XVII

LATER, when the heat of the day was passed and his own work finished, Erik fetched them. Dr. Saunders was sitting alone with Fred, for the skipper, suffering from a violent attack of indigestion, had announced that he didn't want to see no bloody sights and had returned to the lugger. They sauntered through the town. There were more people about than in the morning. Now and then Erik took off his hat to a sunburned Dutchman who walked with a stout and listless wife. There were few Chinese, for they do not settle where no trade is, but a number of Arabs, some in smart tarbouches and neat suits of duck, others in white caps and sarongs; they were dark-skinned, with large shining eyes, and they had the Semitic look of the merchants of Tyre and Sidon. There were Malays, Papuans and half-castes. It was strangely silent. The air was heavy with fatigue. The grand houses of the old perkeniers, in which dwelt now the riff-raff of the East from Baghdad to New Hebrides, had the shamefaced look of respectable citizens who could not pay their rates. They came to a long white wall, all crumbling away, and this once had been a Portuguese monastery; and then to a ruined fort of great grey stones overrun with a wild jungle of trees and flowering shrubs. There was a wide space in front of it, facing the sea, where grew huge old trees, planted it was said by the Portuguese, casuarinas, kanaris and wild figs; and here, after the heat of the day, they had been used to ramble.

Panting a little, for he was somewhat inclined to corpulence, the doctor with his companions ascended the hill on which stood the stronghold, grey and bare, which had commanded the harbour. It was surrounded by a deep moat and the only doorway was high from the ground, so that they had to climb a ladder to enter. Inside the great square walls was the keep, and in this were large and well-proportioned chambers, with windows and doorways of a style that suggested the later Renaissance. Here officers and garrison dwelt. From the upper towers was a spacious and magnificent view.

"It's like Tristan's castle," said the doctor.

The day was softly dying, and the sea was as wine-dark as the sea on which Odysseus sailed. The islands, encircled by the smooth and shining water, had the rich green of a vestment in the treasury of a Spanish cathedral. It was a colour so bizarre and sophisticated that it seemed to belong to art rather than to nature.

"Like a green thought in a green shade," murmured the young Dane.

"They're all right from a distance," said Fred, "those islands, but when you go there—my God! At first I used to want to land. They looked fine from the sea. I thought I'd like to live on one of them for the rest of my life, away from everyone, if you know what I mean, just fishing and keeping my own chickens and pigs. Nichols laughed his head off, said they were lousy, but I insisted on seeing for myself, oh, half a dozen we must have gone to before I gave it up as a bad job. When you got to one of them and went on shore, it all went—I mean, it was just trees and crabs and mosquitoes. It slipped through your fingers, so to speak."

Erik looked at him with his soft beaming eyes, and his smile was sweet with goodwill.

"I know what you mean," he said. "It's always a risk to put things to the test of experience. It's like the locked room in Bluebeard's castle. One's all right so long as one keeps clear of that. You have to be prepared for a shock if you turn the key and walk in."

Dr. Saunders listened to the conversation of the two young men. He was perhaps a cynic and his withers were unwrung at many of the misfortunes that affect men, but he had a peculiar feeling for youth, perhaps because it promised so much and lasted too short a time, and it seemed to him that there was in the bitterness it experiences when reality breaks upon its illusions something more pathetic than in many graver ills. Notwithstanding the clumsy expression he understood what Fred meant and gave the boy's emotion the tribute of a sympathetic smile. As he sat there, in the mellow light, in his singlet and khaki trousers, with his hat off so that you saw his dark curling hair, he was astonishingly handsome. There was something appealing in his beauty so that Dr. Saunders, who had thought him a rather dull young man, felt on a sudden kindly disposed to him. Perhaps it was his good looks that deceived him, perhaps it was due to the companionship of Erik Christessen, but at that moment he felt that there was in the lad a strain of something he had never suspected. Perhaps there was there the dim groping beginning of a soul. The thought faintly amused Dr. Saunders. It gave him just that little shock of surprise that one feels when what looked like a twig on a branch suddenly opens wings and flies away.

"I come up here almost every evening to watch the sunset," said Erik. "To me all the East is here. Not the East of story, the East of palaces and sculptured temples and conquerors with hordes of warriors, but the East of the beginning of the world, the East of the garden of Eden, when men were very few, simple and humble and ignorant, and the world was just waiting, like an empty garden for its absent owner."

He had a way, that hulking, plain young man, of talking in a lyrical manner that would have been disconcerting if you had not had the feeling that it was as natural to him as to talk of pearl shell and copra and *bêche de mer*. His grandiloquence was a trifle absurd, but if it made you smile it was with kindliness. He was strangely ingenuous. The prospect was so lovely, the place they sat in, that gaunt, ruined Portuguese fort, so romantic, that there high strains seemed not unfitting. Erik passed his great heavy hand gently over one of the huge blocks of stone.

"These stones and what they've seen! They have one great advantage over those islands of yours, you can never discover their secret. You can only guess. And you can guess so little. No one knows anything here. Next time I go back to Europe I shall go to Lisbon and see what I can find out of the fellows who lived here."

Of course romance was there, but it was vague, and in your ignorance you could only form pictures as blurred as ill-developed snapshots. It was on those towers that the Portuguese captains had stood, scanning the sea for the ship from Lisbon that brought them blessed news of home, or watched with apprehension the Dutch vessels that came to attack them. In your mind's eye you saw those gallant, swarthy men, in breastplate and hauberk, who carried their adventurous lives in their hands, but they were lifeless shadows, and they owed their substance only to your fancy. There were still the ruins of the little chapel where every day the miracle of transubstantiation took place and whence the priest in his vestments came, during a siege, to administer supreme unction to the soldiers who lay dying on the ramparts. The imagination was tremulous with an indistinct impression of hazard and cruelty and dauntless courage and self-sacrifice.

"Aren't you ever home-sick?" asked Fred presently.

"No. I often think of the little village from which I come, with black-and-white cows in the green pastures, and of Copenhagen. The houses in Copenhagen with their flat windows are just like smooth-faced women with large, short-sighted eyes, and the palaces and the churches look as if they had come out of a fairy tale. But I see it all like a scene in a play, it is very clear, and amusing, but I don't know that I want to step on to the stage. I am quite willing to sit in my dark seat in the gallery and watch the spectacle from far away."

"After all, one's only got one life."

"That is what I think, too. But life is what you make it. I might have been a clerk in an office, and then it would have been more difficult, but here, with the sea and the jungle, and all the memories of the past crowding in upon you, and these people, the Malays, the Papuans, the Chinese, the stolid Dutch, with my books and as much leisure as if I were a millionaire—good heavens, what can the imagination want more?"

Fred Blake looked at him for a moment, and the effort of unaccustomed reflection made him frown. When he understood what the Dane meant, his surprise was evident in his voice.

"But that's all make-believe."

"It's the only reality there is," smiled Erik.

"I don't know what you mean by that. Reality's doing things, not dreaming about them. One's only young once, one must have one's fling, and everyone wants to get on. One wants to make money and have a good position and all that sort of thing."

"Oh no. What does one do things for? Of course one has to work a certain amount to earn one's living, but after that, only to satisfy the imagination. Tell me, when you saw those islands from the sea and your heart was filled with delight, and when you landed on them and found them a dreary jungle, which was the real island? Which gave you most, and which are you going to treasure in your memory?"

Fred smiled into Erik's eager, gentle eyes.

"That's bloody rot, old boy. It's no good thinking the earth of something and when you come down to brass tacks finding out to your cost that it's a wash-out. One doesn't get much forrader by not facing facts. Where d'you expect to get to if you just take things at their face value?"

"The Kingdom of Heaven," smiled Erik.

self-sown in a stone wall that pathetically sought the sun, which excited sympathy and interest. But Fred had not heard a note. He sat, unconscious of his surroundings, staring out of the window. The short twilight of the tropics had darkened into night, and in the blue sky one or two stars twinkled already, but he did not look at them, he seemed to look into some black abyss of thought. The light of the lamp under which he sat threw strange, sharp shadows on his face so that it was like a mask that you hardly recognised. But his body was relaxed, as though a tension had been suddenly withdrawn, and the muscles under his brown skin were loose. He felt the doctor's cool stare and looking at him forced his lips to a smile, but it was a painful little smile, oddly appealing and pathetic. The beer by his side was untouched.

"Anything in the paper?" asked the doctor.

Fred suddenly flushed scarlet.

"No, nothing. They've had the elections."

"Where?"

"New South Wales. Labour's got in."

"Are you Labour?"

Fred hesitated a little, and into his eyes came that watchful look that the doctor had seen in them once or twice before.

"I'm not interested in politics," he said. "I don't know anything about them."

"You might let me have a look at the paper."

Fred took a copy from the bundle and handed it to the doctor. But he did not take it.

"Is that the latest?"

"No, this is the latest," answered Fred, putting his hand on the one he had just been reading.

"If you've done with it I'll read that. I don't know that I'm very keen on news when it's too stale."

Fred hesitated for a second. The doctor held him with smiling but determined eyes. Obviously Fred could think of no plausible way to refuse the very natural request. He gave him the paper, and Dr. Saunders drew forward to the light to read it. Fred did not take up any of the other copies of the *Bulletin*, though certainly there were some he could not have seen, but sat pretending to look at the table, and the doctor was conscious that he was closely watching him from the sides of his eyes. There was no doubt that Fred had read in the paper he now held in his hand something that deeply concerned him. Dr. Saunders turned over the pages. There was much election news. There was a London letter and a certain amount of cabled information from Europe and America. There was a good deal of local intelligence. He turned to the police news. The election had given rise to some disorder, and the courts had dealt with it. There had been a burglary at Newcastle. Some man had received a sentence for an insurance fraud. A stabbing affray between two Tonga Islanders was reported. Captain Nichols suspected that it was on account of murder that this disappearance of Fred had been arranged, and there were two columns about a murder that had taken place at a farmstead in the Blue Mountains, but this arose out of a quarrel between two brothers and the murderer, who had given himself up to the police, pleaded self-defence. Besides, it had taken place after Fred and Captain Nichols had sailed from Sydney. There was the report of an inquest on a woman who had hanged herself. For a moment Dr. Saunders wondered whether there was anything in this. The *Bulletin* is a weekly, of literary tendencies, and it dealt with the matter, not summarily, but in a fashion natural to a paper catering to a public to whom the facts in detail had been made known by the dailies. It appeared that the woman had been under suspicion of the murder of her husband some weeks before, but the evidence against her was too slight for the authorities to take action. She had been repeatedly examined by the police, and this, together with the gossip of neighbours and the scandal, had preyed on her mind. The jury found that she had committed suicide while temporarily insane. The coroner, commenting on the case, remarked that with her death vanished the last chance the police had of solving the mystery of the murder of Patrick Hudson. The doctor read the account again, reflectively; it was odd, but it was too brief to tell him much. The woman was forty-two. It seemed unlikely that a boy of Fred's age could have had anything to do with her. And, after all, Captain Nichols had nothing to go on; it was pure guesswork; the boy was an accountant; he might just as well have taken money that did not belong to him or, pressed by financial difficulties, forged a cheque. If he was connected with some important person politically, that might have been enough to make it advisable to spirit him away for a period. Dr. Saunders, putting the paper down, met Fred's eyes fixed upon him. He gave him a reassuring smile. His curiosity was disinterested, and he was not inclined to put himself to any trouble to gratify it.

"Going to dine at the hotel, Fred?" he asked.

"I'd ask you both to stay and have pot-luck with me here," said the Dane, "but I'm going up to have supper with Frith."

"Well, we'll be toddling."

The doctor and Fred walked a few steps in silence along the dark street.

"I don't want any dinner," the boy said suddenly. "I can't face Nichols to-night. I'm going for a tramp."

Before Dr. Saunders could answer he had turned on his heel and rapidly walked away. The doctor shrugged his shoulders and continued on his unhurried way.

CHAPTER XVIII

HE was drinking a gin pahit before dinner, on the veranda of the hotel, when Captain Nichols strolled up. He had washed and shaved, he was wearing a khaki stengah-shifter, with his topi set at a rakish angle, so that he looked quite spruce. He reminded you of a gentlemanly pirate.

"Feelin' better to-night," he remarked as he sat down, "and quite peckish, to tell you the truth. I don't believe the wing of a chicken could do me any 'arm. Where's Fred?"

"I don't know. He's off somewhere."

"Lookin' for a girl? I don't blame him. Though I don't know what he thinks he's goin' to find in a place like this. Risky, you know."

The doctor ordered him a drink.

"I was a rare one for the girls when I was a young fellow. Got a way with me, you know. The mistake I made was to marry. If I 'ad my time over again . . . I never tell you about my old woman, Doc."

"Enough," said the doctor.

"That's impossible. I couldn't do that, not if I was to tell you about 'er till to-morrow morning. If ever there was a devil in 'uman form, it's my old woman. I ask you, is it fair to treat a man like that? She's directly responsible for my indigestion; I'm just as sure of that as I am that I'm sittin' and talkin' to you. It's 'umiliatin', that's what it is. I'm surprised I 'aven't killed her. I would 'ave, too, only I know that if I was to start anything, and she said to me: 'You put that knife down, Captain,' I'd put it down. Now I ask you, is it natural? And then she'd just start on me. And if I was to edge towards the door, she'd say: 'No, you don't, you stay 'ere till I've said all I've got to say to you, and when I've finished with you, I'll tell you.' "

They dined together, and the doctor lent a sympathetic ear to the recital of Captain Nichols's domestic infelicity. Then they sat again on the veranda, smoking Dutch cigars, and drank Schnapps with their coffee. Alcohol mellowed the skipper, and he grew reminiscent. He told the doctor stories of his early days on the coast of New Guinea and about the islands. He was a racy talker, with an ironic vein of humour, and it was diverting to listen to him, since false shame never tempted him to depict himself in a flattering light. It never occurred to him that anyone would hesitate to diddle another if he had the chance, and he felt just the same satisfaction in the success of a dirty trick as a chess-player might in winning a game by a bold and ingenious move. He was a scamp, but a courageous one. Dr. Saunders found a peculiar savour in his conversation when he remembered the splendid self-confidence with which he had weathered the storm. It had been impossible then not to be impressed by his readiness, resource and coolness.

Presently the doctor found occasion to slip in a question that had been for some time on the tip of his tongue.

"Did you ever know a fellow called Patrick Hudson?"

"Patrick 'udson?"

"He was a resident magistrate in New Guinea at one time. He's been dead a good many years now."

"That's a funny coincidence. No, I didn't know 'im. There was a fellow called Patrick 'udson in Sydney. Come to a sticky end."

"Oh?"

"Yes. Not so very long before we sailed. The papers was full of it."

"He might have been some relation of the man I mean."

"He was what they call a rough diamond. Been a railway man, they said, and worked 'is way up. Took up politics and all that. He was member for some place. Labour, of course."

"What happened to him?"

"Well, 'e was shot. With his own gun, if I remember right."

"Suicide?"

"No, they said 'e couldn't 'a' done it 'imself. I don't know any more than you do what 'appened, on account of my leavin' Sydney. It made quite a sensation."

"Was he married?"

"Yes. A lot of people thought 'is old woman done it. They couldn't prove anythin'. She'd been to the pictures, and when she come 'ome she found 'im lyin' there. There'd been a fight. The furniture was all over the shop. I never thought it was 'is old woman meself. My experience is they don't let you off so easy. They want to keep you alive as long as they can. They ain't going to lose their fun by puttin' you out of your misery."

"Still, a lot of women have murdered their husbands," objected the doctor.

"Pure accident. We all know that accidents will 'appen in the best regulated families. Sometimes they get careless and go too far, and then the poor bastard dies. But they don't mean it. Not them."

CHAPTER XIX

DR. SAUNDERS was fortunate in this, that, notwithstanding the several deplorable habits he had, and in some parts of the world they would certainly have been accounted vices (*vérité au delà des Alpes, erreur ici*), he awoke in the morning with a clean tongue and in a happy frame of mind. He seldom stretched himself in bed, drinking his cup of fragrant China tea and smoking the first delicious cigarette, without looking forward with pleasure to the coming day. Breakfast in the little hotels in the islands of the Dutch East Indies is served at a very early hour. It never varies. Papaia, *œufs sur le plat*, cold meat, and Edam cheese. However punctually you appear, the eggs are cold; they stare at you, two large round yellow eyes on a thin surface of white, and they look as if they had been scooped out of the face of an obscene monster of the deep. The coffee is an essence to which you add Nestlé's Swiss Milk brought to a proper consistency with hot water. The toast is dry, sodden and burnt. Such was the breakfast served in the dining-room of the hotel at Kanda and hurriedly eaten by silent Dutchmen, who had their offices to go to.

But Dr. Saunders got up late next morning, and Ah Kay brought him his breakfast out on the veranda. He enjoyed his papaia, he enjoyed his eggs, that moment out of the frying-pan, and he enjoyed his scented tea. He reflected that to live was a very enjoyable affair. He wanted nothing. He envied no man. He had no regrets. The morning was still fresh and in the clean, pale light the outline of things was sharp-edged. A huge banana just below the terrace with a haughty and complacent disdain flaunted its splendid foliage to the sun's fierce heat. Dr. Saunders was tempted to philosophise: he said that the value of life lay not in its moments of excitement but in its placid intervals when, untroubled, the human spirit in tranquillity undisturbed by the recollection of emotion could survey its being with the same detachment as the Buddha contemplated his navel. Plenty of pepper on the eggs, plenty of salt and a little Worcester sauce, and then when they were finished a piece of bread to soak up the buttery remains, and that was the best mouthful of all. He was intent on this when Fred Blake and Erik Christessen came swinging down the street. They leaped up the steps and, throwing themselves on chairs at the doctor's table, shouted for the boy. They had started for their walk up the volcano before dawn, and were now ravenous. The boy hurried out with papaia and a dish of cold meats, and they finished this before he brought them eggs. They were in great spirits. The enthusiasm of youth had ripened the acquaintance made the day before into friendship, and they called one another Fred and Erik. It was a stiff climb and the violent exercise had excited them. They talked nonsense and laughed at nothing. They were like a couple of boys. The doctor had never seen Fred so gay. He was evidently much taken with Erik, and the companionship of someone only a little older than himself had loosened his constraint so that he seemed to flower with a new adolescence. He looked so young that you could hardly believe he was a grown man, and his deep, ringing voice sounded almost comic.

"D'you know, he's as strong as an ox, this blighter," said he, with a glance of admiration at Erik. "We had one rather nasty little bit of climbing to do, a branch broke and I slipped. I might have taken a nasty toss, broken my leg or something. Erik caught hold of me with one arm, damned if I know how he did it, and lifted me right up and set me on my feet again. And I weigh a good eleven stone."

"I've always been strong," smiled Erik.

"Put your hand up."

Fred placed his elbow on the table and Erik did the same. They put palm to palm and Fred tried to force Erik's arm down. He put all his strength into the effort. He could not move it. Then with a little smile the Dane pressed back and gradually Fred's arm was forced to the table.

"I'm like a kid beside you," he laughed. "Gosh, a fellow wouldn't stand much chance if you hit him. Ever been in a fight?"

"No. Why should I?"

He finished eating and lit a cheroot.

"I must go to my office," he said. "Frith says, will you all go up there this afternoon? He wants us to have supper with him."

"Suits me all right," said the doctor.

"And the captain, too. I'll come for you about four."

Fred watched him go.

"Perfect loon," he said, turning to the doctor, with a smile. "My belief is he isn't all there."

"Oh, why?"

"The way he talked."

"What did he say?"

"Oh, I don't know. Crazy. He asked me about Shakespeare. A fat lot I know about Shakespeare. I told him I'd read *Henry V* when I was at school (we took it one term), and he began spouting one of the speeches. Then he started talking about *Hamlet* and *Othello* and heaven knows what. He knows yards of them by heart. I can't tell you all he said about them. I never heard anyone talk in that way before. And the funny thing was that, although it was all a lot of bunk, you didn't want to tell him to shut up."

A smile lingered in his candid blue eyes, but his face was serious.

"You've never been in Sydney, have you?"

"No."

"We have quite a literary and artistic set there. Not much in my line, but sometimes I couldn't help myself. Women chiefly, you know. They'd talk a lot of tosh about books and then, before you knew where you were, they'd be wanting to pop into bed with you."

"The Philistine dots his i's and crosses his t's with a definiteness that is unbecoming," reflected the doctor, "and when he sees a nail he hits it on the head."

"You get rather leery of them. But, I don't know how to explain it exactly, when Erik talked about all that it was different. He wasn't showing off and he wasn't trying to impress me. He just talked like that because he couldn't help it. He didn't mind if I was bored or not. He was so keen on it all it never struck him, perhaps, I didn't care a damn about it. I didn't understand the half of what he said, you know, but somehow, I don't know, it was as good as a play, if you understand what I mean."

Fred threw out his observations like stones that you dig up in a garden to prepare the ground for planting and cast in a heap one after the other. In his perplexity he vigorously scratched his head. Dr. Saunders watched him with cool, shrewd eyes. The boy was tongue-tied, and it was diverting in his confused remarks to discover the emotion he was trying to put in words. Critics divide writers into those who have something to say and do not know how to say it, and those who know how to say it and have nothing to say. Often it is the same with men, with Anglo-Saxons at all events, to whom words come difficultly. When a man is fluent it is sometimes because he has said a thing so often that it has lost its meaning, and his speech is most significant when he has to fashion it laboriously from thoughts to which he can see no clear outline.

Fred gave the doctor a puckish glance that made him look like a mischievous boy.

"D'you know, he's lending me *Othello*. I don't exactly know why, but I said I wouldn't mind reading it. You've read it, I suppose."

"Thirty years ago."

"Of course I may be mistaken, but when Erik was spouting great chunks of it, it sounded quite exciting. I don't know what it is, but when you're with a chap like that everything seems different. I dare say he's crazy, but I wish there were a few more like him."

"You've taken quite a fancy to him, haven't you?"

"Well, you can hardly help it," answered Fred, with a sudden attack of shyness. "You'd be a perfect damn fool not to see he's as straight as a die. I'd trust him with every penny I had in the world. He couldn't do anyone down. And you know, the funny thing is, though he's such a big hulking fellow and as strong as an ox, you have a sort of feeling you want to take care of him. I know it sounds silly, but you can't help feeling he oughtn't to be allowed about by himself; someone ought to be there to see that he doesn't get into trouble."

The doctor, with his cynical detachment, translated in his own mind the young Australian's awkward phrases into sense. He was surprised and a trifle touched by the emotion that with this shy clumsiness fought for expression. For what emerged from those hackneyed words was the shock of admiration the lad had received when he was confronted with the realisation of something quite startling. Through the oddness of the huge, ungainly Dane, lighting up his complete sincerity, giving body to his idealism and charm to his extravagant enthusiasm, shone, with a warm, all-embracing glow, pure goodness. Fred Blake's youth made him mystically able to see it, and he was amazed by it and baffled. It touched him and made him feel very shy. It shook his self-confidence and humbled him. At that moment the rather ordinary, handsome boy was conscious of something he had never imagined, spiritual beauty.

"Who would have thought it possible?" reflected the doctor.

His own feelings towards Erik Christessen, naturally enough, were more detached. He was interested in him because he was a little unusual. It was amusing, to begin with, in an island of the Malay Archipelago, to come across a trader who knew Shakespeare well enough to say long passages by heart. The doctor could not but look on it as a somewhat tiresome accomplishment. He wondered idly if Erik was a good business man. He was not very fond of idealists. It was difficult for them in this workaday world to reconcile their professions with the exigencies of life, and it was disconcerting how often they managed to combine exalted notions with a keen eye to the main chance. The doctor had often found here cause for amusement. They were apt to look down upon those who were occupied with practical matters but not averse from profiting by their industry. Like the lilies of the field they neither toiled nor spun, but took it as a right that others should perform for them these menial offices.

"Who is this fellow Frith that we're going up to this afternoon?" asked the doctor.

"He's got a plantation. He grows nutmeg and cloves. He's a widower. He lives there with his daughter."

CHAPTER XX

It was about three miles to Frith's house, and they drove out in an old Ford. On each side of the road grew densely huge trees, and there was a heavy undergrowth of ferns and creepers. The jungle began at the outskirts of the town. Here and there were miserable huts. Ragged Malays lay about the verandas and listless children played among the pigs under the piles. It was humid and sultry. The estate had once belonged to a perkenier, and it had a stucco gateway, massive but crumbling, of pleasing design. Over the archway on a tablet was the old burgher's name and the date of erection. They turned down an earth road and bumped along over ruts, hillocks and holes till they came to the bungalow. It was a large, square building not on piles, but on a foundation of masonry, covered with an atap roof and surrounded by a neglected garden. They drove up, the Malay driver sounding his horn with energy, and a man came out of the house and waved to them. It was Frith. He waited for them at the top of the steps that led down from the veranda, and as they came up and Erik mentioned their names, shook hands with them one by one.

"Delighted to see you. I haven't seen any Britishers for a year. Come in and have a drink."

He was quite a big man, but fat, with grey hair and a small grey moustache. He was growing bald and his forehead was imposing. His red face, shining with sweat, was unlined and round, so that at the first glance he looked almost boyish. He had a long yellow tooth in the middle of his mouth, which hung loosely, giving you the impression that with a sharp pull it would come out. He wore khaki shorts and a tennis shirt open at the neck. He walked with a pronounced limp. He led them into a very large room, which served at once as parlour and dining-room; the walls were adorned with Malay weapons, antlers of deer and horns of sladang. On the floor were tiger skins that looked a trifle mouldy and moth-eaten.

When they entered a tiny little old man got up from a chair and without taking a step towards them stood and looked at them. He was wrinkled, battered and bowed. He seemed very old.

"This is Swan," said Frith, with a casual nod of his head. "He's by way of being my father-in-law."

The little old man had very pale blue eyes with red-rimmed, hairless lids, but they were full of cunning, and his glance was darting and mischievous like a monkey's. He shook hands with the three strangers without speaking and then, opening a toothless mouth, addressed Erik in a language the others did not understand.

"Mr. Swan is a Swede," said Erik in explanation.

The old man eyed them one after the other, and in his gaze was a certain suspicion and at the same time, hardly concealed, something of mockery.

"I came out fifty years ago. I was mate of a sailing vessel. I never been back. Maybe I go next year."

"I'm a seafarin' man meself, sir," said Captain Nichols.

But Mr. Swan was not in the least interested in him.

"I been pretty well most things in my day," he went on. "I been captain of a schooner in the slave trade."

"Blackbirding," interrupted Captain Nichols. "There was a nice little bit of money to be picked up that way in the old days."

"I been a blacksmith. I been a trader. I been a planter. I don't know what I haven't been. They tried to kill me over and over again. I got a hernia on my chest, I have. That come from a wound I got in a scrap with the natives in the Solomons. Left me for dead, they did. I've had a lot of money in my time. Haven't I, George?"

"So I've always heard."

"Ruined by the great hurricane, I was. Destroyed my store. Lost everything. I didn't care. Got nothing left now but this plantation. Never mind, it gives us enough to live on and that's all that matters. I've had four wives and more children than you can count."

He talked in a high cracked voice with a strong Swedish accent, so that you had to listen intently to understand what he said. He spoke very quickly, almost as though he were reciting a lesson, and he finished with a little cackle of senile laughter. It seemed to say that he had been through everything and it was all stuff and nonsense. He surveyed human kind and its activities from a great distance, but from no Olympian height, from behind a tree, slyly, and hopping from one foot to another with amusement.

A Malay brought in a bottle of whisky and a syphon, and Frith poured out the drinks.

"A drop of Scotch for you, Swan?" he suggested to the old man.

"Why do you ask me that, George?" he quavered. "You know very well I can't abide it. Give me some rum and water. Scotch has been the ruin of the Pacific. When I first come from Sweden nobody drunk Scotch. Rum. If they'd stuck to rum and stuck to sail, things wouldn't be what they are now, not by a long way."

"We ran into some pretty rough weather on the way 'ere," Captain Nichols remarked, by way of making conversation with a fellow seaman.

"Rough weather? You don't have rough weather nowadays.

You should have seen the weather you had when I was a boy. I remember on one of the schooners I had, I was taking a parcel of labour to Samoa, from the New Hebrides, and we got caught in a hurricane. I told them savages to pop over the side pretty damn quick, and I put out to sea, and for three days I never closed my eyes. Lost our sails, lost our mainmast, lost our boats. Rough weather! Don't talk to me about rough weather, young fellow."

"No offence meant," said Captain Nichols, with a grin that showed his broken, decayed little teeth.

"And no offence taken," cackled old Swan. "Give him a tot of rum, George. If he's a sailor-man he don't want that stinking whisky of yours."

Presently Erik suggested that the strangers would like to walk round the plantation.

"They've never seen a nutmeg estate."

"Take 'em over, George. Twenty-seven acres. Best land on the island," said the old man. "Bought it thirty years ago for a parcel of pearls."

They got up, leaving him, like a little strange bald bird, hunched up over his rum and water, and walked out into the garden. It ended casually and the plantation began. In the cool of the evening the air was limpid. The kanari trees, in the shade of which grew the portly and profitable nutmeg trees, were enormously tall. They towered like the columns of a mosque in the Arabian Nights. Underfoot was no tangle of undergrowth but a carpet of decaying leaves. You heard the boom of great pigeons and saw them flying about with a heavy whirr of wings. Little green parrots in flocks flitted swiftly over the nutmeg trees, screeching, and they were like living jewels darting through the softly sparkling air. Dr. Saunders had a sense of extreme well-being. He felt like a disembodied spirit and his imagination was pleasantly, but not exhaustingly, occupied with image after image. He walked with Frith and the skipper. Frith was explaining the details of the nutmeg trade. He did not listen. There was an idle sensuousness in the air that was almost material, so that it reminded you of the feel of a soft, rich fabric. Erik and Fred were walking a step behind. The declining sun had found a way under the branches of the lofty kanaris and shone on the foliage of the nutmeg trees so that their dense, opulent green glistened like burnished copper.

They strolled along a winding path, made by the accident of people having long followed it, and all at once saw a girl coming towards them. She was walking with eyes cast down, as though absorbed in thought, and it was not till she heard voices that she looked up. She stopped.

"There is my daughter," said Frith.

You might have fancied she had stopped in a momentary embarrassment at the sight of strangers; but she did not move on, she stayed still, watching with a singular calm the men who advanced towards her; and then you received an impression, not exactly of self-assurance, but of tranquil unconcern. She wore nothing but a sarong of Javanese batik, with a little white pattern on a brown ground; it was attached tightly just over her breasts and came down to her knees. She was barefoot. Beside the little smile that hovered on her lips, the only sign she gave that she noticed the approach of strangers was a little shake of the head, almost involuntary, to loosen her hair and an instinctive gesture of the hand through it, for it was long and hung down her back. It spread in a cloud over her neck and shoulders, very thick, and of a fairness so ashy pale that, but for its radiance, it would have looked white. She waited with composure. The sarong tightly wrapped round her concealed nothing of her form; she was very slim, with the narrow hips of a boy, long-legged, and at first sight tall. She was burned by the sun to a rich honey colour. The doctor was not as a rule captivated by feminine beauty; he could not but think the manner in which a woman's frame was made for obvious physiological purposes much detracted from its æsthetic appeal. Just as a table should be solid, of a convenient height and roomy, so a woman should be large-breasted and broad in the beam; but in both cases beauty could only be an adjunct to utility. You might say that a table which was solid, roomy and of a convenient height was beautiful, but the doctor preferred to say that it was solid, roomy and of a convenient height. The girl standing there in an attitude of indolent beauty reminded him of some statue he had seen in a museum of a goddess attaching her peplum; he could not remember it very exactly. Greco-Roman, he thought. She had the same ambiguous slenderness as the little Chinese girls in the flower-boats at Canton, in whose company in his younger days he had on occasion passed moments of somewhat detached amusement. She had the same flower-like grace, and her fairness in that tropic scene gave the exotic sensation that made them so charming. She recalled to his mind the pale, profuse, delicate flowers of the plumbago.

"These are Christessen's friends," said her father as they came up to her.

She did not hold out her hand, but slightly and graciously inclined her head as first the doctor and then Captain Nichols were introduced to her. She gave them both a cool survey in which was enquiry and then swift appraisement. Dr. Saunders noticed that her brown hands were long and slender. Her eyes were blue. Her features were fine and very regular. She was an extremely pretty young woman.

"I've just been having a bathe in the pool," she said.

Her glance travelled to Erik, and she gave him a very sweet and friendly smile.

"This is Fred Blake," he said.

She turned her head a little to look at him, and for an appreciable time her eyes rested on him. The smile died away on her lips.

"Pleased to meet you," said Fred, holding out his hand.

She continued to look at him, not with pertness or brazenly, but as though she were a little surprised. You might have thought she had seen him before and was trying to remember where. But the incident lasted no more than a minute, and no one would have been conscious of a pause before she took the proffered hand.

"I was just going back to the house to dress," she said.

"I'll come with you," said Erik.

Now that he stood beside her you saw that she was not really very tall; it was only her straightness of limb, her slenderness and her carriage, that gave the impression of more than common height.

They sauntered back towards the house.

"Who is that boy?" she asked.

"I don't know," answered Erik. "He's in partnership with the thin, grey one. They're looking for pearl-shell. They're trying to find some new beds."

"He's good-looking."

"I thought you'd like him. He's got a nice nature."

The others continued their tour of the estate.

CHAPTER XXI

WHEN they came in they found Erik sitting alone with Swan. The old man was telling an interminable story, in an odd mixture of Swedish and English, of some adventure he had had in New Guinea.

"Where's Louise?" asked Frith.

"I've been helping her to lay the table. She's been doing something in the kitchen and now she's gone to change."

They sat down and had another drink. They talked somewhat desultorily, as people do when they don't know one another. Old Swan was tired, and when the strangers appeared lapsed into silence, but he watched them, with his sharp, rheumy eyes, as though they filled him with suspicion. Captain Nichols told Frith that he was a martyr to dyspepsia.

"I've never known what it is to have a pain in my tummy," said Frith. "Rheumatism's my trouble."

"I've known men as was martyrs to it. A friend of mine at Brisbane, one of the best pilots in the business, was just crippled by it. Had to go about on crutches."

"One has to have something," said Frith.

"You can't 'ave anythin' worse than dyspepsia, you take my word for it. I'd be a rich man now if it 'adn't been for my dyspepsia."

"Money's not everything," said Frith.

"I'm not sayin' it is. I'm sayin' I'd 'ave been a rich man to-day if it 'adn't been for my dyspepsia."

"Money's never meant anything very much to me. So long as I have a roof over my head and three meals a day I'm content. Leisure's the important thing."

Dr. Saunders listened to the conversation. He could not quite place Frith. He spoke like an educated man. Though fat and gross, shabbily dressed and in want of a shave, he gave the impression, scarcely of distinction, but of being accustomed to the society of decent people. He certainly did not belong to the same class as old Swan and Captain Nichols. His manners were easy. He had welcomed them with courtesy and treated them not with the fussy politeness an ill-bred person thinks it necessary to use towards strange guests, but naturally, as though he knew the ways of the world. Dr. Saunders supposed that he was what in the

England of his youth they would have called a gentleman. He wondered how he had found his way to that distant island. He got up from his chair and wandered about the room. A number of framed photographs hung on the wall over a long book-case. He was surprised to find that they were of rowing eights of a Cambridge college, among which, though only by the name underneath, G. P. Frith, he recognised his host; others were groups of native boys at Perak in the Malay States, and at Kuching in Sarawak, with Frith, a much younger man than now, sitting in the middle. It looked as though on leaving Cambridge he had come to the East as a schoolmaster. The book-case was untidily stacked with books, all stained with damp and the ravages of the white ant, and these, with idle curiosity, taking out one here, one there, he glanced at. There was a number of prizes bound in leather from which he learned that Frith had been at one of the smaller public schools, and had been an industrious and even brilliant boy. There were the text-books that he had used at Cambridge, a good many novels, and a few volumes of poetry which gave the impression that they had been much read, but long ago. They were well-thumbed and many passages were marked in pencil or underlined, but they had a musty smell as though they had for years remained unopened. But what surprised him most was to see two shelves filled with works on Indian religion and Indian philosophy. There were translations of the Rig-Veda and of certain of the Upanishads, and there were paper-bound books published in Calcutta or Bombay by authors with names odd to him and with titles that had a mystical sound. It was an unusual collection to find in the house of a planter in the Far East, and Dr. Saunders, trying to make something of the indications they afforded, asked himself what sort of man they suggested. He was turning the pages of a book by one Srinivasa Iyengar called *Outlines of Indian Philosophy*, when Frith somewhat heavily limped up to him.

"Having a look at my library?"

"Yes."

He glanced at the volume the doctor was holding.

"Interesting. Those Hindus, they're marvellous; they have a natural instinct for philosophy. They make all our philosophers look cheap and obvious. Their subtlety is so amazing. Plotinus is the only fellow I know to compare with them." He replaced the book on a shelf. "Of course, Brahma is the only religion that a reasonable man can accept without misgiving."

The doctor gave him a sidelong glance. With his red, round face, and that long yellow tooth hanging loose in his jaw, his baldish head, he had none of the look of a man with spiritual leanings. It was surprising to hear him talk in this strain.

"When I consider the universe, those innumerable worlds and the vast distances of interstellar space, I cannot think it the work of a creator, and if it were, then I am forced to ask who or what created the creator. The Vedanta teaches that in the beginning was the existent, for how could the existent be born from the non-existent? And this existent was Atman, the supreme spirit, from whom emanated maya, the illusion of the phenomenal world. And when you ask those wise men of the East why the supreme spirit should have sent forth this phantasmagory they will tell you it was for his diversion. For being complete and perfect, he could not be actuated by aim or motive. Aim and motive imply desire and he that is perfect and complete needs neither change nor addition. Therefore the activity of the eternal spirit has no purpose, but, like the frolic of princes or the play of children, is spontaneous and exultant. He sports in the world, he sports in the soul."

"That is an explanation of things that does not entirely displease me," the doctor murmured, smiling. "There is a futility about it that gratifies the sense of irony."

But he was watchful and suspicious. He was conscious that he would have attached more significance to what Frith said had he been of ascetic appearance, and his face, instead of shining with sweat, shone with the travail of urgent thought. But does the outer man represent the man within? The face of a scholar or a saint may well mask a vulgar and a trivial soul. Socrates, with his flattened nose and protruding eyes, his thick lips and unwieldy belly, looked like Silenus, and yet was full of admirable temperance and wisdom.

Frith gave a little sigh.

"For a time I was attracted by Yoga, but after all it's only a schismatic branch of Sankhya, and its materialism is unreasonable. All that mortification of the senses is inane. The goal is perfect knowledge of the soul's nature, and apathy and abstraction and rigidity of posture will not enable you to attain that any more than rites and ceremonies. I've got masses of notes. When I have time I shall get some sort of order in my material and write a book. I've had it in mind for twenty years."

"I should have thought you had time to burn here," said the doctor dryly.

"Not enough for all I have to do. I've been spending the last four years doing a metrical translation of *The Lusiads*. Camoens, you know. I should like to read you one or two cantos. There's no one here who has any critical discernment. Christessen is a Dane, and I can't trust his ear."

"But hasn't it been translated before?"

"Yes. By Burton, among others. Poor Burton was no poet. His version is intolerable. Every generation must retranslate the great works of the world for itself. My aim is not only to render the sense, but also to preserve the rhythm and music and lyrical quality of the original."

"What made you think of it?"

"It's the last of the great epics. After all, my book on the Vedanta can only hope to appeal to a small and special public. I felt I owed it to my daughter to undertake a work of more popular character. I have nothing. This estate belongs to old Swan. My translation of *The Lusiads* shall be her dowry. I am going to give her every penny I make out of it. But that is not all; money isn't very important. I want her to be proud of me; I don't think my name will be very easily forgotten: my fame also shall be her dowry."

Dr. Saunders kept silence. It seemed to him fantastic that this man should expect to get money and fame by translating a Portuguese poem that not a hundred people had any wish to read. He shrugged a tolerant shoulder.

"It is strange how things happen," Frith continued, his face heavy and serious. "It's hard for me to believe that it is only by accident that I have undertaken this task. You know, of course, that Camoens, a soldier of fortune as well as a poet, came to this island, and he must often have watched the sea from the fort as I have watched it. Why should I have come here? I was a schoolmaster. When I left Cambridge I had an opportunity to come to the East, and I jumped at it. I'd longed to ever since I was a child. But the routine of school-work was too much for me. I couldn't bear the people I had to mix with. I was in the Malay States, and then I thought I'd try Borneo. It was no better. At last I couldn't stand it any more. I resigned. For some time I was in an office in Calcutta. Then I started a book-shop in Singapore. But it didn't pay. I ran a hotel in Bali, but I was before my time, and I couldn't make both ends meet. At last I drifted down here. It's strange that my wife should have been called Catherine, because that was the name of the only woman Camoens loved. It was for her he wrote his perfect lyrics. Of course, if there's anything that seems to me proved beyond all doubt it's the doctrine of transmigration which the Hindus call Samsara. Sometimes I've asked myself if perhaps the spark that issued from the fire and formed the spirit of Camoens is not the self-same spark that now forms mine. So often when I'm reading *The Lusiads* I come across a line that I seem to remember so distinctly that I can't believe I'm reading it for the first time. You know that Pedro de Alcaçova said that *The Lusiads* had only one fault. They were not short enough to learn by heart and not long enough to have no ending."

He gave a deprecating smile as a man might to whom an extravagant compliment was addressed.

"Ah, here's Louise," he said. "That looks as if supper was nearly ready."

Dr. Saunders turned to look at her. She was wearing a sarong of green silk in which was woven an elaborate pattern in gold thread. It had a sleek and glowing splendour. It was Javanese, and such as the ladies of the Sultan's harem at Djokjakarta wore on occasions of state. It fitted her slim body like a sheath, tight over her young nipples and tight over her narrow hips. Her bosom and her legs were bare. She wore high-heeled green shoes, and they added to her graceful stature. That ashy blonde hair of hers was done high on her head, but very simply, and the sober brilliance of the green-and-golden sarong enhanced its astonishing fairness. Her beauty took the breath away. The sarong had been kept with sweet-smelling essences or she had scented herself; when she joined them they were conscious of a faint and unknown perfume. It was languorous and illusive, and it was pleasant to surmise that it was made from a secret recipe in the palace of one of the rajahs of the islands.

"What's the meaning of this fancy dress?" asked Frith, with a smile in his pale eyes and a waggle of his long tooth.

"Erik gave me this sarong the other day. I thought it would be a good opportunity to wear it."

She gave the Dane a friendly little smile that thanked him again.

"It's an old one," said Frith. "It must have cost you a small fortune, Christessen. You'll spoil the child."

"I got it for a bad debt. I couldn't resist it. I know Louise likes green."

A Malay servant brought in a great bowl of soup and set it down on the table.

"Will you take Dr. Saunders on your right, Louise, and Captain Nichols on your left?" said Frith, with a certain stateliness.

"What does she want to sit between those two old men for?" cackled the ancient Swan suddenly. "Let her sit between Erik and the kid."

"I see no reason not to conform to the usages of polite society," said Frith in a very dignified manner.

"Want to show off?"

"Then will you sit beside me, Doctor?" said Frith, taking no notice of this. "And perhaps Captain Nichols wouldn't mind sitting on my left."

Old Swan, with a funny quick crawl, took what was evidently his accustomed place. Frith ladled out the soup.

"Pair of crooks they look to me," said the little old man, shooting a sharp glance from the doctor to Nichols. "Where'd you fish 'em from, Erik?"

"You're ginny, Mr. Swan," said Frith, handing him gravely a plate of soup to be passed down the table.

"No offence meant," said Mr. Swan.

"And no offence taken," answered Captain Nichols, graciously. "I'd ever so much sooner somebody said I looked like a crook than I looked like a fool. And I'm sure the doctor'll say the same as me. What does a fellow mean when 'e says you're a crook? Well, 'e means you're cleverer than 'im, that's all; I ask you, am I right or am I wrong?"

"I know a crook when I see one," said old Swan. "I've known too many in my time not to. Been a bit of a crook meself at times." He gave a little cackling laugh.

"And who hasn't?" said Captain Nichols, wiping his mouth, for he ate soup somewhat untidily. "What I always say is, you must take the world as you find it. Compromise, that's the thing. Ask anybody and they'll tell you what made the British Empire what it is, is compromise."

With a deft movement of his lower lip Frith sucked the remains of his soup off his little grey moustache.

"It's a matter of temperament, I suppose. Compromise has never appealed to me. I have had other fish to fry."

"Someone else caught 'em for you, I bet," said old Swan, with a little snicker of senile glee. "Bone-idle, that's what you are, George. Had a dozen jobs in your time and never kept one of them."

Frith gave Dr. Saunders an indulgent smile. It said as clearly as if he had spoken that it was mightily absurd to hurl such charges at a man who had spent twenty years in the study of the highly metaphysical thought of the Hindus and in whom in all probability dwelt the spirit of a celebrated Portuguese poet.

"My life has been a journey in search of truth and there can be no compromise with truth. The Europeans ask what is the use of truth, but for the thinkers of India it is not a means but an end. Truth is the goal of life. Years ago I used sometimes to hanker for the world I had left behind me. I would go down to the Dutch club and look at the illustrated papers, and when I saw pictures of London my heart ached. But now I know that it is only the recluse who enjoys the civilisation of cities to the full. At long last I have learnt that it is we exiles from life who get most value from it. For the way of knowledge is the true way and that way passes every door."

But at that moment, three chickens, the scrawny, pallid, tasteless chickens of the East, were set before him. He rose from his chair and seized a carving knife.

"Ah, the duties and ceremonies of the householder," he said cheerfully.

Old Swan had been sitting silent, hunched up in his chair like a little gnome. He ate his soup greedily. Suddenly, in his thin cracked voice, he began to speak:

"I spent seven years in New Guinea, I did. I spoke every language they spoke in New Guinea. You go to Port Moresby and ask 'em about Jack Swan. They remember me. I was the first white man ever walked across the island. Moreton did it afterwards, unarmed, with a walking-stick, but he had his police with him. I did it by meself. Everyone thought I was dead, and when I walked into town they thought I was a ghost. Been shooting birds of paradise, we had, my mate and me, a New Zealander he was, been a bank-manager and got into some mess-up, we had our own cutter and we sailed along the coast from Merauke. Got a lot of birds. Worth a mint of money they was then. We was very friendly with the natives, used to give them a drink now and then, and a stick of tobacco. One day I'd been out shooting by myself and I was coming back to the cutter, I was just going to give my mate a shout to come and fetch me in the dinghy when I see some natives on it. We never allowed them to come on board, and I thought something was up. So I just hid myself and stood there looking. I didn't half like the look of it. I crept along very quiet and I saw the dinghy pulled up on the beach. I thought my mate had come ashore and some of them natives had swum out to the cutter. I thought I wouldn't half give them what for. And then I bumped against something. My God, it did give me a turn. D'you know what it was? It was my mate's body, with the head cut off, and all a mass of blood from the wounds in his back. I didn't wait to see no more. I knew I'd go the same way if they caught me. They was waiting for me on the cutter, that's what they was doing. I'd got to get away and I'd got to get away damned quick. Rare time I had getting across. The things that happened to me! You could write a book about it. One old fellow, chief of a big village he was, took quite a fancy to me, wanted to adopt me and give me a couple of wives, said I'd be chief after him. I was nippy with my hands when I was a young fellow, having been a sailor and all that. I knew a lot. Nothing I couldn't do. Three months I stayed there. If I hadn't been a young fool I'd have stayed for good. Powerful chief he was. I might have been a king, I might. King of the Cannibal Islands."

He ended with his high-pitched cackle and relapsed into silence; but it was a strange silence, for he seemed to notice everything that was going on around him, and yet live his own life apart. The sudden burst of reminiscence, which had no connection with anything that had been said, had a sort of automatic effect as though a machine controlled by an unseen clock at intervals uncannily shot forth a stream of patter. Dr. Saunders was puzzled by Frith. What he said was on occasion not without interest; to the doctor, indeed, sometimes striking; and yet his manner and appearance predisposed you to listen to him warily. He seemed sincere, his attitude had even nobility, but there was something in him that the doctor found disconcerting. It was odd that these two men, old Swan and Frith, the man of action and the man who had devoted his life to speculation, should have ended up there, together, on this lonely island. It looked as though it all came to very much the same in the end. The end of all the adventurer's hazards, like the end of the philosopher's high thoughts, was a comfortable respectability.

Frith, having to his satisfaction divided three birds among seven people, sat down again and helped himself to boiled potatoes.

"I have always been attracted by the idea of the Brahmans, that a man should devote his youth to study," he said, turning to Dr. Saunders, "his maturity to the duties and ceremonies of a householder, and his age to abstract thought and meditation of the absolute."

He glanced at old Swan, hunched up in his chair and laboriously gnawing a drumstick, and then at Louise.

"It will not be very long now before I am liberated from the obligations of my maturity. Then I shall take my staff and journey out into the world in search of the knowledge which passeth all understanding."

The doctor's eyes had followed Frith's, and they rested for a while on Louise. She sat at the end of the table between the two young men. Fred, as a rule, tongue-tied, was talking nineteen to the dozen. He had lost the slight sulkiness of expression that his features bore in repose and looked frank, care-free and boyish. His face was lit up by the play of his words and his desire to please lent a soft and engaging lustre to his fine eyes. Dr. Saunders, smiling, saw how taking was his charm. He was not shy with women. He knew how to amuse them and you had only to see the girl's easy gaiety, and her animation, to know that she was happy and interested. The doctor caught snatches of his conversation; it was about the races at Randwick, bathing at Manley Beach, the cinema, the amusements of Sydney; the sort of things that young people talk to one another about and because all experience is fresh to them find so absorbing. Erik, with his great clumsy size and his massive square head, a kindly smile on his pleasantly ugly face, sat watching Fred quietly. You could see that he was glad the boy he had brought to the house was going down well. It gave him a little warm feeling of self-satisfaction that he was so charming.

When dinner was finished, Louise went up to old Swan and put her hand on his shoulder.

"Now, Grandpa, you must go to bed."

"Not before I've had me tot of rum, Louise."

"Well, drink it up quick."

She poured him out the considerable amount he wanted, while he watched the glass with cunning, rheumy eyes, and added a little water.

"Put a tune on the gramophone, Erik," she said.
The Dane did as he was bid.
"Can you dance, Fred?" he asked.
"Can't you?"
"No."
Fred rose to his feet, and looking at Louise outlined a gesture of
invitation. She smiled. He took her hand and put his arm round
her waist. They began to dance. They made a lovely couple. Dr.
Saunders, standing with Erik by the gramophone, saw to his
surprise that Fred was an exquisite dancer. He had an unimaginable grace. He made his partner, not more than competent, appear
to dance as well as he did. He had the gift of being able to absorb
her movements into his so that she was instinctively responsive to
the notions as they formed themselves in his brain. He made the
fox-trot they danced a thing of the most delicate beauty.
"You're a pretty good dancer, young fellow," said Dr. Saunders,
when the record came to an end.
"It's the only thing I can do," answered the boy, with a smile.
He was so well aware of his amiable gift that he took it as a
matter of course and compliments upon it meant nothing to him.
Louise looked down at the floor with a serious look on her face.
Suddenly she seemed to rouse herself.
"I must go and put Grandfather to bed."
She went over to the old man, still hugging his empty glass, and,
leaning over him, tenderly cajoled him to come with her. He took
her arm and toddled, a foot shorter than she, out of the room
beside her.
"What about a game of bridge?" said Frith. "Do you gentlemen
play?"
"I do," said the skipper. "I don't know about the doctor and
Fred."
"I'll make up a four," said Dr. Saunders.
"Christessen plays a very good game."
"I don't play," said Fred.
"That's all right," said Frith. "We can manage without you."
Erik brought forward a bridge table, its green baize patched and
worn, and Frith produced two packs of greasy cards. They
brought up chairs and cut for partners. Fred stood beside the
gramophone, alert, as though his body were on springs, and with
little movements kept time to an inaudible tune. When Louise
came back he did not move, but in his eyes was a smile of goodwill.

It had a familiarity that was not offensive and it gave her the feeling that she had known him all her life.

"Shall I put on the gramophone?" he asked.

"No, they'll have a fit."

"We must have another dance."

"Dad and Erik take their bridge very seriously."

She walked over to the table and he accompanied her. He stood behind Captain Nichols for a few minutes. The skipper gave him one or two uneasy glances and then, having made a bad play, turned round irascibly.

"I can't do a thing with someone lookin' over me 'and," he said. "Nothin' puts me off like that."

"Sorry, old man."

"Let's go outside," said Louise.

The living-room of the bungalow opened on to a veranda, and they stepped out. Beyond the little garden you saw in the starlight the towering kanari trees and below them, thick and dark, the massy verdure of the nutmegs. At the bottom of the steps, on one side, grew a large bush and it was alight with fire-flies. There was a multitude of them and they sparkled softly. It was like the radiance of a soul at peace. They stood side by side for a little while looking at the night. Then he took her hand and led her down the steps. They walked along the pathway till they came to the plantation and she let her hand rest in his as though it were such a natural thing for him to hold it that she paid no attention.

"Don't you play bridge?" she asked.

"Yes, of course."

"Why aren't you playing, then?"

"I didn't want to."

It was very dark under the nutmeg trees. The great white pigeons that roosted in their branches were asleep, and the only sound that broke the silence was when one of them for some reason rustled its wings. There was not a breath of wind and the air, vaguely aromatic, had a warm softness so that it surrounded them sensible to the nerves of touch like water to the swimmer. Fire-flies hovered across the path with a sort of swaying movement that made you think of drunken men staggering down an empty street. They walked a little without saying a word. Then he stopped and took her gently in his arms and kissed her on the mouth. She did not start. She did not stiffen, with surprise, or modesty; she made no instinctive movement of withdrawal; she accepted his embrace as though it were in the order of things. She was soft in his arms, but not weak, yielding, but yielding with a sort of tender willingness. They were accustomed to the darkness now, and when he looked into her eyes they had lost their blue and were dark and unfathomable. He had his hand round her waist and an arm round her neck. She rested her head against it comfortably.

"You are lovely," he said.

"You're awfully good-looking," she answered.

He kissed her again. He kissed her eyelids.

"Kiss *me*," he whispered.

She smiled. She took his face in her two hands and pressed her lips to his. He placed his hands on her two small breasts. She sighed.

"We must go in."

She took his hand and side by side they walked back slowly to the house.

"I love you," he whispered.

She did not answer, but tightly pressed his hand. They came into the light from the house, and when they went into the room for an instant were dazzled. Erik looked up as they entered and gave Louise a smile.

"Been down to the pool?"

"No, it was too dark."

She sat down and, taking up an illustrated Dutch paper, began to look at the pictures. Then putting it down she let her gaze rest on Fred. She stared at him thoughtfully, without expression on her face, as though he were not a man but an inanimate object. Now and then Erik glanced across at her and when he caught her eye she gave him a tiny little smile. Then she got up.

"I shall go to bed," she said.

She bade them all good-night. Fred sat down behind the doctor and watched them play. Presently, having finished a rubber, they stopped. The old Ford had come back for them and the four men piled in. When they reached the town it drew up to put the doctor and Erik down at the hotel and then drove on to the harbour with the others.

CHAPTER XXII

". . ?" asked Erik.

"Are you sle͜fy yet," replied the doctor.

"No, it͜'er to my place and have a night-cap."

"Comt."

"Aòctor had not smoked for a night or two and intended to ·that evening, but he did not mind waiting a little. To delay ·pleasure was to increase it. He accompanied Erik along the ·eserted street. People went to bed early at Kanda and there was not a soul about. The doctor walked with a little quick trip and he took two steps to Erik's one. With his short legs and somewhat prominent belly he cut a comic figure beside the striding giant. It was not more than two hundred yards to the Dane's house, but he was a little out of breath when they arrived. The door was unlocked, there was not much fear of thieves on that island where people could neither escape nor dispose of stolen property, and Erik, opening the door, walked in ahead to light the lamp. The doctor threw himself in the most comfortable of the chairs and waited while Erik fetched glasses, ice, whisky and soda. In the uncertain light of a paraffin lamp, with his short grey hair, snub nose and the bright colour on his high cheek-bones, he reminded you of an elderly chimpanzee, and his little bright eyes had the monkey's scintillating sharpness. It would have been a foolish man who thought they would not see through pretence, but perhaps it would have been a wise one who discerned that, however clumsily an awkward address concealed it, they would recognise sincerity. He was not likely to take at its face value what a man said, however plausible, though no more than the shadow of a mischievous smile betrayed his thoughts, but honesty, however naïve, and true feeling, however incongruous, he could repay with a sympathy somewhat ironical and amused, but patient and kindly.

Erik poured out a drink for his guest and a drink for himself.

"What about Mrs. Frith?" asked the doctor. "Is she dead?"

"Yes, she died last year. Heart disease. She was a fine woman. Her mother came from New Zealand, but to look at her you would have said she was pure Swedish. The real Scandinavian type, tall and big and fair, like one of the goddesses in the *Rheingold*. Old Swan used to say that when she was a girl she was better-looking than Louise."

"A very pretty young woman," said the doctor.

"She was like a mother to me. You can't imagine how kind she was. I used to spend all my spare time up there, and if I didn't go for a few days because I was afraid of abusing their hospitality she'd come down and fetch me herself. We Danes, you know, think the Dutch are rather dull and heavy, and it was a godsend to me to have that house to go to. Old Swan used to like talking to me." Erik gave a little laugh. "He'd forgotten most of his talks half Swedish, half English, and Malay words thrown in, bits of Japanese; at first I had a job to understand. Funny how a man can forget his native language. I've always liked the English. It was fine for me to have long talks with Frith. You wouldn't expect to find a man with that education in a place like this."

"I was wondering how he ever found his way here."

"He'd read about it in some old travel book. He's told me he wanted to come ever since he was a kid. It's a funny thing, he'd got it into his head that it was the one place in the world he wanted to live in. And I'll tell you what's strange, he'd forgotten the name of it; he could never find again the book in which he'd read about it; he just knew there was an island all by itself in a little group somewhere between Celebes and New Guinea, where the sea was scented with spices and there were great marble palaces."

"It sounds more like the sort of thing you read about in *The Arabian Nights* than in a book of travel."

"That's what a good many people expect to find in the East."

"Sometimes they do," murmured the doctor.

He thought of the noble bridge that spanned the river at Fuchou. There was a press of traffic on the Min, great junks with eyes painted on their prows so that they could see the way to go, wupans with their rattan hoods, frail sampans and chugging motorboats. On the barges dwelt the turbulent river-folk. In midstream on a raft two men, wearing nothing but a loin-cloth, fished with cormorants. It was a sight you could watch for an hour at a time. The fisherman sent his bird into the water; it dived, it caught; as it rose to the surface he drew it in by a string tied to its leg; then, while it struggled, angrily flapping its wings, he seized it by the throat and made it disgorge the fish it had seized. After all it was just such a fisherman, fishing in his different Arab way, to whom a casual chance brought such amazing adventures.

The Dane continued:

"He came out East when he was twenty-four. It took him twelve years to get here. He asked everyone he met if they'd heard of the island, but you know, in the F.M.S. and in Borneo, they don't know much about these parts. He was a bit of a rolling-stone when he was a young chap and he wandered from place to place. You heard what old Swan said to him and I guess it was true. He never kept a job very long. He got here at last. The skipper of a Dutch ship told him about it. It didn't sound very much like the place he was looking for, but it was the only island in the Archipelago that answered to the description at all, and he thought he'd come and look at it. When he landed he hadn't much beside his books and the clothes he stood up in. At first he couldn't believe it was the right place; you've seen the marble palaces, you're sitting in one of them now." Erik looked round the room and laughed. "You see, he'd pictured them to himself all those years like the palaces on the Grand Canal. Anyhow, if it wasn't the place he was looking for it was the only place he could find. He shifted his standpoint, if you understand what I mean, and forced the reality to tally with his fancy. He came to the conclusion that it was all right. Because they've got marble floors and stucco columns he really thinks they are marble palaces."

"You make him out a wiser man than I thought he was."

"He got a job here, there was more trade then than there is now; after that, he fell in love with old Swan's daughter and married her."

"Were they happy together?"

"Yes. Swan didn't like him much. He was pretty active in those days and he was always concocting some scheme or other. He could never get Frith to get a move on. But she worshipped him. She thought he was wonderful. When Swan got too old, she ran the estate and looked after things and made both ends meet. You know, some women are like that. It gave her a sort of satisfaction to think of Frith sitting in his den with his books, reading and writing and making notes. She thought him a genius. She thought everything she did for him was only his due. She was a fine woman."

The doctor reflected on what Erik told him. What a picture of a strange life this offered to the fancy! The shabby bungalow in the nutmeg plantation, with the immensely tall kanari trees; that old pirate of a Swede, ruthless and crotchety, brave adventurer in the soulless deserts of hard fact; the dreamy, unpractical school-master, lured by the mirage of the East, who, like—like a coster's donkey let loose on a common, wandered aimlessly in the pleasant lands of the spirit, browsing at random; and then, the great blonde woman, like a goddess of the Vikings, with her efficiency, her love, her honesty of mind, and surely her charitable sense of humour, who held things together, managed, guided and protected those two incompatible men.

"When she knew she was dying she made Louise promise to look after them. The plantation belongs to Swan. Even now it brings in enough to keep them all. She was afraid that after she was gone the old man would turn Frith out." Erik hesitated a little. "And she made me promise to look after Louise. It hasn't been very easy for her, poor child. Swan is like a cunning old monkey. He's up to any mischief. His brain in a way is as active as ever it was, and he'll lie and plot and intrigue just to play some silly little trick on you. He dotes on Louise. She's the only person who can do anything with him. Once, just for fun, he tore some of Frith's manuscripts into tiny fragments. When they found him he was surrounded by a snow-fall of little bits of paper."

"No great loss to the world, I dare say," smiled the doctor, "but exasperating to a struggling author."

"You don't think much of Frith?"

"I haven't made up my mind about him."

"He's taught me so much. I shall always be grateful to him. I was only a kid when I first came here. I'd been to the University at Copenhagen, and at home we'd always cared for culture; my father was a friend of George Brandes, and Holger Drachmann, the poet, used often to come to our house; it was Brandes who first made me read Shakespeare, but I was very ignorant and narrow. It was Frith who made me understand the magic of the East. You know, people come out here and they see nothing. Is that all? they say. And they go home again. That fort I took you to see yesterday, just a few old grey walls overgrown with weeds. I shall never forget the first time *he* took me there. His words built up the ruined walls and put ordnance on the battlements. When he told me how the governor had paced them week after week in sickening anxiety, for the natives, in the strange way they have in the East of knowing things before they can possibly be known, were whispering of a terrible disaster to the Portuguese, and he waited desperately for the ship that would bring news; and at last it came, and he read the letter which told him that King Sebastian, with his splendid train of nobles and courtiers, had been annihilated at the battle of Alcacer, and the tears ran down his old cheeks, not only because his King had met a cruel death, but because he foresaw that the defeat must cost his country her freedom; and that rich world they had discovered and conquered, those innumerable islands a handful of brave men had seized for the power of Portugal, must pass under the dominion of foreigners —then, believe me or not, I felt a lump in my throat, and for a little while I couldn't see because my eyes were blurred with tears. And not only this. He talked to me of Goa the Golden, rich with the plunder of Asia, the great capital of the East, and of the Malabar Coast and Macao, and Ormuz and Bassora. He made that old life so plain and vivid that I've never since been able to see the East but with the past still present to-day. And I've thought what a privilege it was that I, a poor Danish country boy, should see all these wonders with my own eyes. And I think it's grand to be a man when I think of those little swarthy chaps from a country no bigger than my own Denmark who, by their dauntless courage, their gallantry, their ardent imagination, held half the world in fee. It's all gone now and they say that Goa the Golden is no more than a poverty-stricken village; but if it's true that the only reality is spirit, then somehow that dream of empire, that dauntless courage, that gallantry, live on."

"It was strong wine for a young head that our Mr. Frith gave you to drink," murmured the doctor.

"It intoxicated me," smiled Erik, "but that intoxication causes no headache in the morning."

The doctor did not reply. He was inclined to think that its effects, more lasting, might be a great deal more pernicious. Erik took a sip of whisky.

"I was brought up a Lutheran, but when I went to the university I became an atheist. It was the fashion, and I was very young. I just shrugged my shoulders when Frith began to talk to me of Brahma. Oh, we've spent hours sitting on the veranda, up at the plantation, Frith, his wife Catherine and me. He'd talk. She never said much, but she listened, looking at him with adoring eyes, and he and I would argue. It was all vague and difficult to understand, but, you know, he was very persuasive, and what he believed had a sort of grandeur and beauty; it seemed to fit in with the tropical, moonlit nights and the distant stars and the murmur of the sea. I've often wondered if there isn't something in it. And if you know what I mean, it fits in too with Wagner and Shakespeare's plays and those lyrics of Camoens. Sometimes I've grown impatient and said to myself: The man's an empty windbag. You see, it bothered me that he should drink more than was good for him, and be so fond of his food, and when there was a job of work to do always have an excuse for not doing it. But Catherine believed in him. She was no fool. If he'd been a fake she couldn't have lived with him for twenty years and not found it out. It was funny that he should be so gross and yet be capable of such lofty thoughts. I've heard him say things that I shall never forget. Sometimes he could soar into mystical regions of the spirit— d'you know what I mean?—when you couldn't follow him, but just watched dizzily from the ground and yet were filled with rapture. And, you know, he could do surprising things. That day that old Swan tore up his manuscript, a year's work, two whole cantos of *The Lusiads*, when they saw what had happened Catherine burst out crying, but he just sighed and went out for a walk. When he came in he brought the old man, delighted with his mischief, but a little scared all the same, a bottle of rum. It's true he'd bought it with Swan's money, but that doesn't matter. 'Never mind, old man,' he said, 'you've only torn up a few dozen sheets of paper; they were merely an illusion and it would be foolish to give them a second thought; the reality remains, for the reality is indestructible.' And next day he set to work to do it all over again."

"He said he was going to give me some passages to read," said Dr. Saunders. "I suppose he forgot."

"He'll remember," said Erik, with a smile in which there was a good-natured grimness.

Dr. Saunders liked him. The Dane was genuine, at all events; an idealist, of course, but his idealism was tempered with humour. He gave you the impression that his strength of character was greater even than the strength of his mighty frame. Perhaps he was not very clever, but he was immensely reliable, and the charm of his simple, honest nature pleasantly complemented the charm of his ungainly person. It occurred to the doctor that a woman might very well fall deeply in love with him and his next remark was not entirely void of guile.

"And that girl we saw, is that the only child they had?"

"Catherine was a widow when Frith married her. She had a son by her first husband, and a son by Frith, too, but they both died when Louise was a child."

"And has she looked after everything since her mother's death?"

"Yes."

"She's very young."

"Eighteen. She was only a kid when I first came to the island. They sent her to the missionary school here, and then her mother thought she ought to go to Auckland. But when Catherine fell ill they sent for her. It's funny what a year'll do for girls; when she went away she was a child who used to sit on my knee, and when she came back she was a young woman." He gave the doctor his small, diffident smile. "I'll tell you in confidence that we're engaged."

"Oh?"

"Not officially, so I'd sooner you didn't mention it. Old Swan's willing enough, but her father says she's too young. I suppose she is, but that's not his real reason for objecting. I'm afraid he doesn't think me good enough. He's got an idea that one of these days some rich English lord will come along in his yacht and fall madly in love with her. The nearest approach so far is young Fred in a pearling lugger."

He chuckled.

"I don't mind waiting. I know she's young. That's why I didn't ask her to marry me before. You see, it took me some time to get it into my head that she wasn't a little girl any more. When you love anyone like I love Louise, a few months, a year or two—well, they don't matter. We've got all life before us. It won't be quite the same when we're married. I know it's going to be perfect happiness, but we shall have it, we shan't be looking forward to it any more. We've got something now that we shall lose. D'you think that's stupid?"

"No."

"Of course, you've only just seen her, you don't know her. She's beautiful, isn't she?"

"Very."

"Well, her beauty's the least of her qualities. She's got a head on her shoulders, she's got the same practical spirit that her mother had. It makes me laugh sometimes to see this lovely child—after all, she is hardly more than a kid—manage the labour on the estate with so much commonsense. The Malays know it's useless to try any tricks with her. Of course, having lived practically all her life here, she has all sorts of knowledge in her bones. It's amazing how

shrewd she is. And the tact she shows with those two men, her
grandfather and Frith. She knows them inside out; she knows all
their faults, but she doesn't mind them; she's awfully fond of
them, of course, and she takes them as they are, as though they
were just like everybody else. I've never seen her even impatient
with either of them. And, you know, one wants one's patience
when old Swan rambles on with some story you've heard fifty
times already."

"I guessed that it was she who made things run smooth."

"I suppose one would. But what one wouldn't guess is that her
beauty, and her cleverness, and the goodness of her heart mask a
spirit of the most subtle and exquisite delicacy. Mask isn't the
right word. Mask suggests disguise and disguise suggests deceit.
Louise doesn't know what disguise and deceit mean. She is
beautiful, and she is kind, and she is clever; all that's she; but
there's someone else there too, a sort of illusive spirit that somehow I think no one but her mother who is dead and I have ever
suspected. I don't know how to explain it. It's like a wraith
within the body; it's like a soul within the spirit, if you can
imagine it; it's like the essential flame of the individual of which all
the qualities that the world sees are only emanations."

The doctor raised his eyebrows. It seemed to him that Erik
Christessen was getting a bit out of his depth. Still, he listened to
him without displeasure. He was very much in love and Dr.
Saunders had a half-cynical tenderness for young things in that
condition.

"Have you ever read Hans Andersen's *Little Mermaid?*" asked
Erik.

"A hundred years ago."

"That lovely flame-like spirit not my eyes but my soul has felt in
Louise seems to me just like that little mermaid. It's not quite at
home in the haunts of men. It has always a vague nostalgia for the
sea. It's not quite human; she's so sweet, she's so gentle, she's so
tender, and yet there is a sort of aloofness in her that keeps you at a
distance. It seems to me very rare and beautiful. I'm not jealous
of it. I'm not afraid of it. It's a priceless possession and I love her
so much that I almost regret that she cannot always keep it. I feel
that she will lose it when she becomes a wife and a mother, and
whatever beauty of soul she has then it will be different. It's
something apart and independent. It's the self which is part of the
universal self; perhaps we've all got it; but what is so wonderful in

her is that it's almost sensible, and you feel that if only your eyes were a little more piercing you could see it plain. I'm so ashamed that I shall not go to her as pure as she will come to me."

"Don't be so silly," said the doctor.

"Why is it silly? When you love someone like Louise it's horrible to think that you've lain in strange arms and that you've kissed bought and painted mouths. I feel unworthy enough of her as it is. I might at least have brought her a clean and decent body."

"Oh, my dear boy!"

Dr. Saunders thought the young man was talking nonsense, but he felt no inclination to argue with him. It was getting late and his own concerns called him. He finished his drink.

"I have never had any sympathy with the ascetic attitude. The wise man combines the pleasures of the senses and the pleasures of the spirit in such a way as to increase the satisfaction he gets from both. The most valuable thing I have learnt from life is to regret nothing. Life is short, nature is hostile, and man is ridiculous; but oddly enough most misfortunes have their compensations and with a certain humour and a good deal of horse-sense one can make a fairly good job of what is after all a matter of very small consequence."

With that he got up and left.

CHAPTER XXIII

NEXT morning, comfortably seated on the veranda of the hotel, with his legs up, Dr. Saunders was reading a book. He had just learnt from the steamship office that news had been received of the arrival of a ship on the following day but one. It stopped at Bali, which would give him the opportunity of seeing that attractive island, and from there it would be easy to get to Surabaya. He was enjoying his holiday. He had forgotten that it was so pleasant to have nothing in the world to do.

"A man of leisure," he murmured to himself. "By God, I might almost pass for a gentleman."

Presently Fred Blake strolled along the road, nodded and joined him.

"You haven't received a cable, have you?" he asked.

"No, that's the last thing I expect."

"I was in the post-office a minute ago. The man asked me if my name was Saunders."

"That's funny. No one has the least notion I'm here; nor do I know anyone in the world who wants to communicate with me urgently enough to waste money on a cablegram."

But a surprise was in store for him. Barely an hour had passed when a youth rode up to the hotel on a bicycle and the manager shortly afterwards came out with him on to the veranda and asked Dr. Saunders to sign for a cable that had just arrived for him.

"What an extraordinary thing!" he cried. "Old Kim Ching is the only man who can even suspect that I'm here."

But when he opened the cablegram he was more astonished still.

"That's a damned idiotic thing," he said. "It's in code. Who in God's name can have done such a silly thing as that? How can I be expected to make head or tail of it?"

"May I have a look?" asked Fred. "If it's one of the well-known codes I might be able to tell you. One's sure to be able to get all the usual code-books here."

The doctor handed him the slip of paper. It was a numeral code. The words, or phrases, were represented by groups of numbers and the termination of each group was clearly indicated by a zero.

"The commercial codes use made-up words," said Fred.

"I know as much as that."

"I've made rather a study of codes. Been a hobby of mine. D'you mind if I have a shot at deciphering it?"

"Not a bit."

"They say it's only a question of time before you can find the secret of any code. There's one fellow in the British service, they say, who can solve the most complicated code anyone can invent in twenty-four hours."

"Go right ahead."

"I'll go inside. I must have pens and paper."

Dr. Saunders suddenly remembered. He reached out.

"Let me just see that cable again."

Fred handed it to him and he looked for the place of despatch. Melbourne. He did not give it back.

"Is it for you by any chance?"

Fred hesitated for an instant. Then he smiled. When he wanted to cajole anyone he could be very ingratiating.

"Well, it is, as a matter of fact."

"Why did you have it addressed to me?"

"Well, I thought that, me living on the *Fenton* and all that, perhaps they wouldn't deliver it, or they might want proof of identity or something. I thought it would save a lot of trouble if I had it sent to you."

"You've got your nerve with you."

"I knew you were a sport."

"And that little realistic detail about your being asked at the post-office if your name was Saunders?"

"Pure invention, old man," Fred answered airily.

Dr. Saunders chuckled.

"What would you have done if I hadn't been able to make head or tail of it and torn it up?"

"I knew it couldn't arrive till to-day. They only got the address yesterday."

"Who's 'they'?"

"The people who sent the cable," replied Fred, with a smile.

"Then it's not entirely for the pleasure of my society that you have been giving me your company this morning?"

"Not entirely."

The doctor gave him back the flimsy.

"You've got the cheek of the devil. Take it. I suppose you've got the key in your pocket."

"In my head."

He went into the hotel. Dr. Saunders began to read again. But he read with divided attention. He could not entirely dismiss from his head the incident that had just occurred. It amused him not a little and he wondered again what was the mystery in which the boy was involved. He was discreet. He had never so much as dropped a hint upon which an agile intelligence might work. There was nothing to go upon. The doctor shrugged his shoulders. After all, the matter was no business of his. He sought to dissipate his baffled curiosity by pretending to himself that he didn't care a damn and made a resolute effort to attend to what he was reading. But after an interval Fred came back on to the veranda.

"Have a drink, Doctor?" he said.

His eyes were shining, his face was flushed, but at the same time he bore an air of some bewilderment. He was excited. He wanted to burst out laughing, but since he could give no reason for hilarity plainly was trying to control himself.

"Had good news?" asked the doctor.

Suddenly Fred could restrain himself no longer. He burst into a peal of laughter.

"As good as all that?"

"I don't know if it's good or bad. It's awfully funny. I wish I could tell you. It's strange. It makes me feel rather queer. I don't quite know what to make of it. I must have a bit of time to get used to it. I don't quite know if I'm standing on my head or on my heels."

Dr. Saunders looked at him reflectively. The boy seemed to have gained vitality. There had always been something hang-dog in his expression that took away from his unusual good looks. Now he looked candid and open. You would have thought a load had been lifted from his shoulders. The drinks came.

"I want you to drink to the memory of a deceased friend of mine," he said, seizing his glass.

"By name?"

"Smith."

He emptied the glass in a draught.

"I must ask Erik if we can't go somewhere this afternoon. I feel like walking my legs off. A bit of exercise would do me good."

"When are you sailing?"

"Oh, I don't know. I like it here. I wouldn't mind staying for a bit. I wish you could have seen the view from the top of that volcano Erik and I went up yesterday. Pretty, I can tell you. The world's not a bad old place, is it?"

A buggy drawn by a small shabby horse came trundling shakily down the road, raising a cloud of dust, and stopped at the hotel. Louise was driving and her father sat by her side. He got out and walked up the steps. He had in his hand a flat brown-paper parcel.

"I forgot to give you the manuscripts last night that I promised to let you see, so I've brought them down."

"That's very kind of you."

Frith untied the string and disclosed a small pile of typewritten sheets.

"Of course, I want an absolutely candid opinion." He gave the doctor a doubtful look. "If you have nothing very much to do at the moment I might read you a few pages myself. I always think poetry should be read aloud and it's only the author who can do justice to it."

The doctor sighed. He was weak. He could think of no excuse that would turn Frith from his purpose.

"D'you think your daughter ought to wait in the sun?" he hazarded.

"Oh, she has things to do. She can go upon her errands and come back for me."

"Would you like me to go with her, sir?" said Fred Blake. "I've got nothing to do."

"I think she'd be very glad."

He went down and spoke to Louise. The doctor saw her look at him gravely, then smile a little and say something. She was wearing this morning a dress of white cotton and a large straw hat of native make. Under it her face had a golden coolness. Fred swung himself up beside her and she drove off.

"I'd like to read you the third canto," said Frith. "It has a lyrical quality that suits me. I think it's about the best thing I've done. Do you know Portuguese?"

"No, I don't."

"That's a pity. It's almost a word-for-word translation. It would have amused you to see how closely I've managed to reproduce the rhythm and music, the feeling, in fact, everything that makes it a great poem. Of course you won't hesitate to criticise, I'm only too willing to listen to anything you have to say, but I have no doubt in my own mind that this is the definitive translation. I can't honestly believe that it will ever be superseded."

He began to read. His voice had a pleasing quality. The poem was in *ottava rima*, and Frith laid an emphasis on the metre that was not ineffective. Dr. Saunders listened attentively. The version seemed fluent and easy, but he could not be sure how much this was due to the measured and stately elocution. Frith's delivery was dramatic, but he put the drama into the sound, rather than the sense, so that the meaning of what he read tended to escape you. He stressed the rhyme so that it reminded Dr. Saunders of a slow train jogging over an ill-laid rail and his body felt a slight jolt as the expected sound at regular intervals fell upon his ear. He found his attention wandering. The rich, monotonous voice hammered on and he began to feel a little drowsy. He stared hard at the reader, but his eyes closed involuntarily; he opened them with a slight effort and frowned with the violence of his concentration. He gave a start, for his head fell suddenly towards his chest, and he realised that for a moment he had dozed. Frith read of gallant deeds and the great men that had made Portugal an empire. His voice rose when he read of high heroical things and trembled and fell when he read of death and untoward fate. Suddenly Dr. Saunders was conscious of silence. He opened his eyes. Frith was no longer there. Fred Blake was sitting in front of him, a roguish smile on his handsome face.

"Had a nice nap?"

"I haven't been asleep."

"You've been snoring your head off."

"Where's Frith?"

"He's gone. We came back in the buggy and they've gone home to dinner. He said I wasn't to disturb you."

"I know what's wrong with him now," said the doctor. "He had a dream and it's come true. What gives an ideal beauty is that it's unattainable. The gods laugh when men get what they want."

"I don't know what you're talking about," said Fred. "You're half asleep still."

"Let's have a glass of beer. That at all events is real."

CHAPTER XXIV

ROUND about ten o'clock that night the doctor and Captain Nichols were playing piquet in the sitting-room of the hotel. They had been driven indoors by the flying ants which the lamp on the veranda attracted. Erik Christessen came in.

"Where have you been all day?" asked the doctor.

"I had to visit a plantation we've got over at the other end of the island. I thought I'd be back earlier, but the manager's just had a son and he was giving a feast. I had to stay for it."

"Fred was looking for you. He wanted to go for a walk."

"I wish I'd known. I'd have taken him with me." He threw himself into a chair and called for beer. "I've had the best part of ten miles to walk and then we had to row back half-way round the island."

"Like to play *chouette*?" asked the skipper, giving him his sharp, foxy look.

"No, I'm tired. Where's Fred?"

"Courtin', I expect."

"Not much chance of that here," said Erik, good-naturedly.

"Don't you be too sure. Good-lookin' young fellow, you know. The girls fall for 'im. At Merauke I 'ad a rare job keepin' 'em away from 'im. Between you and me and the gate-post I should 'ave said 'e clicked good and proper last night."

"Who with?"

"That girl up there."

"Louise?"

Erik smiled. The idea was quite preposterous to him.

"Well, I don't know. She come and 'ad a look at the boat with 'im this mornin'. And I know 'e dolled 'imself up somethin' fierce to-night. Shaved 'imself. Brushed 'is 'air. Put on a clean suit. I ask 'im what it was all about and 'e tell me to mind me own bloody business."

"Frith was down here this morning," said Dr. Saunders. "It may be he asked Fred to go and have supper there again to-night."

"He 'ad supper on the *Fenton*," said Nichols.

He dealt the cards. The players went on with their game. Erik smoking a big Dutch cigar watched them and sipped his beer. Now and again the skipper gave him that sidelong glance of his in which there was something so unpleasant that it sent a shiver down your spine. His little close-set eyes glittered with malicious amusement. After a while Erik looked at his watch.

"I'll go down to the *Fenton*. Maybe Fred'd like to come fishing with me to-morrow morning."

"You won't find 'im," said the skipper.

"Why not? He wouldn't be at Swan's as late as this."

"Don't you be too sure."

"They go to bed at ten and it's past eleven now."

"Maybe 'e's gone to bed, too."

"Rot."

"Well, if you ask me I think that girl looked as though she knew a thing or two. It wouldn't surprise me if they was comfortably tucked up together at this very minute. And very nice too. I wish I was in 'is place."

Erik was standing up. With his great height he towered over the two men seated at the table. His face grew pale, and he clenched his fists. For a moment it looked as though he would hit the skipper. He gave an inarticulate cry of rage. The skipper looked up at him and grinned. Dr. Saunders could not but see that he was not in the least frightened. A blow from that great fist would certainly have knocked him out. He was a mean skunk, but he had pluck. The doctor saw with what a tremendous effort Erik controlled himself.

"It's not a bad plan to judge others by oneself," he said, his voice trembling, "but not if one's a mangy cur."

" 'Ave I said anythin' to offend you?" asked the skipper. "I didn't know the lady was a friend of yours."

Erik stared at him for a moment. His face showed the disgust he felt for the man, and his withering contempt. He turned on his heel and walked heavily out of the hotel.

"Wanting to commit suicide, Skipper?" asked the doctor dryly.

"Known a lot of them big fellows. Sentimental, that's what they are. Never 'it a chap smaller than yourself. Their minds don't work quick, you know. A bit stupid, generally."

The doctor chuckled. It diverted him to think of that rascal making shrewd use of the decent feelings of others to go his crooked, nasty way.

"You took a risk. If he hadn't had himself well in hand he might have hit you before he knew what he was doing."

"What was 'e upset about? Sweet on the girl 'imself?"

Dr. Saunders thought it unnecessary to tell him that Erik was engaged to Louise Frith.

"There are men who object to hearing their girl friends spoken of in that way," he answered.

"Come off it, Doc. Don't pull that stuff on me. It don't go with you at all. If a girl's easy a chap likes to know. If someone else 'as been there, well, there's a chance for 'im, ain't there? Stands to reason."

"You know, you're one of the dirtiest tykes I've ever met, Skipper," said the doctor in his detached manner.

"That's a compliment in its way, ain't it? Funny part is, you don't like me any the less if I am. Seems to me to prove you ain't exactly a saint yourself. And I don't mind tellin' you I've 'eard as much in various quarters."

Dr. Saunders's eyes twinkled.

"Digestion troubling you to-night, Skipper?"

"I ain't exactly comfortable, and it would be a lie if I said I was. I don't say I'm in pain, mind you, but I just ain't comfortable."

"It's a long business. You can't expect to be able to digest a pound of lead after a week's treatment."

"I don't want to digest a pound of lead, Doc, and I don't pretend for a minute I do. Mind you, I ain't complaining. I don't say you ain't done me good. You 'ave. But I got a long way to go yet."

"Well, I've told you, have your teeth out. They're no use to you, and God knows, they don't add to your beauty."

"I will. I give you me word of honour. The minute I'm through with the cruise. I don't see why we can't pop over to Singapore. Sure to be a good American dentist there. The kid wants to go to Batavia now."

"Does he?"

"Yes, 'e got a cable this mornin'. I don't know what it was all about, but 'e's all for stoppin' on 'ere a bit and then goin' to Batavia."

"How d'you know he got a cable?"

"I found it in the pocket of 'is pants. He put on a clean suit to go ashore in, and 'e left his pants lyin' about. Untidy little blighter. That shows you 'e's not a sailor. A sailorman's always tidy. Has to be. It was all Greek to me. The cable, I mean. In cipher."

"I suppose you didn't notice that it was addressed to me?"

"You? No, I can't say I did."

"Well, have another look at it. I just gave it to Fred to decode."

The doctor found it highly diverting thus to throw Captain Nichols off the scent.

"Then what's the reason of all this changin' around? He was always for keepin' away from big places. Naturally, I thought it was on account of the cops. Anyhow, I mean to get to Singapore or sink the ruddy boat in the attempt." Captain Nichols leaned over impressively and looked with deep emotion into the doctor's eyes. "I wonder if you realise what it means to a chap not to 'ave 'ad a beefsteak and kidney puddin' for ten years. Talk of girls. You can 'ave all the girls in the world you like. There's not one I wouldn't give if I could only eat a suet puddin' with plenty of treacle and a good wallop of cream all over it. That's my idea of 'eaven and you can put your golden 'arps where the monkey put the nuts."

CHAPTER XXV

ERIK, with his deliberate stride that seemed to measure the earth as a man might measure a cricket pitch, walked down to the beach.

He was unmoved. He dismissed the skipper's shameless innuendo from his mind. It had left a nasty taste in his mouth and as though he had drunk a nauseous draught, he spat. But he was not devoid of humour and he gave a little low chuckle as he thought of the innuendo's absurdity. Fred was just a boy. He could not imagine that any woman would look at him twice; and he knew Louise much too well to suppose even for an instant that she could give him even a thought.

The beach was deserted. Everyone slept. He walked along the pier and hailed the *Fenton*. She was anchored a hundred yards out. Her light shone like a little steady eye on the smooth surface of the water. He shouted again. There was no answer. But a muffled, sleepy voice rose from below him. It was the blackfellow in the dinghy waiting for Captain Nichols. Erik went down the steps and found it tied to the bottom rung of the rail. The man was still half asleep. He yawned noisily as he stirred himself.

"Is that the *Fenton's* dinghy?"

"Ye'. What you want?"

The blackfellow thought it might be the skipper or Fred Blake, but seeing his mistake was irritable and suspicious.

"Just row me on board. I want to see Fred Blake."

"He ain't on board."

"Sure?"

"If he ain't swum."

"Oh, all right. Good-night."

The man gave a discontented grunt and settled down again to sleep. Erik walked back along the silent road. He thought that Fred had gone to the bungalow and Frith had kept him talking. He smiled as he wondered what the boy would make of the Englishman's mystical discourse. Something. He had taken to Fred. Beneath his pretence of worldly wisdom, and behind all that idle chatter about racing and cricketing, dancing and prize-fighting, you could not but be conscious of a pleasant and simple nature. Erik was not altogether unaware of the lad's feelings toward himself. Hero-worship. Oh, well, there was no great harm in that. It would pass. He was a decent kid. One might make something of him if one had the chance. It was nice to talk to him and feel that, even if it was all strange to him, he was trying to understand. It might be that if you cast a seed on that grateful soil a fair plant would spring up. Erik tramped on, hoping to meet Fred; they would walk back together, they might go on to his house, and they could rout themselves out some cheese and biscuits and have a bottle of beer. He did not feel at all sleepy. He had not many people to talk to on the island; with Frith and old Swan he had mostly to listen. It was good to talk deep into the night.

"Had tired the sun with talking," he quoted to himself, "and sent him down the sky."

Erik was reticent about his private affairs, but he made up his mind to tell Fred of his engagement to Louise. He would like him to know. He had a great desire to talk about her that night. Sometimes love so possessed him that he felt if he did not tell somebody about it his heart would break. The doctor was old and could not understand; he could say things to Fred that it would have embarrassed him to say to a grown man.

It was three miles to the plantation, but his thoughts so absorbed him that he did not notice the distance. He was quite surprised when he arrived. It was funny that he had not met Fred. Then it occurred to him that Fred must have gone in to the hotel during the time he had gone down to the beach. How stupid of him not to think of that! Oh, well, there was nothing to be done about it. Now that he was there he might just as well go in and sit down for a bit. Of course, they'd all be asleep, but he wouldn't disturb anyone. He often did that; went up to the bungalow after they'd gone to bed and sat there thinking. There was a chair in the garden, below the veranda, in which old Swan sometimes rested in the cool of the evening. It was in front of Louise's room and it reposed him strangely to sit there quite quietly and look at her window and think of her sleeping so peacefully under her mosquito curtains. Her lovely ash-blonde hair was spread on the pillow and she lay on her side, her young breast rising and falling softly in deep slumber. The emotion that filled his heart when he thus pictured her was angel-pure. Sometimes he was a little sad when he thought that this virginal grace must perish and that slim and lovely body at last lie still in death. It was dreadful that a being so beautiful should die. He sat there sometimes till a faint chill in the balmy air, the rustle of the pigeons in the trees, warned him that day was at hand. They were hours of peace and of enchanting serenity. Once he had seen the shutter softly open, and Louise stepped out. Perhaps the heat oppressed her or a dream had awakened her and she wanted a breath of air. On her bare feet she walked across the veranda and with her hands on the rail stood looking at the starry night. She wore a sarong round her loins, but the upper part of her body was naked. She raised her hands and shook out her pale hair over her shoulders. Her body was silhouetted in wan silver against the darkness of the house. She did not look a woman of flesh and blood. She was like a spirit-maiden, and Erik, his mind full of the old Danish stories, almost expected her to change into a lovely white bird and fly away to the fabled lands of the sunrise. He sat very still. He was hidden by the darkness. It was so silent that when she gave a little sigh he heard it as though he held her in his arms and her heart were pressed to his. She turned round and went back into her room. She drew the shutter to.

Erik walked up the earth road that led to the house and sat down in the chair that faced Louise's room. The house was dark. It was wrapped in a silence so profound that you might have thought its inmates were not asleep but dead. But there was no fear in the silence. It had an exquisite peace. It reassured you. It was comfortable, like the feel of a girl's smooth skin. Erik gave a little sigh of content. A sadness, but a sadness in which there was anguish no longer, befell him because dear Catherine Frith was there no more. He hoped that he would never forget the kindness she had shown him when, a shy and callow boy, he had first come to the island. He had worshipped her. She was then a woman of forty-five, but neither hard work nor child-bearing had had any effect on her powerful physique. She was tall and full-breasted, with magnificent golden hair, and she held herself proudly. You would have thought she would live to be a hundred. She took the place for him of the mother, a woman of character and of courage too, that he had left in a farmhouse in Denmark, and she loved in him the sons that had been born to her years before and of whom death had robbed her. But he felt that the relation between them was more intimate than it ever could have been if they had been mother and son. They could never have talked to one another so openly. Perhaps it could never have been such a tranquil satisfaction just to be in one another's company. He loved her and admired her and it made him very happy to be so sure that she loved him. Even then he had an inkling that the love he might one day feel for a girl would never have exactly the restful and comforting quality that he found in his very pure affection for Catherine Frith. She was a woman who had never read much, but she had a vast fund of knowledge, lying there like an unworked mine, gathered, you would have said, through innumerable generations out of the timeless experience of the race, so that she could cope with your book-learning and meet you on level terms. She was one of those persons who made you feel as though you were saying wonderful things, and when you talked to her, thoughts came to you that you had never dreamt you were capable of. She was of a practical turn and she had a canny sense of humour; she was quick to ridicule absurdity, but the kindness of her heart was such that if she laughed at you, it was so tenderly that you loved her for it. It seemed to Erik that her most wonderful trait was a sincerity so perfect that it glowed all about her with a light that shone into the heart of all that had communication with her.

It filled Erik with a warm and grateful feeling to think that her life for so long had been as happy as she deserved it to be. Her marriage with George Frith had been an idyll. She had been a widow for some time when he first came to that distant and beautiful island. Her first husband was a New Zealander, skipper of a schooner engaged in the island trade, and he was drowned at sea in the great hurricane that ruined her father. Swan, owing to the wound in his chest unable to do any hard work, was broken by the accident that swept away almost all his life's savings, and together they came to that plantation which with his shrewd Scandinavian sense he had kept for years as a refuge should all else fail. She had had a son by the New Zealander, but he had died of diphtheria when still a baby. She had never known anyone like George Frith. She had never heard anyone talk as he did. He was thirty-six, with an untidy mop of dark hair and a haggard, romantic look. She loved him. It was as though her practical sense, her nobly terrestrial instincts, sought their compensation in this mysterious waif who spoke so greatly of such high things. She loved him not as she had loved her rough, downright sailor husband, but with a half-amused tenderness that wanted to protect and guard. She felt that he was infinitely above her. She stood in awe of his subtle and aspiring intelligence. She never ceased to believe in his goodness and his genius. Erik thought that, notwithstanding Frith's tiresomeness, he would always feel kindly toward him because she had so devotedly loved him and he for so many years had given her happiness.

It was Catherine who had first said that she would like him to marry Louise. She was then a child.

"She'll never be as lovely as you, my dear," he smiled.

"Oh, much more. You can't tell yet. I can. She'll be like me, but quite different, and she'll be better-looking than I ever was."

"I would only marry her if she was exactly like you. I don't want her different."

"Wait till she's grown-up and then you'll be very pleased she isn't a fat old woman."

It amused him now to think of that conversation. The darkness of the house was paling and for a moment he thought with a start that it must be the dawn that was breaking, but then, looking round, he saw that a lop-sided moon was floating up over the tops of the trees, like an empty barrel drifting with the tide, and its light, dim still, shone on the sleeping bungalow. He gave the moon a friendly little wave of the hand.

When that strong, muscular and vigorous woman was inexplicably attacked by a disease of the heart, and violent spasms of agonising pain warned her that death at any moment might overtake her, she spoke to Erik again of her wish. Louise, at school in Auckland, had been sent for, but she could only get home by a roundabout route, and it would take her a month to arrive.

"She'll be seventeen in a few days. I think she's got a head on her shoulders, but she'll be very young to take full charge of everything here."

"What makes you think she'll want to marry me?" asked Erik.

"She adored you when she was a child. She used to follow you about like a dog."

"Oh, that's just a school-girl's *Schwärmerei*."

"You'll be practically the only man she's ever known."

"But, Catherine, you wouldn't wish me to marry her if I didn't love her."

She gave him her sweet, humorous smile.

"No, but I can't help thinking that you will love her." She was silent for a moment. Then she said something that he did not quite understand. "I think I'm just as glad that I shan't be here."

"Oh, don't say that. Why?"

She did not answer. She just patted his hand and chuckled.

It touched him with a sort of sad emotion to reflect how right she had been and he was inclined to attribute her prescience to the strange presentiment of the dying. He was staggered when he saw Louise on her return. She was grown into a lovely girl. She had lost her childish worship of him, but also her shyness; she was perfectly at ease with him. She was, of course, very fond of him; he couldn't doubt that, she was so sweet, friendly and affectionate; but he had the impression, not exactly that she criticised him, but that she coolly appraised him. It did not embarrass him, but it made him feel a little self-conscious. She had acquired the quizzical, humorous look in the eyes that he knew so well in her mother, but whereas in her it warmed your heart because it was so rich with love, with Louise it slightly disconcerted you; you were not sure that she did not find you a trifle absurd. Erik discovered that he had to start with her from the beginning, for it was not only her body that had changed, it was her spirit too. She was as companionable as ever, as jolly, and they took the same long walks together as in the old days, bathed and fished; they talked and laughed together as freely as when he was twenty-two and she fourteen; but he was vaguely conscious that there was in her a new aloofness. Her soul had been transparent as glass; now it was mysteriously veiled, and he was aware that its depths held something he did not know.

Catherine died quite suddenly. She had an attack of angina, and when the half-caste doctor reached the bungalow she was beyond his aid. Louise broke down completely. The years, with the early maturity they had brought, fell away from her and she was a little girl again. She did not know how to cope with her grief. She was shattered. For long hours she lay in Erik's arms on his lap, weeping, like a child who cannot realise that sorrow will pass, and would not be comforted. The situation was more than she could deal with, and she did meekly what he told her. Frith went all to pieces and no sense could be got from him. He spent his time drinking whisky and water and crying. Old Swan talked of all the children he had had and how they had died one after the other. They'd all treated him very badly. There was not one of them left now to look after a poor old man. Some of them had run away and some had robbed him, and some had married he didn't know whom, and the rest had died. One would have thought one of them would have had the decency to stay and look after his father now he wanted looking after.

Erik did everything that had to be done.

"You are angelic," Louise said to him.

He saw the light of love in her eyes, but he contented himself with patting her hand and telling her not to be silly; he did not want to take advantage of her emotion, of the sense of helplessness and of being deserted that just then overwhelmed her, to ask her to marry him. She was so young. It would be unfair to take this advantage over her. He loved her madly. But no sooner had he said this to himself than he corrected it; he loved her sanely. He loved her with all the energy of his solid intelligence, with all the power of his mighty limbs, with all the vigour of his honest character; he loved her not only for the beauty of her virginal body, but for the firm outlines of her growing personality and for the purity of her virginal soul. His love increased his sense of his own strength. He felt there was nothing he could not achieve. And yet, when he considered her perfection, so much more than the healthy mind in the healthy body, the subtle, sensitive soul that so wonderfully corresponded with the lovely form, he felt abject and humble.

And now it was all settled. Frith's hesitations were not serious; he could be induced, if not to listen to reason, at least to yield to persuasion. But Swan was very old. He was failing fast. It might be necessary to await his death before they married. Erik was efficient. The company would not leave him indefinitely on that island. Sooner or later they would move him to Rangoon, Bangkok or Calcutta. Eventually they would need him at Copenhagen. He could never be satisfied, like Frith, to spend his life on the plantation and make a bare living by selling cloves and nutmegs. Nor had Louise the placidity that had enabled her mother to make a lovely idyll of her life on that beautiful island. There was nothing he had admired in Catherine so much as that out of these simple elements, the common round of every day, the immemorial labours of husbandry, peace, quiet, humour and a contented mind, she had been able to make a pattern of such an exquisite and completed beauty. Louise was high-strung as her mother had never been. Though she accepted her circumstances with serenity, her vagrant spirit roved. Sometimes, when they sat on the ramparts of the old Portuguese fort and looked at the sea together, he felt that there was an activity in her soul that craved exercise.

They had often spoken of their wedding journey. He wanted to arrive in Denmark in the spring when all the trees after the long cruel winter were bursting into leaf. The green of that northern country had a fresh tenderness that the tropics never knew. The meadows with their black-and-white cows and the farmsteads nestling among trees had a sweet and tidy beauty that did not

amaze you, but made you feel at home. Then there was Copenhagen, with its wide, busy streets, the prim, dignified houses with
so many windows you were quite surprised, and its churches and
the red palaces King Christian had built that looked as though they
belonged to a fairy story. He wanted to take her to Elsinore. It
was on its battlements that his father's ghost had appeared to the
Danish prince. It was grand on the Sound in summer, the calm
sea grey or milk-blue; life there was very pleasant, then, with
music and laughter; and all through the long northern twilight the
cheerful talk flowed. But they must go to England. There was
London, with the National Gallery and the British Museum.
Neither of them had ever been to England. They would go to
Stratford-on-Avon and see Shakespeare's tomb. Paris, of course.
It was the centre of civilisation. She would go shopping at the
Louvre, and they would drive in the Bois de Boulogne. They
would walk hand in hand in the Forest of Fontainebleau. Italy
and the Grand Canal by moonlight in a gondola! For Frith's sake
they must go to Lisbon. It would be wonderful to see the country
from which those old Portuguese had sallied to found an empire
of which, beside a few ruined forts and here and there a moribund
station, nothing remained but a little deathless poetry and an
imperishable renown. To see all these lovely places with the
person who is all the world to you, what could life offer more
perfect? At that moment Erik understood what Frith meant
when he said that the Primal Spirit, whom you can call God if you
will, was not apart from the world but in it. That great spirit was
in the stone on the mountain side, in the beast of the field, in man
and in the thunder that rolled down the vault of heaven.

The late moon now flooded the house with white light. It gave
its neat lines an airy distinction and its substantial mass a fragile
and charming unreality. Suddenly the shutter of Louise's room
was slowly pushed open. Erik held his breath. If he had been
asked what he wanted most in the world, he would have said just
for one moment to be allowed to see her. She came out on the
veranda. She was wearing nothing but the sarong in which she
slept.

In the moonlight she looked like a wraith. The night seemed on
a sudden to stand still and the silence was like a living thing that
listened. She took a step or two and looked up and down the
veranda. She wanted to see that no one was about. Erik expected
her to come to the rail as she had done before and stand there for a

while. In that light he thought he could almost see the colour of her eyes. She turned round towards the window of her room and beckoned. A man came out. He stopped for an instant as though to take her hand, but she shook her head and pointed to the rail. He went up to it and quickly stepped over. He looked down at the ground, six feet below him, and leapt lightly down. Louise slipped back into her room and closed the shutter behind her.

For a moment Erik was so astonished, so bewildered, that he could not understand. He did not believe his eyes. He sat where he was, in old Swan's chair, stock-still, and stared and stared. The man landed on his feet and then sat down on the ground. He appeared to be putting on his shoes. Suddenly Erik found the use of his limbs. He sprang forwards, the man was only a few yards away, and with a bound seized him by the collar of his coat and dragged him to his feet. The man, startled, opened his mouth to cry out, but Erik put his great heavy hand over it. Then he slowly dropped his hand till it encircled the man's throat. The man was so taken aback that he did not struggle. He stood there stupidly, staring at Erik, powerless in that mighty grasp. Then Erik looked at him. It was Fred Blake.

CHAPTER XXVI

An hour later Dr. Saunders, lying awake in bed, heard steps in the passage and then a scratching on the door. He did not answer and the handle was tried. The door was locked.

"Who is it?" he called out.

The reply came on the top of his cry, quickly, in a low, agitated voice.

"Doctor. It's me, Fred. I want to see you."

The doctor had smoked half a dozen pipes after Captain Nichols had left him to go back on board the *Fenton*, and when he had been smoking he hated to be disturbed. Thoughts as clear as the geometrical designs in a child's drawing-book, squares, oblongs, circles, triangles, flowed through his mind in an orderly procession. The delight he felt in their lucidity was part and parcel of the indolent pleasure of his body. He raised his mosquito curtains and padded across the bare floor to the door. When he opened it he saw the night watchman, hooded with a blanket against the noxious air of the night, holding a lantern, and just behind him Fred Blake.

"Let me in, Doctor. It's frightfully important."

"Wait till I light the lamp."

By the light of the watchman's lantern he found the matches and lit the lamp. Ah Kay, who slept on a mat on the veranda outside the doctor's room, awoke at the disturbance and raising himself on his seat rubbed his dark sloe-like eyes. Fred gave the watchman a tip and he went away.

"Go to sleep, Ah Kay," said the doctor. "There's nothing for you to get up for."

"Look here, you must come to Erik's at once," said Fred. "There's been an accident."

"What d'you mean?"

He looked at Fred and saw that he was as white as a sheet. He was trembling in every limb.

"He's shot himself."

"Good God! How d'you know?"

"I've just come from there. He's dead."

At Fred's first words the doctor had instinctively begun to busy himself, but at this he stopped short.

"Are you sure?"

"Oh, quite."

"If he's dead, what's the good of my going?"

"He can't be left like that. Come and see. Oh, my God." His voice broke as though he were going to cry. "Perhaps you can do something."

"Who's there?"

"Nobody. He's lying there alone. I can't bear it. You must do something. For Christ's sake come."

"What's that on your hand?"

Fred looked at it. It was smeared with blood. By a natural instinct he was about to wipe it on his duck trousers.

"Don't do that," cried the doctor, catching hold of his wrist. "Come and wash it off."

Still holding him by the wrist, with the lamp in his other hand, he led him into the bath-house. This was a little dark, square chamber with a concrete floor; there was a huge tub in the corner and you bathed yourself by sluicing water over your body with a small tin pan which you filled from the tub. The doctor gave a pan full of water and a piece of soap to Fred and told him to wash.

"Have you got any on your clothes?"

He held up the lamp to look.

"I don't think so."

The doctor poured the blood-stained water away and they went back to the bedroom. The sight of the blood had startled Fred and he sought to master his hysterical agitation. He was whiter than ever and though he held his hands clenched, Dr. Saunders saw that he could not control their violent trembling.

"Better have a drink. Ah Kay, give the gentleman some whisky. No water."

Ah Kay got up and brought a glass into which he poured the neat spirit. Fred tossed it off. The doctor watched him closely.

"Look here, my boy, we're in a foreign country. We don't want to run up against the Dutch authorities. I don't believe they're very easy people to deal with."

"We can't leave him lying there in a pool of blood."

"Isn't it a fact that something happened in Sydney that made you leave in a hurry? The police here are going to ask you a lot of questions. D'you want them to cable to Sydney?"

"I don't care. I'm fed up with the whole thing."

"Don't be a fool. If he's dead you can do no good and neither can I. We'd better keep out of it. The best thing you can do is to get away from the island as soon as you can. Did anyone see you there?"

"Where?"

"At his house," said the doctor impatiently.

"No, I was only there a minute. I rushed straight round here."

"What about his boys?"

"I suppose they were asleep. They live at the back."

"I know. The night watchman's the only person who's seen you. Why did you rouse him?"

"I couldn't get in. The door was locked. I had to get hold of you."

"Oh, well, it doesn't matter. There are plenty of reasons why you should rout me out in the middle of the night. What made you go to Erik's?"

"I had to. I had something to say to him that couldn't wait."

"I suppose he did shoot himself. You didn't shoot him, did you?"

"Me?" The boy gasped with horror and surprise. "Why, he's . . . I wouldn't have hurt a hair of his head. If he'd been my brother I couldn't have thought more of him. The best pal a chap ever had."

The doctor frowned with faint distaste of the language Fred used, but his feeling for Erik was very clear, and the shock the doctor's question caused him was plain enough proof that he spoke the truth.

"Then what does it all mean?"

"Oh, my God, I don't know. He must have gone crazy. How the hell should I know he was going to do a thing like that?"

"Spit it out, sonny. You needn't be afraid I shall give you away."

"It's that girl up at old Swan's. Louise."

The doctor sharpened his look, but did not interrupt him.

"I had a bit of fun with her to-night."

"You? But you only saw her for the first time yesterday."

"I know. What's that got to do with it? She took a fancy to me the first moment she saw me. I knew that. I took a fancy to her, too. I haven't had a thing since I left Sydney. Somehow, I can't stick these natives. When I had that dance with her I knew it was all right. I could have had her then. We went out in the garden when you were playing bridge. I kissed her. She was just aching for it. When a girl's like that you don't want to give her time to think twice about it. I was in a bit of a state myself. I've never seen anyone to touch her. If she'd told me to go and throw myself over a cliff I'd have done it. When she came this morning with her old man I asked her if we couldn't meet. She said, No. I said, Couldn't I come up after they'd all gone to bed and we could have a bathe in the pool together? She said, No, but she wouldn't say why not. I told her I was crazy about her. And I was too. My God, she's a peach. I took her down to the ketch and showed her over. I kissed her there. That damned old Nichols wouldn't leave us alone for more than a minute. I said I'd go up to the plantation to-night. She said she wouldn't come, but I knew she would, she wanted me just as much as I wanted her; and sure enough when I got there, she was waiting for me. It was lovely there, in the dark, except for the mosquitoes; they were biting like mad, it was more than flesh and blood could stand, and I said, Couldn't we go to her room? and she said she was afraid, but I told her it was all right, and at last she said, Yes."

Fred stopped. The doctor looked at him from under his heavy eyelids. His pupils, from the opium he had smoked, were like pin-points. He listened and pondered over what he heard.

"At last she said I'd better get a move on. I put on my clothes, all but my shoes, so that I shouldn't make a row on the veranda. She went out first to see the coast was clear. Sometimes when he couldn't sleep old Swan wandered up and down there as if it was the deck of a ship. Then I slipped out and hopped over the veranda. I sat down on the ground and started to put on my shoes and before I knew what had happened someone grabbed me and pulled me up. Erik. He's got the strength of an ox, he lifted me up as if I was a bit of a kid, and he put his hand over my mouth, but I was so startled I couldn't have shouted if I'd wanted to. Then he put his hand round my throat and I thought he was going to choke the life out of me. I don't know, I was paralysed, I couldn't even struggle. I couldn't see his face. I heard him breathing; by God, I thought I was done for, and then suddenly he let me go; he gave me a great clout over the side of the head, with the back of his hand, I think it was, and I just fell like a log. He stood over me for a bit; I didn't move; I thought if I moved he'd kill me, and then suddenly he turned round and walked away at about a hundred miles an hour. I got up in a minute and looked at the house. Louise hadn't heard a thing. I thought, should I go and tell her? but I didn't dare, I was afraid someone would hear me knocking on the shutter. I didn't want to frighten her. I didn't know what to do. I started to walk, and then I found I hadn't put my shoes on, I had to go back for them. I was in a panic because just at first I couldn't find them. I drew a long breath when I got back on the road. I was wondering if Erik was waiting for me. It's no joke walking along a road at night, with not a soul about, and knowing that a great hulking fellow may step out at any minute and give you a hiding. He could wring my neck like a chicken's, and I shouldn't be able to do a thing about it. I didn't walk very quick and I kept my eyes peeled. I thought if I saw him first I'd make a dash for it. I mean, it's no good standing up to a chap when you haven't got a chance, and I knew I could run a lot faster than him. I expect it was only nerves. After I'd walked about a mile I wasn't in a funk any more. And then, you know, I felt I must see him at any price. If it had been anybody else I shouldn't have cared a damn, but, somehow, I couldn't stand him thinking me just a damned swine. You can't understand, but I've never met anyone like him, he's so straight himself, you can't bear he shouldn't think you straight, too. Most people you know—well, they're no better than you are; but Erik was different. I mean, you'd have to be a perfect damned fool not to see that he was one in a thousand. See what I mean?"

The doctor gave his thin, derisive smile, and his lips were drawn back from his long yellow teeth so that you thought of the snarl of a gorilla.

"Goodness. I know, it's shattering. One doesn't know what to do about it. It knocks human relations endways. Damned shame, isn't it?"

"Christ, why can't you talk like everybody else?"

"Go on."

"Well, I just felt I had to have it out with him. I wanted to tell him the whole thing. I was quite ready to marry the girl. I just couldn't help myself with her, I mean. After all, it was only human nature. You're old, you don't know what it is. It's all very well when you're fifty. I knew I shouldn't have a moment's rest till I put myself right with him. When I got to his house I stood outside for I don't know how long, screwing up my courage; it wanted some nerve to go in, you know, but I just forced myself. I couldn't help thinking that if he hadn't killed me then he wouldn't kill me now. I knew he didn't lock the door. That first time we went there he just turned the handle and walked in. But, my God, my heart was thumping when I got in the passage. It was pitch-black when I shut the door. I called his name, but he didn't answer. I knew where his room was and I went along and I knocked at the door. Somehow, I didn't believe he was asleep. I knocked again and then I shouted, 'Erik, Erik.' At least I tried to shout, but my throat was so dry my voice was as hoarse as a raven's. I couldn't make out why he didn't answer. I thought he was just waiting in there, listening. I was in a blue funk, I had half a mind to cut and run, but I didn't. I tried the latch, the door wasn't locked, and I opened it. I couldn't see a thing, I called again and I said: 'For God's sake speak to me, Erik.' Then I struck a match and I gave a great jump. I almost jumped out of my skin, he was lying on the floor, at my feet, and if I'd taken a step more I should have tumbled over him. I dropped the match and I couldn't see a thing. I screamed at him. I thought he'd fainted or was dead drunk or something. I tried to strike another match, but the damned thing wouldn't light, and then, when it did, I held it over him and, my God, the whole side of his head was shot away.

The match went out and I lit another. I saw the lamp and I lit that. I knelt down and felt his hand. It was quite warm. He had a revolver clenched in the other hand. I touched his face to see if he was alive. There was blood all over the place. My God, you never saw such a wound; and then I just came round here as quick as I could. I shall never forget that sight as long as I live."

He hid his face with his hands and in his misery rocked to and fro. Then a sob broke from him and, throwing himself back in the chair, he turned his face away and wept. Dr. Saunders let him cry. He reached out for a cigarette, lit it and deeply inhaled the smoke.

"Did you leave the lamp burning?" he said at last.

"Oh, damn the lamp!" cried Fred impatiently. "Don't be such a bloody fool."

"It doesn't matter. He could just as well have shot himself with the lamp burning as in the darkness. Funny none of the boys should have heard anything. I suppose they would have thought it was a Chinaman letting off a cracker."

Fred put aside all that the doctor said. Nothing of that was of any consequence.

"What in God's name made him do it?" he cried desperately.

"He was engaged to Louise."

The effect of the doctor's remark was startling. Fred sprang to his feet with a bound, and his face grew livid. His eyes almost started out of his head with horror.

"Erik? He never told me."

"I suppose he thought it was none of your damned business."

"She didn't tell me. She never said a word. Oh, God! If I'd known I wouldn't have touched her with the fag-end of a barge-pole. You're just saying that. It can't be true. It can't!"

"He told me so himself."

"Was he awfully in love with her?"

"Awfully."

"Then why didn't he kill me or her instead of himself?"

Dr. Saunders gave a laugh.

"Curious, isn't it?"

"For God's sake don't laugh. I'm so miserable. I thought nothing worse could happen to me than what has. But this. . . . She meant nothing to me, really. If I'd only known I wouldn't have thought of fooling about with her. He was the best pal a chap ever had. I wouldn't have hurt him for anything in the world.

What a beast he must have thought me! He'd been so awfully decent to me."

Tears filled his eyes and flowed slowly down his cheeks. He cried bitterly.

"Isn't life foul? You start a thing and you don't think twice about it, and then there's hell to pay. I think there's a curse on me."

He looked at the doctor, his mouth trembling and his fine eyes heavy with woe. Dr. Saunders examined his own feelings. He did not quite approve of the faint satisfaction he felt in the young man's grief. He had a tendency to feel that what he was suffering served him right. At the same time he was unreasonably sorry to see him unhappy. He looked so young and woebegone he could not help being touched.

"You'll get over it, you know," he said. "There's nothing one doesn't get over."

"I wish I was dead. My old man said I was no damned good and I bet he was right. I make trouble wherever I go. I swear it's not all my fault. The lousy bitch. Why didn't she leave me alone? Can you imagine that a girl who was engaged to a chap like Erik should go to bed with the first man she sees. Well, there's one thing, he was well rid of her."

"You're talking rubbish."

"I may be a stinking bad lot, but, by God, I'm not as bad as she is. I thought I was going to get another chance and now it's all gone to hell."

He hesitated a moment.

"You remember that cable I got this morning? It told me something I didn't know. It was so extraordinary, I couldn't make it out at first. There's a letter for me at Batavia. It's all right for me to go there now. It was rather a shock at first. I didn't know whether to laugh or what. The cable says I died of scarlet fever at the Fever Hospital just outside Sydney. I saw what it meant after a bit. Father's rather important in New South Wales. There was a bad epidemic. They rushed someone to the hospital under my name; they had to explain why I didn't go to the office and all that, and when the chap died I died too. If I know my old man he was damned glad to get rid of me. Well, there's someone who'll lie nice and cosy in the family grave. Father's a wonderful organiser. It's him that's kept the party in power so long. He wasn't going to take a risk if he could help it, and I expect as long as I was above ground he never could feel quite safe. The Government got in

again at the election. Did you see that? A thumping majority.
I can see him with a black band round his arm."

He gave a mirthless chuckle. Dr. Saunders shot a question at
him, abruptly.

"What did you do?"

Fred looked away. He answered in a low, choked voice.

"I killed a chap."

"I wouldn't tell too many people if I were you," said the
doctor.

"You seem to take it pretty calm. Have you ever killed anyone?"

"Only professionally."

Fred looked up quickly and a smile was wrung from his tortured
lips.

"You're a queer fellow, Doc. Blest if I can make you out.
When one's talking to you, somehow nothing seems to matter a
damn. Isn't there anything that makes a difference to you? Isn't
there anything you believe in?"

"Why did you kill him? For fun?"

"A damned lot of fun I got out of it. What I've gone through!
I wonder it hasn't turned my hair grey. You see, I brooded over it.
I could never forget it. I'd be feeling all merry and bright and
having a good time and then suddenly I'd remember. I was afraid
to go to sleep sometimes. I used to dream I was being pinioned
and just going to be hanged. Half a dozen times I've been on the
point of slipping overboard one night when nobody was looking,
and just swimming till I drowned or a shark got me. If you only
knew what a relief it was when I got that cable and understood
what it meant! My God, it was a weight off my mind. I was safe.
You know, I never felt really safe on the lugger and when we
landed anywhere I was always looking for someone to nab me.
The first time I saw you, I thought you were a detective and you
were on my track. D'you know the first thing I thought this
morning? 'Now I shall be able to sleep sound.' And then this had
got to happen. I tell you there's a curse on me."

"Don't talk such rot."

"What am I to do? Where am I to go? To-night, while that
girl and I were lying in one another's arms, I thought: Why
shouldn't I marry her and settle down here? The boat'll be
damned useful. Nichols could have gone back on the same ship
that you're taking. You could have got my letter that's waiting in
Batavia. I expect it's got a bit of money in it. Mother would have

made the old man send something. I thought me and Erik, we could have gone into partnership."

"You can't do that, but you can still marry Louise."

"Me?" cried Fred. "After what's happened? I couldn't stick the sight of her. I hope to God I never see her again. I'll never forgive her. Never. Never."

"What are you going to do, then?"

"God knows. I don't. I can't go home. I'm dead and buried in the family grave. I should like to see Sydney again, George Street, you know, and Manley Bay. I haven't got anyone in the world now. I'm a pretty good accountant, I suppose. I can get a job as book-keeper in some store. I don't know where to go. I'm like a lost dog."

"If I were you the first thing I'd do is to go back to the *Fenton* and try and get a little sleep. You're all in. You'll be able to think better in the morning."

"I can't go back to the boat. I hate it. If you knew how often I've woken up in a cold sweat, with my heart beating, because those men opened the door of my cell, and I knew the rope was waiting for me! And now Erik's lying there with half his head blown away. My God, how can I sleep?"

"Well, curl up on that chair. I'm going to bed."

"Thanks. Go ahead. Will it disturb you if I smoke?"

"I'll give you a little something. There's no object in your lying awake."

The doctor got out his hypodermic needle and gave the boy a shot of morphine. Then he put out the lamp and slipped under his mosquito curtain.

CHAPTER XXVII

THE doctor awoke when Ah Kay brought him a cup of tea. Ah Kay drew back the mosquito curtains and raised the jalousie to let in the day. The doctor's room looked on the garden, tangled and neglected, with its palm trees, its clumps of bananas—their immense flat leaves still shining with the night, its bedraggled but splendid cassias; and the light filtered through, cool and green. The doctor smoked a cigarette. Fred lay on the long chair, sleeping still, and his unlined boyish face, so calm, had an innocence in which the doctor, with a suspicion of sardonic humour, found a certain beauty.

"Shall I wake him?" asked Ah Kay.

"Not yet."

While he slept he was at peace. He must awake to grief. An odd boy. Who would have thought that he could be so susceptible to goodness? For, though he didn't know it, though he put what he felt in clumsy and stupid words, there was no doubt about it, what had knocked him off his feet in the Dane, what had excited his embarrassed admiration and made him feel that here was a man of a different sort, was the plain, simple goodness that shone in him with so clear and steadfast a light. You might have thought Erik a trifle absurd, you might have asked yourself uneasily whether his head were quite equal to his heart, but there was no doubt about it, he had, heaven only knew by what accident of nature, a real and simple goodness. It was specific. It was absolute. It had an æsthetic quality, and that commonplace lad, insensible to beauty in its usual forms, had been moved to ecstasy by it as a mystic might be moved by the sudden overwhelming sense of union with the Godhead. It was a queer trait that Erik had possessed.

"It leads to no good," said the doctor, with a grim smile as he got out of bed.

He went over to the mirror and stared at himself. He looked at his grey hair all disarranged after the night and his stubble of white beard that had grown since he had shaved the day before. He bared his teeth to look at his long yellow fangs. There were heavy pouches under his eyes. His cheeks had an unsightly purple. He was seized with disgust. He wondered why it was that of all creatures man was the only one that age so hideously disfigured. It was pitiful to think that Ah Kay, with his slender ivory beauty, must become nothing but a little shrivelled, wizened Chinaman, and that Fred Blake, so slim, upright and square-shouldered, would be just a red-faced old man with a bald head and a belly. The doctor shaved and had his bath. Then he awakened Fred.

"Come along, young fellow. Ah Kay's just gone to see about our breakfast."

Fred opened his eyes, immediately alert, eager in his youth to welcome another day, but then, looking about him, he remembered where he was, and everything else. His face on a sudden grew sullen.

"Oh, buck up," said the doctor impatiently. "Go and have a wash down."

Ten minutes l-r they were seated at breakfast, and the doctor noticed withou urprise that Fred ate with a hearty appetite. He did not talk. Dr. Saunders congratulated himself. After so disturbed a n he felt none too well. His reflections upon life, then, were a and he preferred to keep them to himself.

When th were finishing the manager came up to them and addressed self to Dr. Saunders in voluble Dutch. He knew the doctor di t understand, but talked nevertheless, and his signs and ges would have made him comprehensible even if his manne ated and distressed, had not made what he was saying quite Dr. Saunders shrugged his shoulders. He pretended he h notion what the half-caste was talking about, and pre exasperation, the little man left them.

w found out," said the doctor.

lo know. I suppose his house-boy went in to take him his

Isn ere anybody who can interpret?"

w all hear soon enough. Don't forget, we neither of us kno thing about it."

T elapsed into silence. A few minutes later the manager ret with a Dutch official, in a white uniform with brass b he clicked his heels together and mentioned an incomble name. He spoke English with a very strong accent.

orry to tell you that a Danish trader called Christessen has self."

stessen?" cried the doctor. "That tall fellow?"

atched Fred out of the corner of his eye.

was found by his boys an hour ago. I am in charge of the . There can be no doubt that it is a case of suicide. Mr. k," he motioned to the half-caste manager, "informs me that here last night to visit you."

hat's quite true."

How long did he stay?"

Ten minutes or a quarter of an hour."

"Was he sober?"

"Quite."

"I never saw him drunk myself. Did he say anything tha suggested he had the intention of doing away with himself?"

"No. He was quite cheerful. I didn't know him very well, you know. I only arrived three days ago, and I' waiting for the *Princess Juliana*."

"Yes, I know. Then you can give no ex nation of the tragedy?"

"I'm afraid not."

"That is all I wanted to know. If I have any ne more from you I will let you know. Perhaps you of anything coming to my office." He glanced at Fred. "And th not mind can tell us nothing?" ntleman

"Nothing," said the doctor. "He was not here. I playing cards with the skipper of the ketch in the harbour just

"I've seen her. I'm sorry for the poor fellow. He was quiet and never gave any trouble. You could not help liking afraid it's the old story. It's a mistake to live alone in I'm this. They brood. They get home-sick. The heat is ke then one day they can't stand it any more, and they st bullet through their heads. I've seen it before, more t o Much better to have a little girl to live with you, and ma hardly any difference to your expenses. Well, gentlem a much obliged to you. I won't take up any more of yo me You have not been to the *Gesellschaft* yet, I believe? We be very glad to see you there. You will find all the most im people of the island there from six or seven till nine. It is place. Quite a social centre. Well, good-morning, gentlemen

He clicked his heels, shook hands with the doctor and and stumped somewhat heavily away.

CHAPTER XXVIII

at hot country not much time was permitted to pass betwee
n's death and his burial, but in this case the examination ha
nducted, and it was not till latish in the afternoon that th
ok place. It was attended by a few Dutch friends of Erik,
Dr. Saunders, Fred Blake and Captain Nichols. This
sion after the skipper's heart. He had managed to
k suit from an acquaintance he had made on the
not fit very well, since it belonged to a man both
than he, and he was obliged to turn up the

trousers and the sleeves, but in contrast with the others, clad in nondescript fashion, it produced a satisfactory effect of respectability. The service was conducted in Dutch, which seemed to Captain Nichols a little out of place, and he could not take part in it, but there was much unction in his deportment; and when it was over he shook hands with the Lutheran pastor and the two or three Dutch officials present as though they had rendered him a personal service, so that they thought for a moment he must be a near relative of the deceased. Fred wept.

The four Britishers walked back together. They came to the harbour.

"If you gentlemen will come on board the *Fenton*," said the skipper, "I'll open a bottle of port for you. I 'appened to see it in the store this mornin', and I always think a bottle of port's the right thing after a funeral. I mean, it's not like beer and whisky. There's somethin' serious about port."

"I never thought of it before," said Frith, "but I quite see what you mean."

"I'm not coming," said Fred. "I've got a hump. Can I go along with you, Doctor?"

"If you like."

"We've all got a 'ump," said Captain Nichols. "That's why I vote we 'ave a bottle of port. It won't take the 'ump away. Not by any manner of means. It'll make it worse if anythin', at least that's my experience, but it means you can enjoy it, if you follow me, you get something out of it, and it's not wasted."

"Go to hell," said Fred.

"Come on, Frith. If you're the man I take you for, you and me can drink a bottle of port without strainin' ourselves."

"We live in degenerate days," said Frith. "Two-bottle men, three-bottle men, they're as extinct as the dodo."

"An Australian bird," said Captain Nichols.

"If two grown men can't drink one bottle of port between them I despair of the human race. Babylon is fallen, is fallen."

"Exactly," replied Captain Nichols.

They got into the dinghy and a blackfellow rowed them out to the *Fenton*. The doctor and Fred walked slowly on. When they reached the hotel they went in.

"Let's go to your room," said Fred.

The doctor poured himself out a whisky and soda and gave one to Fred.

"We're sailing at dawn," said the boy.

"Are you? Have you seen Louise?"

"No."

"Aren't you going to?"

"No."

Dr. Saunders shrugged his shoulders. It was no business of his. For a while they drank and smoked in silence.

"I've told you so much," the boy said at last, "I may as well tell you the rest."

"I'm not curious."

"I've wanted to tell someone badly. Sometimes I could hardly prevent myself from telling Nichols. Thank God, I wasn't such a fool as that. Grand opportunity for blackmail it would have been for him."

"He isn't the sort of man I'd choose to confide a secret to."

Fred gave a little derisive chuckle.

"It wasn't my fault, really. It was just rotten luck. It is bloody that your life should be ruined by an accident like that. It's so damned unfair. My people are in a very good position. I was in one of the best firms in Sydney. Eventually, my old man was going to buy me a partnership. He's got a lot of influence and he could have thrown business in my way. I could have made plenty of money and sooner or later of course I should have married and settled down. I expect I should have gone into politics like Father did. If ever anyone had a chance I had. And look at me now. No home, no name, no prospects, a couple of hundred pounds in my belt and whatever the old man's sent to Batavia. Not a friend in the world."

"You've got youth. You've got some education. And you're not bad-looking."

"That's what makes me laugh. If I'd had a squint in my eye or a hump-back I'd have been all right. I'd be in Sydney now. You're no beauty, Doctor."

"I am conscious of the fact and resigned to it."

"Resigned to it! Thank your lucky stars every day of your life."

Dr. Saunders smiled.

"I'm not prepared to go as far as that."

But the foolish boy was desperately serious.

"I don't want you to think I'm conceited. God knows I've got nothing to be conceited about. But, you know, I've always been able to get any girl I wanted to. Oh, almost since I was a kid. I thought it rather a lark. After all, you're only young once. I didn't see why I shouldn't have all the fun I could get. D'you blame me?"

"No. The only people who would are those who never had your opportunities."

"I never went out of my way to get them. But when they practically asked for it—well, I should have been a fool not to take what I could get. It used to make me laugh sometimes to see them all in a dither and often I'd pretend I didn't notice. They'd get furious with me. Girls are funny, you know, nothing makes them so mad as a chap standing off. Of course, I never let it interfere with my work; I'm not a fool, you know, in any sense of the word, and I wanted to get on."

"An only child, were you?"

"No. I've got a brother. He went into the business with Father. He's married. And I've got a married sister, too.

"Well, one Sunday last year, a chap brought his wife to spend the day up at our house. His name was Hudson. He was a Roman Catholic, and he'd got a lot of influence with the Irish and the Italians. Father said he could make all the difference at the election, and he told Mother she was to do them proud. They came up to dinner, the Premier came and brought his wife, and Mother gave them enough to eat to feed a regiment. After dinner Father took them into his den to talk business and the rest of us went and sat in the garden. I'd wanted to go fishing, but Father said I'd got to stay and make myself civil. Mother and Mrs. Darnes had been at school together."

"Who was Mrs. Darnes?"

"Mr. Darnes is the Premier. He's the biggest man in Australia."

"I'm sorry. I didn't know."

"They always had a lot to talk about. They tried to be polite to Mrs. Hudson, but I could see they didn't much like her. She was doing her best to be nice to them, admiring everything and buttering them up, but the more she laid it on the less they liked it. At last, Mother asked me if I wouldn't show her round the garden. We strolled off and the first thing she said was: 'For God's sake give me a cigarette.' She gave me a look when I lit it for her and she said: 'You're a very good-looking boy.' 'D'you think so?' I said. 'I suppose you've been told that before?' she said. 'Only by Mother,' I said, 'and I thought perhaps she was

prejudiced.' She asked me if I was fond of dancing and I said I
was, so she said she was having tea at the Australia next day and if I
liked to come in after the office we could have a dance together. I
wasn't keen on it, so I said I couldn't; then she said: 'What about
Tuesday or Wednesday?' I couldn't very well say I was engaged
both days, so I said Tuesday would suit me all right; and when
they'd gone away I told Father and Mother. She didn't much like
the idea, but Father was all for it. He said it wouldn't suit his book
at all to have us stand-offish. 'I didn't like the way she kept on
looking at him,' said Mother, but Father told her not to be silly.
'Why, she's old enough to be his mother,' he said. 'How old is
she?' Mother said: 'She'll never see forty again.'

"She was nothing to look at. Thin as a rail. Her neck was
absolutely scraggy. Tallish. She had a long thin face, with hollow
cheeks, and a brown skin, all one colour, rather leathery, if you
know what I mean; and she never seemed to take any trouble with
her hair, it always looked as though it would come down in a
minute; and she'd have a wisp hanging down in front of her ear or
over her forehead. I do like a woman to have a neat head, don't
you? It was black, rather like a gipsy's, and she had enormous
black eyes. They made her face. When you talked to her you
didn't really see anything else. She didn't look British, she looked
like a foreigner, a Hungarian or something like that. There was
nothing attractive about her.

"Well, I went on the Tuesday. She knew how to dance, you
couldn't deny that. You know, I'm rather keen on dancing. I
enjoyed myself more than I expected. She had a lot to say for
herself. I shouldn't have had a bad time if there hadn't been some
of my pals there. I knew they'd rot my head off for dancing the
whole afternoon with an old geyser like that. There are ways *and*
ways of dancing. It didn't take me long to see what she was up to.
I couldn't help laughing. Poor old cow, I thought, if it gives her
any pleasure, well, let her have it. She asked me to go to the
pictures with her one night when her husband had to go to a
meeting. I said I didn't mind, and we made a date. I held her hand
at the pictures. I thought it'd please her and it didn't do me any
harm, and afterwards she said, Couldn't we walk a bit. We were
pretty friendly by then; she was interested in my work, and she
wanted to know all about my home. We talked about racing, I
told her there was nothing I'd like to do more than ride in a big
race myself. In the dark she wasn't so bad, and I kissed her. Well,

the end of it was that we went to a place I knew and we had a bit of a rough and tumble. I did it more out of politeness than anything else. I thought that would be the finish. Not a bit of it. She went crazy about me. She said she'd fallen in love with me the first time she saw me. I don't mind telling you that just at first I was a bit flattered. She had something. Those great flashing eyes, sometimes they made me feel all funny, and that gipsy look, I don't know, it was so unusual, it seemed to take you right away and you couldn't believe you were in good old Sydney; it was like living in a story about Nihilists and Grand Dukes and I don't know what all. By God, she was hot stuff. I thought I knew a thing or two about all that, but when she took me in hand I found I didn't know a thing. I'm not particular, but really, sometimes she almost disgusted me. She was proud of it. She used to say that after a chap had loved her, other women were duller than cold roast mutton.

"I couldn't help liking it in a way, but, you know, I didn't feel easy about it. You don't like a woman to be absolutely shameless. There was no satisfying her either. She made me see her every day, and she'd ring me up at the office and ring me up at home. I told her for God's sake to be careful; after all she had a husband to think of, and there was Father and Mother—Father was quite capable of packing me off to a sheep-station for a year if he had the smallest suspicion that things weren't going right, but she said she didn't care. She said if I was packed off to a sheep-station she'd come with me. She didn't seem to mind what risks she took, and if it hadn't been for me it would have been all over Sydney in a week. She'd telephone to Mother and ask if I couldn't go to supper at her place and make a four at bridge, and when I was there she'd make love to me under her husband's nose. When she saw I was scared she laughed her head off. It excited her. Pat Hudson just treated me like a boy; he never took much notice of me; he fancied himself at bridge, and got a lot of fun out of telling me all about it. I didn't dislike him. He was a bit of a rough-neck, and he could put his liquor away rather, but he was a smart fellow in his way. He was ambitious, and he liked having me there because I was Father's son. He was quite ready to come in with Father, but he wanted to get something pretty substantial for himself out of it.

"I was getting a bit fed up with it all. I couldn't call my soul my own. And she was as jealous as hell. If we were anywhere and I happened to look at a girl it would be: 'Who's that? Why d'you look at her like that? Have you had her?' And if I said I hadn't ever spoken to her even, she'd say I was a damned liar. I thought I'd slack off a bit. I didn't want to chuck her too suddenly in case she got her knife in me. She could turn Hudson round her little finger, and I knew Father wouldn't be very pleased if he did the dirty on us at the election. I began to say I was busy at the office or had to stay at home, when she wanted me to go out with her. I told her Mother was getting suspicious and that we must be careful. She was as sharp as a knife. She wouldn't believe a word I said. She made me the most awful scenes. To tell you the truth I began to get rather scared. I'd never known anyone like that. With most of the girls I'd played about with—well, they'd known it was just a lark, same as I did, and it just ended naturally, without any fuss or bother. You'd have thought, when she guessed I'd had enough, her pride would prevent her from clinging on to me. But no. Quite the contrary. D'you know, she actually wanted me to run away with her, to America or somewhere, so that we could get married. It never seemed to occur to her that she was twenty years older than me. I mean, it was too ridiculous. I had to pretend that it was out of the question, on account of the election, you know, and because we shouldn't have anything to live on. She was absolutely unreasonable. She said, what did we care about the election, and anyone could make a living in America, she said; she'd been on the stage and she was sure she could get a part. She seemed to think she was a girl. She asked me if I'd marry her if it wasn't for her husband and I had to say I would. The scenes she made got me so nervous I was ready to say anything. You don't know what a life she led me. I wished to God I'd never set eyes on her. I was so worried I didn't know what to do. I had half a mind to tell Mother, but I knew it would upset her so frightfully. She never left me alone for a minute. She came up to the office once. I had to be polite to her and pretend it was all right, because I knew she was capable of making a scene before everybody, but afterwards I told her if she ever did it again I wouldn't have any-thing more to do with her. Then she started waiting for me in the street outside. My God, I could have wrung her neck. Father used to go home in a car and I always walked to his office to fetch him, and she insisted on walking there with me. At last things got to such a pitch that I just couldn't stick it any more; I didn't care what happened. I told her I was sick and tired of the whole thing and it had got to stop.

"I made up my mind that I was going to say it and I did. My God, it was awful. It was at her place—they had a little jerry-built house, overlooking the harbour, on a cliff, rather far out—and I'd got off from the office in the middle of the afternoon on purpose. She screamed and she cried. She said she loved me and she couldn't live without me and I don't know what all. She said she'd do anything I liked and she wouldn't bother me in future and she'd be quite different. She promised every sort of thing. God knows what she didn't say. Then she flew into a rage and cursed me and swore at me and called me every name under the sun. She went for me, and I had to hold her hands to prevent her from scratching my eyes out. She was like a mad woman. Then she said she was going to commit suicide, and tried to run out of the house. I thought she'd throw herself over the cliff or something, and I held her back by main force. She kicked and struggled. And then she threw herself on her knees and tried to kiss my hands, and when I pushed her away she fell on the ground and started sobbing and sobbing. I seized the opportunity and made a bolt for it.

"I'd hardly got home before she rang me up. I wouldn't speak to her and rang off. She rang again and again; fortunately Mother was out, and I just didn't answer. There was a letter waiting for me at the office next morning, ten pages of it, you know the sort of thing; I took no notice of it; I certainly wasn't going to answer. When I went out for lunch at one o'clock she was standing in the doorway waiting for me, but I walked right past her, as quick as I could, and got away in the crowd. I thought she might be there when I came back, so I walked along with one of the chaps at the office, who had his dinner the same place that I had lunch. She was there right enough, but I pretended I didn't see her, and she was afraid to speak. I found another chap to walk out with in the evening. She was still there. I suppose she'd been waiting all the time so that I shouldn't slip out. D'you know, she had the nerve to come straight up to me. She put on a society manner.

" 'How d'you do, Fred?' she said. 'What a bit of luck meeting you. I've got a message for your father.'

"The chap walked on before I could stop him, and I was caught.

" 'What d'you want?' I said.

"I was in a flaming passion.

" 'Oh, my God, don't talk to me like that,' she said. 'Have pity on me. I'm so unhappy. I can't see straight.'

" 'I'm very sorry,' I said. 'I can't help it.'

"Then she began to cry, right there in the middle of the street, with people passing all the time. I could have killed her.

" 'Fred, it's no good,' she said, 'you can't throw me over. You're everything in the world to me.'

" 'Oh, don't be so silly,' I said. 'You're an old woman and I'm hardly more than a kid. You ought to be ashamed of yourself.'

" 'What does that matter?' she said. 'I love you with all my heart.'

" 'Well, I don't love you,' I said. 'I can't bear the sight of you. I tell you it's finished. For God's sake leave me alone.'

" 'Isn't there anything I can do to make you love me?' she said.

" 'Nothing,' I said. 'I'm fed up with you.'

" 'Then I shall kill myself,' she said.

" 'That's your trouble,' I said, and I walked away quickly before she could stop me.

"But although I said it just like that, as if I didn't care a damn, I wasn't easy about it. They say people who threaten to commit suicide never do, but she wasn't like other people. The fact is, she was a madwoman. She was capable of anything. She was capable of coming up to the house and shooting herself in the garden. She was capable of swallowing poison and leaving some awful letter behind. She might accuse me of anything. You see, I hadn't only myself to think of, I had to think of Father, too. If I was mixed up in something it might have done him an awful lot of harm, especially just then. And he isn't the sort of man to let you off easy, if you've made a fool of yourself. I can tell you I didn't sleep much that night. I worried myself sick. I should have been furious if I'd found her hanging about the street outside the office in the morning, but in a way I'd have been rather relieved. She wasn't there. There was no letter for me either. I began to get a bit scared, and I had a job to prevent myself ringing up to see if she was all right. When the evening paper came out I just made a grab at it. Pat Hudson was pretty prominent, and if something had happened to her there'd sure to be a lot about it. But there wasn't a thing. That day there was nothing, no sign of her, no telephone message, no letter, nothing in the paper, and the day after, and the day after that, it was just the same. I began to think it was all right and I was rid of her. I came to the conclusion it was all a bluff. Oh, my God, how thankful I was! But I'd had my lesson. I made

up my mind to be damned careful in future. No more middle-aged
women for me. I'd got all nervous and wrought-up. You can't
think what a relief it was to me. I don't want to make myself out
any better than I am, but I have some sense of decency and really
that woman was the limit. I know it sounds silly, but sometimes
she just horrified me. I'm all for having a bit of fun, but, damn it
all, I don't want to make a beast of myself."

Dr. Saunders did not reply. He understood pretty well what the
boy meant. Careless and hot-blooded, with the callousness of
youth, he took his pleasure where he found it, but youth is not
only callous, it is modest, and his instinct was outraged by the
unbridled passion of the experienced woman.

"Then about ten days later I got a letter from her. The envelope
was typewritten or I shouldn't have opened it. But it was quite
sensible. It started, 'Dear Fred.' She said she was awfully sorry
she'd made me all those scenes, and she thought she must have
been rather crazy, but she'd had time to calm down and she didn't
want to be a nuisance to me. She said it was her nerves, and she'd
taken me much too seriously. Everything was all right now, and
she didn't bear me any ill-will. She said I mustn't blame her,
because it was partly my fault for being so absurdly good-looking.
Then she said she was starting for New Zealand next day, and was
going to be away for three months. She'd got a doctor to say she
needed a complete change. Then she said Pat was going to Newcastle that night, and would I come in for a few minutes to say
good-bye to her. She gave me her solemn word of honour that she
wouldn't be troublesome, all that was over and done with, but
somehow or other Pat had got wind of something, it was nothing
important, but it was just as well I told the same story as her if by
any chance he asked me any questions. She hoped I'd come,
because though it couldn't matter to me and I was absolutely safe,
things might be a little awkward for her and she certainly didn't
want to get into any trouble if she could help it.

"I knew it was true about Hudson going to Newcastle because
my old man had said something about it at breakfast that morning.
The letter was absolutely normal. Sometimes she wrote in a scrawl
that you could hardly read, but she could write very well when she
wanted to, and I could see that when she'd written this she'd been
absolutely calm. I was a little anxious about what she'd said about
Pat. She had insisted on taking the most awful risks, though I'd
warned her over and over again. If he'd heard anything it did seem

better that we should tell the same lie, and forewarned is fore-armed, isn't it? So I rang her up and said I'd be there about six. She was so casual over the telephone that I was almost surprised. It sounded as though she didn't much care if I came or not.

"When I got there she shook hands with me as if we were just friends. She asked me if I'd like some tea. I said I'd had it before I came. She said she wouldn't keep me a minute because she was going to the pictures. She was all dressed up. I asked her what was the matter with Pat, and she said it wasn't really very serious, only he'd heard that I'd been at the pictures with her, and he didn't much like it. She'd said it was just an accident. Once I'd seen her sitting by herself and come over and sat by her, and another time we'd met in the vestibule, and as she was alone I'd paid for her seat and we'd gone in together. She said she didn't think Pat would mention it, but if he did, she wanted me to back her up. Of course I said I would. She mentioned the two times he was asking about, so that I should know, and then she began talking about her journey. She knew New Zealand well and she started talking about it. I'd never been there. It sounded fine. She was going to stay with friends and she made me laugh telling me about them. She could be jolly nice when she liked. She was awfully good company when she was in a good temper, I must admit that, and I never realised that time was passing. She was just like what she was when I first knew her. At last she got up and said she'd better be going. I suppose I'd been there about half an hour, maybe three-quarters. She gave me her hand and she looked at me half laughing.

" ' It wouldn't really hurt you to kiss me good-bye, would it?' she said.

"She said it chaffingly, and I laughed.

" 'No, I don't suppose it would,' I said.

"I bent down and kissed her. Or rather she kissed me. She put her arms round my neck and when I tried to break away she wouldn't let me go. She just clung to me like a vine. And then she said, as she was going away to-morrow, wouldn't I have her just once more. I said she'd promised she wouldn't make a nuisance of herself, and she said she didn't mean to but, seeing me, she couldn't help herself, and she swore it would be the last time. After all, she was going away, and it couldn't matter just once. And all the time she was kissing me and stroking my face. She said she didn't blame me for anything, and she was just a foolish woman and wouldn't I be kind to her? Well, it had all gone off so well and I was so relieved that she seemed to accept the situation; I didn't want to be a brute. If she'd been staying I'd have refused at any price, but as she was going away I thought I might just as well send her away happy.

" 'All right,' I said, 'let's go upstairs.'

"It was a little two-storey house, and the bedroom and spare-room were on the first floor. They've been building a lot of them round Sydney lately.

" 'No,' she said. 'The whole place is in a mess.'

"She drew me towards the sofa. It was one of those Chester-fields, and there was lots of room to cuddle up in it.

" 'I love you, I love you,' she kept on saying.

"Suddenly the door opened. I sprang up and there was Hudson. For a minute he was just as startled as I was. Then he shouted at me, I don't know what he said, and jumped. He let out his fist, but I dodged it; I'm pretty quick on my feet, and I've done a bit of boxing; and then he just chucked himself at me. We grappled. He was a big, powerful chap, bigger than me, but I'm pretty strong. He was trying to get me down, but I wasn't going to let him do that if I could help it. We were struggling all over the room. He hit me when he could, and I hit him back. Once I got away from him, but he charged me like a bull and I staggered. We knocked down chairs and tables. We had a hell of a fight. I tried to get away from him again, but I couldn't. He wanted to trip me up. It didn't take me long to find out he was a lot stronger than me. But I was more active. He'd got his coat on and I hadn't got anything but my undies. Then he got me down; I don't know if I slipped, or if he just forced me, but we were rolling over on the floor like a couple of madmen. He got on top of me and began hitting my face; there was nothing I could do then, and I just tried to protect it with my arm. Suddenly I thought he was going to kill me. God, I was scared! I made a hell of an effort and slipped away, but he was on me again like a flash of lightning. I felt my strength giving out; he put his knee on my windpipe and I knew I'd choke. I tried to shout, but I couldn't. I threw out my right arm and suddenly I felt a revolver put in my hand; I swear I didn't know what I was doing, it all happened in a second, I twisted my arm and fired. He gave a cry and started back. I fired again. He gave a great groan and rolled off me on to the floor. I slid away and jumped to my feet.

"I was trembling like a leaf."

Fred threw himself back in his chair and closed his eyes, so that Dr. Saunders thought he was going to faint. He was as white as a sheet and great beads of sweat stood on his forehead. He took a long breath.

"I was in a sort of daze. I saw Florrie kneel down, and though you wouldn't believe it I noticed that she was careful about it so that she shouldn't get any blood on her. She felt his pulse and she pulled down his eyelid. She got up.

" 'I think it's all right,' she said. 'He's dead.' She gave me a funny look. 'It wouldn't have been very nice if we'd had to polish him off.'

"I was horror-struck. I suppose I couldn't have been all there or I wouldn't have said anything so stupid as I did.

" 'I thought he was at Newcastle,' I said.

" 'No, he didn't go,' she said. 'He had a telephone message.'

" 'What telephone message?' I said. Somehow I couldn't understand what she was talking about. 'Who sent it?'

"D'you know that she almost laughed.

" 'I did,' she said.

" 'What for?' I said. Then it suddenly flashed across me. 'You don't mean to say it was a put-up job?'

" 'Don't be silly,' she said. 'What you've got to do now is to keep your head. You go home and have supper quite quietly with the family. I'm going to the pictures like I said I would.'

" 'You're crazy,' I said.

" 'No, I'm not,' she said. 'I know what I'm doing. You'll be all right if you do what I say. You just behave as if nothing had happened and leave it all to me. Don't forget that if it comes out you'll hang.'

"I expect I nearly jumped out of my skin when she said that, because she laughed. My God, the nerve that woman had got!

" 'You've got nothing to be afraid of,' she said. 'I won't let them touch a hair of your head. You're my property, and I know how to look after what belongs to me. I love you and I want you, and when it's all over and forgotten we'll be married. What a fool you were to think I was ever going to give you up.'

"I swear to you that I felt my blood run icy in my veins. I was in a trap and there was no getting out of it. I stared at her and I hadn't a thing to say. I shall never forget the look on her face. Suddenly she looked at my undervest. I hadn't got anything on but that and my drawers.

" 'Oh, look!' she said.

"I looked at myself and saw that on one side it was just dripping with blood. I was just going to touch it, I don't know why, when she caught hold of my hand.

" 'Don't do that,' she said. 'Wait a minute.'

"She got a newspaper and began rubbing it.

" 'Hold your head down,' she said. 'I'll take it off.'

"I bent my head and she skinned me.

" 'Have you got any blood anywhere else?' she said. 'Damned lucky for you you hadn't got your trousers on.'

"My drawers were all right. I dressed myself as quick as I could. She took the vest.

" 'I'll burn it and I'll burn the paper,' she said. 'I've got a fire in the kitchen. It's my washing day.'

"I looked at Hudson. He was dead all right. It made me feel rather sick to look at him. There was a great pool of blood on the carpet.

" 'Are you ready?' she said.

" 'Yes,' I said.

"She came out in the passage with me and just before she opened the door she put her arms round my neck and kissed me as if she wanted to eat me alive.

" 'My darling,' she said. 'Darling. Darling.'

"She opened the door and I slipped out. It was pitch dark.

"I seemed to walk in a dream. I walked pretty quick. As a matter of fact, I had all I could do not to run. I had my hat as far down as it would go and my collar turned up, but I hardly passed anybody and no one could have recognised me. I went a long way round, as she'd said I was to, and took the tram from right away in the neighbourhood of Chester Avenue.

"They were just going to sit down to dinner when I got home. We always had late dinner and I ran upstairs to wash my hands. I looked at myself in the glass, and d'you know, I was absolutely astonished because I looked just the same as usual. But when I sat down and Mother said, 'Tired, Fred? You're looking very white,' I went as red as a turkey-cock. I didn't manage to eat very much. Luckily I didn't have to talk, we never talked much when we were alone, and after dinner Father started to read some reports and Mother looked at the evening paper. I was feeling awful."

"Half a minute," said the doctor. "You said you suddenly felt a revolver in your hand. I don't quite understand."

"Florrie put it there."

"How did she get it?"

"How should I know? She took it out of Pat's pocket when he was on the top of me or else she had it there. I only fired in self-defence."

"Go on."

"Suddenly Mother said, 'What's the matter, Fred?' It came so unexpectedly and her voice was so—gentle, it just broke me. I tried to control myself; I couldn't, I just burst out crying. 'Hullo, what's this?' said Father. Mother put her arms round me and rocked me as if I was a baby. She kept on asking me what was the matter, and at first I wouldn't say. At last I had to. I pulled myself together. I made a clean breast of the whole thing. Mother was frightfully upset, and started weeping, but Father shut her up. She began reproaching me, but he wouldn't let her do that either. 'All that doesn't matter now,' he said. His face was like thunder. If the earth could have opened and swallowed me on a word of his, he'd have said the word. I told them everything. Father had always said the only chance a criminal has is to be absolutely frank with his lawyer, and that a lawyer couldn't do a thing unless he knew every single fact.

"I finished. Mother and I looked at Father. He'd stared at me all the time I was speaking, but now he looked down. You could see he was thinking like hell. You know, in some ways Father's an extraordinary man. He's always been very keen on culture. He's one of the trustees of the Art Gallery and he's on the committee that gets up the symphony concerts and all that. He's gentlemanly and rather quiet. Mother used to say he looked very distinguished. He was always very mild and amiable and polite. You'd have thought he wouldn't hurt a fly. He was everything he seemed, but there was a lot more in him than that. After all, he'd got the biggest lawyer's business in Sydney, and there was nothing he didn't know about people. Of course he was highly respected, but everyone knew it wasn't much good trying on any hanky-panky with him. And it was the same in politics. He ran the party and old Darnes never did a thing without consulting him. He could have been Premier himself if he'd wanted to, but he didn't, he was quite satisfied just to be in the Government and manage the whole shooting match behind the scenes.

" 'You mustn't blame the boy too much, Jim,' Mother said.

"He made a sort of impatient movement with his hand. I

almost thought he **wasn't** thinking about me at all. It sent a chill down my spine. He spoke at last.

" 'It looks very much like a put-up job between those two,' he said. 'Hudson has been rather difficult lately. I shouldn't be surprised if there was blackmail behind it. And she double-crossed him.'

" 'What's Fred to do?' said Mother.

"Father looked at me. You know, he looked just as mild as always and his voice had the same rather pleasant note in it. 'If he's caught, he'll hang,' he said. Mother gave a shriek and Father frowned a little. 'Oh, I'm not going to let him hang,' he said. 'Don't be afraid. He can escape that by going out now and shooting himself.' 'Jim, d'you want to kill me?' said Mother. 'Unfortunately that wouldn't help us much,' he said. 'What?' I asked. 'Your shooting yourself,' he said. 'The thing's got to be hushed up. We can't afford a scandal. We're going to have a stiff fight at the election, and with me out of it and all this we shouldn't have much chance.' 'Father, I'm so awfully sorry,' I said. 'I don't doubt that,' he said. 'Fools and blackguards generally are when they have to take the consequences of their actions.'

"We were all silent for a bit and then I said, 'I'm not sure if it wouldn't be the best thing if I went and shot myself.' 'Don't be so stupid,' he said; 'that would only make things worse. D'you think the newspapers are such fools that they wouldn't put two and two together? Don't talk. Let me think.' We sat like mutes. Mother was holding my hand. 'There's the woman to deal with, too,' he said at last. 'We're in her clutches all right. Nice to have her as a daughter-in-law.' Mother didn't dare say a word. Father leaned back in his chair and crossed his legs. A little smile came into his eyes. 'Fortunately we live in the most democratic country in the world,' he said. 'Nobody is above corruption.' He liked saying that. He looked at us for a minute or two. He had a way of thrusting out his jaw when he'd made up his mind to do something and meant to put it through that I knew as well as Mother did. 'I suppose it'll be in the paper to-morrow,' he said. 'I'll go and see Mrs. Hudson. I think I know what she's going to say. If she sticks to her story, barring accidents I don't think anyone can prove anything. It looks to me as if she'd worked it all out pretty thoroughly. The police will question her, but I'll see they don't interview her without my being present.' 'And what about Fred?' said Mother. Father smiled again. You'd have sworn butter couldn't melt in his mouth. 'Fred'll go to bed and stay there,' he said. 'By a merciful interposition of providence there's a lot of scarlet fever about, an epidemic practically; to-morrow or the next day we'll rush him off to the fever hospital.' 'But why?' asked Mother. 'What's the use of that?' 'My dear,' said Father, 'it's the best way I know of keeping someone out of the way for a few weeks with perfect security.' 'But supposing he catches it?' said Mother. 'He'd be acting natural,' he said.

"In the morning Father rung up my boss and said I'd got a temperature and he didn't half like the look of it. He was keeping me in bed and had sent for the doctor. The doctor came all right. He was my uncle, Mother's brother, and he'd attended me since I was born. He said he couldn't say for certain, it looked like scarlet fever, but he wouldn't send me to the hospital till the symptoms declared themselves. Mother told the cook and the maid that they weren't to come near me, and she'd look after me herself.

"The evening paper was full of the murder. Mrs. Hudson had gone to the pictures by herself, and when she came home and went into the sitting-room she had found the body of her husband. They didn't keep a servant. You don't know Sydney, but the house was a sort of little villa in a quarter they'd been developing; it stood in its own ground, and the next house was twenty or thirty yards away. Florrie didn't know the people who lived in it, but she ran there and battered on the door till they opened it. They were in bed and asleep. She told them her husband had been murdered and asked them to come quickly; they ran along, and there he was lying all heaped up on the floor. The man from the other house remembered after a while that he'd better call up the police. Mrs. Hudson was hysterical. She threw herself on her husband, screaming and crying, and they had to drag her away.

"Then there were all the details that the reporters had managed to pick up. The police doctor thought the man had been dead two or three hours. Strangely enough, he'd been shot with his own revolver, but the possibility of suicide was dismissed at once. When Mrs. Hudson had collected herself a bit she told the police that she'd spent the evening at a picture palace. She had part of the ticket still in her bag, and she'd spoken while there to two people she knew. She explained that she'd decided to go to the pictures that evening because her husband had arranged to go to Newcastle. He'd come home shortly before six and told her he wasn't going. She said she'd stay at home with him and get him his supper, but he told her to go as she'd intended. Someone was coming to see him on important business, and he wanted to be alone. She went out and that was the last she saw of him alive. There were signs of a terrific struggle in the room. Hudson had evidently fought desperately for his life. Nothing had been stolen from the house, and the police and the reporters at once jumped to the conclusion that the crime had a political motive. Passions run pretty high politically in Sydney, and Pat Hudson was known to be mixed up with some very rough characters. He had a lot of enemies. The police were prosecuting their enquiries, and the public were asked to inform them if they had seen a suspicious-looking person, possibly an Italian, in the neighbourhood or in a tram coming away from there who bore signs of having been engaged in a fight. A couple of nights later an ambulance came to our house and I was taken to the hospital. They kept me there for three or four days, and then I was slipped out and brought to the place where the *Fenton* was waiting for me."

"But that cable," said the doctor. "How did they manage to get the death certificate?"

"I know no more than you do. I've been trying to puzzle it out. I didn't enter the hospital as myself, I was told to call myself Blake. I've been asking myself if someone else didn't go in as me. They'd done all they could in the papers to pretend there wasn't an epidemic, but there was, and the hospital was crowded. The nurses were just run off their feet, and there was a lot of confusion. It's pretty clear that someone died and was buried in my place. Father's clever, you know, and he wouldn't stick at much."

"I think I should like to meet your father," said Dr. Saunders.

"It's struck me that perhaps people got suspicious. After all we must have been seen about together, and they may have started asking questions. I expect the police went into it all pretty thoroughly. I dare say Father thought it safer to have me die. I expect he got a lot of sympathy."

"It may be that's why she hanged herself," said the doctor.

Fred started violently.

"How did you know that?"

"I read it in the paper Erik Christessen brought the other night from Frith's."

"Did you know it was anything to do with me?"

"No, not till you began to tell me. Then I remembered the name."

"It gave me an awful turn when I read it."

"Why d'you think she did it?"

"It said in the paper she'd been worried by malicious gossip. I don't think Father would be satisfied till he got even with her. D'you know, I think the thing that made him see red was that she'd wanted to marry into his family. He must have got a lot of pleasure when he told her I was dead. She was horrible, and I hated her, but, by God, she must have loved me to do that." Fred hesitated for a moment reflectively. "Father knew the whole story. I shouldn't put it past him to tell her that I'd confessed before my death and the police were going to arrest her."

Dr. Saunders slowly nodded. It seemed to him a pretty device. He only wondered that the woman had adopted such an unpleasant means of death as hanging. Of course it looked as though she were in a hurry to do what she intended. Fred's supposition seemed very plausible.

"Anyway, she's out of it," said Fred. "And I've got to go on."

"You surely don't regret her?"

"Regret her? She's ruined my life. And the rotten thing is that the whole thing happened by the merest chance. I never intended to have an affair with her. I wouldn't have touched her if I'd known she was going to take it seriously. If Father had let me go out fishing that Sunday, I shouldn't even have met her. I don't know what to make of anything. And except for that I should never have come to this blasted island. I seem to bring misfortune wherever I go."

"You should put a little vitriol on your handsome face," said the doctor. "You are certainly a public danger."

"Oh, don't sneer at me. I'm so awfully unhappy. I've never cared for a chap like I cared for Erik. I shall never forgive myself for his death."

"Don't think he killed himself on your account. You had very little to do with that. Unless I'm greatly mistaken, he killed himself because he couldn't survive the shock of finding out that the person whom he'd endowed with every quality and every virtue was, after all, but human. It was madness on his part. That's the worst of being an idealist; you won't accept people as they are. Wasn't it Christ who said, 'Forgive them, for they know not what they do'?"

Fred stared at him with perplexed and haggard eyes.

"But you're not a religious man, are you?"

"Sensible men are all of the same religion. And what is that? Sensible men never tell."

"My father wouldn't say that. He'd say that sensible men don't go out of their way to give offence. He'd say, it looks well to go to church and you must respect the prejudices of your neighbours. He'd say, what is the good of getting off the fence when you can sit on it very comfortably? Nichols and I have talked about it all. You wouldn't believe it, but he can talk about religion by the hour. It's funny, I've never met a meaner crook, or a man who had less idea of decency, and yet he honestly believes in God. And hell, too. But it never strikes him that he may go there. Other people are going to suffer for their sins and serve 'em damn well right. But he's a stout fellow, he's all right, and when he does the dirty on a friend it isn't of any importance; it's what anyone would do under the circumstances, and God isn't going to hold that up against him. At first I thought he was just a hypocrite. But he isn't. That's the odd thing about it."

"It shouldn't make you angry. The contrast between a man's professions and his actions is one of the most diverting spectacles that life offers."

"You look at it from the outside and you can laugh, but I look at it from the in, and I'm a ship that's lost its bearings. What does it all mean? Why are we here? Where are we going? What can we do?"

"My dear boy, you don't expect me to answer, do you? Ever since men picked up a glimmer of intelligence in the primeval forests, they've been asking those questions."

"What do you believe?"

"Do you really want to know? I believe in nothing but myself and my experience. The world consists of me and my thoughts and my feelings; and everything else is mere fancy. Life is a dream in which I create the objects that come before me. Everything knowable, every object of experience, is an idea in my mind, and without my mind it does not exist. There is no possibility and no necessity to postulate anything outside myself. Dream and reality are one. Life is a connected and consistent dream, and when I cease to dream, the world, with its beauty, its pain and sorrow, its unimaginable variety, will cease to be."

"But that's quite incredible," cried Fred.

"That is no reason for me to hesitate to believe it," smiled the doctor.

"Well, I'm not prepared to be made a fool of. If life won't fulfil the demands I make on it, then I have no use for it. It's a dull and stupid play, and it's only waste of time to sit it out."

The doctor's eyes twinkled and a grin puckered his ugly little face.

"Oh, my dear boy, what perfect nonsense you talk. Youth, youth! You're a stranger in the world yet. Presently, like a man on a desert island, you'll learn to do without what you can't get and make the most of what you can. A little commonsense, a little tolerance, a little good-humour, and you don't know how comfortable you can make yourself on this planet."

"By giving up all that makes life worth while. Like you. I want life to be fair. I want life to be brave and honest. I want men to be decent and things to come right in the end. Surely that's not asking too much, is it?"

"I don't know. It's asking more than life can give."

"Don't you mind?"

"Not much."

"You're content to wallow in the gutter."

"I get a certain amount of fun from watching the antics of the other creatures that dwell there."

Fred gave his shoulder an angry shrug and a sigh was wrung from him.

"You believe nothing. You respect nobody. You expect man to be vile. You're a cripple chained to a bath-chair and you think it's just stuff and nonsense that anyone should walk or run."

"I'm afraid you don't very much approve of me," the doctor suggested mildly.

"You've lost heart, hope, faith and awe. What in God's name have you got left?"

"Resignation."

The young man jumped to his feet.

"Resignation? That's the refuge of the beaten. Keep your resignation. I don't want it. I'm not willing to accept evil and ugliness and injustice. I'm not willing to stand by while the good are punished and the wicked go scot-free. If life means that virtue is trampled on and honesty is mocked and beauty is fouled, then to hell with life."

"My dear boy, you must take life as you find it."

"I'm fed up with life as I find it. It fills me with horror. I'll either have it on my own terms or not at all."

Rhodomontade. The boy was nervous and upset. It was very natural. Dr. Saunders had little doubt that in a day or two he would be more sensible, and his reply was designed to check this extravagance.

"Have you ever read that laughter is the only gift the gods have vouchsafed to man that he does not share with the beasts?"

"What do you mean by that?" asked Fred sullenly.

"I have acquired resignation by the help of an unfailing sense of the ridiculous."

"Laugh, then. Laugh your head off."

"So long as I can," returned the doctor, looking at him with his tolerant humour, "the gods may destroy me, but I remain unvanquished."

Rhodomontade? Perhaps.

The conversation might have proceeded indefinitely if at that moment there had not come a knock on the door.

"Who the devil is that?" cried Fred irascibly.

A boy who spoke a little English came in to say that someone wished to see Fred, but they could not understand who it was. Fred, shrugging his shoulders, was about to go when an idea struck him and he stopped.

"Is it a man or a woman?"

He had to repeat the question in two or three different ways before the boy caught his meaning. Then with a smile brightened by the appreciation of his own cleverness, he answered that it was a woman.

"Louise." Fred shook his head with decision. "You say, Tuan sick, no can come."

The boy understood this and withdrew.

"You'd better see her," said the doctor.

"Never. Erik was worth ten of her. He meant all the world to me. I loathe the thought of her. I only want to get away. I want to forget. How could she trample on that noble heart!"

Dr. Saunders raised his eyebrows. Language of that sort chilled his sympathy.

"Perhaps she's very unhappy," he suggested mildly.

"I thought you were a cynic. You're a sentimentalist."

"Have you only just discovered it?"

The door was slowly opened, pushed wide, silently, and Louise

stood in the doorway. She did not come forward. She did not
speak. She looked at Fred, and a faint, shy, deprecating smile
hovered on her lips. You could see that she was nervous. Her
whole body seemed to express a timid uncertainty. It had, as
much as her face, an air of appeal. Fred stared at her. He did not
move. He did not ask her to come in. His face was sullen and in
his eyes was a cold and relentless hatred. The little smile froze on
her lips and she seemed to give a gasp, not with her mouth, but
with her body, as though a sharp pain pierced her heart. She
stood there, for two or three minutes, it seemed, and neither of
them moved an eyelash. Their eyes met in an insistent stare.
Then, very slowly, and as silently as when she opened it, she drew
the door to and softly closed it on herself. The two men were left
alone once more. To the doctor the scene had appeared strangely,
horribly pathetic.

CHAPTER XXIX

THE *Fenton* sailed at dawn. The ship that was to take Dr. Saunders
to Bali was due in the course of the afternoon. She was to stay
only just long enough to take on cargo, and so, toward eleven,
hiring a horse-cab, the doctor drove out to Swan's plantation. He
thought it would be uncivil to go without saying good-bye.

When he arrived he found the old man sitting in a chair in the
garden. It was the same chair as that in which Erik Christessen had
sat on the night when he saw Fred come out of Louise's room.
The doctor passed the time of day with him. The old man did not
remember him, but he was spry enough and asked the doctor a
number of questions without paying any attention to the replies.
Presently Louise came down the steps from the house. She shook
hands with him. She bore no sign that she had passed through an
emotional crisis, but greeted him with that composed and winning
smile that she had had the first time he saw her on the way back
from the bathing pool. She wore a brown sarong of batik and a
little native coat. Her very fair hair was plaited and bound round
her head.

"Won't you come inside and sit down?" she said. "Dad is
working. He'll be along presently."

The doctor accompanied her into the large living-room. The

jalousies were drawn and the subdued light was pleasant. There was not much comfort in the room, but it was cool, and a great bunch of yellow cannas in a bowl, flaming like the new-risen sun, gave it a peculiar and exotic distinction.

"We haven't told Grandpa about Erik. He liked him; they were both Scandinavians, you know. We were afraid it would upset him. But perhaps he knows; one can never tell. Sometimes, weeks after, he'll let fall a remark and we find out that he's known all along something that we thought we'd better say nothing about."

She talked in a leisurely manner, with a soft, rather full voice, as though of indifferent things.

"Old age is very strange. It has a kind of aloofness. It's lost so much, that you can hardly look upon the old as quite human any more. But sometimes you have a feeling that they've acquired a sort of new sense that tells them things that we can never know."

"Your grandfather was gay enough the other night. I hope I shall be as alert at his age."

"He was excited. He likes having new people to talk to. But that's just like a phonograph that you wind up. That's the machine. But there's something else there, like a little animal, a rat burrowing away or a squirrel turning in its cage, that's busy within him with things we know nothing of. I feel its existence and I wonder what it's about."

The doctor had nothing to say to this, and silence for a minute or two fell upon them.

"Will you have a stengah?" she said.

"No, thank you."

They were sitting opposite one another in easy chairs. The large room surrounded them with strangeness. It seemed to await something.

"The *Fenton* sailed this morning," said the doctor.

"I know."

He looked at her reflectively and she returned his gaze with tranquillity.

"I'm afraid Christessen's death was a great shock to you."

"I was very fond of him."

"He talked to me a great deal about you the night before he died. He was very much in love with you. He told me he was going to marry you."

"Yes." She gave him a fleeting glance. "Why did he kill himself?"

"He saw that boy coming out of your room."

She looked down. She reddened a little.

"That's impossible."

"Fred told me. He was there when he jumped over the rail of the veranda."

"Who told Fred I was engaged to Erik?"

"I did."

"I thought it was that yesterday afternoon when he wouldn't see me. And then when I came in and he looked at me like that I knew it was hopeless."

There was no despair in her manner, but a collected acceptance of the inevitable. You might almost have said that there was in her tone a shrug of the shoulders.

"You weren't in love with him, then?"

She leaned her face on her hand and for a moment seemed to look into her heart.

"It's all rather complicated," she said.

"Anyhow, it's no business of mine."

"Oh, I don't mind telling you. I don't care what you think of me."

"Why should you?"

"He was very good-looking. D'you remember the other afternoon when I met you in the plantation? I couldn't take my eyes off him. And then at supper, and afterwards when we danced together. I suppose you'd call it love at first sight."

"I'm not sure that I would."

"Oh?" She looked at him with an air of surprise, which changed to a quick, scrutinising glance, as though for the first time she paid him attention. "I knew he'd taken a fancy to me. I felt something I'd never felt in my life before. I wanted him simply frightfully. I generally sleep like a log. I was terribly restless all night. Father wanted to bring you his translation and I offered to drive him down. I knew he was only staying a day or two. Perhaps if he'd been staying a month it wouldn't have happened. I should have thought there was plenty of time, and if I'd seen him every day for a week I dare say I shouldn't have bothered about him. And afterwards, I didn't regret it. I felt contented and free. I lay awake for a little while after he left me that night. I was awfully happy, but, you know, I didn't really care if I never saw him again. It was very comfortable to be alone. I don't suppose you'll know what I mean, but I felt that my soul was a little light-headed."

"Have you no fear of consequences?" asked the doctor.

"How d'you mean?" She understood and smiled. "Oh, that. Oh, Doctor, I've lived on this island almost all my life. When I was a child I used to play with the children on the estate. My great friend, the daughter of our overseer, is the same age as me and she's been married for four years and has had three babies. You don't imagine sex has many secrets for Malay children. I've heard everything connected with it talked about since I was seven."

"Why did you come to the hotel yesterday?"

"I was distracted. I was awfully fond of Erik. I couldn't believe it when they told me he'd shot himself. I was afraid I was to blame. I wanted to know if it was possible that he knew about Fred."

"You were to blame."

"I'm dreadfully sorry he's dead. I owe a great deal to him. When I was a child I used to worship him. He was like one of Grandpa's old Vikings to me. I've always liked him awfully. But I'm not to blame."

"What makes you think that?"

"He didn't know it, but it wasn't me he loved, it was Mother. She knew it and at the end I think she loved him, too. It's funny if you come to think of it. He was almost young enough to be her son. What he loved in me was my mother, and he never knew that either."

"Didn't you love him?"

"Oh, very much. With my soul, not with my heart, or with my heart, perhaps, and not with my nerves. He was very good. He was wonderfully reliable. He was incapable of unkindness. He was very genuine. There was something almost saintly in him."

She took out her handkerchief and wiped her eyes, for while talking of him she had begun to cry.

"If you weren't in love with him, why did you become engaged to him?"

"I promised Mother I would before she died. I think she felt that in me she would gratify her love for him. And I was very fond of him. I knew him so well. I was very much at home with him. I think if he'd wanted to marry me just when Mother died and I was so unhappy I might have loved him. But he thought I was too young. He didn't want to take advantage of the feelings I had then."

"And then?"

"Daddy didn't very much want me to marry him. He was always waiting for the fairy prince who would come and carry me off to an enchanted castle. I suppose you think Daddy's feckless and unpractical. Of course I didn't believe in a fairy prince, but there's generally something behind Daddy's ideas. He has a sort of instinct for things. He lives in the clouds, if you know what I mean, but very often those clouds glow with the light of heaven. Oh, I suppose if nothing had happened we should have married in the end and been very happy. No one could have helped being happy with Erik. It would have been very nice to see all those places he talked about. I should have liked to go to Sweden, to the place where Grandpa was born, and Venice."

"It's unfortunate that we ever came here. And, after all, it was only a chance; we might just as well have made for Amboyna."

"Could you have gone to Amboyna? I think it was fated from all eternity that you should come here."

"Do you think our destinies are so important that the fates should make such a to-do about them?" smiled the doctor.

She did not answer and for a little while they sat in silence.

"I'm terribly unhappy, you know," she said at last.

"You must try not to grieve too much."

"Oh, I don't grieve."

She spoke with a sort of decision, so that the doctor looked at her with surprise.

"You blame me. Anyone would. I don't blame myself. Erik killed himself because I'd fallen short of the ideal he'd made of me."

"Ah."

Dr. Saunders perceived that her instinct had come to the same conclusion as his reasoning.

"If he'd loved me he might have killed me or he might have forgiven me. Don't you think it's rather stupid, the importance men, white men at least, attach to the act of flesh? D'you know, when I was at school in Auckland I had an attack of religion—girls often have at that age—and in Lent I made a vow that I wouldn't eat anything with sugar in it. After about a fortnight I hankered after something sweet so that it was positive torture. One day I passed a candy shop and I looked at the chocolates in the window and my heart turned round inside me. I went in and bought half a pound and ate them in the street outside, every one, till the bag was empty. I shall never forget what a relief it was. Then I went back to school and denied myself quite comfortably for the rest of Lent.

I told that story to Erik and he laughed. He thought it very natural. He was so tolerant. Don't you think if he'd loved me he would have been tolerant about the other, too?"

"Men are very peculiar in that respect."

"Not Erik. He was so wise and so charitable. I tell you he didn't love me. He loved his ideal. My mother's beauty and my mother's qualities in me and those Shakespeare heroines of his and the princesses in Hans Andersen's fairy tales. What right have people to make an image after their own heart and force it on you and be angry if it doesn't fit you? He wanted to imprison me in his ideal. He didn't care who I was. He wouldn't take me as I am. He wanted to possess my soul, and because he felt that there was somewhere in me something that escaped him, he tried to replace that little spark within me which is me by a phantom of his own fancy. I'm unhappy, but I tell you I don't grieve. And Fred in his way was the same. When he lay by my side that night he said he'd like to stay here always on this island, and marry me and cultivate the plantation, and I don't know what else. He made a picture of his life and I was to fit in it. He wanted, too, to imprison me in his dream. It was a different dream, but it was his dream. But I am I. I don't want to dream anyone else's dream. I want to dream my own. All that's happened is terrible and my heart is heavy, but at the back of my mind I know that it's given me freedom."

She did not speak with emotion, but slowly and in measured terms, with the collected manner that the doctor had always found so singular. He listened attentively. He shuddered a little within himself, for the spectacle of the naked human soul always affected him with horror. He saw there that same bare, ruthless instinct that impelled those shapeless creatures of the beginning of the world's history to force their way through the blind hostility of chance. He wondered what would become of this girl.

"Have you any plan for the future?" he asked.

She shook her head.

"I can wait. I'm young. When Grandpa dies this will be mine. Perhaps I shall sell it. Daddy wants to go to India. The world is wide."

"I must go," said Dr. Saunders. "Can I see your father to say good-bye to him?"

"I'll take you to his study."

She led him along a passage to a smallish room at the side of the house. Frith was sitting at a table littered with manuscripts and books. He was pounding a typewriter, and the sweat pouring from his fat red face made his spectacles slip down his nose.

"This is the final typing of the ninth canto," he said. "You're going away, aren't you? I'm afraid I shan't have time to show it you."

He had forgotten that Dr. Saunders had fallen asleep while he was reading his translation aloud to him, or if he remembered was undiscouraged.

"I am nearing the end. It has been an arduous task, and I hardly think I could ever have brought it to a successful conclusion but for my little girl's encouragement. It is very right and proper that she should be the chief gainer."

"You mustn't work too hard, Daddy."

"*Tempus fugit,*" he murmured. "*Ars longa, vita brevis.*"

She put her hand gently on his shoulder and with a smile looked at the sheet of paper in the machine. Once more the doctor was struck by the loving-kindness with which Louise treated her father. With her shrewd sense she could not have failed to form a just estimate of his futile labour.

"We haven't come to disturb you, darling. Dr. Saunders wants to say good-bye."

"Ah, yes, of course," said Frith. He got up from the table. "Well, it's been a treat to see you. In this backwater of life we don't often have visitors. It was kind of you to come to Christessen's funeral yesterday. We Britishers ought to stick together on these occasions. It impresses the Dutch. Not that Christessen was British. But we'd seen a great deal of him since he came to the island, and after all he belonged to the same country as Queen Alexandra. A glass of sherry before you go?"

"No, thank you. I must be getting back."

"I was very much upset when I heard. The Contrôleur told me he had no doubt it was the heat. He wanted to marry Louise. I'm very glad now I wouldn't give my consent. Lack of self-control, of course. The English are the only people who can transplant themselves to strange lands and keep their balance. He'll be a great loss to us. Of course he was a foreigner, but all the same it's a shock. I've felt it very much."

It was evident, however, that he looked upon it as much less serious for a Dane to die than for an Englishman. Frith insisted on coming out into the compound. The doctor, turning round to wave his hand as he drove off, saw him with his arm round his daughter's waist. A ray of sun finding its way through the heavy leafage of the kanari trees touched her fair hair with gold.

CHAPTER XXX

A MONTH later Dr. Saunders was sitting on the little dusty terrace of the Van Dyke Hotel at Singapore. It was late in the afternoon. From where he sat he could see the street below. Cars dashed past and cabs drawn by two sturdy ponies; rickshaws sped by with a patter of naked feet. Now and then Tamils, tall and emaciated, sauntered along, and in their silence, in the quiet of their stealthy movement, was the night of a far-distant past. Trees shaded the street and the sun splashed down in irregular patches. Chinese women in trousers, with gold pins in their hair, stepped out of the shade into the light like marionettes passing across the stage. Now and then a young planter, deeply sunburned, in a double-brimmed hat and khaki shorts, walked past with the long stride he had learnt tramping over the rubber estates. Two dark-skinned soldiers, very smart in their clean uniforms, strutted by, conscious of their importance. The heat of the day was past, the light was golden, and in the air was a crisp nonchalance as though life, there and then, invited you to take it lightly. A water-cart passed, slithering the dusty road with a stream of water.

Dr. Saunders had spent a fortnight in Java. Now he was catching the first ship that came in for Hong-Kong, and from there he intended to take a coasting vessel to Fu-chou. He was glad he had made the journey. It had taken him out of the rut he had been in so long. It had liberated him from the bonds of unprofitable habits, and, relaxed as never before from all earthly ties, he rejoiced in a heavenly sense of spiritual independence. It was an exquisite pleasure to him to know that there was no one in the world who was essential to his peace of mind. He had reached, though by a very different path, the immunity from the concerns of this world which is the aim of the ascetic. While, like the Buddha contemplating his navel, he was delectably immersed in his self-satisfaction, someone touched him on the shoulder. He looked up and saw Captain Nichols.

"I was passin' by and saw you sittin' there. I came up to say 'ow-d'ye-do to you."

"Sit down and have a drink."

"I don't mind if I do."

The skipper wore his shore-going clothes. They were not old, but they looked astonishingly seedy. He had two days' growth of beard on his lean face, and the nails on his hands were rimmed with grime. He looked down-at-heel.

"I'm 'avin' me teeth attended to," he said. "You was right. The dentist says I must 'ave 'em all out. Says 'e's not surprised I suffer from dyspepsia. It's a miracle I've gone on as long as I 'ave, according to 'im."

The doctor gave him a glance and noticed that his upper front teeth had been extracted. It made his ingratiating smile more sinister than ever.

"Where's Fred Blake?" asked Dr. Saunders.

The smile faded from the skipper's lips, but lingered sardonic in his eyes.

"Come to a sticky end, poor young chap," he replied.

"What d'you mean?"

"Fell overboard one night or jumped over. Nobody knows. He was gone in the morning."

"In a storm?"

The doctor could hardly believe his ears.

"No. Sea was as flat as a mill-pond. He was very low after we come away from Kanda. We went to Batavia same as we said we was goin' to do. I suspicioned 'e was expectin' a letter there. But if it come or if it didn't I don't know, and it's no good askin' me."

"But how could he go overboard without anyone noticing? What about the man at the helm?"

"We'd 'ove to for the night. Been drinkin' very 'eavy. Nothin' to do with me, of course, but I tell 'im he'd better go easy. Told me to mind me own bloody business. All right, I says, go your own way. It ain't goin' to disturb my night's rest what you do."

"When did it happen?"

"A week ago last Tuesday."

The doctor leaned back. It was a shock to him. It was so short a while since that boy and he had sat together and talked. It had seemed to him then that there was in him something naïve and aspiring that was not devoid of charm. It was not very pleasant to think of him now drifting, mangled and terrible, at the mercy of the tides. He was only a kid. Notwithstanding his philosophy, the doctor could not but feel a pang when the young died.